STEPHEN JONES lives in _____ of
three World Fantasy Awa _____ on
Bram Stoker Awards and th _____ ds
as well as being a sixteen-ti _____ rd
and a Hugo Award nomine _____ tor
and genre movie publicist _____ ser
movies, *Night Life, Night* _____ *ast
Gasp* etc.), he is the co-editor of *Horror:* _____ *or:
Another 100 Best Books, The Best Horror from Fantasy Tales,
Gaslight & Ghosts, Now We Are Sick, H.P. Lovecraft's Book of
Horror, The Anthology of Fantasy & the Supernatural, Secret City:
Strange Tales of London* and the *Dark Terrors, Dark Voices* and
Fantasy Tales series. He has written *Creepshows: The Illustrated
Stephen King Movie Guide, The Essential Monster Movie Guide,
The Illustrated Vampire Movie Guide, The Illustrated Dinosaur
Movie Guide, The Illustrated Frankenstein Movie Guide* and *The
Illustrated Werewolf Movie Guide*, and compiled *The Mammoth
Book of Best New Horror* series, *The Mammoth Book of Terror,
The Mammoth Book of Vampires, The Mammoth Book of Zombies,
The Mammoth Book of Werewolves, The Mammoth Book of
Frankenstein, The Mammoth Book of Dracula, The Mammoth
Book of Vampire Stories by Women, The Mammoth Book of
New Terror, Shadows Over Innsmouth, Weird Shadows Over
Innsmouth, Dark Detectives, Dancing With the Dark, Dark of
the Night, White of the Moon, Keep Out the Night, By Moonlight
Only, Don't Turn Out the Light, Exorcisms and Ecstasies* by Karl
Edward Wagner, *The Vampire Stories of R. Chetwynd-Hayes,
Phantoms and Fiends* and *Frights and Fancies* by R. Chetwynd-
Hayes, *James Herbert: By Horror Haunted, The Conan Chronicles*
by Robert E. Howard (two volumes), *The Emperor of Dreams: The
Lost Worlds of Clark Ashton Smith, Sea-Kings of Mars and Other-
worldly Stories* by Leigh Brackett, *Clive Barker's A–Z of Horror,
Clive Barker's Shadows in Eden, Clive Barker's The Nightbreed
Chronicles* and the *Hellraiser Chronicles*. He was a Guest of Honour
at the 2002 World Fantasy Convention in Minneapolis, Minnesota,
and the 2004 World Horror Convention in Phoenix, Arizona. You
can visit his web site at www.herebedragons.co.uk/jones

Also available

The Mammoth Book of 20th Century Science Fiction
The Mammoth Book of Awesome Comic Fantasy
The Mammoth Book of Best New Erotica 4
The Mammoth Book of Best New Horror 15
The Mammoth Book of Best New Science Fiction 18
The Mammoth Book of British Kings & Queens
The Mammoth Book of Celtic Myths and Legends
The Mammoth Book of Chess
The Mammoth Book of Fighter Pilots
The Mammoth Book of Future Cops
The Mammoth Book of Great Detective Stories
The Mammoth Book of Great Inventions
The Mammoth Book of Hearts of Oak
The Mammoth Book of Heroes
The Mammoth Book of Historical Whodunnits
The Mammoth Book of How It Happened
The Mammoth Book of How It Happened: America
The Mammoth Book of How It Happened: Ancient Egypt
The Mammoth Book of How It Happened: Ancient Rome
The Mammoth Book of How It Happened: Battles
The Mammoth Book of How It Happened In Britain
The Mammoth Book of International Erotica
The Mammoth Book of Jack the Ripper
The Mammoth Book of Jokes
The Mammoth Book of Maneaters
The Mammoth Book of Mountain Disasters
The Mammoth Book of Native Americans
The Mammoth Book of New Terror
The Mammoth Book of Private Eye Stories
The Mammoth Book of Prophecies
The Mammoth Book of Pulp Action
The Mammoth Book of Roaring Twenties Whodunnits
The Mammoth Book of Roman Whodunnits
The Mammoth Book of SAS & Elite Forces
The Mammoth Book of Science Fiction Century Volume 1
The Mammoth Book of Seriously Comic Fantasy
The Mammoth Book of Sex, Drugs & Rock 'n' Roll
The Mammoth Book of Short Erotic Novels
The Mammoth Book of Special Forces
The Mammoth Book of Storms & Sea Disasters
The Mammoth Book of Sword and Honour
The Mammoth Book of The Edge
The Mammoth Book of Travel in Dangerous Places
The Mammoth Book of True War Stories
The Mammoth Book of UFOs
The Mammoth Book of Vampires
The Mammoth Book of War Correspondents
The Mammoth Book of Women Who Kill
The Mammoth Encyclopedia of Extraterrestrial Encounters
The Mammoth Encyclopedia of Modern Crime Fiction
The Mammoth Encyclopedia of Unsolved Mysteries

THE
MAMMOTH BOOK OF
BEST NEW
HORROR

VOLUME SIXTEEN

Edited and with an Introduction by
STEPHEN JONES

ROBINSON
London

Constable & Robinson Ltd
3 The Lanchesters
162 Fulham Palace Road
London W6 9ER
www.constablerobinson.com

First published in the UK by Robinson,
an imprint of Constable & Robinson Ltd 2005

A copy of the British Library Cataloguing in
Publication Data is available from the British Library.

ISBN 1–84529–117–4

Printed and bound in the EU

1 3 5 7 9 10 8 6 4 2

CONTENTS

ACKNOWLEDGMENTS

I would like to thank David Barraclough, Kim Newman, Rodger Turner and Wayne MacLaurin (sfsite.com), Hugh Lamb, Claudia Dyer, Gordon Van Gelder, Barbara Roden, Mandy Slater, Brian Mooney, Sara and Randy Broecker, Del Howison, Douglas E. Winter, Jo Fletcher, David J. Schow, Jay Broecker, Basil Copper, Lucy Ramsey, Andrew I. Porter, Alan Beatts, Andy Cox and, especially, Pete Duncan and Dorothy Lumley for all their help and support. Special thanks are also due to *Locus*, *Variety* and all the other sources that were used for reference in the Introduction and the Necrology.

INTRODUCTION

Horror in 2004

A REPORT RELEASED IN APRIL revealed that British public libraries were in "near-terminal" decline, with visitor numbers falling so sharply that they would barely be used at all by 2020. According to the study by the charity Libri, book-lending had halved in the UK since 1984. It blamed local councils for not spending enough of their budgets on actually buying new books.

However, a government report two months later revealed that 65 per cent of people in Britain are reading for pleasure – up from 55 per cent in 1979. More people apparently prefer to buy their own books, and sales in the UK have risen 19 per cent over the past five years. Demand was so great that charity chain Barnardo's announced it was transforming many of its secondhand clothes shops into used bookstores. In 2003 Barnardo's sold around a million books, while an Oxfam charity shop in Reading reported it sold 1,500 books a week.

Meanwhile, a report in December by the education watchdog Ofsted revealed that a number of British primary schools were failing to teach children to read properly, with many pupils not being encouraged to read for pleasure.

In the United States, it was estimated that a record $3.12 billion would be spent on celebrating Halloween in 2004. Even in Britain, where it was barely glorified a decade earlier, £100 million is spent on the event annually. It is now the UK's third most lucrative festival of the year after Christmas and Easter, and the second-biggest social event after New Year. However, research carried out by the Tesco supermarket chain discovered that a third of all Hallowe'en items in the UK were sold to adults between their late teens and early thirties, not to children.

A school in Puyallup, Washington State, banned Trick or Treating because, as Puyallup School District spokeswoman Karen Hansen explained, Halloween celebrations and children dressed up in costumes may have been offensive to real witches: "Witches with pointy noses and things like that are not respective (sic) symbols to the Wiccan religion and so we want to be respectful of that," she revealed to a number of US newspapers.

Back in Britain, several local councils also produced posters and advertising campaigns to discourage Trick or Treating in their areas, where the number of Hallowe'en-related anti-social incidents had risen over recent years.

In 2004, Avalon Publishing Group, which owns Carroll & Graf amongst other imprints, acquired publisher Four Walls Eight Windows and integrated the list into its expanded Thunder's Mouth Press imprint.

Britain's largest bookseller chain, WH Smith, began selling off most of its overseas operations during the summer and, in early August, the company sold its Hodder Headline publishing division to French publisher Hachette Livre (who also own Orion/Gollancz) for £233 million. The move was seen as an attempt by chief executive Kate Swann to plug a gap in the company's £200 million pension fund and to focus on the company's core retail and news distribution business. It was apparently a success, with shares eventually rising by almost six per cent after the group announced that its profitability had improved "substantially".

Also in August, troubled British broadcaster ITV sold off its loss-making Carlton Books imprint to its management for an estimated £2.5 million.

In February, 38-year-old J.K. Rowling made the Forbes 2004 list of billionaires at #552 with an estimated fortune of $1 billion (£526 million).

Harry Potter and the Order of the Phoenix was released in mass-market format (with a two million first print run in the US), along with various new "adult" editions of the earlier books in the series. Slightly more unecessary were Ancient Greek and Irish translations of the first *Harry Potter* book.

Meanwhile, The Church of England criticized the BBC for showing the movie *Harry Potter and the Philosopher's Stone* on terrestrial television on Christmas Day (watched by 7.9 million people), claiming "It was unsuitable for children at the best of times" because of its depiction of wizards and witchcraft. One wonders what they would make of that perennial holiday favourite *The Wizard of Oz*?

Despite not having a new *Harry Potter* title in 2004, publisher Bloomsbury had a strong year thanks to the success of Susanna Clarke's acclaimed debut novel *Jonathan Strange & Mr Norrell*, about two rival nineteenth century magicians. The book went through multiple printings and became a bestseller in America.

The sixth and penultimate volume in Stephen King's *The Dark Tower* sequence, *Song of Susannah* focussed on the eponymous character raped by a demon in The Waste Lands. King even wrote himself into the narrative as the flawed poet chronicling Gunslinger Roland's life. The book spent one week at the top of some American bestseller lists before being knocked off by Dan Brown's phenomenally successful thriller *The Da Vinci Code*.

The Donald M. Grant edition of *Song of Susannah* featured colour illustrations by Darrel Anderson and was also available in a deluxe signed and boxed edition of 1,400 copies and an "artist edition" of 3,500 copies. Anderson's art was additionally published as a separate portfilio.

The final novel in the sequence, somewhat unimaginatively titled *The Dark Tower*, appeared in September with illustrations by Michael Whelan. In this concluding volume, Roland and his band of pilgrims finally reached the end of their long quest. Once again, the Donald M. Grant edition was also available in a signed, deluxe slipcased edition of 1,500 copies ($225.00) and a 5,000-copy "artist edition" signed by Whelan. In Britain, Hodder & Stoughton produced a proof edition limited to just 100 copies, which quickly became a collector's item.

Thanks to a clause in their contract, the Boston Red Sox's surprise win of the World Series resulted in an increase in the advance payment from Scribner for Stephen King and co-author Stewart O'Nan's *Faithful: Two Diehard Boston Red Sox Fans Chronicle the Historic 2004 Season*, a book that looked at the ups and downs of the "cursed" baseball team that last won the World Series in 1918.

Anne Rivers Siddons' 1978 haunted house novel, *The House Next Door*, was reissued as part of the Science Fiction Book Club's "Stephen King Horror Library" with a 1981 Introduction by King.

Days of Magic, Nights of War was the second volume in Clive Barker's epic *Abarat* quartet that once again featured more than 125 full-colour paintings by the author. This time Candy Quackenbush and rescued slave Malingo explored the fantastical islands, pursued by Christopher Carrion's agents. An audio version was also available from HarperCollins Audio as an unabridged CD. Barker's artwork also featured on a line of clothing produced by Primal Wear's Signature Series for all the family.

Peter Straub's *In the Night Room* was a follow-up to the author's previous book, *lost boy lost girl*, and featured haunted novelist Tim Underhill in an enigmatic piece of metafiction in which creator and creation were brought together in the "real" world.

A small community was cut off by aliens in Dean Koontz's *The Taking*, while a man's future was predicted by his dying grandfather in *Life Expectancy*, from the same author.

Anne Rice's *Blood Canticle* reportedly marked the conclusion of the author's bestselling "Vampire Chronicles" sequence. Unfortunately for Rice, she decided to respond with a 1,200-word rebuttal to criticism of the book posted on Amazon.com: "Your stupid, arrogant assumptions about me and what I am doing are slander," ranted the author. "You have used the site as if it were a public urinal to publish falsehood and lies." It was perhaps not the best method to attract new readers. Meanwhile, Rice's *Interview With the Vampire* and *The Vampire Lestat* were reissued by Ballantine in "special price" editions, and *New Tales of the Vampires* was an omnibus edition of *Pandora* and *Vittorio, the Vampire*.

With the help of compiler Donn Albright, Ray Bradbury's latest collection, *The Cat's Pajamas: New Stories* contained twenty-two tales (two reprints, although around half the stories were written before 1952) and a narrative poem dated 1996–97. Eighty-four-year-old Bradbury received the 2004 National Medal of Arts, the American government's highest honour for artistic achievement, from President Bush at a White House Oval Office ceremony on 17 November. Madeleine L'Engle was awarded the corresponding National Humanities Medal and was represented by her granddaughter.

Brian Lumley's enjoyable 1980 time-travel Egyptian novel *Khai of Khem* was published in a hardcover edition by Tor Books with a superb dustjacket painting by Bob Eggleton.

Richard Laymon's *The Lake* was posthumously published by Headline in the UK. It concerned a mother and daughter and a far from idyllic summer vacation by a haunted body of water.

Greg Bear's *Dead Lines* involved a new telecommunications technology in the near future that put its users in contact with the spirits of the dead. A family moved to a small town with a dark history in John Saul's *Black Creek Crossing*, while F. Paul Wilson's *Crisscross* was the eighth volume in his popular "Repairman Jack" series.

The Lonely Dead (US: *The Upright Man*) was Michael Marshall (Smith)'s follow-up to his previous bestseller *The Straw Men*, as a former CIA agent became involved with a serial killer and dark secrets that should have remained hidden.

A series of prostitute murders centred around a low budget film shoot in Belgium and a British film critic-turned-investigator were at the heart of Nicholas Royle's new thriller *Antwerp*, which came complete with cover quotes from Jonathan Coe and an interview with the author in *Time Out*. Royle also edited *Dreams Never End: New Noir Short Stories* featuring a number of contributions each from Midlands writers Andrew Newsham, Mick Scully and H.P. Tinker.

The Prayer of the Night Shepherd was the sixth volume in Phil Rickman's "Merrily Watkins" series. In Spider Robinson's *Very Bad Deaths*, a journalist with empathic powers found himself on the trail of a serial killer in British Columbia, while Paul McAuley's biotech thriller *White Devils* involved the discovery of genetic engineering, ape-like creatures and a corporate cover-up in the Congo.

Douglas Preston and Lincoln Child's *Brimstone* once again teamed up FBI agent Aloysius Pendergast and former NYPD cop Vincent D'Agosta, who attempted to capture a murderer who left behind the burned impression of a cloven hoofprint.

Cantankerous geriatric detectives Bryant and May were called in to investigate the bizarre death of an elderly woman found drowned inside her London home in their second case, *The Water Room*, by Christopher Fowler.

Caitlín R. Kiernan's novel *Murder of Angels* was a haunted house novel set in Birmingham, Alabama, in which schizophrenic musician Niki Ky heard her dead lover calling to her from another world. In Christopher Golden's *The Boys Are Back in Town*, a man's tenth high school reunion signalled a terrifying shift in reality.

Golden also teamed up with comic book author Thomas E. Sniegoski for *The Nimble Man: A Novel of the Menagerie*, the first in a new series about a group dedicated to fighting the forces of darkness, while *Operation Medusa* was the second volume in Jim Grand's series about paranormal investigators Unit Omega.

The Devil in Gray was a new title from Graham Masterton, while the author's latest "Jim Rook" novel, *Darkroom*, involved spontaneous combustion.

Elizabeth Hand's haunting romantic novel *Mortal Love* revolved around a disturbing Victorian painting and a mysterious and apparently immortal young woman.

The lost prophecies of Nostradamus could possibly save the United States in Jon Land's thriller *The Last Prophecy*, and there were conspiracy theories aplenty in Shaun Hutson's *Necessary Evil*.

The long-deceased V.C. Andrews® (still probably Andrew Niederman) launched the "Gemini" series of Gothic novels with *Celeste* and *Black Cat*.

As always, Dorchester Books' dedicated Leisure imprint had a busy year with the first US edition of Richard Laymon's *Body Rides* following the late author's manuscript and not the edited UK version published by Headline in 1996.

Frank M. Robinson's *The Donor* was a medical thriller about organ harvesting. A man was haunted by his past in *Black Fire* by James Kidman (Brian Freeman), while P.D. Cacek's protagonist could control the wind in *The Wind Caller*.

An old man believed that his death would free a demon in Leah R. Cutter's *The Caves of Buda*, a witch discovered there was a price to be paid for continued immortality in Sèphra Girón's *Borrowed Flesh*, and a run-down dance hall was a home to evil in Simon Clark's *In This Skin*.

Hallows Eve was a new novel in the "Orangefield" series by Al Sarrantonio, and a group of people were trapped by magic in *House of Blood* by Bryan Smith. A woman returned to confront the madness in her Louisiana home in Deborah LeBlanc's *Family Inheritance*, and an inheritance led to *Possessions* by James A. Moore.

Edward Lee's *The Messenger* was a reprint of a novel originally issued by Necro Publications, James Newman's *Midnight Rain* was another mass-market paperback reprint, and other Leisure titles included *MEG: Primal Waters* by Steve Alten and *The Hidden* by Sarah Pinborough.

Scott Nicholson's Southern Gothic *The Manor* was a haunted house novel set in an isolated retreat for *artistes* situated in the heart of the Appalachian Mountains. The Appalachians were also the setting for Stephen Mark Rainey's *The Lebo Crown*, in which a man investigated the mysterious disappearance of his brother from a small town.

Douglas Clegg's *Afterlife* involved a wife's repressed memories and a government-funded research programme for psychic children.

Convicts were possessed by the dead inmates of a former asylum in Patrick R. Gates' *The Prison*, Cambodian ghosts were stirred up by a body-recovery mission in Jeff Long's *The Reckoning*, and a private investigator and martial arts expert confronted the forces of evil in Chandler McGrew's *The Darkening*.

Laura Anne Gilman's *Staying Dead* was the first in the "Retrievers" trilogy and involved a woman finding an angry ghost. A psychic started receiving abusive phone calls from her supposedly comatose ex-husband in Holly Lisle's *Midnight Rain*, and a woman discovered she had healing powers in Edna Ventre-Auefeld's *Penny's Gift*.

Christopher Moore's comedic *The Stupidest Angel: A Heartwarming Tale of Christmas Terror* was set in a small coastal California town with zombies. Meanwhile, a virus turned its victims into homicidal maniacs in Walter Greatshell's *Xombies*.

A girl plagued with nightmares tried to remember her *Missing Monday* by Matthew Costello, the last deposit of dirt from the Biblical Paradise turned up in a rest home in Thomas Sullivan's *Dust of Eden*, and Michael Laimo's *Deep in Darkness* was set in the same world as the author's "Golden Eyes" stories.

Published by Gale Group/Five Star, David Niall Wilson's novel *Deep Blue* was expanded from a short story by the author and involved a blues guitarist whose music had the power to release pain.

Hunters discovered a Sasquatch in Jay Kumar's *Dark Woods*. Rick Hautala published *Looking Glass* under his "A.J. Matthews" pseudonym, and there were more supernatural thrills in *Dark Corner* by Brandon Massey.

Kelley Armstrong's *Industrial Magic* was a sequel to *Dime Store Magic* and featured wild witch Paige Winterbourne on the trail of an unnatural-born killer, while a man used magic to pursue a murderer in Larry Segriff's *Nightmare Logic*.

In the comedic fantasy *Dead Witch Walking* by "Kim Harrison" (Dawn Cook), white witch Rachel Morgan, who worked for a law enforcement agency, teamed up with vampire Ivy and a pixie to become a private investigator. It was followed by *The Good, The Bad, and the Undead*, in which Rachel and Ivy investigated a serial killer murdering witches.

Legend of the Jade Dragon was the second volume in Yasmine Galenorn's "Chintz 'n' China" series of mysteries about witch Emerald O'Brien; *Merilynn* was the second in Tamara Thorne's *The Sorority* trilogy, about a school's secret coven of witches, and Daniel Hecht's *Land of Echoes* was the second novel to feature psychic investigator Cree Black, this time investigating a case of possession in New Orleans.

Koji Suzuki's 1995 novel *Spiral* (*Rasen*), the sequel to *Ring*, was translated by Robert B. Rohmer and Glynne Walley for publisher Vertical. From the same author and imprint, *Dark Water* (*Hono-*

gural mizu no soko kara, 1996) collected seven stories framed by opening and closing sections.

The Ghost and Mrs McClure was the first in Alice Kimberly's "Haunted Bookshop" mystery series, featuring a phantom detective; Nora Roberts' *Blue Dahlia* was the first in the "In the Garden" trilogy, about a haunted house in Memphis, and *Snowbound* was the ninth volume in Nancy Atherton's "Aunt Dimity" supernatural mystery series, set in a haunted abbey.

Mr and Mrs Darcy from Jane Austen's *Pride and Prejudice* investigated a supernatural mystery in Carrie Bebris' *Pride and Prescience, or, A Truth Universally Acknowledged*.

Tor Books moved the launch of its new paranormal romance line from July to October, publishing one title per month. The imprint launched with Constance O'Day-Flannery's *Shifting Love*.

Dark of the Sun by Chelsea Quinn Yarbro was the seventeenth novel about the undead Count Saint-Germain, set against the eruption of Krakatoa. Yarbro's *In the Face of Death* was a vampire novel set during the American Civil War featuring Madelaine de Montalia. Published by BenBella Books, it was previously available only as an e-book.

Under the pen-name "Trystam Kith", Yarbro was also the author of *Trouble in the Forest Book 2: A Bright Winter Sun*, about vampires in Sherwood Forest.

Nancy A. Collins' "Sonja Blue" novel *In the Blood* was published for the first time in a separate North American trade edition by White Wolf Publishing's Borealis inprint.

Involving a frustrated were-leopard and strippers being murdered by vampire serial killers, *Incubus Dreams* was the twelfth volume in Laurell K. Hamilton's erotic "Anita Blake, Vampire Hunter" series. The book was profiled in the September issue of *Publishers Weekly*.

In Tanya Huff's *Smoke and Shadows*, the undead Henry Fitzroy teamed up with a gay production assistant and a special effects wizard (literally) to investigate the evil centred around a vampire detective TV show. Meanwhile, Jim Butcher's wizard-for-hire Harry Dresden became involved with murders in the porn movie business in *Blood Rites*, the sixth book in "The Dresden Files" series.

Charlaine Harris' telepathic waitress Sookie Stackhouse went looking for her missing brother with the help of vampires, were-wolves and Wiccans (oh, my!) in the author's fourth Southern vampire mystery, *Dead to the World*. Harris also had new stories about the character in the anthologies *Powers of Detection* edited by

Dana Stabenow, which featured contributions from Simon R. Green, Anne Bishop and Laura Anne Gilman, and in *Night's Edge*, along with Barbara Hambly and Maggie Shayne.

In Andrew Fox's *Bride of the Fat White Vampire*, a comedic sequel to his first novel, reassembled New Orleans vampire Jules was recruited to hunt down a serial killer preying on the undead. Katherine Ramsland's *The Blood Hunters* was a sequel to the author's *The Heat Seekers*, while *Blood Retribution* by David Thurlo and Aimée Thurlo was the second volume featuring vampire Navajo policeman Lee Nez.

E.E. Knight's "The Vampire Earth" series continued with Book Two, *Choice of the Cat*, while *Thief of Lives* and *Sister of the Dead* were Barb Hendee and J.C. Hendee's sequels to the bestselling *Dhampir*.

Kiss of the Night and *Night Play* were the fourth and fifth volumes, respectively, in the "Dark-Hunters" series by Sherrilyn Kenyon (a.k.a. "Kinley MacGregor"). Both titles were also available in hardcover from the Science Fiction Book Club.

Siege Perilous by actor Nigel Bennett and P.N. Elrod was the fourth volume in the series about a vampiric Lancelot in contemporary Canada, and *Blood Red Dawn* was the seventh book in Karen E. Taylor's "Vampire Legacy" series.

Vampires had taken over the world in David Sosnowski's *Vamped*, in which the undead Martin Kowalski put aside his suicidal tendencies to adopt a mortal daughter. A tough female vampire and a cop teamed up in *Urban Legend* by the unlikely-named Erica Orloff, a vampiric Marquis confronted New Orleans voodoo queen Marie Laveau in Mary Ann Mitchell's *The Vampire De Sade*, and Michael Cross' *After Human* featured more bloodsuckers.

A female hitchhiker encountered a truck-driving serial killer vampire in Edo van Belkom's *Blood Road*. Michael Romkey's *American Gothic* was about American Civil War soldiers turned into vampires, Andrew Niederman's *Deficiency* featured a vitamin vampire, and *The Fraternity* by Stephen Gresham was about a pair of rival undead fraternities.

"Edited" by Allen C. Kupfer, *The Journal of Professor Abraham Van Helsing* was packaged by Bill Fawcett & Associates.

Lynsay Sands' *Love Bites*, a prequel to *Single White Vampire*, was a vampire romance about an undead video game designer and a Toronto coroner stalked by a crazed vampire-slayer.

Chick-lit mixed with the undead in Mary Janice Davidson's *Undead and Unwed*, the first in a series featuring shopping and sucking vampire Betsy Taylor. The character was back in the sequel, *Undead and Unemployed*. There was more of the same in Katie MacAlister's *Sex and the Single Vampire*, when fledgling psychic Allegra Telford discovered that she may be the soul-mate of an arrogant English vampire.

I Thirst for You was Susan Sizemore's vampire romance sequel to *I Burn for You*, while *Dark Destiny* was the latest in Christine Feehan's romantic series about Carpathian vampire hunters.

The second and third volumes in the "Vampire Huntress Legend" series by "L.A. Banks" (Leslie Esdale Banks), *The Awakening* and *The Hunted*, were optimistically billed as "*Blade* meets *Buffy!*"

In "Maggie Shayne's" (Margaret Benson) "Wings in the Night" romance *Edge of Twilight*, a vampire was out for revenge. *Twilight Begins* was an omnibus of Shayne's earlier novels, *Twilight Phantasies* (1993) and *Twilight Memories* (1994).

A government agent seduced a vampire descended from the Knights of the Round Table in Angela Knight's *Master of the Night*, Ria Dimitra's *Fiend Angelical* was a vampire romance from Ragnell Press, and there were more romantic bloodsuckers in *A Whisper of Eternity* by Amanda Ashley.

Despite praise from Caitlín R. Kiernan, Nancy Kilpatrick and Michael Rowe, Patrick Califia's *Mortal Companion* was an erotic novel about bi-sexual vampires that bordered on the pornographic.

Wendy Swanscombe's *Vamp* was a sexually explicit version of *Dracula*, as told through the diaries of Jonathan Harker. Lisette Ashton's *Faith* was the first volume in the erotic "Bloodlust Chronicles" trilogy, while Derek McCormack's *The Haunted Hillbilly* was a humorous story about a gay vampire who controlled the career of a country music singer.

Edited by Angela C. Allen, *Dark Thirst* was an anthology of six vampire stories by African-American writers, while *Midnight Thirsts* from Kensington contained four erotic gay vampire stories by Greg Herren, Michael Thomas Ford, Timothy Ridge and Sean Wolfe.

Immortal Bad Boys included three vampire romance novellas by Rebecca York, Rosemary Laurey and Linda Thomas-Sundstrom, and *Cravings* collected four sensuous supernatural romance stories by Laurell K. Hamilton (a new "Anita Blake" novel extract), Mary Janice Davidson and Eileen Wilks (both humourous), and Rebecca York (a werewolf mystery).

Hot Blooded featured four erotic vampire and werewolf stories by Christine Feehan, Maggie Shayne, Emma Holly and Angela Knight.

Hunter's Moon by C.T. Adams and Cathy Clamp was a werewolf romance involving a lycanthropic hit man who became involved with his target. San Diego homicide detective Lily Yu investigated the killing of a werewolf in Eileen Wilks' *Tempting Danger*, and David A. Page's mystery novel *Surviving Frank* was about a werewolf detective in Boston.

A forest ranger discovered that orphan wolf cubs turned out to be shape-shifters in Edo van Belkom's young adult novel *Wolf Pack*, while Stephen Cole's *The Wereling: Resurrection* was the third book in another YA series. Michelle Paver's *Wolf Brother* was the first volume in the "Chronicles of Ancient Darkness".

Set in New York City in 1919, Sir Arthur Conan Doyle, Harry Houdini, H.P. Lovecraft and voodoo priestess Marie Laveau comprised the eponymous secret group of investigators on the trail of a serial killer and a mysterious tome in screenwriter Thomas Wheeler's debut novel *The Arcanum*.

A serial killer stalked those who could communicate with the dead in Stephen Woodworth's first novel, *Through Violet Eyes*. A tie-in competition web site included a game based on the book and a sequel, *With Red Hands*, followed.

Dan Vining's first novel *The Quick* was a supernatural mystery set in Hollywood. An unemployed Californian woman turned out to be the incarnation of the goddess Kali in Sonia Singh's debut novel *Goddess for Hire*, while a group of mages in San Francisco used magic to battle sunbathing zombies and other monsters in Stephan Zielinski's offbeat debut, *Bad Magic*.

From Jonathan Cape/Harcourt, *The Ghost Writer* by John Harwood was another first novel, about a man who grew up in Australia and discovered clues to his English family's past in a lost manuscript written by his great-grandmother.

In Jonathan Aycliffe's *The Garden Lost in Time*, an old man looked back on his stay at a haunted Cornish manor.

A young boy was taken to a maze-like library of obscure books hidden away in Barcelona's Old City, where he had to adopt a title for life, in Carlos Ruiz Zafon's literary mystery *The Shadow of the Wind*.

The ghost of a murdered woman observed her family through the ages in Neil Jordan's *Shade*, and a man's spirit had to discover why he died before it could find rest in Glen Duncan's *Death of an Ordinary Man*. Narrated by ghosts, Stewart O'Nan's *The Night Country* was a Halloween tale set in a small Connecticut town that owed more than a passing nod to Ray Bradbury's *Something Wicked This Way Comes*.

A Kansas farmgirl named Oz was raised by the walking dead in Wylene Dunbar's *My Life With Corpses*, expanded from the short story of the same title.

In James Hynes' satirical horror novel *Kings of Infinite Space*, a man was haunted by a ghostly cat, amongst other things, while a decapitated corpse returned to life in Percival Everett's satirical novel *American Desert*.

Wakefield was a modern deal-with-the-Devil story by Andrei Codrescu, and an ancient evil waited beneath a Kentucky college town in Robert Wayne McCoy's *The King of Ice Cream*.

With an Introduction by Wesley Stace, *The Haunted House* was a classic collaborative ghost story written between Charles Dickens, Elizabeth Gaskell, Wilkie Collins and others. Collins' own *Sensation Stories: Tales of Mystery and Suspense* was edited with an Introduction by Peter Haining.

Published as part of the "Norton Critical Editions" series, *The Selected Writings of Edgar Allan Poe* contained thirty-three stories, thirty-one poems and a number of non-fiction pieces by and about Poe.

From the University of Nebraska Press/Bison Books, *The Nightmare and Other Tales of Dark Fantasy* collected eight short stories (1917–23) by Francis Stevens, edited and with an Introduction by Gary Hoppenstand and illustrated by Thomas L. Floyd.

Edited with an Introduction and notes by S.T. Joshi for Penguin Classics, *The Dreams in the Witch House and Other Weird Stories* collected twenty-one stories by H.P. Lovecraft, two from newly-discovered manuscripts.

Red Jacket Press launched a series of deluxe facsimile reprints of Gnome Press books with C.L. Moore's classic collection *Judgment Night* and Wilmar Shiras' science fiction novel *Children of the Atom*. Each volume was a reproduction of the original first edition, including colour dust jacket art, issued in an illustrated slipcase.

Edited with an Introduction by Vigen Guroian, *Ancestral Shadows* collected nineteen ghost stories and an essay by Russell Kirk.

Hugh Lamb's 1979 anthology *Tales from a Gas-Lit Graveyard* was reprinted by Dover in an attractive trade paperback edition. It contained seventeen obscure stories by Mrs J.H. Riddell, Ambrose Bierce, Richard Marsh, Guy Boothby, Bernard Capes and others.

Wildside Press reissued the late Hugh B. Cave's superb 1977

retrospective collection *Murgunstrumm & Others* in both hardcover and trade paperback, retaining the original illustrations by Lee Brown Coye.

Wormwood was the second young adult Gothic adventure by former vicar G.P. Taylor. It involved an eighteenth century scientist and his housemaid attempting to recover an ancient book of magic. Forty-five-year-old Taylor, whose first book *Shadowmancer* was originally self-published and went on to sell 300,000 copies in the UK alone, reportedly signed a £3.5 million deal for his next six novels with Putnam in America and British imprint Faber & Faber. Unfortunately for the author, he watched the only updated manuscript of his unpublished third novel, *Tersias*, go up in flames after he accidentally threw it on a bonfire while moving house in October. The manuscripts for Taylor's first two books were also destroyed by the fire.

Terry Pratchett's loveable Granny Weatherwax was forced to intervene in Tiffany Aching's attempts to become a witch in *A Hat Full of Sky*, a sequel to *The Wee Free Men*. Even Death made a cameo appearance.

A destructive relationship between a teenage girl and a homeless boy was at the heart of Kathe Koja's novella *The Blue Mirror*, which featured cover art by the author's husband, Rick Lieder.

A girl could see phantoms thanks to a magic feather in Zilpha Keatley Snyder's *The Unseen*, there was something in the water in Joseph Bruchac's *The Dark Pond*, and a boy lost his reflection to a ghostly double in James Lincoln Collier's *The Empty Mirror*.

A creepy dollhouse was at the centre of *Sweet Miss Honeywell's Revenge* by Kathryn Reiss, three teenagers developed supernatural powers in Melinda Metz's *Raven's Point*, and *The Old Willis Place* was a ghost story aimed at youngsters by Mary Downing Hahn.

Teenage outsiders lived through a "missing" 25th hour in the day in Scott Westerfeld's *Midnighters: The Secret Hour*, the first volume in a new packaged trilogy. Meanwhile, a man discovered that someone else was living his life in a parallel world in Michael Lawrence's *A Crack in the Line*, the first book in the "Aldous Lexicon" trilogy.

R.L. Stine's *Eye Candy* was a new non-supernatural horror novel, while the author's *Dangerous Girls 2: The Taste of Night* was the second volume in the vampire series about twin girls. *Vampire Plagues: London* was the first in a new series by the pseudonymous "Sebastian Rook".

Lord of the Shadows and *Sons of Destiny* were the eleventh and concluding twelfth volumes, respectively, in *The Saga of Darren Shan*, pseudonymously written by Darren O'Shaughnessy. *The Saga of Darren Shan: Vampire Rites Trilogy* was an omnibus of volumes four through six.

In Libba Bray's *A Great and Terrible Beauty*, an English teenager raised in India discovered she had supernatural powers at a London boarding school. James A. Moore's *Newbies* revolved around a series of mysterious disappearances at school, while a girl and her younger uncle found themselves in a haunted school in Edward Bloor's *Story Time*,

A boy granted immortality through voodoo magic began killing others in William Sleator's *The Boy Who Couldn't Die*. Children with psychic powers attempted to save humanity from parasitic creatures in Eoin Colfer's *The Supernaturalist*, and Charles Butler's *The Fetch of Mardy Watt* was another supernatural thriller.

The Ghost of Cutler Creek was the third in the mystery series by Cynthia DeFelice, about a girl who attracts phantoms, and *The Mediator 6: Twilight* by Meg Cabot (a.k.a. "Jenny Carroll") continued the series about a girl who had the ability to talk with the dead.

A boy's Christmas break took an unexpected turn in Anna Dale's *Whispering to Witches*, while *Summer* and *Fall* were the first and second volumes, respectively, in the *Witch Season* quartet by Jeff Mariotte. The *T*witches* series by H.B. Gilmour and Randi Reisfeld continued with #10: *Destiny's Twins*.

From Scholastic's "Point Horror" series, Samantha Lee's *Demon II* continued the story of the Dreamcatcher that granted wishes – but at a price. Linda Cargill's *The Dark 2* appeared from the same imprint.

E. Nesbit's 1902 novel *Five Children and It* was repackaged with a charm necklace.

Double-Dare to Be Scared: Another Thirteen Chilling Tales was published by Cricket books and was a follow-up to author Robert D. San Souci's acclaimed collection *Dare to be Scared*. Featuring young adult stories with a decidely nasty twist, the book was again elegantly illustrated by David Ouimet.

Published by Allen & Unwin Australia, the award-winning *Black Juice* contained ten original young adult stories by Margo Lanagan and was a companion volume to the author's earlier collection *White Time*.

The Ribbajack and Other Curious Yarns collected six young adult horror stories by Brian Jacques.

Edited by Deborah Noyes, *Gothic! Ten Original Dark Tales*

included stories by Neil Gaiman, Joan Aiken and Garth Nix, illustrated by Gary Kelley.

Nightshape collected eight reprint horror stories by David Morrell with an Introduction by the author.

Fears Unnamed was a collection of four novellas by Tim Lebbon that comprised the modern classic "White", "The Unfortunate", "Naming of Parts" and "Remnants", a new story involving the search for a subterranean City of the Dead.

Nightworlds collected twenty-two stories by William F. Nolan with notes by the author. Issued under White Wolf's Two Wolf Press imprint, Nancy A. Collins' *Dead Man's Hand: Five Tales of the Weird West* included an original vampire novella, "Hell Come Sundown", and a Foreword by Joe R. Lansdale (his ownself).

John Connolly's *Nocturnes* was a collection of fifteen short stories, framed by the novellas "The Reflecting Eye" (featuring the author's recurring private detective character Charlie Parker) and "The Cancer Cowboy Rides Again". Some of the stories were reworked from two series broadcast on BBC Radio 4, and publisher Hodder & Stoughton issued an advance sampler containing three of the stories from the collection.

Blackbird House collected twelve linked stories about the eponymous haunted edifice by Alice Hoffman.

A Walk on the Darkside: Visions of Horror was the third volume in editor John Pelan's series of paperback anthologies from Roc. It contained twenty-one original stories by Don Tumasonis, Mark Samuels, Paul Finch, d.g.k. goldberg, Michael Shea, Jeffrey Thomas, Brian Keene, Tom Piccirilli, Caitlín R. Kiernan, Brian Hodge, Brian A. Hopkins, Steve Rasnic Tem and others, including the editor.

Strange Bedfellows was the twelfth volume in "The Hot Blood Series" edited by Jeff Gelb and Michael Garrett. It contained nineteen explicit erotic horror stories by Greg Kihn, Del Howison, Michael Laimo, Christa Faust, Alan Ormsby, Marv Wofman, Michael Garrett, Graham Masterton and others. Both editors featured their own work.

Edited by Jeanne Cavelos and obviously intended to cash-in on the hoped-for success of the Universal film release, *The Many Faces of Van Helsing* collected twenty-one original stories about the legendary vampire-hunter by Thomas Tessier, Kathe Koja, Tanith Lee, Thomas F. Monteleone, Nina Kiriki Hoffman, Brian Hodge and others.

Great Ghost Stories edited by the late R. Chetwynd-Hayes and Stephen Jones showcased twenty-five stories from the classic Fontana paperback series of the 1970s and 1980s. With a Foreword by Jones and an Introduction by Chetwynd-Hayes, the book included stories by Ambrose Bierce, J. Sheridan Le Fanu, F. Marion Crawford, E. Nesbit, Sydney J. Bounds, Stephen King, Steve Rasnic Tem, Ramsey Campbell, Tina Rath, Garry Kilworth, Guy De Maupassant, Brian Lumley, Tony Richards and Chetwynd-Hayes himself and quickly went into a second trade paperback printing from Carroll & Graf. Cemetery Dance also issued a hardcover edition with a Les Edwards cover and illustrated endpapers by Caniglia.

Also edited by Stephen Jones, and a follow-up-of-sorts to a 1991 volume, *The Mammoth Book of New Terror* contained twenty-six stories (four original) by Brian Lumley, Charles L. Grant, Christopher Fowler, Dennis Etchison, F. Paul Wilson, Basil Copper, Ramsey Campbell, Terry Lamsley, R. Chetwynd-Hayes, Karl Edward Wagner, Neil Gaiman, Michael Marshall Smith, Glen Hirshberg, Kim Newman, David Case and many others. A "revamped" edition of Jones' 1992 anthology *The Mammoth Book of Vampires* dropped six stories and a poem and replaced them with thirteen new stories (three original). Both *Mammoth* books were illustrated by Randy Broecker.

Meanwhile, the 1993 anthology *H.P. Lovecraft's Book of Horror* edited by Jones and Dave Carson was reprinted as *The World's Greatest Horror Stories* without the permission or knowledge of the editors.

Edited by Al Sarrantonio, *Flights: Extreme Visions of Fantasy* featured twenty-nine stories, several of which could be considered horror.

Martin H. Greenberg and Russell Davis co-edited *Haunted Holidays*, containing thirteen non-Halloween holiday stories by Nancy Holder, Peter Crowther, Esther Friesner and others.

Edited by Brandon Massey, *Dark Dreams* contained twenty stories of horror, suspense and science fiction by black authors.

McSweeney's Enchanted Chamber of Astonishing Stories, edited by Michael Chabon, included fifteen new stories in various genres by Margaret Atwood, Stephen King, Peter Straub, Roddy Doyle, China Miéville, Poppy Z. Brite, Jonathan Lethem, Joyce Carol Oates and others. The cover reprinted a classic pulp painting by Lawrence Sterne Stevens.

Co-edited by F. Brett Cox and Andy Duncan for Tor Books, *Crossroads: Tales of the Southern Literary Fantastic* was a literary compilation of twenty-five fantasy and horror stories (eleven reprints) set in the American South. Authors included Richard Butner, James Sallis, Gene Wolfe, Scott Edelman, Jack McDevitt, Kelly Link, Don Webb, Michael Bishop, Michael Swanwick, Fred Chappell, Ian McDowell, John Kessel and others, including both editors.

Strokes of Midnight contained four supernatural romance novellas by Amanda Ashley, L.A. Banks, Lori Handeland and Sherrilyn Kenyon, while editor Greg Herren's *Shadows of the Night* from The Haworth Press was aptly subtitled *Queer Tales of the Uncanny and Unusual* and included fifteen nominally gay horror stories.

With *The Year's Best Fantasy and Horror: Seventeenth Annual Collection*, the husband and wife team of Kelly Link and Gavin J. Grant took over from Terry Windling to share the editing chores with the irrepressible Ellen Datlow. The book contained thirty-nine stories, five poems, and various surveys by the editors plus packager James Frenkel, Edward Bryant, Charles Vess, Charles de Lint and Joan D. Vinge.

Edited with an extensive introductory essay by Stephen Jones and a necrology by Jones and Kim Newman, *The Mammoth Book of Best New Horror Volume Fifteen* included twenty-five stories and novellas. The two annual "Best of" anthologies overlapped with five stories, by Marc Laidlaw, Dale Bailey, Scott Emerson Bull, Mike O'Driscoll and Glen Hirshberg.

From Brian A. Hopkins' Lone Wolf Publications, *Carnival* was an electronic anthology edited by Jean Rabe that featured original stories by Robert E. Vardeman, Gene DeWeese, James S. Dorr, John Urbancik and others, along with art by M.W. Anderson and music by John Everson.

Lone Wolf subsequently announced that it was ceasing operations immediately with all future titles cancelled. "I think it's been obvious for quite some time now that my heart was no longer in it," Hopkins was quoted as saying. Founded in 1999, sales figures did not justify his continued investment in Lone Wolf. "Clearly, the genre has little interest in electronic formats," he observed.

Written five years earlier but unable to find a publisher, Douglas Clegg offered his first vampire novel, *Priest of Blood*, only to those who ordered it through an online horror bookstore. It came with the somewhat optimistic restriction that single customers could order no more than five copies each of the $45.00 self-produced hardcover.

Christopher Golden and actress Amber Benson (*Buffy*) teamed up again for *Ghosts of Albion: The Adventures of Tamara Swift* for

BBC Online in November, featuring the talents of Anthony Daniels and Emma Sams, amongst others.

Lindisfarne Press released *The Mlandoth Myth Cycle and Others: The Complete Cthulhu Mythos Tales* of Walter C. DeBill, Jr. edited by Kevin L. O'Brien as an e-book.

Editor Ellen Datlow's online *SciFiction* site featured new stories by Andy Duncan, Marc Laidlaw, Chelsea Quinn Yarbro, Susan Palwick, Howard Waldrop ("The Wolf-man of Alcatraz") and Kim Newman, along with welcome reprints from Tom Reamy, Fredric Brown, Manly Wade Wellman, Theodore Sturgeon, Charles L. Grant and Eric Frank Russell.

The old *Terror Tales* online site, which was taken over by Hertzan Chimera, was renamed *Horror Quarterly*.

Australia's *Shadowed Realms* online magazine announced that it had narrowed its focus to "flash" stories only (up to 1,000 words). The first issue featured fiction from Stephen Dedman, Stephanie Gunn, Kurt Newton and others.

Hellnotes edited by Judi Rohrig, *The HWA's Internet Mailer* edited by Mary SanGiovanni, *The British Fantasy Society Newsfeed* edited by Gary Couzens, and *DarkEcho* edited by Paula Guran all regularly kept readers up-to-date electronically with news, reviews and signing information.

Print-on-demand Prime Books was acquired by Wildside Press as a separate imprint run by Sean Wallace.

By Reason of Darkness was a collection of twenty-three stories (twelve original) by William P. Simmons from Prime/House of Dominion. It featured an Introduction by Gary Braunbeck and an Afterword by T.M. Wright.

From Wildside Press, *Satan's Daughter and Other Tales from the Pulps* was a collection of thirteen stories by veteran author E. Hoffman Price, while *The Maker of Gargoyles and Other Stories* contained seven tales by Clark Ashton Smith. Both PoD books had introductions by Darrell Schweitzer.

Fritz Leiber and H.P. Lovecraft: Writers of the Dark collected letters, essays, stories and a poem illustrating HPL's influence on Leiber's writing. Ben J.S. Szumskyj supplied an Introduction and the Afterword was by S.T. Joshi.

Paul G. Tremblay's *Compositions for the Young and Old* collected twenty stories (seven original).

On a lighter note from Wildside, *That Darn Squid God* by Nick Pollotta and "James Clay" (Phil Foglio) was a Victorian-set parody of Lovecraft, H.G. Wells, Jules Verne and others. Pollotta's series of *Bureau 13* books, based on the roleplaying game, were also reissued by the publisher.

Richard A. Lupoff's 1978 Oriental novel of the supernatural, *Sword of the Demon*, was reissued by Wildside's Cosmos Books imprint in an attractive print-on-demand edition. Cosmos also continued to put out new issues of Philip Harbottle's *Fantasy Adventures*, a tribute to the British pulp magazines of the past, with original stories from such old hands as Sydney J. Bounds, E.C. Tubb, Brian Ball, John Glasby, Philip E. High, John Russell Fearn and others.

The Worm in Every Heart collected fifteen stories (three original) by Gemma Files, along with an Introduction by Nancy Kilpatrick and an Afterword in which the author interviewed herself. Also from Wildside, Jay Lake's *Dogs in the Moonlight* contained sixteen stories (seven original) from the John W. Campbell Award-winning author, with an Introduction by Ray Vukcevich.

From Hippocampus Press, S.T. Joshi's *Primal Sources: Essays on H.P. Lovecraft* collected twenty-three articles, most of them originally published in *Crypt of Cthulhu* or *Lovecraft Studies*.

Two volumes of the *Collected Essays of H.P. Lovecraft*, covering *Amateur Journalism* and *Literary Criticism* contained nearly 200 pieces of non-fiction between them, edited with notes by Joshi.

Again edited by Joshi with David E. Schultz, *Out of the Immortal Night* collected 6 stories, nearly 200 poems and 14 essays by Lovecraft's associate Samuel Loveman.

Joshi's seminal *The Evolution of the Weird Tale* was reissued by Hippocampus in a new edition with revised essays on eighteen authors, including Fritz Leiber, Poppy Z. Brite, Robert W. Chambers and, of course, Lovecraft.

Algernon Blackwood's 1914 collection *Incredible Adventures* was reprinted as part of Hippocampus' "Lovecraft's Library" series with an Introduction by Joshi, who also introduced *The Sword of Zagan and Other Writings*, a collection of ten previously-unpublished early stories, fourteen poems and nine fragments by Clark Ashton Smith, edited by Dr W.C. Farmer and illustrated by Jason C. Eckhardt.

Edited by Kevin L. O'Brien, *Eldritch Blues: Love & Sex in the Cthulhu Mythos* was a print-on-demand anthology of twenty erotic Lovecraftian stories and a poem by HPL, Ramsey Campbell, Stephen Mark Rainey and others, along with an Introduction by Robert M. Price. It was published by Lindisfarne Press/Cairnsford Tome.

From Rainfall Books, editors John B. Ford and Paul Kane followed up the first edition of their revived *Terror Tales* anthology with a second volume featuring work from Michael Marshall Smith, Paul Finch, Stephen Gallagher, Gemma Files, Jeffrey Thomas and John Skipp (a novel extract), along with a look at James Herbert's work and an interview with Earthing Publications founder Paul Miller.

Also published by Rainfall, Sue Phillips' *The Waldorf Street Paradox* contained ten stories (seven reprints) illustrated by Karl Owens. Published in 200 trade paperback copies, *Charnel Wine* collected twenty-three short stories (eighteen reprints) by Richard Gavin with an Introduction by John B. Ford and illustrations by Steve Lines, while Lines also illustrated Ford's Sargasso Sea novella *The Haunted Ocean*, published in an edition of just 100 hardcover copies.

Published by California's Friendly Firewalk Press, *Conscience* by former "splatterpunk" John Skipp contained the short serial killer novel of the title, along with six short stories and an unproduced film script.

The prolific Steve Burt followed his PoD young adult collections *Odd Lot* and *Even Odder* with *Oddest Yet: Even More Stories to Chill the Heart*, containing eight stories and a subtle ghost novella, illustrated by Jessica Hagerman.

Edited by Garrett Peck and Keith Gouveia, *Small Bites* from Canada's Coscom Entertainment contained almost 200 mostly original short-short stories involving zombies, animal attacks and were-creatures by Mark McLaughlin, Wayne Allen Sallee, Scott Nicholson, Edward Lee, Lois Tilton, Nancy Kilpatrick, Simon Clark, Graham Masterton, Michael Arnzen, Tim Lebbon, F. Paul Wilson, Rick Hautala, Christopher Golden, Kealan Patrick Burke, Karen E. Taylor, Charles Gramlich and numerous others. Proceeds from the sale of the book were donated to the medical fund established for writer Charles L. Grant.

From Wheatland Press, *American Sorrows* contained four long stories (two original) by Jay Lake, with an Introduction by James Van Pelt. Edited by Lake and Deborah Layne, *Polyphony Volume 4* featured twenty-four original "slipstream" stories by Lucius Shepard, Jeff VanderMeer, Michael Bishop, Bruce Holland Rogers, Ray Vukcevich and others.

Thirteen Ways to Water collected a baker's dozen of stories by Bruce Holland Rogers and was jointly published in trade paperback by Wheatland Press and Panisphere Books & Audio. It was apparently the author's first print collection.

All-Star Zeppelin Stories edited by David Moles and Jay Lake was co-published by Wheatland and All-Star Stories and contained twenty stories (one reprint) by Howard Waldrop, Richard A. Lupoff, James Van Pelt, Leslie What, David Brin and others.

Paula Guran launched her new Infrapress imprint with two worthwhile PoD paperback reprints from the now-defunct Stealth Press: Peter Atkins' serial-killer novel *Morningstar* and Dennis Etchison's celebratory collection *Talking in the Dark*.

J.F. Gonzalez's novel *Survivor* was expanded from the author's novella "Maternal Instinct" and available from Midnight Library, while Egerton House published John Kaiine's novel *Fossil Circus*, which was set in a Victorian asylum.

Meisha Merlin Publishing began distributing books published by Marietta Publishing. Both Atlanta-based imprints were founded in 1996. Former punk musician Stephen L. Antczak's novel *God Drug* came from Marietta with a cover quote by Michael Moorcock and was nicely illustrated by Andy Lee. *Underground Atlanta*, from the same imprint, collected twenty-three stories by Gregory Nicoll. Four were original to the book, and another appeared in its complete form for the first time.

From Canada's Double Dragon Publishing, *Scary! Holiday Tales to Make You Scream* edited by Paul Melniczek featured twenty-nine stories about different holidays by Michael A. Arnzen, Quentin S. Crisp and others.

Bulletproof Soul contained twenty tales by Steven L. Shrewsbury featuring albino covert agent Dick Shannon. Published by KHP Industries/Black Death Books, most of the stories had previously been published online. Philip Henry's novel *Vampire Dawn* was available from the same publisher, as was Michael McBride's lazily-titled *Species*, T.M. Gray's *The Ravenous* and Drew Williams' *Art & Becoming*, the latter with an Introduction by Joe Nassise.

From Stark Publishing, *One Hand Screaming* collected sixteen stories (three original) and seven poems by Mark Leslie (Mark Leslie Lefebvre).

A Dirge for the Temporal from Raw Dog Screaming collected thirty-four stories (eleven original) by Darren Speegle. From the same imprint, *100 Jolts: Shockingly Short Stories* collected 100 short-short stories (forty-seven original) by Michael A. Arnzen, along with an interview with the author.

Everybody Scream! was a new "Punktown" novel by Jeffrey Thomas, Ronald Damien Malfi's *The Fall of Never* involved a young woman's estranged family and a suppressed memory, while *Last*

Burn in Hell by John Edward Lawson was a surreal and sexy look into one man's complicated life.

Sick: An Anthology of Illness edited by John Edward Lawson from Raw Dog contained thirty-six "existential splatterpunk" stories (eleven reprints) from C.J. Henderson, Jeffrey Thomas, Michael A. Arnzen, Mark McLaughlin, Kurt Newton and others.

From the same print-on-demand imprint, Kevin L. Donihe edited volumes #5 and #6 of his *Bare Bones* anthology series, which contained mostly new fiction and poetry by Trey R. Barker, Kurt Newton, James S. Dorr, Donald R. Burleson, Gary Fry, Don Webb, Dareen Speegle, C.J. Henderson, Steve Rasnic Tem, Charlee Jacob, Mark McLaughlin, Michael A. Arnzen and numerous others.

James C. Glass' first collection, *Matrix Dreams & Other Stories*, was published by Fairwood Press and contained twenty-one reprint stories along with an Introduction by John Dalmas.

Something in a river devoured its victims in Elizabeth Blue's *Drown in Fear*, from PublishAmerica, while William Pillow's *Grave Convictions* from Gate Way Press was a murder mystery involving reincarnation.

Edited by Frank J. Morlock, *Lord Ruthven the Vampire* from Black Coat Press featured Lord Byron's fragment, two French plays and an original story about Ruthven, Dracula and Sherlock Holmes. *The Return of Lord Ruthven* from the same PoD imprint and editor contained Alexandre Dumas' 1851 play *Le Vampire* and a new story in which Ruthven and Dumas met in Paris.

The Scaffold and Other Cruel Tales and *The Vampire Soul and Other Sardonic Tales* were two collections from Black Coat of stories by Villiers de l'Isle-Adam, translated from the French with notes and Introductions by Brian Stableford. *Artahe: The Legacy of Jules de Grandin* was about the grandson of Seabury Quinn's supernatural detective. Written by "Phillipe Ward" (Phillipe Laguerre), it was translated by David Kirshbaum from the 1997 French novel *Artahe*.

From the same imprint, Donald Sidney-Fryer adapted and translated French poet Aloysius Bertrand's 1842 book of macabre prose ballads *Gaspard de la nuit*. The paperback included an extensive Introduction and Afterward by Sidney-Fryer, a Foreword by T.E.D. Klein, cover illustration by Gahan Wilson and interior illustrations by Bertrand himself. The book was also available in a collector's edition.

From Colorado's Centipede Press, Stephen King's *Salem's Lot* was a signed and numbered slipcased edition limited to just 315 copies for

$470.00. Along with the original novel, it featured fifty pages of alternative manuscript material, the short stories "One for the Road" and "Jerusalem's Lot", photographic illustrations by Jerry Uelsmann, and an Afterword by the author.

Peter Schneider and Peter Atkins' revived Hill House imprint reissued Neil Gaiman's award-winning 2001 novel *American Gods* as "The Author's Preferred Edition" with an additional 12,000 words in a handsome signed, slipcased numbered edition limited to 750 copies. A fifty-two-copy lettered edition was also available. Subscribers also received a free matching numbered trade paperback "Reader's Copy", a signed hardcover of *A Screenplay* (for *Good Omens*) by Gaiman limited to 500 numbered and fifty-two lettered copies, and *The Christmas Booklet*, a chapbook story by Gaiman that was originally written as part of the novel, limited to a 500-copy signed edition.

Also issued as a "Christmas card" by Hill House in an edition of just 400 copies, Gaiman's short apocalyptic poem *Melinda* was a beautifully designed hardcover, profusely illustrated with black and white art and tipped-in colour plates by Dagmara Matuszak.

In Adam L.G. Nevill's *Banquet for the Damned* from Peter Crowther's PS Publishing, a dark magic returned to the Mediaeval streets of a Scottish town. It boasted an Introduction by Ramsey Cambell.

Campbell's own new supernatural novel, *The Overnight*, appeared from PS with an Introduction by Mark Morris. It was set in a failing bookshop built in a haunted business park, where the employees were menaced by a malevolent fog.

Stephen Gallagher's collection *Out of His Mind* contained eighteen stories (one original) and three novelettes along with a brief Introduction by scriptwriter Brian Clemens and an Afterword and notes by Gallagher.

Trujillo was a hefty new collection of eleven novellas (including the titular original) by Lucius Shepard with an Introduction by Michael Swanwick.

All PS hardcovers were published in signed and numbered editions of 500 copies and 200-copy deluxe slipcased editions signed by all the contributors.

In the PS novella series, a writer discovered that her life was inextricably linked with that of an old woman whose biography she was writing in Lisa Tuttle's elegant and elliptical ghost story, *My Death*, introduced by Thomas Tessier. Featuring a fantastic array of were-creatures in a post-Apocalyptic Britain, Tim Lebbon's

Changing of Faces was a sequel to his zombie novella *Naming of Parts*, with an Introduction by Simon Clark. Introduced by Mark Chadbourn, Gary Greenwood's novella *Jigsaw Men* was a detective mystery set in a world of the reanimated dead where Shelley's Frankenstein created his Monster, Wells' Martians invaded Earth and the British Empire still existed, while Paul Park's *No Traveller Returns* was set in the afterlife and had an Introduction by Elizabeth Hand. All PS novellas were published in signed and numbered trade paperback editions of 500 copies and 300-copy hardcover editions.

From Richard Chizmar's Cemetery Dance Publications, *Madman Stan and Other Stories* collected twenty stories by Richard Laymon with a very brief Introduction by Stanley Wiater and an Afterword by Leisure editor Don D'Auria. Bizarrely, none of the reprint stories carried individual copyright information and the author notes read as if Laymon – who died in 2001 – was still alive and writing.

Available in a deluxe hardcover edition, *Fearful Symmetries* was the second CD collection by Thomas F. Monteleone, containing twenty-six reprint horror stories, a Foreword by the author and an Introduction by Rick Hautala.

Ray Garton's *Scissors* was a new novel about child abuse, while his 1991 erotic novel *The New Neighbor* was finally issued in an affordable hardcover edition. Both books were published in deluxe editions limited to 1,000 signed copies.

Edited by Richard Chizmar, *Shivers III* was the latest volume in CD's trade paperback anthology series containing eighteen original stories by Thomas F. Monteleone, Douglas Clegg, Elizabeth Massie, Al Sarrantonio, Tom Piccirilli, Edward Lee, John Maclay and others, including a collaboration between F. Paul Wilson and his daughter Meggan.

The Devil's Wine edited by Tom Piccirilli was an anthology of dark poetry by Stephen King, Ray Bradbury, Peter Straub, Graham Masterton, Steve Rasnic Tem, Peter Crowther, Brian Hodge, Elizabeth Massie and many others (including far too much by the editor himself), published in an attractive hardcover edition by Cemetery Dance and illustrated by Caniglia.

Although written twenty-five years earlier, the Sarob Press edition of Basil Copper's *Solar Pons versus The Devil's Claw* marked the short novel's first publication anywhere in the world. With a historical Introduction from the late Conan Doyle expert Richard Lancelyn Green and wraparound dust jacket art by Les Edwards, the small-sized limited edition hardcover was also available in a signed and slipcased deluxe edition of just fifty copies.

Also from Sarob, Tony Richards' *Postcards from Terri* was a supernatural novella about a modern haunting, introduced by Ramsey Campbell. It was published in an edition of 210 limited hardcovers and a forty-copy deluxe signed and slipcased version.

From the same imprint, Paul Finch's *Darker Ages* contained two historical horror novellas set in Viking times, along with an Introduction by Mike Ashley. *Howling Hounds: The Haunting Tales of Phil Locascio* collected thirteen stories (nine reprints). Both were published in limited editions and forty-copy deluxe signed hardcovers.

Falling Into Heaven collected fourteen stories (ten original) by L. H. Maynard and M.P.N. Sims with an Introduction by William P. Simmons. It was also available in hardcover and as a signed and slipcased deluxe edition limited to forty copies.

Published especially for Halloween by Paul Miller's Earthling Publications, Glen Hirshberg's haunted house novella *Mr Dark's Carnival* was reprinted with a new Introduction by the author in a fifteen-copy quarter leatherbound hardcover that sold out within three hours of being announced, and as a forty-two copy numbered presentation chapbook.

James Newman's debut novel *Midnight Train*, a coming-of-age serial killer tale set in the 1970s, was published by Earthling in a 250-copy signed and numbered hardcover edition and a lettered and slipcased edition of ten copies, with a Foreword by Ed Gorman, an Afterword by the author, and illustrations by Alex McVey.

Apocalypse Now, Voyager by Jay Russell was the latest adventure of occasional detective Marty Burns, who teamed up with a crazy street woman and a man who thought he was a dog for a surreal journey up the Los Angeles River without a paddle. It was available as a 400-copy numbered softcover and fifteen lettered hardcovers, with art by J.K. Potter.

Conrad Williams' *Game* was a novella about a woman who could see various possible futures. It was also available as a signed, fifteen-copy slipcased leatherbound edition.

The fourth volume of D.F. Lewis' *Nemonymous: A Megazanthus for Parthenogenetic Fiction and Late-Labelling* contained seventeen more anonymous stories and revealed that contributors to the previous edition had included Brendan Connell, Lavie Tidhar, Joe Murphy, Monica O'Rourke, Len Maynard and Mick Sims, Rhys Hughes, David Mathew and others.

Elvisland was a welcome new collection of thirteen stories (three original) by John Farris, published by California's Babbage Press. The same imprint was also responsible for *Crypt Orchids*, a reprint of David J. Schow's 1997 collection with an additional Afterword by the author.

Andrew Hook's Elastic Press published *The Alsiso Project*, an anthology of twenty-three stories all with the typo title "Alsiso" written by K.J. Bishop, Justina Robson, Christopher Kenworthy, Allen Ashley, Nicholas Royle, Steve Savile, John Grant, Gary Couzens, Conrad Williams and others (including editor Hook), along with an Introduction by Christopher Fowler. From the same imprint came Allen Ashley's collection *Somnabulists*.

Edited by Tina L. Jens and John Everson for Twilight Tales, *Spooks!* was an attractive-looking anthology of twenty-five stories (eight reprints), two poems, a haiku and an interview by Jay Bonansinga, Charlee Jacob, Maria Alexander, James S. Dorr, Viki S. Rollins, Janet L. Hetherington, Laura Anne Gillman, Jody Lynn Nye, Lawrence Schimel and others, including both editors.

Coming with glowing quotes from Peter Straub, Poppy Z. Brite, F. Paul Wilson, Norman Patridge, Peter Crowther and Forrest J Ackerman, Twilight Tales also presented an expanded edition of Martin Mundt's 1999 collection *The Crawling Abattoir*, containing thirteen stories (four original) and an Introduction by Jay Bonansinga.

Published in trade paperback by iUniverse, *Beyond Reason: 11 Dark Stories of Human Discovery* collected new tales by California writer E.A. Salisbury.

Tom and Elizabeth Monteleone's Borderlands Press had a busy year with signed and numbered editions of Peter Straub's novels *In the Night Room* and its companion volume *lost boy lost girl* limited to just 350 copies each, with the twenty-six lettered editions sold out before publication.

Borderlands continued its reprint of F. Paul Wilson's "The Adversary Cycle" with *The Touch* and *The Tomb*, featuring a spine mural by Caniglia, while a hardcover of Tim Lebbon's collection *Fears Unnamed* was limited to 350 signed and numbered copies.

A Little Purple Book of Peculiar Stories by Craig Shaw Gardner, *A Little Blue Book of Rose Stories* by Peter Straub, *A Little Gray Book of Alien Stories* by John DeChancie and *A Little Brown Book of Bizarre Stories* by Thomas F. Monteleone were limited to 500 signed and numbered copies apiece.

Also from Borderlands, the *12 Scary Guys Calendar* featured Peter Straub (Mr January), Graham Joyce (Mr February), Geoff Cooper

(Mr March), Thomas F. Monteleone (Mr April), F. Paul Wilson (Mr May), Rick Hautala (Mr June), Douglas E. Winter (Mr July), Kealan Patrick Burke (Mr August), Richard Chizmar (Mr September), Jon F. Merz (Mr October), Jack Ketchum (Mr November) and Stephen King (Mr December).

From Small Beer Press, Sean Stewart's *Perfect Circle* was about an unemployed man whose life was complicated by ghosts.

San Francisco's Tachyon Publications issued Suzy McKee Charnas' first print collection, *Stagestruck Vampires & Other Phantasms*, as an attractive trade paperback featuring eight reprint stories and two original essays, with an Introduction from Paul Di Filippo and cover art by John Picacio. From the same publisher, *Stable Strategies and Others* collected twelve stories by Eileen Gunn along with introductions by William Gibson and the author, a poem by Michael Swanwick and an Afterword by Howard Waldrop.

Bumper Crop from Golden Gryphon was a collection of twenty-six "best" stories by Joe R. Lansdale, selected with a Foreword by the author. With an Introduction by Jeffrey Ford, *Secret Life* was another attractive "best" collection, containing twenty-three tales (three original) by Jeff VanderMeer, including a new story set in the author's fictional world of Ambergris. In the UK, the author's earlier Ambergris collection, *City of Saints & Madmen*, was reprinted in a "definitive" version by Tor that added two new stories.

Breathmoss and Other Exhalations collected seven long stories and an Introduction by Ian R. MacLeod. The 100-copy limited slipcased edition was signed by the author and cover artist Bob Eggleton and contained an additional chapbook.

Charles Stross' *The Atrocity Archives* featured the previously serialized novel about a covert branch of British Intelligence battling Lovecraftian monstrosities, along with a bonus novella-length sequel, "The Concrete Jungle".

It was also a busy year for Night Shade Books. Nick Mamatas' debut novel *Move Under Ground* involved "Beat Era" authors Jack Kerouac, Neal Cassady, Allen Ginsberg and William S. Burroughs battling the minions of Lovecraft's Cthulhu Mythos in the California of the early 1960s. The book was also available in a signed edition of 100 copies.

Conrad Williams' collection *Use Once, Then Destroy* contained seventeen stories (three original), while *The Banquet of the Lords of Night & Other Stories* featured eighteen stories (one original) by Liz Williams. An additional story was available in the signed hardcover limited to 100 copies.

The discovery of a wrecked ship sent men mad in Lucius Shepard's short novel *Viator*, published in a trade edition and a 150-copy limited edition. With an Introduction by John Clute, *The New Universal History of Infamy* contained nineteen stories by Rhys Hughes. It was additionally available in a signed edition limited to 100 copies.

Edited by Forrest Aguirre, *Leviathan 4: Cities* contained ten stories (one reprint) by Jay Lake, K.J. Bishop and others.

The House on the Borderland and Other Mysterious Places was the second volume in Night Shade's matching "The Collected Fiction of William Hope Hodgson" set, edited by co-publisher Jeremy Lassen. Besides the title novel, the attractive volume included nine stories about Carnacki the Ghost-Finder and a further eleven tales of mystery and suspense, along with a historical Introduction by the editor and notes on the text.

Night Shade's reissue of M. John Harrison's 1992 novel *The Course of the Heart* was also available in a 150-copy signed edition that included an added story.

From Headpress imprint Diagonal, *Ports of Hell* was a picaresque novel by punk musician Johnny Strike that came with praise from William S. Burroughs, Geoff Nicholson and John Shirley.

Edited and introduced by Bill Sheehan, *Night Visions 11* from Subterranean Press featured three original novellas by Kim Newman (a new "Richard Jeperson" tale), Tim Lebbon and the always-excellent Lucius Shepard. A 250-copy limited edition was signed by the contributors.

Partial Eclipse and Other Stories was the first short fiction collection by Graham Joyce, while *Songs of Leaving* contained twelve reprint stories by Peter Crowther, along with an Introduction by Adam Roberts and extensive story notes by the author. It was published in signed editions of 500 numbered copies and twenty-six lettered copies.

Caitlín R. Kiernan's *The Dry Salvages* was a short dystopian science fiction novel set in a bleak and frozen Paris at the beginning of the twenty-fourth century, where the last survivor of an interplanetary mission was forced to confront her repressed and fragmented memories. It was also available in a 250-copy signed edition with an additional chapbook.

Poppy Z. Brite and Christa Faust's *Triads* was a fix-up novel that involved two Asian boys and a vengeful ghost. It was available in a signed hardcover edition and a 250-copy limited edition containing an extra story by each of the authors.

The Girl in the Basement and Other Stories collected five tales by Ray Garton in a signed edition of 400 copies. A fifty-two copy limited edition contained an additional vampire novella.

Also from Subterreanean, *Brian Lumley's Freaks* was a slim but attractive hardcover volume that collected four obscure reprint tales and a new story, along with a brief Introduction by the author and illustrations by Allen Koszowski. It was published in signed editions limited to 750 numbered and twenty-six lettered copies.

Another slim volume from Lumley was *The House of the Temple*, the second volume in the Endeavor Press Novelette Series. Containing the 1980 Lovecraftian novella and another reprint story, illustrated by Koszowski with a cover by Alan Clark, the nicely-produced hardcover was available in both a 300-copy signed limited edition or a signed lettered edition for $150.00.

From Haffner Press, *Seventy-Five: The Diamond Anniversary of a Science Fiction Pioneer* celebrated 97-year-old Jack Williamson's first publication with eleven stories, four novel excerpts, numerous articles by and about the author, and various photos, cover reproductions and even a comic-strip adaptation in an oversized hardcover volume. Featuring a Foreword by Connie Willis, an Introduction by Arthur C. Clarke and an Afterword by Williamson himself, it was available in a trade edition, a signed slipcased limited edition, and a deluxe lettered edition limited to twenty-six copies and costing $2,000.00!

Despite being mistakenly copyrighted 2002 by Canada's Red Deer Press, *Iterations* was Robert J. Sawyer's first short story collection, containing twenty-two reprint tales, an Introduction by James Alan Gardner and story notes by the author.

Swamp Witch Piquante and Scream Queen Bisque (Over a Bed of Rice) collected a short novel, "The White Trash Witches' Coven" and the novella "Pavane for a Scream Queen" by M.F. Korn. The book was issued in both an electronic edition and as a trade paperback by Silver Lake Publishing.

Published by Canada's Ash-Tree Press, *Acquainted With the Night* was the latest anthology edited by publishers Barbara and Christopher Roden. Containing twenty-seven original stories by Don Tumasonis, Ramsey Campbell, Reggie Oliver, Melanie Tem, Steve Rasnic Tem, Jessica Amanda Salmonson, Chico Kidd, Joel Lane, John Whitbourn, Steve Duffy, Rick Kennett, Paul Finch, John Pelan, Stephen Volk, Glen Hirshberg and others (including one of the editors), it appeared in a hardcover edition of 400 copies and an unlimited trade paperback edition with an eerie wraparound cover painting by Jason Van Hollander.

Acquainted With the Night also included a story by Simon Best-wick, and Ash-Tree published the British author's first book, *A Hazy Shade of Winter*. It collected fourteen ghostly stories (five reprints), along with an enthusiastic Introduction by Joel Lane, and was issued in an edition of 500 copies.

Tales of the Uneasy was the first of two volumes edited by John Pelan that will reprint the complete supernatural fiction of Violet Hunt (1866–1942). The volume featured all nine stories from her 1911 collection of the same title, including a revised novella, along with a historical Introduction by the editor.

Limited to 500 copies, *Dancing on Air and Other Stories* was a collection of ten ghost stories by Frances Oliver. From Ash-Tree Press' series of "Classic Macabre" paperbacks, Oliver's mystery novel *Children of Epiphany* was reprinted in a matching edition with a new Introduction by the author.

Edited with an Introduction by James Doig, *The Devil of the Marsh and Other Stories* collected fifteen obscure tales by Austra-lian-born author H.B. Marriott Watson (1863–1921).

Edited with an Introduction by Barbara and Christopher Roden and limited to 600 copies, *The Captain of the "Pole-Star": Weird and Imaginative Fiction* by Arthur Conan Doyle contained thirty-seven stories of the mysterious and the macabre and included a Preface by Michael Dirda. Featuring an Introduction by Mark Valentine, *The Nebuly Coat* was a 500-copy reprint of the 1903 mystery novel by John Meade Falkner (1858–1932), the author of *Moonfleet*.

Also limited to 500 copies from Ash-Tree, with an Introduction by Christopher Roden, *Satan's Circus* collected thirteen stories by Lady Eleanor Smith (1902–45).

Living up to its title, Quentin S. Crisp's collection *Morbid Stories* contained eight tales and a Foreword by Mark Samuels, from Tartarus Press. Limited to 300 copies, David Lindsay's *The Haunted Woman* originally appeared in 1922 and contained a new Afterword by Douglas A. Anderson, while Arthur Machen's *Ritual & Other Stories* collected a representative group of tales. From the same imprint came a new edition of M.P. Shiel's 1901 novel *The Purple Cloud*, with an Introduction by Brian Stableford, and Frank Baker's humorous 1940 fantasy *Miss Hargreaves*, introduced by Glen Ca-valiero and limited to 300 copies.

Originally published in 1889 as *Stories Weird and Wonderful* by "Dick Donovan", J.E. Muddock's *The Shining Hand & Other Tales of Terror* added a novelette to the twenty-three stories and an Introduction by editor John Pelan.

Edited by the legendary Forrest J Ackerman, *Dr Acula's Thrilling Tales of the Uncanny* was an anthology from publisher Sense of Wonder Press featuring stories by Gustav Meyrink, Arthur J. Burks, Hannes Bok and others. From the same imprint came a welcome reprint of Ackerman's film book about Lon Chaney, Sr., *Lon of 1000 Faces!*.

Yvonne Navarro's *Mirror Me* was a supernatural serial killer novel limited to 500 copies from Overlook Connection Press. Published by Overlook in a trade edition, Lucy Taylor's collection *The Silence Between the Screams* included four original stories and a reprint novella. It was also released under the title *A Hairy Chest, A Big Dick, and a Harley* in a signed edition limited to 1,000 copies and available only through specialty bookstores. The special edition featured original art for each story by Glenn Chadborne.

Douglas Clegg's *The Attraction* was about a roadside attraction that boasted an Aztec mummy. It was published in a signed edition of 500 copies and a twenty six-copy deluxe leatherbound edition by Delirium Books.

Brian Keene's *Fear of Gravity* collected eleven stories (four reprints) with an Introduction, Afterword and story notes by the author. It was published by Delirium in a 400-copy signed edition, along with a $175.00 deluxe leatherbound slipcased edition limited to twenty-six copies.

Dreadful Delineations collected thirty stories (five original) by John Maclay, with an Introduction by William F. Nolan. In John Everson's debut novel *Covenant*, a reporter investigated a series of teen suicides, while a man's nightmares started to invade his waking world in Michael Laimo's *Sleepwalker*. All three titles were published in signed editions limited to 250 copies.

Two erotic-themed collections from Delirium were *Honey is Sweeter Than Blood* (seven stories, two reprints) and *Shadows of Flesh* (fifteen stories, nine reprints) by brothers Jeffrey Thomas and Scott Thomas, respectively. Both books were published in 250-copy signed editions and available together in a deluxe traycase limited to twenty-six copies for $300.00.

From Florida's Necro Publications, Patrick Lestewka's novel *The Preserve* was about a group of Vietnam veterans hunting (and being hunted) by supernatural monsters in the wilds of northern Canada. It was published in a signed and numbered edition of 300 trade paperback copies and 100 hardcovers.

Edited with an historical Introduction about the imprint by Necro founder David G. Barnett, *Damned: An Anthology of the Lost* contained twelve original "hardcore horror" stories by Gerard Houarner, Charlee Jacob, Jack Ketchum, Brian Hodge, Tom Piccirilli, Jeffrey Thomas, Edward Lee, Gary Bruanbeck and others, including a short novel by Doc Solammen. It was published in a hardcover edition of 400 signed and numbered copies and a thirteen-copy lettered deluxe edition.

Apparently derived from a movie treatment, Christopher Fowler's novella *Breathe: Everyone Has to Do It* from Telos Publishing was a rollicking good read about a corporate office block that was turning its workforce into homicidal, sex-crazed zombies. Billed as "*The Office* meets *Night of the Living Dead*" it was published in paperback and as a signed and numbered deluxe hardcover.

Telos' series of original horror novellas continued with Steve Savile's *Houdini's Last Illusion*, which was set at the end of the haunted magician's life and expanded from the author's award-winning short story.

"Edited and annotated" by R.J. Carter and presented as if it were a lost manuscript by Lewis Carroll, *Alice's Journey Beyond the Moon* featured the debut illustrations of Lucy Wright. Published as part of Telos' *Doctor Who Novellas* series, Simon Clark's *The Dalek Factor* featured a Foreword by Christopher Fowler, while the deluxe edition added a frontispiece illustration by Graham Humphreys.

Lee Driver's *The Unseen* was the third horror-mystery featuring Chase Dagger, from Full Moon Publishing, while *Abandon All Hope* was a first novel set in Hell by Tony L. Ford, published by Nephilim Books.

The sixteen stories (seven reprints) in Darren Speegle's *Gothic Wine*, from Aardwolf Press, all involved the juice of the grape and were set in Europe.

From Medusa Press, Frank Chigas' *The Damp Chamber and Other Bad Places* contained nineteen original stories illustrated by the author. F. Greg Gifune's horror novel *Saying Uncle* was expanded from the short story of the same name and published by December Girl Press.

Published by The Canberra Speculative Fiction Guild, *Encounters: An Anthology of Australian Speculative Fiction* edited by Maxine McArthur and Donna Maree Hanson contained twenty-two original stories by Richard Harland, Cat Sparks and others in a trade paperback illustrated by Les Petersen and Shane Parker.

From Patrick Swenson's Darkwood Press, *Waiting My Turn to Go Under the Knife* collected sixty poems by Bram Stoker Award-winning poet Tom Piccirilli. Illustrated by Caniglia with an Introduction by T.M. Wright, the attractive hardcover volume was published in a 250-copy signed and numbered edition.

Meanwhile, *The Women at the Funeral* was a slim softcover volume of new and reprint poetry by Corrine De Winter, published by Space & Time Press.

Published by Durto Press in an edition of just 333 copies, *Death Poems* by Thomas Ligotti came with marbled endpapers, gilt edges, a marker ribbon and a free Carpe Diem enamel badge produced especially for the book.

Edited by Tom Roberts and published by Black Dog Books in association with Tattered Pages Press, *A Memorial Tribute to Hugh B. Cave* was a handsome sixty-four page chapbook limited to just 350 copies and distributed free at Ohio's Pulpcon 33 in July. Contributors included Jack Adrian, Mike Ashley, Stephen Jones, Dave Drake, Milt Thomas, Bob Weinberg, Brian Lumley, Stefan Dziemianowicz and others, and the booklet also included a previously uncollected story by the late pulp author.

Mercury (Atlanta, 1986) was a chapbook story by Caitlín R. Kiernan featuring her character Deacon Silvey, published by Subterranean Press. From the same imprint, the novella *The Feast of St Rosalie* by Poppy Z. Brite was limited to 750 chapbooks and 100 hardbound copies signed by the author.

Available from Haunted Library Publications, *Occult Sciences* was the first appearance in print of a paper read by M.R. James in February 1881 at a meeting of the College Literary Society at Eton School.

Don Koish's Necessary Evil Press launched a series of signed, limited edition novellas with *Dead Man's Hand*, the first book in the annual "Assassin Series" by Tim Lebbon (not to be confused with the Nancy A. Collins collection of the same title). A weird Western about a demon-hunting gunfighter, it had an Introduction by Tom Piccirilli and an Afterword by the author. The first book in another new series from Kealan Patrick Burke, *The Turtle Boy* with artwork by Caniglia and an Introduction by Norman Partridge, was about a haunted community pond. Both titles were available in oversized 450-copy numbered hardcover editions and twenty-six metal traycased lettered editions signed by all the contributors.

Horses Blow Up Dog City and Other Stories from Small Beer Press collected five stories (two original) by Richard Butner, while the same imprint distributed *Family Reunion*, a free comic written by Sean Stewart and beautifully illustrated by Steve Lieber to celebrate the publication of Stewart's novel *Perfect Circle*.

Chicago's Iguana Publications launched a new series of no-frills chapbooks with *Masque of the Small Town Oddball*, edited by publisher John Weagly and featuring seven original stories by Adam Pepper, Tim Curren and others, including the editor. Only 100 copies were printed.

Richard E. Dansky's story *Shadows in Green* was available as a chapbook from Yard Dog Press, while *Eschersketch* by Stephen L. Antczak and James C. Bassett was published by Nth Degree/Big Blind Productions.

Edited by Rabe Phillips, *Darker Than Tin . . . Brighter Than Sin* contained six original stories and two poems about angels and was published in support of the OWW-SF/F/H Scholarship Fund.

From Wormhole Books' "Contemporary Chapbooks" series, Bret Bertholf's horror story *Alfred Bester is Alive and Well and Living in Winterset, Iowa* was illustrated by the author and featured an Introduction by Edward Bryant. Bryant also supplied the Introduction to Stewart O'Nan's *Something Wicked*, a ghostly novella for Halloween excerpted from his novel *The Night Country*. It was illustrated with photographs by Thomas Meek and contained an interview with O'Nan and an Afterword by the author. Both titles were available in signed editions limited to 750 copies, 250-copy numbered hardcovers and 52-copy lettered editions.

The 500-copy signed Wormhole Fourth of July patriotic card contained the short SF story "In the Memory of Dogs" by the aptly-named John Kennedy, while the Greetings and Happy Holidays card featured Edward Bryant's disturbing "The Letter Before Christmas".

Guy N. Smith's *Come in and Join Us* was the first volume in "The Horror Express Chapbook Series", limited to 100 signed and numbered copies. Editor/publisher Marc Shemmans followed it with his own story, *The Forest*, published in an edition of just fifty signed copies, illustrated by Teresa Tunaley.

The Hydrocephalic Ward from California's Dark Regions Press collected fifty poems by Steve Rasnic Tem, while *Bone Sprockets* from the same imprint contained thirty poems by G.O. Clark.

The tireless Peter Crowther launched a new "quarterly" magazine, *Postscripts*, under his PS Publishing imprint. The first perfect-bound issue boasted fine fiction by Ramsey Campbell, Stephen Gallagher, Adam Roberts, Ed Gorman, Jay Lake, Gene Wolfe, Allen Ashley, Eric Brown, Joyce Carol Oates, Brian Aldiss, James Lovegrove and Peter F. Hamilton, plus a dreadful horror story from TV producer

Lawrence Gordon Clark. Along with poetry by Ray Bradbury and non-fiction from Christopher Fowler and Mike Ashley, there was also an interview with James P. Blaylock.

The second volume, dated "Summer 2004", continued to display the same high quality fiction with contributions from Jack Dann, Rhys Hughes, Jeff VanderMeer, Iain Rowan, Michael Marshall Smith, Brian Stableford, Brian A. Hopkins, Robert B. Parker (a reprint) and others, along with Robert Silverberg's article on the 1957 World SF Convention in London and an interview with Kage Baker. Both issues featured wraparound cover paintings by "Edward Miller" (Les Edwards) and were also available in signed and numbered hardcover editions, limited to just 150 copies.

Another new title was *Allen K's Inhuman Magazine*, edited and illustrated by Allen Koszowski and devoted to "monster" stories by Donald R. Burleson, Jeffrey Thomas, Paul W. Finch and others, including reprints from Robert Silverberg and film director John Carpenter. The debut issue of the perfect-bound periodical also featured movie and DVD reviews, along with a limerick by Darrell Schweitzer.

Richard Chizmar and Bob Morrish's *Cemetery Dance Magazine* celebrated its fifteenth year of publication with stories by Stewart O'Nan, Tim Waggoner, David B. Silva, Nancy Holder, Tony Richards, Gerard Houarner and others; interviews with O'Nan, Silva, Holder, David Morrell and Richard Matheson, and the usual columns from Bev Vincent, Thomas F. Monteleone, Paula Guran, Michael Marano, John Pelan and Ed Gorman. The title's "Special 50th Issue" included interviews with Stephen King, Elizabeth Massie, artist Mike Mignola and film director Mick Garris, plus fiction from Douglas Clegg, Glen Hirshberg, Ramsey Campbell, Bentley Little, Norman Partridge and Gary A. Braunbeck, plus a poem by Ray Bradbury. From 2005, *Cemetery Dance* will also be released in a 200-copy signed and numbered hardcover edition available on subscription.

George H. Scithers and Darrell Schweitzer's *Weird Tales* only managed three thin issues in 2004 due to changes in distributors. These editions included fiction and (too much) poetry by co-publisher John Gregory Betancourt, co-editor Darrell Schweitzer, Ian Watson, Tanith Lee, Michael Bishop, Alan Dean Foster and the late Jane Rice, along with "classic" reprints from W.C. Morrow, Richard Middleton and F. Marion Crawford. Boasting some stunning cover paintings by Rowena Morrell and Tom Kidd, there was also a reviews column by Douglas E. Winter and an interview with Terry Pratchett (which was mostly about Neil Gaiman).

The same distribution problems hit companion title *H.P. Love-craft's Magazine of Horror*. After the "Special Collector's Issue" of 2003, the magazine only produced a new half-sized edition, numbered 1.5 and limited to 2,000 copies, that was distributed as a bonus to subscribers. Along with fiction and poetry by Charles Coleman Finlay, C.H. Sherman, Scott E. Green and others, it included book reviews by Craig Shaw Gardner, a convention report, a letters column and numerous advertisements for Wildside Press books.

The first issue of Wildside's semi-annual *Adventure Tales*, edited by John Gregory Betancourt, featured pulp stories and poetry by Hugh B. Cave, Harold Lamb, Vincent Starrett, F. Marion Crawford, H.P. Lovecraft, Robert E. Howard and Clark Ashton Smith, along with an interview with Cave. It was available in both magazine and expanded book versions.

Under the psuedonym "Abner Gibber", Darrell Schweitzer was also the editor of the one-shot *Weird Trails: The Magazine of Supernatural Cowboy Stories*, a "facsimile" from Wildside Press of the alleged April 1933 issue which combined Wild West fiction with the Cthulhu Mythos. (Apparently somebody still remembered Tom Reamy's 1970s magazine *Nickelodeon*, and its "M.M. Moamrath" spoof.) It featured thirteen stories by Ron Goulart, Ray Faraday Nelson, P.D. Cacek, Mike Resnick and others.

The June 1931 *Ghost Stories*, January 1933 *Strange Tales* and February 1937 *Spicy Mystery Stories* were all facsimile reprints of actual pulp magazines from Wildside.

Gordon Van Gelder's always-reliable *The Magazine of Fantasy & Science Fiction* featured the usual offbeat mix of fiction by such authors as Michael Shea, Nancy Etchemendy, Steven Utley, Chet Williamson, Charles Coleman Finlay, Alex Irvine, David Gerrold, Robert Sheckley, Ray Vukcevich, Peter S. Beagle, A.A. Attanasio, Esther M. Friesner, Carol Emshwiller, Gene Wolfe, Dale Bailey, Michael Bishop, Sydney J. Van Scyoc, and a final story by the late Jack Cady. The July edition was a "Special All-American Issue", while the double issue appeared, as usual, in October/November. Bud Webster, David Langford, F. Gwynplaine MacIntyre, John Kessel, Jason Van Hollander, Paul Di Filippo and Bill Sheehan all contributed to the "Curiosities" book review page, and there were columns by Charles de Lint, Robert K.J. Killheffer, Lucius Shepard, Elizabeth Hand, James Sallis, Kathi Maio, Michelle West and Di Filippo.

After twenty years, Gardner Dozois announced that he was stepping down as editor of *Asimov's Science Fiction* to pursue other projects. He remained with the magazine as a contributing editor. Meanwhile, Sheila Williams was named as the new editor, beginning with the January 2005 issue.

David Pringle also resigned as editor of the struggling British science fiction magazine *Interzone*, which he helped co-found twenty-two years earlier. With Pringle's departure with issue #193, the title became a publication of Andy Cox's TTA Press. Unfortunately, along with the new publisher came a design revamp that left the bi-monthly magazine looking a total mess. The two TTA issues published before the end of the year featured fiction from the ubiquitous Jay Lake and others, plus interviews with Pringle and Ken MacLeod, and the usual media reviews and features.

Meanwhile, Andy Cox's *The 3rd Alternative* celebrated its tenth anniversary with a Hugo nomination and the opportunity to give the title yet another design overhaul. Disappointingly, this left it looking a bit too much like its revamped stable-mate *Interzone*. The four issues that took it up to its fortieth number included some fine fiction from Joe Hill, Tim Pratt, John Grant, Joel Lane, Nina Allan, Mike O'Driscoll, Christopher Barzak, Jay Lake and others, interviews with Ursula Le Guin, Joanthan Lethem, Russell Hoban, Christopher Fowler, Clive Barker and Bryan Talbot, plus the usual columns by Allen Ashley, Christopher Fowler, Stephen Volk and Peter Tennant. Guest editors Liz Williams, Graham Joyce, Paula Guran and Nicholas Royle debated the "New Weird" and other literary movements.

Plans to print each issue of *The 3rd Alternative* on a different colour paper in 2004 were abandoned when the Spring issue's "siskin green" was deemed "potentially vomit-inducing" by editor Andy Cox, who had most of the run pulped and the magazine reprinted on the usual white stock. However, 120 copies of the rare "absinthe" edition were held back and subsequently offered for sale.

Also from TTA Press, the eighth issue of *The Fix* contained the usual A-Z reviews of magazines and anthologies, along with an interview with Gardner Dozois.

Editor and publisher Marc Shemmans launched his new British glossy magazine *The Horror Express* with three issues featuring original and reprint fiction and poetry by Graham Masterton, Storm Constantine, Shaun Hutson, Simon Clark, Darrell Schweitzer and Jason Van Hollander, Tom Piccirilli, Guy N. Smith, Christopher Fowler, Jill Bauman and others, including Shemmans himself. There were also book and film reviews, articles on collecting Masterton's and Fowler's work, and interviews with writer and artist James R.

Cain, publisher Gabriel Strange, actor Bruce Campbell, plus authors Constantine, Masterton, Fowler and Hutson.

The third issue of Paul Calvin Wilson's eclectic *Lighthouse Magazine* was a "Robert Weinberg Special" featuring interviews with Weinberg, David Gemmell, Poppy Z. Brite, Hugh B. Cave, Frank Kelly Freas, Anne Bishop, W. Paul Ganley and artist Dave Kendall, along with fiction by Cave, Weinberg, Brian Lumley, Gary Fry and others.

After the distribution problems with its first edition, the second issue of the revived *Argosy* was published in two editions – a slipcased two-volume "Connoisseur Edition" and the single "Proletarian Edition" for news stands and chain stores. Featuring artwork by Dr Seuss, the second issue was once again beautifully produced, with fiction by O'Neil De Noux, Carol Emshwiller, Kevin J. Anderson, Jeff VanderMeer, Mike Resnick and others, along with a bonus novella by Charles Stross and Cory Doctorow illustrated by John Picacio. Unfortunately, some copies of the magazine suffered from a binding problem, with missing pages replaced by duplicates. Before a third issue could appear, Lou Anders resigned as Senior Editor of the title to concentrate on the new Pyr SF and fantasy imprint from Prometheus Books.

The seventh issue of John O'Neill's perfect-bound *Black Gate: Adventures in Fantasy Literature* contained stories by Todd McAulty, Don Bassingthwaite, Mark Summer and others, plus an appreciation of the old *Planet Stories* pulp by Rich Horton.

Editor Pitch Black's *Horror Garage* reached its ninth issue with fiction by Norman Partridge and interviews with Dennis Etchison, Brian Keene and Herschell Gordon Lewis.

Gordon Linzner's *Space and Time* included stories and poetry by Darrell Schweitzer and others.

Edited by Michael D. Pederson and available free of charge, *Nth Degree: The Fiction and Fandom 'Zine* featured fiction and poetry by Peter Huston, C.J. Henderson and others, along with the usual convention and book reviews, and an interview with fan cartoonist Alexis Gilliland.

Billed as "writing with attitude", Shar O'Brien's professional-looking *NFG* published two issues from Canada, featuring fiction, poetry and art from contributors in America, Canada, Britain, Australia and Japan, including Bruce Holland Rogers and Brendan Duffy, along with interviews with A.C. Crispin and Michael Moorcock.

After a three-year hiatus, the world's oldest science fiction magazine, *Amazing Stories*, was resurrected in yet another new incarnation by Paizo Publishing as a monthly large format fiction/media title. Edited by Dave Gross, issue #603 included fiction by Bruce Sterling, Ray Vukcevich, Gene Wolfe and Harlan Ellison, interviews with Robert Silverberg, Larry Niven and George R.R. Martin, along with plenty of reviews and features on films and TV. However, the magazine was put on "hiatus" again after only a handful of issues. Gross was replaced by Jeff Berkwits, who left his position as Senior Writer at Wolfson Public Relations to take the helm after Gross moved to computer game company Bioware.

Christopher M. Cevasco's *Paradox: The Magazine of Historical and Speculative Fiction* contained stories by Paul Finch and Charles Coleman Finlay, while Shawna McCarthy's bi-monthly *Realms of Fantasy* included Tanith Lee's revisionist vampire story "Israbel", plus work by Liz Williams, Jay Lake, Nina Kiriki Hoffman, Ian McDowell, Bruce Holland Rogers and a profusely illustrated article on artist Les Edwards/Edward Miller by Jane Frank.

Now firmly established as the one-shop stop for everything to do with horror (especially the gory and the Gothic), Canada's *Rue Morgue* published its usual six glossy colour editions, including a perfect-bound "Seventh Anniversary Halloween Issue" featuring cover and interior art by Clive Barker. Packed with media and book reviews, plus interviews with Barker, Mike Mignola, David Cronenberg, Marilyn Chambers, Brian Keene, Takashi Shimizu, Sam Raimi, Sean Cunningham, Jack Ketchum, Tobe Hooper, Gunnar Hansen and Forrest J Ackerman, the magazine announced that it would be increasing its schedule to ten issues per year in 2005.

Tim and Donna Lucas' *Video Watchdog* maintained its monthly schedule and even added laminated covers to an already attractive package. Along with all the usual DVD, video and book reviews, there were special articles on Japanese director Nobuo Nakagawa, Lon Chaney, Sr., Roman Polanski (by Kim Newman), Sherlock Holmes, the *Alien* Quadrilogy (sic), Universal Monsters, Jonny Quest (by David J. Schow), Tarzan, and Euro Lounge Soundtracks, plus interviews with French actress Édith Scob and director Georges Franju (*Eyes Without a Face*), and Tom Weaver's rambling talk with "lost" horror star Donnie Dunagan, the curly-haired child in *Son of Frankenstein*. Dunagan also "personally signed" copies of a variant "Signature Edition" with an alternative cover design. However, Lucas' long-promised Mario Bava book *still* failed to appear.

With the slightly expanded title *Filmfax Plus*, Michael Stein's

fascinating historical movie magazine incorporated its sister publication *Outré* with issue #101. The in-depth periodical included
interviews with Hugh B. Cave and Richard Matheson, comics artists
Will Eisner and Jack Davis, actor John Saxon, composer Vic Mizzy,
plus a multi-part look at the career of special effects pioneer Paul
Blaisdell by artist Vincent Di Fate (who also contributed a superb
cover painting of The She-Creature).

Scott Edelman's *SciFi: The Official Magazine of the Sci Fi Channel*
continued to run puff-pieces on all the latest Hollywood releases and
TV shows, with far too much space wasted on the derisory *Van
Helsing*.

Craig Miller's *Spectrum* produced a very attractive "Super Special" issue devoted to Robert E. Howard and Conan in books,
comics and movies. Gary Gianni, Mark Schultz and an opinionated
Barry Windsor-Smith were among those interviewed, and there were
plenty of illustrations and cover reproductions.

The third issue of Michael Ambrose's informative *Charlton Spotlight: Exploring the History of Charlton Magazines* was a special
issue remembering late horror comics writer and artist Tom Sutton
(who died in 2002), with memoirs, commentary and artwork by
Nicola Cuti, Steve Skeates, Bill Pearson, Jim Amash, Bhob Stewart,
Stefan Petrucha, Mark Burbey, Batton Lash and Sutton himself.

The Winter 2003 edition of the academic journal *Extrapolation*
from The University of Texas at Brownsville and Texas Southmost
College included a survey of the work of Ramsey Campbell, while
Alice K. Turner looked at recent books about female werewolves in
the July issue of *The New York Review of Science Fiction*.

The 8 March issue of *Publishers Weekly* featured "Tomes of
Terror and Trepidation", a five-page spotlight on the current state
of horror publishing written by Paula Guran with commentary by
Ellen Datlow, Douglas E. Winter, Stefan Dziemianowicz, Neil Gaiman, Peter Straub and various editors, speciality publishers and
booksellers.

The 9 May issue of Britain's *The Sunday Express* weekly magazine
S:2 was a "horror special" timed to tie-in with the release of *Van
Helsing*. Along with articles on the new film and the classic monsters,
it also included an interview with Sara Karloff about her father Boris.

The May/June issue of *OP*, the magazine of book culture, collectors and commerce, included an interesting article by Girasol Col-
lectables publisher Neil Mechem about the inevitable disintegration
of pulp magazines.

Stephen King's occasional but always-entertaining "The Pop of

King" column in *Entertainment Weekly* covered such eclectic subjects as our attraction to the *National Enquirer*, *The Passion of Christ* ("Sam Peckinpah does Good Friday"), the MPAA's movie rating system, good books for the summer, the death of Elvis, the failure of *Kingdom Hospital*, critical gradeflation, his pet peeves of 2004 (including Dr Phil) and a dozen things to be thankful for (including Jack Ketchum for being "the scariest guy in America").

King also contributed an article to the 30 July issue of *Entertainment Weekly* about favourite movie lines, while the 30 April edition featured an interview with Poppy Z. Brite about her new food novel *Liquor* ("I never really set out to be a horror writer").

In the March issue of *Paper Collectors' Marketplace*, William J. Felchner looked at the collectibility of Stephen King material, including books, magazines and movie items.

The June issue of *Fortean Times: The World of Strange Phenomena* contained an extensive article on H.P. Lovecraft by Daniel Harms.

For Christmas 2004, *Book and Magazine Collector* celebrated its 250th issue with a "Horror Special". Featuring some nice colour cover reproductions, Richard Dalby contributed articles on "The Top 20 Horror Authors" and the centenary of M.R. James' *Ghost Stories of an Antiquary*. There was also a profile of British comics artist Robert Forrest, and an interview with special effects wizard Ray Harryhausen about his friendship with Ray Bradbury, amongst other things.

All Hallows, the award-winning Journal of The Ghost Story Society, produced another three excellent, perfect-bound issues edited by Barbara and Christopher Roden. Along with some subtle fiction from Paul Finch, Phil Locascio, Michael Dirda, Don Tumasonis, Tina Rath, Iain Rowan and others, there was the usual mix of regular columns and articles by Ramsey Campbell, Richard Dalby, Michel Parry, Roger Dobson, Reggie Oliver and John Howard.

Edited by Becky Probert for The London Vampyre Group, *The Chronicles* was a regular digest-size magazine that for presentation put most other society's journals to shame. The four issues published in 2004 included articles on Aleister Crowley, Algernon Charles Swinburne and Marilyn Manson, along with trip reports and book and film reviews. The LVG also published a Poetry and Fiction Supplement #1.

The quarterly *Bulletin of the Science Fiction and Fantasy Writers of America* continued to offer important advice for writers. Although it contained another unconvincing attempt to justify the existence of e-books, there was also a strong and eloquent case put forward by Mike Resnick and Barry Malzberg for including such often overlooked names as Ian Ballantine, Avram Davidson, Robert A.W. Lowndes, Julius Schwartz, Donald A. Wollheim and others amongst a list of the "Heroes" of the genre.

The multiple Hugo Award-winning news and reviews magazine *Locus* featured interviews with Gwyneth Jones, Robert Silverberg, Gordon Van Gelder, Charles Coleman Finlay, Terry Pratchett, Liz Williams, Michael Swanwick, Jeffrey Ford, Stephen Baxter, Stephen R. Donaldson, David G. Hartwell, Anne McCaffrey, Michael Bishop and Michael Chabon, amongst others. The paper quality of the monthly title was markedly reduced with the May issue, and Jennifer A. Hall resigned as editorial director at the end of that month, causing founder Charles N. Brown to return from his brief "retirement".

The British Fantasy Society's *Prism* changed editors from Marie O'Regan back to Debbie Bennett and downsized from a quarterly perfect-bound magazine to a much more useful bi-monthly newsletter. The multimedia periodical included numerous reviews, features on Edgar Rice Burroughs and Alan Garner, articles by Christopher Fowler and Tony Richards, plus interviews with John B. Ford, Neil Gaiman, K.J. Bishop, Tony Richards, Stuart Young, Stephen Gallagher and Jon George. Bennett also edited two issues of the BFS magazine *Dark Horizons*, which featured fiction by Chris Naylor, Allen Ashley, Mike Chinn, Tony Richards, Tina Rath and others.

Despite boasting an Introduction by Clive Barker, short contributions by Neil Gaiman, China Miéville, Graham Joyce, Kim Newman, Mark Chadbourn, Chaz Brenchley, Steve Lockley and others, the *British Fantasy Society 2005* calendar edited by Paul Kane and Marie O'Regan was a credit to nobody. Based around the legend of Sir Gawain and The Green Knight, Les Edwards' cover art was the only featured painting to achieve a professional standard.

Edited by Roger Dobson and Mark Valentine, *The Lost Club Journal* included a look at August Derleth's Solar Pons character, M.P. Shiel's Prince Zaleski, the books of Michael Arlen and John Gawsworth, and other "unheralded" works.

To commemorate the fiftieth anniversary of the death of James Hilton, the author of *Lost Horizon* (1933), The Lost Club produced a beautifully designed Shangri-La postage stamp in a limited edition of just 200, illustrated by artist Colin Langeveld. Depicting the remote lamaserie from the classic novel, the stamps were used by the James Hilton Society for postage to its membership.

Also edited by Valentine, the second issue of *Wormwood* from Tartarus Press included articles on Oliver Onions, Clark Ashton Smith, Francis Stevens, Robert Louis Stevenson and others, with contributions from Brian W. Aldiss, Scott Connors, Brian Stableford, Philip Pullman and Mark Samuels.

Editor David Longhorn published two editions of *Supernatural Tales*, featuring stories by Paul Finch, Iain Rowan, Geoffrey Warburton, Joel Lane, Simon Bestwick, Michael Chislett and others, along with an article on Robert Aickman's "The Stains", an interview with D.F. Lewis, reviews and letters. From 2005 the title will become an annual, double-sized anthology.

As always, the two issues of Patrick and Honna Swenson's perfect-bound *Talebones: A Magazine of Science Fiction & Dark Fantasy* featured an impressive line-up of writers and poets, including Tom Piccirilli, Louise Marley, Charlee Jacob, Bruce Boston and Darrell Schweitzer, along with interviews with Kay Kenyon and Piccirilli, and numerous book reviews.

The third issue of James R. Beach's *Dark Discoveries* spotlighted the work of Gary A. Braunbeck, Simon Clark and Tim Lebbon with interviews, excerpts and reviews. The magazine also featured interviews with Earthling publisher Paul Miller, Tom Piccirilli and Bev Vincent.

Produced by Manchester's Comma Press and supported by the Arts Council of England, the first issue of Tane Vayu's *Liverpool Stories* included reprint fiction from Ramsey Campbell and Martin Edwards.

The fourteenth and fifteenth issues of Jack Fisher's *Flesh & Blood* included stories by Douglas Clegg, Gerard Houarner and others, along with interviews with Peter Crowther and China Miéville.

Studies in Modern Horror: A Scholarly Journal for the Study of Contemporary Weird Fiction included articles on Clive Barker's *The Thief of Always*, China Miéville's *The Scar* and Fritz Leiber's *Our Lady of Darkness*, along with an annotated short story by John Pelan.

From Small Beer Press, Kelly Link and Gavin J. Grant's *Lady Churchill's Rosebud Wristlet* featured experimental fiction, poetry and articles by Susan Mosser, James Sallis, Jay Lake and others, while the second and third issues of Heather Shaw and Tim Pratt's comparable *Flytrap* included work by Benjamin Rosenbaum, Jay Lake and Sonya Taaffe.

John Klima's *Electric Velocipede* featured stories and poetry by Liz Williams, Christopher Rowe, Kiel Stuart and Steve Nagy, amongst others.

Then there was the usual erotic Lovecraftian horror in Michael A. Morel's *Cthulhu Sex* #17, while the third issue of Brian Lingard's *Mythos Collector* featured an interview with Peter Scartabello and an article on Lovecraftian audio adaptations.

From Pentagram Publications, John Navroth's *Lovecraft's Weird Mysteries* included fiction by R. Michael Burns, James S. Dorr and others, along with a reprint from the pre-Code *Tomb* comics plus articles on how to shrink a head and the 1959 film *The Four Skulls of Jonathan Drake*.

The third issue of William Jones' *Book of Dark Wisdom: The Magazine of Dark Fiction and Lovecraftian Horror* contained ten short stories by Don D'Ammassa and others, including a collaboration between Richard Gavin and D.F. Lewis.

Published by Edgewood Press, Steve Pasechnick's *Alchemy* featured six stories from Dale Bailey and others, while the two issues of John Benson's *Not One of Us* included fiction and poetry by Kevin Anderson, Sonya Taffe and Terry Black.

The first two issues of Andrew Hannon's *Thirteen* contained new fiction by Lee Betteridge, David Turnbull, Hugh Cook and the editor himself. The debut edition of Jamie Rosen's *Irregular Quarterly* included stories from Jay Caselberg, D.F. Lewis and Jay Lake, amongst others. Regrettably, the magazine's shoddy production did not live up to the quality of the fiction.

The prolific Lake was also one of the contributors to the third issue of Gary Fry's *Fusing Horizons*, which also featured stories from Peter Tennant, Iain Rowan, John D. Rosenman and others, along with an interview with Stephen Gallagher.

Lake was also sponsored by San Francisco's Borderlands Books to create a short story in-store during an interactive process with artist Alan M. Clark and sculptor Paul Groendes. The combined result, "At the City of Rectified Errors", was distributed in a signed and numbered edition of just fifty manuscript copies.

Issues #33–35 of *Aurealis: Australian Fantasy & Science Fiction* were published as a single paperback volume by Chimaera Publications, edited by Keith Stevenson. The book contained twenty stories and various articles and reviews, along with an interview with author Hal Colebatch.

Harlan Ellison's irregular newsletter *Rabbit Hole* continued to supply information about the irrepressible author's upcoming projects and appearances, along with four "6 Degrees of Separation" between Ellison and actor Kevin Bacon. In a joint statement issued in June, Ellison and America Online, Inc. announced a settlement of their four-year-old copyright infringement dispute for undisclosed terms.

The Winter 2004 edition of Florida Atlantic University's *Journal of the Fantastic in the Arts* featured an article on the Anglican/Catholic influence in James Herbert's novel *Shrine*.

In *The Road to The Dark Tower: Exploring Stephen King's Magnum Opus*, Bev Vincent did just that with plot summaries, themes and motifs discussed, examined and explained.

Hanging Out With the Dream King: Conversations With Neil Gaiman and His Collaborators from Fantagraphics Books was a collection of illustrated interviews by editor Joseph McCabe with Dave McKean, Kim Newman, Stephen Jones, Charles Vess, P. Craig Russell, Bryan Talbot, Tori Amos, Alice Cooper, Terry Pratchett, Gene Wolfe and others who have collaborated with Gaiman over the years in books and comics. The volume also included two interviews with Gaiman himself.

Published by Kent State University Press, *Ray Bradbury: The Life of Fiction* by Jonathan R. Eller and William F. Touponce was a critical evaluation of Bradbury's career, including a chronological bibliography, extracts from a 2002 interview and a Foreword by William F. Nolan. Aimed at younger readers, Wendy Mass' biography *Ray Bradbury: Master of Science Fiction and Fantasy* was part of the "Authors Teens Love" series from Enslow Publishers.

Edited by Steven L. Aggelis for the University Press of Mississippi, *Conversations With Ray Bradbury* collected a number of interviews with the author.

In *Muggles and Magic: J.K. Rowling and the Harry Potter Phenomenon*, George Beahm took a look at the popular children's books, with photos, quotes and illustrations by Tim Kirk. *A Muggle's Guide to the Wizarding World: Exploring the Harry Potter Universe* by Fionna Boyle covered similar ground, while *The Sorcerer's Companion: A Guide to the Magical World of Harry Potter, Second Edition* was a revised and expanded edition of Allan Zola Kronzek and Elizabeth Kronzek's 2001 non-fiction study.

Edited by David Baggett and Shawn E. Klein, the sixteen critical essays in *Harry Potter and Philosophy: If Aristotle Ran Hogwarts* were probably not aimed at Rowling's usual readership.

A Serious Life by D.M. Mitchell was a comprehensive history of maverick publisher Savoy Books, offering a fascinating insight into the imprint's trials (literally!) and tribulations over the past thirty years. Produced in an attractive, illustrated deluxe edition, the book featured the first-ever extended interviews with the company's founders, David Britton and Michael Butterworth.

From the Texas-based MonkeyBrain Books, which specializes in non-fiction genre studies, came four attractively-produced trade paperbacks: *Why Should I Cut Your Throat?: Excursions Into the Worlds of Science Fiction, Fantasy & Horror* was a collection of essays and reviews by Jeff VanderMeer, while *A Blazing World: The Unofficial Companion to The League of Extraordinary Gentlemen Volume Two* by Jess Nevins featured an Introduction by and interview with Alan Moore, plus a striking cover design by John Picacio.

Picacio also produced the cover art for MonkeyBrain's revised reissue of Michael Moorcock's 1987 study *Wizardry & Wild Romance: A Study of Epic Fantasy* that included a new Introduction by China Miéville and a new Afterword by Jeff VanderMeer. Edited by Lou Anders, *Projections: Science Fiction in Literature & Film* contained twenty-nine essays by Michael Moorcock, John Clute, Tim Lebbon, Lucius Shepard, Robert Silverberg, David Brin and others, and Anders also contributed the Introduction to a new edition of *The Discontinuity Guide*, a deconstruction of the *Doctor Who* mythos by Paul Cornell, Martin Day and Keith Topping, with a Foreword by Terrance Dicks.

As the Ambassador of Ireland to the Republic of Korea, there was no denying that Paul Murray knew his Irish history. Unfortunately, his dull biography *From the Shadow of Dracula: The Life of Bram Stoker* not only failed to achieve its title's avowed purpose, but probably left anyone unfamiliar with the rest of Stoker's work wondering what all the fuss was about. Richard Dalby's 1983 *Bram Stoker: A Bibliography* appeared in an expanded edition from Desert Island Books.

Donald Tyson's *Necronomicon: The Wanderings of Alhazred* purported to be the legendary book of magic created by H.P. Lovecraft.

Margaret L. Carter's study *Different Blood: The Vampire as Alien* was a print-on-demand title, while Beth E. McDonald's *The Vampire as Numinous Experience: Spiritual Journeys With the Undead in British and American Literature* from McFarland was another critical examination of the myth.

Edited by Glenn Yeffeth, *Five Seasons of Angel: Science Fiction and Fantasy Authors Discuss Their Favorite Vampire* contained twenty-one essays by Chelsea Quinn Yarbro, Peter S. Beagle and others.

Michael Marshall Smith: The Annotated Bibliography, compiled by Lavie Tidhar, was an attractive illustrated listing of the author's works, with notes by Smith himself. The first in a proposed new series of author bibliographies from PS Publishing, it appeared in a slim edition of 200 signed and numbered hardcovers and 300 numbered paperbacks.

From McFarland & Company, Thomas Mann's *Horror and Mystery Photoplay Editions and Magazine Fictionizations* was an attractive reference guide to more 500 movie tie-in "photoplay" editions published before 1970. Leon E. Nielsen's *Arkham House Books: A Collector's Guide* was available from the same publisher as a trade paperback. With a Foreword by Barry Abrahams, it was a guide to collecting, buying and selling Arkham, Mycroft & Moran and Stanton & Lee books, featuring around sixty photos and a bibliography.

Milt Thomas' *Cave of a Thousand Tales: The Life & Times of Hugh B. Cave* was a biography of the legendary pulp writer, who died a few weeks before the book's publication from Arkham House.

Ronin Ro's *Tales to Astonish* looked at the career of late comics artist Jack Kirby and his struggle to receive a fairer return for the many characters he helped create for Marvel and other publishers.

Produced by Cummington Co. and only available through mail-order, *Ray Guns, Robots and Rocket Ships* was Ken Weiss' guide to every American science fiction sound serial up to 1993, containing almost 250 stills.

Compiled by Nancy Kilpatrick, *The Goth Bible: A Compendium for the Darkly Inclined* included everything any black-clad outcast needed to know to tell a Christian Goth from an Übergoth.

Based loosely on a BBC Radio 4 series, *Tolkien's Gown & Other Stories of Great Authors and Rare Books* amusingly detailed book dealer Rick Gekoski's involvement with such titles as *The Hobbit*, *Lord of the Flies*, *The Picture of Dorian Gray*, *Animal Farm*, *The Satanic Verses*, *Harry Potter and the Philosopher's Stone* and other volumes and their authors.

James Swallow adapted the time-travel movie *The Butterfly Effect*, while Stephen Hand novelized the redundant remake of *The Texas Chainsaw Massacre*.

More interestingly, *The Day After Tomorrow* was novelized by

Whitley Strieber, upon whose 1999 non-fiction book *The Coming Global Superstorm* (co-written with Art Bell) the disaster movie was loosely based.

Other film tie-in titles of the year included *Van Helsing* by Kevin Ryan, *The Punisher* by D.A. Stern, *The Chronicles of Riddick* by Alan Dean Foster, *Spider-Man 2* by Peter David, *Catwoman* by Elizabeth Hand, *Sky Captain and the World of Tomorrow* by K. (Kevin) J. Anderson, *AVP: Alien vs. Predator* by Marc Cerasini, *Resident Evil: Apocalypse* by Keith R.A. DeCandido, *The Final Cut* by Robert Westbrook, *Exorcist: The Beginning* by Steven Piziks, *Blade: Trinity* by Natasha Rhodes and *Elektra* by Yvonne Navarro.

Navarro also wrote the *Hellboy* novelisation, while Christopher Golden's earlier comic book tie-ins, *Hellboy: The Lost Army* and *Hellboy: The Bones of Giants*, both illustrated by Mike Mignola, were also reissued in paperback.

Resident Evil: Genesis by Keith R.A. DeCandido, *Resident Evil: Zero Hour* by S.D. Perry, *Terminator 3: Terminator Hunt* by Aaron Allston and *Underworld 2: Blood Enemy* by Greg Cox were all original sequels set in various movie milieus, while Sholly Fisch's *Ghostbusters: The Return* was a belated sequel to the 1984 film.

The remake tie-in of Ira Levin's *The Stepford Wives* included a 2002 Introduction by Peter Straub as an Afterword, while Richard Condon's 1959 cold war thriller *The Manchurian Candidate* and Michael Crichton's 1999 novel *Timeline* were both reissued in new movie editions.

Although the TV show was finished, the *Buffy, the Vampire Slayer* novelisations proved as popular as ever with *Apocalypse Memories* by J. Laura Burns and Melinda Metz, *Heat* by Nancy Holder and Yvonne Navarro's *Wicked Willow* trilogy (*I: The Darkening*, *II: Shattered Twilight* and *III: Broken Sunrise*), along with the anthology *Tales of the Slayer, Vol. 4*.

Companion show *Angel* also came to an end, but that did not put a stop to the tie-in books, including *Nemesis* by Scott Ciencin and Denise Ciencin, *Dark Mirror* by Craig Shaw Gardner, *Monolith* by John Passarella, *Book of the Dead* by Ashley McConnell and *Love and Death* by Jeff Mariotte.

The *Charmed* series – both books and TV show – continued to thrive with *Luck Be a Lady* by Scott Ciencin, *Inherit the Witch* by Laura J. Burns, *A Tale of Two Pipers* by Emma Harrison, *The Brewing Storm* by Paul Ruditis, *Survival of the Fittest* by Jeff Mariotte and *Pied Piper* by Debbie Viguie.

The *Smallville* novelisation *Temptation* by Suzan Colón was mysteriously retitled *Control* in the UK. It was followed by *Curse* by Alan Grant, *City* by Drevin Grayson and *Sparks* by Cherie Bennett and Jeff Gottesfeld.

Inspired by Stephen King's limited ABC-TV series *Kingdom Hospital*, *The Journals of Eleanor Druse: My Investigation of the Kingdom Hospital Incident* was purported to be written by the pseudonymous psychic, but was reportedly the work of co-producer/scriptwriter Richard Dooling.

Anonymous Rex/Casual Rex was an omnibus edition of Erica Garcia's 1999 and 2001 novels about a velociraptor PI, published to tie-in with the likeable Sci Fi Channel movie.

From ibooks came *The Twilight Zone: Book 3: Deep in the Dark* by John Heffers, while stories from a more recent incarnation of the show appeared in the form of *The Twilight Zone: Upgrade/Sensuous City* by Pat Cadigan, *Memphis/The Pool Guy* by Jay Russell and *Into the Light/Sunrise* by Paul Woods.

Based on the DC Comics series created by Neil Gaiman and John Bolton, *The Books of Magic: Consequences* and *Lost Places* by Carla Jablonski were the fourth and fifth volumes, respectively, in the young adult series about the magical adventures of Tim and his best friend Molly. *Reckonings* was the sixth and final volume in the series.

The Unquiet Grave by Peter J. Evans was the first in a series based on the exploits of vampire agent Durham Red from *2000 AD*.

Lara Croft, Tomb Raider: The Lost Cult by E.E. Knight and *Lara Croft, Tomb Raider: The Man of Bronze* by James Alan Gardner were based on the video games.

White Wolf's "World of Darkness", the contemporary horror setting for the majority of the company's games and fiction, continued with *Vampire: The Puppet-Masters* by Tim Dedopulos, third in the "Clan Brujah Trilogy", while Greg Stolze's *A Hunger Like Fire* was based on the "Vampire: The Requiem" role-playing game.

Vampire: The Clan Novel Saga, Vol.2 The Eye of Gehenna and *Vol.3 Bloody September*, both edited by Stewart Wieck, were omnibus/anthologies using material from various novels, anthologies and stories re-arranged chronologically. They were followed by *Vol.4 End Games*, edited by Philippe Boulle.

Novels based on the "Clan" role-playing game included *Dark Ages: Toreador* by Janet Trautvetter, *Dark Ages: Gangrel* by Tim Waggoner, *Dark Ages: Tremere* by Sarah Roark, *Dark Ages: Venture* by Matthew McFarland and *Dark Ages: Tzimisce* by Myranda Kalis, the thirteenth and final volume in the series.

White Wolf brought an end to the "World of Darkness" in a series of books called the "Time of Judgment". The first volume, *Vampire: Gehenna: The Final Night* by Ari Marmell, sold out its entire print-run of 10,000 copies before publication. It was followed by *Were-wolf: The Last Battle* by Bill Bridges and *Mage: Judgment Day* by Bruce Baugh.

From UK specialist press Telos Publishing, Keith Topping's idiosyncratic *A Vault of Horror* was a hefty paperback subtitled *A Book of 80 Great* (*and not so great) British Horror Movies from 1956–1974*. Profusely illustrated with black and white stills and a nice colour poster section, the volume broke each title down into handy bite-sized chunks of information.

Beasts in the Cellar: The Exploitation Film Career of Tony Tenser by John Hamilton looked at the man who ran Tigon Films and produced such movies as *Repulsion*, *Witchfinder General* and *Naked as Nature Intended*.

From Dark Horse Books, *Hellboy: The Art of the Movie* contained the final shooting script of the movie plus concept artwork and behind-the-scenes shots from the film, with an Introduction by director Guillermo del Toro.

Titan Books published an expanded edition of *Hellraiser* star Doug Bradley's 1996 volume as *Behind the Mask of the Horror Actor* with an improved cover design and the original Foreword by Clive Barker.

As Timeless As Infinity: The Complete Twilight Zone Scripts of Rod Serling, Volume One collected nine television scripts, two in alternate versions. Published by Gauntlet Press in an edition of 750 copies signed by Carol Serling, the hardcover included commentary by editor Tony Albarella, appreciations by Richard Matheson and Rockne S. O'Bannon, and cover art by Harry O. Morris.

Edited and written by Stefano Piselli and Riccardo Morrocchi, the Italian published *La Dolce Paura* (Sweet Fear) was subtitled *1960s Sexy Horror in Italian Movies & Popular Publications* and featured artwork from movie posters and book and magazine covers.

Stephen King's 1999 book *The Girl Who Loved Tom Gordon* was adapted into a children's pop-up book by Peter Abrahams with artwork by Alan Dingman. It had a first printing of 250,000 copies from Simon & Schuster/Little Simon, backed by a $250,000 marketing campaign.

Featuring many classic cartoons and commentary by the artist, *The Best of Gahan Wilson* was edited by Cathy and Arnie Fenner for Underwood Books. From the same publisher and editors, the annual *Spectrum 11: The Best in Contemporary Fantasy Art* featured more than 400 colour works from 2003 by over 250 artists, including John Jude Palencar, Donato Giancola, John Berkey, Phil Hale, Todd Schorr, Jim Burns, William Stout, Rick Berry and many others, along with a profile of 2004 Grand Master Award recipient Michael Whelan.

Published by Shocklines Press, *As Dead as Leaves: The Art of Caniglia* showcased the work of the talented young artist with a Foreword by George Pratt, an Introduction by the illustrator and remarks by Phil Hale. It was available as a trade paperback plus a limited hardcover edition with an added art print.

The Paint in My Blood: Illustration and Fine Art by Alan M. Clark was a full-colour compendium of the artist's work (including collaborations with other illustrators), commentary by Clark and an afterword-of-sorts by Jack Hunter Daves. The book was available from IFD Publishing as a large-size paperback, a 500-copy limited edition hardcover, and in a twenty-six copy lettered state that came in a metal traycase and included a matted sketch ($175.00). Both of the limited editions also contained a CD-R in which the artist demonstrated painting techniques and animations of several of the paintings in the book.

Published by Last Gasp Press, *Dreamland: The Art of Todd Schorr* featured the artist's surreal pop culture paintings with text by Paul Di Filippo.

Darrell C. Richardson's *Those Macabre Pulps* from Adventure House looked at twenty-five titles published between 1910 and 1970, with full-colour cover reproductions and listings of stories by author.

Neil Gaiman and Dave McKean's 1997 book *The Day I Swapped My Dad for Two Goldfish* was reissued in a larger deluxe edition with a new cover, two additional pages of art, a new Afterword by the author and a limited edition enhanced CD of Gaiman reading the story.

Artist Gris Grimley adapted four stories by Edgar Allan Poe for the young adult *Tales of Mystery and Madness*.

From Titan Books, *Modesty Blaise: The Gabriel Set-Up*, *Mister Sun* and *The Black Pearl* by Peter O'Donnell and Jim Holdaway were three welcome oversized softcovers reprinting the black and white newspaper strips from the *London Evening Standard* of the mid-1960s. Beautifully reproduced in full-colour hardcover format, *Dan Dare Pilot of the Future: Voyage to Venus Parts 1 and 2* reprinted Frank Hampson's 1950–51 strip from *Eagle* comic and associated material in two volumes. Far less impressive was *Amazona*, a collection of inferior pin-up paintings by Chris Achilléos and the first in a proposed new series of hardcover art books from Titan.

Published by Paper Tiger, *The Deceiving Eye* showcased the stunning comics, film poster and book cover art of Richard Hescox, with text by Randy M. Dannenfelser.

Produced by the redoubtable team of writer Les Daniels and designer Chip Kidd for publisher Harry N. Abrams, *The Golden Age of DC Comics: 365 Days* was a hefty, if eccentric, trip down memory lane for comics fans.

Revenue at Marvel increased 73 per cent to $155.5 million across the entire company, mostly thanks to tie-in toy sales linked to *Spider-Man 2*. Meanwhile, Marvel Comics created Marvel Press, to expand the Marvel Universe into prose books aimed at both young adult and older readers.

Lovecraft was an original hardcover graphic novel from DC Comics/Vertigo, written by screenwriter Hans Rodionoff with Keith Griffen and painted by Argentinian artist Enriqué Breccia. This heavily fictionalized life of Howard Philips Lovecraft was introduced by film director John Carpenter.

DC's *Elric: The Making of a Sorcerer* was a four-issue prestige format miniseries in which writer Michael Moorcock and artist Walter Simonson revealed the origin of the albino warrior.

George Romero returned to the world of his zombie films in the six-part story arc "The Death of Death!" in DC's *Toe Tags*, which debuted at Halloween. Illustrated by Tommy Castillo and Rodney Ramos, with cover art by Bernie Wrightson, the political satire was set in a world of the living dead.

Christopher Golden's *Justice League of America: Exterminators* and Mark Schultz's *Justice League of America: The Flash: Stop Motion* were both based on the DC series, while Kevin J. Anderson combined comics and pulps in DC's *JSA Strange Adventures*, a six-issue miniseries featuring the Golden Age Justice Society of America, illustrated by Barry Kitson and Gary Erskine.

B.P.R.D.: Plague of Frogs was a *Hellboy* spin-off written by Mike Mignola and illustrated by Guy Davis for Dark Horse Comics that continued the exploits of the Bureau for Paranormal Research and Defense (sic).

The Song of Red Sonja and Other Stories, *The Shadow in the Tomb* and *The Curse of the Golden Skull* were the fourth, fifth and sixth volumes, respectively, in Dark Horse Books' beautifully remastered series *The Chronicles of Conan*, written with always fascinating new Afterwords by Roy Thomas and illustrated by Barry Windsor-Smith, John Buscema, Neal Adams and others. The three volumes included adaptations of Robert E. Howard's short novel "Red Nails", a posthumous collaboration with Lin Carter, an original plot by Mike Resnick, and Norvell W. Page's originally non-Conan novel *Flame Winds*.

The revised and expanded Second Edition of Eureka Productions' *Graphic Classics Volume One: Edgar Allan Poe* dropped work by Clive Barker and Gahan Wilson and added more than eighty new pages of art. *Graphic Classics Volume Nine: Robert Louis Stevenson* featured twenty-one graphic adaptations, including "The Bottle Imp" and "Dr Jekyll and Mr Hyde", while *Graphic Classics Volume Ten: Horror Classics* contained twelve adaptations of stories by H.P. Lovecraft, Edgar Allan Poe, Clark Ashton Smith and others.

The Inklings – J.R.R. Tolkien, C.S. Lewis and Charles Williams – confronted Aleister Crowley in Micah Harris' graphic novel *Heaven's War*, illustrated by Michael Gaydos from Image Comics.

Writer Kris Oprisko and artist Gabriel Hernandez adapted Clive Barker's 1992 young adult novel about Mr Hood's mysterious Holiday House in *Clive Barker's The Thief of Always*, a limited series from IDW Publishing.

A young boy believed that the classic old monsters still had the ability to frighten in Steve Niles' one-shot from IDW, *The Very Big Monster Show*, illustrated by Butch Adams. From the same publisher, Niles also adapted George A. Romero's zombie film *Dawn of the Dead* with painted art by Chee, while Ian Edgington adapted *Richard Matheson's Hell House* as a bi-monthly black and white title, with art by Simon Fraser. Artist Scott Hampton's *Spookhouse: Book Two* included adaptations of work by Clive Barker, Robert E. Howard and others in full colour, also from IDW.

Based on the board game from Human Head Studios, *Dracula's Revenge* #1 from IDW Publishing was written by Matt Forbeck with art from Szymon Kudranski.

Scripted by Max Allan Collins and illustrated by Gabriel Rodriguez, *CSI: Crime Scene Investigation: Serial* was a graphic novel collection of the first five issues of the IDW comic based on the popular CBS-TV series. It concerned a copycat serial killer in Las Vegas who thought he was Jack the Ripper.

1950s TV horror host Zacherley launched his own comic book from Chanting Monks Press with *Zacherley's Midnite Terrors*, featuring a cover painting by Basil Gogos. The second issue was also available in a limited edition of 250 copies signed in silver by cover artist William Stout.

From the same imprint, *Road Kills* featured a cover by Bernie Wrightson and included three original stories by Hart D. Fisher, Christa Faust and Joseph M. Monks and was produced exclusively for the International Festival of Fantasy & Terror in Mexico City. Joe Martino's *Ripperman* was about a mysterious stranger and a series of child killings, while the second issue of *Agony in Black* featured work by Wayne Allen Sallee, amongst others.

From ibooks/Milk & Cookies Press, *Gonna Role the Bones* was a graphic adaptation of Fritz Leiber's award-winning story, written by Sarah L. Thomson and illustrated by David Wiesner.

Mister Negativity and Other Tales of Supernatural Law was the latest graphic collection from Batton Lash, which parodied everything from Harry Potter to Stephen King.

The American summer box office once again broke records with ticket sales hitting $3.9 billion, narrowly beating the record $3.8 billion of 2003. However, the 2004 total was boosted by inflation, as audience numbers dropped slightly from the previous year.

Sequels again proved to be the key to success, with *Shrek 2*, *Spider-Man 2* and *Harry Potter and the Prisoner of Azkaban* all breaking the $200 million barrier. *The Incredibles* and *The Day After Tomorrow* rounded out the top five films of the year.

With an opening weekend of over $100 million and an eventual take of more than $440 million, DreamWorks' fairy tale *Shrek 2* reunited the original voice cast and became the top grossing animated movie ever.

Sam Raimi's superior *Spider-Man 2* had a record-breaking opening day gross of $40.5 million, as Tobey Maguire's angst-ridden web-spinner was pitched against Alfred Molina's grasping Dr Octopus.

Alfonso Cuaron's *Harry Potter and the Prisoner of Azkaban* enjoyed an opening weekend take of $93.69 million, beating both the previous films in the series. In the UK the movie took more than £5 million in 535 venues, breaking the record for biggest opening day and best single day take. The darkest entry in the series to date, it featured Michael Gambon (replacing the late Richard Harris) as Dumbledore, and David Thewlis as a werewolf.

A group of superheroes were called out of retirement to save the world in Brad Bird's animated *The Incredibles*, the biggest hit yet for Pixar Animation Studios/Disney, while Roland Emmerich's spectacular *The Day After Tomorrow* saw the northern hemisphere plunged into a new Ice Age because of a shift in the Earth's climate due to global warming.

They all featured in the UK top ten movies as well, along with the disappointing *Scooby-Doo 2: Monsters Unleashed*, as Britons spent a record £839 million on cinema tickets.

Meanwhile, the British film industry was thrown into turmoil in February when a sudden change in the tax law by the Inland Revenue, closing a tax loophole used to fund movies, resulted in the cancellation or restructuring of up to an estimated forty films.

Seven months later a new tax deal was announced by the Treasury, which would cover a higher percentage of increased production costs. Another change would be that the money would be paid directly to the film makers, rather than a third party investor. Unfortunately it was too little, too late, and the number of films produced in the UK plummeted by 40 per cent in 2004.

Also in September, a partnership headed by the Japanese Sony group bought Hollywood studio Metro-Goldwyn-Mayer in a deal estimated to be worth $4.8 billion (£2.7 billion). Time Warner withdrew a competitive bid at the last minute. Included in the deal was MGM's library of more than 4,000 films.

2004 got off to a good start, with the previous year's *The Lord of the Rings: The Return of the King* going on to take more than $300 million at the American box office and passing the £50 million mark in Britain.

Probably the biggest disappointment of the year was Stephen Sommers' much hyped *Van Helsing*, in which Hugh Jackman's bland monster hunter encountered Dracula, Frankenstein's Monster, a CGI wolfman and Kate Beckinsale's swashbuckling princess in basically a rip-off of Hammer's *Captain Kronos Vampire Hunter* (1972). *Van Helsing: The London Assignment* was an animated prequel for children, with Jackman voicing the titular monster hunter, while *The Adventures of Young Van Helsing: Quest for the Lost Scepter* was an unconnected live action cash-in, also aimed at younger viewers.

Wesley Snipes' undead vampire slayer teamed up with two new

helpers to destroy a reincarnated Dracula (Dominic Purcell) in David S. Goyer's flashy *Blade Trinity*, based on the Marvel Comics character.

Thomas Janes played another Marvel hero in Jonathan Hensleigh's *The Punisher*, as the eponymous vigilante took revenge on John Travolta's crime boss. Even the 1989 adaptation with Dolph Lundgren was an improvement over the new version.

Halle Berry was as embarrassed as the audience about her title role in the pretentiously-named Pitof's *Catwoman*, loosely inspired by the DC Comics character.

Based on Mike Mignola's Dark Horse comic, Guillermo del Toro's enjoyable *Hellboy* pitted Ron Perlman's horned hero against a resurrected Rasputin who wanted to create a new Third Reich using Lovecraftian monsters from another dimension.

Kerry Conran's pulpy *Sky Captain and the World of Tomorrow* was unfairly overlooked despite its all-star cast, stunning CGI effects and knowing nods to 1930s genre classics.

The curse of *The Exorcist* struck again: Despite opening at #1, *Exorcist: The Beginning* barely managed to scrape past $30 million at the box office. Following John Frankenheimer's death, Paul Schrader was brought in as a replacement, but the $35 million film was then re-shot from scratch by Renny Harlin and original star Liam Neeson was replaced by Stellan Skarsgård. Original director William Friedkin described the new prequel, set in Africa in the late 1940s, as "pointless".

Although it died at the box office, the remake of *Dawn of the Dead* took twice as much money when subsequently released as an unrated DVD. Meanwhile, Edgar Wright's low brow and low budget "Rom-ZomCom" (romantic zombie comedy) *Shaun of the Dead* became something of a cult hit on both sides of the Atlantic without taking much money.

Milla Jovovich returned to zap more flesh-eating zombies in a ravaged Raccoon City in Alexander Witt's witless sequel *Resident Evil: Apocalypse*, based on the computer game.

Despite featuring Lance Henriksen, Paul W.S. Anderson's long-awaited *Alien vs. Predator* proved to be the worst of both series.

Following the sleeper success of *Pitch Black*, Vin Diesel was back as the titular anti-hero in David Twohy's overblown *The Chronicles of Riddick*, and future cop Will Smith hunted down a deadly droid in Alex Proyas' *I, Robot*, "suggested by Isaac Asimov's book" (sic).

Julianne Moore seemed to be the only person who remembered her missing 9-year-old son as Joseph Ruben's *The Forgotten* strayed into *X Files* territory, while Greg Kinnear, Rebecca Romjin-Stamos and, especially, Robert De Niro were obviously slumming in Nick Hamm's box-office dud *Godsend*, about evil cloning experiments.

After opening at #1 in the US, M. Night Shyamalan's *The Village* proved to be a twist too far when it dropped sixty-eight per-cent in its second week.

In Dwight H. Little's belated follow-up *Anacondas: The Hunt for the Blood Orchid*, a group of pharmaceutical researchers were squeezed out of the Borneo jungle by giant CGI serpents.

Despite the presence of Johnny Depp as a successful author accused of plagarism by a scary John Turturro, David Koepp's adaptation of Stephen King's *Secret Window* was not a hit. Unfortunately, the year's other King adaptation, Mick Garris' *Riding the Bullet*, fared even worse at the box office in a limited release.

Ashton Kutcher travelled back and forth in time in New Line's *The Butterfly Effect*, which was considered a box-office flop, despite opening at #1 in the US. The film's title was inspired by a story from Ray Bradbury, who publicly complained that film-maker Michael Moore "stole" his title for the award-winning anti-George Bush documentary *Fahrenheit 9/11*, a surprise box-office hit during the summer.

Don Mancini's self-referential *Seed of Chucky*, the fifth entry in the patchy series, had killer dolls Chucky and Tiffany (voiced by Brad Dourif and Jennifer Tilly) revived from the dead and menacing actress Jennifer Tilly while she was filming a *Chucky* movie! John Walters had a fun cameo.

With its emerging importance as a key release date, some industry insiders pegged Halloween as the new Christmas with the success of Takashi Shimizu's remake of his overrated 2002 film, *The Grudge* (*Ju-On*), and James Wan's low budget debut *Saw*. The latter gorefest cost $1 million to make and grossed more than $50 million in the US.

Shimizu's original version of *Ju-On* was heavily influenced by other recent Asian horror movies and received a limited American theatrical release, as did Takashi Miike's bizarre *Gozu*.

Jee-woon Kim's spooky Korean thriller *A Tale of Two Sisters* ran rings around the other Asian releases.

Starring Denzel Washington and Meryl Streep, Jonathan Demme's unnecessary remake of the cold war thriller *The Manchurian Candidate* was released in America to tie in with the Democratic Convention.

After finally reaching the screen after nearly fifteen years, Joel Schumacher's version of Andrew Lloyd Webber's hit musical *The Phantom of the Opera* actually wasn't worth the wait.

Frank Oz's critically-panned remake of *The Stepford Wives* starred Nicole Kidman as a robotic male fantasy in an ill-conceived spoof of Ira Levin's book, and Kidman decided her dead husband had been reincarnated in the body of a 10-year-old boy (Cameron Bright) in Jonathan Glazer's controversial *Birth*.

Tobe Hooper's career dropped another notch with a pointless remake of *The Toolbox Murders*, while two cousins raped and murdered women in 1970s Los Angeles in the unpleasant thriller *The Hillside Strangler*.

In Chris Smith's derivative *Creep*, a woman (Franka Potente) fell asleep on a London Underground platform and ended up taking the wrong train into a nightmare world of cannibal mutants.

From Robert Harmon, director of the much better *The Hitcher*, revenge-seeking widower Jim Caviezel hunted down a monocular maniac in *Highwaymen*.

Two women were menaced by a psychopath with a cut-throat razor and wood saw in Alexandre Aja's French/Romanian slasher film *Switchblade Romance*, but Colin Firth and Mena Suvari were as comatose as the audiences who saw Marc Evan's long-delayed psychological thriller *Trauma*.

Despite starring Angelina Jolie as an unlikely FBI profiler and Ethan Hawke as her prime suspect, D.J. Caruso's *Taking Lives* was a mundane thriller. An unrated "Director's Cut" was subsequently issued on DVD. In E. Elias Merhige's *Suspect Zero*, a pair of telepathically trained FBI agents (Aaron Eckhart and Carrie-Anne Moss) tracked down Ben Kingsley's crazy killer.

A group of holidaymakers on an island off Costa Rica fell victim to a silly serial killer in Jay Chandrasekhar's dumb comedy *Club Dread*. The only surprise was Bill Paxton's involvement.

The Lost Skeleton of Cadavra was Larry Blamire's low budget spoof of bad "B" movies, while James Woods and Nick Nolte turned up in Michael Polish's monochromatic fantasy *Northfork*.

Based on a true story, a pair of abandoned scuba divers were menaced by hungry sharks in Chris Kentis' shaky docudrama *Open Water*.

Isabelle Huppert discovered that the world was slowly coming to an end due to a psychic plague in Michael Haneke's thoughtful *Time of the Wolf*, while Jan Kounen's weird Western *Blueberry* was based on a French comic book and featured Michael Madsen, Juliette Lewis, Geoffrey Lewis, Eddie Izzard and veteran Ernest Borgnine.

Robin Williams and Mira Sorvino starred in *The Final Cut*, which was about downloading the memories of dead people.

Hayao Miyazaki's animated version of Diana Wynne Jones' *Howl's Moving Castle* (*Hauru no ugoku shiro*) set records in Japan in November, achieving more than a million admissions in just two days.

Jim Carrey had fun as the evil Count Olaf, a ham actor out to bump off a trio of orphaned children for their inheritance, in Brad Silberling's superb-looking Gothic comedy *Lemony Snicket's A Series of Unfortunate Events*.

Jennifer Garner found herself all grown-up in *13 Going on 30*, Gary Winick's take on *Big* for young girls.

Frank Coraci's redundant remake of *Around the World in 80 Days* was more Jackie Chan than Jules Verne, and comedian Harry Enfield played the evil Fairy Hunter in Edouard Nammour's disastrous children's fantasy *Tooth*.

Kenneth Branagh starred in John Stephenson's *5 Children & It*, based on E. Nesbit's 1902 fantasy story for children, while Johnny Depp portrayed *Peter Pan* author J.M. Barrie in Marc Foster's Oscar-nominated *Finding Neverland*.

Bill Murray voiced the fat cat star of the animated *Garfield the Movie*, and the title characters from *Boo, Zino & the Snurks* were snatched from their TV world by a mad inventor in the German-made CGI adventure.

An uncredited Richard Curtis (*Four Weddings and a Funeral*, etc.) was apparently brought in by Working Title to "beef up" the dialogue for Lady Penelope (Sophia Myles) in Jonathan Frakes' misguided $70 million live-action version of *Thunderbirds*, based on the 1960s puppet TV series. Despite taking a respectable £4.41 million in the UK, with a worldwide box office total of just $26 million, the film was one of the biggest flops of the summer.

Based on the children's picture book by Chris Van Allsburg, Robert Zemeckis' *The Polar Express* took more than $155 million and pushed the envelope for computer "performance capture" animation. The film was also released in a special polarized 3-D IMAX version.

Shown at various conventions around the world, Robert Pratten's low budget *London Voodoo* was about an American family moving into a cursed terrace house with a psychotic nanny. It featured a soundtrack by Steven Severin of Siouxsie & The Banshees.

To celebrate its fiftieth anniversary, the original 1954 version of *Godzilla* was released theatrically in America for the first time with forty minutes of previously cut footage restored. At the end of

November, Godzilla also received his own star on the Hollywood Walk of Fame.

Peter Jackson's *The Lord of the Rings: The Return of the King* made a record-breaking clean sweep at the seventy-sixth Academy Awards, held in Hollywood at the very end of February, when it won all eleven categories it was nominated in. The final part of the trilogy collected Oscars for Art Direction, Costume Design, Visual Effects, Make-up, Sound Mixing, Film Editing, Original Song, Original Score, Adapted Screenplay, Director and the coveted Best Picture (the first time a fantasy film had done so). South African actress Charlize Theron won Best Actress for her role in the serial killer film *Monster*, and *Finding Nemo* picked up the award for Best Animated Film.

Over November and December, London's National Film Theatre programmed "A History of the Horror Film", an eclectic selection of titles that included Universal and Hammer classics along with several silents, some low budget schlock, Asian horrors and even a few titles projected in 3-D. Co-curator Mark Kermode also interviewed director Ken Russell about his controversial 1971 film, *The Devils*.

"Lady in Red" singer Chris De Burgh paid £30,000 for the "chestburster" from *Alien* (1979) at an auction in London in mid-July. The sixteen-inch latex model came complete with controls.

Neil Gaiman's *A Short Film About John Bolton* was released on DVD containing more than two hours of bonus material. Along with the short vampire film of the title (which included Judith Clute, Michel Parry, Stephen Jones and the real John Bolton among the extras), there was a commentary track, a feature-length benefit performance, an audio recording and an interview with writer/ director Gaiman. A John Bolton photo gallery and various biographies rounded out the package.

Christopher Lee's missing scenes were finally restored to the special extended DVD edition of *The Lord of the Rings: The Return of the King*, which was issued in a four-disc set loaded with extra features. The gift set featured a collectable Minas Tirith keepsake box and a bonus DVD.

Giorgio Ferroni's 1960 film *Mill of the Stone Women* (*Il Mulino delle donne di pietra*) was released for the first time on DVD in its full-length uncut version by Mondo Macabro.

Released on the back of the dire *Van Helsing*, Universal yet again repackaged its classic horror movies in "The Monster Legacy" DVD gift sets devoted to Dracula, Frankenstein, The Wolf Man, The

Creature from the Black Lagoon, The Mummy and The Invisible Man.

Michael Gross starred in *Tremors 4: The Legend Begins*, a prequel to the giant worm series set in the Old West.

From Guerrilla Productions, *H.P. Lovecraft's The Dream-Quest of Unknown Kadath* limited edition DVD was signed by director Edward Martin III and comics artist Jason Thompson, on whose work the animated feature was based. The numbered DVD also included two bonus short features: *The Call of Cthulhu* and *The Testament of Tom Jacoby*.

EI Independent Cinema relaunched its Shock-O-Rama Cinema label with six new horror films, all produced in-house. Beginning in March with the release of Brett Piper's *Screaming Dead* starring the ubiquitous Misty Mundae, they continued with Piper's *Bite Me!*, also featuring Mundae and an army of mutant killer bugs, and Jon Keeyes' *Suburban Nightmare*, about a psychotic couple portrayed by Trent Haaga and Brandy Little. Mundae also wrote, directed and starred in the six-minute short *Voodoun Blues*, which came with numerous extras in an edition limited to 5,000 copies.

Under the EI Seduction Cinema logo, Darian Caine, Misty Mundae and Julian Wells starred in *Lust for Dracula*, Anthony Marsiglia's modern reworking of the classic vampire story, while Caine also turned up as Countess Dracula in "Max Von Diesel's" less-than-subtle comedy *The Sexy Adventures of Van Helsing*, also featuring A.J. Khan, Tina Krause, Chelsea Mundae and Debbie Rochon.

Brad Watson's incompetent and amateurish blend of vampires, psychos and comic policeman, *Asylum Night* was a shot-on-video disaster that was released directly to Britain's The Horror Channel before receiving a DVD release in the UK.

Hell Breeder was about a woman who suffered from nightmares and featured Darren Day.

Artisan's *Kindred: The Embraced* two-disc set collected all eight original episodes of the 1996 TV series based on the role-playing game.

The *Kolchak: The Night Stalker* double feature disc from MGM Home Entertainment contained the 1970s pilot TV movies *The Night Stalker* and *The Night Strangler*, both scripted by Richard Matheson and starring Darren McGavin as the seersucker-suited investigative reporter.

For Halloween, Universal offered the complete first seasons of Rod Serling's underrated *Night Gallery* and the classic comedy series *The Munsters* (including the unaired pilot) on DVD.

MPI Home Video's two-volume *The Sherlock Holmes Collection* contained "digitally restored" prints of Universal's 1940s series of low budget adventures starring Basil Rathbone and Nigel Bruce. Meanwhile, BBC DVD's *The Sherlock Holmes Collection* collected five classic TV episodes from the 1960s starring Peter Cushing as Sir Arthur Conan Doyle's consulting detective. *A Study in Scarlet*, *The Boscombe Valley Mystery*, *The Sign of Four*, *The Blue Carbuncle* and *The Hound of the Baskervilles* were available on three DVDs or as a boxed set.

A&E Home Video's four-disc set of *The New Avengers* collected all thirteen episodes from the series' second season.

You may not be able to watch them on television any more due to complaints from ethnic pressure groups, but MGM Home Entertainment's "Chanthology" three-disc DVD set collected six of Monogram's 1940s *Charlie Chan* features starring Sidney Toler.

Although the promise of "three alternative endings" was not strictly true, the much-anticipated DVD release of Tod Browning's seminal *Freaks* also featured a new documentary entitled *Freaks: Sideshow Cinema*.

October saw the premier of two new TV versions of *Frankenstein*. William Hurt, Donald Sutherland and Julie Delpy starred in a miniseries version of Mary Shelley's classic on the Hallmark Channel with Luke Goss as the Monster, while Dean Koontz's modern-day adaptation on the USA Network had the evolved 200-year-old Monster (Vincent Perez) teaming up with New Orleans detectives Parker Posey and Adam Goldberg for a silly series pilot involving a mad scientist (Thomas Kretschmann) creating a race of super-beings from harvested organs. Koontz took his name off the project and subsequently developed it as a series of novels in collaboration with Kevin J. Anderson.

TNT's two-part, $12 million adaptation of Stephen King's *Salem's Lot* was a pointless remake of the superior 1979 version. It starred a bland Rob Lowe, Donald Sutherland, and Rutger Hauer as Barlow the vampire, while the ending was left open for a possible series.

The Sci Fi channel churned out a raft of made-for-TV "B" movies in 2004: John Savage played a crazy scientist who mutated an alien reptile in *Alien Lockdown*; Bruce Boxleitner hunted mutated killer fish in *Snakehead Terror*; Costas Mandylor saved a small town from a prehistoric crocodile in *Dinocroc*; David Hewlett's geneticist witnessed the battle between a mutant *Boa vs. Python*; Eric Lutes had to prevent an Alaskan town being overrun by ravenous soldier ants in *Marabunta: Terror in Burline Pines*; Tim Abell's scientist investigated mutant Komodo dragons in *Curse of the Komodo*; cave explorers Trevor Murphy and Larry Casey encountered carnivorous creepy-crawlies in *Centipede!*; Navy SEAL Lorenzo Lamas battled dinosaurs on *Raptor Island*, and mutated fish fed on humans in the wittily titled *Frankenfish*.

Also on Sci Fi, Cameron Bancroft played a shape-shifting commando in *Code Name: Eternity*; Nicole Eggert investigated a series of bizarre killings by alien babes in *Decoys*; Shiri Appleby portrayed a remorseful demon in *Darklight*, and Sunny Mabrey was Eve's alien spawn in the series pilot *Species III*.

From the same channel, Kevin Dillon's depressed cop was bitten by an acid-bleeding vampire in *Out for Blood*; the offbeat *Anonymous Rex* co-starred Sam Trammell and Daniel Baldwin as a pair of dinosaur private eyes working for Faye Dunaway, and *Puppet Master vs Demonic Toys* featured Corey Feldman in the ultimate doll smackdown.

Supposedly disowned by its subject, Nathaniel Kahn's *The Buried Secret of M. Night Shyamalan* on the Sci Fi Channel in July was a much too long *Blair Witch*-style spoof documentary about the director of *The Village* that shouldn't have fooled anybody.

Ursula K. Le Guin's classic fantasy *Earthsea* premiered on the Sci Fi channel as a miniseries starring Shawn Ashmore as sorcerer-in-training Ged and Danny Glover as his legendary mentor, the wizard Ogion. The author really did disown it.

MTV's original made-for-cable movie *Monster Island* was a tongue-in-cheek spoof of classic 1950s creature features. A group of high school competition winners found themselves trapped on a Pacific island with Carmen Electra in a fur bikini, Adam West's Dr Harryhausen and various stop-motion giant insects.

Noah Wyle went searching for a lost artifact in TNT's *The Librarian: Quest for the Spear*, while New Orleans lawyer Anne Heche was given an antique engagement ring by her fiancé and started seeing dead people in CBS' *The Dead Will Tell*, inspired by the readings of real-life medium James Van Praagh.

Nicolette Sheridan starred in yet another version of the old "eyes of Orlac" scenario for the Lifetime movie *Deadly Visions*, in which a woman's eyesight was restored by a transplant that had the unpleasant side effect of visions of the donor's demise.

Shelved since 2003, *Doctor Sleep* from BBC Films starred Goran Visnjic as a telepathic American psychologist investigating a series of occult murders linked to a 500-year-old French heretic seeking immortality. It was released theatrically in America under the point-less title *Close Your Eyes*.

John Nettles returned as unflappable DCI Tom Barnaby with John Hopkins as his loyal sergeant to investigate a series of spontaneous combustion deaths in the typically bizarre and convoluted *Midsomer Murders* film *The Straw Woman*, while in *Things That Go Bump in the Night* the duo investigated a number of murders linked to a local séance group.

A combination of extreme weather conditions wiped out Chicago in the CBS movie *Category 6: Day of Destruction* starring Thomas Gibson, Randy Quaid, Dianne Wiest and Brian Dennehy, and NBC's *10.5* trotted out all the usual clichés as a series of earthquakes led to the destruction of Los Angeles and the breaking away of the California coastline.

The Hollow was an updating of the Washington Irving story about the headless horseman, starring Kaley Cuoco, Nick Carter and Stacy Keach. It was shown as part of ABC-TV's "13 Nights of Halloween".

The Disney Channel's *Halloweentown High* was the third in the series featuring young witch Marnie (Kimberly J. Brown) and her eccentric grandmother (veteran Debbie Reynolds), while ABC-TV's long-shelved *A Wrinkle in Time* was based on Madeleine L'Engle's 1962 classic children's novel and shown on "The Wonderful World of Disney".

Kelsey Grammer starred as Scrooge in NBC-TV's version of the New York stage musical of Charles Dickens' *A Christmas Carol*, which also featured Jason Alexander as Jacob Marley along with Jesse L. Martin, Jane Krakowski, Geraldine Chaplin and Jennifer Love Hewitt. Peter Falk reprised his role as Max the angel for the third time in the CBS Christmas movie *When Angels Come to Town*, and a grumpy Santa (Tom Cavanagh) lost his reindeer in the ABC Family channel movie *Snow*.

Scooby-Doo and the Loch Ness Monster premiered on the Car-toon Network.

Benjamin Britten's opera *Turn of the Screw*, based on the novella by Henry James, was broadcast in the summer by BBC-TV with music performed by the City of London Sinfonia.

ABC's US network television premiere in May of *Harry Potter and the Sorcerer's Stone* contained never-before-seen footage and an exclusive ten-minute sneak preview of *Harry Potter and the Prisoner of Azkaban*.

The Horror Channel launched in May on Britain's BSkyB satellite platform as a limited movie channel showing old and obscure (i.e. cheap or out-of-copyright) films. Original programming consisted of talking head interviews with British film stars and directors of the 1960s and 1970s.

Although *Smallville*'s lead-in helped *Angel* with viewing figures, and the show reached its 100th epsiode (without the hoped-for cameo from *Buffy*'s Sarah Michelle Gellar, although Charisma Carpenter returned for one last time as Cordelia), it was still cancelled after five seasons by The WB due to poor ratings. A write-in campaign and online petitions failed to save the series.

The fifth and final season included the irritating Fred (Amy Acker) being "killed" by resurrected demon god Illyria, while Angel (David Boreanaz) travelled back in time to 1943 and was turned into a puppet on a demonic TV show.

In the final episode, "Not Fade Away", broadcast in May, Angel signed away his last chance of becoming human again as the vampire-with-a-soul and his team took on the Circle of the Black Thorn and Wolfram & Hart's Senior Partners in a final showdown that revealed some genuine surprises and included the deaths of two major characters.

One of the hottest new shows of 2004 was ABC-TV's *Lost*, which premiered in September. Created by J.J. Abrams (*Alias*), the survivors of a plane crash found themselves trapped on a mysterious Pacific island menaced by unseen forces, including what appeared to be a monster.

Also on ABC, Craig Baxley directed every episode of Stephen King's ambitious thirteen-part, fifteen-hour *Kingdom Hospital*, loosely based on Lars von Trier's 1990s Danish TV series about a haunted hospital. With talking animals, headless zombies and a central plot built around the author's own near fatal hit-and-run incident, audiences stayed away in droves and viewing figures plunged from fourteen million to just five million in three weeks. As a result, the network quickly moved the show to an impossible time slot opposite *CSI* and *Will & Grace*, before temporarily putting it on summer hiatus in May and then airing the final four episodes from the end of June.

"I realize now, we were asking viewers to give us a week or two, maybe three," revealed King, "and that was more time than most were willing to give."

Bill Paterson starred as the leader of a Glasgow-based parasychology research team in *Sea of Souls*, a dull co-production between BBC

Scotland and Sony Pictures. The three two-part episodes involved identical twins with a psychic link, a child who remembered a previous life and voodoo magic.

A co-production between Sky and Sony, *Hex* was a silly five-part series set in an English boarding school where psychic teenager Cassie (Christina Cole) unleashed an ancient voodoo curse. She inadvertently called up seductive fallen angel Azazeal (Michael Fassbender), much to the chagrin of the ghost of her lesbian friend Thelma (Jemima Rooper).

Even worse was Channel 4's *Garth Maranghi's Darkplace*, a six-episode sit-com set in the cursed Darkplace Hospital. Incredibly, this lame spoof of 1970s and 1980s TV shows, starring the supposed bestselling horror author (Richard Ayoade), was even more unfunny than the stage show that inspired it.

CBS' *CSI: Crime Scene Investigation* and NBC's *Crossing Jordan* both had episodes featuring fake vampires, while CBS' futuristic legal series *Century City* was set in 2030 and quickly came and went.

Five Days to Midnight was a Sci Fi Channel original miniseries in June in which Timothy Hutton's physics professor was sent a police file from the future detailing his own murder. Premiering in July, the USA Network's "event series" *The 4400* was a trite blending of *The X Files* and *Taken*, as government agents Joel Gretsch and Jacqueline McKenzie investigated the sudden return of the eponymous number of abductees. The rambling plot eventually turned out to have something to do with time travel.

There was a definite nod to Barbara Eden and *I Dream of Jeannie* when Phoebe (Alyssa Milano) became a genie in a bottle in the sixth season of the WB's *Charmed*. Having killed his mentor to save his and Piper's newborn devil-child, Whitelighter Leo (Brian Krause) began the seventh season in a bad way. Meanwhile, *Angel*'s Charisma Carpenter turned up in the recurring role of a scheming seer, and Nick Lachey (Mr Jessica Simpson) joined the cast as a romantic attachment for Phoebe.

The third season of UPN's *The Dead Zone* opened in June with Johnny Smith (Anthony Michael Hall) being arrested for murder and ended with him discovering that his telepathic powers may be killing him. Meanwhile, time-traveller Christopher Wey (Frank Whaley) from the year 2016 shed some light on the roles Rebecca (Sarah Wynter) and Greg Stillson (Sean Patrick Flanery) would play in the forthcoming Armageddon.

The sharply written *Dead Like Me* returned to Showtime for a welcome second, but final season in July, in which 18-year-old slacker George (Ellen Muth) was still dead and still a not-so-grim "Reaper". In the Halloween series finale, George recalled fond childhood memories while a serial killer kept the soul-takers busy.

In the two-hour season finale of Fox's struggling *Tru Calling*, Eliza Dushku's character discovered that her friend Jack (mid-season addition Jason Priestly) was actually a Grim Reaper working against her ability to turn back time to help dead people. In the second season, Priestly's character teamed up with Tru's evil father, after knocking off her boring boyfriend Luc (Matthew Bomer).

In Fox's quirky *Wonderfalls*, inanimate objects began talking to store clerk Jaye (Caroline Dhavernas), urging her to help others by surrendering to her own destiny. Even executive producer Tim Minear's attempts to stir up support on the Internet failed to save the critically-acclaimed show, which was cancelled after just four of its thirteen episodes were aired.

In September, the second season of CBS' *Joan of Arcadia* continued on from Joan (Amber Tamblyn) discovering she had Lyme disease and believing that she hallucinated all her conversations with the many guises of God. The star's father, Russ Tamblyn, guest-starred in the first series as a dog-walker God.

After a welcome return appearance by Christopher Reeve as reclusive scientist Dr Virgil Swann, the third season of The WB's *Smallville* ended on a cliffhanger with the apparent death of Chloe (Allison Mack), while the fourth season opened with Lex Luthor (Michael Rosenbaum) surviving being poisoned and Lois Lane (Canadian newcomer Erica Durance) arriving for thirteen episodes to help Clark (Tom Welling) investigate her cousin's supposed demise. As the show thankfully returned to its supernatural roots, other guest stars included another *Superman* alumna, Margot Kidder; Michael Ironside as Lois' father, and Jane Seymour as an uncharacteristically evil mother.

After the Enterprise tracked down the alien Xindi responsible for attacking Earth, UPN's disastrous *Enterprise* sent Captain Archer (Scott Bakula) back in time to a Nazi-occupied United States for a desperate fourth season. Meanwhile, *Family Guy* creator Seth Mac-Farlane turned up in a cameo, Robert Foxworth and Joanna Cassidy played Vulcan adversaries, and *The Next Generation*'s Brent Spiner guest-starred in three episodes as Dr Arik Soong, the scheming ancestor of Data's creator. Reports suggested that Paramount reduced the amount it charged UPN for the show so that it would have enough episodes for syndication.

While *Stargate SG-1* entered its eighth season on the Sci Fi

Channel with Richard Dean Anderson's Jack O'Neill promoted to
general, the new spin-off series *Stargate Atlantis* introduced the
vampiric blue-skinned Wraith as the major menace to the human
explorers stranded in the Pegasus galaxy.

The Sci Fi Channel's "re-imagining" of the 1970s series *Battlestar
Galactica* (shown on UK television before its American debut),
proved to be the most gripping new SF show of the year, as sinister
cyborg cylons returned to wipe out the twelve colonies of man.

Replacing Gloria Reuben, Vivica A. Fox joined Caterina Scorsone
and newcomer Mark Consuelos on the second season of Lifetime's
psychic-FBI series *Missing* (originally titled *1-800-Missing*), which
premiered in July.

When he died for ten minutes after being shot in the head by a man
in a ski mask, San Francisco Organized and Serial Crimes Unit
detective David Creegan (Jeffrey Donovan) woke up with horrific
visions in the USA Network's *Touching Evil*, based on the UK
miniseries of the same title. The show's executive producers included
the Hughes brothers and actor Bruce Willis.

For soap opera fans, Leigh Taylor-Young and Richard Steinmetz
joined NBC-TV's goofy *Passions* as two previously-dead characters.
Arch-villain Alistair Crane was almost killed by a poisoned cigar,
and androgynous axe-wielding psycho Norma escaped from the
asylum and tried to murder Tabitha in a Christmas homage to
EC comics.

Meanwhile, both NBC's *Days of Our Lives* and ABC's *One Life
to Live* featured rival serial killing sprees.

Martin Clunes and Fay Ripley were among the live-action stars of the
BBC's three-part animated British/Canadian co-production *Fungus the
Bogeyman*, based on the classic children's book by Raymond Briggs.

The Simpsons "Treehouse of Horror XV" opener to season sixteen
on Fox featured a *Fantastic Voyage* spoof, in which the dysfunctional
family explored Mr Burns' insides to rescue a miniaturized Maggie;
Ned Flanders had premonitions of death and destruction in "The Ned
Zone", while the Holmesian Eliza Simpson and her sidekick Dr Bartley
investigated the mystery of London's Ripper-like Mutton Chop Murderer in "Four Beheadings and a Funeral".

Timid teen Danny Fenton was transformed into a half-human, half-
phantom who used his superpowers to protect his friends and family
from ghosts in Nickelodeon's animated series *Danny Phantom*.

The Batman arrived on the Kids WB! Saturday morning line-up
and featured a grim animated caped crusader in his twenties battling
a dreadlocked Joker and other foes. Nineteen sixties live-action

Batman Adam West voiced Gotham City's mayor. The Cartoon Network's *Justice League Unlimited* teamed-up Superman, Batman, Wonder Woman, Supergirl and Green Arrow.

Comedy Central's *Drawn Together* combined cartoon characters and reality TV for an adults-only audience.

As part of the Fox Movie Channel's "13 Nights of Fright" leading up to Halloween, a bearded Neil Gaiman played horror host (complete with coffin and vampish assistant) to introduce such films as *Tales from the Crypt*, *The Alligator People*, *The Fly* remake, *Edward Scissorhands*, *The Norliss Tapes*, *Phantom of the Paradise* and other titles. The comedy may have been lame, but viewers were also offered the opportunity to win signed Gaiman books from the station's web site every night.

For its eight-day "Monsterfest" over Halloween, AMC presented *Entertainment Weekly's Scariest Movies*, hosted by Bruce Campbell and featuring the magazine's choice of the top twenty horror films of all time. Campbell also hosted *Boogeymen II: Masters of Horror*, another clip-heavy Halloween show on Sci Fi Channel featuring interviews with Tobe Hooper, George Romero, Wes Craven and all the usual suspects.

Meanwhile, over on E!, *True Hollywood Story: Scream Queens* was hosted by Elvira, Mistress of the Dark (Cassandra Peterson). Along with interviews with Sarah Michelle Gellar, Jennifer Love Hewitt, Brinke Stevens, Jennifer Tilly, Dee Wallace Stone, Julie Adams, Janet Leigh, Linda Blair, Jamie Lee Curtis, Ashley Laurence and many others, the show also contained (often brief) contributions from writers Nancy Kilpatrick, David Skal, Stephen Jones, Clive Barker, Séphera Girón and Edward Bryant.

The busy Elvria also hosted *Hollywood's Creepiest Creatures* and *Nature's Vampires*, two documentaries shown on Animal Planet, as well as *Elvira's Movies to Die For* on Lifetime.

On Starz! *Hare-Raising Halloween Marathon*, rabbits appeared in spoofs of *Freddy vs. Jason*, *Scream* and *The Texas Chainsaw Massacre* in-between the films.

Made for the Discovery Channel, *True Horror With Anthony Head* was a short-lived series that featured the *Buffy* actor wandering around Eastern Europe investigating the historic proof for vampires and werewolves. Among those he consulted were Dr Tina Rath and the Reverend Shaun Manchester.

In BBC Radio 4's half-hour show *Fear at the Flicks*, comedian Michael Roberts took a personal look at horror film history with the help of his impersonations of Boris Karloff, Vincent Price and Peter Lorre.

Eponymous peasant *Mort* became Death's unlikely apprentice in Radio 4's four-part adaptation of Terry Pratchett's fourth "Discworld" novel, dramatized by Robin Brooks and narrated by Anton Lesser.

Cathy Sara starred in Neville Teller's dramatization of Henry James' *The Turn of the Screw* for Radio 4.

Miriam Margolyes portrayed Annie Wilkes, who kept her favourite author Paul Sheldon (Nicholas Farrell) prisoner in an adaptation of Stephen King's *Misery* broadcast on the BBC World Service in September.

Emma Fielding read an eight-part adaptation of Shirley Jackson's *The Haunting of Hill House* on digital station BBC 7 for Hallowe'en. Over the same period, Radio 4's *Ghost Stories* featured five tales by mystery author John Connolly, about a haunted inkpot, pagan gods, creepy clowns, a spinster vampire and a haunted house, read by Freddie Jones, Ian McDiarmid, Alun Armstrong, Jacqueline Pearce and Niall Buggy.

In December, BBC Radio 4 broadcast a ten-part abridged version of Mary Shelley's *Frankenstein*, read by actor David Rintoul (the werewolf in the 1974 film *Legend of the Werewolf*), while the same month also found Dougray Scott reading an eight-part abridgement of Wilkie Collins' Gothic thriller *The Woman in White* on BBC Radio 2.

Over Christmas, Radio 2 broadcast *Christopher Lee's Fireside Tales*, a late-night collection of five fifteen-minute readings of Edgar Allan Poe's "The Black Cat", Jerome K. Jerome's "The Man of Science", E. Nesbit's "John Charrington's Wedding", Ambrose Bierce's "The Man and the Snake" and W.W. Jacobs' "The Monkey's Paw".

During October, "The Rolling Darkness Revue 2004" was a performance book tour of American West Coast stores by authors/musicians Peter Atkins, Dennis Etchison and Glen Hirshberg. Issued to coincide with the tour by Dog Run Studios, Hirshberg's *Flowers on Their Bridles, Hooves in the Air* was a handsomely-packaged CD of the novella read by the author, illustrated with an evocative series of photographs by Jonas Yip and a booklet containing the complete story. It was limited to just seventy-five copies.

Meanwhile, *Don't Turn on the Lights! The Audio Library of Modern Horror, Vol. 1* was the first in a new digitally recorded CD series. It featured Dennis Etchison reading his stories "The Dog Park" and "Inside the Cackle Factory". Produced by Dark Country Productions, a special signed and numbered "Preview Edition" was limited to 100 copies.

From The Hollywood Theater of the Ear and Blackstone Audiobooks on CD, actor John de Lancie starred in a full-cast audio play of *The Cabinet of Dr Caligari* written, produced and directed by Yuri Rasavsky and inspired by the classic 1919 silent film. With a running time of around eight hours, and also issued by Blackstone and compiled by Rasavsky, *Tales for a Stormy Night: A Pandora's Box of Classic Chillers* was a seven CD set of fourteen stories by Henry James, H.P. Lovecraft, H.H. Munro, Ambrose Bierce, Edith Wharton, Edgar Allan Poe, Lafcadio Hearn, Robert Louis Stevenson, Guy de Maupassant and others.

Despite being first published in 1975, it took almost three decades for Stephen King's *Salem's Lot* to be turned into an unabridged, seventeen-hour audio book, read by Ron McLarty.

The National Theatre's epic adaptation of Philip Pullman's trilogy *His Dark Materials* finally opened to mixed reviews in London in January after technical difficulties resulted in a delay of two weeks. The two-play, six-hour marathon starred Timothy Dalton as Lord Asriel and Patricia Hodge as Mrs Coulter.

In early February, a week after its sixteenth anniversary, Andrew Lloyd Webber's *The Phantom of the Opera* became the second-longest running musical in Broadway history. Webber's latest production, *The Woman in White*, was loosely based on the Gothic novel by Wilkie Collins and directed by Sir Trevor Nunn. It opened in London in September to decidedly mixed reviews and featured Webber's original *Phantom* star Michael Crawford as the obese Count Fosco, all but unrecognisable beneath a fat suit.

Tom Hewitt starred as the undead Count in Frank Wildhorn's critically-panned *Dracula: The Musical*, which opened at New York's Belasco Theater in August under the direction of Des McAnuff. Meanwhile, Paul Nicholas toured the UK in the title role(s) of Wildhorn's earlier Broadway adaptation of *Jekyll and Hyde: The Musical*.

Inspired by a *National Enquirer* cover and first mounted off-Broadway in 2001, potholers discovered a half-man, half-bat creature (a pointy-earred Deven May) in Laurence O'Keefe's *Bat Boy: The Musical* at the Shaftesbury Theatre, London.

Diana Rigg starred in a revival of Tennessee Williams' *Suddenly*

Last Summer at London's Albery Theatre. Dennis Potter's 1976 drama *Brimstone and Treacle*, which was banned by the BBC for eleven years, was revived at London's Bridewell Theatre in July, while Penelope Keith played medium Madame Arcati in a generally well-received revival of Noël Coward's classic 1941 comedy *Blithe Spirit*, which premiered in Bath in August before moving to London's Savoy Theatre.

In an echo of Britain's "Video Nasty" fiasco of two decades ago, there were calls from the right-wing media in July to ban the ultra-violent *Manhunt* game on PlayStation 2, following the conviction of a 17-year-old boy for the fatal stabbing of a 14-year-old in Leicester. Although the killer was said to have been obsessed by the game, the police and the courts maintained that it had no connection with the case. The victim's parents planned a £50 million lawsuit against *Manhunt*'s Edinburgh-based creators and console maker Sony.

Meanwhile, id Software's science fiction/horror game *Doom 3* was described as the most bloodthirsty computer game yet made. In early August a pirate copy of the eagerly awaited game was leaked on Internet file-sharing networks and newsgroups. Set on Mars, it involved Marines battling demons accidentally released from Hell by a scientific experiment.

The Japanese-inspired *Forbidden Siren* was set in a small town where the dead walked the streets, while two teenage sisters found an abandoned village filled with vengeful spirits in *Project Zero II: Crimson Butterflies*.

The Suffering was another horror survival game, about a prisoner trying to escape a correction facility invaded by creatures from Hell, and players were trapped in a locked apartment with a gateway leading to other dimensions in *Silent Hill 4: The Room*.

In *Beyond Good and Evil*, female photographer Jade had to get pictures of aliens to make money, while *Curse: The Eye of Isis* was set in Victorian London and involved some Ancient Egyptian arte-facts in the British Museum turning victims into zombie-like killers.

First launched in 1987, the latest in the *Castlevania* series, *Lament of Innocence*, pitted the player against Count Dracula in a castle full of monsters.

Take 2's *The Haunted Mansion* was based on the Disneyland theme ride, featuring timid ghost-hunter Zeke.

The *Van Helsing* game for PlayStation 2 and X-Box was as disappointing as its cinematic inspiration, while *Catwoman* from

EA Games was even worse than its big-screen version, despite utilising the voice of Halle Berry.

Actor Vin Diesel's Tigon Studios collaborated with Starbreeze on the Vivendi Universal film tie-in game *The Chronicles of Riddick: Escape from Butcher Bay*. Vin Diesel, along with Ron Perlman, Dwight Schultz, Cole Hauser and rapper Xzibit contributed their voices to an impressive prequel to the two movies.

Harry Potter and the Prisoner of Azkaban was a tie-in to the movie that allowed the player to control all three of the juvenile characters for the first time. However, *Harry Potter* games maker Argonaut Games encountered problems when cash reserves became so low that the firm was brought to the edge of closure.

For the first time since the movie *Moonraker* (1979), genre veteran Richard Kiel returned as the metal-toothed assassin Jaws in the EA computer game *James Bond 007: Everything or Nothing* featuring the voices and likenesses of series regulars Pierce Brosnan, Dame Judi Dench and John Cleese, plus Willem Dafoe, model Heidi Klum and singer Mya. The game was available for PlayStation 2, X-Box, GameCube and GBA formats.

Although the TV series was no longer around, *The X Files: Resist or Serve* for PlayStation 2 featured actor David Duchovny and involved a series of mysterious murders linked to paranormal activity.

California governor Arnold Schwarzenegger settled his lawsuit against a toy company that produced a bobbing-head of him carrying a gun. The former actor apparently wanted to appear more "child-friendly".

To tie-in with Universal's disappointing movie, the *Van Helsing* twelve-inch action figures included the eponymous hero, Dracula, Frankenstein's monster and a Velkan/Wolf figure with removable latex skin. There were also various playsets available with slightly different figures. A series of hand-numbered bobble heads featured the same four main characters.

The *Van Helsing* limited edition Cookie Jars featured Dracula, Frankenstein's monster and the Wolfman.

Jakks Pacific's line of seven-inch Classic Monsters kicked off with Universal's Frankenstein Monster, Count Dracula and The Wolf Man. Each came with "transformation" parts and a diorama setting.

Limited to 2,000 pieces from Japan, the pre-painted Universal Monsters Resin Bust Statues were almost eight inches tall and featured Bela Lugosi as Dracula, Boris Karloff as the Frankenstein

Monster and The Mummy, and Lon Chaney, Jr. as The Wolf Man. From the same company came a twelve-inch pre-painted Bust Coin Bank of Karloff's Monster.

Meanwhile, a twelve-inch figure of Karloff's revived sorcerer Ardeth Bey from *The Mummy* had more than thirty points of articulation and came with mummy scroll, sacrificial knife and display stand.

A quarter-scale limited edition figure of Bela Lugosi as the original Count Dracula cost $199.99, and "Dracula's Castle", "Franken-stein's Monster" and "Wolfman's Curse" were each available as hand-painted lighted porcelain façades.

Universal's Dracula, Frankenstein, The Mummy, The Wolf Man and Creature from the Black Lagoon were available as eight-inch tall resin bobble heads. The Universal Monsters 3D Movie Poster Wall Art Sculptures featured hand-painted sculptures based on the classic movie posters for *Dracula*, *The Mummy* and *Creature from the Black Lagoon*.

From Legendary Casts, 3D Movie Poster Sculptures in cold cast resign featured classic designs for Universal's Dracula, *Frankenstein* and the advance poster for *Van Helsing*. Meanwhile, *The Creature from the Black Lagoon* poster was available as a tin sign.

The *Creature from the Black Lagoon* mugs and tin box also featured artwork from the movie poster, while a fiftieth Anniversary poster used a montage of three different images of the Gill Man.

A Creature from the Depths and The Mummy resin mini-busts, signed by designer John DiCicco and sculpted by The Kucharek Brothers were limited to just 750 individually numbered pieces.

A company called Classic TVToys.com reissued eight-inch action figures from the 1970s of the classic "Mad Monsters" (with glow-in-the-dark eyes and hands), plus TV's *The Munsters* and *Space: 1999*.

Grampa's "Dragula" dragster from *The Munsters* was available as a 1:18th scale die-cast replica, while werewolf Eddie's "Woof Woof" doll from the same show came in two thirty-inch high replicas encased in a coffin-shaped box.

For fans of *The Munsters*, sets of the trading cards from Ritten-house Archives included randomly inserted autograph cards signed by the surviving cast members.

The British-made Hammer Horror Collection featured a twelve-inch articulated figure of Christopher Lee's Dracula with flaming candlestick and Jonathan Harker Diary accessories.

Frederic March's Mr Hyde from the Academy Award-winning 1932 movie was recreated as a fully articulated twelve-inch figure.

Or for those with a more historical outlook, you could get a Vlad the Impaler figure that came with spear, sword, scabbard and a chalice filled with blood.

An *Attack of the 50-Foot Woman* coaster set and tin box featured images from the 1950s sci-fi film, while a *War of the Colossal Beast* vinyl figure from the 1958 AIP film was available with diorama base from Japan. In the same "AMC Monsterfest" series was the three-eyed mutant from *Day the World Ended*, *The She-Creature* and *Cat Girl*.

The *Hellraiser* Series 3 action figures from Reel Toys included Skinned Frank, Femail Cenobite, Bloodline Twins and Hell on Earth Pinhead. Each figure came with a section of an eighteen-inch Leviathan Diamond. The first *Hellraiser* Deluxe Boxed Figure was Dr Channard from *Hellraiser II*, complete with fifteen inch-tall tentacles and a variety of attachable snake tools. The *Hellraiser* acrylic paperweight had Pinhead's head in its centre.

Sota Toys' "Now Playing" series included seven-inch articulated action figures from *The Toxic Avenger*, *An American Werewolf in London* and *Darkman*.

The *Army of Darkness* Splitting Ash two-pack included a figure of Ash splitting in two, a repainted version of the Deadite Scout figure and various accessories and weapons.

The *Trilogy of Terror* Zuni Warrior Doll was based on the homicidal figure in the 1975 TV movie scripted by Richard Matheson and came with real hair, cloth skirt and ceremonial spear.

Based on Larry Cohen's cult 1974 film, the *It's Alive!* life-size baby puppet had a blanket to hide the hand-control.

Mezco Toyz's popular range of Living Dead Dolls offered collectors a Graf Orlok/Nosferatu and his Victim with a bloody neckwound. Both came packaged in a coffin built for two with a "Death Certificate" of authenticity. Meanwhile, the second series of Mezco's Monster Mez-itz featured a mad scientist, a cloaked skeleton, the Invisible Man and a ghoul.

For fans of Japanese monsters, a small Godzilla plush was licensed by Toho Studios, while the Rodan mini-plush had wire in its wings to allow them to be shaped as needed. Even better were a series of four-inch resin statues of Godzilla, Gigan, Mothra and Super Mechagodzilla.

The Cthulhu plastic action figure stood three-and-a-half inches tall, while the ten-inch articulated Jack the Ripper action figure came complete with cape, top hat and appropriate accessories.

During October at the Camden County College in Blackwood, New Jersey, the American Library Association mounted an exhibition entitled "Frankenstein, Penetrating the Secrets of Nature", which showcased the largest private collection of Frankenstein and Boris Karloff memorabilia in the world. On the Friday before Halloween, The Franky Award was presented to James Warren, the controversial publisher of the original *Famous Monsters of Filmland*.

The fourteenth World Horror Convention returned to Phoenix, Arizona, from 8–11 April with an eclectic Guest of Honour list that included writer Douglas Clegg, artist Caniglia, editor Stephen Jones and toastmaster David Morrell. Twisted Sister singer Dee Snider was the media guest, author Adam Niswander was special guest, and Mort Castle and Nancy Kilpatrick conducted writer and editor workshops, respectively.

The International Horror Guild Awards were presented on the Saturday evening to Peter Straub's *lost boy lost girl* for Novel and Matthew B.J. Delaney's *Jinn* for First Novel. *Louisiana Breakdown* by Lucius Shepard won for Long Form, "Dancing Men" by Glen Hirshberg (from *The Dark*) won for Intermediate Form and "With Acknowledgements to Sun Tzu" by Brian Hodge (from *The Third Alternative*) won for Short Form. Collection was a tie between Glen Hirshberg's *The Two Sams* and Michael Marshall Smith's *More Tomorrow & Other Stories*. The Anthology award went to *The Dark* edited by Ellen Datlow, while *The Devil in the White City: Murder, Magic, and Madness at the Fair that Changed America* by Erika Larson won in the Non-fiction category.

Eric Powell's *The Goon* Issues 1–4 won for Graphic Narrative, The Ghost Story Society's *All Hallows* won for Periodical, and Caniglia won for Art. David Cronenberg's *Spider* collected the Film award, and HBO's *Carnivàle* picked up the award for Television. Stephen King and F. Everett Bleiler were recipients of Living Legend Awards, and the late Jack Cady received a posthumous Special Award for writing and teaching.

The Winners of the (far too many) 2003 Bram Stoker Awards were announced on 5 June at the HWA Annual Conference held at the Park Central Hotel in Manhattan. The Novel award was presented to *lost boy lost girl* by Peter Straub, while Brian Keene's *The Rising* won for First Novel. The Long Fiction award went to "Closing Time" by Jack Ketchum (from *Peaceable Kingdom*) and the Short Fiction award went to "Duty" by Gary A. Braunbeck (from *Vivisections*). Ketchum also picked up the Fiction Collection award for *Peaceable Kingdom*, the Anthology award went to *Borderlands 5* edited by Elizabeth and Thomas F. Monteleone, and Monteleone's book of essays *The Mothers and Fathers Italian Association* won for Non-fiction.

The winner of Illustrated Narrative was *The Sandman: Endless Nights* by Neil Gaiman, the Screenplay award went to *Bubba Ho-Tep* by Don Coscarelli, and *Harry Potter and the Order of the Phoenix* by J.K. Rowling won the award for Work for Young Readers. Bruce Boston's *Pitchblende* won for Poetry Collection, the Alternative Forms award went to Michael Arnzen's e-mail newsletter *The Goreletter*, and Lifetime Achievement Awards were announced for Martin H. Greenberg and Anne Rice.

Special Awards were also presented to Paul Miller's speciality press, Earthling Publications, and Lee Thomas for Outstanding Contribution to the genre and HWA, while Robert Weinberg was given the Trustee Award for over-all contribution and many years' service to HWA.

The British Fantasy Society's annual Fantasycon 2004 was held in Walsall, in England's West Midlands, from 24–26 September. Guests of Honour were Robert Holdstock and Muriel Gray. The British Fantasy Awards were presented at the Sunday banquet to Christopher Fowler's *Full Dark House* for Best Novel (The August Derleth Fantasy Award) and the same author's "American Waitress" (from *Crimewave 7: The Last Sunset*) for Best Short Fiction.

The Mammoth Book of Best New Horror Volume Fourteen was awarded Best Anthology, while Best Collection was won by Ramsey Campbell's *Told by the Dead*. Best Artist was Les Edwards, the Best Small Press Award went to Peter Crowther's PS Publishing, and the winner of the Special Award (Karl Edward Wagner Award) was announced as Peter Jackson, for his *The Lord of the Rings* trilogy of films.

The 30th World Fantasy Convention was held in Tempe, Arizona, from 28–31 October with a Guests of Honor list that included author Gwyneth Jones, artist Janny Wurts, editor Ellen Datlow, publisher Betty Ballantine and Toastmistress Jennifer Roberson.

The World Fantasy Awards were presented at the banquet on Halloween afternoon to Jo Walton's *Tooth and Claw* for Best Novel, Greer Gilman's "A Crowd of Bone" (from *Trampoline: An Anthology*) for Best Novella, and Bruce Holland Rogers' "Don Ysidro" (from *Polyphony 3*) for Best Short Fiction.

Rosalie Parker's *Strange Tales* from Tartarus Press was voted Best Anthology, the Best Collection Award went to Elizabeth Hand's

Bibliomancy: Four Novellas from PS Publishing, and Best Artist was a tie between Donato Giancola and Jason van Hollander.

The Special Award, Professional went to Peter Crowther for PS Publishing, while the Special Award, Non-Professional was won by Ray Russell and Rosalie Parker for Tartarus Press. Stephen King and Gahan Wilson were both announced as recipients of Life Achievement Awards.

While attending the World Fantasy Convention in Tempe, I ended up at a room party sponsored by a well-known print-on-demand publisher. During the course of the evening, I found myself involved in a somewhat heated discussion about the use of apparently copyrighted material in PoD publications.

As the editor of numerous anthologies, I have always ensured that I secure copyright clearance where it is required before using a story. However, it appears that some editors and publishers are not quite so scrupulous.

It should be pointed out that since the legal term of copyright was extended to life plus seventy years, the rights of some authors whose work was brought back into copyright has been, at best, in question. This is because the law is subtly different between the European Union and the United States.

In America, all works created on or after 1 January 1978 are protected by copyright for life plus seventy years. However, any material published before that date which was under a renewed copyright on 27 October 1998, had its term extended by an additional twenty years. This means that many older works are still protected, while others have fallen into the public domain.

As I prefer to err on the side of caution, I ensure that rights have been acquired before publishing any material on either side of the Atlantic. So do many publishers. That is why, for example, Robert E. Howard's work only enters the public domain next year. H.P. Lovecraft follows in 2007, while Clark Ashton Smith continues to be protected until 2031.

Yet what surprised me most about the altercation in Arizona was that a couple of experienced editors (who I have known for years and greatly admire), firmly argued against the seventy year rule, claiming it was unfair to publishers.

In an article in the January-February 2004 *Weird Tales*, John Gregory Betancourt – publisher of PoD imprint Wildside Press and an author himself – argued somewhat disingenuously that copyright for books should actually be reduced to life plus twenty years so that

"People can publish them cheaply, or make them available in other media like TV shows, movies, radio, films, etc. without going through a maze of contractual red tape."

Or, to put it another way: To allow people with no creative stake in an author's work to exploit it as quickly as possible after that author's death.

Betancourt claimed that it is only because such writers as H.G. Wells, Jules Verne and Arthur Conan Doyle had fallen into public domain under American law that they are remembered today. This is, of course, nonsense. It is due to the quality of their work that these (and many other) authors will continue to have their writings published for many, many decades to come. And while they are protected by the period of copyright – Wells died, incidentally, in 1946 – then their heirs and estates will continue to reap the benefit of their labour. Surely that is something that any author would wish to see happen, in return for all the effort – and often hardship – endured during their lifetime?

It seems to me that people who argue for a reduction in the term of copyright – or in rare cases, simply ignore it – are merely trying to make a hasty profit at the author's expense. Why shouldn't a writer's descendants and successors continue to earn money from a work, for at least one generation (or approximately seventy years) after their death? After all, many authors are still poorly reimbursed for their efforts during their lifetimes, and the copyright law allows their estates to finally receive some recompense if that work continues to remain in print.

It may well be that some writers who die intestate could be in danger of disappearing, but this is only likely to happen in a few very rare cases. Usually, if an author has not actually named a literary executor, then the rights automatically revert to the next of kin.

If anything, I would argue that the American copyright laws should be brought into line with those in Europe, which would result in some anomalous loopholes finally being closed. At the moment we have the absurd situation where some publishers pay for the rights to reprint an author's work, while others are simply using it free of charge.

There is no doubt that the copyright rules are a minefield. But when it comes to print-on-demand publishers – whose books are available around the world at the press of a button – have they even considered that they may be in breach of another country's laws if they print or export their "public domain" titles to the majority of those countries that respect international copyright protection?

I suspect not. They are probably more interested in making a quick buck off the back of a deceased author than worry too much about such minor and ethical concerns . . .

The Editor
May, 2005

NEIL GAIMAN

Forbidden Brides of the Faceless Slaves in the Nameless House of the Night of Dread Desire

DESCRIBED BY THE AUTHOR as "a magical-horror-thriller-ghost-romantic-comedy-family-epic," *Anansi Boys* is the first adult novel Neil Gaiman has had out since the bestselling and multiple award-winning *American Gods* in 1999. His other novels include *Good Omens* (with Terry Pratchett), *Neverwhere* (a novelisation of his BBC-TV miniseries) and *Stardust* (an expansion of a graphic novel).

Amongst Gaiman's other books are *Ghastly Beyond Belief* (with Kim Newman), *Now We Are Sick* (with Stephen Jones), *Book of Dreams* (with Ed Kramer), *Don't Panic: The Official Hitchhiker's Guide to the Galaxy Companion* and the short story collections *Angels and Visitations: A Miscellany* and *Smoke and Mirrors*. He wrote and directed *A Short Film About John Bolton*, which was recently released on DVD in a special collector's edition, and is currently co-scripting (with Roger Avary) an adaptation of *Beowulf*, which will be filmed in "performance capture" animation by director Robert Zemeckis for a proposed October 2007 release.

As the author explains: "'Forbidden Brides . . .' was written for *Gothic!*, an anthology of Gothic stories for teens, a couple of years ago. Well, actually, it was written almost twenty years ago late at night on East Croydon station: I showed it to a few people, nobody liked it, and I put it away and forgot about it.

"When I was asked for a Gothic story I went up to the attic and pulled it out, wondering if there was anything good in there that could be rescued, and found myself laughing at many of the jokes.

The re-write felt oddly collaborative, as if I was collaborating with the 'me' who wrote that story twenty years ago. He had the manic energy, while I had the technique. It's a love story to the Gothic novels, or any book with a lady in a nightie clutching a candelabra on the cover."

The story that follows is the first of two literary-themed contributions that Gaiman has in this volume . . .

I

SOMEWHERE IN THE NIGHT, someone was writing.

II

Her feet scrunched the gravel as she ran, wildly, up the tree-lined drive. Her heart was pounding in her chest, her lungs felt as if they were bursting, heaving breath after breath of the cold night air. Her eyes fixed on the house ahead, the single light in the topmost room drawing her toward it like a moth to a candle flame. Above her, and away in the deep forest behind the house, night-things whooped and skrarked. From the road behind her, she heard something scream, briefly – a small animal, that had been the victim of some beast of prey, she hoped, but could not be certain.

She ran as if the legions of hell were close on her heels, and spared not even a glance behind her until she reached the porch of the old mansion. In the moon's pale light the white pillars seemed skeletal, like the bones of a great beast. She clung to the wooden doorframe, gulping air, staring back down the long driveway, as if she were waiting for something, and then she rapped on the door – timorously at first, and then harder. The rapping echoed through the house. She imagined, from the echo that came back to her that, far away, someone was knocking on another door, muffled and dead.

"Please!" she called. "If there's someone here – anyone – please let me in. I beseech you. I implore you." Her voice sounded strange to her ears.

The flickering light in the topmost room faded and vanished, to reappear in successive descending windows. One person, then, with a candle. The light vanished into the depths of the house. She tried to catch her breath. It seemed like an age passed before she heard footsteps on the other side of the door, and spied a chink of candle-light through a crack in the ill-fitting doorframe.

"Hello?" she said.

The voice, when it spoke, was dry as old bone – a desiccated voice, redolent of crackling parchment and musty grave-hangings. "Who calls?" it said. "Who knocks? Who calls, on this night of all nights?"

The voice gave her no comfort. She looked out at the night that enveloped the house, then pulled herself straight, tossed her raven locks, and said, in a voice that, she hoped, betrayed no fear, "Tis I, Amelia Earnshawe, recently orphaned and now on my way to take up a position as a governess to the two small children – a boy, and a girl – of Lord Falconmere, whose cruel glances I found, during our interview in his London residence, both repellent and fascinating, but whose aquiline face haunts my dreams."

"And what do you do here, then, at this house, on this night of all nights? Falconmere Castle lies a good twenty leagues on from here, on the other side of the moors."

"The coachman – an ill-natured fellow, and a mute, or so he pretended to be, for he formed no words, but made his wishes known only by grunts and gobblings – reined in his team a mile or so back down the road, or so I judge, and then he shewed me by gestures that he would go no further, and that I was to alight. When I did refuse to do so, he pushed me roughly from the carriage to the cold earth, then, whipping the poor horses into a frenzy, he clattered off the way he had come, taking my several bags and my trunk with him. I called after him, but he did not return, and it seemed to me that a deeper darkness stirred in the forest gloom behind me. I saw the light in your window and I . . . I . . . ." She was able to keep up her pretence of bravery no longer, and she began to sob.

"Your father," came the voice from the other side of the door. "Would he have been the Honourable Hubert Earnshawe?"

Amelia choked back her tears. "Yes. Yes, he was."

"And you – you say you are an orphan?"

She thought of her father, of his tweed jacket, as the maelstrom seized him, and whipped him onto the rocks and away from her forever.

"He died trying to save my mother's life. They both were drowned."

She heard the dull chunking of a key being turned in a lock, then twin booms as iron bolts were drawn back. "Welcome, then, Miss Amelia Earnshawe. Welcome to your inheritance, in this house without a name. Aye, welcome – on this night, of all nights." The door opened.

The man held a black tallow candle; its flickering flame illuminated his face from below, giving it an unearthly and eldritch appearance. He could have been a Jack O'Lantern, she thought, or a particularly elderly axe-murderer.

He gestured for her to come in.

"Why do you keep saying that?" she asked.

"Why do I keep saying what?"

"*On this night of all nights*. You've said it three times so far."

He simply stared at her for a moment. Then he beckoned again, with one bone-coloured finger. As she entered, he thrust the candle close to her face, and stared at her with eyes that were not truly mad, but were still far from sane. He seemed to be examining her, and eventually he grunted, and nodded. "This way," was all he said.

She followed him down a long corridor. The candle-flame threw fantastic shadows about the two of them, and in its light the grandfather clock and the spindly chairs and table danced and capered. The old man fumbled with his key-chain, and unlocked a door in the wall, beneath the stairs. A smell came from the darkness beyond, of must and dust and abandonment.

"Where are we going?" she asked.

He nodded, as if he had not understood her. Then he said, "There are some as are what they are. And there are some as aren't what they seem to be. And there are some as only seem to be what they seem to be. Mark my words, and mark them well, Hubert Earnshawe's daughter. Do you understand me?"

She shook her head. He began to walk, and did not look back. She followed the old man down the stairs.

III

Far away and far along the young man slammed his quill down upon the manuscript, spattering sepia ink across the ream of paper and the polished table.

"It's no good," he said, despondently. He dabbed at a circle of ink he had just made on the table with a delicate forefinger, smearing the teak a darker brown, then, unthinking, he rubbed the finger against the bridge of his nose. It left a dark smudge.

"No, sir?" The butler had entered almost soundlessly.

"It's happening again, Toombes. Humour creeps in. Self-parody whispers at the edges of things. I find myself guying literary convention and sending up both myself and the whole scrivening profession."

The butler gazed unblinking at his young master. "I believe humour is very highly thought of in certain circles, sir."

The young man rested his head in his hands, rubbing his forehead pensively with his fingertips. He sighed. "That's not the point, Toombes. I'm trying to create a slice of life here, an accurate representation of the world as it is, and of the human condition. Instead, I find myself indulging, as I write, in schoolboy parody of the foibles of my fellows. I make little jokes." He had smeared ink all over his face. "Very little."

From the forbidden room at the top of the house an eerie, ululating cry rang out, echoing through the house. The young man sighed. "You had better feed Aunt Agatha, Toombes."

"Very good, sir."

The young man picked up the quill pen and idly scratched his ear with the tip.

Behind him, in a bad light, hung the portrait of his great-great grandfather. The painted eyes had been cut out most carefully, long ago, and now real eyes stared out of the canvas face, looking down at the writer. The eyes glinted a tawny gold. If the young man had turned around, and remarked upon them, he might have thought them the golden eyes of some great cat or of some misshapen bird of prey, were such a thing possible. These were not eyes that belonged in any human head. But the young man did not turn. Instead, oblivious, he reached for a new sheet of paper, dipped his quill into the glass inkwell, and commenced to write:

IV

"Aye . . ." said the old man, putting down the black tallow candle on the silent harmonium. "He is our master, and we are his slaves, though we pretend to ourselves that it is not so. But when the time is right, then he demands what he craves, and it is our duty and our compulsion to provide him with . . ." he shuddered, and drew a breath. Then he said only, " . . . with what he needs."

The bat-wing curtains shook and fluttered in the glassless casement as the storm drew closer. Amelia clutched the lace handkerchief to her breast, her father's monogram upwards. "And the gate?" she asked, in a whisper.

"It was locked in your ancestor's time, and he charged, before he vanished, that it should always remain so. But there are still tunnels, folk do say, that link the old crypt with the burial grounds."

"And Sir Frederick's first wife . . .?"

He shook his head, sadly. "Hopelessly insane, and but a mediocre harpsichord player. He put it about that she was dead, and perhaps some believed him."

She repeated his last four words to herself. Then she looked up at him, a new resolve in her eyes.

"And for myself? Now I have learned why I am here, what do you advise me to do?"

He peered around the empty hall. Then he said, urgently, "Fly from here, Miss Earnshawe. Fly while there is still time. Fly for your life, fly for your immortal *aagh*."

"My what?" she asked, but even as the words escaped her crimson lips the old man crumpled to the floor. A silver crossbow quarrel protruded from the back of his head.

"He is dead," she said, in shocked wonderment.

"Aye," affirmed a cruel voice from the far end of the hall. "But he was dead before this day, girl. And I do think that he has been dead a monstrous long time."

Under her shocked gaze, the body began to putrefy. The flesh dripped and rotted and liquefied, the bones revealed crumbled and oozed, until there was nothing but a stinking mass of foetidness where once there had been a man.

Amelia squatted beside it, then dipped her fingertip into the noxious stuff. She licked her finger with her tongue, and she made a face. "You would appear to be right, sir, whoever you are," she said. "I would estimate that he has been dead for the better part of a hundred years."

V

"I am endeavouring," said the young man to the chambermaid, "to write a novel that reflects life as it is, mirrors it down to the finest degree. Yet as I write it turns to dross and gross mockery. What should I do? Eh, Ethel? What should I do?"

"I'm sure I don't know, sir," said the chambermaid, who was pretty and young, and had come to the great house in mysterious circumstances several weeks earlier. She gave the bellows several more squeezes, making the heart of the fire glow an orange-white. "Will that be all?"

"Yes. No. Yes," he said. "You may go, Ethel."

The girl picked up the now-empty coal-scuttle and walked at a steady pace across the drawing room.

The young man made no move to return to his writing-desk; instead he stood in thought by the fireplace, staring at the human skull on the mantel, at the twin crossed swords that hung above it upon the wall. The fire crackled and spat as a lump of coal broke in half.

Footsteps, close behind him. The young man turned. "You?"

The man facing him was almost his double – the white streak in the auburn hair proclaimed them of the same blood, if any proof were needed. The stranger's eyes were dark and wild, his mouth petulant yet oddly firm.

"Yes – I! I, your elder brother, who you thought dead these many years. But I am not dead – or perhaps, I am no longer dead – and I have come back – aye, come back from ways that are best left untravelled – to claim what is truly mine."

The young man's eyebrows raised. "I see. Well, obviously all this is yours – if you can prove that you are who you say you are."

"Proof? I need no proof. I claim birth-right, and blood-right – and death-right!" So saying, he pulled both the swords down from above the fireplace, and passed one, hilt first, to his younger brother. "Now guard you, my brother – and may the best man win."

Steel flashed in the firelight and kissed and clashed and kissed again in an intricate dance of thrust and parry. At times it seemed no more than a dainty minuet, or a courtly and deliberate ritual, while at other times it seemed pure savagery, a wildness that moved faster than the eye could easily follow. Around and around the room they went, and up the steps to the mezzanine, and down the steps to the main hall. They swung from drapes and from chandeliers. They leapt up on tables and down again.

The older brother obviously was more experienced, and, perhaps, was a better swordsman, but the younger man was fresher and he fought like a man possessed, forcing his opponent back and back and back to the roaring fire itself. The older brother reached out with his left hand and grasped the poker. He swung it wildly at the younger, who ducked, and, in one elegant motion, ran his brother through.

"I am done for. I am a dead man."

The younger brother nodded his ink-stained face.

"Perhaps it is better this way. Truly, I did not want the house, or the lands. All I wanted, I think, was peace." He lay there, bleeding crimson onto the grey flagstone. "Brother? Take my hand."

The young man knelt, and clasped a hand that already, it seemed to him, was becoming cold.

"Before I go into that night that none can follow, there are things I must tell you. Firstly, with my death, I truly believe the curse is lifted from our line. The second . . ." His breath now came in a bubbling wheeze, and he was having difficulty speaking. "The second . . . is . . . the . . . the thing in the abyss . . . beware the cellars . . . the rats . . . the – *it follows*!"

And with this his head lolled on the stone, and his eyes rolled back and saw nothing, ever again.

Outside the house, the raven cawed thrice. Inside, strange music had begun to skirl up from the crypt, signifying that, for some, the wake had already started.

The younger brother, once more, he hoped, the rightful possessor of his title, picked up a bell and rang for a servant. Toombes the butler was there in the doorway before the last ring had died away.

"Remove this," said the young man. "But treat it well. He died to redeem himself. Perhaps to redeem us both."

Toombes said nothing, merely nodded to show that he had understood.

The young man walked out of the drawing room. He entered the Hall of Mirrors – a hall from which all the mirrors had carefully been removed, leaving irregularly-shaped patches on the panelled walls, and, believing himself alone, he began to muse aloud.

"This is precisely what I was talking about," he said. "Had such a thing happened in one of my tales – and such things happen all the time – I would have felt myself constrained to guy it unmercifully." He slammed a fist against a wall, where once a hexagonal mirror had hung. "What is wrong with me? Wherefore this flaw?"

Strange scuttling things gibbered and cheetled in the black drapes at the end of the room, and high in the gloomy oak beams, and behind the wainscoting, but they made no answer. He had expected none.

He walked up the grand staircase, and along a darkened hall, to enter his study. Someone, he suspected, had been tampering with his papers. He suspected that he would find out who later that evening, after the Gathering.

He sat down at his desk, dipped his quill pen once more, and continued to write.

VI

Outside the room the ghoul-lords howled with frustration and hunger, and they threw themselves against the door in their ravenous fury, but the locks were stout, and Amelia had every hope that they would hold.

What had the wood-cutter said to her? His words came back to her then, in her time of need, as if he were standing close to her, his manly frame mere inches from her feminine curves, the very scent of his honest labouring body surrounding her like the headiest perfume, and she heard his words as if he were, that moment, whispering them in her ear. "I was not always in the state you see me in now, lassie," he had told her. "Once I had another name, and a destiny unconnected to the hewing of cords of firewood from fallen trees. But know you this – in the escritoire, there is a secret compartment, or so my great-uncle claimed, when he was in his cups . . ."

The escritoire! Of course!

She rushed to the old writing desk. At first she could find no trace of a secret compartment. She pulled out the drawers, one after another, and then perceived that one of them was much shorter than the rest, which seeing she forced her white hand into the space that the drawer had been, and found, at the back, a button. Frantically, she pressed it. Something opened, and she put her hand on a tightly-rolled paper scroll.

Amelia withdrew her hand. The scroll was tied with a dusty black ribbon, and with fumbling fingers she untied the knot, and opened the paper. Then she read, trying to make sense of the antiquated handwriting, of the ancient words. As she did so, a ghastly pallor suffused her handsome face, and even her violet eyes seemed clouded and distracted.

The knockings and the scratchings redoubled. In but a short time they would burst through, she had no doubt. No door could hold them forever. They would burst through, and she would be their prey. Unless, unless . . .

"Stop!" she called, her voice trembling. "I abjure you, every one of you, and thee most of all, oh Prince of Carrion. In the name of the ancient compact, between thy people and mine."

The sounds stopped. It seemed to the girl that there was shock in that silence. Finally, a cracked voice said, "The compact?" and a dozen voices, as ghastly again, whispered "The compact," in a susurrus of unearthly sound.

"Aye!" called Amelia Earnshawe, her voice no longer unsteady. "The compact."

For the scroll, the long-hidden scroll, had been the compact – the dread agreement between the Lords of the House, and the denizens of the crypt in ages past. It had described and enumerated the nightmarish rituals that had chained them one to another over the centuries – rituals of blood, and of salt, and more.

"If you have read the compact," said a deep voice from beyond the door, "then you know what we need, Hubert Earnshawe's daughter."

"Brides," she said, simply.

"The brides!" came the whisper from beyond the door, and it redoubled and resounded until it seemed to her that the very house itself throbbed and echoed to the beat of those words – two syllables invested with longing, and with love, and with hunger.

Amelia bit her lip. "Aye. The brides. I will bring thee brides. I shall bring brides for all."

She spoke quietly, but they heard her, for there was only silence, a deep and velvet silence, on the other side of the door.

And then one ghoul-voice hissed, "Yes, and do you think we could get her to throw in a side-order of those little bread-roll things?"

VII

Hot tears stung the young man's eyes. He pushed the papers from him, and flung the quill pen across the room. It spattered its inky load over the bust of his great-great-great grandfather, the brown ink soiling the patient white marble. The occupant of the bust, a large and mournful raven, startled, nearly fell off, and only kept its place by dint of flapping its wings, several times. It turned, then, in an awkward step and hop, to stare with one black bead eye at the young man.

"Oh, this is intolerable!" exclaimed the young man. He was pale and trembling. "I cannot do it, and I shall never do it. I swear now, by . . ." and he hesitated, casting his mind around for a suitable curse from the extensive family archives.

The raven looked unimpressed. "Before you start cursing, and probably dragging peacefully dead and respectable ancestors back from their well-earned graves, just answer me one question." The voice of the bird was like stone striking against stone.

The young man said nothing, at first. It is not unknown for ravens to talk, but this one had not done so before, and he had not been expecting it. "Certainly. Ask your question."

The raven tipped its head onto one side. "Do you *like* writing that stuff?"

"Like?"

"That life-as-it-is-stuff you do. I've looked over your shoulder sometimes. I've even read a little here and there. Do you enjoy writing it?"

The young man looked down at the bird. "It's literature," he explained, as if to a child. "Real literature. Real life. The real world. It's an artist's job to show people the world they live in. We hold up mirrors."

Outside the room lightning clove the sky. The young man glanced out of the window: a jagged streak of blinding fire created warped and ominous silhouettes from the bony trees and the ruined abbey on the hill.

The raven cleared its throat.

"I said, do you enjoy it?"

The young man looked at the bird, then he looked away and, wordlessly, he shook his head.

"That's why you keep trying to pull it apart," said the bird. "It's not the satirist in you that makes you lampoon the commonplace and the humdrum. Merely boredom with the way things are. D'you see?" It paused to preen a stray wing feather back into place with its beak. Then it looked up at him once more. "Have you ever thought of writing fantasy?" it asked.

The young man laughed. "Fantasy? Listen, I write literature. Fantasy isn't life. Esoteric dreams, written by a minority for a minority, it's—"

"What you'd be writing if you knew what was good for you."

"I'm a classicist," said the young man. He reached out his hand to a shelf of the classics – *Udolpho*, *The Castle of Otranto*, *The Saragossa Manuscript*, *The Monk* and the rest of them. "It's literature."

"Nevermore," said the raven. It was the last word the young man ever heard it speak. It hopped from the bust, spread its wings and glided out of the study door into the waiting darkness.

The young man shivered. He rolled the stock themes of fantasy over in his mind: cars and stockbrokers and commuters, housewives and police, agony columns and commercials for soap, income tax and cheap restaurants, magazines and credit cards and streetlights and computers . . .

"It is escapism, true," he said, aloud. "But is not the highest impulse in mankind the urge towards freedom, the drive to escape?"

The young man returned to his desk, and he gathered together the pages of his unfinished novel, and dropped them, unceremoniously, in the bottom drawer, amongst the yellowing maps and cryptic testaments and the documents signed in blood. The dust, disturbed, made him cough.

He took up a fresh quill; sliced at its tip with his pen-knife. In five deft strokes and cuts he had a pen. He dipped the tip of it into the glass inkwell. Once more he began to write:

VIII

Amelia Earnshawe placed the slices of wholewheat bread into the toaster and pushed it down. She set the timer to dark brown, just as George liked it. Amelia preferred her toast barely singed. She liked white bread, as well, even if it didn't have the vitamins. She hadn't eaten white bread for a decade now.

At the breakfast table, George read his paper. He did not look up. He never looked up.

I hate him, she thought, and simply putting the emotion into words surprised her. She said it again in her head. *I hate him*. It was like a song. *I hate him for his toast, and for his bald head, and for the way he chases the office crumpet – girls barely out of school who laugh at him behind his back, and for the way he ignores me whenever he doesn't want to be bothered with me, and for the way he says "What, love?" when I ask him a simple question, as if he's long ago forgotten my name. As if he's forgotten that I even have a name.*

"Scrambled or boiled?" she said aloud.

"What, love?"

George Earnshawe regarded his wife with fond affection, and would have found her hatred of him astonishing. He thought of her in the same way, and with the same emotions, that he thought of anything which had been in the house for ten years and still worked well. The television, for example. Or the lawnmower. He thought it was love.

"You know, *we* ought to go on one of those marches," he said, tapping the newspaper's editorial. "Show we're committed. Eh, love?"

The toaster made a noise to show that it was done. Only one dark brown slice had popped up. She took a knife and fished out the torn second slice with it. The toaster had been a wedding present from her Uncle John. Soon she'd have to buy another, or start cooking toast under the grill, the way her mother had done.

"George? Do you want your eggs scrambled or boiled?" she asked, very quietly, and there was something in her voice that made him look up.

"Any way you like it, love," he said amiably, and could not for the life of him, as he told everyone in the office later that morning, understand why she simply stood there holding her slice of toast, or why she started to cry.

IX

The quill pen went *scritch scritch* across the paper, and the young man was engrossed in what he was doing. His face was strangely content, and a smile flickered between his eyes and his lips.

He was rapt.

Things scratched and scuttled in the wainscot but he hardly heard them.

High in her attic room Aunt Agatha howled and yowled and rattled her chains. A weird cachinnation came from the ruined abbey: it rent the night air, ascending into a peal of manic glee. In the dark woods beyond the great house, shapeless figures shuffled and loped, and raven-locked young women fled from them in fear.

"Swear!" said Toombes the butler, down in the butler's pantry, to the brave girl who was passing herself off as a chambermaid. "Swear to me, Ethel, on your life, that you'll never reveal a word of what I tell you to a living soul . . ."

There were faces at the windows and words written in blood; deep in the crypt a lonely ghoul crunched on something that might once have been alive; forked lightning slashed the ebony night; the faceless were walking; all was right with the world.

IAIN ROWAN

Lilies

IAIN ROWAN LIVES IN the north-east of England, near the sea but not near enough. He has had short stories published in a number of magazines and anthologies, including *Postscripts, Ellery Queen's, Alfred Hitchcock's, Black Gate, The Thackery T. Lambshead Pocket Guide to Eccentric & Discredited Diseases* and other titles. He is currently finishing revisions to his first novel.

According to Rowan: " 'Lilies' came from the image of the city that it's set in – a vague half-daydream of an idea that lurked around in my subconscious for a month or so. Then I sat down to explore it in writing, and much to my surprise a story poured out in one sitting.

"A story that, with some editing, ended up as the one that's published here. It's the only time that I can say that I've produced a story that seemed to have written itself. Which, as I'm naturally lazy, is a bit of a shame."

I T WAS AUTUMN, and the city was at war. As the pavements glistened slick with damp yellow leaves, the hills to the north talked to each other in low rumbling voices. Soldiers clattered into the city in trains, spent their money in a whirl of drink and women, and left for the hills. Fewer returned. Those that did, drank more quietly, eyes on the floor, worn coats patched up against the spiteful wind. The leaves fell, the war carried on, and every day the night stole in a few minutes earlier. It was autumn, and the city was at war, and Alex was afraid.

He was one of the lucky ones. He had spent fourteen days on the front, cowering in holes in the ground while the earth erupted around him and men that he had spoken to just hours before lost arms, legs, lives. His entire world had been mud. He had lived in mud, tasted mud, pressed himself against the mud as if it could shelter him from the world being ripped apart around him. Then his sergeant had crawled up to him one morning, spat in his face, and told him that his daddy must have lined somebody's pocket: he was to report to the back lines for transport to the city, and when – not if, when – he returned to the front the sergeant would make it his personal mission to ensure that Alex was first in the firing line.

He was assigned duties couriering messages back and forth, from civil servant to general to minister to anonymous civilian. It was tiring, it was tedious, and it was safe, but Alex was still afraid and often when he ate all he could taste was mud. He spent hours shivering outside closed doors, shuffling his feet in the rotting autumn slush. He hurried from one side of the city to the other, two stops on the train, six stops on the rattling tram, hours of getting lost in strange streets, and everywhere, the dead.

Alex tried not to look at them, conscious of the impulse to stare, embarrassed by it. He had seen the occasional dead person back in the village, as had every child. He'd even slept under the same roof as one, when his grandfather came back. None of this prepared him for the city. In the village, custom was that families kept their dead to themselves, that the week was a time for private moments, not public display. In the city, Alex thought at times that the dead outnumbered the living. If the war went on much longer, maybe they would.

As he searched an elegant row of tall houses for the address on the letter in his hand, he passed one of the dead. The man stood on the pavement, looking at the houses, slowly moving his head from side to side in an unconscious mockery of Alex's own search. It struck Alex that the reason there were so many dead in the city was that they could not find their families. They were cut off by the dislocation of wartime, everything in motion. Perhaps the man standing in the street, vacantly considering doorways, belonged to a family who had all died together, and now they all wandered the streets with the same cold stare, looking for one another, never finding each other, always lost.

Alex was only nine the day that his grandfather came back. The old man had been ill for weeks, sweating and wheezing in his bed. Alex had spent dutiful hours by his bedside, alternating between fear and boredom. It had seemed that his grandfather was over the worst and would live to sit glowering by the fireside another year, but then he sat up in bed, said something about last year's apples, and died. He was buried the next day. Alex stood uncertain in the soft rain while his mother cried and the village priest stumbled through his words. Then the mourners walked away, Alex's uncle putting a hand on his shoulder to guide him. Halfway across the graveyard he looked back.

The graveyard workers stood around the shallow mound while the black-coated priest knelt in front of it. His coat tails flapped around him, and for a moment Alex thought that he was not a man at all, just a swirl of crows, come to reclaim their graveyard from the intruders. Then the priest thrust his hands into the soil and pulled, and Alex saw the thin white legs of his grandfather appear, heard the priest muttering the blessings.

"This isn't for you," his uncle said softly, and the pressure of his hand kept Alex walking. He still looked back though, and he saw his grandfather's rebirth from the ground, the soil falling from him like black snow. When the priest had brought the body back into the world again, he nodded his head and the graveyard workers draped a shroud over it, and carried it slowly into the place of rest. "Now we wait, son," Alex's uncle said. "Wait for the miracle."

Three days later, as Alex steered his dinner from one side of his plate to the other, there was a heavy knock at the door. Alex's mother gasped and closed her eyes. His father stood up and said "Well. Well." Alex took the opportunity to drop several vegetables under his chair.

"You go to your room now, Alex," his mother said.

He looked up cringing, thinking that she'd caught him, but saw that her eyes were still shut.

"No," his father said as he walked to the door. "No, the boy should stay. He's old enough." Standing outside in the rain was one of the workers from the graveyard, and just behind him stood Alex's grandfather, looking confused, as if there were something very important that he should remember that he could not. Alex's father handed over the customary couple of coins and the worker nodded and then walked away.

"Come in, father."

The old man shuffled into the house and stood in the middle of the kitchen as if he were unsure what to do. Alex stared at him, fascinated. He was the same grandfather to look at as always, but his skin was pale and his eyes were clouded, the way fields were by the early morning mist. Alex's father ushered the old man to his usual seat by the fire, his mother cried, and the boy hung back by the door, wondering, uncertain.

*   *   *

Alex climbed worn stone steps and knocked on a dark green door. An elderly man in an ornate servant's uniform cracked the door open and raised a trembling eyebrow.

"Message for the colonel."

The old man held out his hand, and Alex gave him the letter. Noise came from the end of the street, a brief scuffle, the sound of running feet, but no voices. Both Alex and the servant turned to look into the gathering darkness, but a voice bellowed from inside the house and distracted them.

"Who's that? Who is it there, eh?"

"A messenger, Colonel," the old man said. "Message for you. I have it here, I will bring it up."

They both looked out at the street again, but whatever the noise was, it had stopped.

"A courier, eh." The colonel had come down the stairs, and stood in the hallway red-faced, breath wheezing, looking at Alex. "Know what the message is about, son?"

"No – no, it's sealed sir, I wouldn't read it—"

"Don't have to read it, son. Know what it's about. Know what they're all about. All about how little by little we are trying our hardest to lose the war. Don't look so shocked lad, you think that's treasonous talk, you should hear what the generals say. A drink for the cold, eh."

The servant creaked off towards a side-table in the hall.

"No, my orders—" Alex said.

"Bugger your orders. Who gave you your orders?"

"My sergeant."

"Bugger your sergeant. I'm a colonel, still counts for something. A drink for the cold." The servant had returned with two shot glasses. The colonel handed one to Alex.

"You been there, have you son? At the front?"

"Yes," Alex said.

"Thought so. See it in your eyes." He raised his glass in a toast. "To the end of the war."

"End of the war." The raw spirit burnt Alex's throat and made his eyes water. He bit down on his tongue, desperate not to cough. The servant took the glass back, and Alex began to retreat down the steps.

"Yes, the end of the war," the colonel was staring out into the dusk, one hand tugging at his beard, seeing a landscape that wasn't the city. "Don't go back there, lad."

Alex saluted and hurried away down the street. Just before he reached the main road, he saw a dark huddle on the pavement. It was the body of the dead man. Alex looked around, wandering what to do, who to contact. The man had obviously been searching for his family or old friends, and had not found them. Now his week had passed, and he was gone for ever. Given another chance, and it was wasted. Sad. Alex bent down over the body, and then he saw the white petals of the lily that had been placed on the man's stomach.

The fire of the alcohol in his stomach turned to a sour swell of fear. He looked up and down the street, saw no-one, and hurried away towards the main road, towards the light. Alex knew what the lily meant: it meant that this was none of his business, and that he should leave now, before those responsible saw him there, considered him a witness to their crime. It had never happened in his village, but he had heard the stories, knew what the lily, flower of mourning, meant. It meant political support for the enemy over the hills, it was a mark of rebellion against everything – the government, custom and tradition, all the old ways. Those who left the lilies were subversives who put into practice the ways of the enemy. They committed the strangest of murders, they killed the already dead.

The night after his grandfather came back, Alex's father took the boy for a walk in the long field. They said nothing until they reached the river. The night was cold and clear, and Alex stood and looked at the stars which gleamed hard in the sky, pins pushed through black velvet. He could hear his father breathing hard beside him.

"You know that he's not back for ever," he said at last. "You remember what I told you."

"One week," Alex said.

"Right, lad. One week."

"That's not a very long time, father."

"Not long enough son, not long enough." A silence stretched out between them, and they thought words that were snatched away by the dark water of the river, carried off before they could say them. At last his father sighed, and spoke. "But one week is what God has given us, and we must be thankful for that, a chance to say our goodbyes, fix your grandfather in our minds. It's our way, and we must be thankful and respect it. It's one of the things that sets us apart from the godless filth on the other side of the mountains."

"I thought the dead came back everywhere?"

"They do son, they do."

"So why don't they—"

"They stop them."

"How?"

He stared out into the darkness, shuffled his feet. "There are ways, son. There are ways." Alex knew from his tone of voice that he should drop the subject.

"And after a week, will granda go away again?"

"That he will, to the day, to the same hour he rose again."

"And where will he go then?"

His father turned and walked away across the field, back towards the house, one hand up at his face. Halfway across, he stopped and waited for Alex to catch up. He put a hand around his son's shoulders, and they walked back to the house together. A week later he was in his room, lost worlds away in a book, when his mother cried out. Alex never saw his grandfather again.

Days passed, the last few leaves fell from the trees, and the lonely routine of Alex's work took him back into its arms and made everything outside it seem unreal. He felt that it was a city of shadows that at times only existed street by street, that the graceful terraces that lined whatever street he was walking down were all that there was, and beyond them there was nothing. From the window of a tram halted at a stop he saw a dark-haired woman waiting to cross the road. The simple beauty of her face was the only thing in that whole time that felt real to him. Then the tram juddered back into motion and she was gone. One night he dreamt of her, pale skin framed by falls of black hair, and even in the dream she had more substance than anything else he saw when awake. The war went on in the hills, the guns still rumbled, and everywhere Alex went he saw the distracted stares of the dead, as they stumbled lost along misty streets.

The sky was bruising with evening when he returned to the office from his last assignment. There was no-one else there but the sergeant, who sat next to the stove smoking one of his stinking cigarettes.

"No more today. You're done."

Alex sat on a stool, warmed his hands, rested his aching legs. "I'll get away in a minute. Think I'll just sleep the whole night through."

The sergeant twisted the stub of his cigarette out on the dark iron of the stove. "I'd get out if I were you. Get out, get drunk, spend your wages on some whore."

"Don't have that much to spend, not if I'm going to eat the rest of the week."

"Don't worry about the rest of the week, son, live for today. I been talking to an old mate of mine, works as a valet to one of the generals. Rumour is, any day now they're going to pass this work on to some civil servants—" he spat, and it sizzled on the hot coals – "and send you poor bastards back to the front. Count yourself lucky, you've had it good here, thanks to whoever pulled the strings for you – no bastard trying to kill you apart from the tram drivers, private room, not in some flea-ridden barracks. You've escaped the front this long, must have known you'd end up back there one day, fit young lad like you. They're running out of fit young lads. They'd send me, if I had two legs. Get out, son. Live life, while you have one."

Alex walked back to his small room. He thought about the mud and the terror and the choir of the dying who lay sobbing in no man's land, he thought about the sergeant's missing leg, he thought about the dead. He considered desertion for a while, melting away into the city, but he knew that he would be caught. And if he was caught, he would be taken to the moor to the west of the city, shot by a bored soldier no older than himself, and thrown in a pit of lime. No resurrection, no chance for his parents to say their sad goodbyes. He had hardly lived life, how could be accept that it could soon be over? He sat on his hard bed for a while, head in his hands, grieving for his future. Then he left, not bothering to lock the door.

All the light had seeped out of the sky, and the night was still and cold. It felt as if the whole world was waiting, holding its breath, because something important was about to happen. Thin fingers of fog wavered up from the motionless dark water of the canals. Alex walked towards the heart of the city. He didn't know where he was going, but the sergeant's suggestions held little attraction for him. What was the point of getting drunk in an anonymous bar, sliding slowly down a rough wooden counter as the night went on? What was the point in spending the night with a woman who found only his money attractive? Alex had never been with a woman, his head was full of the things he had read in books and poems, stories about passion and love set in worlds that seemed so much more real than that of the cold streets, the quiet small rooms with a bed and a chair and the silence of despair.

As Alex reached a square near the centre of the city, the streets became busier. Soldiers on leave, the officers of the general staff in their never-seen-blood finery, the prostitutes and petty thugs who preyed upon them, the ordinary men and women of the city, trying to lead a normal life amidst the chaos, putting on a pretence of peacetime in a city at war. Alex felt a stranger to them, a stranger to them all. There was so much that he wanted to do in life, so many places he wanted to visit, so many things he wanted to feel, and because a man he had never met had signed a piece of paper he would end up wandering the streets of the city, one of the slow-witted dead, looking in vain for the family that lived two day's journey away by train. A tram sparked through the square, metal grinding on metal. As it passed him, it slowed, and Alex jumped on to the footplate at the back, not knowing where it was going, not caring.

He bought a ticket to the last stop on the line, and settled back on the hard seat, content to let the sway and rattle take him to the place that he always went to while travelling, a place that was neither where he had come from nor where he was going. The tram jolted its way out from the centre of the city, heading for the suburbs. People got on, people got off, Alex paid them no attention. They stopped at a railway station, and all of the passengers left the tram apart from Alex and a short man who flapped and rustled at his newspaper. After a few moments the tram jerked and moved a few feet, and then stopped again. The back door of the tram opened and closed and Alex felt a gust of cold night air on the back of his neck. A dark-haired woman brushed past him, and the tram started moving again. As she passed, Alex smelt her scent. He could not identify it, but it made him think of falling leaves and the embers of bonfires and all the autumnal thoughts of things that he had meant to do and never done, things he meant to say but had left unsaid.

She sat facing Alex, a few seats in front of him on the other side of the tram. It was the woman he had seen a few days earlier. Even though he had only seen her for a few seconds, her face had stayed in his mind like a picture in a locket. She was more beautiful than any woman he had ever seen, even though if looked at part by part her features were no more than conventionally attractive. She had a fragile quality, translucent, like delicate china lit from within. The woman turned her head slightly to look out of the window, and the collar of her coat fell away to reveal her neck, slightly arched, a perfect curve. Alex felt a regret that made his fears seem an irrelevance. What happened tomorrow, or the day after, or the day after that, was immaterial. What mattered now, more than anything ever would matter, was that he had seen beauty, and in another stop or two the woman would get off the tram and walk into the darkness. By luck he might survive the war, live his life, meet a thousand other people, and then die an old man knowing that he had lost something in his youth which he had never been able to find again.

She looked back in Alex's direction, and he dropped his gaze. After a while, he looked up again. She was watching him, and he wanted to turn away again in embarrassment but for a few seconds he could not do so. Then he looked out of the window beside him, his mouth dry, his hands clenched. The shadows of the city flickered past. He could see her reflection in his window. She was still watching him. He found the courage to look at her again, but as he did, she looked away. Alex thought that she in turn was now watching his reflection, that they both looked not at each other, but at an image of the other.

The tram slowed and came to a halt. The woman stood up, and walked towards the door at the front. As the door opened, she looked back down the tram. Alex looked back at her. Then she walked down the steps of the tram and out onto the street. The door closed and the tram started off again.

Alex jumped up, ran to the back of the tram, threw open the door, and jumped down to the street from the footplate, nearly falling flat on his face. They were in an old part of the city, close to the river, where the streets narrowed and sloped down towards the dark water. The woman had crossed the road, but she must have heard him jump from the tram because she stopped and turned, looked at him crouching in the road between the cold metal tramlines. The warm red lights of the tram receded into the mist, then it turned a corner, and was gone. She looked at him, said nothing.

"Don't be scared, please," he stammered. "I don't mean – I just – I had to talk to you."

She stayed on the other side of the street, but didn't walk away, didn't look around in alarm for help. He crossed the road towards her, hands held wide, making trembling circles in the air.

"Please, you must be freezing. Let me just walk with you, wherever you're going. Just – just let me just walk with you a little while, and then I'll go, I promise."

She smiled, a slow sad smile, and nodded. Alex knew that whatever happened in the next few days, whether he was sent to the front or not, whether he lived or not, he would remember that smile until he had memory no longer. She began to walk, and he fell in beside her, talking more than he knew he ought to, but desperate to try and say in a few minutes what it could take a lifetime to tell.

The road came to an end facing the high brick wall of a warehouse that overlooked the river. An alley ran off alongside the warehouse. The woman hesitated, as if she were uncertain of the direction to take. She turned towards the alley, and then stopped, and looked at Alex for a moment. Her perfection made him want to cry. The autumn air was cold on his face, the night was still, everything was quiet and perfect. Everything was sharp, the world more real than Alex had ever known it, beauty and meaning in every damp brick, in every tree that reached dark fingers towards the night. She held out her hand to him, and he took it. Her skin was like the most delicate statue carved from ivory, unblemished, pale, cold as stone.

Alex wasn't sure if he had known that she was dead when they were on the tram, or whether he had realized in the moments that they had walked together. He did not know, he did not care. In this city, amongst the rotting leaves and the distant thundering of the guns, the difference between the dead and the living did not seem very important to him any more.

"Let's walk," he said to her, "I'll help you find them. Your family. I'll help you find them." Her fingers tightened on his, and they walked on together. Halfway down the alley, Alex heard footsteps behind them. He turned, and saw three men. One of them carried a large knife, the sort a butcher would use to cut joints of meat. Another swung something in his hand, something that was white and indistinct in the soft mist that rose from the river. As they came closer, Alex saw that it was a bunch of lilies.

He looked around the alley. If they ran, the men would catch them before they reached the end. A yard or two away, a solid door was set into the brick of the warehouse. It was padlocked and barred, there was no way through, but leaning in the doorway was an old iron shovel, its edges corroded and half-eaten away with rust. Alex picked it up.

"Go," he said to the woman. "Go. Find your family. Be as quick as you can. Do you understand? And thank you. Do you understand? Thank you."

She looked at him and he could not tell if she knew what he was saying or not. Then there was a slight squeeze of her fingers on his, and his hand was holding nothing but air and she was walking away down the alley.

"We're going to pass," the man with the knife said in a conversational voice. "Whether you stand there or not. You know what she is. Move."

"Who is he?" the man carrying the lilies said, sounding nervous. "I don't know him. He's not her family, I told you, I know the family, that's how come I knew she'd be coming back. They're all waiting for her in the house. It's only on the next street, if we don't take her now, here . . ."

The three men kept walking towards Alex. The man with the knife was slapping it gently against his free hand.

"Get out of the way," he said. "We've got no quarrel with you. Walk away and let us put nature back how it ought to be. It's the new way. Way things ought to be. Soon the war will be over and it will all be like this. You're either with us, and the future, or you're with them, and the past. Stay where you are, and we'll make you like her. What do you care anyway? Why are you bothering? She'll be dead inside a week."

Alex thought of his grandfather, of the way that the river at home curved between the fields and shone secret and silver in the light of the moon, of the trains full of soldiers that rattled off up into the hills towards the mud and the fear, of the dead that walked the city, and he thought about the gentle curve of her neck and the feel of her hand upon his.

"So will I," he said, and raised the shovel.

RAMSEY CAMPBELL

Breaking Up

RAMSEY CAMPBELL IS A REGULAR contributor to the *Best New Horror* series. Described by *The Oxford Companion to English Literature* as "Britain's most respected living horror writer," he has been named Grand Master by the World Horror Convention and received a Lifetime Achievement Award from the Horror Writers Association.

Campbell's most recent novels include *Secret Stories* and *The Overnight*, while a new edition of his Arkham House collection *The Height of the Scream* was recently reissued by Babbage Press. The author is currently at work on a new novel, *The Communications*.

"I'd already written one macabre tale about a mobile phone," reveals the author, "and then it occurred to me that there could be another. I suspect all this is my mental preparation for owning one of the things."

A S KERRY GLANCED THROUGH the display window at the street that was bony with frozen snow, a mobile rang. "Will that be him?" Harvey said.

At first she wasn't certain it was hers – more than one of the thousands of phones they sold might play that disco tune – and then she realized the sound was muffled by her handbag on the counter. It stayed a little indistinct when she slipped the phone out of the bag. She read the displayed number and terminated the call. "Not him," Harvey said as if she needed to be told.

"Just a customer," she almost said, remembering how Russell had waited for her to be free so that he could ask whether she thought he was too old for a mobile. "Just someone I used to know," she said.

"Never a stalker, is it? Would you like me to stick with you till Jason picks you up?"

"I'm sure he would have rung if he wasn't nearly here."

"I'd be happy to, all the same. Then if he doesn't show up I could run you wherever you like."

She suspected the manager had somewhere that he liked in mind. His hair was dyed a shade too black, and a sunbed and a gym also kept up his appearance, but his jowls were starting to bag his age. "I thought you had someone to go home to," she said.

"Nowt wrong with being friendly as well, is there?"

"I normally am, I think." His voice had taken on some of the edge he used for second warnings to staff, and she didn't want to be alone with that either. She gave her scarf another turn around her throat and tugged her gloves on before picking up her bag. "You lock up," she said. "I'll be fine."

The first thing she saw on stepping outside was her breath. The cold set about making a mask of her face at once. Along both sides of the deserted street the shop windows were dusty with frost, glass cases in an abandoned museum. The pale mounds with which the glittering pavements were heaped seemed to glow from within. A wind from somewhere even colder sent a shiver through her, which lent Harvey an excuse to look concerned as he withdrew the key from the door. "Really, I could—"

"Really, don't." She was about to put some distance between them when her mobile intervened. As soon as she extracted it she was able to say "This is him."

She keyed the phone but didn't speak until Harvey made for the car park, skidding as he reached the alley between the shops and righting himself with a penguinish flap of his arms. She heared his walled-in curse at a second tumble as she said "Where are you?"

"I'm bloody—" Jason paused to reclaim some of his temper. "I was on my way," he complained.

"Aren't you still?"

"Would I be talking to you if I was? You know what I think of these clowns that talk on their phones while they're driving."

"Not the ones that sell them, I hope."

"There ought to be a law that says you have to tell your customers how to use them. You know that's what I think. Save it, all right? I don't need an argument just now."

She could miss Russell's politeness after all. "You still haven't told me where you are."

"Some bloody place in the middle of nowhere. I've come off the road."

"Are you lost, do you mean?"

"Off the side. In a bloody snowdrift and a ditch. I'm waiting for a tow."

"You sound as if you're blaming me."

"I wouldn't have been going so fast if you didn't get in a panic whenever I'm a minute late."

"Hold on, I don't panic. I haven't been panicking now."

"A huff, then. You make me feel I've let you down and it's a major insult even if you don't say anything."

"Well, please don't feel obliged to meet me tonight."

"You're doing it now. I don't know if I can," Jason added less apologetically than she thought the conversation warranted. "I'll let you know what's happening."

"Don't put yourself to any extra trouble. I'm going home."

"I'll call you there, then."

She didn't quite advise him not to bother. She broke the connection and was stowing the phone when it stirred, a vibration muffled by her glove. As the disco melody began to tick she blinked at the digits through the whitish glow with which a streetlamp coated the display. It was Russell's number.

For an instant she was tempted to agree to dinner at a restaurant or a chat over drinks, except that he would end up pleading gently for more, every plea primed with the expectation of refusal. She might have given him the option of leaving a message, but she wanted to deal more decisively with him than she had with Jason. "Kerry," she said, turning along the path between the huddled mounds.

"Russell."

He sounded uncertain, presumably of her response. "I can see that," she told him.

"Can you?"

She took his surprise as a joke not much less feeble than he was making his voice. "On the call display," she explained nonetheless.

"You're up on these things, not like us oldsters. That's why I came to you."

"Haven't you charged your battery?" she said or, if she was honest, hoped. "You're starting to break up."

"Oh, don't say that." His voice surged, hissing and fragmenting in her ear, then subsided. "What would do that? Would the cold?"

"This much might. Why were you calling, Russell? I'm outside and I don't want mine to die on me."

"Mustn't." He might have been talking to himself until he said "I think it's even colder up here."

Kerry's gaze was drawn beyond the shops to the darker streets that climbed increasingly steeply to the glimmering ridge a thousand feet above the town. "Where's that?" she felt required to ask.

"Home."

She had no more idea where he lived than she had let him have about her; she'd found him a little too eager for that information. "Then I should do something about it," she said.

"Oh, will you? I knew you'd still be kind. Anything you feel you can. Just come and see me if you like."

"I'm sorry, Russell, but it's over. You must know that." Kerry hadn't finished when she heard a rattle and a sprinkling of static that put her in mind of a shower of ice. "Are you still there?" she said and, convinced of the opposite, shut the mobile in her handbag.

She'd reached the end of the shops without encountering a solitary person. She might as well have called in sick like several of her colleagues; the shop had hardly seen a customer all week, and none in the last three hours despite staying open late. Kerry heard the distant clatter of a garage door, and somewhere else uphill a woman was shouting to a child or a dog. Whatever the name was, it seemed to shatter on the sharpness of the air. The low moan that had occupied the pauses in Russell's speech must have been the note of Harvey's car as it laboured up into the dark.

Since the pavements of the first road homewards had been turned into slides by children or less wilfully by adults, she kept to the middle of the road. The light of the floppy-capped streetlamps fell short of her path, and it was only by treading gingerly on it that she established which of the blackness was ice. All the windows of the cars parked on both sides of the slope were either encased in frost or spread with the local newspaper, every visible page of which mentioned someone's death. The windows of the staggered houses were hermetically curtained even if dark, and Kerry felt as though the entire town apart from her was hiding from the weather. She'd tramped as far as the lowest crossroad when her phone began to clamour.

Was it wearing out, or had it caught a chill? Once she managed to fumble it out of her bag she was unable to read the faltering digits in the greenish window. She halted on the intersection, pinning down the hour hand of her shadow and a less distinct minute one while she located the key with a clumsy finger. "On the way?" she said.

"I think you are."

Before he spoke she knew he wasn't Jason, from a rush of static like an effort to breathe. "Russell, can you please stop. I'm expecting a call."

"Anyone but me." For as long as it took him to say this he seemed hardly even to be talking to himself. "I wasn't asking what you think," he said.

To begin with he always had; it had been much of his appeal. "Don't you care about that now?" she was disappointed enough to retort.

"Didn't mean that. Don't confuse me," he protested so harshly that his voice grew almost shapeless. "I meant all I want is for us to see each other."

"I told you once, Russell. I'm sorry if it was rude of me not to answer all your messages, but you did leave a lot after I kept telling you I couldn't meet you. And now I've told you it's over."

"Don't say that." His voice sounded close to disintegrating altogether. "Once more is all I ask. You can see me at least."

"Find someone else, Russell. I'm sure you will. You deserve someone more—"

"More my own age?" he said, not so much interrupting as filling the pause. "There's nobody. I only know your number."

Perhaps he'd stored none except hers. Empty roads loomed on both sides of her vision, and she was aware of another at her back. She was making for the street ahead and trying to find words that would be as civil as final when he spoke. "If it's something I said, please say. Just remember I've never met anyone like you."

He'd ended up repeating that too often and too intensely, along with exhorting her not to waste herself on her job or on such of his friends as he'd met, but his insistence on introducing himself as her uncle had been worst of all. It had started as a joke, then turned into a plea for her not just to contradict him but to reassure him that everyone knew he was teasing. Although striving to hearten him exhausted her, she made a last effort. "You will," she said. "You'll meet someone better, you'll see. Now I'm—"

"Never." Before she could tell him not to be silly he said "No time."

"Look, Russell, is something really wrong? Because if there is you should call—"

"I just need you. You're coming. I can hear."

Kerry closed her fingers around the mobile and strained her ears until they ached with more than the temperature. The phone muttered in her fist – she even seemed to feel it wriggling feebly – but she couldn't hear him in any of the houses. He must be pretending to locate her, unless he was deluding himself. When the crushed voice stopped trying to slip through her fingers she returned the mobile to her bag. She quickened her pace uphill, and a whitish figure peered around a hulking gatepost at her. The token face had fallen askew on its way to leaving the head.

At least half a dozen other snowmen were lying in wait as she toiled up the road. She was in danger of feeling surrounded by them and very little else, as if the townsfolk had been replaced with frozen snow. Of course she was simply nervous that the glazed silence might be interrupted by the shrilling of her phone, but the knowledge didn't help. At least there was a pub across the intersection at the top of the slope she was conquering. Even if she didn't go in, its presence would be company for her. The drinkers beyond the lit windows must be keeping their voices down; perhaps just a few would have ventured out of their houses on a night like this. She was sure that she was hearing muted conversation until she stepped onto the level cross-road and saw that ice had transformed the windows into marble slabs. Their light was borrowed from the nearest streetlamp.

Now that she was denied the chance she couldn't avoid realising she would have liked to be among people if she received another call. She could only make for home as fast as was safe. The rest of the route was yet steeper, and she crossed to the pavement, which consisted of giant steps with a railing to help her climb.

Despite her glove, the rail felt like a handful of ice. To her right, lumps of snow had been gouged out of the crests of the hedges for snowballs or by someone's desperate clutch. Beyond the hedges on both sides of the road, pale figures no more shapely than a child's first drawing appeared to mark her progress. She might almost have fancied they were watching her, even those that had least with which to do so. When a phone jangled, she was near to imagining that it related to a dim hunched shape with the sloughed remains of a face. The sound was in the house belonging to the snowman. She hauled herself past it in a rage at her nerves. It fell silent, and her phone rang.

She snatched it out so furiously that she was barely able to keep hold of it. A few indecipherable scraps of digits like traces of a fossil glimpsed through moss were visible in the window. She poked the key and clapped the mobile to her face. "Who's there?"

"Don't go too fast. Don't hurt yourself."

"I'm not going to." This wasn't enough of a retort or a challenge. "You can't see me," she said in case that made Russell betray he could.

"I don't need to. We've got a rapport, you and I." If that seemed to bring his voice closer, she wasn't about to let it persuade her of anything; he must be holding the mouthpiece against his lips to blur his words so much. Before she could deny his claim he said "We aren't as different as some people like to think."

By people, did he mean her? She shouldn't care; if she kept him talking, perhaps she could locate him. She hung her bag on her left arm and gripped the railing as she forged uphill. "Why are you saying that?" she had to ask.

"We both stayed where our roots are, didn't we? We never sought our future elsewhere."

"I stayed for my parents."

"So did I."

Could they still be alive? Kerry doubted it, given how much older than she'd taken him to be he'd finally owned up to being. "I thought you were going to write some more books about the countryside," she said.

"That was the plan."

"Why, have you given up?"

"I wouldn't be talking to you if I had."

This sounded more like a plea than she welcomed. "You don't need me, Russell. You were writing long before we met."

A whisper of restlessness made her think she'd scored a point until he said "Why did you start going out with me?"

His voice was disintegrating so much that she could hardly detect the tone, never mind the relevance. "Because you asked me," she said and didn't add "Because you kept asking."

"You took pity on me, you mean. Couldn't you again?"

"No, Russell, because you had class. Can't you have some now?"

"There isn't much to me any more."

"You know that isn't true. You write books people want to read. I've seen them all over the place."

"If we're finished, so are they."

Was he saying anything that came into his head? As she clambered up the next step, through a tree's sparkling shadow that felt like the threat of being buried under an avalanche, she said "I don't believe you mean that. You must have got over me by now. It's been months."

"Is that all? I can't tell."

Was this another bid for sympathy? Presumably it was the transmission rather than his voice that sounded near to shivering to pieces, but it dismayed her. "Russell, if you're truly feeling so bad you ought to call—"

At once the phone was dead as ice. If he'd given up pestering her, she would let that be enough. She fumbled the mobile into her bag and flexed her stiff fingers before entrusting the bag to them. A dozen clutches at the rail, and twice as many paces as there were slippery steps, brought her to her road.

It stretched left, iced with light under three streetlamps partly masked with snow. The scene might have been embedded in the amber of the night sky. Perhaps it was the silence that rendered it unreal as a Christmas card. The house where she lived was part of the emptiness, since the couple on the ground floor had gone abroad for the winter. She would be happy just to switch on the fires and draw the curtains and have nothing else that she absolutely had to do, she vowed, and was heading left when her mobile came to life.

It could have been Jason, but when she succeeded in wielding the phone her voice felt cold and heavy as the spiked caps of the roofs. "Yes," she said.

"Not far now."

Russell's voice made her feel as if his lips were trying to keep their shape against her ear. "So tell me where," she said.

"Up here."

Suppose he was unable to be any more specific and nervous of admitting it? "Just talk as you walk. I'll hear you," she gathered he was saying despite shedding several consonants.

She couldn't leave the situation unresolved. If he needed help, she ought to find out where to send it. She turned away from her house and grasped the uphill railing. "Just talk," he repeated, though the first word almost dissolved into a hiss.

This street was even steeper. She had to keep hold of the rail, though her gloved hand ached with its iciness. At the end of every pace the handbag on her wrist blundered like a blind but affectionate creature against her hip. Beyond their plots of white the houses appeared to be holding themselves still for fear of inundation by the burdens on their roofs. A wind like the essence of the frozen dark groped at her face as though searching for the bones. She licked her stiff lips to release her voice. "What do you want to talk about?"

"Can't you think of anything?"

His voice must be shivering with static, not with panic. "The weather," she said less than wholly as a joke.

"About us. Times we had together." The silence that ensued might have signified exhaustion or a wordless plea until he said "When we went dancing. I did enjoy myself, you know."

It had been the beginning of their end. Once he'd finished shouting above the disco uproar that he was her uncle, he'd set about dancing with a violence that seemed designed to compete with everyone else in the room. She could almost see the thin figure jigging and jerking as if he'd borrowed all the artificial vigour of the strobe light, his sleeves and trousers flapping like flags in a gale. When he'd panted to a standstill he had subsided into a chair and watched her dance, his eyes flickering with resignation that might have concealed a plea. Now she could have hoped he would ask anything other than "Didn't you?"

"I'm remembering. I don't do everything aloud."

"Don't you want to talk about it?"

"I thought it didn't matter what I talk about as long as I keep talking."

"It doesn't," he might have finished saying if his voice hadn't collapsed into a flood of static.

In a moment the phone was lifeless. A wind drifted down from the white ridge that was gnawing the black sky. The gust lingered behind a hedge to disturb a newspaper or a bank of loose snow – something white that whispered, at any rate. As the wind fastened on her, Kerry shivered and nearly dropped the mobile, which had twitched in her hand. That was a preamble to playing the tune she might have heard at the disco with Russell. "I'm here," she told the blank phone.

"I know. You're outside."

The house beyond the gate to her right seemed to advance from the rank, although it was no taller or thinner than any of its neighbours. A few sets of footprints smudged by last week's brief false thaw led to a front door unconcerned with any colour. The house was beetle-browed with icicles, and as far as she could see, it was unlit. "Well, are you going to let me in?" she said.

"Sorry." He sounded worse than that. "If you could find your own way," he said, dropping several consonants.

Kerry fumbled to thumb the key and then to snap her bag shut on the mobile. As she ventured up the path she felt as if the ill-defined prints were directing her course. If he didn't answer the doorbell she would certainly phone for help. She planted one foot on the doorstep bloated with snow and poked the bellpush in the middle of the door. It rattled more than rang, and at once the door swung inwards.

Light fanned along the hall in time to catch the white mass that swelled into her face. Could the house be colder than the street? The enervated glow through the puffy branches of a tree revealed half of the hall, the lower reaches of a staircase, two open doorways with a light switch between them. On her way to the switch a shiver overwhelmed her. She thought this and her glove were hindering her fingers until she saw that the switch wouldn't budge because it was encased in ice.

She was distracted by the notion that the house was somehow less defined than it ought to be. She peered into the rooms on either side of the switch and saw why. The first would be a sitting-room, the second for dining, but the furniture was close to unidentifiable. Though the windows were shut now, they had been open to the blizzard; the rooms and their contents were deep in snow. As she gazed at the dim pallid heaps, which barely referred to the shapes of a chair and a table and sideboard, Russell said "Up here."

She mustn't have switched off her mobile. His muffled voice was more fragmented than ever, and quite devoid of consonants. She wanted to finish whatever needed to be done, and so she hurried upstairs almost fast enough to outdistance a shiver, gripping the banister that felt cold and slippery enough for metal. "Where?" she called.

She gained the upper floor without hearing any answer. All the doors off the landing were open. While the bathroom appeared to be clear of snow, icicles glimmered beneath the taps. Next was a room so cold that its darkness put her in mind of black ice. Around the door she caught sight of the foot of a bed. She was hoping that he didn't plan to entice her in that direction when his crumbling voice said "Not there, here."

That could only apply to one room. As she stepped over the threshold she saw the town draped in pallor under a sky of brass flawed with stars. Russell's desk must overlook the view, but the desk was buried in a snowdrift. All the same, a form was slumped or crouched in the snowbound chair in front of it. Kerry hurried forward, angry as much as dismayed. "Russell, what have you—"

She was falling towards the chair. She regained her footing barely in time not to clutch at the chair and swing it around or worse. Whatever she'd slipped on, it wasn't ice. She blinked at the floor and tried not to believe what she was seeing. It was scattered with paper – with pages. The empty objects scattered among them were bindings, and she recognized the covers. He'd torn up all his books.

Had he done it for her to find? She wasn't going to feel guilty, but her eyes grew wet and unfocused as she leaned over the chair. "Russell, what did you think—"

She almost planted an unwary hand on the object in the chair for support as she began to make it out. She could only assume he'd ensured for some reason that he couldn't sit at his desk. He'd built his version of a snowman, which was near to collapsing. The lump on top contained more holes than a head should, while the body had thawed and refrozen into such contortions it reminded her of a dead spider. The items like pale glistening sticks that appeared to be exposed here and there must be ice. She started to blink before deciding that she'd seen enough. She turned away hastily and picked her way over the waste of paper.

There was only the bedroom now. She was tempted to walk past and out of the house, but she was too anxious for him. She would have worried about anybody in the state of which she'd seen so much evidence. She pushed the door wide and strode into the room. "Russell, I've had—"

She didn't even manage to utter all of that. For a moment – far too brief – she thought he'd wrapped a heavy quilt around him as he sat propped up against the pillows on the bed under the open window. It was snow, which filled his open mouth. His eyes were doughy wads. He looked no thinner than when she'd last seen him – and then she understood that he owed much of his substance to snow. The little she could distinguish of him was naked, and was that a withered icicle protruding from his fist between his legs? She was trying desperately to grasp how recently he must have lost the power of speech when she heard him. "Not that," he said.

Though each word was in shreds, the voice wasn't on her mobile. She didn't know where it was, and so she almost couldn't move. A shudder helped release her, and she staggered out of the frozen room. "Don't go," Russell said.

His voice was emerging from one of the rooms, and not only his voice. She was nearly at the stairs when whatever was behind her touched the back of her neck. Its grasp was so icy that although it almost instantly disintegrated, the feeling of it lingered like a brand. She would have fallen headlong if she hadn't seized the banister. She fled downstairs and along the unlit hall, and heard a whisper at her back that might have been an attempt to speak or the best her pursuer could do in the way of footsteps. She groped at the latch and dragged the door open and slammed it behind her so hard that it dislodged snow from the roof. She skidded along the path and slithered downhill, clinging to the rail, as fast as carelessness would take her. She wasn't out of sight of Russell's house when her mobile rang.

She had to force herself to halt and dig in her handbag, though the sound of any of her friends would be reassuring. She couldn't identify the unfinished digits that appeared to be struggling into view. "Jason," she almost hoped aloud, but the dogged incomplete voice wasn't his. "You tried," it said. "My turn."

BRIAN KEENE

"The King", in: *Yellow*

BRIAN KEENE IS A two-time Bram Stoker Award-winning author. His books include *The Rising*, *Terminal*, *City of the Dead*, *Fear of Gravity* and the upcoming *Earthworm Gods*, *The Rutting Season* and *War Pigs* (co-written with Tim Lebbon). Many of Keene's novels and short stories are slated for film, comic book, and video game adaptations.

About the following story, which would have fitted perfectly into Karl Edward Wagner's late and lamented *Year's Best Horror Stories* series, he recalls: "I got the idea while walking around Fell's Point in Baltimore, after a budding young horror writer told me he'd never read Robert W. Chambers' 'The King in Yellow'.

"My story is, of course, a tribute to that classic tale. But you already knew this because you've read the original, right? If not, you need to correct that. Horror fiction has a rich history, and it is your heritage as a fan, a reader, and especially if you're a writer. Seek it out. Learn from it. Machen. Hodgson. Dunsany. Blackwood. Bierce. Clark Ashton Smith. Edward Lucas White. Read them. You'll be glad you did . . ."

T HE MAN STOOD ROTTING on the corner. Frayed rags hung from his skeletal frame and ulcerated sores covered his exposed flesh, weeping blood and pus. He stank. Sweat. Infection. Excrement. Despair.

Finley considered going the long way around him, but Kathryn waved impatiently from across the street. He shouldered by; head down, eyes fixed on the pavement. Invisible.

He can't see me if I can't see him.

"Yo 'zup," the rotting man mumbled over the traffic. "Kin you help a brutha' out wit' a quarta'?"

Finley tried ignoring him, then relented. He didn't have the heart to be so cold, although Kathryn's yuppie friends (they were supposed to be *his* friends too, but he never thought of them that way) would have mocked him for it. He raised his head, actually *looking* at the bum, meeting his watery eyes.

They shone.

Finley glanced across the street. Kathryn's expression was incredulous.

"Sorry, man." Finley held his hands out in a pretence of sympathy. "I'm taking my girl to dinner." Feeling like an idiot, he pointed at Kathryn, as if proving he spoke the truth. "Need to stop at an ATM."

"S'cool," the vagrant smiled. "Ya'll kin hit me on da way back."

"Okay, we'll do that."

Finley stepped off the curb. The man darted forward, grasping his shoulder. Dirty fingernails clawed at his suit jacket.

"Hey!" Finley protested.

"Listen," the bum croaked. "Have ya'll seen *Yellow*?"

"N-no, I don't think so," Finley stammered, clueless.

"Afta' ya' eat, take yo' lady t' see it."

Cackling, the homeless man shambled off toward the waterfront. Finley crossed the street.

Kathryn shook her head. "So you met the Human Scab?"

"Only in Baltimore," he grinned.

"Fucking wildlife," she spat, taking his arm. "That's why I take my smoke breaks in the parking garage. I don't know what's worse – the seagulls dive-bombing me, or the homeless dive-bombing me."

"The seagulls," Finley replied. "How was your day?"

"Don't try to change the subject, Roger. Christ, you've become so liberal. What happened to the conservative I fell in love with?" She paused and let go of his arm, lighting a cigarette. In the early darkness, the flame lit her face, reminding Finley why he'd fallen in love with her. "But since you asked, it sucked. How was yours?"

"Okay, I guess. Pet Search's web site crashed, so I had to un-fuck that. Fed-Ex dropped off my new back-up server. On *Days of Our Lives*, John is still trying to find Stefano and Bo found out about Hope's baby."

"Wish I could work from home and watch soap operas all day. But one of us has to make money."

"Well isn't that why we're going out to dinner? To celebrate your big bonus?"

They crossed Albemarle Street in silence. Ahead, the bright lights of the Inner Harbour beckoned with its fancy restaurants and posh shops. The National Aquarium overlooked the water like an ancient monolith.

Kathryn's brow furrowed.

"Beautiful night," Finley said, tugging his collar against the cold air blowing in across the water. "You can almost see the stars."

Kathryn didn't reply.

"What's wrong?"

She sighed, her breath forming mist in the air. "I feel – I don't know – old. We used to do fun things all the time. Now it's dinner on the couch and whatever's on satellite. Maybe a game of Scrabble if we're feeling energetic."

Finley stared out across the harbour. "I thought you liked coming home every evening with dinner made, and spending a quiet night around the house."

She took his hand.

"I do, Roger. I'm sorry. It's just – we're both thirty now. When was the last time we did something *really* fun?"

"When we were twenty-one and you puked on me during the Depeche Mode concert?"

Kathryn finally laughed, and they walked on, approaching Victor's. "So why did your day suck?"

"Oh, the lender won't approve the loan on the Spring Grove project because the inspector found black mould in some of the properties. Of course, Ned told him we were going to rip out the tiles during the remodelling phase, but he—"

Finley tuned her out, still nodding and expressing acknowledgement where applicable. After ten years, he'd gotten good at it. When *was* the last time they'd really done something fun? He tried to remember. Didn't this count? Going out to dinner? Probably not. He tried to pinpoint exactly *when* they'd settled into this comfortable zone of domestic familiarity. By mutual agreement, they didn't go to the club anymore. Too many ghetto fabulous suburbanites barely out of college. They didn't go to the movies because she hated the cramped seating and symphony of babies crying and cell phones ringing.

"—so I don't know what I'm going to do," Kathryn finished.

"You'll be fine." Finley squeezed her hand. "You can handle it."

She smiled, squeezing back.

The line outside Victor's snaked around the restaurant. Finley manoeuvred them through it; thankful he'd had the foresight to make reservations.

The maitre d' approached them, waving a manicured hand.

"Hello, Ms Kathryn," he said, clasping her hand. "I'm delighted you could join us."

"Hello, Franklin," she curtsied, smiling as the older man kissed both her cheeks. "This is my boyfriend, Roger."

The maitre d' winked. "A pleasure to make your acquaintance, sir. I've heard much about you."

Finley grinned, unsure of how to reply.

"Give them a good view," Franklin told the hostess, and turned back to them. "Sheila will seat you. Enjoy your meal."

"I come here a lot for lunch," Kathryn explained as they followed Sheila to their table. "I told Franklin we'd be coming in tonight. He's a nice old guy; a real charmer."

"Yes, he does seem nice," Finley mumbled, distracted. Not for the first time, he found himself surprised by how little he knew about Kathryn's life outside their relationship. He'd never thought to wonder where she spent her lunches.

In many ways, they were different. Strangers making up a whole. She was the consummate twenty-first century yuppie – a corporate lioness intent upon her career and nothing else. He was the epitome of the Generation X slacker, running a home-based web-hosting business. They'd been together almost ten years, but at times, it seemed to him as if they were just coasting. The subjects of marriage and children had been broached several times, and usually deflected them both. He needed to devote time to developing his business. She wasn't where she wanted to be in her career.

Despite that, he thought they were happy. So why the disquiet? Maybe Kathryn was right. Maybe they needed to do something fun, something different.

"—at night, isn't it?"

"I'm sorry," he stammered. "What'd you say hon?"

"I said the harbour really is beautiful at night." They were seated in front of a large window, looking out towards the Chesapeake Bay. The lights of the city twinkled in the darkness.

"Yeah, it sure is."

"What were you thinking about, Roger?"

"Honestly? That you're right. We should do something *fun*. How about we take a trip down to the ocean this weekend? Check out the wild horses, maybe do a little beach combing?"

"That sounds great," she sighed. "But I can't this weekend. I've got to come in on Saturday and crunch numbers for the Vermont deal. We close on that next week."

"Well then, how about we do something Sunday? Maybe take a drive up to Pennsylvania and visit some of the flea markets, see the Amish, or stop at a produce stand?"

"That's a possibility. Let's play it by ear, okay?"

They studied their menus, basking in the comfortable silence that only long-time partners share.

That was when Roger noticed the woman.

She and her companion sat at the next table. The flickering candlelight cast shadows on her sallow face. She was thin, almost to the point of emaciation, and there were dark circles under her eyes.

Heroin, he wondered, *or maybe Anorexia?* She obviously came from money. That much was apparent from her jewellery and shoes. Her companion looked wealthy, too. Maybe she was a prostitute? No, they seemed too familiar with each other for that.

What caught Finley's attention next was the blood trickling down her leg. Her conversation was animated, and while she gestured excitedly with one hand, the other was beneath the table, clenching her leg. Her fingernails clawed deep into the flesh of her thigh, hard enough to draw blood. She didn't seem to care. In fact, judging by the look in her eye, she enjoyed the sensation.

Finley glanced at Kathryn, but she was absorbed with the menu. He turned back to the couple, and focused on what the woman was saying.

"And then, the King appears. It's *such* a powerful moment, you can't breathe. I've been to Vegas, and I've seen impersonators, but this guy is the real thing!"

Her companion's response was muffled, and Finley strained to hear.

"I'm serious, Reginald! It's like he's channelling Elvis! The King playing the King! The whole cast is like that. There's a woman who looks and sounds just like Janis Joplin playing the Queen, and a very passable John Lennon as Thale. The best though, next to the King of course, is the guy they cast to play the Pallid Mask. I swear to you Reginald, he's Kurt Cobain! You can't tell the difference. It's all so realistically clever! Actors playing rock stars playing roles. A play within a musical within a play."

Her voice dropped to a conspiratorial whisper, and Finley leaned towards them.

"The special effects are amazing. When the Queen has the Pallid Mask tortured, you can actually see little pieces of brain in Cobain's hair. And they have audience participation, too. It's different every night. We each had to reveal a secret that we'd never told anyone. That's why Stephanie left Christopher. Apparently, he revealed a tryst he'd had with a dog when he was ten. She left him after the performance. Tonight, I hear they'll be having the audience unmask along with the actors, during the masquerade scene."

Finley jumped as Kathryn's fingertips brushed his hand.

"Stop eavesdropping," she hissed. "It's not polite."

"Sorry, dear. Have you decided what you're going to have?"

"Mmmm-hmmm," she purred. "I'm going with the crab cakes. How about you?"

"I think I'll have the filet mignon. Rare. And a big baked potato with lots of sour cream and butter."

Her eyes widened. "Why Roger, you haven't had that since your last visit to the doctor. What happened to eating healthy, so that you don't end up like your father?"

"The hell with my hereditary heart disease and cholesterol!" He closed the menu with a snap. "You said we need to start having more fun. Red meat and starch is a good start!"

She laughed, and the lights of the bay reflected in her eyes. Underneath the table, she slid her foot against his leg.

"I love you, Kathryn."

"I love you, too."

The woman at the other table stood up, knocking her chair backward, and screamed.

Kathryn jumped. "I think somebody has had too much wine."

Silence, then hushed murmurs as the woman tottered back and forth on her heels. Her companion scooted his chair back, cleared his throat in embarrassment, and reached for her. She slapped his hand away with a shriek.

"Have you seen the Yellow Sign?" she sang. "Have you found the Yellow Sign? Have you seen the Yellow Sign?"

She continued the chorus, spinning round and round. Her flailing arms sent a wine glass crashing to the floor. Her date lunged for her. She side-stepped, and in one quick movement, snatched her steak knife from the table and plunged it into his side. He sank to his knees, pulling the tablecloth and their meals down with him. Screaming, several patrons dashed for the exit, but no one moved to stop her.

Finley felt frozen in place, transfixed by what occurred next.

Still singing, the woman bent over and plucked up her soup spoon from the mess on the floor, then used it to gouge out her eyes. Red and white pulp dribbled down her face.

Voice never wavering, she continued to sing.

Franklin the maitre d', and several men from the kitchen rushed towards the woman.

Kathryn cringed against Finley. He grabbed her hand, pulling her toward the exit.

As he hurried Kathryn out the door, he heard the woman cackling.

"I found it! I can see it all! Yhtill, under the stars of Aldebaran and the Hyades! And across the Lake of Hali, on the far shore, lies Carcosa!"

Then they were out the door and into the night.

Kathryn sobbed against him, and Finley shuddered. The image of the woman digging into her eye sockets with the soup spoon would not go away.

After they'd given their statement to the police, they walked back to Kathryn's building.

Kathryn shook her head. "How could a person *do* something like that?"

"Drugs maybe?" Finley shrugged. "She looked pretty strung out."

"This city gets worse every year."

They arrived back at her office building, and Finley walked around to the side entrance leading into the parking garage. He'd taken the bus, so that they could drive her car back home. Kathryn didn't follow, and he turned to find her stopped under a streetlight.

"What's wrong?"

"I don't think I'm going to be able to sleep tonight, Roger."

"Yeah, me either. Let's go home and get you a nice hot bubble bath. Maybe you'll feel better after that."

"I need a drink."

"We can stop off at the liquor store—"

"No," she cut him off. "I need to be around *people*, Roger. I need to hear music and laughter and forget all about that insane bitch."

"You want to hit a club?" He heard the surprised tone in his voice.

"I don't know what I want, but I know that I don't want to go home right now. Let's walk over to Fell's Point and see what we can find."

Part of Baltimore's harbour district, the buildings in Fell's Point had been old when Edgar Allan Poe was new to the city. By day, it was a tourist trap; six blocks of antique shops and bookstores and curio dealers. Urban chic spawned and bred in its coffee shops and cafés. At night, the college crowd descended upon it, flocking to any of the dozens of nightclubs and bars that dotted the area.

They strolled down Pratt Street, arms linked around each other's waist, and Finley smiled.

A figure lurched out of the shadows.

"Have ya'll seen *Yellow*?"

Finley groaned. He'd forgotten about the homeless man – the Human Scab.

He thrust his hand into his pants pocket, pulled out a rumpled five, and offered it to the rotting man. "Here. I promised you I'd get you on the way back. Now, if you don't mind, my girlfriend and I have had a rough evening."

"Thanks, yo. Sorry t' hear 'bout yo night. I'm tellin' ya', take yer girl ta' see *Yellow*. Dat'll fix ya right up."

With one dirty, ragged finger, he pointed at a poster hanging from a light pole.

"Ya'll have a good 'un."

The bum shuffled off into the darkness, humming a snatch of melody. Finley recognized the tune as *Are You Lonesome Tonight*. He shuddered, reminded of the crazy woman at the restaurant, raving about the Elvis impersonator that she'd seen. He tried to remember what it was she'd been singing, but all that came to mind was the image of her gored face.

The eight by ten poster that the bum had pointed out was made to look like it was printed on a snake's skin. Overtop the scales, pale lettering read:

Hastur Productions Proudly Presents:

YELLOW
(The Awful Tragedy of Young Castaigne)

Banned in Paris, Munich, London, and Rome, we are proud
to bring this classic 19th century play to Baltimore, in its
only U.S appearance! Filled with music, emotion and dark
wonder, YELLOW is an unforgettable and mystifying tale!
Not to be missed!

Starring:
Sid Vicious as Uoht
John Lennon as Thale
Mama Cass as Cassilda
Janis Joplin as The Queen
Karen Carpenter as Camilla
James Marshall Hendrix as Alar
Jim Morrison as Aldones, the Lizard King
Kurt Cobain as The Pallid Mask, or, Phantom of Truth
and

Elvis Presley as The King
Also featuring: Robert Johnson, Johnny Cash, Bon Scott,
Roy Orbison, Freddy Mercury, Cliff Burton, and more.

One Week Only!
Nightly Performances Begin Promptly at Midnight

The R. W. Chambers Theatre
Fell's Point, corner of Fedogan St. & Bremer Ave.
Baltimore, MD

Finley shivered in the breeze coming off the harbour. This was what the crazy woman at the restaurant had been talking about – actors depicting dead musicians depicting characters in a play. *This* play. The coincidence was unsettling.

"Sounds like fun, doesn't it?" Kathryn asked. "You should have tipped him more money."

"Only in Baltimore can the homeless get jobs as ushers. Come on, let's find a pub."

"No, let's go see this! Look, they've got actors pretending to be dead musicians playing actors. How cool is that?" She giggled, and looked at him pleadingly.

He told her what he'd overheard the woman say.

"Then that's all the more reason," she insisted. "Once people read about the connection in tomorrow's *Baltimore Sun*, we won't be able to get tickets because of the demand. People love morbid stuff like that!"

"Don't you think it's odd that this all happened in the same night? You said you wanted to forget about what happened. Don't you think that attending a play that this same woman went to will just make it that more vivid?"

"Roger, you said that you agreed with me; that we never do anything fun anymore, that we're not spontaneous. Here's our chance! How much more spur-of-the-moment can we get?"

"Kathryn, it's almost eleven-thirty! It's late."

"The poster says it doesn't start until midnight."

Finley sighed reluctantly.

"Okay, we'll go to the play. You're right, it might be fun." He allowed her to lead him down the street and into Fell's Point.

The R. W. Chambers Theatre wasn't just off the beaten path – it was far, far beyond it. They picked their way through a maze of winding, twisting streets and alleyways, each more narrow than the previous.

The throng of drunken college kids, and office interns vanished, replaced by the occasional rat or pigeon. Kathryn's heels clicked on the cobblestones, each step sounding like a rifle shot.

This is the old part of the city, Finley thought. *The oldest. The dark heart.*

The very atmosphere seemed to echo his discomfort, accentuating it as they went further. There were no streetlights in this section, and no warm glow in the windows of the houses. The buildings crowded together, crumbling monuments to nineteenth century architecture. The street stank of garbage and urine, and the only sound was that of dripping water, and of something small scuttling in the darkness.

Kathryn gripped his hand tightly, and then—

– they emerged onto the corner, and the lights and noise flooded back again. A crowd milled about in front of the theatre. Finley's apprehension dissipated, and he chided himself for being silly. At the same time, Kathryn's grip loosened.

"Look at this crowd," she exclaimed. "It's more popular than we thought!"

"Word of mouth must have spread fast."

"Maybe your homeless friend's been pimping it."

Finley grinned. "Maybe."

They took their place at the end of the line, behind a young Goth couple.

The theatre had seen better days. The water-stained brickwork looked tired and faded. Several windows on the second floor had been boarded over, and the others were dark. Some of the light bulbs in the marquee had burned out, but HASTUR PRODUCTIONS' YELLOW and the show time and ticket prices were prominently visible. One side of the building was plastered with paper billboards promoting the play. Others advertised bands with names like Your Kid's On Fire, Suicide Run, and I, Chaos.

The line snaked forward, and finally it was their turn. Finley stared at the man behind the glass window of the ticket booth. His skin was pale, almost opaque, and tiny blue veins spider-webbed his face and hands. Grey lips flopped like two pieces of raw liver as he spoke.

"Enjoy the performance."

Finley nodded. Placing his arm around Kathryn's waist, he guided them into the building.

The usher in the lobby had the same alabaster complexion, and was slightly more laconic than his sullen ticket booth counterpart. Without a word, he took their tickets, handed back the stubs and two programs, then silently parted a pair of black curtains and gestured for them to enter.

The theatre filled quickly. They found a spot midway down the centre aisle. The red velvet-covered chairs squeaked as they sat down.

"I can't get over it," Kathryn whispered. "Look at all these people!"

Finley studied the program booklet. Like the posters, it was designed to appear as if it had been bound in serpent skin. He struggled to read the pale lettering:

YELLOW was written in the late 19th century by a young playwright named Castaigne. Tragically, Castaigne took his own life immediately upon completing the work. When YELLOW was first published and performed, the city of Paris banned the play, followed by Munich and London, and eventually most of the world's governments and churches.

It was translated in 1930 by the scholar Daniel Mason Winfield-Harms; who, in a strange twist of fate echoing that of the original author, was found dead in Buffalo, New York after finishing the adaptation.

YELLOW takes place, not on Earth, but on another world, in the city of Yhtill, on the shore of the Lake of Hali, under the stars of Aldebaran and Hyades.

Kathryn stirred next to him. "You know what this reminds me of?"

"What?"

"When I was in high school. At midnight on Saturdays, we'd go to see *The Rocky Horror Picture Show*. It has that feel to it."

"Maybe they'll sing 'The Time Warp'."

She reached over and squeezed his hand, and Finley felt good. Happy. Then the lights dimmed, plunging them into darkness.

The crowd grew silent as a burst of static coughed from the overhead speakers. Then, an eerie, unfamiliar style of music began. A light appeared at the back of the theatre. The performers entered from the rear, each of them carrying a single candle. The troupe walked slowly down the centre aisle, singing as they approached the stage.

"Have you seen the Yellow Sign? Have you found the Yellow Sign?"

As they passed by, Finley resisted the urge to reach out and touch them. The resemblance to their dead alter egos was uncanny. The actress playing Janis Joplin (playing the Queen) was a *perfect* duplicate, down to the blue-tinged skin that must have adorned her face in death. Following her were Jim Morrison (a bloated Aldones) and John Lennon (a Thale with fresh bloodstains on his clothing). Mama Cass, Jimi Hendrix, Sid Vicious, Johnny Cash – the procession continued, until two-dozen actors had taken the stage.

"Look at that!" Kathryn pointed to the quarter-sized drops of blood left in the Lennon actor's wake. "Gruesome. I can't wait to see what they did with Kurt Cobain . . ."

Finley shuddered. "Good special effects, that's for sure."

The singing swelled, the upraised voices echoing like thunder.

"Have you seen the Yellow Sign? Have you found the Yellow Sign? Let the red dawn surmise what we shall do, when this blue starlight dies and all is through. Have you seen the Yellow Sign? Have you found the Yellow Sign?"

They repeated the chorus two more times. On the last note, the candles were extinguished and the lights on the stage grew brighter.

The first part of the play concerned the intrigue of the royal court. The ageing Queen was pestered and plied by her children: Cassilda, Alar, Camilla, Thale, Uoht, and Aldones, all claimants for the throne to Yhtill. They vied for the crown, so that the dynasty would continue, each one claiming to be the rightful successor. Despite their efforts, the Queen declined to give the crown away.

Mama Cass began to sing a strange, lilting melody, and Finley's skin prickled.

"Along the shore the cloud waves break. The twin suns sink behind the lake. The shadows lengthen, in Carcosa. Strange is the night where black stars rise, and strange moons circle through the skies. But stranger still is lost Carcosa. Songs that the Hyades shall sing, where flap the tatters of the King, must die unheard in dim Carcosa. Song of my soul, my voice is dead, die though, unsung, as tears unshed shall dry and die in lost Carcosa."

The crowd applauded, enraptured with her performance. Then the Cobain character appeared on stage, his face hidden beneath a pallid mask. When he turned his back to the audience, the crowd gasped. Hair and skull were gone, offering a glimpse of grey matter.

Finley had trouble following the plot after that. Cobain's character, the Phantom of Truth, pronounced doom upon the Queen and her subjects. The threat apparently came from a non-existent city that would appear on the other side of the lake. Reacting to this news, the Queen ordered him tortured.

Though Kathryn seemed enraptured, Finley grew more and more restless as it continued. He found the story incoherent to the point of absurdity. One moment, a character professed their love for another. The next, they discussed a race of people who could consume only milk, lacked anuses, and evacuated their waste through vomiting.

The characters rambled on, and Finley slipped into a half conscious state – his mind adrift with other matters but the actor's lines droned on in the back of his head.

"There are so many things which are impossible to explain! Why should certain chords of music make me think of the brown and golden tints of autumn foliage?"

"Let the red dawn surmise . . ."

"Aldebaran and the Hyades have aligned, my Queen!"

"What we shall do . . ."

"Sleep now, the blessed sleep, and be not troubled by these ill omens."

"When this blue starlight dies . . ."

"The City of Carcosa has appeared on the other side of Lake Hali!"

"And all is through . . ."

Finley wasn't sure how long he stayed like that; head drooping and eyes half shut. Kathryn's light laughter and the chuckles coming from the rest of the audience startled him awake again. He checked his watch; then glanced around at the other patrons. His attention focused on a couple behind them. The woman's head was in her lover's lap, bobbing up and down in the darkness.

Before he could tell Kathryn, he noticed another display – this one in their row. A man at the end was lovingly biting another man's ear, hard enough to draw blood. His partner licked his lips in ecstasy.

"Kathryn—" he whispered.

She shushed him and focused on the play, her face rapt with attention. Her cheeks were flushed, and her nipples stood out hard against her blouse. Without a word, she put her hand into his lap and began to stroke him through his pants. Despite the bizarre mood permeating the theatre, Finley felt himself harden.

Just then, there was a commotion at the back of the theatre, as another actor entered. The crowd turned as the actors on stage pointed with mock cries of shock and dismay.

The new player wore a gilded robe with scarlet fringes, and a clasp of black onyx, on which was inlaid a curious symbol of gold. Though his face was hidden beneath a pallid mask identical to the one Cobain was wearing, there was no mistaking the trademark swagger. He swept down the aisle, pausing as the crowd burst into spontaneous applause.

"Thank you. Thank you very much."

He bowed to the audience, and then took the stage in three quick strides.

"Behold, the Yellow Sign upon his breast," cried the Queen. "It is the King of Carcosa, and he seeks the Phantom of Truth!"

Hendrix, Lennon, and Vicious entered the audience, each with a burlap bag slung over their shoulders.

"Masks!" they called. "Everyone receive your masks! No pushing. There's plenty for everyone!"

Finley's eyes widened in alarm, and he pushed Kathryn's hand away. They were passing out *knives* – real knives, rather than stage props. The lights glinted off the serrated blades.

"Kathryn, we—"

His statement was cut short as her mouth covered his. Greedily, she sucked at his tongue, her body filling his lap. The scene replayed itself throughout the theatre – men and women, men and men, women and women. Couples, threesomes, and more. Clothes were discarded, and naked, glistening bodies entwined around each other in the seats and on the floor. All the while, the dead rock stars waded through the crowd, dispensing knives.

"Kathryn, stop it!" He pushed her away. "Something is really fucked up here."

Her breath came in short, excited pants. "Have you found it, Roger? Have you seen the Yellow Sign?"

"What?"

She slapped him. Hard. Then, grinning, she slapped him again.

"Now, you slap me," she urged. "Come on, Roger. You said you wanted to do something different. Make me wet. Hit me!"

"No!"

"Coward! Pussy! You limp dick mother-fucker. Do it, or I'll find someone else here who will!"

"Kathryn, what the hell is wrong with you?"

It's like she's hypnotized or something. All of them are! What the fuck happened while I was asleep?

On stage, what appeared to be a masked ball scene was underway.

"You have questioned him to no avail!" Elvis' voice rang out through the hall, echoing over the mingled cries of pain and ecstasy. He was addressing the actors, but at the same time, the audience as well. "Time to unmask. All must show their true faces. All! Except for myself. For indeed, I wear no mask!"

As one, the crowd picked up their knives and began to flay the skin from their faces. Some laughed as they did it. Others helped the people sitting next to them.

Finley turned, just as Kathryn slid the blade through one cheek. A loose flap of skin hung down past her chin.

"Kathryn, don't! Give me that."

He grabbed for the knife and she jerked it away, then slashed at his hands. Blood welled in his palm as he dodged another slice. Finally, he slapped her, leaving a bloody handprint on her cheek.

"That's it baby," she shrieked. "Let me finish taking my mask off, and then I'll help you with yours."

"All unmask!" Elvis boomed again, and Finley turned to the stage, unable to look away. The King removed the pallid mask concealing his face, and what he revealed wasn't Elvis. It wasn't even human. Beneath the mask was a head like that of a puffy grave worm. It lolled obscenely, surveying the crowd, then gave a strange, warbling cry.

Kathryn's skin landed on the floor with a wet sound.

The thing on stage turned toward Finley, and then he saw.

He saw it. He found it.

Roger Finley screamed.

"Excuse me?" The bum shuffled forward.

"Just ignore him, Marianne. If we give him money, he'll hound us the whole way to the harbour."

"Don't be ridiculous, Thomas," the woman scolded her husband. "The poor fellow looks half starved. And he's quite articulate for a street person. We should help him."

The bum shuffled eagerly from foot to foot while she reached within her purse and pulled out a five-dollar bill. She placed it in his outstretched hand.

"Here you go. Please see to it that you get a hot meal. No alcohol or drugs."

"Thank you. Much obliged." The vagrant smiled sadly. "Since you folks were so kind, let me help you out."

The husband stiffened, wary of the homeless man's advances. "We don't need any help, thank you very much."

"Just wanted to give you a tip. If you like the theatre, you should take your wife to see *Yellow*." He pointed at a nearby poster.

The couple thanked the bum and walked away, but not before stopping to read the poster for themselves.

Roger Finley pocketed the five dollars, and watched them disappear into Fell's Point, in search of the Yellow Sign.

He wondered if they would find it, and if so, what they would see.

TINA RATH

A Trick of the Dark

TINA RATH SOLD HER first dark fantasy story in 1974. Since then her short fiction has appeared in such magazines and anthologies as *Ghosts & Scholars, All Hallows, The Magazine of Fantasy & Science Fiction, The Fontana Book of Great Ghost Stories, The Fontana Book of Horror Stories, Midnight Never Comes, The Year's Best Horror Stories: XV, The Mammoth Book of Vampire Stories by Women, The Mammoth Book of Vampires* and *Great Ghost Stories.*

An actress, model and Queen Victoria look-alike, she lives in London with her husband and several cats. Rath is currently working on two collections of short stories, plus a young adult novel and a fantasy trilogy.

"The genesis of 'A Trick of the Dark' was a postcard showing an early *Dracula* cover and a notice outside a public park, announcing that it closed at sunset," the author explains. "What if, I wondered, a stranger was seen passing a certain window every day at around sunset?

"He could, of course, be a park keeper going off duty, but . . . he might not. And why was someone around to notice him every day? Well, perhaps she was confined to bed, that cosy bed with its pretty bedside lamp and plump eiderdown shown on the *Dracula* cover which conjured up, for me, the comfortable middle-class suburban world of the early 1920s: comfortable, but with brooding threats of worse than vampires hovering over it."

Although she is something of a vampire expert, having written her doctoral thesis for the London University on "The Vampire in Popular Fiction", Rath has not written many vampire stories.

"In fact, 'A Trick of the Dark' may not really be a vampire story at all," she adds, "in spite of its first incarnation.

"I would like the reader to judge . . ."

"WHAT JOB FINISHES JUST at sunset?"

Margaret jumped slightly. "What a weird question, darling. Park keeper, I suppose." Something made her turn to look at her daughter. She was propped up against her pillows, looking, Margaret thought guiltily, about ten years old. She must keep remembering, she told herself fiercely, that Maddie was nineteen. This silly heart-thing, as she called it, was keeping her in bed for much longer than they ever thought it would, but it couldn't stop her growing up . . . she must listen to her, and talk to her like a grown-up.

Intending to do just that she went to sit on the edge of the bed. It was covered with a glossy pink eiderdown, embroidered with fat pink and mauve peonies. The lamp on Maddie's bedside table had a rosy shade. Maddie was wearing a pink bed-jacket, lovingly cro-cheted by her grandmother, and Maddie's pale blonde hair was tied back with a pink ribbon . . . but in the midst of this plethora of pink Maddie's face looked pale and peaky. The words of a story she had read to Maddie once – how many years ago? – came back to her: "Peak and pine, peak and pine." It was about a changeling child who never thrived, but lay in the cradle, crying and fretting, peaking and pining . . . in the end the creature had gone back to its own people, and, she supposed that the healthy child had somehow got back to his mother, but she couldn't remember. Margaret shivered, wonder-ing why people thought such horrid stories were suitable for chil-dren.

"What made you wonder who finishes work at sunset?" she asked.

"Oh – nothing," Maddie looked oddly shy, as she might have done if her mother had asked her about a boy who had partnered her at tennis, or asked her to a dance. If such a thing could ever have happened. She played with the pink ribbons at her neck and a little, a very little colour crept into that pale face. "It's just – well – I can't read all day, or—" she hesitated and Margaret mentally filled in the gap. She had her embroidery, her knitting, those huge complicated jigsaws that her friends were so good about finding for her, a notebook for jotting down those funny little verses that someone was going to ask someone's uncle about publishing . . . but all that couldn't keep her occupied all day.

"Sometimes I just look out of the window," she said.

"Oh, darling . . ." she couldn't bear to think of her daughter just lying there – just looking out of the window. "Why don't you call me when you get bored? We could have some lovely talks. Or I could telephone Bunty or Cissie or—"

It's getting quite autumnal after all, she thought, and Maddie's friends won't be out so much, playing tennis, or swimming or . . . You couldn't expect them to sit for hours in a sick-room. They dashed in, tanned and breathless from their games and bicycle rides, or windblown and glowing from a winter walk, and dropped off a jigsaw or a new novel . . . and went away.

"I don't mind, mummy," Maddie was saying. "It's amazing what you can see, even in a quiet street like this. I mean, that's why I like this room. Because you can see out."

Margaret looked out of the window. Yes. You could see a stretch of pavement, a bit of Mrs Creswell's hedge, a lamp-post, the post-box and Mrs Monkton's gate. It was not precisely an enticing view, and she exclaimed, "Oh, darling!" again.

"You'd be amazed who visits Mrs Monkton in the afternoons," Maddie said demurely.

"Good heavens, who—" Margaret exclaimed, but Maddie gave a reassuringly naughty giggle.

"That would be telling! You'll have to sit up here one afternoon and watch for yourself."

"I might," Margaret said. But how could she? There was always so much to do downstairs, letters to write, shopping to do, and cook to deal with. (Life to get on with?) She too, she realized, dropped in on Maddie, left her with things to sustain or amuse her. And went away.

"Perhaps we could move you downstairs, darling," she said. But that would be so difficult. The doctor had absolutely forbidden Maddie to use the stairs, so how on earth could they manage what Margaret could only, even in the privacy of her thoughts, call "the bathroom problem"? Too shame-making for Maddie to have to ask to be carried up the stairs every time she needed – and who was there to do it during the day? Maddie was very light – much too light – but her mother knew that she could not lift her let alone carry her by herself.

"But you can't see anything from the sitting-room," Maddie said.

"Oh darling—" Margaret realized she was going to have to leave Maddie alone again. Her husband would be home soon and she was beginning to have serious doubts about the advisability of re-heating the fish-pie . . . She must have a quick word with cook about cheese omelettes. If only cook wasn't so bad with eggs . . . "What's this about sunset anyway?" She said briskly.

"Sunset comes a bit earlier every day," Maddie said. "And just at sunset a man walks down the street."

"The same man, every night?" Margaret asked.

"The same man, always just after sunset," Maddie confirmed.

"Perhaps he's a postman?" Margaret suggested.

"Then he'd wear a uniform," Maddie said patiently. "And the same if he was a park keeper I suppose – they wear uniforms too, don't they? Besides he doesn't look like a postman."

"So – what does he look like?"

"It's hard to explain," Maddie struggled for the right words, "but – can you imagine a beautiful skull?"

"What! What a horrible idea!" Margaret stood up, clutching the grey foulard at her bosom. "Maddie, if you begin talking like this I shall call Dr Whiston. I don't care if he doesn't like coming out after dinner. Skull-headed men walking past the house every night indeed!"

Maddie pouted. "I didn't say that. It's just that his face is very – sculptured. You can see the bones under the skin, especially the cheekbones. It just made me think – he must even have a beautiful skull."

"And how is he dressed?" Margaret asked faintly.

"A white shirt and a sort of loose black coat," Maddie said. "And he has quite long curly black hair. I think he might be a student."

"No hat?" her mother asked, scandalised. "He sounds more like an anarchist! Really Maddie, I wonder if I should go and have a word with the policeman on the corner and tell him a suspicious character has been hanging about outside the house."

"No, mother!" Maddie sounded so anguished that her mother hastily laid a calming hand on her forehead.

"Now darling, don't upset yourself. You must remember what the doctor said. Of course I won't call him if you don't want me to, or the policeman. That was a joke, darling! But you mustn't get yourself upset like this . . . Oh dear, your forehead feels quite clammy. Here, take one of your tablets. I'll get you a glass of water."

And in her very real anxiety for her daughter, worries about the fish-pie and well-founded doubts about the substitute omelettes, Margaret almost forgot about the stranger. Almost, but not quite. A meeting with Mrs Monkton one evening when they had both hurried out to catch the last post and met in front of the post-box, reminded her and she found herself asking if Mrs Monkton had noticed anyone "hanging about".

"A young man?" that lady exclaimed with a flash of what Margaret decided was rather indecent excitement. "But darling, there are no young men left." Margaret raised a hand in mute protest only to have it brushed aside by Mrs Monkton. "Well, not nearly enough to go round anyway. I expect this one was waiting for Elsie."

Elsie worked for both Mrs Monkton and Margaret, coming in several times a week to do "the rough", the cleaning that was beneath Margaret's cook and Mrs Monkton's extremely superior maid. She was a handsome girl, with, it was rumoured, an obliging disposition, who would never have been allowed across the threshold of a respectable household when Margaret was young. But nowadays . . . Mrs Monkton's suggestion did set Margaret's mind at rest. A hatless young man – yes, he must be waiting for Elsie. She might "have a word" with the girl about the propriety of encouraging young men to hang about the street for her; but, on the other hand, she might not . . . She hurried back home.

Bunty's mother came to tea, full of news. Bunty's elder sister was getting engaged to someone her mother described as "a bit n.q.o.s., but what can you do . . ." N.q.o.s. was a rather transparent code for "not quite our sort". The young man's father was, it appeared, very, very rich, though no one was quite sure where he had made his money. He was going to give – to give outright! – (Bunty's mother had gasped) a big house in Surrey to the young couple. And he was going to furnish it too, unfortunately, according to his own somewhat . . . individual taste . . .

"Chrome, my dear, chrome from floor to ceiling. The dining room looks like a milk bar. And as for the bedroom – Jack says—" she lowered her voice, "he says it looks like an avant-garde brothel in Berlin. Although how he knows anything about them I'm sure I'm not going to ask. But he's having nothing to do with the wedding," she added, sipping her tea as if it were hemlock. "I wonder my dear – would dear little Maddie be well enough to be a bridesmaid? It won't be until next June. I want to keep Pammy to myself for as long as I can . . ." She dabbed at her eyes.

"Of course," Margaret murmured doubtfully. And then, with more determination, "I'll ask the doctor."

And, rather surprising herself, she did. On his next visit to Maddie she lured him into the sitting-room with the offer of a glass of sherry and let him boom on for a while on how well Maddie was responding to his treatment. Then she asked the Question, the one she had, until that moment, not dared to ask.

"But when will Maddie be – quite well? Could she be a bridesmaid, say, in June next year?"

The doctor paused, sherry halfway to his lips. He was not used to being questioned. Margaret realized that he thought she had been intolerably frivolous. "Bridesmaid?" the doctor boomed. And then thawed, visibly. Women, he knew, cared about such things. "Bridesmaid! Well, why not? Provided she goes on as well as she has been. And you don't let her get too excited. Not too many dress fittings, you know, and see you get her home early after the wedding. No dancing and only a tiny glass of champagne . . ."

"And will she ever be well enough . . . to . . . to . . . marry herself and to . . ." but Margaret could not bring herself to finish that sentence to a man, not even a medical man.

"Marry – well, I wouldn't advise it. And babies? No. No. Still, that's the modern girl isn't it? No use for husbands and children these days—" and he boomed himself out of the house.

Margaret remembered that the doctor had married a much younger woman. Presumably the marriage was not a success . . . then she let herself think of Maddie. She wondered if Bunty's mother would like to exchange places with her. Margaret would never have to lose her daughter to the son of a *nouveau riche* war profiteer. Never . . . and she sat down in her pretty chintz-covered armchair and cried as quietly as she could, in case Maddie heard her. For some reason she never asked herself how far the doctor's confident boom might carry. Later she went up to her daughter, smiling gallantly.

"The doctor's so pleased with you, Maddie," she said. "He thinks you'll be well enough to be Pammy's bridesmaid! You'll have to be sure you finish her present in nice time."

Margaret had bought a tray cloth and six place mats stamped with the design of a figure in a poke bonnet and a crinoline, surrounded by flowers. Maddie was supposed to be embroidering them in tasteful naturalistic shades of pink, mauve and green, as a wedding gift for Pammy, but she seemed to have little enthusiasm for the task. Her mother stared at her, lying back in her nest of pillows. "Peak and pine! Peak and pine!" said the voice in her head.

"Do you ever see your young man any more?" she asked, more to distract herself than because she was really concerned.

"Oh, no," Maddie said, raising her shadowed eyes to her mother. "I don't think he was ever there at all. It was a trick of the dark."

"Trick of the light, surely," Margaret said. And then, almost against her will, "do you remember that story I used to read you? About the changeling child?"

"What, the one that lay in the cradle saying 'I'm old, I'm old, I'm ever so old?'" Maddie said. "Whatever made you think of that?"

"I don't know," Margaret gasped. "But you know how you sometimes get silly words going round and round your head – it's as if I can't stop repeating those words from the story, 'Peak and pine!' to myself over and over again." There, she had said it aloud. That must exorcize them, surely.

"But that's not from the changeling story," Maddie said. "It's from 'Christabel', you know, Coleridge's poem about the weird Lady Geraldine. She says it to the mother's ghost 'Off wandering mother! Peak and pine!' We read it at school, but Miss Brownrigg made us miss out all that bit about Geraldine's breasts."

"I should think so, too," Margaret said weakly.

Autumn became winter, although few people noticed by what tiny degrees the days grew shorter and shorter until sunset came at around four o'clock. Except perhaps Maddie, sitting propped up on her pillows, and watching every day for the young man who still walked down the street every evening, in spite of what she had told her mother. And even she could not have said just when he stopped walking directly past the window, and took to standing in that dark spot just between the lamp-post and the post-box, looking up at her . . .

"Where's your little silver cross, darling?" Margaret said, suddenly, wondering vaguely when she had last seen Maddie wearing it.

"Oh, I don't know," Maddie said, too casually. "I think the clasp must have broken and it slipped off."

"Oh, but—" Margaret looked helplessly at her daughter. "I do hope Elsie hasn't picked it up. I sometimes think . . ."

"I expect it'll turn up," Maddie said. Her eyes slid away from her mother's face and returned to the window.

"How's Pammy's present coming along?" Margaret asked, speaking to that white reflection in the dark glass, trying to make her daughter turn back to her. She picked up Maddie's work-bag. And stared. One of the place mats had been completed. But the figure of the lady had been embroidered in shades of black and it was standing in the midst of scarlet roses and tall purple lilies. It was cleverly done: every fold and flounce was picked out . . . but Margaret found it rather disturbing. She was glad that the poke bonnet hid the figure's face . . . She looked up to realize that Maddie was looking at her almost slyly.

"Don't you like it?" she said.

"It's – it's quite modern isn't it?"

"What, lazy daisies and crinoline ladies, modern?" How long had Maddie's voice had that lazy mocking tone? She sounded like a world-weary adult talking to a very young and silly child.

Margaret put the work down.

"You will be all right, darling, won't you?" Margaret said, rushing into her daughter's room one cold December afternoon. "Only I must do some Christmas shopping, I really must . . ."

"Of course you must, mummy," Maddie said. "You've got my list, haven't you? Do try to find something really nice for Bunty, she's been so kind . . ."

And what I would really like to give her, Maddie thought, is a whole parcel of jigsaws . . . and all the time in the world to see how she likes them . . . She leaned against her pillows, watching her mother scurry down the street. She would catch a bus at the corner by the church, and then an underground train, and then face the crowded streets and shops of a near-Christmas west-end London. Maddie would have plenty of time to herself. She knew (although her mother did not) that cook would be going out to have tea with her friend at Mrs Cresswell's at half-past three, and for at least one blessed hour she would be entirely alone in the house.

She pulled herself further up in the bed, and fumbled in the drawer of her bedside table to find the contraband she had managed to persuade Elsie to bring in for her. Elsie had proved much more useful than Bunty or Cissie or any of her kind friends. She sorted through the scarlet lipstick, the eye-black, the face-powder, and began to draw the kind of face she knew she had always wanted on the blank canvas of her pale skin. After twenty minutes of careful work she felt she had succeeded rather well.

"I'm old, I'm old, I'm ever so old," she crooned to herself. She freed her hair from its inevitable pink ribbon, and brushed it sleekly over her shoulders. Then she took off her lacy bed-jacket and the white winceyette nightie beneath it. Finally she slid into the garment the invaluable Elsie had found for her (Heaven knows where, although Maddie had a shrewd suspicion it might have been stolen from another of Elsie's clients – perhaps the naughty Mrs Monkton). It was a night-dress made of layers of black and red chiffon, just a little too large for Maddie, but the way it tended to slide from her shoulders could have, she felt, its own attraction.

All these preparations had taken quite a long time, especially as Maddie had had to stop every so often to catch her breath and once to take one of her tablets . . . but she was ready just before sunset.

She slipped out of bed, crossed the room, and sat in a chair beside the window. So. The trap was almost set (but was she the trap or only the bait . . .?) Only one thing remained to be done.

Maddie took out her embroidery scissors, and, clenching her teeth, ran the tiny sharp points into her wrist . . .

The bus was late and crowded. Margaret struggled off, trying to balance her load of packages and parcels and hurried down the road, past the churchyard wall, past Mrs Monkton's redbrick villa, past the post-box – and hesitated. For a moment she thought she had seen something – Maddie's strange man with the beautiful skull-like face? But no, there were two white faces there in the shadows – no . . . there was nothing. A trick of the dark . . . She dropped her parcels in the hall and hurried up the stairs.

"Here I am, darling! I'm so sorry I'm late . . . Oh, Maddie . . . Maddie darling – whatever are you doing in the dark?"

She switched on the light.

"Maddie. Maddie, where are you?" she whispered. "What have you done?"

LESLIE WHAT

The Mutable Borders of Love

LESLIE WHAT LIVES in Oregon, where she is married and has two children, both taller than she is. A Nebula Award-winner writer and the author of the comic novel *Olympic Games*, she has published more than sixty short stories in such magazines and anthologies as *The Magazine of Fantasy & Science Fiction*, *Asimov's Science Fiction*, *Realms of Fantasy*, *The Third Alternative*, *SciFiction*, *The Mammoth Book of Tales from the Road*, *Bending the Landscape: Horror*, *All-Star Zeppelin Stories* and *Polyphony*. Her work has been translated into Greek, Spanish, German, Japanese and Klingon.

"It's hard to think of anything more terrifying than love," admits the author. "A friend commented that breaking-up with her partner was like watching her true love die and was surprised by the depth of her grief.

"It got me thinking about how we're haunted by our failed relationships and the metaphor climbed the next step once I sat down to write. The game goes on every day. Players know the risks.

"My thanks to Dave Gross for his excellent editing suggestions. Also, this is not my first story featuring scary fabric."

T HOUGH MARIETTA'S EYES ARE closed, she is wide-awake, fingering the new sheets she gave Asher as part of his six-month anniversary present. The other parts were dinner, followed by multiple sexual favours. She has already thought ahead, to the seven-month anniversary, when she will trade dinner for breakfast, a languorous night of sex for a quickie. She worries to be thinking so far ahead, to have expectations about things she cannot fully control. Is this the way love is supposed to feel?

Asher's bed is a California King. It is out of place, too big for the eight-by-ten room. The sheets cost almost double the price of her queen-size, but she bought these for herself as much as him. Asher's new sheets are crisp and cool dense cotton that makes them feel shiny. Marietta is obsessed by their smooth texture, the fine weave. She can't stop fidgeting with the fabric between her forefinger and thumb. The old sheets were a remnant from a previous relationship. No matter how many times they were laundered, the Hawaiian ginger scent favoured by the woman Marietta has replaced lingered like old smoke. Marietta hated sleeping over, until tonight.

Asher snores contentedly beside her, something she calculates will continue another ten minutes before he fades into a deep and heavy sleep, at which time he might call out names of women he dated before she met him. Marietta knows these women are all dead, just as her past sweethearts have all died, but it bothers her all the same, maybe because it's an unwelcome reminder that not everyone is strong enough to survive love.

In most relationships, someone wins and someone loses. Marietta has been fortunate, so far, to have won them all. She gazes over at the lump in the bed that is Asher. He has been fortunate, too. They are successful competitors in the contest of love. She isn't jealous, just insecure. Is love ever worth the risk? So far, for both of them, the answer has been no.

Street lamplight filters through the shaded windows of his apartment. In the dim light, the delicate pastel blue of the sheets dulls to computer grey. Outside, the wind rattles branches and pushes cool air through cracks in the window frames. Go to sleep, she tells herself, sweet dreams. It takes every effort to keep her eyes shut and lie motionless. She's waiting for what seems inevitable, for a ghost to appear as he has nearly every night for the past few weeks.

Her ghost's name is Lenny; he was her first lover. They were eighteen – late for her, early for him. If she were honest, she would admit that she used him, that she saw him as a means to an end. She was anxious to get it over with, to cede her virginity to her past. It wasn't until long after that she realized Lenny viewed her deflowering with more gravity.

Asher murmurs something in his sleep, a name perhaps, but not one that she recognizes. Asher is dark-skinned and dark-haired, stocky enough to spill over onto her side of the bed. The California King is oversized, and he's used to taking up more than his share. She doesn't mind. Lying beside him is oddly comforting, given that he has passed out and she is fretting. They are both naked; the warmth from their bodies forms a placid layer that stays trapped between the sheets.

The weather has changed to those days just before fall, the only time of year an apartment feels comfortable without either heat or air conditioning. It is man-messy here, with a ring around the toilet bowl, no counter space, and a yeasty aroma leeching from bags filled with beer bottles, bottles unsuccessfully hidden in the closet, awaiting redemption. Asher doesn't leave much room for her to fit into his life. In this way they're well suited. She doesn't understand women who sacrifice their independence for their men. Women like that die young. Asher's apartment reminds her of a foreign country, one she's welcome to visit, so long as her belongings fit inside a backpack.

"Go away," Asher says in his sleep.

A tickle of doubt crosses her mind that he might be thinking of her, but she tells herself that that's out of the question. They have been together long enough that she's certain she loves him, yet short enough that she worries things might fall apart, that one of them will move on, that their time together will be defined by memories and smells loitering in the furniture and bedding. Marietta is twenty-six and ready for this to be the real thing. She thinks Asher feels the same, especially since he is thirty-three, at that age where many men think it's now or never.

Her ghost, Lenny, is late. Maybe he's decided to respect the mutable borders of love and not show up, here, in her lover's bed, in the new sheets that mark a new beginning. The waiting makes her anxious. She's about to give up on sleep, slip into the other room to watch television, when she feels a slight sensation tugging at the covers just below her left foot. Her gut twists, relaxes. Her eyes flick open and adjust to the darkness. A ghost perches on the edge of the bed, staring at Asher. Marietta knows that it's a ghost because she can see through its lithe body to a cherry wood chest of drawers propped against the wall. Transparency is a ghostly quality she greatly admires. Mystical, yet honest. Intriguing. There is no human equivalent.

This is not her Lenny. This ghost is a woman she doesn't know, no doubt one of Asher's old lovers. The apparition looks to be in her early twenties, wearing a sheer negligee that's about as thick as a window screen. She sits as if posing for an art class, hands crossed at the knee, torso twisted slightly. She's a lovely thing, only the littlest bit scary because of her ghost-white hair, which is thin and patchy like the packaged spider webs sold at Halloween. Her face is bathed in fluorescent green light and she's smiling, a beatific, disarming expression. Marietta isn't sure what to say to someone else's ghost. "Hi," she says at last. "You didn't wake me."

The ghost answers with a condescending look that conveys both boredom and disapproval at finding her ex-boyfriend in bed with another woman.

"This is awkward," Marietta whispers, because it's always better to acknowledge a problem instead of ignoring it. Obviously, this affair is over and Asher succeeded in moving on. Too bad about the woman, but these things happen when love doesn't go your way. Should she wake Asher? Or would that just make things worse?

The ghost shrugs. "He doesn't like to be awakened," she says.

"Can you read my thoughts?" asks Marietta.

"Sorry about that," says the ghost. "I forgot how that spooks y'all."

Keeping her mind blank takes concentration. Marietta is slightly afraid, an emotion only a step up from vague anxiety. "When did you two hook up?"

"Two-thousand two," says the ghost.

The answer provides relief because it's unlikely that the latest set of sheets belonged to this ghost. "Did you love him?" Marietta asks.

"More than you can understand. He really hurt me."

He must not have loved her much, Marietta thinks, or things would have worked out.

"I was better than you in bed," the ghost whispers.

It shouldn't, but this boast hurts and Marietta cannot keep from fretting that the ghost is speaking the truth. She pushes back her insecurity. "You're dead now," she retorts. "So how good could you be?"

"Don't underestimate me," says the ghost, rising from the bed. When she stands, her body extends from the floor nearly to the ceiling, elongated, like she is made of taffy.

Marietta hears primitive noises, growling and snorts. At first she thinks the sounds emanate from the ghost, but the growling moves closer, accompanying a change in the texture of the sheets. The fabric roughens from smooth water to broken glass. The growling and snorts are sound effects, a cheap parlour trick. Ghosts are good at effects, better than people. Marietta's arms itch – the more she scratches, the worse it gets – until hot, itchy bumps crop up through her skin. The temperature in the room rises; Marietta breaks into a sweat. Sandy granules cling to her skin.

"What do you want from me?" Marietta asks. She climbs from the bed, sweat dribbling down her face, temporarily blinding her. Her shoulders grow raw from scratching. Her skin burns. It itches behind her ears, between her thighs, inside her mouth. She can't stop raking herself with her nails. "This isn't fair," she protests. "Take it out on him. I didn't do anything to you."

"Good point." Ghosts enjoy showing off their powers. They're quite human in that respect. "Listen," the ghost says. "Sorry, things got out of hand. I just came to warn you. So you don't end up like me."

"Don't worry," Marietta says. "I won't end up like you."

"There are worse things," the ghost says with a dismissive wave.

Marietta's skin dries and the itchy feeling passes as quickly as it began. She's annoyed. This ghost isn't from her past; she's from Asher's. Marietta shouldn't be responsible for his mistakes, as well as her own. As if on cue, Asher calls out in sleep, "Inez!"

"It's good to know he still thinks about me," says the ghost.

"No," says Marietta because Asher should be thinking of her. "It's just a dream."

"Yes, of course," says Inez. "I didn't mean to hurt you or get you so worked up."

"Is that an apology?" asks Marietta.

Inez laughs. "Sure," she says. "Sort of."

Marietta cracks a smile and senses some barrier breaking between them. She trusts this ghost, senses she means well. " 'Inez' is rather old-fashioned."

"It's a family name."

Family names seem like gloating. Marietta thinks of all the family lines she's ended by being the lone survivor. How sad. She's sorry to have been so inconsiderate.

"Asher is afraid of commitment. You two will have another week, two at most. He'll win, you know. Asher's very strong. He's never lost."

"Neither have I," says Marietta.

"You haven't played against Asher."

"It's not a game."

"Not exactly, no. But there's always a loser. Don't you worry that your luck will run out?"

Inez is right: rarely do both parties survive intact. But it can happen, if both want it enough. Maybe it's not the norm, but she knows of people who love *for keeps*. "Why are you telling me this?"

"It's complicated," says Inez.

"You're still angry."

"Not with you. Just with him. I can't forgive what he did to me."

"It won't happen to me," says Marietta. "I'm strong."

"That's what I used to say," says Inez. "By the time you under-stand it all, you're already dead."

"I'm fairly experienced," Marietta says.

"Experience doesn't help," says Inez.

"I asked you before: why are you telling me?"

"I don't want you to die," says Inez. "This might sound funny, but I've found someone else."

"Good to know there's love after death."

"The weird thing is you knew him. His name's Sheldon Perri-cone."

"I know him," says Marietta. She corrects herself. "Knew him." Good old Sheldon. Somewhere between Lenny and Asher. It turns out that a man she abandoned on the altar has found love with Asher's old girlfriend. "Small world," says Marietta.

"Sheldon loves me, but I can't take a chance that he loves me more than you. Not just yet. If you die . . . We need more time to make it work. That's why I want to warn you. I'm not being nice – just cautious."

Marietta nods. This makes sense, in a weird, metaphysical, love-sick sort of way.

"Promise you'll be careful. Asher is sneaky," says Inez.

"So am I."

Next, there's a loud yawn and a stirring as Asher lifts himself to a sitting position on his side of the bed. He rubs his eyes. "Are you talking to someone?" he asks.

They are alone.

Inez has vanished.

"What's the matter?" Asher asks.

Marietta snuggles beside him and wraps her long legs around his muscular ones. She kisses his neck, while he strokes her back. He's so warm, so dark and substantial, nothing like a ghost. Her body-warmth returns. "It was nothing," she says. "I couldn't sleep."

"I don't mind," he says, and she can feel him growing hard beneath her touch.

The next morning, while in her office catching up on e-mail, Marietta gets an instant message from someone named SP. Caught off guard, she answers and soon finds herself corresponding with her old, dead boyfriend, Sheldon Perricone, the ghost who is now partnered with Inez.

    <Marietta> So, do you have a fast connection up there?
    <SP> LOL. How about you?"

She agonizes over what to say next, feeling both curiosity and dread at continuing the conversation. She's just about to type "I'm okay," when her monitor goes dark and a voice from behind her says, "It's better if we talk in person. I was never a good typist."

And there is Sheldon Perricone, whom she had loved and left so long ago it seems like another life. She hadn't meant to be cruel. She never meant to be cruel. With any of them. Human interaction is not an exact science, so there's bound to be mistakes along the way.

Sheldon stands naked in the middle of a plant stand. Philodendron leaves surround his abdomen like a tutu. She sees straight through his chest, though his face seems more solid. His eyes, no longer an intense ocean blue shade, have dulled to grey, with milky quartz crystals as their centres. He's watching her, waiting.

"You're forgetting something," he says, and old memories wash over her. He had hinted of a plan to propose one morning and at night, instead of meeting him for dinner, she had gone out drinking, met someone new, enjoyed a very fun, very sexy one-night stand with a stranger. She remembers telling Sheldon it was over, remembers a face that grew angry, then despondent, remembers watching him fade away before her eyes. It was horrible. Her guilt has come and gone, but at the moment, the feeling pulses strong. "Sorry," she says. "I guess I wasn't very nice."

His expression is sorrowful and vast; she's first to break away from eye contact.

"Should I say more?" she asks.

"Mistakes were made. It won't help to talk about the past."

"I was young."

"Don't make excuses," Sheldon says. "I was young, too. I forgive you. Just don't make excuses."

She wills herself to be quiet, sensing that she seeks something from him, something she cannot fairly ask. She would like to be pardoned for all mistakes, not just those mistakes she made with Sheldon. She doesn't want to be a bad person. It's just that being a good one is too costly. Sheldon, for example. What did being good buy him? He lost. "You have to move on," she says. It's a vacuous statement, one she immediately regrets. "How have you been?" she asks, though the answer is obvious.

"You've met Inez, I hear," he says. "I love her very much. I think she's my soul mate."

Her jaw drops, and while she's tempted to contradict him, she cannot believe what he has said. Does true love only happen after you're dead?

"No," he says, reading her thoughts. "Not always. We find love where we can. I just wanted to warn you. Asher loves you. Don't mess up. Not everyone gets another chance."

She's recovered her cynicism. "Are you afraid I'll dump Asher? Is he that much of a threat?" she asks.

"You've got it all wrong," he says. "You're worrying about the wrong things." He disappears without so much as a subtle whoosh.

On the bus ride home from work a man across the aisle gives her a look that could be interpreted as simple friendliness, or could be interpreted as an invitation. Isn't he worried about what she'll do to him if she gets the chance? Is the urge to pair up so strong it would make a reasonable person risk his life? She has power over men, something they all recognize. It never stops them. It doesn't stop her, either. Everyone thinks they are in control the situation.

The man stands up and moves across to sit beside her. "Hey," he says.

"Do you want to die?" she asks and flashes a look she hopes signifies contempt. She stares ahead, refusing to meet the stranger's glance.

She notices she's fidgeting. The ghosts of her past have unnerved her. She accidentally skips her stop and has to backtrack several blocks. Breaking up is hard to do, though she is better at it than most. But she really does love Asher. She's sure he loves her, though if she's wrong, it will be the end of one or the other. She wants more than anything to be right.

Later, she'll meet Asher at her place to watch *Survivor*, which now holds an especially ironic twist. She's running late enough there will barely be time to call for pizza, let alone shave and straighten up. No choice but to settle for a spit bath and quick rubdown with a towel. She has already picked out a silk shirt to match her jeans. The bell chimes, signalling Asher has arrived.

"Coming," she yells, wishing she'd had time to change her bedding. Her sheets are old and threadbare, a suddenly significant fact. She can't ignore all the ghosts who have slept beside her in her bed. Some part of them still lingers in her life. They get in her way, make it difficult for her to fully commit to love.

She sets her towel on the bed and pulls up her panties and jeans, dabs Must de Cartier perfume at her pulse points, and wonders if it's worth the effort to wear heels that will come off the second she sits on the couch. She picks up the shirt, no bra. The doorbell rings again.

From behind her, she hears conspiring whispers. She turns around. Lying on their backs, smoking cigarettes, pale and naked, are three gossamer men she once thought she loved: Lenny, Sheldon, and a one-night stand whose name is hidden just a bit lower than the tip of her tongue. The worn sheet covers the lumps of their genitals.

Terrific. Her ghosts have hard-ons.

"Hey there," says Lenny. When he exhales, his smoke has more substance than does he. He points to her shirt and moves his fingers in increasingly small circles. Her silk shirt flies up from her side and hangs fluttering in the air like a fabric kite.

"Come sit beside me," says Sheldon with a tap on the sheet. "Plenty of room," he says. "I could use some company." When he nudges the pillow his elbow passes straight through it.

"You were something," says the one-night stand. "But you said you'd call. Why didn't you call?"

They mean to scare her. But they are dead and she's alive. The scariest thing that could happen has already happened, to them. "What do you want?" she asks. "It's over. I won." It sounds harsh when she says it straight out, yet true.

Her ghosts smile with hollow lips. They act as if they don't believe she's the victor.

Sheldon blows her a smoke kiss. "It's not over 'til it's over." The room grows ominously cold.

There's a knocking at the door. In the distance, Asher shouts her name. He's a punctual man who expects no less from the woman he dates.

She checks her watch. "This has been fun but I gotta go."

"Stay," says Lenny, his cold stare pricking like nettles.

She stands up, feeling shaky, says, "Go away!"

"Make us," says Sheldon.

They think she's to blame, but she didn't make up the rules. They knew what they were getting into when they hooked up with her. She tried to love them. It just wasn't meant to be. She wasn't ready. That's not the kind of thing you know until it happens. She snaps her towel and the spectres disappear one by one, pop back up, and disappear again. Flustered, she throws her shoe. It passes through Lenny and bangs against the wall.

"Come back with us," says the one whose name she has forgotten.

"Too late," she says.

Lenny sniffles. "You sure know how to hurt a guy's feelings."

"Tell me something I don't know," she says and pulls the old sheet from the bed to wrap around her shoulders. She styles the sheet over her head and looks out at a room that is daytime foggy, with just enough light peeking through the blinds that her furniture looks like boxes. Her hands appear almost transparent. A creepy effect, but one that makes her laugh. Who says that being a ghost isn't fun? She rushes from the room, toward the front door.

She hears them rummaging through her things, hears their footsteps follow her into the living room. They make the lights dance and topple books from the shelves, but their efforts fall short. She's made up her mind to forget them. They can't touch her. "It's too late," she says. She says it again, louder. Shadows appear through the fabric of her sheet. The shadows lengthen and twist like jungle vines. She trips on something she cannot quite see and pitches forward. "You can't get me," she says. She's stronger than they are; she's stronger than any of them. She's proved that by surviving this long.

Still, her pulse races.

She anticipates what will happen when she opens the door. Asher will smile when she answers, when he sees his lovely, ghostly girl, hidden beneath her sheet. He'll pull away the fabric, notice she isn't wearing a shirt. They'll make love on the carpet. Sex, when it's good, makes her forget about the problematic things, like love. She's afraid of love but with good reason. Loving can be dangerous. Is it really worth the risk? Fear is an icy river coursing through her veins. Fear is a dust devil in her throat that makes her cough and choke for air. Fear is the stabbing pain in the gut that comes from uncertainty. Marietta is afraid because she cannot know if it's worth the risk until too late.

The ghosts laugh and groan. Their voices strangle and then sputter out like a fire doused with sand. When she turns the ghosts are faint ripples. Their steps slow, come to a halt. Their rustling movements fade to silence. As suddenly as they appeared, their spirits vanish.

She's won again. It should feel good, but it doesn't.

Knocking.

Asher waits for her to let him in.

She can barely make out the frame of the door through the worn sheet. She stumbles forward, twists the lock open, pulls back the door. A dark form wavers on the other side of the threshold.

Relief floods through her as she recognizes him. She hesitates before speaking. "Hey," she says.

"Hey," he answers. Once he steps inside he winds his arms around her. The door closes softly behind him. "Missed you," he says.

There's a slight warble to his voice, like he's worried. He holds her so tight it's difficult to breathe. He nuzzles her neck through the sheet, breathing in the sweet scent of her laundry soap, her spicy perfume, the salty fragrance of her skin. He's told her how much he adores these things. "I love you," he says. He waits for her response.

It would be easy to comfort him, to say that she loves him. It would be easy to lose herself in love. Because she does love him. And that terrifies her. She wants to tell him, but she can't make her mouth form the words. It's too dangerous to admit how she feels. She can't do it.

He brushes her lips with his.

She pulls away from his kiss. "I'm sorry," she says.

His arms stiffen. He lifts the sheet from her face and stares into her eyes. His complexion has the clarity of old bath water. His effect is flat. "Why?" he asks.

"Asher," she says. She doesn't want to explain. She leans her weight into him, pressing her breasts flat against his chest, unable to feel the thrum of his heartbeat through her skin. A slow chill trickles like a tear along her spine. "Sorry," she says. "I really tried."

"Congratulations. You won."

"I didn't think this would happen," she tells him, but that's not exactly true. She suspected it would end this way. It always does. She feels bereft, alone, empty. For the first time in her life, she understands love, how it is best defined by loss, by what is missing, not by the transience of joy.

"It hurts," Asher says.

She holds him tight, not to comfort him but more to hold her own feelings of regret. In the end, he slips through her grasp and floats upward, to a place where love has no boundaries, where it floats like the memory of artefacts trapped in amber.

"I love you," she says, too late for him to hear.

L.H. MAYNARD &
M.P.N. SIMS

Flour White and Spindle Thin

LEN MAYNARD AND MICK SIMS have written many books in the supernatural genre, and edited several more, as well as having numerous stories published in a variety of anthologies and magazines.

Their collections include *Shadows at Midnight* (1979, revised and enlarged 1999), *Echoes of Darkness*, *Incantations*, *Falling Into Heaven*, the forthcoming *When Darkness Answers*, and two retrospective collections of their stories, essays and interviews: *The Secret Geography of Nightmare* and *Selling Dark Miracles*.

Their novellas *Moths*, *The Hidden Language of Demons* and *The Seminar* have been published separately while, as editors, they have worked on seven *Darkness Rising* anthologies and co-edited and published *F20* with The British Fantasy Society. As editors/publishers they also ran Enigmatic Press in the UK, which produced *Enigmatic Tales*, amongst other titles.

According to Maynard and Sims: " 'Flour White and Spindle Thin' was written on a palm-held organizer, during a few train journeys between Letchworth Garden City and Kings Cross, London. Revisions were made in a pub in Bishops Stortford, during possibly three pints of IPA bitter.

"The theme of a reluctantly childless marriage is a personal one we have both experienced."

D AWN THE COLOUR OF honey rose slowly over the verdant expanse of Flatland Marsh. Tom Henderson breathed in the crisp morning air, pulled a packet of cigarettes from his pocket and lit one, sucking in the tobacco smoke and rolling it around his mouth before drawing it deeply into his lungs. His first morning in his new job of marsh-warden and already he was grateful for his redundancy from the electronics company. The redundancy had given him an opportunity to reassess his life. With his wife Louise making enough money from book illustrating to cover most of their needs, his role as breadwinner had become more and more superfluous. It was time for a complete break, and he'd grabbed this chance to escape the rat race with both hands. Now he was glad he had done so.

He surveyed the landscape, taking in the rough tussocks of scrubby grass and the torpid pools of water that harboured all manner of wildlife. To the west were outcrops of granite, dark soldiers standing guard over the marsh; to the east the town of Risley. And beyond the marsh, the cold grey waters of the North Sea, separated from the land by mud flats.

He ground the cigarette under the thick rubber sole of his boot and headed back. The house that came with the job was nothing grand, no more than a two bedroomed cottage sitting in half an acre of land. There was a garden, an orchard and a large ornamental pond, but the garden was unkempt and running to weed, the orchard just a handful of diseased apple trees, with a couple of pears to give variety, and the pond was choked with weed and harboured undernourished frogs and newts, the fish having long died off. His predecessor obviously had no time for maintenance, either that or couldn't be bothered, and the decor in the house mirrored the sad state of the garden with peeling wallpaper, chipped and browning paintwork, and the dishevelled feel of an old man long since past his prime.

Louise saw the place as a challenge and had set about stripping walls and repainting doorways with all the passion of a zealot. She'd always supported him, always been there to bolster his confidence, and to embrace his sometimes hare-brained schemes, and he loved her for it.

As he approached the house through the orchard, he picked up a windfall apple from the ground beneath one of the stunted trees, rubbed it on his jacket until the skin shone, then bit into it, spitting the flesh out quickly as sour juice filled his mouth. He tossed the apple away with a grimace. Perhaps he could use them to make cider. As he passed the large weather-beaten shed that occupied space to the right of the pond he noticed the door was slightly ajar. He could see the padlock that once secured it lying on the grass, the hasp hanging loose from the door.

Inside the shed everything seemed much as it had the day before when he'd been looking for some shears. Nothing appeared to have been stolen, but there was something different about the place. In the corner a muddy tarpaulin was wrapped around a sleeping form.

He approached silently, just getting a glimpse of a head poking out from under the tarpaulin. The sleeping figure was a young boy, who looked no more than twelve years old, with pale skin and a shock of white-blond hair. The tarpaulin rose and fell gently with the boy's breathing, but other than that there was no movement.

A sudden gust of wind caught the door and slammed it into the frame, making Tom jump. He spun around at the noise, caught a small tower of terracotta pots on the shelf with his arm and sent them crashing to the floor. When he looked back the boy was awake and on his feet, staring at him wildly.

He was tall for his age, almost as tall as Tom, and was dressed in clothes that were nothing more than rags. His feet were bare, scratched and muddy, the toenails filthy and unclipped. The pale hair flopped over a face as white as flour, and the boy's limbs were spindle thin, looking as if they might snap at the slightest touch. Obviously malnourished and uncared for the boy presented a sorry sight. He regarded Tom with frightened eyes, looking past him at the door and his means of escape.

"It's all right," Tom said. "I won't hurt you."

Still badly frightened, the boy cocked his head to one side at the sound of Tom's voice, puzzlement jostling with fear in his eyes, almost as if he'd never heard a human voice before, and was trying to ascertain what the strange sound was.

Tom tried again. "What's your name?" he said, and took a step towards him.

The boy bared a row of brilliantly white teeth and growled deep in his throat, and then, with a movement so quick it took Tom completely by surprise, darted past him. Tom reached out and caught an arm, his fingers encircling thin flesh and bone. The boy ducked his head and bit Tom's exposed wrist, the teeth cutting through the soft skin. Tom imagined them grinding against his bones. He cried out and swore, pulling his arm away and clutching it to his chest.

The boy crashed through the door, sending it careening back against the shed wall. Tom screwed his eyes tight with the pain from his wrist and tried to follow, but his foot rolled over one of the fallen pots and he stumbled, falling down, one knee taking his full weight and sending fresh paroxysms of pain lancing through his body.

By the time he got to his feet and stumbled outside, the boy was nothing but a pale shape disappearing through the trees towards the marsh. Tom rubbed at his bruised knee and limped back to the house.

"You should go to Casualty," Louise said as she swabbed disinfectant into the bite. The teeth marks were red and angry, the skin around each puncture puckered and swollen. "Human bites are more poisonous and bacteria-filled than most other animals."

"Thanks. You're making me feel better by the minute. Just disinfect it and wrap a bandage round it. It'll be fine."

"I wonder where he came from," she said, pressing a gauze pad over the wound. "I know there's an orphanage over Hepton way. Perhaps he came from there."

Tom shook his head. "No, I don't think so. I told you, he was dressed in rags. He's been living rough for some time."

"Perhaps we should notify the police."

"And face all those questions? No, there's probably a family of travellers in the area – gypsies. He was probably on a foraging mission and decided to bed down here for the night rather than try to find his way back in the dark." It was an unlikely scenario and Tom knew it, but he wanted a quick answer to the problem of the boy. He wanted nothing to interfere with the peace and quiet of his newly discovered idyllic lifestyle.

Louise tore off two strips of sticking plaster and taped them over the bandage to secure it. "I still think you should get it looked at."

He grinned reassuringly. "I'll live; besides, I've got loads to do. There's the fence to repair."

"That's not going to take you all day," she said.

He reached up and stroked her neck fondly. "No it won't, but I can think of better ways of spending the afternoon than sitting in Casualty, can't you?"

His finger tickled the base of her hairline and she felt warmth spread through her body. She shuddered slightly and kissed the top of his head. "I've got to work too, you know?" she said, but the thought of spending the afternoon curled up in bed together was a strong temptation. "You'd better get on then," she said, returning his grin.

The fence was on the west side of the marsh, where the boggy ground bordered a field that once belonged to a neighbouring farm. The farm suffered badly in the last foot and mouth outbreak, the farmer losing all his stock. After seeing his livelihood, and indeed his complete way of life, decimated by the disease and the draconian prevention methods of the Ministry of Agriculture, the farmer took a shotgun to his wife and children, and finally himself. It was a tragic, but not a unique case. Tom could only guess at the despair the man felt.

In the time the farm had stood empty nature stepped in and started to reclaim the land that was once grazing for the herd of Friesians, and the field now resembled a meadow, with poppies, campion and other wild flowers vying for space with the long grass that waved softly in the morning breeze.

Tom crouched down in front of the first post and tapped a heavy staple into the wood, threaded the end of a coil of wire through the eye and twisted it around itself. Then he hammered the staple flush, securing the wire, picked up the coil and carried it to the next post, letting the wire trail out behind him.

Repairing the fence was necessary. The field was now a popular place for local children. Games of cowboys and Indians and cops and robbers could easily end in tragedy should one of the participants stray too far into the greedy marsh.

He crouched down at the next post, positioned the wire and surrounded it with a staple, and then, using a length of wood twisted into the wire to serve as a lever, he stretched it until it was as taut as a guitar string and drove the staple home. He plucked the wire, listening with satisfaction to the deep, tense note it produced.

He was about to move on when he stopped and looked around. It was a familiar tingle down his spine: a sensation he always got when he felt he was being watched. For a moment he thought Louise had come out to join him on the marsh, but he looked back towards the house and there was no sign of her. He pushed himself upright and turned 360 degrees, his eyes scanning the land in all directions, but there was nobody to see. The marsh and surrounding areas were deserted, with not even a rabbit or deer to be seen.

It was unusual for his instincts to play him false, but for the next two hours as he worked, he'd stop and stand every so often, convinced he could feel someone watching him.

Louise propped herself up on her elbow and looked at her sleeping husband. The lines that had been etched into his face by strain and worry were smoothing out, the dark circles under his eyes gradually fading. It was everything to do with the new job and moving here. It was as though ten years had been wiped from his features. He slept now with a peaceful, almost beatific look on his face. She smiled at him fondly and swung her legs to the floor, careful not to wake him, and went to shower.

His renewed interest in sex was also a sign the new position was having a restorative effect. At thirty-five she had begun to feel that this aspect of her life was in suspended animation. His lack of enthusiasm for the physical side of their relationship almost caused her to look elsewhere. Almost, but not quite. She'd had the opportunity – an opportunity almost too tempting to resist, but was now grateful she hadn't succumbed to the temptation. She loved Tom with a passion undimmed in the years since they'd got together at university, and now that carefree, sexy man was finally returning to her.

She had few regrets in their marriage. The absence of children was one but, as she grew older, even that was beginning to fade. The miscarriages were now ancient history, and she was beginning to accept the doctor's prognosis that she would never be able to have children. It was painful at first, devastatingly painful, difficult to deal with, and the strain it put on the marriage was intense. Gradually the pain eased, and the hormonal thrust that fuelled her desire to reproduce dimmed, like a guttering candle using up the last of the oxygen in a sealed jar.

Besides, she had nieces and nephews now, and her friends had children. There was plenty of opportunity to indulge the maternal side of her nature, if only by proxy – at least that's what she told herself.

She went downstairs and made coffee, pouring herself a cup and taking it back to the spare bedroom they'd already converted into a studio for her. Taped to the drawing board was a pencil sketch she'd been working on while Tom was outside fixing the fence. She picked up a pencil and shaded a couple of areas, then went across to the window and picked up the binoculars, lying on the sill where she'd left them. She put them to her eyes and scanned the area where the granite outcrops jutted rudely up from the surrounding countryside.

He was no longer there, the subject of her picture – the painfully thin boy with white hair who'd sat cross-legged on top of one of the monoliths, watching Tom as he worked. It didn't matter that he had gone because she'd captured his likeness perfectly, and when Tom awoke she'd show him the picture and ask him if this was the lad he'd encountered in the shed.

She took a sip of coffee and went back to the drawing board.

Staring hard at the boy's face, wondering what elements of life could bring such a look of sadness to one so young.

"It looks just like him."

She hadn't heard Tom come up behind her, but he was there, his arms around her waist, nuzzling her neck and staring over her shoulder at the sketch. He took her coffee cup from her and filled his mouth. She nudged him in the ribs with her elbow. "Get your own," she said.

"So this is what you get up to while you're supposed to be working," he said, peering out through the window at the granite monolith. "So that's why I kept getting the feeling I was being watched. How long was he there?"

"Long enough for me to do this. He sat there perfectly still, an hour, maybe more, and watched you while you worked. It was as if he was modelling for me."

"You should have come and told me."

"And have you haring after him. He was too good a subject to miss. I can use this image in the fairy book I'm doing next. Don't you think he looks a bit fairy-like?"

"Nah, the ears aren't pointed enough. Looks bloody weird though . . . as if he hasn't been out in the sun for years. Flour white and spindle thin. That's the phrase that repeats itself in my mind whenever I think about him.'

"It's a great title for the picture," Louise said. "I'll suggest it. You never know, Marion might write a story about him." Marion Wheeler was a writer of children's books. Louise had illustrated every one to see print and they'd developed a mutually beneficial working relationship. They trusted each other, and that was important.

He kissed her neck again. "Come back to bed."

"You're insatiable. No. I've wasted enough time today. Go back out onto the marsh and do what marsh-wardens are supposed to do."

"Spoilsport," he said, and gave her a final squeeze before going back to the bedroom to dress.

When she was alone, Louise went back to the window and picked up the binoculars again, raking the countryside with the high magnification lenses, hoping to see a flash of white hair, a glimpse of pale skin. Something to reassure herself that he was still out there. Somehow it was important to her, but she hadn't yet begun to fathom out why.

*   *   *

The evening was spent in front of the television. She'd finished work about six, in time to prepare a lasagne for their dinner, and they'd eaten it off trays on their laps, watching the unlikely scenarios being played out in a popular soap opera.

He put down his knife and fork and set the tray at his feet. "What's wrong?" he said.

"Wrong? Nothing's wrong. Why?"

"You seem to be in another place. For the past half hour you've been glancing up at the window as if you're expecting to see something there."

She smiled ruefully. It was true, but she hadn't realized she was being that obvious. "It's the boy. I can't seem to get him out of my mind. What if he's still out there? It's a filthy night." Late that afternoon black storm clouds rolled in from the sea. They'd done nothing for an hour or so, except to growl menacingly, as if showing their displeasure. Then the first flash of lightning fizzed across the sky and the heavens unleashed a downpour causing Tom to take shelter under a nearby hornbeam. Not a sensible move in an electrical storm, but he figured the hornbeam was lower than the surrounding trees and was unlikely to be struck, and its dense crown afforded at least some protection from the torrent hammering down from the sky.

"Well if he is still out there, which I doubt, I dare say he's got enough savvy to find some shelter."

"Did you leave the shed open?"

"No. I fixed the hasp and padlocked it again. It's a shed not a doss house."

"But . . ." she started to protest, but left the rest unsaid. She didn't want to make an issue of it. She didn't really want to let Tom know just how much the pale boy had come to dominate her thoughts over the last few hours. "As you say, he's probably used to being outdoors. I like my comfort too much to begin to contemplate what it must be like to sleep under the stars. That's why I never joined the girl guides."

"I'll keep a look out for him tomorrow . . . and if he shows himself again, and you see him, come and tell me."

"Yes," she said thoughtfully, gathering up the trays and taking them through to the kitchen. "Yes I'll do that."

But the boy didn't appear the next day, or the day after that. On the Saturday morning they drove into Risley to shop. The larder was alarmingly depleted, and they had virtually cleared the stocks in the freezer. Laden with bags from the supermarket they returned to the car park, where they'd left Tom's Land Rover, to find the window on the passenger side smashed. A pool of small glass cubes littered the floor and seat.

"How can they get away with this in broad daylight?" Tom said angrily. "I thought this car park was patrolled."

Louise was looking in through the broken window. "But what were they after? There was nothing in here to tempt them except the CD player, and they haven't touched it."

"Perhaps they were disturbed before they had a chance to grab it."

Louise ran her hand through her short dark hair. "My jacket's gone."

"Jacket?"

"The Barbour I keep on the back seat . . . in case the weather turns. It's gone."

"I can't see there'd be much resale value in a waxed jacket, can you?" Tom said, his mind still weighing up the cost of a replacement window. "You're sure it's not hanging up at home?"

"Definitely. I wore it last week when we went to that furniture auction. Don't you remember? By the time we got there the weather had brightened up. I distinctly remember taking it off and slinging it onto the back seat. I didn't put it back on, and I certainly never took it back to the house."

Tom was using a piece of cardboard torn from one of their boxes to scrape the glass from the seat. "I'll tidy it up more thoroughly when we get back. This'll do for now. I still can't believe that someone would break in to a car just to steal a jacket."

"They might if they were cold . . ." she said. Or if the only clothes they possessed were rags, she thought, but kept the thought to herself. It came unbidden into her mind and she tried to turn it away, but it remained, niggling at her during the blustery journey home. The image of the pale boy, huddled under a tree somewhere, hugging her waxed jacket tightly around him to stave off the elements was strangely comforting. At least I'm doing something, she thought, then immediately chided herself for being so ridiculous. The chances of the pale boy being the one who'd broken into the Land Rover were remote. More likely it was a local tearaway, disturbed, as Tom speculated, before he had a chance to get away with anything more valuable. Perhaps he thought the coat would contain some money, or even a packet of cigarettes – muggings had taken place for less.

As they pulled into the drive she shook the thoughts away, and tried to concentrate on the meal she was going to cook for them both tonight.

*   *   *

Tom stood at the sink in the bathroom and slid the nail scissors under the edge of the bandage. The wound was throbbing and itching like mad. He guessed it was probably infected, but said nothing to Louise, fearing a reprimand for not going to the hospital as she suggested. He snipped at the bandage, careful not to nick his skin, wincing as he saw the angry pus-filled bite mark.

He touched it gingerly with his finger and winced again as a hot pain shot up his arm. "Damn it!" he said under his breath, and reached into the medicine cabinet on the wall for some antiseptic. The yellow liquid made contact with the wound, and for a moment he though he would pass out. It was like pouring acid onto raw flesh. He gripped the edge of the sink, waiting for the searing pain to ease, beads of sweat popping out like tiny moonstones on his forehead.

Gradually the pain abated and he took a deep breath, mopping the perspiration from his brow with a towel. Louise kept the bandages in a small first aid box under the sink. He took out a fresh bandage and tore off the wrapper, then put his hand flat against the wall and started to twist the dressing around his wrist. He figured he'd be able to manage without Louise's attention, but fumbled once and the bandage dropped to the floor, spilling out like a party streamer. He swore, gathered it up and started the laborious process again.

He'd been concentrating on wrapping the wound, and it was only when he'd finished and was reaching for a strip of sticking plaster that he noticed the hand itself.

The skin from his wrist down was almost bleached of colour, dead looking. He held both hands out under the light above the vanity unit. His other hand looked normal, pink and healthy, making the other one look significantly worse by comparison. He flexed the fingers of the pale hand. Was it his imagination, or was there a slight numbness there? His fingers moved when he wanted them to move, but the movements seemed sluggish, uncoordinated.

"What are you doing in there?" Louise called from outside the door.

"Won't be a moment," he called back and hurriedly stuck the plaster over the edge of the bandage, rolling down the sleeve of his shirt to hide it. "Sorry," he said, opening the door. "Didn't know you were waiting."

"You look warm," she said, almost an accusation.

"Do I? Must be the central heating. I'll check the thermostat."

Her eyes narrowed and she shook her head. "Feels fine to me," she said, and pushed past him into the bathroom. He heard the lock click and went to pour himself a stiff drink.

His hand shook slightly as he raised the glass to his lips. The whisky burnt his throat and he gave an involuntary shudder as the liquid reached his stomach. He wasn't a drinker these days, though it had been different several years ago when he was getting through three or four bottles of whisky a week, But those were troubled times. Hospitalisation and countless tests for Louise, and the endless recriminations and tears that had threatened to blow their marriage apart.

The taste of the scotch on his tongue brought the memories of that time flooding back. He screwed the cap back on the bottle and put it back in the cupboard, then went through to the kitchen and rinsed out the glass. Then he switched on the coffee machine, brewing up a strong espresso to remove the taste of alcohol from his mouth. He had no wish to revisit those times. They were bleak and depressing years. The tedious monthly ritual of taking temperatures, judging the ovulation cycle, and the mechanical, passionless sex. Baby making. Relentless and unsuccessful baby making.

He heard Louise moving about upstairs and glanced down at his hand. She'd notice before much longer and she'd recommend a trip to the hospital, or the doctor's at least. And he couldn't really tell her of his aversion to anything medical; couldn't begin to explain the emotions visiting such places stirred in him.

The books Louise read focussed on the woman, her body, her emotions; how she could cope with the loss of a child, of the endless, unpitying struggle to conceive. The male partner was seen very much as a necessary adjunct to that struggle. A seed supplier, nothing more. How could he tell her that his drive to reproduce was almost as strong as hers? He was an only child, the last of his line. The family name stopped with him, and while her hormones and that indefinable thing called maternal instinct drove her, his need was more pragmatic. He didn't want to be the last, the end of the chapter. He wanted his genes perpetuated. He wanted the immortality a child would have provided. The crushing monthly disappointment when her period started affected him just as deeply as it did her. And while she cried and he held her, being strong for her, so his mind screamed in despair. The drink silenced the scream and deadened the pain. And it had also nearly destroyed him.

He took another sip of coffee and swilled it around his mouth, getting rid of the final lingering taste of scotch. Why he should be dredging up those memories again he wasn't sure. He hadn't thought about them for years. But now they were back pushing their way to the forefront of his mind, and he wondered what had triggered them.

*   *   *

Louise didn't see the boy again for a number of days, though she continued to pick up the binoculars on occasion and search the marsh and beyond, hoping to catch sight of him.

The following Thursday Tom took the Land Rover into town to get the window fixed. He'd repaired it with a sheet of thick poly-thene, but that was only a stopgap, and as autumn gradually eased its way towards winter, he couldn't delay the inevitable. The Land Rover window would take a hefty chunk out of their monthly budget, and these days they had to be careful with their money. The marsh warden's job paid a good deal less than his previous position, and Louise's income was, by its nature, sporadic; but the vehicle was not only necessary in his job, it was also their lifeline, their means of getting to town to bring supplies back to the isolated cottage. It had to be attended to.

Once the window of the Land Rover was fixed he intended to go and see his employer at the local council office to discuss plans for a picnic area that the council, in their wisdom, had decided would draw sightseers to the area. "To their death, more like," Tom grumbled when he told Louise about the plan.

She watched him go, waving from the gate, until he turned the corner at the end of the lane, then she went back to the house. In her study she taped a fresh piece of paper to the drawing board and sat for a moment waiting for inspiration to strike. She picked up her pencil and made a few exploratory lines on the page, but her mind remained exasperatingly barren.

Pushing herself away from the board in frustration she went across to the filing cabinet in the corner to rummage through the folders of photographs and clippings from magazines – her source material. But she could find nothing to inspire her. She couldn't remember the last time she was blocked like this. Usually the muse that sat on her shoulder rose to the challenge of virgin paper and fed her something with which to fill it. But today the muse was obstinately silent. Perhaps she was asleep.

Louise slid the drawer back into the cabinet and crossed to the window. She reached for the binoculars and stopped.

The boy was standing in the back garden, staring up at the window. She smiled slightly when she saw he was wearing her waxed jacket. Her instincts had been right.

She hurried from the room and down the stairs, hoping he would still be there when she reached the garden.

He was.

He took a step backwards as she opened the back door and

stepped outside, but other than that he didn't seem alarmed by her appearance.

She stood still, facing him. She'd never seen anybody with skin so white and hair so fair. Almost albino, but the eyes were dark – deep black pools that regarded her with something like wry amusement.

"Hello," she said softly, worried that if she raised her voice much above a whisper the boy might take flight.

He said nothing but continued to stare for a moment then made a quick beckoning motion with his hand, turned and walked slowly to the gate that led onto the marsh. At the gate he stopped, turned to look at her and beckoned again.

"I can't go with you," she said. "I've work to do," she added unconvincingly.

He didn't move.

"Let me get my coat and lock the house," she continued, curiosity beating her reservations into submission.

When she returned to the garden he hadn't moved, but as she drew close he turned and strode out into the marsh.

He moved with a curious grace, like a pale deer, sure-footed, without effort, picking his way between the muddy pools and hopping from tussock to tussock with the confidence that comes from long familiarity.

Louise followed as best she could, trying to keep in his footsteps, trying hard to avoid the murky pools that threatened to suck the shoes from her feet, to grab her legs and draw her down into the mire.

A mist had blown in from the sea, and the further she got into the marsh the thicker the haze became. Occasionally she lost sight of him altogether and she had to call out, to urge him to wait for her. He'd appear out of the swirls of drizzle, a small smile playing on his lips, waiting for her to almost, but never quite, catch up to him.

I must be mad, she thought, as she picked her way through the morass. Tom would be furious if he knew what she was doing. But Tom would be away all morning, and probably much of the afternoon.

She stopped and looked back, but the mist had closed in behind her like thick gauze curtains, hiding the house. She had no choice now. She had to follow the boy. She'd never find her way back home, and the thought of wandering around in the lethal marsh frightened her.

Ahead of her appeared a small wooden-built hut. It was ramshackle, its palings worn and rotted, the roofing-felt split and curling over the front of the hut. There were no windows but a narrow horizontal slit at the front gave away its purpose. It was a bird-watcher's hide. A place for avian enthusiasts to decamp and mount their cameras and binoculars in the hope of catching a glimpse of the rare and endangered birds that made the marsh their home.

The boy was standing in front of the hide, his arms hanging loosely at his sides, waiting for her. When she was within six feet of him he ducked around the side of the hut and disappeared.

She jumped over a small boggy pool, stumbled and reached out to the wall of the hut to steady herself. The rough wood split under her touch and tiny splinters embedded themselves in her hand. She sucked in her breath and then swore. Finding the ground firm under her feet, she moved round in the direction the boy had taken.

There was no sign of him. It was as if the mist had swallowed him.

She called out and strained to hear a reply, but the air was silent, oppressively silent, as if a blanket had been thrown over the world, killing all sound. She reached the door of the hut and pushed it open, but it was empty; the only sign of human habitation being a discarded crisp packet and several empty soft drink cans. She fought down a swell of panic and hurried outside. She called again, and this time there was a response.

A small girl stepped out. She was five or six years old, her hair as white as the boy's and her limbs as thin, if not thinner than his. She looked emaciated and Louise felt a surge of pity. "Oh, you poor thing," she said, crouching down to the girl's level, trying to reassure her with her body language that she presented no threat to her.

The child stood, unmoving, watching her with a mildly curious expression. Like the boy she was dressed in rags, the material threadbare and filthy, torn in places, allowing Louise to catch glimpses of the unnaturally pale flesh beneath.

The girl wound a strand of white hair around her thumb and pushed the whole lot into her mouth.

"I won't hurt you," Louise said, and held out her arms. She just wanted to hug the child, to reassure her, and to carry her back home. She needed to report this to the proper authorities. For a child of this age to be allowed to get in this state was nothing short of criminal. If the parents were around here, she would have no compunction in telling them exactly what she thought of their parenting skills.

The little girl moved forward so gracefully it was almost as if she was gliding over the muddy grass. To her horror Louise noticed the little girl's feet were bare, wet mud squelching up between her toes.

When she was within reach, Louise closed her arms around the girl in a tight embrace and stood upright, lifting the child off her feet. She was feather-light, insubstantial like the mist that surrounded them. The girl wrapped her arms around Louise's neck, pulling herself in closer, as if craving the warmth of Louise's body. She buried her face into the protective shoulder, nuzzling close against Louise's breast.

The bite, when it came, was so shocking and so painful, that for a moment Louise just stood there, feeling the pain, and the tickling motion of a tiny tongue flicking over the wound.

With a cry she pushed the child away from her, holding her at arm's length, staring questioningly into the watery blue eyes. The expression on the little girl's face was serene as she licked her blood-specked lips. There was no malice there, no malevolence.

And suddenly Louise understood why she'd been brought here. With tears streaming down her face she hugged the child close to her again and let her feed.

Tom arrived home at about 2:00 p.m., slamming the door behind him, and walked into the lounge, a string of expletives issuing from his mouth. The meeting with the council had not gone well. Their decision to site the picnic area on the edge of one of the most treacherous stretches of marsh was, in his opinion, sheer folly, but his protests were met with bland bureaucratic platitudes. "After all, Mr Henderson, you are only warden on the marsh. Should anything happen, which we sincerely doubt will, you would not be held responsible. And we must look at the broader picture. The shops and cafés in the area that would undoubtedly benefit from an influx of fresh revenue."

He'd given up at that point. He knew that financial kickbacks and promises of favours had been made, and that the decision had already been taken.

Louise listened to his tirade of several minutes before saying, "Why don't you sit down, calm down, and I'll make us a cup of tea?"

He flopped into an armchair with a sigh. She was right, as usual. He'd taken this job to escape stress, not to immerse himself again in battles he had no hope of winning. "How's your day been?" he called.

"Interesting," she called back from the kitchen. She was wearing a high rolled-neck sweater to hide the bite marks on her chest and neck, but the chenille was irritating the wounds, making them itch. "I'll tell you about it later," she added.

He sank back in the chair and closed his eyes, letting the tension ebb from his body.

"You're going grey," she said. She was standing behind him holding two steaming mugs of tea.

He glanced up at her. "Is it any wonder, after the day I've had?" He held her eyes for a moment. "You're being serious, aren't you?"

She nodded. "I'd never noticed before, but there are definitely a few silver ones threading their way through now."

"Shit!" he said, and pushed himself to his feet, crossing to the mirror and pulling his hair this way and that. It was more than just a couple of stray premature greys. Silver strands made up about a quarter of the brown untidy thatch that covered his head. He was sure they hadn't been there this morning when he'd been drying his hair after the shower, but then he hadn't been looking for them.

"But I'm only thirty-five. It's a bit young for all this."

"I think it's dead sexy," she said, coming up behind him and wrapping her arms around his waist. "After you've had your tea, do you fancy coming for a walk?"

"A walk? Where?"

"On the marsh. I made an interesting discovery today. I'd like to show you."

He shrugged. "Fine." Then he thought for a moment. "You haven't been walking around out there on your own, have you? I did warn you . . ."

"It's all right. I had company. Finish your tea. I'll tell you as we walk."

An east wind had kicked up and blown the mist back out to sea. As they picked their way through the marsh Tom checked his watch. "This'd better not take long. We've only got two hours of daylight at the most. We'll never find our way back in the dark, and I really don't fancy calling the rescue services to come and find us." He patted his jacket pocket, feeling the reassuring bulge of his mobile phone. He'd brought it along as a precaution, but he hoped he wouldn't have to use it.

"Not far now. I wasn't sure I'd be able to find it on my own, but it all seems so familiar."

He slipped from a tussock of grass and buried his boot in the mud to the ankle. He swore savagely and yanked it free, groaning as water seeped over the top of the leather and soaked his sock. "You still haven't explained what we're doing here."

She glanced back at him, an annoyingly enigmatic smile on her face. "No, I didn't, did I? Wait and see."

"Bugger that!" he said and stopped walking. "You either explain or I'm going back."

She looked at him steadily, trying to decide whether or not he was bluffing. There was steel in his eyes and his chin jutted forwards pugnaciously. She decided not to call his bluff. "It was the boy," she said simply. "He came to the house earlier . . . He was wearing my Barbour," she added, a fond smile spreading over her lips.

"So he *was* the lout who smashed my window. When you see him again you might like to get the money out of him to pay for it."

"That doesn't matter now," she said. The wind was cold, and cut through the thin material of her jacket, but she didn't feel cold. A mixture of excitement and adrenaline was warming her from within. "It's all so perfectly clear to me."

"What is?"

"The reason we're here. The real reason you took the job."

He sighed. "I took the job because it was the only thing I could find that would take me completely out of the rat race. And that's the reason . . . the real reason."

"But we were guided. Call it providence, fate, whatever you like, but you were destined to find and take that job, and we were destined to come to this place together. Come on," she said, starting to walk again. "Just a little bit further."

He shook his head but followed.

"And don't think I haven't noticed your hand," she said as she walked. "I know you've been trying to hide it from me. But that's all part of it, don't you see?"

He flexed the fingers of the hand that was completely numb now, and almost bleached white.

"And your hair. Can't you see what's happening to us?"

"All I can see is that you're leading us on some wild goose chase, and that you're starting to sound deranged."

She laughed. "O ye of little faith," she said. "Look, just up ahead."

The hide was a few hundred yards ahead of them.

"That old place," he said incredulously. "But it's derelict. I checked it out a few days ago. You haven't seriously brought me out here to see . . ."

She hushed him. "Keep your voice down. You'll scare her."

"Scare who?" he said, but she was starting to run now and the wind whipped the words from his lips and carried them across the marsh and out to sea. He was sure she hadn't heard him.

They reached the hide together, Tom having to sprint to catch up with her. She held out her arm to stop him going any further. "Quiet now," she said, putting her finger to her lips.

He said nothing, alarmed at her behaviour, but curious to see how this was going to resolve itself. He felt a wetness in his palm and looked down. The bandage on his wrist was crimson where the wound had opened and started to bleed again. He brought his wrist up and hugged it to his chest, but there was no pain, just a curious pulling sensation, as if unseen hands were plucking at the bandage.

Louise was calling softly. "It's me. I've come back, just like I said I would. Are you there?"

For a moment there was absolute stillness and absolute silence. Then came the sound of a footfall from behind a stand of trees. Louise reached back and gripped his arm excitedly. "She's here." Then she slipped off her jacket and pulled off her sweater.

He saw the bite marks for the first time. "Louise!" he said, but a movement in front of them distracted his attention as a small, filthy girl stepped out from behind the shelter of the trees. She was dressed in rags and her white hair hung in rat's tails. Louise sank to her knees and held out her arms. The girl ran forward, casting furtive glances at Tom who stood, open-mouthed, hardly daring to believe what he was seeing.

The girl fell into Louise's embrace, buried her face into Louise's neck, tongue reaching for the raw flesh.

With a cry Tom lashed out with his foot, catching the girl in the chest and knocking her out of his wife's arms. The girl landed on her back on the spongy ground, and with a guttural snarl rolled over onto her hands and knees, poised, ready to leap at him.

He grabbed Louise roughly by the arm and hauled her to her feet. "Run!" he said, striding out onto the marsh. "Run now!"

She was resisting him, sobbing. "Tom, no!"

He took no notice. All he wanted to do was to get them as far away from this place as possible. He was dragging her along behind him, oblivious to her protests, yanking her impatiently if she stumbled. "It's why we're here," she cried. "Don't you see?"

He glanced back at her and stopped dead. The colour had drained from her hair, leaving it a stark white. Even as he watched, the weight seemed to be falling away from her body. He stared, transfixed, as her skin bleached and grew translucent. He let go of her arm, as if it were something alien.

She stood erect, tossing back her pale hair. "Don't you see?"

He felt a sharp pain in his thigh. The little girl had attached herself to his leg, gnawing through the denim of his jeans, seeking out the life-giving flesh beneath. He knocked her away and started to run again, but had gone no more than two paces when bony hands exploded from the mud and gripped his ankles.

Around him the marsh bubbled and heaved as figures emerged from its depths. Pale, skeletal figures, their parchment skin streaked with earth and weed. Ten, twenty of them, rising from the mud pools to stand, surrounding him.

He looked back at Louise imploringly, but she hadn't moved and her face was impassive. Next to her stood the boy he'd discovered in the shed, flour white and spindle thin. His impossibly gaunt body draped incongruously in Louise's waxed jacket. He was smiling, his white skin almost glinting in the late afternoon sun, as Louise draped a maternal arm across his shoulders.

Dusk was drawing in over the verdant expanse of Flatland Marsh, coating the swaying figures with a deathly paleness that began to mask them from view. In the barely visible distance Tom could just about make out more thin figures, bleached of colour as if washed up on a shore, swaying like reeds over the flat land.

Louise was all but invisible now, and as Tom looked down at his own body he realized that he too was losing his natural colour; becoming one with the children of the marsh.

CHRISTA FAUST

Tighter

CHRISTA FAUST LIVES IN Los Angeles with her Boston Terriers and too many high-heeled shoes.

She has been writing dark fiction for over ten years, and her novels include *Control Freak*, *Hoodtown*, *Triads* (with Poppy Z. Brite) and media tie-in projects such as *A Nightmare on Elm Street: Dreamspawn*, *The Twilight Zone: Burned/One Night at Mercy* and *Friday the 13th: The Jason Strain*. Faust's short fiction has appeared in several anthologies, including *Millenium* (aka *Revelations*), the *Hot Blood* series and *The Mammoth Book of Vampire Stories by Women*.

"I originally wrote this story for Jeff Fazio when he was working on the Showtime television series *The Hunger*," reveals the author. "He had optioned my other *Hot Blood* story 'Skin Deep' and was interested in more erotic horror.

"I have always been leery of the intensely punitive attitude in most so-called erotic horror and stories that consistently punish bedroom adventurers for straying from the sexually correct seem both dull and narrow minded. I wanted to give Jeff a story that involved SM and bondage, but not in a purely negative light.

"In 'Tighter', things go horribly awry, not because bondage is wrong and bad, but because we perverts are susceptible to human flaws like greed and selfishness just like the average norm. Unfortunately (but unsurprisingly), it was too intense for *The Hunger*. Luckily, Jeff Gelb and Michael Garrett snapped it up for *Strange Bedfellows: The Hot Blood Series*."

V EGAS AT NIGHT, all glitter and neon like smashed candy scattered across the desert's endless dark. Visual cacophony of a thousand billboards, all competing for the mayfly attention span of feckless tourist hordes. A thousand entertainers, a thousand hustles. Comedians and singers, wannabes and used-to-bes. Animal acts and acrobats. Strippers and showgirls and drag queens. And Persephone.

In one of the older casinos, a tarnished relic from the days when Vegas was still strictly for grownups, Persephone does Monday, Wednesday and Friday. Two shows on Saturday. In the dimly lit lounge, she appears with flashpots, clad only in a golden g-string and tiny, star shaped pasties. Her makeup is theatrical, all eyes and lips, and her body is fiercely muscled, slicked with oil and dusted with glitter. Over the ageing PA system, a honey-voiced announcer speaks.

"Ladies and gentlemen, prepare yourselves for the most daring, death-defying escape ever witnessed. Just as her ancient namesake descended into the underworld and returned unscathed, so will our modern day goddess kiss death on the cheek before your very eyes!"

A curtain is parted to reveal a large water-filled tank, hypnotically backlit by hidden green and blue spotlights. Then a single golden light washes over Persephone as a pair of young men nearly identical in their forgettable perfection approach her from either side. They are oiled and glittered like Persephone and just as close to naked. Each bears an armful of heavy steel chains and thick, locking cuffs. The audience watches in uncomfortable silence as Persephone is meticulously bound, arms locked behind her back, torso wrapped in unyielding steel, legs woven together and ankles locked and fastened to a heavy hook lowered from the ceiling. Her face is serene, but her eyes glisten with some manic ecstasy in the seconds before she is blindfolded by a gold silk scarf. One of the boys lifts her in his arms as the other turns a large, theatrical crank to raise the hook, higher and higher until she dangles upside-down, suspended above the audience's expectant heads. The tank rolls automatically forward until it is positioned directly beneath her.

"Now as we all know, it takes only three minutes for the human brain to die from lack of oxygen. But in as little as two short minutes . . ." A dramatic pause. ". . . irreversible damage may be sustained."

An oversize stopwatch is unveiled. The space on the clock between two and three is painted blood red and the number three has been replaced with a skull and crossbones.

"In 1953, the Great Gambini attempted this very stunt. They

pulled him out after two-and-a-half minutes . . ." Another dramatic pause, stretching out to infinity in the hot space above the audience's expectant heads. "But it was too late. Will the lovely Persephone make the history books, or will she just be history?"

A drum roll and Persephone plunges, headfirst, into the water.

The clock starts, a sharp, metronomic ticking like a nervous heartbeat while a subtle web of low, disquieting music insinuates itself between the seconds.

All around her video screens light up. Each screen shows a close-up of a different body part. Her narrow, elegant hands. Her chain-wrapped midriff. Her sculpted ankles and delicate feet. Her lips, spangled with tiny silver bubbles.

Persephone struggles beneath the water. Her skin is pale, gleaming and her blonde hair floats, weightless around her face. The chains that bind her glint and flash. Time continues to pass and she seems to tire. The audience is on the edge of their seats. It is as if no one dares to breathe until she can breathe with them. Inside the tank, she has gone completely still. Her attendants sell it with nervous faces and hands tightly clenched, one eye on her motionless form and one eye on the ever-advancing clock. The ticking hand hits the red and the audience's hearts are pounding, palms sweating. A full thirty seconds pass. One of the boys starts toward the tank as if to free her but his companion restrains him. Then, in a single, serpent-smooth move, her muscles flex and ripple and the chains fall away, sinking to the bottom of the tank. She bursts upward in a rush of bubbles and frantic applause as she rips off the blindfold, triumphant.

In the front row to her left is a young man. Hard eyes set in a rough, ugly-sexy face. Bald head and thick sinewy arms ending in blunt wrestler's hands. From the stage, Persephone fixes him with a gaze resonant with hunger and frank invitation and he holds it, doesn't look away. She gives him a small, suggestive smile and slips behind the curtain.

Backstage, Persephone sits before a mirrored vanity, burning. An insistent heat boils beneath her skin, radiating outward from the deep pink grooves left behind by the cold steel chains. Desire pounds its fists between her legs and she has to clutch the edges of the vanity, stealthy sparkles dancing at the corners of her vision. It is always like this, has been since the first time young Persephone (just plain old Peggy back then) wound a piece of oil-stained rope around her wrists in her father's tool shed, heavy, honey-thick sunlight pouring in through the dusty windows to caress her sweat-glossed flesh as she strained against her bonds, pretending. Pretending that she was captured, pretending that she could not escape, that her bones could not fold up and flatten like the bones of a weasel sliding under the hen-house door. She would wind the fraying rope around her hips, down between her legs and she would lay on the cold and filthy cement struggling, straining against the rope, until the friction brought its own fierce release.

But it was never enough. Sitting here now in her sad little dressing room with desire devouring her from the inside out, she knows that pretending will never be enough. The sharp, firecracker orgasms that hit her like rabbit punches as she struggled against the cruel chains on stage only made it worse. She pulls her gold satin kimono tighter around her body. It seems to take far too long for her assistant to fetch the man from the front row.

When he arrives, she does not let him speak. A glitter-nailed finger against his thin lips, and then her own hungry mouth, and he responds with harsh strength, sledgehammer hard against her belly. There is an impatient wrenching of clothing and then his chest is bare and her kimono is pooled like golden water around her feet. A touch of glitter remains on her skin, flashing under his rough, clutching hands. She sighs and grips his wrist, moving his hand from her breast to the grooves the chain has left across her ribs. When he runs his fingertips experimentally over the corrugated surface, she shudders, a thick sound welling up like blood in her throat. Her heart is pounding between her legs as her hand flashes out like a cat's paw, nails raking across his chest, across the face of a grinning tattooed demon.

"Bitch!" He grabs her wrist, grip vice-tight, but not tight enough. She slips loose, too easy. Showing her teeth, she lashes out at his face.

He is fast, catches both hands and wrenches them behind her back. She is faint with desire, wet flush of heat between her legs.

"Tighter," she whispers, grinding her hips against his muscular thigh.

His fingers dig into her flesh, forcing her arms up higher behind her back.

"More," she breathes, nearly begging.

"Are you crazy?" He frowns. "You want me to break your wrists?"

"You can't," she says, and before he knows what is happening, she is free again, slipping away to dig through a drawer in her vanity. When she turns back, she is holding a length of rope.

"Tie me up," she says.

His frown deepens and she is afraid that she is losing him. She pulls him close and kisses him again, deliberate fingers teasing him back to full erection.

"Don't you want to fuck me?" This a throaty whisper punctuated by a flick of her tongue over the curve of his ear.

"Hell yeah." His voice is thick with lust, his dark eyes mean and hungry.

She holds the rope out to him. Breathing like a bull about to charge, he takes it in one hand, gripping her upper arm with the other. He turns her away from him and begins winding the rope around her wrists.

"Tight," she says between clenched teeth.

His fingers are clumsy with the knots. She slips loose as if shrugging off a too-big jacket.

"Come on!" she says. There is an edge of desperation in her voice. "Do it tighter."

He tries again, but she can tell his patience is rapidly eroding. Frustration like broken glass in her throat as she finds the rope slipping off like water, even though she was willing to hold on, to pretend.

He is angry now. He throws the rope away.

"Fuck this," he spits. "I don't have time for this bullshit."

"Please." She is begging now, hating herself for it but begging anyway. "Please. I need it."

He shakes his head.

"You need help," he says, grabbing his rumpled T-shirt and buttoning his jeans. "How can you want to be tied up when so many women are abused for real? It's crazy."

"What does that have to do with anything?" She knows she has already lost, but she's angry now. Angry at him for making her feel like some kind of pervert. "I like to be tied up because it makes me feel good. It's that simple. How can it be wrong to make somebody feel good?" She steps closer, giving it one last shot. Still naked, she pitches her voice low and seductive. "We're both consenting adults. How can it be wrong if we both want it?"

"You want it, not me." He turns away. "I'm outta here."

She wraps her kimono around her body and rushes after him. "Wait, please . . ."

But he is gone, down the long dim corridor and she is yelling after him, cursing and then fighting tears as she leans her forehead against the wall.

"Your clock is fast," a voice says and Persephone turns, startled to see a man leaning against the wall beside her. He is not handsome, strange green eyes amplified by clunky glasses and a body too thin beneath unfashionable clothes. She can see a long, shiny scar inside his left wrist, suicide ghost peeking out from the cuff of his ugly jacket. He holds what appears to be an artist's portfolio.

"What?" She frowns and looks away from him, wondering how much of the scene he witnessed, feeling the thin heat of shame crawling under her skin.

"Your clock, in the show. It says three minutes, but it was really only two minutes and forty one seconds." He smiles and she creases her brows, annoyed.

"Yeah, well, I can hold my breath for much longer than that," she says. "It's just that these days, three minutes is a long time for the marks to sit there waiting. I want to make it long enough for them to think it's dangerous but not long enough for them to get bored. What's it to you anyway?"

He shrugs. She notices that his eyes are not just green, as they seemed at first glance, but actually a strange kaleidoscopic cluster of emerald and pale grey. Fascinating, but she looks away, still shrouded in her own frustration and shame.

"My name is Kevin," he says shyly, looking down and away. "I really enjoyed your act and I wanted to show you some of my work."

He starts unzipping the portfolio when one of her security guys shows up.

"What the fuck?" The muscle takes Kevin's elbow. "I thought I told you to get lost, pal."

Persephone isn't sure how to feel about this but hey it's just as well since he's probably some kind of weirdo stalker. Then the unzipped portfolio spills photos out onto the ground between them and everything changes.

Each photo shows a naked woman bound. But more than bound, they are works of art, sculptures in the medium of glossy red rope and tender flesh. The designs and patterns formed by the complex knotwork flows over their skins like the symmetrical characters of some exotic forgotten language. She kneels down and touches the image of a particularly intricate design, heart gunning in her chest and between her legs. Although she doesn't know what she was expecting, she is disappointed when her fingertips find only the flat slick texture of a photograph.

"Leave him," she tells the guard.

The guard's eyes ask her if she's sure, but she dismisses him with a quick nod of her head. When they are alone, Kevin kneels down beside her and starts gathering up the photos.

"Did you do this?" She licks her lips

He nods.

"The knots, I mean . . ."

He nods again. His quick green eyes have not missed her reaction but he seems nervous, blushing.

"Can you . . .?"

He reaches out and takes her hand, running his thumb over the ligature marks across her wrist and looking into her eyes.

"Is there somewhere we can go?" he asks.

Her apartment is small but meticulously neat, generic, like a hotel room. Posters for her act are the only personal touch.

He has a tightly woven, lidded basket like the sort a charmed snake might rise out of. When he sets it down on her bed and lifts the lid he sees that it is full of rope. Not the cheap cotton clothesline that she keeps hidden in a drawer beside her bed, but an amazingly rich, reddish-purple cord like something an 18th century madam might use to tie back her velvet curtains. She plunges her fingers into the neat coils, their texture fine as satin, as the tender skin inside her mouth.

"Undress," he tells her.

She obeys, stripping down in seconds and standing naked and trembling as he lifts the rope from the basket, seeming to test its weight in his hand and draw strength from its heft. She is amazed to see that it is all one length.

His shyness seems to have evaporated as he assesses her body with a speculative eye. She can see the possible knots mating and combining in his head. Long minutes pass and she grows restless, impatient, until finally he pulls her to him and begins to weave a complex web across her torso. She loses herself in the beauty of the design, hypnotized by his nimble fingers.

The rope caresses her, squeezing her breasts and her waist and tormenting her swollen clit with a single fat knot that grinds against her with the slightest movement. He wraps a tight cinch around her elbows, pulling them together behind her back until they touch and she gasps, shamelessly working her hips against the rope. Her wrists are last, tighter than ever and as he steps away from her, there is a moment of explosive joy, a moment where she strains and struggles and cannot get free. But it is a fleeting moment as her rubber joints twist and shift beneath her skin and she can feel it slipping away as she pulls, pulls, pulls and then the ropes around her wrists fall away and a thick spike of disappointment slams through her as tears fill her eyes, the beautiful design gone to useless slack around her. She wants to scream, to smash everything. She wants to tear into her own flesh and rip out her flexible, treacherous bones. But then something happens, something that makes her scalp crawl and her eyes go wide.

The rope is moving, flexing and tensing, gliding over her with amazing speed, faster than his fingers, wrapping her up like a constrictor's prey. And the knots, twisting and reforming into exquisite designs and haunting symmetry like the blueprints for some profane cathedral. Tighter, too. Tighter than ever and she is breathless, burning. The final knot winds itself, macramé perfection against her pounding heart and she is caught again. There are scant inches for struggle but as she strains and pulls and thrashes, the rope moves with her, seeming to anticipate every escape, only to wind her tighter. For the first time, after a lifetime of escape, she is really, truly caught and it feels so good, safe somehow, like a lover's arms. Her heart and her pussy and her soul open wide as the most exquisite surrender washes over her, washing her clean like the tears that he kisses from her cheeks. She is in love. She is his.

Later, she is sleeping beside him and although his arm is going numb beneath her, he doesn't want to move. Like when a beautiful and arrogant cat curls up in your lap, he is afraid to disturb her for fear that she will go away and never return. He still can't believe that she is here at all, his beautiful golden goddess. The woman whose insatiable hunger for restraint had drawn him to her like a plant growing toward the sun. She was everything he ever wanted, as if his own missing half had sprung fully formed, Venus-like, from the chaos of his darkest fantasies. After a lifetime of women who laughed at him, horrified women who called him a freak and a monster, here was Persephone, now and forever. She is curled against him, satiated and smelling of sweat and sex and honey, and he knows that all the years of deprivation and shame really have been worth it. When he'd been spent but still inside her and tasting her tears on his lips, she had told him that she loved him. Now looking into her sleeping face, he is finally able to answer.

"I love you, too, Persephone," he tells her, the words sounding so small and awkward, barely audible in the hot space between them.

"Again," she says, eyes too bright, breathless.

Kevin looks down at the basket, frowning. He sets it aside. They have been together for three months and her desperate need for the rope's embrace has increased exponentially until she is not satisfied with less than seven or eight times a day. Her hunger is a black hole, desire that is never satiated. Of all the women he has been with, all the women that he has tied, she is the only one who can never get enough and at first it was perfect, true love. But now, it is as if she doesn't even see him. She only sees the knots.

"Do we have to?" He reaches out as if to take her into his arms and she steps back, wary. "Please. I just want to hold you for a while."

"After, okay?" She is acting like a junkie, desperate. It makes him feel invisible and he is overwhelmed with a desire to hit her, to keep on hitting her until she really sees him. He still loves her so much, and the love feels like its own kind of crushing bondage.

"Persephone," he says. "I can't do this anymore."

Her head swivels sharply.

"What?"

He looks away, pain and resignation in the corners of his mouth.

"Look, you don't love me." His voice is soft and hopeless. "You never did. You love the rope."

There is a moment of anger flashing hot and fierce across her features, then it submerges and she slides her arms around him, all cooing and seductive lies.

"That's not true, baby," she whispers. "You know how much I love you."

She guides him to the bed, takes him down. He knows that she is lying, but her touch, her mouth feels so good and he lets himself pretend, knowing inside that it really is over.

After, she slips out of his embrace. Moving cat-burglar silent, she pulls on clothes and takes the basket. He lays in the bed with his back to her, eyes wide and glinting with angry tears. He does not stop her.

In her dim dressing room, she strips naked and opens the basket. The rope is coiled inside like a sleeping cobra, but when she lifts it out, it lays inert in her hands, lifeless. She winds it around her wrists, but it is as limp as the bunched-up cotton clothesline in her vanity drawer.

"Come on," she whispers through clenched teeth, frustration a nest of angry hornets in her belly. "Come on, come on, come on."

Nothing. Just a length of fancy satin rope. She flings it away, furious. So it only works with him. No problem. He's probably still sleeping. She could sneak back in and be there to lovey-dovey him into making it work for her.

"It's dead."

She turns and sees Kevin poking the rope with the toe of his boot.

"Dead?" Fear ignites in her throat. "It can't be . . ."

"Oh, don't worry, baby." His voice is cruel, caustic. He pulls out a stubby little pocket knife and thumbs it open. "There's plenty more where that came from."

He plunges the knife into the inside of his scarred wrist.

"Jesus, Kevin!"

She rushes to him, filled with a sudden terrible fear that he will die bleeding on her carpet and the rope's secret will die with him. But it is not blood that oozes from the quivering slit in his flesh. It is something more solid, stealthy, glistening like a newborn snake. A wet length of the gore-red rope struggles free from the wound, fat as a vital artery and pulsing and Persephone backs away, nausea churning in her belly. Its blind head elongates like an earthworm, straining toward her and she screams, clawing through her vanity drawer until her shaking fingers close over the cold grip of her .38.

"Keep it away from me," she says, drawing a bead first on the languidly flexing rope, then up to Kevin's forehead. The idea that she allowed one of those things to touch her skin, to wind down between the lips of her pussy, sickens her and brings a cold crawling sweat to the back of her neck. But her fear is underscored by the stealthy flush of desire, her body's memory of that inescapable embrace.

"Come on, baby," Kevin says, too-green eyes narrow and hot with anger. "What's wrong? I thought you loved this."

The rope-like creature finally wriggles free, plopping with a dull smack onto the floor between them and humping, sidewinder swift, toward her feet. With a shriek of disgust, she fires at it, cutting it smartly in half. The halves flop noiselessly around, thick sluggish blood splattering the carpet.

Kevin takes another step and she stumbles backward against her vanity.

"Stay the fuck away from me," she hisses. "Freak!"

The anger in his eyes flares into bright, killing hatred, and when he takes that last step, she shoots him, again and then three times.

He crumples and she instantly regrets her actions, rushing to take him in her arms. It is not love that wrenches high wailing sobs from her twisting belly, but the realisation that she has killed the golden goose, that she will never feel that ultimate surrender again.

When a hundred slick ropy tentacles boil up from the bullet holes and seize her, she is almost grateful. As they wind around her throat, crushing her oesophagus and cutting off her air, she fights against them, twisting. She cannot break loose. Every time she moves, they move with her, complex constrictor embrace shifting and tightening and she begins to grey out, world going red and muddy around the edges. In her mind she sees a clock ticking relentlessly into the red, red like the pulsing spots that obscure her vision, red like they are, those horrible wormy things that cinch tighter, tighter around her and she wonders how long it's been. Has it been three minutes? Longer? Is she dying? She imagines a vast, dark, blank-faced audience waiting in excruciating expectation while the clock inches closer and closer to the oversized, cartoony skull that marks the number three. Black starts to swallow the pulsing red and she feels sure that it is really over when the coils around her begin to slacken, subtly at first, then relaxing exponentially around her. One by one they begin to fall away like the chains in her act and she tries to hold on, teeth digging into the raw flesh inside her mouth and realisation filling her like the blood rushing back into her numb extremities. Her vision returns in slow, gauzy stages and she becomes aware of her cheek pressed against the cold floor inches from her dead lover's face. The fleshy ropes that still connect them like a dozen corrupt umbilici are slowly liquefying around her and she clutches frantically at them, trying to wrap them back around her wrists but her desperate fingers punch through their slick, disintegrating skins. She was willing to hold on, to pretend, but in the end she has escaped again, just like always.

STEPHEN GALLAGHER

Restraint

STEPHEN GALLAGHER LIVES IN Blackburn, Lancashire, with his wife and daughter. While working for Yorkshire Television's documentaries department, he scripted two serials for BBC-TV's *Doctor Who* series – *Warrior's Gate* and *Terminus* (both of which he subsequently novelized under the pseudonym "John Lydecker").

Gallagher's subsequent novels include *Valley of Lights*, *Down River*, *Rain*, *Nightmare With Angel*, *Red Red Robin* and *White Bizango*, while his short fiction has recently been collected in PS Publishing's *Out of His Mind*.

He adapted his own novels *Chimera* (aka *Monkey Boy*) and also directed *Oktober* as TV miniseries, along with scripting episodes of *Chillers* and *Murder Rooms: The Dark Beginnings of Sherlock Holmes*.

His latest novel is *The Spirit Box* from Subterranean Press, and he is the creator and writer of the science-and-suspense TV series *Eleventh Hour*.

"The opening scene of this story links to a very specific memory," Gallagher recalls. "I can picture it still. It's 1984, it's night, and I'm on an examination couch in a curtained booth in the Accident and Emergency department of Bolton General Hospital.

"I'm sitting there in my underpants waiting for the doctor, feeling very vulnerable as I hear the business of A&E going on just a few feet away . . . and I'm bright yellow. Real yellow. Van Gogh yellow. With my goose-pimples I look just like a plucked corn-fed chicken.

"Only a couple of weeks before I'd been in Russia, researching my novel *The Boat House*. I was about to be told that I'd contracted a bout of Hepatitis A and that the virus was most commonly transmitted via the fecal/food chain. That's right, the fecal/food chain.

Some bastard of a Russian cook had effectively been wiping his arse on my breakfast.

"Hope that doesn't spoil the story for you. I can tell you that it didn't do much for the rest of my year."

"**D**ID YOU GET A look at the driver who forced you off the road?"

The woman in uniform had pulled up a chair to put herself right alongside Holly's hospital trolley, so that she could speak close and keep her voice low.

Holly made the slightest movement of her head, not even a shake, and was instantly sorry.

The policewoman spoke again.

"Your son thinks it was your husband's car. Could that be right? We've called your house and there's nobody there."

Holly meant to speak, but it came out in an unrecognisable whisper.

"Where are the children?"

"Out in the waiting room. They've been checked over and neither of them's hurt. Your neighbours said you left after some kind of an argument."

"I'd like some water."

"I'll have to ask if that's all right."

Holly closed her eyes, and a moment later heard the sound of metal rings sliding as the policewoman stepped out of the cubicle. Only a curtain separated her from the Saturday night crowd out in Casualty, and a pretty lively crowd they sounded.

She lay with a thin blanket covering her. They'd brought her back here after the X-rays. It was a relief to hear that the children were unhurt, even though it was what she'd half-expected. That short trip down the embankment would have shaken them up, but it was only their stupid mother who'd neglected to put on her own seat belt after making sure of theirs.

That car. It had come out of nowhere. But if there was one thing that Holly knew for certain, it was that Frank couldn't have been at the wheel.

Why? Because she and Lizzie had struggled to lift him into the boot of their own car, not forty-five minutes before. And assuming he hadn't leaked too much and no-one had lifted the lid for a look inside, he had to be lying there still.

He certainly wouldn't be going anywhere on his own.

The young policewoman was back.

"I'm sorry," she said. "I had to stop an argument. I forgot to ask about your water."

"Where's the car?" Holly croaked.

"Still in the ditch," the policewoman said. "The accident unit can get it towed away for you, but you'll have to sort out the rest with your insurers."

This was seductive. The linen smelled clean, and felt fresh. Holly was all but exhausted. She'd been lifted, laid down, tended to. It would be so easy to drift. The racket right outside was almost like a lullaby.

But her husband's dead body was in the boot of her car, and the police were all over it even as she lay there.

"Can I get that drink now?" she said.

As soon as the policewoman was gone, Holly tried to rise up on her elbows. The effort it called for surprised her at first, but she made it on the second attempt.

She was in her underwear, her outer clothing piled on a chair that stood against the wall. She started to climb off the trolley and it hurt, but it wasn't too bad; nothing grated and nothing refused to take her weight. Her head ached and she felt a great overall weariness, but there was no one part of her that screamed of special damage.

The floor was cold under her bare feet. She stood for a moment with her hand resting on the trolley, and then she straightened.

At least she could stand.

She tweaked open the side-curtain and put her face through the gap. In the next cubicle sat a young man on a chair, holding a spectacularly bloodstained dressing to the side of his head. He was in formal dress, with a carnation in his buttonhole and his tie all awry. He looked like the type who owned one suit and wore it for all his weddings, funerals, and court appearances.

"I wouldn't call you a shitsucker," Holly said.

He blinked at her, uncomprehending.

"The man you came in with just did," she said.

He was up on his feet in an instant, and as he flung back the outer curtain she got a glimpse of the scene beyond it. The rest of the wedding party was out there, arguing with the staff and with each other. The bride in her gown could be seen in their midst. They rose in a wave as the bloodied guest was spotted hurtling toward them, and then the curtain fell back as if on the world's most energetic Punch and Judy show.

That ought to keep her policewoman occupied for a while.

Holly could feel the adrenaline pumping now, flushing her of all weariness and pain, leaving her wired and edgy and ready to roll. She dressed as quickly as she could, and then instead of emerging into the open she started to make her way through one dividing curtain after another toward the end of the row. In the next occupied cubicle, an elderly West Indian man lay huddled under a red blanket. In the last sat a scared-looking woman with a small boy. They looked up apprehensively as she appeared out of nowhere.

"Sorry to disturb you," Holly said. "Where's the children's waiting room?"

It was around a corner and separated from the main area by a short passageway and a couple of vending machines. Under a mural of mis-shapen Disney characters stood a basket of wrecked toys, some coverless picture books, and some undersized chairs across which a sleeping form lay. She woke up Lizzie, and dragged Jack protesting out of the corner playhouse in which he'd made a den. He quietened suddenly when he looked at her face. She took them both by the hand and they followed a yellow line on the hospital floor toward the exit.

As they approached the automatic doors, Holly saw herself in the glass. But then the doors slid apart, and they sailed out into the night to look for a taxi.

In the presence of the driver they asked her no questions, and they gave her no trouble. Lizzie was twelve. She was dark, she was pretty, good at her lessons and no good at games. Jack was only six, a beefy little fair-haired Tonka truck of a boy.

The roads were quiet and the taxi got them to the place on the ring road in twenty minutes. It was a good half-mile on from where she'd expected it to be. The police were gone but the car was still there.

"Do you want me to wait?" the cab driver said, but Holly said no and paid him off.

She waited until the cab was out of sight before she descended to her vehicle.

The children hung back on the grass verge, by the deep earth-gouges that marked the spot where their car had left the carriageway. Spray-painted lines on the grass and on the tarmac showed where the accident unit had taken measurements. Down in the ditch, they'd left a big POLICE AWARE sticker on the back window of her Toyota.

The Toyota was old and it wasn't in the best of shape, but it was a runner. Usually. Right now it was stuck nose-first in the bushes along with all the windblown litter at the bottom of the embankment.

The keys had been taken, but Holly groped around in the wheel arch where she kept a secret spare. As she crouched there, she glanced up at the children. They were watching her, two shapes etched against the yellow sodium mist that hung over the road.

Her fingertips found the little magnetic box right up at the top of the arch, deep in the crusted road dirt.

"Got them," she said. "Come on."

Lizzie was nervously eyeing the Toyota as she and Jack came scrambling down.

"What are we going to do?" she said. "It's stuck here. We can't go anywhere."

"We don't know that for certain yet," Holly said, tearing off the police notice and then moving around to open the doors. She didn't know what the procedure was, but they couldn't have looked inside the boot. However quick the glance, Frank would have been hard to miss.

Jack climbed into the back, without an argument for once, and Lizzie got into the passenger seat.

Once she was behind the wheel, Holly checked herself in the rearview mirror. At least when she'd hit her head on the roof, her face had been spared. Her vision had been blurred in the ambulance, hence the need for an X-ray, but that had mostly cleared up now.

Still, she looked a sight. She ran her fingers through to straighten her hair and then she rubbed at her reddened eyes, but of course that only made them worse.

"Here goes," she said, and tried the engine.

It started on the second try. It was sluggish and it didn't sound at all right, but it caught just the same.

There was no point in trying to reverse up the banking, but she tried it anyway. The wheels spun and the car went nowhere. So instead she put it into first gear and tried going forward, squeezing on through the bushes.

For a moment it looked as if this wasn't going to work either, but with a jarring bump they lurched forward into the leaves. Switches bent and cracked as the Toyota forced its way through. She glanced in the mirror and saw Jack watching, fascinated, as foliage scraped and slid along the window only inches from his face. God alone knew what it was doing to her paintwork.

They came out onto what looked like a narrow limestone track, which was actually a soakaway at the bottom of the ditch. Staying in low gear, she began to follow its irregular line. After about a hundred yards she was able to transfer across to a dirt road, which led in turn to a lane. The lane took them under the ring road and then around and back onto it.

Once they were on hard tarmac again, Holly permitted herself to breathe. But not too much. There was the rest of the night still to be managed.

And then – perhaps even more of a challenge – the rest of their lives thereafter.

She hadn't seen it happen. She hadn't even been in the house. She'd come home to find Frank lying awkwardly at the bottom of the stairs and Lizzie sitting with her head in her hands at the top of them. It might have passed for an accident, but for the letter-opener stuck in Frank's neck.

He wasn't supposed to be in the house. The restraining order was meant to take care of that. He wasn't even supposed to come within a hundred yards of his daughter, regardless of where she might be.

So, technically speaking, by being in the boot of the car he was in breach of the order right now.

Holly's first thought had been to pick up the phone and call the police. Her second had been that perhaps she could first wipe off the handle and put her own prints onto it and take all the blame. Then a sudden rage had risen within her. She'd looked down on his twisted body and felt no horror, no awe. No anguish or dismay. Just cheated. Frank had contrived to poison their existence while he was around; was there to be no end to it even with him gone?

She'd made the decision right then. They would not enter that process. If they moved quickly enough, they could put him right out of their lives and make a clean beginning. It would be a credible move; Frank could make an enemy in the time it took him to buy a newspaper, and any suspicion would be dispersed among the many. She'd looked at Lizzie and told her exactly what she had in mind.

We can't, Lizzie had said.

So Holly had sat her down and for ten solid minutes had laid out the choices for her, making sure that she understood how much depended on the next few hours. What was done was done, she'd said to her, and there's no changing it now. Don't feel you're to blame. It isn't a matter of right or wrong. Your father made all the choices that caused this to happen.

It had worked. Kind of.

They couldn't use Frank's car. Being in the motor trade he'd use whatever vehicle was going spare on the lot, and of late he'd been favouring a red coupé that was hardly practical for the job in hand.

So Holly had backed her Toyota into the garage on the side of the house, lined the boot with a plastic decorating sheet, and together they'd dragged Frank through the connecting door and manhandled his body into it. Handling him was less of a problem than Holly had expected. In the unpleasantness stakes, Frank dead was hard-pressed to match up to Frank in life.

Once he was safely stowed and covered in a couple of old towels, they'd driven out to collect Jack from school and then set off for the coast. Fish and chips on the pier, Jack. It's a surprise treat. We just have to make a call somewhere, first. Somewhere quiet. You'll stay in the car.

And then the accident, and the plan forced off-course.

But back on it, now.

From the ring road, they got onto the motorway. The traffic was heavier here, and it slowed when the carriageway narrowed to a single lane. For a long time there was no visible reason for it, and then suddenly they came upon a surfacing crew laying down new tarmac under bright worklights; a colossal rolling tar factory that belched and stank like a dragon as it excreted a lane-wide ribbon of hot road, men with shovels and brushes working furiously in its wake, supervisors in hard hats chatting by their vehicles.

"Look, Jack," Lizzie said. "Big trucks."

"Big, big trucks!" Jack said with awe, and turned in his seat to watch through the back window as they left the staged drama behind.

"You like the big trucks, don't you, Jack?" Holly said as the lanes cleared and the Toyota picked up speed again, but Jack didn't answer.

Holly couldn't put a finger on it, but the Toyota didn't feel quite right after the accident. She could only hope that it wouldn't let them down, and that the outside of the car wasn't messed up too much. A police stop was something that she didn't dare risk.

The next time she checked on Jack, he was asleep. His mouth was open and his head was rocking with the rhythm of the car. He slept the way he did everything else . . . wholeheartedly, and with a 100 per cent commitment.

For a moment, Holly experienced a sensation in her heart that was like a power surge. This was her family. Everything that mattered to her was here, in this car.

And then she remembered that Frank was in the car with them, too. Good old Frank. Consistent as ever. Bringing a little touch of dread into every family outing.

They left the motorway, took a back road, and drove through a couple of darkened villages. There was a place that she had in mind. Out to the north and west was a great bay whose inland fields and marshes were almost unknown beyond the region. At low tide, saltings and sand-flats extended the land almost to the horizon. Much of what was now solid ground had once been part of the sea. In places the sea was claiming it back, pushing the coastline inland so that fields and even some roads were being lost forever. Hide something well enough in the part that was disappearing, and . . .

Well, she'd have to hope. It was the best she could come up with.

Somewhere along here there was a causeway road that had once led to a farm, long-abandoned. People had trekked out to it for a picnic spot when there was something to see, but then the shell had become unsafe and it had all been pulled down. Now there was just rubble and the lines of a couple of walls, and that only visible at a low spring tide.

They crawled along, following the causeway with the Toyota's dipped beams. It didn't so much end as deteriorate steadily for the last couple of hundred yards. The concrete sections of the road had become tilted and skewed as the ground beneath them had given up any pretence of permanence. The sections had drifted, and in places they'd separated completely.

She had to stop the car and get out to locate the cesspit. When she turned back, Lizzie was out of the car and standing beside it.

She was looking around and she said, "Have I been here before?"

"Once," Holly said. "Before Jack was born. I brought you out here to show it to you, because it was a place my mother and father used to bring me. But it had all changed."

Lizzie tried to speak, but then she just nodded. And then her control went altogether, and her body was suddenly convulsed with an air-sucking sob that was shocking both in its violence, and in its unexpectedness.

Holly moved to her quickly and put her arms around her, holding her tightly until the worst of it passed. There in the darkness, out on the causeway, with the moon rising and this thing of such enormity to be dealt with. It would be no easy night, and no easy ride from here. Holly was only just beginning to appreciate how hard her daughter's journey would be.

"I can't do this," Lizzie whispered.

"Yes we can," Holly told her.

They got him out of the car into the pool and he floated, just under the surface, a hand drifting up into the pale shaft of dirtwater light from the Toyota's beams. The first stone sank him and then they added others, as many as they could lift. A sudden gout of bubbles gave them a fright. Holly was convinced that it caused her heart to stop beating for a moment.

They stood watching for a while to be sure of their work, and Holly sneaked a glance at Lizzie. Her face was in shadow and impossible to read.

"We should say a prayer," Lizzie said.

"Say one in the car," Holly said. "We need to get back and clean up the stairs."

Back on the motorway she watched for police cars, but she saw none. She *did* become aware of some lights that seemed to pace her for a while, but when she slowed a little the vehicle drew closer, and she was able to see that it lacked the telltale profile of roof bar and blue lights.

They had unmarked ones, of course. There was always that risk.

After a while, the headlamps in her mirror began to irritate her. She slowed even more to let the car pass, but it didn't. So then she picked up speed and tried to leave it behind; two minutes later and as many miles on, it was still there.

It surely meant nothing, but now it was making her nervous. Lizzie seemed to pick up on this. She saw Holly's frequent glances in the mirror and turned herself around in her seat, straining at her belt to look out of the back window.

"It's the same car," she said.

"What do you mean?"

"The one that pushed us off the road."

"It can't be," Holly said.

Lizzie clearly wasn't certain enough to argue the point.

"Well, it's similar," she said.

Holly increased her speed even further, up and over the limit, and the wheel began to vibrate in her hands as if the Toyota was beginning to shake itself apart. It couldn't be the same car. She couldn't imagine who'd want to follow her, or why.

It seemed to be working. They were leaving the other car behind, but then she saw something out of the corner of her eye. She looked down. The oil light was on, the brightest thing on the dash, and the one thing she knew about a car's oil light was that on a screaming engine it signalled imminent disaster.

She slowed, but it didn't go out. Other warning lights started to flicker on around it. So Holly quickly put the car out of gear and indicated to move off the motorway and onto the hard shoulder.

They coasted to a halt. The engine was already silent by the time they reached a stop. It had died somewhere during the deceleration, she couldn't be sure when. As they sat there, the cooling engine block ticked and clanked like coins dropping into a bucket.

In the back, Jack was stirring.

"Fish and chips on the pier," he said suddenly.

"I'm sorry, Jack," Holly said. "It's got too late. Another time."

The other car was pulling in behind them, hazard lights flashing. Right then a big bus passed them at speed in the inside lane, and its slipstream rocked the Toyota on its wheels.

"Who is it, then?" Lizzie said, peering back as the other car came to a halt about fifty or sixty yards back.

"I don't know," Holly said. "Nobody."

Jack said, "Is it daddy?"

Holly looked at Lizzie, and Lizzie looked at her. There was a risk that Jack might have picked up on something then, but all his attention was on the road behind them. The following driver was getting out. Just as the car was an anonymous shape behind the glare of its own headlights, the driver's figure was a slip of shadow against the liquid stream of passing traffic.

"No, Jack," Holly said, an inexplicable anxiety rising up within her. "It can't be your daddy." She glanced down at the dash. All of the warning lights were on now, but that meant nothing. Everything always came on when the engine stalled.

"It *is*," Jack said.

Holly could tell him it wasn't. But she couldn't tell him why.

She heard Lizzie draw in a deep and shuddering breath, and let it out again. She found her daughter's hand in the dark and squeezed it once.

Traffic flew by, and the driver kept on coming. He was silhouetted against the flashing hazard lights of his own vehicle, pulsing like an amber heart.

Maybe he was your regular Good Samaritan, coming to offer them a hand.

Or maybe he was one of any number of things, as yet unrecognized and uncatalogued.

"He's been in the rain," said Jack.

Forget the oil pressure. Forget the ruinous cost of a thrown piston or a seized-up engine. Suddenly it was far more important to get herself and the children away from this spot.

But all the Toyota's power seemed to have gone. The engine turned over like an exhausted fighter trying to rise after a long count. She tried turning off the lights, and as their beams died, the sound of the starter immediately improved.

It barked, it caught. All the warning lights on the dash went out, including the oil. She crashed the gears, checked her mirror once, and pulled out. Right now her only concern was to get moving again.

Jack was turned around in his seat, straining to see.

"Who is it, if it isn't daddy?" he said.

"It's nobody," Holly said. "Face forward."

"He's running after us."

"Jack," she said sharply, "how many times have I got to tell you?"

She was expecting him to give her an argument. But something in her tone seemed to make him decide, and he complied without another word.

Nothing that she was supposed to hear, anyway.

"It *was* daddy," she heard him mutter.

She knew it wasn't, but the thought was planted now and it spooked her. The sooner this was over with, the better. She wondered how they'd recall this night. Would it be etched in their minds so they'd relive it, moment by moment, or would it move to the distance of a remembered nightmare?

Jack must never know the truth. For him, the story would have to be that his daddy had gone away. He'd keep on looking forward to his father's return, but in time he'd grow and the hope would fade and become part of the background noise of his life.

For Lizzie it was going to be a lot trickier. But at least she was safe from her father now. Whatever problems she might have in dealing with the deed and its memory, that was the thing to keep in mind.

Over a wooded hill, down into a valley, heading for home. Out there in the darkness were the lights of all those small towns that didn't rate exits of their own, but were linked by the road that the motorway had replaced.

That following car was back in her mirror. Or perhaps it was some different car, it was impossible to say. All she could see was those anonymous lights. This time they were staying well back.

Here came the roadworks again. Same stretch, opposite direction. Again, one lane was coned off and the carriageway lights were out. A few moments after they'd crossed into this darker territory, the driver behind her switched on his beams. They were the pop-up kind. She saw them swivel into view like laser eyes.

Just like on Frank's coupé.

Jack said, "Can we have the radio?"

"Not right now," Holly said.

"It was working before."

"I'm trying to concentrate."

He was closing the distance between them. Holly knew she couldn't go any faster.

She looked down and saw that her ignition lights were flickering and that, once again, her oil warning light was full on.

They passed what remained of a demolished bridge, with new concrete piers ready to take its wider replacement. Beyond the bridge site, just off the road, stood a mass of caravans and portable buildings. It was a construction village, a shantytown of churned up mud and giant machines. A temporary sliproad had been bull-dozed into the embankment to give access to works traffic.

Holly waited until it was almost too late. Then she swerved across the lanes and into the sliproad.

Something thumped against the car, and in the mirror she saw one of the cones go tumbling in her wake. The car behind her was swerving to avoid it. It made him overshoot the turnoff, so he couldn't follow her. Now he'd be stuck. The traffic wouldn't allow him to stop and back up again. He'd be heading in the same direction for miles and miles.

Good Samaritan? Good riddance.

All the lights in this temporary settlement were on, yet nothing moved. Jack was craning, eagerly looking around the various site office buildings as they entered the main area. But Holly got in first.

"Yes, Jack," she said. "They have big trucks here."

It was almost as bright as day, and completely deserted. The yard was floodlit and every portakabin office had its lights on. Holly could see through all the uncurtained windows that every one of the offices was empty.

She slowed, and stopped, and looked around.

A few vans, a couple of big diggers. Some concrete bridge sections waiting to be trucked out and assembled elsewhere. The site had the look of a frontier fort, obviously not intended to be here for ever; but it was hard to believe that the scars it would leave on the land could ever easily heal.

They would, of course. The big machines would simply put it all back when they'd finished. It wouldn't quite be nature, but every-body would be going by too fast to notice.

She got out. There was the sound of a generator, banging away somewhere in the background.

"Hello?" she called out, and then glanced back at the car.

Jack and Lizzie were watching her through the side-windows. Pale children, out on the road past their bedtimes. They looked hollow-eyed and tired. Jack with his little round face, Lizzie like a stick-version of the teenager she'd soon be.

Holly gave them a brief smile, and then moved out to look for someone. She didn't want to get too far from the car. She didn't want to let them out of her sight.

She called again, and this time someone came out from behind one of the buildings.

He stood there, and she had to walk over to him. He looked like a toothless old shepherd in a flat cloth cap, knuckly hands hanging down by his sides. He could have been any age, from a well-preserved seventy down to a badly done-by fifty. Too old to be one of the road gang, he looked as if he'd been on road gangs all his life.

She said, "Is anyone in charge around here?"

"Never, love," the man said. "They all do what they sodding well like."

"Well . . . what do *you* do?"

"I'm just the brewman."

Holly looked around her at some of the heavy plant that stood under the lights, looking as if it had all been airdropped in to remodel the face of Mars.

She said, "I've been having trouble with my car. Is there anyone who could have a look at it for me? I've got some money."

"Andy's the mechanic," he said.

"Is he here?"

"He's never here."

"Is it worth me waiting for him? Can I do that?"

"You can do whatever you want," and then added, as if it was his all-purpose charm to ward off evil, "I'm just the brewman." And then he trudged off.

She went back to the car.

"I'm fed up of this," Jack said.

"I can't help it, Jack," Holly said. "Try to understand."

"No," he said, barking it out like a little dog with all the passion and venom he could manage.

Rather than argue or get angry, Holly got out of the car again to watch for Andy the Mechanic.

The site wasn't quite as deserted as it looked, but it took a while to become attuned to it and to pick up the signals; the sound of a door opening and closing somewhere, a glimpse of a figure passing from one building to another.

She paced a little. She looked toward the motorway. For something to do, she raised the Toyota's bonnet and took a look at the engine in the vague hope that her car problems might have some blindingly obvious solution. But it looked like engines always did to her, grimy and complex and meaningless. There was a smell as if something had been burning, and when she held her hand out over the block she could feel the heat rising from it. She poked at a couple of the leads, to no effect other than to get her hands dirtier than they already were.

A voice called out, "Are you looking for someone?"

A man was walking across the open ground toward her. He was short, dark, powerfully built. He had at least six upper teeth missing on one side, but from the way that he grinned the loss didn't seem to trouble him.

"Would you be Andy?" she said.

"I might."

"Then I'm looking for you."

She quickly explained her problem in case he started to get the wrong idea, and he moved her out of the way so that he could take a look. It didn't take him long.

"Look at your fan belt," he said. "If your drawers were that slack, they'd be down around your ankles. When that starts to slip, your battery runs down and you run out of power."

"Is it hard to fix?"

"If I said yes, you'd be more impressed," he said, and it was then that he noticed the two children inside the car. They were staring out at him.

"Yours?" he said.

"Yes," Holly said. "We've been to the seaside."

He looked at her, and then he looked at the car.

And then he said, "You take the kids and wait in the brew hut while I have a go at this. Tell Diesel to make you a cup of tea."

"Is Diesel the brewman's name?"

"It's what his tea tastes like, as well."

The brew hut was the oldest-looking and most battered of the site buildings. It was up on blocks, and reached by three stairs. The floor sagged as they stepped inside. There were about a dozen folding card tables with chairs around them, and a sense of permanent grime everywhere; it was as if engine oil had been ground into the floor, rubbed into the walls, coated onto the windows.

The brewman was sitting by a plug-in radiator, reading a copy of *The Sun*. It wasn't a cold night, but the radiator was turned up high and the air inside the hut was stifling. He looked up as they entered.

Holly said, "Andy told us to wait in here. Is that all right with you?"

"Whatever you like," the brewman said. "I'm Matty."

"He said you were called Diesel."

Matty's face fell, and he looked out of the window.

"The bastard," he said, and he got up and stamped off.

Given his mood and the likely state of his crockery, Holly decided not to press him about the tea. She ushered the children onto grimy plastic seats that stood against the wall. On the wall itself was tacked a selection of yellowing newspaper cuttings, all of them showing the debris of spectacular motorway crashes.

Jack said, "It stinks in here."

"Shh," Holly said.

"It *does*."

She couldn't tell him it didn't, because it did. And she couldn't agree that it did in case Matty was listening. So she only said, "It won't be for long."

They waited. There was a clock on the wall, but it was wrong. Jack swung his feet, Lizzie stared at the floor. Outside, a massive engine began to rev up somewhere close behind the building, making their chairs vibrate.

Jack said, "I'm bored."

"Play I-spy," Holly suggested.

"I'm not playing with him," Lizzie said. "He can't spell."

Holly said, with an unexpected tightness in her tone, "Then why don't we all just sit here quietly?"

There was silence for a while and then Lizzie muttered, rebelliously, "It's true. He can't."

And Jack agreed with her. "I've got a giant brain," he said, "but I can't spell."

Holly covered her eyes. She wasn't sure whether she was laughing or crying and the two children, equally uncertain, were watching her closely for clues.

This night would pass. It would somehow all be fine.

Keep thinking that, she told herself, and it might even come true.

"Mum . . ." Lizzie said.

Holly looked at her and saw the unease and the apprehension in her eyes. She might be sharp, but she was still only twelve years old.

"When this part's over," she said, "what then?"

She was choosing her words carefully because of Jack, but Holly knew what Lizzie was trying to say.

"We'll carry on as normal," she said.

"Can we do that?"

"We'll have to," Holly said.

There was a tap on the window. Andy was standing there outside, raising himself up on tiptoe so that he could look in, and he beckoned to her.

She went out, and they walked over to the car together. He told her he'd left the keys inside it.

"Best I can do," he said. "I've tightened your fan belt and cleaned off your plugs. They were blacker than Matty's fingernails."

"Thanks, Andy."

"You've got a lot of oil down there. I don't know where it's coming from. You might need a new gasket."

He showed her what he'd done and got her to feel the difference in the fan belt, which she pretended to appreciate. She offered him twenty quid and he took it with no embarrassment. Then she went back for the children.

The brew hut door was open. Lizzie was alone inside.

Holly said, "Where's Jack?"

Lizzie had slumped down into her coat as if it was a nest, hands in her pockets and legs outstretched, looking at the toes of her shoes as she clacked them together. She said, "He followed you outside."

"I didn't see him."

"He wanted to look at the big trucks."

Holly went out. Jack hadn't gone over toward the car, or she'd have seen him. She stood in front of the brew hut and called out his name.

Nothing.

Lizzie was in the doorway behind her now.

"It's not my fault," she said defensively.

Holly went around by the side of the brew hut and found herself in an area lit by the most powerful of the overhead floodlights. Under the lights stood a few parked cars and a variety of dormant machines. She could hear the massive engine whose note had been shaking the brew hut's foundations, and could tell that it was somewhere close.

She looked back and saw that Lizzie had followed her some of the way.

"You look around the buildings," Holly said. "I'll look here."

She didn't wait to see how Lizzie responded, but started to make her way through the machine yard. It was like a giant's bazaar of heavy engineering, the night sun casting deep, dark shadows under the gear. These were machines for ripping up the land, and they had spikes and claws and teeth on a saurian scale. Encrusted with clay and battered by hard use, they stood like bombed-out tanks.

She hauled herself up and looked in the cab of a well-rusted bulldozer on tracks. Jack wasn't in it, but by hanging on she could look out over the yard. Down the next row, a wagon was being inched up onto a flatbed trailer by some driver she couldn't see. The tyres on the wagon were enormous, and the ramps were bending under its weight.

She looked all around and called Jack's name, but she had little chance of being heard. The big engine roared and the great tonnage slowly rolled. In her mind's eye she saw Jack crushed or falling or struggling to get free of some unexpected snare. She saw gears turning, teeth meshing, pulling him in.

She called his name again, louder, and then hopped down to continue the search. She stumbled a little when she landed. The ground here was nothing more than churned-up dirt into which stones had been dumped to give it some firmness. It was no playground.

"Jack!" she called, moving forward.

As she came around by the bulldozer onto a firmer stretch of concrete road, she saw him. She could see all the way to the perimeter fence, where he was climbing.

Climbing? What was he *doing*?

And then she understood, and started to run.

It was a storm fence, about eight feet high. Jack was already over the top of it, and climbing down the other side. The fence rocked back and forth under his weight as the concrete posts shifted in their holes, but he clung to it like a bug; its close weave offered ideal purchase for his small feet and fingers.

Holly stumbled on the rough ground, but caught herself and went on. On the other side of the perimeter fence was an unlit country lane.

Out on the country lane stood the red coupé with the pop-up headlights.

"Hey," she shouted. "Hey, Jack, no!"

He was descending with his face set in a look of utter concentration. Behind him, the car was making a low purring sound with its engine off but its electric fan sucking in the cool night air. The driver hadn't stepped out, and she could barely see anything of him. She could only guess that he was watching her.

Holly reached the fence, looking through it and up at him. "Jack," she said. "Come down, Jack, please. You can't go over there. That's not your daddy. Believe me. There's no way it could be."

But Jack didn't look at her, and didn't even show any sign of having heard. He was moving like a monkey. He reached down with his foot, found another space in the diamond pattern, and hooked his scuffed trainer into it before lowering the rest of his weight.

She could touch his fingers as they hooked through, right in front of her eyes; her breath through the wire could fall onto his face. "Jack," she said, "no!"

But he wouldn't look at her, and although he was only inches away she couldn't reach him. She was powerless.

"Jack," she said, "Look at me, please. Don't do this. Don't go to him."

She made a move as if to try and catch his hands through the wire, but it was pointless. She couldn't hold him if she caught him. All she could do was risk hurting him.

"Lizzie's looking for you as well," she pleaded. "Oh, *Jack* . . ."

He jumped, and hit the dirt on the far side with a thump. Holly made a leap at the wire and felt the entire fence lean before her, but she didn't have his agility and couldn't begin to climb the way that he had.

He was running for the car, now, and the car's passenger door was opening to receive him.

Holly was screaming, although she didn't immediately realize it. The car door slammed and its laser eyes opened. The engine started, and its nose swung around as it began to turn in the narrow lane.

Her hands were up at the sides of her head. She'd heard of people tearing at their hair, but she'd always thought it was just an expression. She looked around wildly.

Then she started to run along the inside of the fence, ahead of the turning car.

The country lane ran close on the other side. If there was a gap anywhere, she'd get through it. The car wouldn't pass her. No way was she going to let that happen.

Here was a gate. It was a back way into the site, little-used. A big double gate, wide enough for a lorry but chained and padlocked in the middle. There was enough play in the chain to make a gap of a foot or so.

It was a squeeze, but not an impossible one. She came out on the other side and all that she could see were the twin lights, the laser eyes of the beast that she had to impede.

She put on a burst and dived into its way, sliding to a halt in the middle of the lane and raising both of her hands. When it hit her, she felt nothing other than her own sudden acceleration; no impact, no pain, just the instantaneous switch from rest into motion as her legs were knocked from under her and she was spun down the side of the car.

Afterwards she'd never know whether she really saw it or only imagined the memory, but Holly went down hard in the wake of the moving car with a mental picture of her son's blank face only inches away on the other side of the glass.

She lay there.

She couldn't move. She could hear that the car had stopped and she wanted to lift her head to look, but nothing happened. Oh God, she was thinking, I'm paralysed. But then when she made an enormous effort, her hand came up and braced itself against the ground. As she was doing it, she heard a car door opening.

She wasn't paralysed, but she'd no strength. When she tried to push down with her hand to raise herself, her arm trembled and nothing happened.

Someone was walking up behind her.

Before she could muster the energy to turn and look, strong fingers gripped the back of her head and thrust her face down into the mud. In an instant, she was blinded and choking.

She found her strength now, all right, but it did her no good as a sudden knee in her back pinned her further to the ground. She struggled and flapped like a fish, but her face stayed under. The blood roared in her ears and lights exploded before her eyes.

Then in an instant, the pressure was off.

That first deep breath nearly drowned her on the spot, as she sucked in all the mud that had filled up her mouth. She retched and coughed, blowing it out of her nostrils and heaving up what she'd both swallowed and inhaled.

She felt a lighter touch on her shoulder and lashed out, only to hear a cry from Lizzie. She was there when Holly's vision cleared, keeping back and holding her arm where she'd been struck.

"I'm sorry, mum," she said.

Holly stared dumbly for a moment before an understanding started to form. Lizzie was backing toward the waiting car.

"No, Lizzie!" she said. She tried to rise, but one of her legs wouldn't support her.

"I know how you want me to feel about it, but I can't. I wish I could. I'm sorry. It's never going to be right after tonight, whatever we do. Ever."

Holly made another massive effort and this time made it up and onto her feet, putting all of her weight onto the uninjured leg.

"Wait," she managed.

Lizzie had reached the car.

"I'm the one that he wants," she said. "But he'll take Jack if I don't go with him."

The passenger door popped open about an inch.

"I'm sorry," she said again, and she reached out and opened it all the way.

Holly wasn't close enough to see how it worked, but Jack popped out of the vehicle as if propelled on a spring. He landed on both feet, and Lizzie quickly slipped around behind him and into the car.

The door closed like the door on a well-fitting safe, and the car's engine started to rev. It was all as swift and as decisive as that.

Holly started toward them, half-hopping, half-limping, but the car was already moving off and starting to pick up speed.

"Frank!" she shouted. "You bastard! Give her back!" and at the sound of her voice, Jack seemed to wake as if from a daze.

He looked about, as if suddenly remembering something, and spotted those red tail lights receding off into the darkness.

He gave a strangled cry.

"Dad!" he called out, and started to run down the lane after the car, slapping down his feet so hard that the ground almost shook.

Holly hadn't yet reached him, and her cries couldn't stop him. Neither of them had any chance of catching the car. But both of them tried.

She caught up with him a full ten minutes later, still standing on the dark spot where his breath and his hopes had finally given out.

"He forgot me!" he wailed. Holly dropped to her knees and pulled him to her.

For once, he let her hold him.

TANITH LEE

Israbel

TANITH LEE LIVES WITH her husband, the artist, photographer and writer John Kaiine, on the south-east coast of England.

She began writing at the age of nine and published three children's books with Macmillan in the early 1970s, becoming a full-time author in 1975, when DAW Books published her novel *The Birth-grave*.

Lee has now written and published around seventy novels, nine collections and more than 200 short stories, and her work has been translated into sixteen languages. She also scripted two episodes of the cult BBC-TV series *Blake's 7*. Her short fiction has twice won the World Fantasy Award and she was awarded the British Fantasy Society's August Derleth Award in 1980 for her novel *Death's Master*.

Her more recent books include two pirate novels for young adults, *Piratica* and *Piratica II: Return to Parrot Island. Lionwolf: Cast a Bright Shadow* and *Here in Cold Hell* are the first two volumes in an adult fantasy series, while *Metallic Love* is a sequel to her 1981 novel *The Silver Metal Lover*. She also has new stories appearing in such magazines and anthologies as *Weird Tales, H.P. Lovecraft's Magazine of Horror, Winter Moon* and *The Ghost Quartet*.

"The dawn of this story happened at night," explains the author. "John and I were eating dinner. We often talk about work and ideas at meals. This time he held up a piece of artwork he had that day created.

"It showed a girl with curious dark, yet gilded, somehow *feathered* hair. She had beautiful eyes – and no other features. The rest of her face was an exquisitely shaped blank. And he challenged me, smiling: 'Tell me who she is'.

"Instantly Israbel, complete with name, was in the room with us. And so I told him – literally as the story tells of her. Let's hear it for a bottle of wine and a tomato omelette!"

For John Kaiine, who showed me her image
more clearly than any mirror could.

I SRABEL RAN THROUGH THE STREETS of Paris. The cobbles were slick with filth and wet, the city was made of thick grey rain. Israbel was sixteen – probably, who could be quite sure? Her mother was long dead, her father always unknown. Somewhere behind her waited a man with his belt drawn off, like a sword to smite her with. Israbel ran.

The narrow streets were mostly empty now, for night was coming. A fellow with a torch went by, to light the lamps along the front of some tavern. Wet cats, thin as strings, shot across the alleys, or slunk over the roofs above.

When Israbel turned a corner into the Place du Coeur, she did not know where she was, but in the deepening dusk one further cat came slinking out to cross her path. This cat was not like the others. It was very big, the size, she was afterwards to believe, of a horse. Though the light was gone, some peculiar sheen on the darkness showed her the faint dapplings along its back, its neck, which was longer than that of any ordinary feline, the narrow ruff about its head. Its eyes were luminous, and grey as the death of the light. It stopped.

She too, the running girl, had halted.

She thought, confusedly, *It's escaped from the great circus up at Montmartre.*

Israbel had heard of a circus, and that it had many curiosities, including both people and beasts of weird appearance and characteristics.

She was not afraid of the cat. That is, not more afraid of it than of the darkness, the sadist she had escaped, the world, everything. And so, she did not, now, run away, only stood, watching it, as it stood also watching *her*.

A hundred years later when Israbel, still sixteen, rich, lovely, and, in her own way, dangerous, came occasionally to explain about the great cat, she would always add, "Its pelt was so soft and warm, so smooth and plush, like the double velvets of Venice. Like my hair, you say? Well, perhaps very like that. But truly, its pelt was much better than my hair."

"She is the woman I intend to be my wife."

Plinta stared, a moment. He thought, *Your wife?* And then, *She looks like an insect. Oh, a beautiful insect – some sort of exquisite beetle, with gilded black wings*.

"Really?" he said.

"You don't approve."

Plinta shivered – but unseen: inside his mind.

"Does it matter to you that I approve?"

"Well, no."

By then, the woman – the *creature* – was approaching them, slipping between the candlelit marbles of the salon.

Dumière held out his hands. She paused, smiling, and took neither.

"Good evening, my love," said Dumière. "May I present my friend, Monsieur Plinta, the painter."

She looked at Plinta.

Her eyes were like a flash of blackness seen through blue smoke.

Yes, she was beautiful. A perfect, sculpted face, large dark eyes – blue? – black? – whose lids were just barely touched with kohl, a long aquiline nose (perhaps she was a Jewess?), a wonderful mouth, not large – yet full, and capable of lengthening its shape – blushed either with rouge or uncommon good health.

She was not young. That is, she was about twenty-five, or so Plinta thought. Not that, physically, she seemed much older than sixteen. Yet her eyes knew things. Perhaps her clear and unlined eyes were even older – thirty, forty – *fifty?*

Plinta, the artist, now realized why he had thought of her pictorially and specifically as a beetle. Her black dress wrapped her closely, thrusting up a velvet glimpse of breasts, holding her corsetted waist like two tight ebony hands ringed with gold. Her hair, too, which she wore partly loose, was quilled and rayed with gold – wings.

He thought, distinctly, *She is a vampire*.

"Madame," he said, and bowed.

"Oh, but, Monsieur," she said, "I'm not married."

"Not yet," agreed Dumière. Now he reached out and took hold of her, like the tight hands of her dress on her waist. "Come on, let's dance."

As he led her away, she glanced back once, and directly into Plinta's eyes.

What was her name? Had Dumière not told him?

*   *   *

The next evening, as Plinta, who had just left his bed, lay on the sofa, reading the morning's journals and drinking bitter coffee, his shambling servant Colas showed Israbel into the studio.

Plinta did not get up. Then he thought he had better, to be rude was too obvious. So he rose. But, when he did that, she laughed at him.

She said, "I saw last night, Monsieur Plinta, you'd penetrated my disguise."

Today she wore very dark blue-green, with a lemon plume in her hat. She was still like a beautiful beetle. Or maybe a lizard . . .?

"Disguise? I didn't know you'd worn fancy-dress, madame."

"Oh yes, of course. Always. But you saw right through to me, didn't you? As if I were naked."

Plinta felt at once an unmistakable and vivid surge of lust. Positioned high in his own brain, he looked down at the lust, tingling and flaring about in his body, and said, cautiously, "I don't know what you mean, madame."

"I'm not 'madame'. I have only one name. Israbel. Under that name I sometimes sing and act at the *Opèra*."

"Very well," he said. "Please sit down."

She too, he sensed, saw right through *him*. She knew what he felt, still felt. She knew, too, he was still in command of himself.

Israbel seated herself. She drew off the plumed hat, and her hair fell all around her, down to her waist. Though there were no longer golden quills and spangles in it, yet it glittered with strange gilding.

"I want you," she said, "to paint my portrait."

"You honour me. Alas, I'm very busy."

"No, you are not. You haven't had a commission, nor any paid work, for eighteen months. You mustn't forget, I know Dumière, who knows *you*."

"Dumière doesn't know everything about me, I'm afraid."

"No. You're a secretive man. But your painting is interesting. Wouldn't you like me to sit for you?"

"Frankly, Madame Israbel—"

"You wouldn't," she finished for him.

The door opened. In blundered Colas, with more wood for the stove, for it was a chilly evening. Israbel watched Colas, then she turned back her eyes on to Plinta. And, annoyed, he realized he had been hungry for their return to him, sulky in the split second of her looking away.

Colas banged the stove door shut again and lumbered out. Like two interrupted lovers, they resumed their murmured conversation.

"Dumière may have told you, monsieur, I'm well-off. I can pay you handsomely for your portrait of myself."

"Why do you want such a portrait?"

She said, without hesitation, "I'd like to look at it. I'd like to see myself in it."

And, before he could quite stop himself, if he had even meant to stop himself, Plinta added, "That being because a portrait is the only way you ever *could* see yourself. Am I correct, madame? You don't reflect in mirrors."

Israbel smiled once more. It was difficult to take your gaze away from her mouth – unless you looked into her eyes; and then you could only look at those . . .

"I note you understand my predicament, monsieur," she said, as if they had spoken of something dull.

Plinta decided not to reply.

Israbel got up, and as she did so, even clothed in her fashionable Parisian dress, something fell from her like a seventh veil.

"Others are fooled, of course," she remarked. "It's commonly thought no one can make out a vampire in a mirror. But naturally anyone can see us reflected there – save only we, ourselves."

"Then you have kindred?" said Plinta, between wonder and alarm.

"Perhaps – but I've met none of them. No, no, I'm quite alone. I speak of them only in the historical and mythic sense. I belong, you understand, monsieur, to an ancient sisterhood, brotherhood, packed with persons. Except I've never met any of them."

"Then how did you become what you are?" Plinta asked, inevitably.

"If I tell you that, will you paint me? Will you give me my mirror, Monsieur Plinta?"

He turned his back and walked off to the window.

Standing by the frozen glass, he gazed down at the icy, barely-lit streets running towards the River Seine, the bell-clanging local church, then to the sky like black lead. But talking to her was a game he seemed unable to give up playing.

"Why do you want to see yourself, madame? Anyone else's face can tell you how beautiful you are."

"Not yours," she said.

Plinta lurched inside his skin. In utter silence, she had drawn physically close to him. Her narrow hand was on his shoulder. Almost as tall as he, she leaned to his ear: "I'll tell you my story anyway," she murmured, "perhaps . . ."

Plinta did not move. He wondered if she would sink her teeth, or some other blood-letting implement, into his neck. But he felt only her perfumed warmth, and then a coldness, and turning, he saw she was once more seated far off across the studio, her feet stretched out to the stove, drinking coffee, like an ordinary human woman.

She did not appear at the *Opèra* very often. When she did, she always took some small cameo part, usually limited to a single appearance lasting maybe five minutes, during which she sang an aria by Handel, Rameau, or Voulé. Her voice was good, if not especially brilliant, but nevertheless, a great hush would grip the theatre while she voiced her lines and sang her music. She was always rapturously applauded, and flowers rained on the stage.

She was said to have slept with some of the richer or more notorious patrons – bankers, poets, that sort. None of them had ever seemed any the worse for it. That is, none of them mysteriously died or otherwise disappeared. None of them, perhaps, more to the point, metamorphosed in any way. They merely went on with their own earthbound lives, long after they parted from her.

Men did become infatuated, of course. One had drowned himself, Plinta thought. Plinta had never paid her name much attention, nor even seen her, until Dumière became in turn obsessed by her.

Dumière took Plinta to dinner at the Café d'Orléans. Here they ate oysters and various roast meats, and drank wine and liqeurs. Dumière spoke mostly – solely – of Israbel. Plinta, to his own consternation, listened with interest and completely failed to be bored. He had already agreed with Israbel to paint her. There had seemed to be nothing else he could do. He did not tell Dumière, however, as if this were a guilty secret. He sensed Dumière would call him out over it to a dawn duel in the Bois, and perhaps shoot him dead in jealousy.

Dumière was not really Plinta's friend. Dumière used Plinta as a sort of social musical instrument, a piano perhaps, coming up to him and playing him with enthusiasm for a few hours now and then, even in public, in restaurants and salons, then forgetting Plinta again entirely for months – years – on end.

Plinta watched Dumière all through the dinner. Even over the crystalized fruits, brandy and cigars. Dumière seemed the same as ever, handsome, spoiled and charming.

Finally, when they were drunk enough, Plinta said to him, "Have you had her yet?"

"*Had* her?"

"The kiss that is more than a kiss."

"Why, Plinta! What do you think? Aren't I irresistable? Isn't *she*?"

"You have, then."

"You prude! Do you want me to describe it?" Amused in victory, Dumière glowed above the glowing cigar. "Well? I will if you like."

Plinta thought he *would* like, that his *body* would have liked to hear every detail. Conversely his clever appraising mind was also highly curious.

"No, thank you."

"I'll tell you this, Plinta, she isn't like any other woman I've ever known."

"Doesn't the new lover always think that?"

"No, of course he doesn't. How absurd. We *pretend* we do, but we don't."

"Then—" cautious still, Plinta leaned back, "—then how is she *different*? Is she perverse?"

"No such luck. Not that anything like that is necessary with her. Oh, her skin's soft and smooth, her hair's a marvel, she has a special scent she wears – like spice. Her body is lithe as a snake's. It isn't any of that."

"And *do* you mean to marry her?" said Plinta, as Dumière fell silent, hypnotized by absorbing thoughts of Israbel.

"I might. I wouldn't mind it. Just to keep her to myself."

"Do you think you could?"

"Yes. I'd put her in a cage. Like a panther. She only lets me visit her at night. She's nocturnal, like most panthers."

"A *cage*—" despite himself, Plinta was shocked, mostly at Dumière's suddenly active imagination.

"Oh, I mean a house, man, a big, glorious house – but I'd have the only key. I'd keep her there. Do you know," he added abruptly, "the strangest thing is when she looks into a mirror. I bought her one, you see, a gorgeous thing from Italy, silvered glass, gilt cupids – she stood in front of it nearly half an hour. Staring in at her reflection. She had such a puzzled look – a *sad* look – as if she were searching for something she couldn't find. I wonder what . . .?"

Her soul, Plinta thought.

Worse than Dumière's invented cage-house, a door slammed in Plinta's heart, then, trapping him inside with Israbel.

Israbel told Plinta at once she wished to pose for him in the nude.

This, rather than excite, made cool sense to him. After all, if she wanted to see *herself* – which no mirror could now ever show her –

she wanted to see her flesh, *not* her *clothes*. She need only look into her wardrobe to behold those.

When she came out naked to the lamplight from behind the studio screen, he noted, unsurprised, her body was beautiful. But Plinta had seen the beautiful unclad bodies of women – and men – often in his trade.

What moved him was Israbel herself. Her gestures, expressions. Even the sound of her voice. For she would talk to him as he began his sketches.

Her voice was pleasant, restful. It was elusive, too. Neither young nor old, barely even feminine. A slightly-tarnished silver voice, to vie with the gold glints in her eyes and hair.

He found her easy to capture on paper, and presently on canvas. Even her colours were simple – cream and black, with highlights of turquoise, navy, and warmer tones, like shining metals. But her red mouth burned for him.

What would it be like – not to kiss – but to be *bitten* by the teeth of that burning mouth.

Plinta recalled that awareness he had had before, of the casting of a seventh veil – less the provocative act of a dancing Salomé – it had been as if Israbel *cast a skin*.

She had not yet, despite her pledge, told him the tale of how she became what he knew she was, a vampire, who lived on the blood of others. But, for that matter, he did not know when or how she took blood. She had never approached him in any way, either in seduction or attack. Naturally, she would want the portrait completed to her satisfaction first. However. One day he would finish.

He actually considered, twice, following her when she left the studio, to see her method of predation. Yet he never did.

What would he do if she suddenly turned her attentions on him? Would he allow her his blood? Would he be able to prevent her?

He was not afraid of Israbel. He was not in love with her. But obsessed he *was*. Intellectually and artistically at least as much as physically and in his emotions.

A winter dusk brought her early, while a thick sun-fall bubbled behind the church like sweet apricot preserves.

The painting was almost done, and he permitted her, when she asked, to see it. She had never asked before.

She stood a long while staring at it, just as Dumière – whom, now, Plinta had not seen for two months – had described with the costly cupid mirror. For one awful second, Plinta thought perhaps she could not see herself in the painted picture, *either* – it was a very exact likeness.

Then she said, "Oh thank God. There I am again. Oh, yes. Thank God.

"Do you know, can you guess," she whispered presently, when he had sat her down, wrapped her furs about her, given her cognac, "what it's like – *never again to see your own self*? Oh, there are whole peoples, I know, who never have mirrors and so never look into them but, even so, they may see a reflection in some surface. And here in this city – a polished table-top, window, a pool. Think of me, I was so young. Gazing instead at my hands, my feet, my *shadow* – because my shadow I still have – trying to remember myself from that. I pulled my hair across my eyes, too, and looked at my hair. But myself – my face, my eyes, my mouth – for ever gone. All of *you* could see them, *all of you*. All save I myself! And they were *mine*."

"The penalty for everything else you've gained," he said. Was this harsh? No, only a fact.

And "True," she said. "Nevertheless, I have outwitted the penalty, or I *shall* do so. With the help of Plinta the Painter. Do you know, Plinta, the oddest thing – I'd only seen myself four or five times in any case, before I lost the ability to view my own reflection. In my – shall I even say *home*? – in the slum where I was born, there were few mirrors. Despite that, as I've said – once in a windowpane, and once a table polished with my hand – and once in a pool of rain-water in a gutter, and once in the side of a bottle – but once a man gave me a piece of looking-glass. I looked, and truly saw myself, and he said, *now you do as I say, or I'll cut that face you see across with my razor*. I did what he said. He still took off his belt to beat me. I hadn't pleased him, you understand. That was when I ran. This, Plinta, was about a hundred, a hundred and seven years ago. It was in the era just before the Revolution. Paris was raw and smarting, not yet seething – I didn't notice. The city was like a model made of wet newspaper. Unreal. And I must only escape. So, I escaped, as you see."

He said, "You became what you are now."

Then she told him.

The great cat in the Place du Coeur had approached her so suddenly and so swiftly, seeming to move as if on wheels, that Israbel had had no time to think, or to decide after all once more to run away. Next second its body touched hers.

The body of the cat was warm, she said, as a hearth, or a summer stone, and its pelt was smooth, velvet-soft, yet prickling with electric life. The instant they were in contact, a vast soothing, in fact a feeling of *content*, flooded Israbel. "It was like the first time I ever tasted good brandy."

The Place du Coeur was now, she said, long felled, its yards and hovels squashed and built over. Alleys attenuated from it however, then and still, creeping towards the Isle of the City.

Israbel remembered only this, walking very fast with the great leopard, whose neck was long and who was tall as a horse, both it and she unseen and incredibly unnoted, through shadows and night. Here and there bleary lights shone in the rain. Sometimes loud displays of inebriation, rage or merriment flowed round the edges of their progress. For everything like that seemed divided by their passage, like a river, which they swam together, she and the cat, effortlessly. They came eventually out on to the open spaces before the Cathedral.

Notre Dame, Our Lady of Paris, was that night herself lit to gold and smoky red. In her windows dark blue fires, and rubies. Far above, her demonic gargoyles craned, peering over and down at the city, their wings locked until midnight should strike in some other dimension, and let them loose.

But the leopard drew Israbel away down a sort of slope, and into a cavern under the street. She could not say exactly *how* it drew her. It was as if she had become invisibly connected to its skin, the vibrant *spirit* of its short dense fur, which led her along like a benevolent leash.

"What did I think or feel? I was only happy. I felt quite safe, going down into the dark. If instead it had somehow drawn me up the very heights of the Cathedral, I couldn't have been afraid."

In the cavern – no, she had sometimes, in later years, looked for this spot by Notre Dame, never found it, nor any entrance to it – was the leopard's lair. The stone floor was dry and thick with straw and rushes and scraps of material. The air was warm yet clean, faintly tinged with the incense of Notre Dame, freshened by little cracks and other apertures. She smelled the river, too, wholesome as the rest.

She lay down against the cat, which held her between its great, muscled forelegs, the paws resting around her, without a hint of talons. It breathed into her face. And its breath was healthy and clean, and smelled only a little salty.

"Some of those I tell this story, ask if the cat then ravished me, as lions can be trained to do with human women. Yet no such thing happened at all. Oh it wasn't like that. It was as if I lay again, a child, in the arms of my mother, or a father who loved me tenderly. I never felt so secure, nor have I ever, after. So I slept, my head on one of the huge arms, against the breast of dappled fur, to the rhythmic hymn of its breathing."

Israbel paused. This hiatus went on and on.

Plinta said finally, "And then?"

She sighed. "I woke up. It was twilight. I felt well and strong, as if I'd eaten a nourishing meal and drunk a little wine. And as if I'd bathed in hot scented water – that was how I now smelled. I wasn't under the city any more. I was on a back street against a wall, out of sight, where it must have taken me when it was done. I might have dreamed everything, but for knowing I was glad it wasn't daytime, and for the sense of well-being, of *vitality* – neither of which have ever left me since. Even so, I started to cry. I ran about, trying to find the way back down to my beloved friend – for yes, the great cat had become my only friend, and all the family I had. Of course, I detected no way and not a single clue. I never saw my leopard again. Presently, instead, my own – no, *human* kind – discovered me. And so I learned my powers over them, what I could do and gain. What I had become."

"A vampire."

"An immortal thing. Naturally limited to the night, but otherwise able to exist as she wishes. And fed – *cherished* – by mortal blood."

Plinta roused himself. He felt cold and sleepy, inert and depressed, all the opposites of what she had described her own feelings to be.

"But how had – this cat – taken *your* blood. How had it re-fashioned you?"

"Do you really wish to know?"

"*Yes—*"

Israbel lowered her eyes of black turquoise. "The pelt," she said, simply, in a sad low voice, "the beautiful fur of it – every fibre leached every atom of my blood away, and filled me in return with the ichor of the vampire race."

"Its *fur*!"

Plinta surged up. He strode up and down the studio, rubbing circulation back into numbed arms and hands, stopping only to shovel more wood into the stove. The room seemed hot – yet he was freezing.

When he happened to glance at the clock, he was astounded: two hours had passed since Israbel had first arrived.

The moment he looked at her now, she too got up. She had not anyway taken off any but her outer garments, the furs. It seemed she did not, tonight, mean to pose for her portrait.

Certainly she did not, for she said then, "Monsieur, your picture of me is all I could ever hope for. You've given me a very special gift. Now I shall pay you."

"It isn't finished!" Plinta exclaimed. He himself heard the panic in his tone. It was not only the unfinished painting that troubled him. It seemed their commerce, hers and his, was at an end.

But Israbel only nodded gravely.

"Not quite finished, I agree. But that's as it should be – as it *must* be, don't you think? For neither am I, monsieur, *finished*. Nor, perhaps, can I ever be. The picture has reached the very stage I myself am at. Like me, it must remain there, or how can I see myself in it?"

Plinta stood still. He stared at Israbel, memorizing her, her grace, elegance and otherness.

"And so," she said gently, "let me settle my account with you."

"I don't know," he said, "what this picture can be worth."

"Everything."

"Do I ask everything of you, then?"

"You know that I'm rich."

"Don't pay me," he said, "in money."

"Then how?"

As she questioned him like that, Plinta saw in her a total fatal innocence. It had nothing to do with naivety or foolishness. *I must never lose her*. Aloud he said, "Show me."

"Ah."

"Show me how – *pelt* – can take blood. *How you feed yourself*."

The crudeness of the words he had used, and his desire to find out, both appalled him. He was humiliated by himself, and trembling, but even so, would not deny what he had said.

She answered, "If you wish. But – I'm hungry, Plinta, Monsieur Plinta the Painter. If it's to be you—"

"*Me*. Who *else*?"

"Then, I shan't hold back. You must become as I am. Do you want such a thing?"

Plinta thought about it. But he had been thinking of it constantly, behind a screen of debate, arguing with himself that in fact, it was not possible. But it was.

"Madame Israbel, I have so much to learn of my trade. That alone would need immortality. I'd like the time. I don't subscribe to the idea that, being always myself, I must become less. I think one must be able to *evolve* – even in the same continuing body. Yes, I'd give up the daylight. But I too am already partly nocturnal. I sleep through a day, rise at sunset. But more than that – I want to *know*."

Israbel turned her head. This was as if she listened, obediently, to some angel at her right shoulder, who now told her what she must do. It seemed she knew the angel of old. Its advice was always sound.

Before, he had seen a seventh veil fall from her.

Now Israbel touched the bodice of her dress, and the yellow silk parted and dropped, like a veil, and all else with it. As before, she stood in front of him naked. Her hair, loose and gleaming, framed her face, neck and upper body.

Plinta felt a stab of sexual appetite so intense it hurt him. Then he grasped it was not sexual at all.

She came to him as her kind did, as the great cat had come to *her* – sudden and swift, gliding as if over burnished ice.

And as she came, her hair, her *hair*, lifted up on her head in two wide, black-flaming wings, glittering with tines and prisms of diamond, topaz and gold, and as it fastened on him, and her flesh met his own clothed body, he felt the touch of her, hair, skin, her eyes, her lips. Oh, not like mother or father. This was like the meeting of mortal man with god.

Plinta seemed to lie that night high up on the roofs of the Cathedral, among the army of gargoyles which, as a white moon rose, flew back and forth, scratching their claws on the parapets, their eyes full of misty smoulderings.

Here, Israbel took his blood, not biting but through her skin and her hair, the soft persuasive caresses ebbing and swelling like a symphony.

He understood that, in the future, he too must also take sustenance in this way. But *her* hair, so long and thick, had become two wings, like those of some giant Egyptian hawk, and she too, he saw, as he lay quiet between the delicious bouts of her feeding, flew off the roof, into the sky and stars. Sometimes she even gripped the gargoyles, held them, while both they and she soared across the moon, her hair coiling them, their tails wrapped around her. Did she take blood also from their carved stone, replacing it with immortal vampiric essences? Of course, how else were they able to fly?

Near dawn she closed his eyes with her lips, a kind of kiss.

"Sleep now. Be at peace. Asleep, the sun can't harm you. Tomorrow night you will be changed."

"Then tomorrow, where shall I meet you?" he said. But Plinta discovered he could not, now she had shut them, open his eyes, and she did not reply, and had drawn away. A colossal slumberousness stole over him. He sank into it, not minding.

In the dream then, asleep, which itself held a dream. In this second trance, he saw Israbel after all, her face framed now by the velvet and silk curtains of a stage. Wings flew out from her skull. Her eyes were highly reflective – like a pair of looking-glasses. Otherwise, her face had no features at all. It was a *faceless* face, a perfect, blind face, of fabric stretched taut on bone.

Colas found him the next evening. Plinta lay stiff and marble cold, and looking bloodless as marble, there on the studio rug, splashed by the dregs of a sunset.

Colas gave a yowl. Howling and yelping like a wolf, he rolled Plinta about the floor, and when neighbours rushed up the stairs, wailed that Plinta had died, was dead, and now Colas would be slung out on the street – Colas's only actual concern.

"No, you dolt. Look, he's waking up. *Dead*? *Plinta*? Only drunk—"

Plinta woke. He stretched, and Colas, who genuinely had seen him minutes before dead as the deadest corpse, backed away gibbering.

But Plinta himself felt wonderful, like a prince who is in love and has, besides, dined on a banquet. He threw a boot at Colas, and Colas, at last reassured his patron was the same as ever, tramped off to fetch the coffee.

Already the marvellous dream – of the Cathedral, the gargoyles, the vampire and her attentions – was fading. Of the dream-within-the-dream did anything remain? Maybe not. But Plinta soon noticed Israbel had taken her portrait away with her. Why not, when she had bought it, and at an excellent price. Next time he saw it, the picture, he would be again with her.

One last splinter of dream-memory did linger, however. He had asked her where he should meet her, Israbel his sister, now, in blood. But he had been stupid to ask, for Plinta had not needed to. Tonight, as much of Paris knew, Israbel was due to act and sing her glimmering five minutes at the *Opèra*.

Plinta threw his mirror into the cupboard before he left the studio. Now a vampire, he could never again see himself reflected, and had duly proved as much with one or two contemptuous glares at the glass. Others though *would* see him in mirrors, and not suspect, just as Israbel had explained.

Would she be glad, at last, of his company? They were brethren, and she had admitted she had discovered no kindred, just as never again had she located the supernatural cat.

Two moods possessed Plinta, as he walked the glacial streets of

Paris, moving towards the golden ornament of the theatre. One was an elation not unmixed with eager fear. The other was a deep melancholy, a sort of shadow. The first state he comprehended. The second puzzled him. Was he in mourning then for his purely *human* life, now ended? What did that matter? Nothing, not at all. But no, it was not that.

He stood in the light-spiked dark, and thought. Perhaps immortality is only formed, for *us*, from those countless days we may never now experience. A life of nights, doubled.

All things are paid for. Even Israbel had paid for the painting he had made of her.

Plinta took a box at the theatre, a rare extravagance. He soon glimpsed Dumière across the auditorium in a box of his own, with other friends. Dumière saluted Plinta, pleased to see him at a distance. But how jealous Dumière would be, if only he knew. Had he offered Israbel marriage? Israbel and Plinta *were* married, in more than religion or legality. *One flesh*.

Where shall I feed? Plinta thought, as the curtain rose on some spectacular unimportance. *She will show me. She will be my teacher.* Then he sat back, watching the acts of the play through half-closed eyes, and all about the theatre rustled and murmured, whistled and called, alienly alive. He imagined it was like being in the zoological gardens. He had never felt a part of them, the human race, and now was not.

To great clapping and calls, Israbel came out in the fifth act, as the programme stipulated, to perform her part, and sing her aria, which that night was by Rameau.

Plinta sat forward. His eyes widened. His heart, or some more profound mechanism, slammed high into his chest, then leapt away, down in to a chasm. Tears rolled, helpless to save themselves, from his eyes.

If he had been able, in those minutes, like the Biblical Samson, he would have risen, grabbed vast pillars of the *Opéra* temple, and brought it crashing down.

Samson had lost all. Plinta too, had lost.

Now he could never know, he who must learn *everything*, whether or not he had loved her. Instead he would be, like the rest of his kind, bereft, and quite unique.

On the stage Israbel sang, and the audience hung in wild suspense until the last note, then bellowed its applause and flung its flowers. And across the theatre, Dumière sprang up and raced, fever-flushed from his box, to seek her in the dressing-rooms.

But Plinta stayed where he was, still as when Colas had found him and thought him, rightly, dead. Only the mobile tears ran on from Plinta's eyes.

For she had warned him, had she not? Even his mirror, in its own cruelly amusing way, had done so. Certainly his inner dream of facelessness. No vampire could see itself in reflection – only human things could see it there. But that was not *only* in mirrors. No vampire could see *any* vampire – themselves or another, either in a mirror – or anywhere in the whole crystal globe of the heartless, lonely, reflective world. On the stage, Israbel was taking her bow. Plinta alone did not applaud. To him she was now entirely inaudible and invisible, just as he was now entirely inaudible and invisible to Israbel, and to all their kind.

MICHAEL SHEA

The Growlimb

AFTER DISCOVERING A BATTERED copy of Jack Vance's *The Eyes of the Overworld* in a cheap hotel in Juneau, Alaska, Michael Shea wrote a sequel to the book as a homage. Shea then wrote to Vance, asking if he would help get the sequel published and split the take.

Although Vance graciously declined the offer, or to even read another author's addendum to his own work, he did invite Shea to get the work published on his own. The result was *A Quest for Simbilis* (1974).

Since then the author has published more than two dozen stories and novellas, along with such books as the World Fantasy Award-winning *Nifft the Lean*, *In Yana the Touch of Undying*, *The Color Out of Time* (a sequel to H.P. Lovecraft's "The Colour Out of Space"), *Fat Face*, *The Mines of Behemoth*, *The A'rak* and the World Fantasy Award-nominated collection *Polyphemus*.

"I guess I can say I knew this story at least a decade before I wrote it down," Shea reveals. "It's a story I'd learned not just from the haunting terrain of Northern California, but also from the harsher, equally haunting chaparral hills and mountains around my natal Los Angeles."

I N THE OFFICES OF HUMANITY INCORPORATED, Marjorie, Program Director of Different Path, had her own cubicle. From her desk she could look across the floor directly into the corner nook – not a cubicle really, with only a standing screen to half partition it off – where Carl Larken had his desk.

Larken was on the phone, his chair tilted back, his outthrust feet toed under his desktop, his body poised almost horizontal to the floor. In cut-offs and worn Nikes, a brambly grey beard and raked-back grey locks tendrilled on his neck, the man's toughness showed. A lean and sunburned man in his fifties.

Marjorie tried to decide why Larken stood out so. It wasn't his dress. Humanity Inc. was a sizeable human services non-profit, and didn't insist on office drag – most of its program managers had social activist backgrounds and liberal views. What nagged at her was the man's . . . tautness. He was a very personable, articulate guy, sociable on demand, but he had an agenda, an undistracted inwardness. He could be talking to you about your program, deep in the details of a write up with you, showing perfect grasp and sensitive awareness, and you would suddenly know he wasn't really there, was working his tongue and his face like a puppet, flawlessly managing his half of the exchange, lightyears away in his mind. Over the months, she had formed the whimsical but persistent notion that Carl Larken was insane.

She recognised that this secret alienation she saw in him could be a reflection of her own lack of real involvement in her work. She was rich. Her parents owned a flourishing winery.

After her B.A. in Fine Arts, a sense of aimlessness had overtaken her. This job was her Term of Involvement with Reality, an immersion in the hard and hurting strata of the world. Different Path was a criminal-justice diversionary program, counselling and community services for the drug-riddled, the sick and the desperate. She worked it, pulled her Beemer into the lot at eight sharp, waded into her case files, made her house calls, networked with the D.A.'s office – the whole 9 yards.

But ultimately, she didn't believe it made any difference. Didn't believe counselling and community service did a thing for the already-damaged, the already-damned. And her own underlying contempt for her work made her sure of Larken's. It was a felt thing, a sympathetic vibration between them.

Being indifferent, though, was a far cry from being insane. What *was* there about him, when she studied him from a distance like this, that always ended by sending that cold thrill of suspicion up her spine? This conviction that the man was not really here, was deeply, utterly somewhere else?

She had to go meet with a counselling group. On impulse, she went over and leaned into Larken's nook on her way out.

"Hi Carl."

"Hey, Marjorie. The *Press Republican* says they'll run a feature for us."

"Super! Just put the copy on my desk."

"It's done. Take it with you. I'm going for a run soon. If you're out on the road, don't run me over."

A little standing joke. Larken worked a loose schedule, often taking long mid-day runs in the nearby countryside. She'd passed him a number of times, smiling and waving, wondering at what drove the guy – far from young, but every inch of him honed down to sinew and vein and tireless muscle. Heading out, she glanced at the copy of his feature:

> *For those stricken by chemical addictions, shoplifting and other petty property misdemeanours are more the symptoms of an affliction than the acts of a real criminal. At Different Path, with the generous co-operation of the Superior Court of Sonoma County, we take these afflicted folks out of the criminal justice loop, and into a circle of care, counselling, and rehabilitation.*

And so on. The usual. She paused at the exit to the parking lot and glanced back at Larken, balanced on his chair, murmuring into the phone. Those humanitarian homilies that he composed so glibly— they didn't really fit the man at all. He had all the standard smiles, the affable, earnest expressions. But the whole shape and aura of him . . . he looked about as compassionate as a coyote.

Larken's phone interview with "Dan G." was going well. It was amazing what people would just tell you about themselves. Back when he had taught at the Junior College, he'd been delighted by how much personal revelation he could draw from his students with his writing assignments. He was always struck by how *faintly* these kids seemed to feel their own existence. They had to squint to see their own feelings. They had to strain to remember the things they had seen with their own eyes in the course of a single day. But when driven by an instructor, and the need of a grade, they could scrape some of it together, report what life was like for them.

"So Guy, if I have this straight . . ." Guy Blankenship was "Dan G.'s" real name, which Larken had gotten out of him easily enough, ". . . the meth cost you your wife and kids first, and then your house, and now, because you started spiking it, it's given you AIDS. And you're what? Only twenty six?"

"It did a major number on me." This was spoken solemnly, almost with a kind of satisfaction.

"Well I have to tell you that your story is one of the most moving ones I've ever heard, Guy. I want to suggest something to you. I want you to bear with me for a minute here, because I want to suggest an idea to you, and I need to work up to it a little, okay?"

"Sure. I don't mind." And you could hear his comfort with the conversation; Guy was well along in the morphine phase of his AIDS-related cancer.

"Okay. When you look out your window, what do you see? I want to get a feel for your neighbourhood."

"Well. Mim's Market is right across the street, like a mom and pop. And boy, those kids with their skateboards and earrings, they like *live* on the sidewalk in front of it I swear."

"You're on Prince over towards the Fairgrounds, right?"

"Right"

"And if you head down Prince you hit Crestview. You probably turn on Crestview when you go down to the hospital, right?"

"That's right."

"So Guy, did you ever keep going up Crestview, into the hills behind the Fairgrounds?"

"Yeah. Marjorie took us up there to a picnic like just a few days ago."

"Oh right, she told me that. That's a great view up there, isn't it, Guy? Those big crooked oak trees down on the slope below that turnout there? Four centuries old, minimum, those oaks. You remember them, don't you? Huge big crooked old trees?"

"Big trees, yeah, sure."

"Well, just imagine this, okay Guy? Imagine a bluejay landing on one of those trees' branches. Just fluttering down, and landing, pecking up a couple little bugs, *peck, peck*, and then flying right off again. Say he's there four seconds. Imagine how brief, how short, his time in that tree was, compared to the whole span of that tree's life. That bird is just a quick blue blip that scarcely touches the tree at all. And the idea that I want to get across to you, is that's how short your life on this earth will have been, Guy, when you check out a year or so from now. Your whole stay on this glorious green globe will be like that bird's landing and flying off again. It'll hardly have happened at all."

". . . What're you . . . you're sayin', like . . ." The man's morphine patches defintely had him on glide. You could hear him trying to hook in to this idea, startled by suddenly realising that his own existence, and his own death, were the focus of this conversation.

"I'm just telling you I feel for you, man. I wanted to share with you the *poignance* I feel in your situation. My good thoughts go out to you. I'm going to write up what you gave me. We'll talk soon, okay?"

". . . Okay . . ." Guy was more than morphine vague now. You could hear him struggling to bring these imponderables into focus. His own existence. His own death.

Larken gently hung up the phone. He very much craved a run. A couple hours chugging down the country blacktop would bring him back to a nearly empty building, and he could put the last few touches on the corporate newsletter. He slipped into his sleeveless running jersey, its once-black laundered to a light grey. Out the back, he broke into an easy trot across the parking lot.

For a mile or so it was all body shops and strip malls, gas stations and burger chains – lots of cars and mucho monoxide . . . But after that, the street became a county two-lane which ran past rural lots and sprawling fields, some orchards and dairy farms still surviving here and there, but increasingly, grapevines out to the horizons.

He had an easy lope that ate the miles and never tired. He cruised in the tough vehicle of his bone and muscle, lightly oiled with sweat, and thought of his words to Blankenship. Reckless words if the guy should wake up enough to resent them. Reckless if Larken wanted to keep this job.

His problem was this exaltation, this high and reckless humour in his heart. For days now it had filled him, sneaked into him at odd moments as he worked, and set his heart floating. A foretremor of hope. A limbic tingle of something approaching – something approaching at long, long last!

His meditation as he ran was what it always was out here: Behold the visible world! How simply impossibly beautiful it was! The fields, the far-flung quilt of tree-lines over the hills, giant hermit oaks, swollen and crooked with vegetal muscle! Those towering wind-breaks of eucalyptus, cascading with silver applause for the wind! Those hillsides of cattle gorgeously mottled black and white like antique ceramics. Those turkey-vultures hanging on man-sized wing-spans above the roadkill feasts which were spread on the two-lane by the hustling Mercedes, Beemers, and SUVs, above all the pizza-ed possums and skunks decorating the webbed highways . . .

Life! All its parts mortal, but in their aggregate, immortal and unstoppable. Life the star-conqueror. It spread and spread every-where, slipping itself like a green glove over the bare, steaming bones of the universe.

All living things were dangerous miracles. Each tree brimmed with majesty as it wore the light, and the wind moved through it, but anything that lived could blow up in your face. And if you *did* win your own immortality, then you must live it in the web of these mortal lives, and you must endure all of their deaths, death after death after death. And if the beauty of it all – fields farms trees skies suns stars – was almost unendurable now, must not immortality itself kill you if you did attain it? Kill you with all that excruciating beauty?

His run had passed the two-hour mark, and he decided to push to three. First, a piss. In recent years, with San Francisco fortunes being pumped into the wine country, new fencelines and country estates had stripped the roadsides of the margins of old-growth trees and weedy coverts wherein a man might duck to pee concealed. Bleeding your lizard now required thought, and retention skills. He chose a crossroad towards a spot he knew.

There it was. A rank of big old eucalypti stood between the margin of the road and the fence of a vineyard. In a little strip of brush behind the trees stood the roofless ruin of a little cinderblock hut.

Several well-trod footpaths crossed the poison oak and foxtail and blackberry vines, threading through the litter of trash in the weeds outside the hut: cast-off shirts and shoes, a torn, stained mattress. He stepped through the concrete doorframe. In the centre of the heavily littered concrete floor was a little grass-choked drain-grate. He stood there, downloading hours of coffee into it, while high over his unroofed head the cascade-shaped eucalypti splashed and glittered in the breeze.

He liked the square solidity of this cinderblock hull, which he guessed had been a tool shed. Its simple shape, tucked in this green nook, made him think of a little country temple in ancient Greece.

It was surprising how much of the litter in here was discarded clothing. Many a fieldworker who had tended the adjacent vineyard had surely found free sleep-space here in the warm months, and free drinking space, to judge by the beer cans and flattened cardboards of six-packs. Clothes, thrift-store stuff, were something the poor seemed to have in abundance. He noticed, as he was zipping up, that there was one little snarl of clothing, isolated slightly from the rest, that possessed the most amazing suggestion of personality.

Here lay a pair of khaki workpants whose legs seemed to leap, and just above the pants' waist a red-and-black checked flannel shirt, its sleeves wide-flung, which seemed to be the top half of the same leap. To provide the clinching touch, one black tennis shoe lay just below one of the pants leg's cuffs. The shoe presented its sole to the cuff, but in every other respect it was oriented perfectly to become the leading foot of this clothes-fossil's leap. Just rotate the tennie one-eighty around its long axis and the effect would be perfect . . .

With a sense of ceremony, of an augmented silence surrounding him, he bent, and inverted the shoe.

The result was remarkably expressive. This was a grand, balletic leap, an outburst of eloquence and power, a leap of jubilation . . . or an explosive *escape*? A surge of will to be shut of it all, to shed the body with one fierce shake, burst free and clear of the shabby garment of bone and skin.

The strangest surge of inspiration welled up in Larken. He'd noted a roadkilled possum a little way back down he road. Suppose he . . .

Don't weigh it, spontaneity was everything. With a leap of his own, he bolted from the hut, and ran back down the two-lane, retracing his approach.

Here was the possum, flat as a puddle, and baked crispy by several days of summer sun. It was a Cubist possum, where inner and outer possumparts – front, back, left, right – all shared the same plane. Hair, intestine, a ten-key piano-fragment of flattened vertebrae, a spill of teeth surrounding one raisin eye, a parenthesis of sinewy tail as naked as a rat's – all sides of the animal could be possessed at a glance without the trouble of walking around it.

Careful not to pause but to move fluidly at the prompting of his imagination, he took out his Buck knife and sawed through one leathery drumstick, obtaining a hind paw, and then he sawed and peeled free the tail's sharp comma. With his trophies he trotted back to the cinder block hut, feeling surer with each stride, more convinced he had found something real.

Stepping back inside the hut, Larken felt he was stepping into a pool of waiting silence, a tension of expectation. He knelt, and tucked the bone of the leg into the cuff of the hinder pants leg, so the possum's little clawed foot was providing the thrust for the leap. Then he tucked the root of the tail through the rearmost belt loop of the slacks.

This was a decisive, perfecting touch. The little up-curving tail-spike clarified the clothes-fossil's leap. Its emotion was both gleeful and savagely furious. This was a demon's frolicsome, vengeful leap.

And then, as if his enhancements themselves opened his eyes to a further one, he saw something he had not noticed. A little, flattened hat lying not far above the shirt's collar. He darted his hands out, half unfolded the hat, tilted it by half an inch – perfect!

It was one of those small-brimmed fedoras that bookies in old movies wore, and it was now cocked at just the exact angle to be perched upon the clothes-fossil's invisible head.

Larken was captivated. For a long moment he could only stand

and gaze at what he had made. The original fossil was a ghost, and full of a ghost's haunting questions. And these marsupial parts Larken had given it were an answer, a new touch of evolution.

And then he felt a stirring somewhere near . . . and realized there was someone else in the little roofless room with him.

Though the knowledge crackled through him like lightning, he did not move by the slightest fraction. This Someone Else felt far nearer than anything visible could feel. This Someone's presence was like a chord struck ever so lightly, a fugitive coherence that reached his nerves without identifiable route through any of his senses.

Once long before, bellying cautiously up towards some possibly occupied bump in the jungle, Larken had heard (except he could not possibly have really *heard*) the faint *thrumm* of a claymore's tripwire, as the guy off to that side of him tripped it – Harry Pogue, that had been – and Larken had slammed his face in mud with only that precious nano-second of micro-noise for warning, and in consequence, Larken had lived, while Pogue's head had been brightly sprayed across an acre of green.

Not a sound he had heard, no. He'd known it even then. A Someone who had warned, had thrown him a fine filament of intimation, a slender bridge across the abyss of Annihilation Everlasting.

A Someone who was with him now.

What must Larken do? What was wanted? And because he had framed these panicky questions, instead of acting with instant instinct, and drawing understanding after, because in his heart, in his awe, he had hesitated . . . he could not grasp what must be done, could not capture the deep, veiled prompting. The moment passed, and then Larken knew that what this Someone wanted was solitude in this shrine. It wanted his withdrawal.

He backed out of the hut, slowly, ceremoniously, eyes downcast. He should speak something, some acknowledgement, some valediction. Again, his instincts failed him, no inspiration came, and he completed his withdrawal feeling the silence hanging there sullenly behind him, feeling his tongue-tied failure of grace in this first encounter.

Marjorie gave her cell phone number to some of her clients at Different Path. She was wryly aware of a certain insincerity in this "personal touch", because she always left the phone in her Beemer, so she surrendered none of her real privacy with the gesture. It rang as she pulled into the parking structure of the downtown mall. She thought it would be Pat Bonds, her currently significant other, and so Guy Blankenship's vague, whiny voice disoriented her for a moment. She carried Guy and her conversation with him out of the parking structure and into the mall.

"It was like . . . it was un*real*. It suddenly hit me, he was like saying my life, my whole life. It was like this blue bird landing on a branch and pecking twice. My whole life was that short! He just . . . told me that. He just *said* that to me . . ."

Marjorie, making tracks towards the mall's central fountain, where she and Pat were to decide on their dinner destination, was saying things like, "Well that's ridiculous, Guy! You've got your whole life still ahead of you!" but meanwhile the image of those massive old oak trees, of the bluejay's quick flutter and flash among their leaves, struck her imagination indelibly as she strode past windows where Technicolor jellybeans gleamed in barrels, and Technicolor lingerie flaunted on headless white mannequins. And just as vividly, she visualized Guy Blankenship then: his plump red underlip, so slack and unprepared; his narrow, tufted eyebrows—minimal, as if the man was drawn in haste, and economy in materials was a priority.

That this poor, simple guy, his past and his memory of it so abbreviated by childhood abuse and hard drugs' erasure, and his future so short . . . that this Guy should also be seeing that same bird dance on that green bough, that he should be looking at his existence for the first time in his life like a wise man – it struck Marjorie as a minor miracle that Carl Larken had planted this vision in Guy Blankenship's mind.

And this made her see Larken again as she had once seen him, loping along in the dusk past orchards where the gloom had begun to gather under the tangled branches. He was a wolf-lean, muscled shape in her headlights who turned at her honk and waved as she passed. His face was a shadow-holed mask, the brambly hair thick on his brow like undercover he lurked in. She had feared him then, and she feared him now because she realized that something in her applauded the little mental cruelty he had done to Guy Blankenship, that soft little twit from whose fingers the gift of life was leaking so swiftly away.

"I'm going to talk to Carl tomorrow, Guy, about that upsetting kind of talk."

". . . Well . . ."

"I'll call you tomorrow, Guy." She clicked off. There was Pat sitting handsomely ankle-on-knee, on one of the ornate benches

MICHAEL SHEA

surrounding the fountain. He was the picture of understated class. He saluted her with a white-capped Latte, and handed her one of her own as she joined him on the bench.

"Fifty more acres of Zin," he told her. "A done deal."

He was just Marjorie's age, a bright, mellow guy, with a clarity of ambition beyond his years, who unlike her had no trouble with his class identity: a Wine Yuppie and proud of it. Bankrolled by his dad, a corporate attorney in San Francisco, Pat's lack of intellectual pretensions had made him content with the local Junior College for the first two years of his B.A. in Business, and he'd had Carl Larken for an English instructor five or six years ago.

When Marjorie had first described her co-worker to Pat, and they had discovered this funny little piece of common ground, it had struck her that Pat was covertly amused, that he had instantly perceived her hidden interest in the older man. Herself still unsure what that interest was, she told him now how Larkin had tweaked Guy's imagination. "On one level it's kind of a raw thing to do," she offered in conclusion.

"Telling some terminal guy how short his life's gonna be? I guess you could call it that," Pat smiled. "He'd get on that note in class I remember. Mortality, I guess you'd call it."

"I guess you would." Smiling back at him. "Would you say, Pat, that Larken was, well, insane? Like quietly insane?"

There it was, the thing that kept bringing Larken up between them. She thought Pat's eyes confirmed her question, even while he was saying, "I don't know. Everyone's had one or two teachers like that, right? They've got a crazy routine, but they can be really entertaining too sometimes."

She let a beat go by. "Would you say, Pat," (batting her eyes like the question was occuring to her for the first time) "that Larken is, like, quietly insane?"

She wrung a laugh out of him with that. "Well, I remember one time in class, one thing he told us. He compared a guy being blown apart by a mine to a guy dying of old age. He said the years hit the old guy just like the frags hit the soldier – the years blew the old guy to a fog too, they just took longer to impact him . . . But hey, the man acts like he's got a purpose. I see him on the road chuggin' away. Could an insane guy stay in the kind of shape he's in?"

"You still haven't answered me, but screw it. Let's eat. How bout sushi?"

"Sushi rocks."

*　　*　　*

The sun was declining when Larken locked the offices' back door behind him, unlocked his ten-speed, and mounted it.

He didn't head straight home. He pedalled for hours through town, ricocheting randomly through the city's maze, whirring down long ranks of streetlamps, down streets of houses and treed lawns, down streets of neons and flashing signals – trying to wear out the eagerness and fear that struggled inside him.

At last it was time to aim his flight out toward the darkness surrounding the city. Along four miles of lampless two-lane, the last two miles winding through gentle hills, he sped deep into the crickety country night. The waxing moon, well up, said nearly midnight when he steered into the narrow gravel driveway that branched from the road up into his seven acres of wooded slope.

He dismounted and shouldered the bike, and carried it up the drive amidst the tree-shadows. He had spread with his own spade this blue-shale gravel. He practised the skill of silently treading it – liked to come soundless into his property. As he climbed the slope, the leafy gloom chirred with buglife, and breathed down on him the dry scents of bay and manzanita and oak and madrone. Something at least coon-sized skittered in dry leaves upslope of him. A pair of owls were trading their tentative syllables.

He branched from his driveway onto a much narrower deer-trail that crooked its way up, steeply up. Near the crest of his property, on a crescent of levelish ground, a slant-grown oak laid the dome of its branches partly on the grass. Under this crook-ribbed canopy Larken had his sleeping bag. His little aluminium food locker dangled from a branch above his Sierra trail-stove: a number-10 can with its ends cut out and a flap cut in its rim for feeding sticks through. It channelled enough heat from a few handfuls of twigs to boil his oatmeal, and the fire was near invisible at any distance.

He unrolled his leather mat and sleeping bag, and lay half-curled around the little stove and its bubbling one-quart pot of porridge studded with nuts and dried fruits. He garnished his meal with blackstrap molasses and ate it with a spoon, eating faster as it cooled.

Afterwards he lay on top of his bag, looking up at the stars that blazed thick through his oak-leaf dome. These hills were a maze of little valleys – in all directions were pocket vineyards, small ranches, country houses. Here and there, faint in the distance, dogs sometimes barked, taunted perhaps by fox, coyote, coon or bobcat.

His body lay slumped in fatigue, but his senses ate up the wide-flung night. Homecoming tires hissed down on the two-lane, coming fewer and fewer as the stars blazed more thickly. Four-legged things were afoot in several places on his own acres. The peremptory little tearing sounds of what had to be coon paws were shredding something down in the old overgrown garden where potatoes and tomatoes thinly persisted. A clumsier more faintly heard scrabbling, from just about down at the compost heap . . . that would be possum.

The thought conjured the clothes-fossil, never far from his mind these eight hours past. It dawned on him only then. He had found it a footless, anchored thing, but he had left it clawed and shod. And those claws, whose awkwardness on asphalt made the possum the commonest species of road-pizza, made him a nimble traveller up in the trees, a nomad of the arboreal highway.

The Someone Else who joined him in that hut today . . . could he *follow* Larken now?

He lay there on the little piece of earth he owned, trying to detect something like a footfall, or a faint, faint click of claw on branch. Joy and terror hammered at his heart. Could he be on the threshold at last, the threshold of the thing he had sought all his life? He had exiled himself from so much, left his precious family behind – Jolly, his wife, sweet Maxie and sweet little Jack, his daughter and son . . .

He could not bear to think of them, of leaving them behind forever. How many years now? More than three. From that moment of departure, he had stepped into this absolute solitude . . .

Perhaps a half-mile off, coyote voices began kindling, as if in direct answer to his train of thought. Of course the settling in of the midnight chill – as now – was often the signal for their song. Larken was wary of seeing omens everywhere, the mark of the lunatic. Still . . . It had been coyotes who had conveyed to Larken his first revelation – had shown him the promise for whose sake he had left his dearly beloved ones behind. The animals' ghostly sound was wholly undoglike. It was a giddy wailing and hooting, a sardonic gibbering – the music of exiled demons begging for readmittance to the underworld.

Larken had long made a practice of extended moonlit treks through the hills. All this land was owned of course, and so there would be fences even in the deepest hills – fences around the vineyards, around the more sprawling yellow-grass ranches where cattle grazed, around the country estates. He carried a small bolt-cutter for the stubborn few fences he could not otherwise penetrate. When he had to pass near houses, he found it amusing to revive his jungle patrol skills, learned so well in Vietnam, modified for this sparser cover.

His goal was the entry of the hills themselves, to move through them as their inhabitant, as linked to the earth as any fox, as roofed by the sky. His night vision, given only a strong moon to work with, was excellent, as were his skills for quiet movement, and he had surprised many a deer on his travels, a silver fox, and twice a wildcat, but never, before that night, a coyote.

It seemed they caught your slightest move a mile away, and politely, invariably declined contact. And yet they went everywhere in these hills. They fed from men's very decks and porches, fearlessly devouring unwary cats and small dogs practically from their owners' laps. The coyotes filled their world to the brim without once confronting the simian squatters who claimed every foot of it, and roared up and down their roads killing every other natural denizen – even, rarely, the foxes – but never, to Larken's knowledge, claiming a single coyote as roadkill. Like colliding galaxies, the two nations drifted right through each other – or theirs drifted through ours.

It had been a windy night, that night where his life had taken its turning. The atmosphere, in flood, was trying to wash the trees right off the hills. The big oaks twisted and shuddered like black flames in the moonlight, and the white grass rippled and bannered.

The wind that night made him feel his chronic longing. The wind, trying to stampede the trees, was roaring for a grand, universal departure to another solar system, a better deal, and the grass struggled to join the rootless giant of the air. All that lives strives to fly, to master time. All tribes of beings strain to rise in insurrection, all knowing their time is short, all, when the wind blows, wanting to climb aboard.

He climbed in the wind's teeth, up to the last ridgeline before the plain, where the city glowed. He rounded a hill-shoulder towards a vantage point he liked when, completing the curve, he stopped just short of walking into three coyotes who were oppositely bound. All four of them froze, and stood staring at each other.

The gibbous moon, declining at Larken's back, put a glint in the six canine eyes. He looked at each in turn, and settled on the eyes, not of the largest, but of the one who stood foremost, a lean bitch with a jaw that was slightly crooked.

He was moved by their beauty, not at all uncomfortable. At first he thought they were shocked, embarrassed even at this direct discovery. Animal etiquette would call for a slow side step, a careful withdrawal that avoided any signal of a wish to flee, but the bitch, head low, stood planted, fixedly regarding him. Though the wind was contrary, she dabbed her nose towards him. The two males flanking her then did the same, were probably her big-grown pups, still in training for all their size.

The fixity of their stare became fascinating to him. He dabbed his own face at them, snuffed their air, in case this was a necessary greeting. Snuffed, and a whiff of something ice-cold came to him.

It was a scent of . . . terror. Awe. The coyotes reeked of it . . . it was raising their hackles, was causing them to crouch and tense . . .

He watched enraptured, until it dawned on him, *finally* came to him. He turned – the turning seemed to take forever – turned to look behind him.

Hovering above the wind-whipped grass, revealed against the distant fields of city lights behind it, something towered in the air, a transparent something that twisted the light-field into a snarled weave, as if the lights were a coloured net just barely containing the fight of a huge translucent catch.

Even as he struggled to make out its giant form . . . it was no more. The moonlight dissolved it. The city lights gleamed undisturbed.

The wild dogs stirred now, shaking off their holy awe. They gazed at Larken a moment, perhaps with interest. Then they turned, wet muzzles glinting in the moonlight, and melted into the grass.

Larken stood there. All his life – long before 'Nam, which had just clarified it – all his life he had longed to find this doorway, this path that could lead him off the treadmill of time and death.

His legs buckled under, he dropped like lead and sat in the deep grass, staring at the lightfield where that Someone had stood. He found himself slowed to a synchrony with the earth-clock itself, and sat there unmoving as the starfield inched across the sky. He then knew that when he returned to his wife and children, it would be to take his leave of them forever.

He knew he had been mocked in this revelation. Here he'd been tramping through the night, the earnest searcher, while the power and glory he was dogging followed him unperceived.

How long had this Someone mocked him? Back through the decades, had every cloud of crows that burst in flight before him been, in reality, exploding in mirth at oncoming Larken with his giant follower, the derisive god behind him unperceived?

Well, it was the gods' prerogative to mock. Larken had been shown at last. He had accrued fifty years of spiritual hunger, poverty and nonentity and finally, it seemed, had amassed his down payment on eternity.

Oh the price! It was an unending agony to pay, to be denied forever dear Jolly, sweet, sweet Maxie and Jack. But it was a father's place to die before his children, to show them, with his calm as he steps out into the great Dark, that they have nothing to fear, that their own path will be bearable. How could he abide with them while they aged year by year, and he aged no further? Far easier for them to know no more of him beyond tonight, than to learn that he was not of their world, and was to live beyond even his own memory of their existence.

So when that morning's sun rose, Carl Larken had turned forever onto his present path, and lived in solitude.

He smiled a barbed smile now that tore his heart, and he felt the scald of bitter tears. He'd put down everything he had that very day – turned aside from his life. And the careless god, having beckoned him, had left him hanging, utterly alone, these three years since.

But what are years to a god? What are a man's tears? And now the god, or perhaps the god's messenger, had touched him between the eyes, and run a finger down his spine. Said *Yes. I am here.*

Larken crushed out his coals, washed out his oatmeal pan from the jug of water in his food locker – locked everything up and rehung it from the branch. Then he carried his mat and sleeping bag out from under the oak to a level spot, and lay down, still clothed, on top of the bag, lay scanning the thick strew of stars.

And heard, or almost heard, that faint, clawed tread – the clothes-ghost he had conjured, coming now, drawing nearer, coming to offer Larken what he had lived for. Coming to tell him the price.

He realized it didn't matter whether he actually heard this or not. Because now, after fifty-five years, he was about to step up to his threshold, and confront the god. This had now been granted. He knew it in his spine.

Strangely, the most immediate effect on him was not jubilation, but a renewed agony at the price he had paid for this victory. Dear Christ, his precious Jolly! His precious Maxie, and little Jack! Eternal exile from them! How had he mustered the strength, the resolution?

They were his only riches, a fortune he had stumbled blindly into, undeservingly. His and Jolly's first years together, after he had come back, drugged and raging, from the war, had been dissolute years. They drank and drugged and fucked and fought. On the wings of substances, as they took wobbly flight together, he had tried to show her his most private faith – his mad hope that time could be broken like shackles, and a soul, a fiercely desiring sould, could burn forever.

But then priceless, accidental Maxie befell them, and Jolly became wholly Mother overnight. Larken himself took three more years, sullenly sucking booze and powders, before turning to at last, and taking on his fatherhood. By then, equally accidental Jack had arrived, and the rusty doors of Larken's heart were forced all the way open.

In that deep, tricky torrent of parental love and nurturing, the next fourteen years fled away. The immortal fire persisted in Larken's inmost self, but he could not share it with his children. He found it a faith too perilous to speak – a magic he would lose if he tried to bestow it. His children's minds grew strong and agile, but he could not find the words. Before he knew it, Maxie was in middle school, Jack just graduating elementary. Behold, they had friends, passionate interests, lives laid out before them in the world! They had already left him when at last the god vouchsafed to beckon him. Only that made it possible for him to renounce them.

He wiped his tears and listened to the night. The price he had paid was past counting, but his purchase was vast. He had bought nothing less than this whole world, night and day, north and south, now and forever. Was he insane, to feel this reckless certainty? Wasn't this blasphemy? Hubris? Wouldn't it cost him his prize?

He could not think so. This bitter joy refused to leave him. He listened to the night, deep night now, where living things moved quietly about their mortal business. Upslope of him, deer moved very carefully, small-footed through the scarcely rustling oak leaves. Far down on the two-lane he heard the faint, awkward *scritch* of a skunk (awkward as possums, skunks) beginning to cross the asphalt.

Whoops. Far down the two-lane, the beefy growl of a grunt-mobile. Enter Man on the stage of night, roaring high, wide and handsome in a muscle-truck – a tinny sprinkle of radio music above the roar. Closing fast, with a coming-home-from-the-bar aura. It must be just after two . . .

Larken listened to the tires as it roared near, roared past – and yes, there it came, that *whump-crunch-thumpa-thumpa* as the skunk was taken for a high-speed dribble down the court beneath the 60-mile-an-hour underframe of the truck.

He lay listening. All the dyings! Everywhere, all the time. The coyotes announced themselves, very far off now, but with the gibbering intensity of a group kill. Webbed wings made a tiny, soft commotion – a bat, zig-zagging bugs from the air. All the mulch, all the broken, gutted things settling down to decay . . . He felt a shift in his bowels.

He rose and got his little entrenching tool, and a small canteen of water – set out slantwise up the hill, and upwind of his camp.

High on the slope, he crouched on a crescent of deep soil, and a fine, round shit came loose from him. Filling his cupped hand from the canteen, he washed and rinsed himself, and washed his hands. He buried his accomplishments, thinking how coyotes and foxes left their skat right on the trail. When those animals retraced their steps at later times, they nosed the skats and knew themselves, sniffed the ghosts of previous meals. Each time they nosed the fading map of former days, the ever-fainter proofs of their own being, dwindling to rumours. Was this their sense of Time?

Men, more murderous animals, secreted their shit, hiding the lees of their innumerable victims . . . fearing vengeance?

Larken must make an offering to the clothes-ghost. Tomorrow. Must give it . . . something for a heart.

Precisely at the sun's first kindling on the eastern hills, Larken, his bike propped by a tree, stood again before the little cinderblock shrine.

He had pedalled for an hour in the dawn's light, scouting the country roads for a fit offering. He had hoped for the rare luck to find something he'd happened on before: a road-struck animal whose life had not yet left it. He remembered once running, and coming up eye to eye with a possum that had not yet finished dying. There was still a little bit of him left there in his inky little possum's eyes. The beast was looking back forgetfully at life, looking into Larken's eyes forgetful that he was human, seeming to struggle to remember something they had in common long ago . . .

Had he been given such a find it would have amounted to an omen from the god that his improvised ritual was welcomed. As it was, he found a rare enough thing indeed – a silver fox, whose bush, ruffled by the breeze, had caught his eye. The fox was beautifully intact – back-broken, not mauled – and dead not very many days.

This was much, he reflected as he eased it into his old khaki knapsack. Enough to be a kind of warrant from the god. Foxes, these sharp-muzzled tricksters, were almost never nailed by monkey Man's grunting pig machines. Larken had to pedal hard to bring this rarity to the shrine before the sun's rising, and he made it there just at the instant that the first light struck the grey wall.

He knew, seeing that, that this rite of his was welcomed, and the god was present to receive his offering.

He stepped inside, his knapsack cupped before him in both hands. The clothes-ghost seemed to float on the floor, to glow, so full of feral insolence, of fierce and graceful glee its posture was. Under the hat's slanted bill, the spark of an eye almost glinted. The jauntiness of that up-hooked tail, the sinewy thrust of that clawed foot . . . It *knew*!

Larken knelt down slowly on one knee. He felt the ghost's seething aura of energy, waiting for Larken to find the awakening magic to give it form and force.

He drew the reeking fox-that-was from the sack. Sun had shrunk its tendons, and there was a stiffness that made the little corpse more wieldy. He gripped the grey pelt at the spine just below the neck, and with his other hand, lifted one flap of the ghost's shirt. He felt no need for words. He shrouded the fox inside the ghost's shirt, willing spirit into this inhuman gatekeeper. His hidden hand felt in an alien space, felt the heat and menace of a hostile dimension.

Just as he withdrew his hand, it was powerfully, searingly bitten. Torn to the bone, both the palm and the back of his hand. Blood, its astonishing crimson, welled blazing out of him in the morning light.

He stood staring at his hand full of blood.

Was this a message?

What was the message?

He became aware that an engine, something big and huffy, was idling not far off. Larken had to stand a moment, struggling to decide if the sound came from that eternal world where his hand had been torn, or from this one his feet were planted on.

He seized up a sun-bleached fragment of T-shirt from one corner, bound his hand and knotted it with his teeth. The bandage went instantly red as he thrust the hand inside the light windbreaker he wore. His bike outside already declared him. He stepped out into the slanting sun, picked up his bike with his left hand, and stepped through the trees to the road with it. A young man stood by a black Jeep Cherokee, arm draped on the roof.

Larken smiled easily at him, straddled his bike with his hand still tucked away, stood on one pedal and slowly coasted over to him.

"The pause that refreshes," he said to the young man who, looking surprised, said:

"Mr Larken!"

Larken, when teaching junior college, had infallibly Mistered and Mized all his students, and after a beat, he said, "Mr Bonds! This *is* a pleasure! Is this your . . . estate you're viewing?"

Pat was remembering Marjorie's question yesterday. No doubt about it, there was something subtly but deeply not normal about this guy. He steps out of a ruined shed at dawn, steps smiling out of the trees with his hidden hand making what looked like it might be a bloodstain in the armpit of his jacket, then cruises over to Pat, totally suave and smiling. And not only does he remember Pat after what, six years? But he even remembers the little standing jokes between them about Pat's pragmatism, his fiscal realism, his good-humoured disinterest in big ideas.

The old man had a real . . . charisma. A complete self-possession. But sitting here with a bloodstain spreading across his jacket, having just stepped out of a fucking abandoned shed at sunrise . . . his self-possession looked more than a little unreal.

"I don't own these grapes themselves. I'm in the development sector of the viticulture industry. We design acquisitions, financing. We're going to get fifty more acres of zin out of this field."

Larken looked across a sea of grapes from fence to fence. "Where are you going to get it?"

"Here and there along the margins. We'll get a good ten acres here when we tear out that shed and this border strip."

At this Larken just nodded, but he let a beat go by. "Are you leaving any eucalyptus?"

"Just one line at the roadside. We'll take those out later this year. They create a shadowing problem for the new acres." Pat found himself getting a little stiffer as he went on. He still *amused* Larken on a level he didn't get. That was okay when he was the guy's student – a teacher is supposed to run some attitude on you, poke at your perspective. But this man, this whacko old man with his chickenfeed job, found something genuinely funny about the way Pat was, after all, engineering this entire environment here.

And Larken seemed to sense his thought. "A world-shaper," he smiled at Pat. "I saw it long ago."

"Well, every generation *shapes* things, right? Every generation makes what they can, builds what they can make use of."

"You are absolutely right, Mr Bonds. You can't take a single step on this old globe without changing it. So when are you clearing this section?"

"Tomorrow." And Pat had scored something, he felt it. Where's your contempt for money and power now, he asked the old man in his mind. There's something he values here, and just twenty-four hours from now I'm making it disappear.

Then Larken smiled again. "Time is on the wing, isn't it? On the *wing*. Which reminds me, I've got to get to work. Good to see you!"

When Larken had pedalled off, right hand still tucked beneath his arm, Pat entered the weedy margin behind the trees. He wondered how he'd failed to ask Larken how he hurt his hand. He stepped into the cinderblock shed.

Nothing. Trash and discarded clothing everywhere. Just a useless eyesore. A perfect place to be scraped clean. Developed.

As he climbed back in his jeep, he thought of Larken's eyes, grey eyes under shaggy brows. There was an intention behind those eyes, something fixed and unyielding. What might a trashy nook like this one here mean to a war-scarred old guy like that, a bookish man of the kind who brooded about big ideas. Who could tell? The fact remained that, just meeting Larken's eyes as he'd emerged from that shed, Pat Bonds had felt like a trespasser here.

Marjorie was northbound on 101. The 3:00 p.m. traffic was clotting and creeping around her, still five miles south of town, where she was already fifteen minutes late for coffee with Pat at Espresso Buono. When she reached him on his cell phone, she could tell that he too was carbound.

"Where are you Pat?"

"101. I'm just above Novato."

"Christ you're thirty miles behind me. I'm just north of Rodent Park."

"Things ran late at the title company."

"It's kind of romantic, Pat, the two of us just cruising the traffic-stream together, trading sweet nothings."

"Are you actually *cruising* that close to town?"

"Actually no, it's creep and crawl . . ." Should she tell him? On the phone like this? "I was just down in Petaluma. I had to go see the mother of the guy I told you about, Guy Blankenship? He had morphine patches, right? Well he, like, put on half a dozen of them last night. He overdosed. He's dead. He left a note, or he started a note. It said *tell Carl*."

"Whoa."

"Right. Well the police asked me about it. It's a wrongful death, right? I said I didn't know who it was. I said I'd look into it and maybe get back to them."

"Did you tell Larken?"

"He didn't come to work today, and he doesn't have a phone."

A little silence passed between them. Marjorie was picturing Carl Larken out for a run along some two-lane. She pictured the city ahead of her and thought of it semi-abstractly as an environment, as the habitat of Larken. That gaunt greybeard, implacable as Jeremiah. Picturing him like this, it seemed incredible to her that she had not seen his madness sooner. He was no longer a creature of civilization. He was like an animal that infiltrated the city by day, and returned to the hills by night. The man was almost auraed with otherness.

"Hey Marjo? Tell the police. It's no harm to Larken. They'll hard-time him a little is all, and maybe he needs a little accountability check here."

Marjorie laughed, thinking of the vivid Mrs Blankenship, whose ramshackle house she had just left – the woman a bleached, cigarette-throated, leather-vested speedfreak. "No harm? If they told his mother, and she found someone smart enough to help her with it, she'd sue the Humanity Incorporated's socks off."

"You know, I ran into him this morning . . ."

Larken lost himself in an endless patrol, bee-lining across the hills. He carried his little bolt-cutter for the stubbornest fences. He crossed pasture and vineyard and tree-choked stream course. Carefully void of intention, he chose his course as randomly as he could.

In these hills he had at last been shown, invited. Now, as Time closed in on him, these hills must show him his next step. He gripped this faith and patrolled them, hour after hour.

The sun had begun to wester. When he was startled out of his walking reverie, he was amazed to realize just how oblivious he'd been. Aware of nothing but these acres of rolling pasture dropping away before him, when close behind him, a voice said, "I see you have a bolt-cutter there. Is that what you used to cut through my fence?"

When he turned, here was a frail old woman walking towards him from a Jeep – the old fashioned military-looking kind – parked a short way down the fire-break path his feet had been treading so automatically.

The lady wore khaki work clothes, and a grey canvas hat with a little circular brim. She was so frail; hair as wispy as web escaped the hat. She was frail and there was something else about her – a scent he could almost pick up. "You've done it before too, haven't you?" she urged, her voice very level, though age made it waver slightly. "You like to follow a bee-line across people's property."

Larken smiled gently. "You've determined to call the devil by his name, right to his face, hesitation be damned," he said with admiration. "From now on you're not going to waste time with caution."

"I never have. You talk about caution. Am I in danger here from you?"

He had been honestly absorbed in her. She would be an omen, of course! Part of the answer he was after. But when she asked him this question, it stunned him for a moment, the alienness of the notion that he should lift his hand against her frailty. And in that moment he identified that faint scent she had. Chemotherapy.

"You are correct, Ma'am," he was saying, "I do make bee-lines. I damage as little fence as possible, but sometimes I need to follow the route I'm feeling. You are in absolutely no danger from me. I'm afraid I might have a pretty uncouth appearance, but I'm a good person. I did two tours in Vietnam, a lot of them in-country, and I guess it's left me a little reclusive."

The slopes of dried grass below them were growing golder in the slanting sun. That rich light flooded her face with such detail! Blue veins across her forehead, the fine-china translucence of her wrinkled eyelid, her hair's sparseness betrayed by the looseness of her hat . . . She watched him as he spoke, not so much listening to his words as following her own train of thought about him. "You tell me I've decided not to waste time on caution. You seem to be telling me that I'm obviously someone with not much time left. Suppose that's true. Why should that make me care any less about vandalism to my property?"

"When I ventured that description of your state of mind, Ma'am, I meant to express my admiration. I don't dispute the wrongness of damaging your fence. My trespass was totally impersonal, and I did no harm to your property—"

"Except to its boundary!"

"Except to its fence. May I guess, Ma'am? Are you that little beef ranch, a hundred acres or so, triple-strand barbed wire?" Her icy look was as good as a nod. "I will of course pay you whatever damages you see fit."

Again she seemed – rather than listening – to be struggling to digest him. "I've seen you on the roads, you know, over the years – running, cycling. I've seen you running out of your driveway. You call yourself a recluse, and I've had exactly that thought about you as I drove past, that you were a kind of hermit. Completely in your own world."

"But aren't you completely in yours?"

"Are you hinting again? That you know I'm dying?"

"I'm just trying for an understanding. I'm dying too."

"Not as fast as I am." Almost wry here, her fragile, skull-stretched face. He could sense her mood exactly. She was partly lured by an unlooked-for understander of her plight, but equally was stung by his understanding. In the pinch, she reverted to legalities. "I called the sheriff on my cell phone as soon as I found the damage, and I told them I suspected you. I felt a little bad about that, not being positive, but then I took the jeep out, and found you practically red-handed."

Understanding flooded Larken. This woman was not an omen to him, she was more than that. She was *in herself* a gift, a token of passage. He understood now the garish Sign that had been given him, in return for his morning's offering: his right hand full of blood.

"I'm sure, of course," she was saying, "that the officers, after writing up a report, will let us settle it between ourselves."

All this golden light! It was beginning to shade over to a voluptuous red-gold. Hills rolled away on all sides, and the two of them stood bathed in this ocean of light, and at the same time, they were utterly unwitnessed by another human being. Perfectly alone together in all this big emptiness, with the royal sun alone looking on. Larken, before setting out on his day's quest, had made and properly tied a bandage for his right hand, though the red stain had seeped through even this one. Perhaps because she sensed his own sudden awareness of it, she took note of his wound for the first time. "How did you hurt your hand?"

He smiled apologetically. "I was bitten."

"Bitten by what?"

"I was bitten by a god. A god who is about to break out from these hills. Is about to hatch from them. He has promised me . . . immortality."

He had her full, bemused attention. He pulled the bandage off his hand. Out of the deep tear in his flesh, black-scabbed though it was, the naked tendons peeked.

The setting sun gilded the trenched meat, and it glowed like a sacrament.

Deep night. The county road far below him had at last gone quiet and empty.

The darkness, even after these long hours of it, still felt like a balm to Larken, as if the bright work of blood-spilling that he had done today had scorched his retinas, and made sunlight agony to them.

He lay far upslope under one of his oak trees, his own hillside rock-solid under his back. He lay perfectly still, wholly relaxed, so that the vast crickety sound of the night felt like a deep lake he sank in, deeper with each heartbeat into the creaking, trilling music of the earth's nocturne.

And then, woven into that vast music, it began to be faintly, sinisterly audible.

So far off at first, so sketchy: a jostle of leaves . . . a friction against bark. An approach. Something moving through the leafy canopy, something small and very far, picking its way from branch to branch. It meandered, finding its path through contiguous trees, but it was seeking him.

To Larken's ears this faint advance might as well have been thunder, for there was nothing else in the world but it. Because the earth was opening beneath him. This visitation he had bought with human blood would leave him changed forever, would actually begin his removal from this world, and his advance toward eternity. He lay there, waiting as he had waited all his conscious life, to step off of the earth, and into the universe.

It wasn't as small as it had sounded, now that it was working its way up the slopes of Larken's property. He began to hear a muscular agility, which had helped to mute its approach but, nearing, betrayed a solid mass laddering its way through the branches and boughs.

Just a short way down the slope from where he lay, his visitant came to a stop. In the short silence that followed, Larken felt an alien intent grow focussed on him.

Sssssssst

It was a summons, and its echo changed the air as it drifted up among the oaks and madrones. The night mist grew more spacious, its very molecules drawing apart, as if mimicking the separations of the stars themselves.

He got to his feet, and doing so took forever, his legs, hands, arms slow travellers across the interstellar emptiness that had entered each cubic foot of the night air. He threaded downslope through bushes-manzanita, scrub oak, bay, scotch broom – that were abstract silhouettes, like archetypes, but whose odours, rich and distinct, filled him with a terrible nostalgia for that mortal world that he was now abandoning.

He stopped, doubting that he dared, after all, all, all . . . to do this. It spoke again instantly, in answer to his hesitation:

Sssssssst

Down he walked, dazed but footsure, stepping down through eons of mist and shadow . . .

Here was the big oak tree that marked an arc of level ground where Larken's long-defunct compost patch lay. Up in its branches was where his caller awaited him. It seemed that from the tree's overarching mass a fine, impalpable panic rained down. As if the tree itself, that crooked old leafy mortal, radiated its terror at what this man was bent on doing. Larken stood in this faint rain of fear, like a warning breathed down by the tree.

Though his fear was dire, his hesitation had left him. His legs had carried him too many miles and years on this path to retreat from its terminus.

Its terminus, this compost patch – a sunken crust now which the oak's canopy overhung. A dried, sunken vegetal crust which to Larken was terror itself, a patch of Absolute Zero. He came to the brink of the worst place on earth.

There was a small, energetic commotion in the oak's lower branches. Feet, shod in something like track shoes but gaudier, dangled into view from a lower branch. These shoes were blazoned with stripes and chevrons in sweeping curves of some glossy material coloured copper and silver, and dully luminous, burnished, giving off an inner light. Short legs followed, too-short legs sheathed in baggy cholo-pants whose excess material stacked in bulges on the shoes' tops.

This was the dreadful ripening of what Larken had lived to summon, and only the combined weight of his whole past life – though such a frail, slight weight it seemed now! – sufficed to hold him steady on his legs, sufficed to plant him to confront this strange fruit's falling, at long last.

The visitant dropped to the ground and stood entire upon the crusty mat. He was a natty little monster three feet high. The whiskered, 'gator-toothed snout of a possum was likest to the face he thrust forth with a loll-tongued leer of greeting. He was jauntily hatted with a snap-brimmed bookie's fedora of straw – or woven brass? For it glowed like dirty dull gold. The hat was cocked arrogantly over one beady black eye. His baggy black sports coat was hung up at the back on the upthrust sickle of his tail, a huge rat's tail, a stiff, dried tail, a comma of carrion whose roadkill scent Larken caught on the cold air of this eternity.

The visitant hissed, *Feeeed me* – its tongue, a limber spike of black meat, stirring in its narrow nest of canines.

Larken discovered at his side something he had not noticed: a shovel standing upright, stabbed into the earth.

Stepping out of an airplane into an alien night sky above Vietnam had been nothing to this, but Larken did it in the same kind of here-I-go instant: he took up the shovel, and stabbed it into the scab of compost.

He dug, knowing without thinking exactly where to dig.

It was his own heart he shovelled out chunks of and spilled to one side.

The shovel was heavy and cold, did not warm to his hands. It was time's tooth, chewing up lives and spitting them out. It bit out his heart, and dumped it to one side.

He had not understood. He would not have done it if he had known how they were to serve.

Careful, very careful he was near the depth that he knew. He knelt at the last, and scraped the soil away with his hands.

He uncovered a little arm, the slender, bow-and-arrow arc of two bones, the flesh all but mouldered away. He stood up and turned away, his tears streaming down for those precious bones, that little arm.

The visitant's steps crunched across the compost. Something much more massive than that dapper little monster it sounded like. The monster's littleness was so dense with greed, as dense as the heart of a neutron star.

Larken stood with his back turned, tears streaming, as the Messenger feasted behind him, as it ripped at the compost and soil in a horrid undressing of the precious bodies sleeping in their garment of earth. The sound of its feeding, the gnashing and guttural guzzling, long it lasted, and he would carry that sound into eternity.

When the meal was done, the visitant spoke again.

The price is two more. They are here . . .

And Larken heard a distant purr and crackle, car tires crunching up his drive. He turned and saw glints of headlights far below, and the beam of a patrol car's searchlight climbing the twisted ribbon of gravel.

The first officer said, "Christ. It's abandoned." Their headlights, as they pulled up onto the narrow plateau where the driveway ended, flooded against a little house walled in weeds and vines, its roof a thick sloping scalp of dead leaves a foot deep sprouting grass also dead now in the dry fall.

They got out and splashed their flashlight beams across windows opaque with rain-spotted dust. They approached the gaping front door, and poured their beams inside, across furniture blurred by dust and leaves and cobwebs.

"Christ," echoed the second officer. "We're not gonna find him here."

The first shrugged. "Some indications of whereabouts, maybe."

They moved farther into the house, and the floor felt the same underfoot as the ground had. Their beams woke a startling scuttle and scramble of animal paws. They tried light switches that didn't work. Kitchen and living room conjoined with no wall between. The second officer began to search these rooms.

The first officer followed a short hallway farther inside. The hallway was festooned with dusty cobwebs, and behind this dust, was walled with books, books, books, their ranked titles like muffled shouts and exclamations choking in the dark.

Insanity. Right here. If the guy's brain was packed with all these mummified shouts, then the missing woman was dead. The officer, though he tingled with this intuition, dismissed it as ungrounded, at least so far. There was no denying, though, that to leave a house like this, just abandon it with everything in it, indicated some kind of insanity, if it didn't prove homicide. The door to the bathroom opened off this hall.

Tacked to the bathroom door was a drawing. It was clearly a very old one, done with pencils and colored markers. It was divided in panels on an oversize sheet of art paper. In each panel the father, small daughter and smaller son appeared to be self-drawn. The panels presented a narrative: the trio find their cat nursing five kittens. The family dog licks the kittens while the mother cat stands by with raised hackles and fluffed-out tail. They carry the kittens in a box. They stand in front of a supermarket with the box, the little girl handing a kitten to another little girl. The kittens look like slugs with pointed ears and tails. Dad is clownishly self-drawn with big ears and wild hair, the little girl very precisely drawn with pony tail and bangs and a pretty dress, the boy drawn with barely controlled energy, head and limbs various in size from panel to panel, hair all energetic spikes.

The officer heard a shift of mass, a sigh.

"Ted?"

A big, sinewy shape stood in his flashlight beam. The officer struggled to clear his sidearm.

"I'm sorry," the shape said sadly, and cut his throat.

Up before sunrise. Marjorie hated getting out of bed in the dark, but loved the payoff once she was dressed and rolling down the country roads in the first light, cruising and owning them almost alone. The countryside here used to be a lot more interesting, though. She remembered it in her girlhood – orchards, small ranches, farmhouses, each one of these houses a distinct personality . . . Money, she thought wryly, scanning the endless miles of grapevines, all identically wired and braced and drip-lined, mile after mile – money was such a powerful organizer.

As the dawn light gained strength, and bathed the endless vines in tarnished silver, it struck her that there was, after all, something scary about money, that it could run loose in the world like a mythic monster, gobbling up houses and trees, serving strictly its own monstrous appetite.

But there was Pat and his crew ahead. A bright red Japanese

earthmover – skip-loader in front, back-hoe behind – had already
bladed out the wide strip of bramble and weed between the vineyard
fence and the roadside rank of eucalyptus. The mangled vegetation
had already been heaped in a bright orange dump-truck which was
now pulling out for the dump, passing Marjorie as she approached.
The next load the truck would be returning for had not yet been
created, but Marjorie could see what it would be. The earthmover,
with its backhoe foremost now, stood confronting the cinderblock
shed. The hydraulic hoe's mighty bucket-hand rested knuckles-down
against the earth, like the fist of a wrestling opponent, awaiting the
onset. Its motor idled while its short, stolid Mexican operator had
dismounted to confer with Pat.

And instantly Marjorie forgave money, loved and trusted it again,
seeing all this lustrous sexy powerful machinery marshalled to
money's will. And just look at that cleanness and order it had
created. Where there had been tangle and dirtiness and trash before,
was now clean bare dirt, reddish in the rising light, beside the
columned trees.

Pat stepped smiling out to the road. "Good morning! You look
radiant!"

"I look that tired, huh?"

"Nothing some Espresso Buono won't fix when we head out of
here. I didn't expect you'd actually come out."

They hadn't been able to make yesterday's date, Marjorie going
instead to make her report to the police, but they'd agreed she might
meet him for this morning's early business. Why exactly had she
come? "I figured," she said sweetly, "that if we grabbed a date this
early, we'd actually get to see each other."

He nodded, but added, "Did you have the thought that Larken
might show up?"

"Yeah. You've had the thought too?"

"I guess I have. Look, pull off into that drive down there. This
won't take half an hour. Come watch this Nipponese brute do its
stuff."

She pulled off about a hundred feet downroad, in the driveway of
the fieldhands' little house. As she parked she saw Pat in her rearview, lifting his arm in greeting to someone beyond him. She got out
and saw, about a hundred feet uproad of Pat, Carl Larken come
coasting on his bike, a pack on his back, one bandaged hand raised in
salute.

He dismounted still a little distance off, leaned his bike on a tree,
and began walking towards the men and their machine.

Marjorie had to gather herself a moment before approaching. She must tell Carl simply and honestly about the report she'd made. It was not, after all, a criminal matter, but there would have to be discussions with the police. There were accountability issues here. She began to walk towards them, had taken three steps, when she felt a wave of nausea move up into her through her legs.

She froze, utterly disoriented by the sensation. The ground beneath her feet was . . . feeding terror up into her body. She stood, almost comically arrested in mid-stride. What was this panic crawling out of the earth? It had something to do with Carl Larken down there, approaching the men from the opposite direction, something to do with the impact of his feet on the fresh-scraped earth.

Look at his slow liquid gait, all muscle up his legs and arms. He was so *here*, he pressed with impossible mass against the earth. Suddenly all this regimented greenery, this whole army of rank-and-file vegetation, seemed to belong to him, while Pat and his helper and their bright machine had a slightly startled, caught-in-the-act air.

Marjorie gripped the trunk of a eucalyptus, but even the hugeness of the tree against her felt flimsy in this radioactive sleet of fear that was blazing from the ground beneath them both.

Pat and the operator stood slack-shouldered beside the red steel monster. Larken came to within fifteen feet or so, and stopped. It seemed to Marjorie, even at her little distance, that the mass of him dented the earth, putting the two lighter men in danger of falling towards him. His voice was gentle.

"Good morning, Mr Bonds. Señor." (a faint smile for the operator) "I'm really sorry to intrude. I have to make use of this . . . land you own. It is a purely ceremonial thing, and executed in mere moments. Would you bear with me, Mr Bonds? Indulge an addled old pedagogue for just a moment?"

"You say you want to perform a *ceremony*, Mr Larken?" It was odd how much frailer Pat's voice sounded than Larken's. The idling earthmover half drowned him out with a surge in its engine's rumble.

"A simple ceremony, Mr Bonds. An offering, plainly and briefly made."

"You want to do it . . . in that shed?" Again the earthmover engine surged, and half-erased Pat's words, his little laugh at the strangeness of his own question.

"This spot of earth, right here, is all I need. The god I'm praying to is here, right underfoot of us."

The man's utter madness was out, it loomed before them now. But in that moment it was the others who seemed unreal to Marjorie.

Hugging her tree, melted by her terror out of any shape to act, she found Pat and the operator, the Jeep and the 'dozer, all too garish to be real – like bright balloons, all of them, taut, weightless, flimsy.

Pat, helpless before Larken's perfect nonsense, made a gesture of permission that was oddly priest-like, an opening-out of hands and arms.

Larken unslung his knapsack, and cupped it in both hands before him, tilted his head back slightly, his eyes searching inwardly. Marjorie, stuck like lichen to the tree's trunk, a limbless shape, a pair of eyes only and a heart with the earthquake-awe in it – Marjorie understood that the strange man was searching for the right words. Understood too now that the rumbling of that 'dozer's engine was awakening this sensation of earthquake underfoot.

Larken chose his words. "I have been your faithful seeker, your faithful servant, forsaking all others! All others! I make you now your commanded offering. Open to me now the gates of eternity!"

He opened the knapsack, lifted it high, and sent its contents tumbling down through the silver air – two pale spheroids, two human heads, jouncing so vividly on the ground, their short-barbered hair looking surreally neat against the red dirt, their black-scabbed neck-stumps glossy as lacquer.

Their impact with the earth set off the earthquake. There was a shrieking of metal as the 'dozer flung its great arm in the air, a gesture galvanic as some colossal scorpion's. The whole machine came apart with the fury of this straightening, the steel sinews spraying asunder in red shards, and revealing a darker sinew within, a huge, black hatchling of tarry muscle clotted on long bone. Two crimson eyes blazed above its black snout, as its crooked paw, prehensile, seized Pat and the operator together. The men cried out, their bones breaking in the grip that lifted them up to the mad red moons of eyes, lifted them higher still, and flung them powerfully at the earth. They struck the ground, impossibly flattened by the impact, transformed, in fact, to roadkill, to sprawling husks of human beings, bony silhouettes postured as if they were running full tilt toward the core of the planet.

"Thank you! Thank you! Oh, thank you!" Larken's gratitude sounded as wild as grief. His wail brought the god's paw down to him in turn. In turn he was seized up and lofted high, and was held aloft a moment while the god's eyes bathed him in their scarlet radiation.

And Marjorie, who had not guessed that she had voice left in her, screamed, and screamed again, because the earth beside the monster was no longer earth, but was a ragged-edged chasm of blackness, an infinite cauldron of darkness and stars.

The brute god held Larken high above this abyss. She could make out his face clearly above the crooked claw that gripped him. He was weeping with wonder and awe.

The god flung him down. His arms wind-milling, down Larken plunged. The god gave one furious snort that wafted like roadkill through the morning air, and leapt after his acolyte, dwindling down toward the starfields.

The earth closed over them, and Marjorie hugged the tree, quivering, staring at that resealed earth. It seemed to her the spot was not quite healed. The soil seemed sneakily transparent, thinly buried stars trying to burn through it like diamond drill-bits. The planet felt hollow underfoot, the great tree sustaining her seemed to feel it too. They huddled together, feeling the planet-bone resonate under them, like the deck of a ship in high seas.

She straightened and started forward, a starship traveller negotiating the gravity of an alien world. The ship had crashed . . . there were the twisted shards of bright red metal . . . right here was where it had happened, the red dirt solid now, supporting her, supporting the black-stumped heads like thrown dice, their dulled snake-eyes aimed askew of one another, looking in different directions for the sane earth they had known, Marjorie had known . . .

The sane world that lay that way . . . didn't it? Down this narrow country road here she could find her way back to freeway on-ramps and off-ramps that channelled directly to shopping malls that sold Technicolored candy and underwear, and to Humanity Incorporated with its computers and telephones and case files full of lost souls dying on their feet . . .

But how could this road lead *there* from such a starting-point as this? Here on the asphalt sprawled two human husks. She gazed on the distorted profile of Pat Bonds, crushed bone clad in sun-baked parchment. Older than Egypt he looked, the eye a glazed clot of mucus, a canted half-grin of teeth erupting from a leathery cheek. Crazed Cubist face, yet so expressive. He stared at eternity with outrage, with furious protest.

Go back down this road. Take the first step and the next will follow . . . See? Now the next. You're doing fine, Marjorie. Soon you'll reach your Beemer, and your Beemer will reach the city. Just keep moving. It'll all come back to you . . .

MICHAEL MARSHALL SMITH

This is Now

MICHAEL MARSHALL SMITH grew up in the United States, South Africa and Australia before moving to north London, where he lives with his wife Paula, his son and two cats.

He spent some time as a comedy writer and performer for BBC Radio before winning the 1991 British Fantasy Award for Best Newcomer and for his debut story, "The Man Who Drew Cats". He followed those with two more for his short fiction, some of which is collected in *What You Make It* and the International Horror Guild Award-winning *More Tomorrow & Other Stories*.

The author of three science fiction novels, *Only Forward* won the August Derleth and Philip K. Dick Awards, *Spares* was translated into seventeen languages, and *One of Us* was optioned by Warner Brothers. Writing as "Michael Marshall" he has recently completed a trio of dark thrillers – *The Straw Men*, *The Lonely Dead* (aka *The Upright Man*) and *Blood of Angels*. He has also written a number of film and television scripts for companies in Hollywood and London.

"Once in a while you get the opportunity to write a story for a market with a specific theme," explains Smith, "which gives you the freedom to play around a little, to take an oblique view.

"It has often struck me how most of our banner fears are entertaining distractions for the real horrors of life, and how some of those horrors are small, creeping, and insidious in their effects. This story is about one of them: about Time, and how it kills."

"**O** KAY," HENRY SAID. "So now we're here."

He was using his "So entertain me" voice, and he was cold but trying not to show it. Pete and I were cold too. We were trying not to show it either. Being cold is not manly. You look at your condensing breath as if it's a surprise to you, what with it being so balmy and all. Even when you've known each other for over thirty years, you do these things. Why? I don't know.

"Yep," I agreed. It wasn't my job to entertain Henry.

Pete walked up to the thick wire fence. He tilted his head back until he was looking at the top, 4 feet above his head. A 10-foot wall of tautly criss-crossed wire.

"Who's going to test it?"

"Well, hey, you're closest." Like the others, I was speaking quietly, though we were half a mile from the nearest road or house or person.

This side of the fence, anyhow.

"I did it last time."

"Long while ago."

"Still," he said, stepping back. "Your turn, Dave."

I held up my hands. "These are my tools, man."

Henry sniggered. "You're a tool, that's for sure."

Pete laughed too, I had to smile, and for a moment it was like it was the last time. Hey presto: time travel. You don't need a machine, it turns out, you just need a friend to laugh like a teenager. Chronology shivers.

And so – quickly, before I could think about it – I flipped my hand out and touched the fence. My whole arm jolted, as if every bone in it had been tapped with a hammer. Tapped hard, and in different directions.

"Christ," I hissed, spinning away, shaking my hand like I was trying to rid myself of it. "Goddamn Christ that hurts."

Henry nodded sagely. "This stretch got current, then. Also, didn't we use a stick last time?"

"Always been the brains of the operation, right, Hank?"

Pete snickered again. I was annoyed, but the shock had pushed me over a line. It had brought it all back much more strongly.

I nodded up the line of the fence as it marched off into the trees. "Further," I said, and pointed at Henry. "And you're testing the next section, bro."

It was one of those things you do, one of those stupid, drunken things, that afterwards seem hard to understand. You ask yourself why, confused and sad, like the ghost of a man killed through a careless step in front of a car.

We could have not gone to The Junction, for a start, though it was a Thursday and the Thursday session is a winter tradition with us, a way of making January and February seem less like a living death. The two young guys could have given up the pool table, though, instead of bogarting it all night (by being better than us, and efficiently dismissing each of our challenges in turn): in which case we would have played a dozen slow frames and gone home around eleven, like usual – ready to get up the next morning feeling no more than a little fusty. This time of year it hardly matters if Henry yawns over the gas pump, or Pete zones out behind the counter in the Massaqua Mart, and I can sling a morning's home fries and sausage in my sleep. We've been doing these things so long that we barely have to be present. Maybe that's the point. Maybe that's the real problem right there.

By quarter after eight, proven pool-fools, we were sitting at the corner table. We always have, since back when it was Bill's place and beer tasted strange and metallic in our mouths. We were talking back and forth, laughing once in a while, none of us bothered about the pool but yes, a little bit bothered all the same. It wasn't some macho thing. I don't care about being beat by some guys who are passing through. I don't much care about being beat by anyone. Henry and Pete and I tend to win games about equally. If it weren't that way then probably we wouldn't play together. It's never been about winning. It was more that I just wished I was better. Had assumed I'd be better, one day, like I expected to wind up being something other than a short order cook. Don't get me wrong: you eat one of my breakfasts you're set up for the day and tomorrow you'll come back and order the same thing. It just wasn't what I had in mind when I was young. Not sure what I did have in mind – I used to think maybe I'd go over the mountains to Seattle, be in a band or something, but the thought got vague after that – but it certainly wasn't being first in command at a hot griddle. None of ours are bad jobs, but they're the kind held by people in the background. People who are getting by. People who don't play pool that well.

It struck me, as I watched Pete banter with Nicole when she brought round number four or five, that I was still smoking. I had been assuming I would have given it up by now. Tried, once or twice. Didn't take. Would it happen? Probably not. Would it give me cancer sooner or later? Most likely. Better try again, then. At some point.

Henry watched Nicole's ass as it accompanied her back to the counter. "Cute as hell," he said, approvingly, not for the first time.

Pete and I grunted, in the way we would if he'd observed that the moon was smaller than the earth. Henry's observation was both true and something that had little bearing on our lives. Nicole was twenty-three. We could give her fifteen years each. That's not the kind of gift that cute girls covet.

So we sat and talked, and smoked, and didn't listen to the sound of balls being efficiently slotted into pockets by people who weren't us.

You walk for long enough in the woods at night, you start getting a little jittery. Forests have a way of making civilization seem less inevitable. In sunlight they may make you want to build yourself a cabin and get back to nature, get that whole Davy Crockett vibe going on. In the dark they remind you what a good thing chairs and hot meals and electric light really are, and you thank God you live now instead of then.

Every once in a while we'd test the fence – using a stick now. The current was on each time we tried. So we kept walking. We followed the line of the wire as it cut up the rise, then down into a shallow stream bed, then up again steeply on the other side.

If you were seeing the fence for the first time, you'd likely wonder at the straightness of it, the way in which the concrete posts had been planted at ten yard intervals deep into the rock. You might ask yourself if national forests normally went to these lengths, and you'd soon remember they didn't, that for the most part a cheerful little wooden sign by the side of the road was all that was judged to be required. If you kept on walking deeper, intrigued, sooner or later you'd see a notice attached to one of the posts. The notices are small, designed to convey authority rather than draw attention.

NO TRESPASSING, they say. MILITARY LAND.

That could strike you as a little strange, perhaps, because you might have believed that most of the marked-off areas were down over in the moonscapes of Nevada, rather than up here at the quiet Northeast corner of Washington State. But who knows what the military's up to, right? Apart from protecting us from foreign aggressors, of course, and The Terrorist Threat, and if that means they need a few acres to themselves then that's actually kind of comforting. The army moves in mysterious ways, our freedoms to defend. Good for them, you'd think, and you'd likely turn and head back for town, having had enough of tramping through snow for the day. In the evening you'd come into Ruby's and eat hearty, some of my wings or a burger or the brisket – which, though I say so myself, isn't half bad. Next morning you'd drive back South.

I remember when the fences went up. Thirty years ago. 1985. Our parents knew what they were for. Hell, we were only eight and we knew.

There was a danger, and it was getting worse: the last decade had proved that. Four people had disappeared in the last year alone. One came back and was sick for a week, in an odd and dangerous kind of way, and then died. The others were never seen again. My aunt Jean was one of those.

But there's a danger to going in abandoned mine shafts, too, or talking to strangers, or juggling knives when you're drunk. So . . . you don't do it. You walk the town in pairs at night, and you observe the unspoken curfew. You kept an eye out for men who didn't blink, for slim women whose strides were too short – or so people said. There was never that much passing trade in town. Massaqua isn't on the way to anywhere. Massaqua is a single guy who keeps his yard tidy and doesn't bother anyone. The tourist season up here is short and not exactly intense. There is no ski lodge or health spa and the motel frankly isn't up to much.

The fence seemed to keep the danger contained and out of town, and within a few years its existence was part of life. It wasn't like it was right there on the doorstep. No big-city reporter heard of it and came up looking to make a sensation – or, if they did, they didn't make it all the way here.

Life went on. Years passed. Sometimes small signs work better than great big ones.

As we climbed deeper into the forest, Pete was in front, I was more-or-less beside him, and Henry lagged a few steps behind. It had been that way the last time, too, but then we hadn't had hip flasks to keep us fuelled in our intentions. We hadn't needed to stop to catch our breath so often either.

"We just going to keep on walking?"

It was Henry asked the question, of course. Pete and I didn't even answer.

At quarter after ten we were still in the bar. The two guys remained at the pool table. When one leaned down, the other stood silently, judiciously sipping from a bottled beer. They weren't talking to each other, just slotting the balls away. Looked like they're having a whale of a time.

We were drinking steadily, and the conversation was often two-way while one or other of us trekked back and forth to empty our bladder. By then we were resigned to sitting around. We were a little too drunk to start playing pool, even if the table became free. There was no news to catch up on. We felt aimless. We already knew that Pete was ten years married, that they had no children and it was likely going to stay that way. His wife is fine, and still pleasant to be with, though her collection of dolls is getting exponentially bigger. We knew that Henry was married once too, had a little boy, and that though the kid and his mother now lived forty miles away, relations between them remained cordial. Neither Pete nor I are much surprised that he has achieved this. Henry can be a royal pain in the ass at times, but he wouldn't still be our friend if that's all he was.

"Same again, boys? You're thirsty tonight."

It was Pete's turn in the gents so it was Henry and I who looked up to see Nicole smiling down at us, thumb hovering over the REPEAT button on her pad. Deprived of Pete's easy manner (partly genetic, also honed over years of chatting while totting and bagging groceries), our response was cluttered and vague.

Quick nods and smiles, I said thanks and Henry got in a "Hell, yes!" that came out a little loud.

Nicole winked at me and went away again, as she has done many times over the last three years. As she got to the bar I saw one of the pool-players looking at her, and felt a strange twist of something in my stomach. It wasn't because they were strangers, or because I suspected they might be something else, something that shouldn't be here.

They were just younger guys, that's all.

Of course they're going to look at her. She's probably going to want them to.

I lit another cigarette and wondered why I still didn't really know how to deal with women. They've always seemed so different to me. So confident, so powerful, so in themselves. Kind of scary, even. Most teenage boys feel that way, I guess, but I had assumed age would help. That being older might make a difference. Apparently not. The opposite, if anything.

"Cute just doesn't really cover it," Henry said, again not for the first time. "Going to have to come up with a whole new word. Supercute, how's that. Hyperhot. Ultra—"

How about just beautiful?

For a horrible moment I thought I'd said this out loud. I guess in a way I did, because what pronouncements are louder than the ones you make only in your own head?

Pete returned at the same time as the new beers arrived, and with him around it was easier to come across like grown-ups. He came back looking thoughtful, too.

He waited until the three of us were alone again, and then he reached across and took one of my Marlboro: like he used to, back in the day, when he couldn't afford his own. He didn't seem to be aware he'd done it. He looked pretty drunk, in fact, and I realized that I was too. Henry is generally at least a little drunk.

Pete lit the cigarette, took a long mouthful of beer, and then he said:

"You remember that time we went over the fence?"

The stick touched, and nothing happened.

I did it again. Same result. We stopped walking. My legs ached and I was glad for the break.

Pete hesitated a beat, then reached out and brushed the thick black wire with his hand. When we were kids he might have pretended it was charged, and jiggered back and forth, eyes rolling and tongue sticking out.

He didn't now. He just curled his fingers around it, gave it a light tug.

"Power's down," he said, quietly.

Henry and I stepped up close. Even with Pete standing there grasping it, you still had to gird yourself to do the same.

Then all three of us were holding the fence, holding it with both hands, looking in.

That close up, the wire fuzzed out of focus and it was almost as if it wasn't there. You just saw the forest beyond it: moonlit trunks, snow; you heard the quietness. If you stood on the other side and looked out, the view would be exactly the same. With a fence that long, it could be difficult to tell which side was in, which was out.

This, too, was what had happened the previous time, when we were fifteen. We'd heard that sometimes a section went down, and so we went looking. With animals, snow, the random impacts of falling branches and a wind that could blow hard and cold at most times of year, once in a while a cable stopped supplying the juice to one ten yard stretch. The power was never down for more than a day. There was a computer that kept track, and – somewhere, nobody knew where – a small station from which a couple of military engineers could come to repair the outage. But for now, a section was down.

We stood, this silent row of older men, and remembered what had happened back then.

Pete had gone up first. He shuffled along to one of the concrete posts, so the wire wouldn't bag out, and started pulling himself up.

As soon as his feet left the ground I didn't want to be left behind, so I went to the other post and went up just as quickly.

We reached the top at around the same time. Soon as we started down the other side – lowering ourselves at first, then just dropping, Henry started his own climb.

We all landed silently in the snow, with bent knees.

We were on the other side, and we stood very still. Far as we knew, no-one had ever done this before.

To some people, this might have been enough.

Not to three fifteen-year-old boys.

Moving very quietly, hearts beating hard – just from the exertion, none of us were scared, not exactly, not enough to admit it anyway – we moved away from the fence.

After about twenty yards I stopped and looked back.

"You chickening out?"

"No, Henry," I said. His voice had been quiet and shaky. I took pains that mine sound firm. "Memorising. We want to be able to find that dead section again."

He'd nodded. "Good thinking, smart boy."

Pete looked back with us. Stand of three trees close together there. Unusually big tree over on the right. Kind of a semi-clearing, on a crest. Shouldn't be hard to find.

We glanced at each other, judged it logged in our heads, then turned and headed away, into a place no-one had been for nearly ten years.

The forest floor led away gently. There was just enough moonlight to show the ground panning down towards a kind of high valley lined with thick trees.

As we walked, bent over a little with unconscious caution, part of me was already relishing how we'd remember this in the future, leaping over the event into its retrospection. Not that we'd talk about it, outside the three of us. It was the kind of thing which might attract attention to the town, including maybe attention from this side of the fence.

There was one person I thought I might mention it to, though. Her name was Lauren and she was very cute, the kind of beautiful that doesn't have to open its mouth to call your name from across the street. I had talked to her a couple times, finding bravery I didn't know I possessed. It was she who had talked about Seattle, said she'd like to go hang out there some day. That sounded good to me, good and exciting and strange. What I didn't know, that night in the forest, was that she would do this, and I would not, and that she would leave without us ever having kissed.

I just assumed . . . I assumed a lot back then.

After a couple of hundred yards we stopped, huddled together, shared one of my cigarettes. Our hearts were beating heavily, even though we'd been coming downhill. The forest is hard work whatever direction it slopes. But it wasn't just that. It felt a little colder here. There was also something about the light. It seemed to hold more shadows. You found your eyes flicking from side to side, checking things out, wanting to be reassured, but not being confident that you had been after all.

I bent down to put the cigarette out in the snow. It was extinguished in a hiss that seemed very loud.

We continued in the direction we'd been heading. We walked maybe another five, six hundred yards.

It was Henry who stopped.

Keyed up as we were, Pete and I stopped immediately too. Henry was leaning forward a little, squinting ahead.

"What?"

He pointed. Down at the bottom of the rocky valley was a shape. A big shape.

After a moment I could make out it was a building. Two wooden storeys high, and slanting.

You saw that kind of thing, sometimes. The sagging remnant of some pioneer's attempt to claim an area of this wilderness and pretend it could be a home.

Pete nudged me and pointed in a slightly different direction. There was the remnants of another house further down. A little fancier, with a fallen-down porch.

And 30 yards further, another: smaller, with a false front.

"Cool," Henry said, and briefly I admired him.

We sidled now, a lot more slowly and heading along the rise instead of down it. Ruined houses look real interesting during the day. At night they feel different, especially when lost high up in the forest. Trees grow too close to them, pressing in. The lack of a road, long overgrown, can make the houses look like they were never built but instead made their own way to this forgotten place, in which you have now disturbed them; they sit at angles which do not seem quite right.

I was beginning to wonder if maybe we'd done enough, come far enough, and I doubt I was the only one.

Then we saw the light.

After Pete asked his question in the bar, there was silence for a moment. Of course we remembered that night. It wasn't something you'd forget. It was a dumb question unless you were really asking something else, and we both knew Pete wasn't dumb.

Behind us, on the other side of the room, came the quiet, reproachful sound of pool balls hitting each other, and then one of them going down a pocket.

We could hear each other thinking. Thinking it was a cold evening, and there was thick snow on the ground, as there had been on that other night, when we were fifteen. That the rest of the town had pretty much gone to bed. That we could get in Henry's truck and be at the head of a hiking trail in 20 minutes, even driving drunkard slow.

I didn't hear anyone thinking a reason, though. I didn't hear anyone think why we might do such a thing, or what might happen.

By the time Pete had finished his cigarette our glasses were empty. We put on our coats and left and crunched across the lot to the truck.

Back then, on that long-ago night, suddenly my heart hadn't seemed to be beating at all. When we saw the light in the second house, a faint and curdled glow in one of the downstairs windows, my whole body suddenly felt light and insubstantial.

One of us tried to speak. It came out like a dry click. I realized there was a light in the other house too, faint and golden. Had I missed it before, or had it just come on?

I took a step backwards. The forest was silent but for the sound of my friends breathing.

"Oh, no," Pete said. He started moving backwards, stumbling. Then I saw it too.

A figure, standing in front of the first house.

It was tall and slim, like a rake's shadow. It was 100 yards away but still it seemed as though you could make out an oval shape on its shoulders, the colour of milk diluted with water. It was looking in our direction.

Then another was standing near the other house.

No, two.

Henry moaned softly, we three boys turned as one, and I have never run like that before or since.

The first 10 yards were fast but then the slope cut in and our feet slipped, and we were down on hands half the time, scrabbling and pulling – every muscle working together in a headlong attempt to be somewhere else.

I heard a crash behind and flicked my head to see Pete had gone down hard, banging his knee, falling on his side.

Henry kept on going but I made myself turn around to grab Pete's hand, not really helping but just pulling, trying to yank him back to his feet or at least away.

Over his shoulder I glimpsed the valley below and I saw the figures were down at the bottom of the rise, speeding our way in jerky blurred-black movements, like half-seen spiders darting across an icy window pane.

Pete's face jerked up and I saw there what I felt in myself, and it was not a cold fear but a hot one, a red-hot meltdown as if you were going to rattle and break apart.

Then he was on his feet again, moving past me, and I followed on after him towards the disappearing shape of Henry's back. It seemed so much further than we'd walked. It was uphill and the trees no longer formed a path and even the wind seemed to be pushing us back.

We caught up with Henry and passed him, streaking up the last 100 yards towards the fence. None of us turned around. You didn't have to. You could feel them coming, like rocks thrown at your head, rocks glimpsed at the last minute when there is time to flinch but not to turn.

I was sprinting straight at the fence when Henry called out. I was going too fast and didn't want to know what his problem was. I leapt up at the wire.

It was like a truck hit me from the side.

I crashed to the ground fizzing, arms sparking and with no idea which way was up. Then two pairs of hands were on me, pulling at my coat.

I thought the fingers would be long and pale and strong but when I realized it was my friends and they were pulling me along from the wrong section of the fence, dragging me to the side, when they could have just left me where I fell and made their own escape.

The three of us jumped up at the wire at once, scrabbling like monkeys, stretching out for the top. I rolled over wildly, grunting as I scored deep scratches across my back that would earn me a long, hard look from my mother when she happened to glimpse them a week later.

We landed heavily on the other side, still moving forward, having realized that we'd just given away the location of a portion of dead fence.

But now we had to look back, and what I saw – though my head was still vibrating from the shock I'd received, so I cannot swear to it

– was at least three, maybe five, figures on the other side of the fence. Not right up against it, but a few yards back.

Black hair was whipped up around their faces, and they looked like absences ill-lit.

Then they were gone.

We moved fast. We didn't know why they'd stopped, but we didn't hang around. We didn't stick too close to the fence either, in case they changed their minds.

We half-walked, half-ran, and at first we were quiet but as we got further away, and nothing came after us, we began to laugh and then to shout, punching the air, boys who had come triumphantly out the other side.

The forest felt like some huge football field, applauding its heroes with whispering leaves.

We got back to town a little after two in the morning. We walked down the middle of the deserted main street, slowly, untouchable, knowing the world had changed: that we were not the boys who had started the evening, but men, and that the stars were there to be touched.

That was then.

As older men we stood together at the fence for a long time, recalling that night.

Parts of it are fuzzy now, of course, and it comes down to snapshots: Pete's terrified face when he slipped, the first glimpse of light at the houses, Henry's shout as he tried to warn me, narrow faces the colour of moonlight. They most likely remembered other things, defined that night in different ways and were the centre of their own recollections. As I looked now through the fence at the other forest I was thinking how long a decade had seemed back then, and how you could learn that it was no time at all.

Henry stepped away first. I wasn't far behind. Pete stayed a moment longer, then took a couple of steps back. Nobody said anything. We just looked at the fence a little longer, and then we turned and walked away.

Took us 40 minutes to get back to the truck.

The next Thursday Henry couldn't make it, so it was just me and Pete at the pool table. Late in the evening, with many beers drunk, I mentioned the fence.

Not looking at me, chalking his cue, Pete said that if Henry hadn't stepped back when he did, he'd have climbed it.

"And gone over?"

"Yeah," he said.

This was bullshit, and I knew it. "Really?"

There was a pause. "No," he said, eventually, and I wished I hadn't asked the second time. I could have left him with something, left us with it. Calling an ass cute isn't much, but it's better than just coming right out and admitting you'll never cup it in your hand.

The next week it was the three of us again, and our walk in the woods wasn't even mentioned. We've never brought it up since, and we can't talk about the first time any more either. We killed it. I think about it sometimes, though. I know I could go out walking there myself some night, and there have been slow afternoons and dry, sleepless small hours when I think I might do it: when I tell myself such a thing isn't impossible now, that I am still who I once was. But I have learned a little since I was fifteen, and in the end I just go smoke another cigarette on the porch, or out back of the diner, because in my heart of hearts I know that was then, and this is now.

TIM LEBBON

Remnants

TIM LEBBON IS THE winner of two British Fantasy Awards, a Bram Stoker Award and a Tombstone Award. His novels include *Face*, *The Nature of Balance*, *Mesmer*, *Hush* (with Gavin Williams), *Until She Sleeps*, *Desolation* and *Berserk*.

White, *Naming of Parts*, *Changing of Faces*, *Exorcising Angels* (with Simon Clark), *Dead Man's Hand* and *Pieces of Hate* are separately published novellas, and his short fiction is collected in *Fears Unnamed*, *As the Sun Goes Down* and *White and Other Tales of Ruin*.

Forthcoming titles include *The Dead of Night: Dusk and Dawn*, *Hellboy: The New Ark*, and more books with Cemetery Dance, Night Shade Books and Necessary Evil Press, amongst other imprints.

"When I wrote 'Remnants' I'd just come off a bit of an Algernon Blackwood reading frenzy," Lebbon reveals. "I love Blackwood's wide range of themes, his fearlessness, and I also like the classic idea of a stranger being drawn into a story from outside: the protagonist receiving a telegram from a long-lost friend, saying 'Come quickly! Something *terrible* has happened!'

"I suppose there's an element of autobiography here as well (isn't there always?), in that sometimes I wish I was the one scampering across deserts, through mountain ranges, delving beneath the surface of things . . . and in real life, instead of through my writing.

"But then I get all sensible and middle-aged, and I realize that doing it this way is far safer, less wearing on the joints, and the kettle's never far away."

S COTT ALWAYS LOVED DIGGING down to history. When we were nine years old we would spend time in the local woods, me climbing trees and searching for birds' nests and damming the local stream, Scott excavating through the accumulated carpet of leaves and other forest debris in his search for hidden things. Usually he found nothing but mud, muck and crawling things, but on those rare occasions when he went home happy instead of dejected, he would be carrying something of interest. A small skeleton once, easily identifiable were we to ask our parents, though we did not because we preferred the mystery. He also found a buried box, about the size of a house brick, and we undertook to smash the lock with a rock. Those few seconds were a magical time – the impact of stone on metal reverberating through the woods, the endless possibilities rich and coloured by our childish imaginations – and even when the lid flipped open to reveal nothing but rust, we weren't truly disappointed. It was empty of treasure or maps or hidden truths, but the box itself was still there, and that was good enough for us. Scott walked home that day happier than I had ever seen him, the box tucked beneath one arm, his small trowel dirtying his trousers where it protruded from a pocket. He was beaming. "There's always something there," he said. "Everyone reckons that what we see is it. They forget about all the buried stuff."

His progression from school, to university, to a career in archaeology was no surprise to anyone. We kept in touch, even though my work took me on a vastly different route. Scott would disappear from my life for years on end, and then I would receive an e-mail or letter out of the blue, inviting me to join him in Bolivia or Uzbekistan or Taiwan. More often than not I would have to decline, but several times a rush of excitement grabbed me. It was often his young, enthusiastic face I thought of as I sat there in my office at home, dreaming, persuading myself that I should go. The wonder in his eyes. The knowledge that when I saw him again, that wonder would still be there.

I was a jealous friend. Jealous when we were nine, and jealous when we were thirty-nine. Scott had always known what he wanted from life, and he pursued it with vigour. I lived my life unfulfilled, and worse, felt that I had no potential *to* fulfil.

So I would talk to my wife and children and, with their blessing, jet off to some far-flung corner of the world to spend two weeks in a tent with my old friend. He never changed, only became fuller. Each time I saw him he seemed more alive and I felt more dead, ground down by life and work, impulsiveness slaughtered by necessity. And each time, Scott seemed to be digging much deeper than even he knew. It was not only lost things he was looking for, but things unknown, and even things that had never been. He was looking past history and into the abyss of unadulterated truth.

He sometimes told tell me what he had unearthed. I was no longer a child, so I often found it difficult to believe, a leap of imagination that I was not able to make. He would smile and shake his head, and that simple gesture hurt me to the core. He was so used to miracles.

His final calling came in a series of brief, enigmatic e-mails.

I've found a city that no one has dreamed of in centuries, the first said. I smiled at the words on the screen, my heart quickening in unconscious sympathy with the excitement bleeding from them. I imagined Scott's eyes wide and child-like in their amazement.

The following night: *it must be a city of ghosts*. A thrill went through me. Scott could imbue text on a screen with so much emotion and feeling . . . but then I knew that my memories of him were providing that effect. He gave me sterile, blank words, and I fleshed them out with his passion.

Matthew is here.

Matthew was Scott's son. Scott had had a brief, passionate affair when he was twenty, and six years later he learned from his ex-lover that he had a child. She only told him because the boy was dying of leukaemia.

This wasn't even funny.

What the hell are you talking about? I mailed back, angry and disturbed at the same time. Scott was a dreamer, a thinker, someone whose imagination led him places not only unheard of, but long forgotten. I had never thought of him as a fool.

Come to me, Peter, Scott mailed back. *Please*. It was the 'please' that convinced me I had to go. I was certain that Scott needed my help, though perhaps not in the way he believed. Perhaps, somewhere deep inside me where I did not care to look, there was a smugness. Here was the great adventurer – glamorous, passionate, so rich in intellect and enthusiasm – asking for my help. Not outright, but I could read between his digital lines, perceive a desperation that I had never expected to find. A desperation, and perhaps a fear. Up until now he had always invited my presence, not requested it.

Matthew is here, he had said.

What could that mean?

I stood from my computer desk after receiving that last message and walked around my home. My wife was at work, my two children in school, and I should have been working through some submissions. But Scott's words had fired my comatose imagination, their mystery setting a fire in the dried out landscape of my mind and struggling to light its shadowed corners. I walked from room to room, bathing in the history of my life as it lay revealed in photographs. Here was Janine and me standing by Victoria Falls, our glasses splashed with spray, wide smiles as magical as upside-down rainbows. And here, the two of us in hospital with our daughter a bloody bundle at her breast, suckling her way into the world. Another picture sat on the dresser in the hallway showing us on our honeymoon, sheltering beneath a heavy palm tree while a tropical storm thundered its ways across the small island. Neither of us could remember who had taken the photo.

There was an old shelf of books in the living room, various first editions I had collected over the years. I liked to think of myself as something of a detective, hauling out my guide to British bookshops every time we found ourselves in a strange town or city, exploring a few here and there, searching old cobwebbed shelves and delving deep into overflowing bargain bins in my search for that elusive rare time. My collection filled one glass-fronted shelf and was worth over ten thousand pounds.

Worthless. Meaningless. If this was all I had to show for a life . . .

A dried nut, as large as my fist, sat on the fireplace. I had climbed a tree for it in Australia, supposedly braving spiders and snakes to grab a piece of that country for myself. Janine had been watching, camera at the ready in case I slipped and fell. I had been in no danger at all.

I tried to think of the most daring thing I had ever done. I had abseiled over 300 feet down the side of a cliff. It was raining, the rock was slippery and, in places, loose. I had a safety line attached, and an expert climber stood on top of the cliff slowly feeding me rope. I had raised £500 for charity. At the time, I had felt on the edge.

Scott once showed me his collection of scars. Shark off the coast of South Africa, snake in Paraguay, a goring from running with the bulls in Spain, a bullet in his hip from a brush with Chinese soldiers in Tibet, the ragged wound in his throat where he had given himself a tracheotomy after being stung by a deadly scorpion, airways closing, life fading away in his poisoned blood, his knife so sharp and sure. He had a tattoo on one shoulder-blade, put there by an old woman in Haiti who claimed it would keep him alive when death came knocking. On the other shoulder, a gypsy woman in Ireland had painted a bird, hugely feathered and colourful, the carrier of Scott's soul. The ink had never faded, and sometimes it still looked wet. Scott could not explain that, but it did not concern him. He simply accepted it. He had a wooden mask dating from one of the great Egyptian Dynasties, a Roman soldier's spear-tip found in Jerusalem and dating from around the time of Christ's crucifixion, and around his neck hung a charm, diamond inset in white gold, the heart of the diamond impossibly black with the sealed blood of a saint.

I had some photographs and memories, trinkets, meagre evidence showing that the most adventurous thing I had done was to go on holiday and book the hotel and flights myself.

"Damn you, Scott," I whispered at the empty house. I closed my eyes and tried to imagine the memories and dreams he must have every single night of his life. When Janine came home I would talk to her, and she would give me her blessing to go and stay with Scott for a week or two.

Perhaps the fact that I wanted to steal a dream sealed the fate of that journey from the start.

Scott was waiting for me at what passed as the airport. I had changed three times since Heathrow, each transfer resulting in me sitting aboard a smaller, more dilapidated aircraft, and I finally flew into an airport somewhere in Ogaden in an antique that must have begun service before World War II. There were eighteen seats in the cabin, fifteen of which remained empty. The other two passengers spared me not a glance. They were enrapttured in the frantic conversation that came through the open doorway from the flight deck. Not understanding the language, I watched them for any reaction that should give me cause for concern. I had the distinct impression that the whole flight skirted the brink of disaster, and that the intermittent shouts of glee from the pilot or co-pilot marked another severe problem somehow overcome. As the propellers spun down and the tang of burning filtered into the cabin, the two other passengers swapped strangers' smiles.

"Peter!" Scott shouted as I descended the rickety set of steps. He ran across the landing strip, kicking up puffs of dust. "Peter! Christ mate, it's bloody good to see you!"

I could only smile. Here he was again, my old friend who somehow instilled a very private, very deep jealousy in me, and I couldn't help but love him.

"You too," I said. I held out my hand for a shake but he dodged it, ducking in for a hug, his arms strong, his scent that of someone used to a hard life. I hugged him back, certain that my ribs would rupture within seconds.

"How's Janine?" he asked. "The kids? How are they?"

"Janine sends her love," I said, even though she had not. "Gary's starting comprehensive school this year, and Sandy's taking her exams."

"Shit me. Time eh? Time, my old mate. Time slips away."

I looked at Scott then, really looked at him, and though his skin was leathered by the sun, his hair greying and thinning rapidly, his jowls drooping lower and lower each time I saw him, he had the manner and bearing of someone much younger. I felt old, even though I tried to keep in shape. Scott had a sense of awe to keep him youthful, and he found wonder every day, in everyday things.

"Yeah," I said. "Nice fuckin' life."

Scott smiled at our old catchphrase, but he did not respond. He was looking at me, appraising me much more openly than I had just assessed him. "You need to see what I've found, Peter," he said.

Someone shouted behind us, one of the other passengers, and a group of people standing at the edge of the runway waved and shouted back. The laughter belonged in the hot dry air, but so did the sudden sense of import between Scott and me, hanging there with the laughter like its solid, immovable counterpoint. Scott's eyes did not shift from mine. I waited for him to say more, but he was silent. He smiled, but there was a sadness there as well, so deep that I wondered if he was aware of its existence.

"What is it?" I asked.

Scott seemed to snap out of a brief trance. He looked around, pointed out the ramshackle shed that served as an airport arrivals and departures lounge, the watchtower where an old man sat with a table-top radio, the collection of huts and shelters that lined the airport perimeter on both sides, people wandering amongst them like shadows ignoring the sun. The whole place looked run-down, wasting away, and as Scott spoke he was exuberant, a brighter spark in the glow of the day.

"This is no place for wonders," he said quietly. "This country has its paradise, but it's a distance from here. I can't mention it until we're closer." And then he turned and started walking away.

"Scott!" I said. "Why did you ask me to come?"

"You'll see," he said, almost dismissively. He did not even turn to me when he spoke. "This is the cradle of civilization, you know. This place." He waved his arm around and moved on.

I looked around at the 'plane, the pilots gesticulating at one of the steaming engine compartments, the joyful reunion over by the airport buildings. In the sky dark shapes rode the currents. They were too high to make out properly, and I frowned at the childish memories of vultures in old films, circling, waiting on a fresh death.

My luggage had been unceremoniously dumped on the ground beneath the open luggage compartment. I grabbed the holdall, snapped open the handle on the suitcase and followed Scott towards the potholed car park. The heat had hit me. I was melting.

"Thanks for the help with my luggage!" I called lightly, hoping for an abusive response, hoping for normality.

But Scott only raised his hand and waved back at me without turning around. "I'll tell you when we get nearer," he said. "I can't tell you yet. Not yet. Not here."

The family watched me walk from the runway, but they ignored Scott. Perhaps they knew him. More likely, he looked like he belonged.

Scott had an old World War II jeep, left over from that conflict and probably not serviced since. It screeched at us as he started it up, a high-pitched whine intermingled with the sound of something hard spinning around inside the engine, ricocheting, trying to find its way out. A cloud of smoke erupted from the vehicle's back end.

"Shit," I said.

"Don't worry," Scott said, "I've cursed it. Wouldn't dare let me down." He grinned madly, smashed the gearstick into first, and slammed his foot on the gas.

My first instinct was to look for a seatbelt, but if there had ever been one it was long since gone. Instead I grabbed on to my seat with one hand, the rusted window frame with the other, trying to ride out the jolts and bounces. The road was rough as a ploughed field, not even bearing the ruts of frequent use.

"Fun, eh?" Scott shouted, laughing as the underside of the jeep crunched against the ground and sent a solid judder through the whole chassis.

Perhaps we were in a town, but there was not much to see. The most salubrious building we passed was an old church, its tower tall and bell-less, walls rough-rendered and pocked here and there with what could have been bullet holes. Empty windows hid a dark interior, untouched by the strong sun. Contrasting this seemingly unused shell was the church's garden, fenced in with a clean white picket fence. It held a profusion of bright shrubs, lush and thriving even through the dust that had settled on their leaves, gorgeous orchids nestling at the bases of thick green stems; green and purple, blue and red. They could have been artificial, such were the colours.

An incredibly old man approached the church as we passed by, carrying a plastic water container on his shoulder, its contents spewing from a rent in its base. He looked our way but did not appear to see us.

"Where are we going?" I shouted.

"The desert!" Scott replied. "Hot as Hell, beautiful as Heaven! Hope you brought your sun-block."

I nodded, though he was paying little attention. I had coated myself on the 'plane, drawing a single amused glance from one of my fellow passengers. Perhaps the sun was the least I had to worry about, and maybe he knew.

We soon passed out of the small settlement. The shacks and rubbish-strewn streets ended abruptly, as did any sign of cultivation. What few sad fruit trees and root crops I had seen had no place past the town's outer boundary; now, there was only the wilds. The road suddenly seemed to smooth out and calm down, as if pleased to be leaving civilization behind, and before us lay the desert.

I had been aware of its presence for some minutes. It could be seen beyond the town, hunched down, spread as far as the eye could see. Its smell permeated the air; hot and dry, barren and cruel. I could even feel its weight, its distance, its vastness affecting my emotional tides like the sky at night, or the sea on a stormy day. But now for the first time I really *noticed* it. I saw its beauty and danger, its mystery and shapely curves. And I perceived the sharp edges that waited for those unacquainted with its harsh truth.

Now that the road had levelled to merely uncomfortable – and Scott had dropped his speed as if mourning the potholes left behind – I had a chance to talk.

"Scott, you have me confused."

"It'll all become clear," he said. "Or . . . clearer. More obvious." He shook his head, trying to rattle loose whatever he was trying to say. "Just wait and let me show you, Pete."

I nodded, tried to return his smile, but the sun must have stretched my skin. I uncapped the lid of my sun-block and coated my face and arms once more, taking off my cap and rubbing it into my scalp. It grated and scratched. Glancing at the mess on my hand, I saw that a thousand grains of sand had become mixed in, turning the cream into an effective exfoliant.

"Hah!" Scott laughed. "Just like being at the beach. You get used to the sand eventually, just like you get used to being thirsty, sweaty, tired. You can get used to anything, really. Remember going to the beach as a kid? That time when our families went together, you wanted to go canoeing but I dragged you over to explore the rock pools and caves?"

"You got me into so much trouble."

"I was a kid, what was I supposed to know about tides?" He laughed again, wild, uninhibited, untempered by normal worries like mortgages and jobs and love. I loved him and hated him, and for the thousandth time I wondered how that could be.

"We could have died."

"We should have gone further into the caves. But you were scared."

I shook my head. "You didn't know what was there. We could have died."

"You never find out unless you look." If I didn't know him better, I may have imagined mockery in his smile.

"You said you'd found a city," I said. "A city of ghosts?" He glanced across at me, handed over a bottle of water, looked ahead again.

The road had effectively ended as we left town, cross-country evidently being a more comfortable ride. This desert was not as I had always imagined it to be – the high, sharp-ridged dunes of 'Lawrence of Arabia' – but rather flat, hard-packed, supporting sparse oases of vegetation that seemed to sprout from the bases of rocky mounds or in shallows in the ground. Leaves were dark green and thin, their ends sharp, threatening and unwelcoming. If these plants did flower, now was not their season. The sun was high, the heat intense, and mirage lakes danced across the horizon. Ghost water, I thought, and the idea made Scott's silence even more frustrating.

"What city could be hidden out here?" I asked. "It's the desert, but it's hardly wilderness."

"Hardly?" he repeated, raising his eyebrows. "What's wilderness?"

"Well . . . the wilds. Somewhere away from civilization."

Scott lifted a hand from the wheel and swept it ahead of him, as if offering me everything I could see. "This is as wild as it gets," he said. "Civilisation? Where? Out here there are scorpions and snakes and spiders and flies, and other things to do you mischief. It's easy to die in the desert."

"And?" I asked. There had been no feeling to his words, no sense that he meant it. Spiders and snakes did not frighten him, nor turn his desert into a wilderness. There was something else here for him.

"And history," he said. The jeep began to protest as we started up a shallow, long rise. Scott frowned down at the bonnet, cursing under his breath, and then with a cough the engine settled into its old rumble once more.

I looked around, searching for ruins or some other evidence of humanity, of history. But I saw only compacted sand and plants, and a shimmering mirage which made me ever more thirsty.

"The sands of time," Scott said. "Blown around the world for the last million years. Parts of every civilization that has ever existed on Earth are here. Shards of the pyramids. Flecks of stone from the hanging gardens of Babylon. Dust from unknown obelisks. Traces of societies and peoples we've never known or imagined. All here."

I looked across the desert, trying to perceive anything other than what my eyes told me were there. Yet again I envied Scott his sense of wonder. He could take a deep breath and know that a million people before him had inhaled part of that lungful. I could see or feel nothing of the sort.

"Time has ghosts," he said. "That's what time is: the ghost of every instant passed, haunting the potential of every moment to come. And sometimes, the ghosts gather."

"The city of ghosts?"

Scott drew to a halt atop a low ridge. Ahead of us lay a staggering expanse of nothing: desert forever, the horizon merging with the light blue sky where distance blurred them together. Heat shimmered everything into falseness.

"Further in," he said quietly. "A couple of hours' travel. I have plenty of water, and there's spring at my camp. But here. I found this. Take a look. Gather your thoughts, and when you're ready tell me what you think."

He dug down under his seat and handed me something. For a couple of seconds I drew back and kept my hands to myself, afraid that it would be deadly. Not an insect, nothing poisonous, nothing so banal; something *dangerous*. Something that, were I to accept it from Scott, would have consequences.

"Here," he said, urging me. "It won't hurt you. That's the last thing it'll do."

I took in a deep breath and held out my hand.

The bundle of cloth was small, and it had no weight whatsoever. I was holding a handful of air. It was old, crumbled, dried by the intense heat until all flexibility and movement had been boiled away. It lay there in my hand, a relic, and as I turned it this way and that I saw what was inside.

Bones. Short and thin, knotted, disjointed. Finger bones. One of them had a shred of mummified flesh still hanging on for dear, long-departed life.

I gasped, froze in my seat, conscious of Scott's gaze upon me. I hefted the bundle, still amazed at how light it seemed, wondering if the climate had done something to my muscles or sense of touch. And for a moment so brief I may have imagined it in a blink, I saw this person's death.

Cold. Wet. Alone. And a long, long way from here.

"It's old," Scott said. "Very old. Before Christ. Before the Minoans, the Egyptians, Mesopotamia."

"How do you know?" I whispered.

"It's hardly there," he said. "Touch it."

I pointed a finger and reached out, aiming between the folds of ancient cloth at the dull grey bone wrapped inside. Closer, closer, until my finger felt as though it had been immersed in water of the exact same temperature as our surroundings. But that was all.

I pushed further, but there was no sense of the bone being there. It was not solid.

"Mirage?" I said. But I knew that was wrong. "What is this?" I hefted the package again, squeezed it, watched as it kept its shape and did not touch my skin. "What the bloody hell . . .?"

"Sometimes I guess even ghosts fade away," Scott said. He started the Jeep again and headed down the slope, out into the great desert.

I dropped the cloth bundle and kicked it away from my feet, watching, waiting for it to vanish or change. It did neither. But by the time we reached Scott's encampment, I thought perhaps it had faded a little more.

There were six tents scattered around a boggy depression in the ground. This was Scott's "spring". As we pulled up in the Jeep a flock of birds took off from the watering hole, darting quickly between the tents, moving sharply like bats. There was movement on the ground too; lizards shimmied beneath rocks, and a larger creature on four legs – too fast to see, too blurred for me to make out – flickered out of sight over the lip of the depression and into the desert.

"Quite a busy place," I said.

"It's the only spring for miles in any direction. I don't mind sharing it."

"You have others on the dig?" I asked. The tents looked deserted, unkempt, unused, but there was no other reason for them to be there.

"I used to," he said. "The last one left three weeks ago."

"You been skimping on their wages again?" I was trying to be jolly, but it could not reach my voice, let alone my smile.

"Frightened off," he said casually. He jumped from the Jeep, slammed the door and made for one of the tents.

I sat there for a while, trying to make out just what was different about this place compared to the other camps I had visited over the past two decades. The sun scorched down, trying to beat sense out of me. I closed my eyes, but still it found its way through, burning my vision red.

There were no people here, but that was not the main difference. There were fewer tents than most digs. Those that were here looked older, more bedraggled, as if they had been here for a lot longer than usual.

Scott stood staring back at me, hands on his hips. "I have a solar fridge," he said. "I have beer. We need to wash up, catch up, and then talk some about what I've found out here. You ready for some wonder, Pete?"

You ready for some wonder, Pete? He could have been reading my mind. And yet again, only my closeness to Scott prevented me from taking his comment as ridicule.

"Where's the dig?" I asked. "Where's the equipment? The washers, the boxed artefacts, the tools?"

"Ah," Scott said, throwing up his hands as if he'd been caught cheating at cards. "Well . . . Pete, please mate, I'm not trying to deceive you or catch you out. I just wanted you here to *share* something with me. Come on, into my tent. We'll crack a few, then I'll tell you everything. The time needs to be right."

"Matthew," I said. It was the first time I had mentioned Scott's most baffling e-mail since my arrival.

His face dropped and he looked down at his feet. We stayed that way for some time – me sat in the Jeep, slowly frying in the sun; Scott standing a few steps away examining the desert floor – and then he looked up.

"I haven't found him yet, but he's here."

I shook my head, frowned.

"I just need to look further . . . deeper . . ."

"Scott, has the sun—?"

"No, it hasn't, the sun hasn't touched me!" He almost became angry, but then he calmed, relaxed. "Pete, Matthew is here somewhere, because every dead person who has ever been wronged is here. Somewhere. Under our feet, under this desert. I've found the City of the Dead."

He turned and walked into one of the larger tents, leaving me alone in the Jeep. *The City of the Dead.* "A real city?" I said, but Scott seemed not to hear. I may have been alone. Tent flaps wavered for a few seconds in a sudden breeze, snapping angrily at the heat. I looked around and felt the immensity of the place bearing down, crushing me into the small, insignificant speck of sand I was. I was lost here, just as lost as I was at home, and though it was a feeling I had never grown used to, at least here I could find justification. Here, I was lost because the desert made light of so many aspects of life I took to be important. Here there was only water, or no water. Here too there was life, or death . . . and perhaps, if Scott's weird story held any trace of truth, something connecting the two.

But I could not believe. I did not have the *facility* to believe.

The sun must have driven him mad.

I jumped from the Jeep and followed him into his tent. Its interior was more well-appointed than it had any right to be, being compartmented into four by hanging swirls of fine material, and carpeted with an outlandish collection of rugs and throw cushions. In one quarter there was even some rudimentary furniture; a cot, a couple of low-slung chairs, and the solar fridge. He was pulling out two bottles of beer, their labels beaded with moisture.

He popped the caps and offered me a bottle. "To us!" he said. "Nice fuckin' life!"

"Absolutely," I said. We clinked bottles and drank. Only he could use that phrase and sound like he actually meant it.

"So tell me," I said. "This city? A real city? Why have you dragged me a million miles from home? Other than to sit and drink beer and see if you're still a pansy when it comes to booze."

"Three bottles and I'm done," he said, slurping noisily, wiping his chin, sighing in satisfaction. "I wonder if the dead spend their time mourning their senses?"

"The dead."

"Wouldn't you? If you died and could still think, reason, wouldn't you miss the sound of a full orchestra or a child's laugh? Miss the taste of a good steak or a woman's pussy? Miss the smell of fresh bread or a rose garden?"

I shrugged, nodded, not knowing quite how to respond.

"I would," he said. "Life is so lucky, you just have to wonder at it, don't you? Even thinking about it makes everything sound, taste and smell so much better." He looked at me. "Apart from you. Didn't you shower before you left home? Stinking bastard."

"And I suppose the showers are out of action," I said.

"Yes, but the Jacuzzi is in the next tent, and the Jacuzzi maids have been told to treat you special."

We shared a laugh then, for the first time this visit, and we sank wearily into the low chairs.

"The city," I said again. For someone so keen to drag me out here, he was being infuriatingly reticent about revealing his discovery.

"The city." He nodded. "I don't know if it's a real city, Pete. It's really here, really under our feet, and later I'll show you how I know that. The relic I handed you in the car is one of a few I've found, all of them . . . the same. Distant."

"It didn't feel all there."

"I think it was a ghost," he said, frowning, concentrating. "I think it was a part of someone who died a long time ago, but a piece that was buried or lost to the ages. The other things I've found point to that too."

"But have you actually *found* this place? Or are you surmising?"

"I've found enough to tell me that it's really here. For sure."

"These bits of ghosts?" I felt slightly foolish verbalising what Scott had said. It was patently wrong, there was some other explanation, but he could state these outlandish ideas comfortably. They did not sound so real coming from my sceptical self.

"Them, and more. I saw a part of the city revealed by a sink hole. Haven't been able to get close yet, the sand is too fluid. But there's nothing else it can be other than a buried ruin. Blocks, joints. I'll show you soon." He stared at me, challenging me to doubt.

"But why hasn't anyone else ever come here, found this stuff?"

Scott took another long drink from his bottle, emptying it, and then tilted his chair back and stared up at the tent ceiling. The sun cast weird shapes across the canvas, emphasising irregularities in its surface and casting shadows where sand had blown and been trapped, gathered in folds and creases. Scott looked as though he was trying to make sense.

"Scott?"

"I don't know," he said. "I don't know why no one has found those scraps of things before, or seen the ruin, or pieced together the evidence that's just lying around for me to find. And for a while, this made me doubt the truth of what I'd discovered. It couldn't be so easy, I thought. I couldn't have just stumbled across it. The evidence was so *real*, and the existence of the city here is so *right*, that others must have come to the same conclusions. A hundred others, a thousand."

"Are you quite sure no one has?"

"No," he said. "Not positive. Perhaps others have found the place, but never had a chance to reveal any of their findings."

I drank my beer and glanced around the tent. The closer I looked, the more I saw Scott's identity and personality stamped on the interior. A pile of books stood in one corner, all of them reference, no fiction. *What's the point of reading something that isn't true?* he'd once said to me, and I'd hated myself for not being able to come up with a good reason. Me, someone who worked in publishing, incapable of defending the purpose of my life. A belt lay carelessly thrown down on the rugs, various brushes, chisels and other implements of his trade tied to it. And the rugs themselves, far from being locally made, seemed to speak a variety of styles and cultures. Some told stories within their weaves, others held only patterns, and one or two seemed to perform both tasks with deceptive simplicity. The realisation that this man, my friend, did not actually have a home hit me then, strong and hard. He carried his home with him. After all these years, all this time, I guessed that I had assumed Scott would "come home" one day, not realising that he lived there every day of his life.

I missed my wife and kids then, sharply and brightly. But the feeling, though intense, was brief, and it soon faded into a background fog as Scott opened another bottle for each of us.

"I think I found this place for a reason," he said at last. "I can't say I was led here – I led myself if anything, looking, delving, searching into old histories and older tales – but I think it was meant to be."

"Don't tell me you've started to believe in fate."

"Only if it's self-made," he said, grinning. "I was fated to find this place, and you were fated to join me here, to search more fully. But only because that's what both of us wanted. Me to find Matthew, and you to give your life an injection of *life*."

I felt slighted, but I knew that he was right. In what he said about me, at least. As to Matthew, I could not begin to imagine.

"Where better for the city of the dead than nestling in the cradle of humanity?" he said. "Ethiopia is where the first people walked, where Homo Sapiens came into being. What better place?"

Something slammed against the side of the tent, sending the canvas stretching and snapping against the poles. I jumped to my feet and Scott glanced up, bottle poised at his mouth. "Sounds like we're in for a bit of a blow," he said.

"What the hell was that?"

"Wind. Storm coming in. You'd best get your things inside, we'll share this tent. Sand storms can be a bit disconcerting the first time you're caught in one, especially in a tent. Magnifies sound."

"You never said anything about sand storms." I felt the familiar fear rising inside, the one that hit me keen and hard when I was removed from my normal place, the company of normal people. The fear that said I was lost.

"Didn't say much at all," he said. "If I had, would you have come?"

"Of course!" I said. "Of course I would."

"Even though you think I've lost the plot?"

I considered lying to my friend then, but he would have known. He already knew the truth. "That was the main reason."

He smiled. "You're a good mate. I'm a lucky man. I may only have a few possessions to my name, but I'm rich in friends."

I was unfeasibly flattered by his comment, and I went on to say something trite in response – *thanks*, or *so am I* – when another gust of wind hit the tent. It seemed to suck the air from inside, drawing in the tent walls, pulling down the ceiling, shrinking the canopy as if to allow the desert sand and air to move closer. The whole structure leaned and strained for a few seconds that seemed like minutes, and then the gale lessened, the tent relaxed, and I glared down at Scott.

"Are we likely to be left homeless by this?" I said.

"Nope. Tent's meant to move and shift with the wind." His eyes were wide, seeing something far more distant than I knew, and I saw the familiar excitement there, the knowledge that there was more going on than we could ever hope to understand. That kind of ignorance never offended Scott. It merely gave him more cause to wonder.

I ducked outside to drag in my luggage, squinting against the sand being blown around by the rising wind. I stood there for a while, hand shielding my eyes, looking out towards the horizon to see whether I could see the storm. All around, the skies seemed to have darkened from light blue to a grubby, uniform grey. The sun was a smudge heading down to the western horizon, a smear of yellow like a daffodil whipped in the wind. Out past the camp I could see dust dancing above the ground, playing in spirals across the plain where the wind was being twisted by the heat. They flicked to and fro. Snapping at the ground. Whipping up more dust and sand to add to their mass.

And then, in the distance, floating above the horizon, there was a ghastly flash of light that lit the insides of the grey mass.

I gasped, felt grit on my teeth and in my eyes, and a few seconds later a long, low roar rolled in across the desert. It started subdued as a rumbling stomach, but increased in volume until it shook the ground beneath my feet and smashed my ears. Another flash displayed just how dark it had suddenly become. The resultant thunder merged with the first. The sky was screaming at me.

Just as I turned to go back into the tent the wind came down with a vengeance. What I had thought a gale was only a precursor to this onslaught. Sand was ripped up and blasted into my face, my ears, my hair and eyes and mouth. The sound was tremendous; wind, thunder, and grit coursing across the tent walls.

Inside, Scott had stood up and was opening two more bottles of beer. "Bit of a howler!"

"Is it always like this?" I had to shout just to be heard, and even then I could have been mumbling.

"Never seen one like this before! Here. More beer!" He held out the bottle and I went to him, accepting it, grateful for the dulling effect of the alcohol.

The storm came down. It was so loud that we could not hear ourselves talk, let alone each other, so we sat together and listened. I was terrified. The aural onslaught was so extreme that I wanted to scream, challenge its ferocity with some of my own. It beat into the tent, seemingly increasing in volume all the time, and it was all for me, aimed at me, targeted at me and me alone.

Scott sat wide-eyed and astonished, an inscrutable smile on his face as he stared at the canopy shifting above us.

It went on for a long time, becoming more fearsome with each passing minute. The roar turned into something that sounded alive, a snarling thing, crunching down into the ground in a hideous rhythm. The storm was running towards us across the desert, legs so long that the footfalls were minutes apart. It was not an image that I relished, but deep down I found some satisfaction in the stirring of my mostly dormant imagination. Thousands of tons of sand picked up by the storm abraded the whole landscape. It was powered against the canvas, setting the whole structure vibrating into a blur.

Something hit the tent. It slid slowly across the surface, visible as a dark shadow against the slightly lighter background. Its edges shimmered in the wind, and it took several long seconds to pass over the tent's domed roof, finally being sucked away into the storm with a whip-like crack.

"What the hell was that?" I shouted

"One of the other tents, I guess."

"I thought you said they were meant to bend, could withstand this?"

"We weren't in that one." His comment made no sense. I guessed I had misheard.

We attempted some more shouted conversation, but two out of every three words were stolen by the storm. I imagined these lost thoughts blown together, mixed and matched into things neither of us had ever meant to say. Scott's tent seemed to be withstanding the battering, its poles bending and twisting just as he'd said they were designed to, though I never once felt safe. As far as I was concerned we were forever on the verge of doom. The tent would be whipped away into the grey storm and we would be left bare, exposed, tumbling across the desert in a cloud of rugs and cushions and clothes, sand scoring our skin until the flesh showed through, blinded, deafened, eventually buried wherever the storm chose to dump us.

Scott never looked anything less than amazed. His excitement did not flicker. He continued drinking, and to my surprise so did I, still able to enjoy the beer even in such desperate circumstances. Part of it was the lulling effect of the alcohol, but perhaps I was also taking on some of Scott's awe through our companionable silence.

The lightning flashes continued, shimmering across the tents outer walls and casting strange shadows, swirling, dancing dust devils celebrating the wind. The thunder came almost immediately. It was a long time before the period between lightning and thunder began to grow again. I imagined the storm waiting above our tent, examining us, interested in these petty humans that had decided to pitch against its power.

Still the sands scoured the tent, driven by the horrendous gales. I shouted at Scott several times to ask whether the canvas could withstand such a battering, but he did not answer. He knew I was asking something but he merely smiled, eyes sparkling, bringing the bottle to his lips once more. He existed in his own little space.

There was no point in trying to sleep. I checked my watch regularly, but day and night had become confused, and when the time began to make no sense I stopped checking. Perhaps night fell, because the dark storm became that much darker, but lightning gave us brief moments of illumination here and there. Scott lit some electric lanterns around the tent, solar batteries charged during the day to keep the day with us through the long, dark desert nights. And it grew perceptibly cooler. I opened my luggage and rummaged around for a jumper and a pair of combat trousers, standing to change, with my head only inches from the convex canvas ceiling. For some reason it seemed so much louder than when I was sitting down.

Eventually, after hours that felt like days, the storm began to abate. We only realized how much it had lessened when we found that we could converse comfortably by raising our voices only slightly.

"How long do these usually last?" I asked.

Scott shrugged. "As I said, never seen one like this before. But I think that was short."

I looked at my watch, but still it made no sense.

"Hours," he said. "Maybe six." He glanced at the empty beer bottles strewn around the floor of his tent. "Maybe more."

I suddenly realized how much I needed to urinate. I looked around the tent but there was no sign of a bucket or a partitioned toilet area.

"Two tents along," Scott said. "If it's still there." He pointed the way without standing. He suddenly looked very drunk, even though minutes before he had been alert and observant.

I stared at him. I was scared, terrified of the desert and the prospect of leaving the tent on my own, but I could not articulate that idea.

He knew. "Come on," he said, standing and swaying slowly towards me. "Shit, listen to that. Like it never was."

The storm had all but died down. There was a continuous, low hissing of sand slipping slowly from the dome tent. But even that faded away after only a few more seconds, and we were left with our own heavy breathing.

The silence was shocking. My stomach rumbled, and I was ridiculously embarrassed.

"Like it never was," Scott said again. "Let's go and see what it's left us."

We exited the tent into a blood-red dusk.

And we saw what the storm had left behind.

The landscape had changed beyond recognition.

Where the watering hole had been, a sand dune now lay. Where the neighbouring tents had been pitched there was now a wind-patterned expanse of loose sand. And the horizon that had once been apparent, viewed across packed sand and low, gentle mounds, was now hidden behind something new.

Rising out of the desert, a city.

I fell to my knees. I could not take in the immensity of what we were viewing. My mind would not permit it. It did not fit within the confines of my imagination, the limits of my understanding.

Scott was amazed, but not surprised. That was something that terrified me even more. He was not surprised.

"There it is," he said. "There it is, at last." He walked across the altered landscape, ignoring the fact that ours was the only tent left standing. There was no sign of the others. They could have been anywhere.

"Scott?" I whispered at last. He turned and looked, smiling, but not at me. "Scott, what's going on?"

"City of the Dead," he said. "The storm gave it to us. Pete, you have to come and see it with me. Don't just stay here."

"I'm afraid. It shouldn't be there, it's too . . . big."

"Out of the desert, that's all. *Please* Pete. You'll always regret it if you don't come. You'll think about it forever, it'll haunt you . . . *believe* me, I know. Live a little."

Live a little. Yes, that was what I wanted to do. Scott had lived a lot, and I only wanted to live a little. But still, I was terrified. I could conceive of no way that this could be happening. I looked past him at the ruins revealed by the storm. They seemed to begin just over a wide, low dune created at the western extremes of the old camp, and if they were as close as I believed they probably rose about 20 feet above the desert level. Only 20 feet.

But before the storm, there had been nothing there at all.

"They shouldn't be there . . ." I said.

Scott shrugged. "The desert is deceiving. Messes with perspective. Come on."

He was lying. But somehow I stood and followed.

The sand underfoot was loose and treacherous; more than once we both slipped and slid several steps down the side of the new dune. I could not take my eyes from the ruin rising before me. I tried to convince myself that I had been misled by Scott's certainty; that the structure was naturally formed, carved from solid stone by millennia of scouring wind. But it could only be artificial. There were the joints between blocks, the blocks themselves huge and probably each weighing several tons. And the windows, squared at the base, curved inward at their head, like traditional church windows back home. Around the windows, still visible here and there, ornamentation. Scrolls. Patterned carvings that may have been some sort of writing. And in one place, staring out at us as we approached, guarding the ancient ruin it formed a part of, the face of a gargoyle.

I tried not to look, but my gaze was drawn there. It had three eyes, two mouths, and though its edges had been worn by eons of erosion, still its teeth looked sharp.

"Scott," I whispered.

"I know!" he said, excitement to my fear. "Come on! I think this is just a part of it."

We walked slowly up the low slope of the new dune. I glanced back once or twice at the remains of the camp we left behind. Only the single large tent was visible now, with a few sand-covered mounds here and there which may have been scattered equipment. Ahead of us, the old ruin revealed itself more and more with each step.

I was afraid to reach the top. Afraid to see whether this was just a part of it, or if there was so much more beyond. I so wanted this to be a single tall wall.

When we crested the hill, the world became a different place. Everything I had held true shifted, much of it drastically. My beliefs, my faith took a gut-punch and reeled against the assault. Scott touched my shoulder and then held on; he knew what I was feeling. I looked at him, and his eyes were ablaze with the thrill of discovery.

The ruins lay in a wide hollow in the desert. There was not only one high wall. It was not even a single building. Spread across the floor of the depression in the land, seemingly growing from the ground, lay the remains of several large and dozens of smaller buildings. Sand and grit was skirted around bases and against walls, drifted up and through openings that may have been windows, may have been wounds. Some of the ruins rose above the level of the desert floor, but many more had been revealed below, shown the sunlight for the first time in eons when the terrible sand storm had opened them up to view. The hollow must have been a mile across.

"Let's go down," Scott said.

"Why?"

"I want to see. I want to know where the dead live. Look, over there!" He pointed over to our left, and before the dark stone of the first tumbled building there was something in the sand, something dark, moving.

At first I thought it was a scorpion or small lizard. But as we moved closer I saw the reality. It was a foot, still clod in the remains of a sandal, bones stripped of flesh and dangling with scraps of skin, snapped or broken at the ankle. The delusion of movement stopped as we came closer, but I blinked several times and wiped sand from my eyes, waiting for it to move again.

Scott hesitated momentarily before picking it up. "Here," he said, offering me the relic. "Touch something timeless."

Before I could refuse he grabbed my hand and placed the skeletal foot there. It had no weight. Lighter than a feather, little more than a memory, it lay across my palm and fingers, yet seemed not to touch them. It felt warm, though that may have been the sun beating through its nothingness—

And the sun struck down as this person walked, endlessly, herded with a thousand more, driven from one old land and taken towards another. Soldiers and settlers accompanied them on their way, using guns and boots if any of the ragged tribe lagged behind. This person was old by now, crying, leaving a trail of tears as she was torn away from her own lands for the first time ever, and she died from thirst and sorrow on strange soil—

I dropped the thing back into the sand and it landed with a thud. It sat there motionless, and at any second I expected it to strike out.

"There's more," he said. "Signs of habitation."

I shook my head, trying to dispel whatever it was I had imagined. *Hallucination? Vision?* "You really believe this place is what you said it is?"

"Of course!" he said. "And there's more, much more. This is just the surface. I want to go down inside. Matthew is inside!"

"If that were true – if everything you're saying, all this madness, has an ounce of truth – do you know what this would do to the world? To religion, belief, faith?"

"I don't care," Scott said.

"Why?"

"Because caring can't change the truth."

I stared over Scott's shoulder at the ruined city risen from the sands.

"I want to go *deeper*," Scott said, and he turned and walked down towards the ruins.

I followed, sliding once or twice, starting a small avalanche that preceded us both down the slope. There were several more dark shapes in the sand, shapes with glimpses of white within, old bones, ready to crumble in the heat. I wondered if they were light and insubstantial like the foot. Light, but filled with memories waiting to be relived. I had no wish to touch them.

Scott reached the first ruin. He stood very close, hand held up in front of him, palm out, almost touching the wall. The stone sported some elaborate designs, letters or images, numbers or figures.

"Old," Scott said. "These are so old."

"What language is that? Is that hieroglyphics?"

"An earlier form, perhaps. Though initiated separately. I've seen variations of this before, many times all across the world. I've been searching for so long, it's almost my second tongue."

"What does it say?"

Scott turned to me and smiled, and his hand touched the rock for the first time. He sighed and blinked heavily, as if suddenly tired or drunk. "You don't want to know," he said. "Come on."

Scott and I circled the stone ruin. It was built from huge flat blocks, far too large to possibly be moved by hand, and old though it was, burial in the sands must have protected it from erosion by the winds of time. As well as the strange markings there were several more of the gruesome gargoyle-things at various points on its upper surface, not corresponding at all with any opening or any particular spacing. I glanced back, and our footprints seemed to have disappeared into the desert. The sand was so smooth, so fine, that it had flowed back in to fill the depressions, leaving little more than dents in the surface. It was as though the buried city were swallowing our presence. Or wiping it away.

"I think this may be a temple," he said.

"May *have* been," I said.

"No." He shook his head, frowning and smiling at me at the same time. "This may be the city of the dead, but it can never be deserted."

"What do you mean?"

"Come on," he said. "Deeper."

Further down in the depression stood the remains of more buildings. They looked ruined to me, ancient and ruined, but what Scott had said stuck with me, forced me to view them in a different light. So there was no roof on these four tumbled-down walls, but what need of a roof buried in the sands? The doorway was blocked with the tumbled stone arch that had once held it open, but do the dead need true doorways? I looked around at our feet and saw more of the scattered remains, some of them still wrapped in old cloth, some of the bones white in the glaring sun, bleached and seemingly brittle as if they had been exposed for eons, not hours. The wind must have danced and spun between these barely-standing walls, because the stone floor was revealed in places, sand swept aside. It held patterns, coloured rocks inlaid in the stone so perfectly that their edges seemed to merge, offering no cracks for time to prise apart. Scott tried to brush away more sand, reveal a larger pattern, but the more that was on display the less sense it made.

He revelled in the mystery, while it made me more nervous.

"Is that a language?" I asked. "Same as the wall markings?"

Scott shook his head. "Not a language as we know it," he said. "I think it's meant to inspire feelings. True art. We could carry on, uncover it all. Find out *which* feelings."

I shook my head. "Let's move on."

"Good man!" Scott said, slapping my shoulder and hurrying on ahead.

There was a maze of long, low walls at the base of the depression, spreading maybe three hundred feet from side to side. Scott paused at its perimeter for a few moments, looking around, kicking at the sand. He stooped and picked up a badly eroded bone. It may have been a skull, but it was full of unnatural holes. He closed his eyes.

The air around us seemed to shimmer, as if stirred by an invisible breeze. I felt no breath against my sweating skin, but the ruined walls and the high ridge of sand around us flickered as if through a heat haze. And though I felt no breath, I seemed to hear a whisper.

Scott dropped the relic, glancing back at me. "Murder," he said.

I looked at the tangled mess of cloth and bone. And then I surprised myself. I must have shocked Scott as well, because he raised his eyebrows and took a step back.

I reached out and picked up the skull—

And it was dark by the sea, windy and wet, stinking of rotting sea life as beaches always do. This person stood with their back to the cliffs, staring out, watching the bursts of effervescence as waves broke and captured the moonlight. In one hand there was a gun, in the other a torch, and when the small rowing boat came ashore both would be pointed outward this night, and both used. But that chance did not arrive. The waves hid the sound of the shape creeping up behind him, out of the cave where it must have been waiting all day. When the knife curled around his throat and slid through the skin, the moon caught the spurting blood, bright as breaking waves, and the betrayal tasted of salt—

I dropped the bundle and watched it sink into the sand. The sudden change from vision to real life – darkness and wet, to dryness and blazing sun – startled me, but not as much as it should have. I squinted at Scott, and for the first time I saw a fleck of fear in his eyes, a dark, fiery look that floated there like the sun reflected in negative.

"Did you see?" he whispered.

I nodded.

"You saw what ties that person to this city," he said. "Why they can't let go."

"Murder?"

"Unfinished business."

I looked down at where the old skull had fallen and sunk. I felt observed.

"I'm going down," Scott said,

"What?"

"I'm going down, into the city. For every ghost with unfinished business, there's someone accountable."

"Matthew," I said, but Scott chose not to answer. He was already walking away, across the boiling sand, past ruins that should not be, past the mysterious language carved into these stone walls, his footprints being swallowed by the desert behind him, eschewing the sun for darker depths. When he reached another pile of stone protruding from the ground he turned and looked back at me.

"I'd like you to come," he said. Perhaps he feigned the fear. Maybe he was playing me even then, luring me to his own ends. But I was his friend, and his fear I thought I heard in those few words somehow enabled me to better my own.

I followed him into the ground.

The way down should never have been there. After the storm, and after the eons which the desert had had to fill this place with its own, there should have been no clear route underground. The fluid sand should have seen to that. It was as if while the gale thundered above, so too had a storm raged down below, powerful enough to expel the sand like the cork from a shaken bottle of Champagne. And Scott had found the way.

"Down there," he said. "Down there we'll find ghosts, Pete. Wraiths never given a chance to rest. Are you sure you want to come with me?"

"I've come all this way," I said, failing to understand my own skewed logic.

"I knew I could count on you. Say goodbye to the sun!" He looked up and squinted at the sun, blazing and hot even though it was dipping into the west.

I looked as well, but not for long. I did not want to imbue the moment with too much ceremony. That would be admitting that I may never see the sun again.

The hole was just wide enough for our entry. It opened up beneath a wall, smashed through the buried foundations by some ancient cataclysm, leading in and down like an opened throat waiting to swallow us whole. Scott slipped quickly inside on his stomach, but I lay there for a while in the hot sand, looking at the perimeter of the hole and wondering just what was holding it up. It looked like compacted sand, little more. The wall passed above it and pressed down, but there was no lintel, no supporting stone. A trial of danger before entering the City of the Dead.

I squeezed through, scraped my back against the edge, felt sand crumble down the neck of my shirt, and then I was inside.

Scott was rummaging around at the base of a wall, cursing and shaking his head. Enough light filtered in for me to see him there, moving stuff aside with his foot, bending, grabbing something, dropping it again. He groaned and sighed, spat and whimpered.

"Scott!"

"We need a torch," he said. "We need some light." And I saw what he was doing. There were more segments of skeletons piled against the wall, as if blown there by some subterranean wind, and Scott was sorting them until he found a bone long enough to use as a torch. And every time he touched a bone . . .

"Here," he said. "Not so bad. Love rejected. Hell of a reason to miss out on Heaven." He held a long thigh bone, knotted a wad of material about its smashed joint, twisting and tying it hard so that the fire would take its time eating through. He slipped a lighter from his pocket and gave us light.

We were in a long corridor, its floor sloping down quite steeply, its far end lost in darkness.

"I guess we go down," he said.

"No other way. Scott, do you really think"

"Shhh!" he hissed. "Hear that? Do you *hear that*?"

I listened intently, breathing out slowly through my nose, and perhaps I heard the echoes of his voice. They seemed to go on for a long time, and they grew closer again before fading away into the stone walls.

"Let's go," he said. "They know we're here."

He headed off into the corridor and I could only follow. The light from his make-do torch was very weak, but it bled back far enough to touch the ground around my feet, casting sad reflections from the bones Scott had rooted through. They were mixed, but I was sure they would not match. A dozen remains here, two dozen, and I accidentally kicked one aside with my sandaled foot—

The ship was going, sinking quickly, and this person was trapped inside, searching for an air trap, trying to force his way through the deluge, pushing aside floating things, food, ropes, bodies, cursing at those that had shut them down here, cursing until his mouth opened and emitted a final bubbling gasp that no one would ever hear—

Scott would have felt every one of those remains. Every death, each betrayal or sin or deceit, telling its story as he shuffled the remains.

"It's all so unfair." I had no idea what I was seeing, and no idea why.

"It's life," he said. "Or death."

Scott went on, and the slope began to dip down even steeper than before. I glanced back frequently, just to reassure myself that the glow of sunlight was still behind us. That small entrance grew smaller and fainter, from a false sun into little more than a smudge in the dark. And then, as I knew had to happen, we turned a bend in the corridor and the daylight vanished.

I stopped and called out to Scott. "We're alone."

He paused and looked back over my shoulder. The torch he carried was growing fainter as the fire consumed the ancient material. I reached out to take it from him but there was nothing there. No bone to touch, no friction, no heat when I held my hand in the guttering flames. Nothing.

"Scott," I said. "Just where the hell are you taking us?"

"There'll be light," he said. "Every place I've read of this, there's the light of the dead. We just have to get there. This is the route to the city, not the city proper. We should find it soon, Pete. Soon! And then perhaps I can lay Matthew to rest."

"This is madness," I said. Our voices were peculiarly dead in that subterranean place, consumed by the rock walls and the weird hieroglyphs. The etchings writhed in the weak light from Scott's insubstantial torch, given a life of their own.

"Stay with me, Pete," he said. He turned away and continued along the tunnel, heading down and away from the vanished light, perhaps leading us into places and dangers neither of us could truthfully imagine. "You're my best friend."

I followed because it was the only thing I could do. I like to think I stayed on his tail because of my devotion to my friend, my burgeoning sense of adventure, my excitement at what we may discover around the next curve in the corridor, or the next. But in reality I think I was simply scared. I could not face the walk back out on my own. Uphill. Past those strange markings on the wall, those bones that had no weight or touch.

I had no choice but to follow. We walked for what felt like hours. Scott's torch had guttered down to little more than a blue smudge in the utter darkness. The new light that manifested came so slowly, so gradually, that for a while I could not understand how that failing torch was throwing out so much illumination. But this new light was growing and expanding, dusty and blue, originating from no single source. The walls of the passage began to glow, as if touched by the sticky early morning sun, and the shapes and tales carved there told differing stories as the shadows writhed and shifted. None of them were clear to me.

"Scott," I said, afraid, more afraid than I had been since those first blasts of the storm had assaulted the tent walls.

"The light of the dead," he said. "They need it to see. I guess they don't like the dark. We're almost there, Pete."

Ahead of us the passage narrowed, walls closing in and ceiling dipping until we had to stoop to pass by. The ceiling touched my head once and I did not like the sensation; the rock was smooth and as warm as living flesh. I could not shake the idea that we were walking willingly into the belly of a beast, and now here we were at the base of its oesophagus, deep deep down, about to enter its stomach and submit ourselves to digestion.

There were more remains around our feet here, scattered across the ground offering no resistance as we waded through. The bones tumbled aside, clanking silently together, some falling into dust as soon as they were disturbed and others rolling together as if coveting their former cosy togetherness. I could not feel them. It was like kicking aside wafts of smoke. I wondered if they could feel me.

Scott was ahead of me. When I heard him gasp, and I walked into him, and his gasp came again as a groan, I knew that things were about to change. The claustrophobic passage opened out on to a small ledge, strewn with skeletal parts that seemed to dance away as we both came to a stunned standstill, looking forward, out, ahead of us at the place we had come down here to find.

I once stood on the viewing platform at the top of the Empire State Building in New York, looking down at the city surrounding me, the myriad streets and blocks crawling with people and cars, the mechanical streams spotted yellow with frequent taxis, sirens singing up out of the city like long-lost wailing souls, other high buildings near and far speckled with interior lights, the city rising in three dimensions, not just spread out like the carpet of humanity I imagined. I could look east towards the river and see a hot dog vendor stand at a road junction, and then south towards Greenwich Village, where through one of the telescopes I could just make out someone hurrying across a street with a dog tugging them along, and I knew that these two people may never meet. In a city of this size, there was a good chance that they would pass their lives without ever exchanging glances. And I, at the top of this huge tower, could see it all. I could see a fire to the east of Central Park, follow the course of fire engines screeching intermittently through the traffic, but wherever the owners of the burning building were I could not tell them. I had a strange feeling of being lifted way above the city, an observer rather than a player, and as I descended in the express elevator and exited once more on to the streets, I experienced a dislocation that lasted for the rest of the day. I glanced back up at the tower, and wondered just who was looking down at me right then.

What I saw in that place way below the desert was larger, older, and far less explicable.

The City of the Dead lay spread out before us. It was flat and utterly without limit, stretching way out farther than I could see, and it was sheer distance rather than anything else that faded it into the horizon. No hazy atmosphere, no darkening of the air – the light of the dead was rich and pure and all-encompassing, much more revealing and honest than mere sunlight – but pure, unbelievable distance. The city went on forever, and I could only see at the speed of light. It spread out left and right and ahead, the only visibly defined border being the high cliff from which we had emerged. The wall fell down to the city and rose up higher than I could see, and it faded similarly as I looked left and right. It did not seem to curve around, perhaps enclosing the city, but stood on a straight line, and here and there I spied other ledges and darker smudges which may have been the mouths of other tunnels. In the distance I thought I saw another shocked individual standing on one of these ledges, but I blinked and the image was taken away.

I looked down, trying to judge how far below the ground lay. *Too far to climb but close enough to fall*, I thought, and though I had no idea where the idea came from I looked at Scott, caught his eye, knew that he was thinking the same awful thing.

Together we stepped forward and tipped slowly over the lip of the ledge, leaning into space, somehow welcoming the plunge that would immerse us in this city.

The fall lasted long enough for me to make out plenty more detail. I did not dwell upon the strangeness of what was happening – right then, it did not seem important – and though I knew that things had changed irrevocably as Scott and I had set foot on that ledge, I took the opportunity offered to view this place. Here was the supposed City of the Dead. The buildings were hugely diverse, ranging from small shacks made of corrugated tin spread across branch uprights, to golden-domed offerings of love; steel and glass towers, to complex timber-clad settlements; frosty ice-sculptured homes, to hollows in the ground, caves, deep holes heated by the boiling insides of the hot earth itself. There was no order, no design to the city, no blocks or arrangement, merely buildings and the spaces in between. Here and there I saw wider areas that may have been parks, though there was no greenery to be seen. The things in these parks may have been dead trees, or simply much taller skeletons than any I had seen before. Some buildings had windows and some did not, and only some of those with windows retained their glazing. It was only as we fell closer to the city – and that fall, that plunge, was still accepted by both of us – that my attention was drawn more to the spaces in between the buildings.

In those spaces, things moved.

Until now I had seen this as a city of the dead, and I was falling towards it, and that did not matter.

Now, seeing this movement in the streets and roads and alleys and parks – seeing also the flittering movements behind the windows of the taller buildings, shadows denying the strange, level light that this place possessed – I came to dwell upon exactly what was happening to us. We fell, though there was no sensation of movement; no wind past my ears, no sickness in my stomach, no velocity. And soon, looking down, I knew that there was an impact to come. Directly below us was a collection of smaller, humped buildings, rising from the ground like insect hills, surrounded by taller constructions which even now we began to fall past.

"Scott!" I yelled, but even though I felt no breeze my voice was stolen away. He was next to me, spread-eagled in the air, and when he caught my eye he looked quickly away again. What that signified, I did not know.

The impact came closer, and then it was past. It did not hurt, and I had no memory at all of having landed. One second we were falling by tall buildings, flitting past windows which each seemed to hold a shadowy face observing our descent, and the next we were on the ground. Dust rose around us and floated in the still air, drifting up, up, as if eager to trace the paths of our recent descent. We lay there, watching the dust form ghostly shapes around us. Somehow, at the end of our fall, we had flipped over to land on our backs.

"We're here," Scott whispered. "Look."

He did not point and I did not turn my head to see where he was looking. I did not need to. Because one of those ambiguous shapes suddenly became more real, emerging from the dust like sunbeams bursting through cloud cover, carrying a bluish light and forming a very definite shape as it passed first over Scott's body, and then my own. The shape of a woman in long, flowing robes, her hair short and cropped, her hands held out before her as if forever warding off some horrible fate, and her foot touched my arm—

She sees it coming at her, the dog, the animal, whatever it is, she sees it and she sees the faces of those behind it, and they could be grimacing or laughing. She brings up her hands, as if that will do any good, and before the thing crashes into her in a rage of teeth and claws, she catches sight of the face of someone she had once loved in the gleeful crowd—

I scurried back, pushing with my feet until I was leaning against a stone wall, shaking my head to loosen the image. The wraith drifted away down the street and eventually faded into the uniform blue light that smothered this place. The wall at my back should have felt good, but it was merely more confirmation that this was somewhere that should not be, as was the solid ground, the ground that I had hit after minutes of falling. I glanced up, but the cliff wall was nowhere to be seen. Only that blue light.

"Are we alive?" I said, a sick fear suddenly sending me cold.

"Of course," Scott said. "Do you remember dying?"

"No. But that doesn't mean we didn't. We fell!"

"Everyone here remembers dying," he said. "That's why they're here."

"But why."

"No more questions, Pete," he said. "Just open your eyes to it all."

"I'm not sure I want to."

Scott reached down to help me up. His firm grip was comforting, and we held on to each other for a second or two as we stood there together, looking around. He was real to me and I was real to him, and right then that was very important. These buildings were real too. I kicked at the stone wall I had been leaning against. There was a dull *thud* and dust drifted from my tatty shoe. And I realized then, for the first time, how utterly silent it was.

Wherever we were, however deep below the ground or submerged in disbelief, there were no voices, no gusts of air, no sounds of a city, no movements, no breaths. My own heart started to sound excessively loud as it continued on its startled course, busy pumping oxygen through veins to dilute my fear and cool the heat of my distress. I was not used to existence without noise of some kind. At home, with a wife and two children sharing the house, there was always a raised voice or a mumbled dream, music or television adding a theme, toys being crashed or musical instruments adding their tone-deaf lilt to the air. Even at work, reading and editing, the voices in my mind were loud enough to be audible. Here, in this city larger than any I had ever seen or imagined, the complete silence was incongruous and unfair. And it made things so obviously false.

"We're not really here," I said. Scott ignored me. Perhaps in silence he was dealing with this in his own way.

There was an opening in the stone wall a few metres along, and I went to it and looked inside. I saw a room, large and high-ceilinged, bereft of anything – furniture, character, life. Four walls, a floor, a ceiling, nothing more. There were no signs of it ever having been used. There was a doorway in the far wall without a door, no glass in the window I looked through, no light fitting in the ceiling; the same uniform blue light lit every corner of the room, top and bottom, revealing nothing but slight drifts of dust. Shadows had no place here. I stood back slightly and looked up, realising that the building was maybe fifteen storeys tall, all of them identically holed with glassless windows, and I was certain that each room and floor was the same sterile, deserted emptiness.

Scott nudged against me as he walked by, and when I glanced down I realized that he had done so on purpose.

There were several more wraiths moving along the street. Two of them walked, strutting purposefully together, their expressions and facial features similar. They wore bathing shorts and nothing else, their torsos and limbs dark with suntan, faces young and strong and long, long dead. They did not touch each other as they strode by, and they exuded contempt, staring straight ahead and doing nothing to acknowledge the other's closeness. Another shape seemed to float and spin through the air, but as she passed by I realized that she was falling horizontally, clothes ripped from her body by the invisible wind that whipped her hair around her head, face and shoulders. She may have been beautiful, but the forces crushing her this way and that were too cruel to tell. She passed over the heads of the striding brothers and cornered at the end of the street, her fall unimpeded. Two more shapes came by separately, neither of them appearing to notice us. One shouted silently and waved fists at the sky, and the other struggled on footless legs, stumping his way along and swinging his arms for balance, as if pushing through mud. One of his hands brushed mine, I saw it but did not feel it—

He was in the sea, trapped there by a giant clam that had closed around both feet, his muscles burning acid into his bones as he struggled to keep his nose high enough to snort in a desperate breath between waves, and even though the salt water was doing its best to blind him he could see the boat bobbing a few feet away, the faces peering over the edge, laughing so much as their tears of mirth fell to quicken his fate—

I gasped and pressed myself back against the wall, watching the dead man hobble away.

Scott had remained in the centre of the narrow street, staring about him as the new shapes breezed by. Perhaps they touched him, but he seemed not to have noticed. With the taste of brine still on my own lips I went to him, desperate to feel someone real again. I clapped my hand to his shoulder, held on hard, followed his gaze. High buildings, that blue light, no sign of where we had come from . . . and high up, sometimes, darker blue shapes sweeping by.

"What are they?" I asked.

"I don't know. But Pete, Matthew is here. He has to be! I have to find him, and however long it takes . . ." He left the sentence unfinished, ominous with possibilities.

"These aren't just ghosts," I said.

"Not ghosts, no!" He shook his head as if frustrated at my naïveté. "Dead people, Pete."

"There's nothing to them!"

"Do you have to feel them for them to be real or mean anything? Can you touch your dreams, taste your imagination? They're as real as we are, just not in quite the same place, the same way. And they're here because they were wronged."

"How could you know all this?"

"You think I haven't been looking for this place?" he said. "Interrogating every scrap of ancient script I've discovered, or uncovered in some godforsaken old library somewhere? Tearing apart whole digs by hand to find a fragment of writing about it, a shred of evidence? Ever since I first got wind of this place the year Matthew died, it's been my only reason to keep on living."

"Matthew? Why . . .?"

He looked at me then, a quick glance, as if he was unwillingly to relinquish sight of our unbelievable surroundings. "I wasn't there when he died."

"He died of leukaemia, Scott," I said.

"I should have been there."

"You couldn't have done anything! He died of leukaemia, just tell me what you could have done?"

He stared at me, but not for effect. He really could not understand why I was even asking. "I could have held his hand," he said.

"You think your young son could hold that against you?"

"No, but I could. And that's enough to keep him here."

"You can't know any of this!" I said, shaking my head, looking around at the impossible buildings with the occasional impossible shape floating, striding or crawling by. "You might think you do, but you've been—"

"Misled?" He said it mockingly, as if anyone could draw any sane idea from this place.

"No," I said. "Not misled. Maybe just a little mad."

"Do you see all this?" he asked.

"I don't know *what* I see. It's madness. My eyes are playing tricks, I'm drunk, I'm dreaming, I'm drugged. All of this is madness and—"

"*You see the City of the Dead*!" He grabbed my lapels and propelled me back against a wall, dust puffing out around me in an uneven halo. His shout tried to echo off between the buildings, but it was soon swallowed or absorbed, and it did not return. He did not shout again.

"Scott, please . . ." I felt a little madness closing in on myself. Some vague insulating layer of disbelief still hung around me, blurring the sharp edges and dangerous points of what I saw and what I could not believe. But beyond that layer lay something far more dangerous. I wondered if Scott was there already.

"Don't 'please' me!" he said. "Matthew is here, *trapped* here, because of *me*! He could be there!" He pointed along the street at a large domed building, ran there, peered in through one of several triangular buildings. I followed after him and looked inside. There were shadows moving about, writhing across the floor like the dark echoes of snakes, passing through the blue light and somehow negating it with themselves.

"There's only—"

"He could be there!" Scott said, running away from me again, dodging around a grey shape that stood wringing its hands. He passed by a row of squat-fronted buildings and ducked into a gap in the block, disappearing from view. I followed quickly and found him leaning over a low wall, looking down into the huge basement rooms that it skirted. "Down there, see?" Scott said. "He could so easily be down there!" I saw several shapes sitting on rough circular seats, each of them gesticulating and issuing silent shouts and pleas.

"Is he?" I asked.

"No," Scott said, "not there. But there! He could be there!" Yet again he ran, heading between two buildings, and the lonely pad of his footsteps sounded like a riot in that silent place.

I ran after him, terrified that he would lose me in a maze of alleys and streets, parks and squares. "Matthew!" he called, still running, calling again. His voice came back to me and guided me on.

I did not want to be lost. I'd spent my whole life being lost and found, lost and found again, sometimes the same day, emotionally tumbled and torn down by the doubt and fear that time was running away from me. My mind could not cope with the complexity of life, I had often thought, and while others found their escape in imagination and wonder, I wallowed, lost in a miserable self-pity. Now, in this place, lost was the last place I wanted to be.

I spun around a corner and straight into the figure of a lady of the night standing against a wall, smiling at me, making some silent offer as I ducked by. Her fingers snagged my sleeves and brushed against my skin, and in that brief instant I saw abuse more terrible than I could have imagined. I gasped, fell to my knees and crawled forward, desperate to escape this dead woman's cursed touch. I turned and glanced back at her. She was laughing, pointing at me as if that could touch and show me again. I stood and ran, wondering just how mad a dead person could become.

Scott's shouts drew me on. I was darting around corners blind, not knowing what would be revealed beyond. A long alley once, the blue light of the dead faded here as if swallowed by the walls. Then a square courtyard, filled with so many wandering shapes that I could not help but touch several of them as I ran by, sensing them stroke my skin but unaware of any weight, any substance to their presence. At each touch, I saw something of their reasons for being here. This place was an unbalanced concentration of pain and suffering, I knew, but before long I began to despair that there was any good left anywhere in the world.

I wondered what these dead things saw or felt when *I* touched *them*.

"In here!" Scott called. "Or over there!" His voice angled in from several directions at once now, the city juggling it to confuse me. I passed from the courtyard into another narrow alley, this one turning and bearing downward, no square angles, only curved walls to enclose its sloping floor. There were shapes sitting in doorways like black-garbed Greek women, but they all looked up at me with pale, dead faces. Some reached out to show me their stories, most did not. One of them turned at my approach and passed through a doorway into the building behind it, and I could not help but stop and look inside. There were things apparently growing in there, strange dark fungi breaking from the floor and reaching for the ceiling, but when one of them moved and cast its dead gaze upon me, I turned and fled.

Some dead people walked, some ran. And some stood still or sat down, forgetting to move at all.

Scott's voice rang out again, and for the first time I realized that it was only his voice. Footsteps no longer accompanied his cries. He had either stopped running, or he was too far away for me to hear them. Yet still he was crying out for Matthew, and somewhere he looked upon ghosts and did not see his dead son's face, because his call came again and again. I ran on, but with every step, and whichever direction I took, his voice grew fainter.

I came across a district of timber buildings, most of them squared and severe looking with their ancient saw marks, a few seemingly made from the natural shapes of cut trees; curved roofs, irregular walls, windows of bare branches where leaves may have chosen to grow, once.

There was no greenery, only dead wood.

I wondered who had built this place.

The ground was scattered with fine sawdust, ankle deep in places, and I saw no footprints of any kind. My own were the first, and I imagined them as prints on the moon, no air movement to take them away, destined to remain for as long as time held them. Yet the dead were here too, though leaving no trace. Remains were scattered against the timber walls, just as they had been in the caves and tunnel leading down from the surface, and as I accidentally kicked a skull out of my way I had a brief inkling of its owner's fate—

Standing in the woods as strange sounds came in, weird visions lighting their way between the trees as the hunt drew closer, the air grew warmer, and the fear became an all-encompassing thing as the first of the arrows *twanged* into trees and parted the air by his head. The voices called in a language he could not know, though he recognized the universal sound of laughter, vicious laughter, and that made him turn to run. The knowledge of his own death was there already, as if he had seen what I was seeing many times over—

I kicked the holed skull away just as I heard the sound of an arrow parting the air.

The place was utterly silent once more as I looked down into the sightless sockets. *Where was his ghost?* I wondered. *Is this it? Do even ghosts fade away in the end?* And as I mused on this, wondering where I was and why and just how I would ever escape, I realized that Scott's voice had bled away to nothing, and that I was alone and lost.

I despaired. My breath came heavy and fast, and the air tasted of the blue light, cool and devoid of life. I could not be here, or anywhere like this, because cities like this did not exist. I saw and smelled this place, but I was lying to myself. In fleeing, Scott had taken his open mind with him, leaving me with my own weak, insipid perception of things.

I found a small courtyard, the fossilized remains of plants clinging solidly to the walls. The well at the centre was dry as my mouth. There were no dead here and no remains on the ground, so for a time I could pretend that I was alone. I sat beneath an overhanging balcony. There was no shade from the unvarying bluish light, but the balcony gave me the psychological impression of being hidden away from prying eyes. So I sat there, held my head in my hands and looked down at my feet, striving to forget that the dust around them was in a place that could not be.

There were dead people all around me. And the blue light, the light of the dead, giving me no day or night, brightness or darkness, cold or heat . . .

I believed none of it, because I *could* not. I was more willing to accept that I was mad, or dead myself.

My breathing became slower, gentler and more calmed, and eventually I fell asleep.

Upon waking there was no telling how much time had passed. I was still not hungry or thirsty. I had not dreamed. I was in the same position in which I had dropped off. Time eluded me.

"Scott!" I shouted once, loud, but the sound terrified me more than being alone. It felt so wrong. Even though my voice sailed away I had the distinct sense that it was ricocheting from walls and angles I could not see, not from these buildings that stood around me. The resonance sounded wrong.

My old friend did not answer. Perhaps he'd been as dead as this place all along.

I leaned back and closed my eyes, and a sudden breeze blew a handful of dust across my face, a hundred images screaming in and destroying the relative peace of the moment, assaulting my sense with smells and sounds and views from too many different places and times to take in. Each scrap of dust stung, and each sting was a past life striving to make itself and its suffering known. I opened my mouth to cry out and felt grit on my tongue and between my teeth. Held there by my saliva, these old ghosts had time to make themselves and their reasons for being here known—

She runs along the dock, the animals chasing her, jeering and laughing and tripping as they try to drag their trousers down, readying themselves—

Where had that breeze come from?—

A man stands against a wall and stares down the barrels of a dozen guns, hating them, hating what they are doing, hating their uncaring eyes as they see a rat in front of them, not a man, not a human being—

Something must have caused it!—

She should never have left him, never, not when he could do this, not when he could stroke his wrists this way and open the skin, the flesh, the veins, she should never have left him, never—

There had been no movement before, nothing, and now a wind to blow the dust over me?—

The rattle of machine-gun fire tears the air above him, just as his stomach has been torn asunder, and the sand is soaking up his life as he cries out for help that will not come—

There were more, more, so many images crowding in and flooding my mind that for some time, seconds or days, I forgot just who I was. I stood and ran and raged, shaking my head, running blind, and each impact with a wall only gave me more painful deaths to see, more wronged lives ripped away by unfairness at best, evil at worst. I remember faces watching me, and for a time these faces seemed even more alive than I felt, true observers rather than mere echoes of who and what they had once been.

For a while, I was just like them.

Perhaps that was their way of trying to chase me away.

I walked. Through the city, past the barren buildings, dodging fleeting shapes of dead people where I could. Some of them glanced at me, one even smiled. I always tried to look the other way.

Eventually, after hours spent walking, I found myself at the base of a cliff, and without thinking I began to climb. Up must be good, I reasoned, we had come *down* here so *up* must be good. Hand over hand, feet seeking purchase, fingers knotting with cramps, muscles twisting and burning as I heaved myself higher, higher. I refused to look back down, because I knew that silent city was below me, watching, and that somewhere Scott still pursued his own wronged ghost. I could not bear to see him.

I had no thoughts of trying to find him in a place so endless.

Time lost its meaning. The blue light of the dead lit my way. I went up, and up, and though I once thought of sleep there was nowhere to rest. I moved on, never pausing for more than a few seconds to locate the next handhold or footrest, weightless. I did not tire. My heavy breathing fled into the massive space behind me, swallowed away without echo. I wondered how far the sound would travel before fading away. Perhaps forever.

I was hardly surprised when I tumbled on to the same ledge Scott and I had fallen from. I had no idea how long had passed since then. I was not hungry or thirsty and did not need to urinate, but I was certain that I had been in the city for days. Its grime seemed to cling to my skin, giving glimpses of the multifarious fates its inhabitants had suffered. And much as I thought of my wife and children right then, they seemed like memories from ages ago, the past lives of someone else entirely. It was the city that had taken the bulk of my life.

I plunged into the tunnel without a backward glance. If I turned I may have seen something impossible to ignore, a sight so mind-befuddling that it would petrify me, leaving me there to turn slowly to stone or a pillar of salt. I simply ducked away from that impossible place and entered the real world of darkness once again.

The blue light abandoned me immediately. I was in pitch blackness. I must have kicked through the shapes at my feet, though I could only visualize them. I kept one hand held out, fingertips flitting across the stone wall to my right. Perhaps it was because I could imagine nothing worse than that place I was leaving behind – and the fate that must surely await Scott there, given time – but I walked forward without fear, and with a burning eagerness to see the sun once more.

I walked, and walked, and all the time I thought back to Scott running from me, wondering what had made him do so, why he had not turned to say goodbye.

He should never have left me like that. Never. Not on my own down there.

The tunnel seemed far longer than it had on the way down. The slope was steeper, perhaps, or maybe I had taken a branch in the darkness, a route leading somewhere else. I walked on because that was all I could do.

As light began to bleed in, its manifestation was so subtle that it took me a while to notice. I could not see and then I could see, and I did not discern the moment when that changed. My fear was dwindling, fading away with the darkness. We are all energy after all, I thought. There's nothing to us but space and power. Our thoughts are an illusion, and the world around us even more so.

An illusion . . .

"Where is *that* coming from?" I whispered, and my voice was curiously light. Those ideas, those images and concepts, all so unlike me. Given time perhaps I could have thought them, but it had only been a while since I had left the city, only a while.

He should have never left me alone . . .

I heard Scott calling my name. His voice floated to me from afar, nebulous and ambiguous, and it could have been a breeze drifting through the tunnels from above. I made out carved symbols on the walls, recognized them from our journey down here. In the bluish light issuing from my skin, eyes and mouth, the ancient words were beginning to make some kind of sense.

I heard Scott again from up ahead, but his voice was fainter now, fading, retreating somewhere and some place lost to me forever.

Voices rose behind me to call me back, and sounds, and the noises of a city coming to life.

At last I could hear the dead.

GLEN HIRSHBERG

Safety Clowns

GLEN HIRSHBERG LIVES in the Los Angeles area with his wife and children. He has won two International Horror Guild Awards and received four World Fantasy Award nominations. Both *The Two Sams*, a collection of ghost stories, and *The Snowman's Children*, his debut novel, are published in the United States by Carroll & Graf.

Hirshberg's fiction has appeared in numerous magazines and anthologies, including *The Mammoth Book of Best New Horror*, *Trampoline*, *The Year's Best Fantasy and Horror*, *Cemetery Dance*, *The Mammoth Book of Best New Terror*, *Acquainted With the Night*, *Shadows & Silence*, *Dark Terrors 6* and *The Dark*, as well as online at SciFi.com.

He has just completed both a new novel, *Sisters of Baikal*, and a second story collection, *The Muldoon*.

"I have also driven an ice-cream truck, for one day, with an ex-marine named Randy," recalls the author, "and that's all I'm prepared to say about that particular experience.

"Louboland is an actual place, though a very different kind of place, and the proprietor really did once seem that remote, that driven by a code of ethics entirely of his own devising.

"The clowns, meanwhile, got in my dreams and then down on paper thanks to a mug my dastardly son, then barely two-years-old, selected and kept sticking in my face during a visit to the circus that sometimes seems never to have ended . . ."

> "*and*
>
>   *the*
>
>   *goat-footed*
>
> *baloonMan* *whistles*
>
> *far*
>
> *and*
>
> *wee*"
>
>   —E.E. Cummings

A S SOON AS I SPOTTED THE AD, I knew I'd found what I wanted. LIKE BEING THE GOOD GUY? LIKE HAPPY FACES? SAFE DRIVER? SAFETY CLOWN NEEDS YOU.

One phone call and thirty seconds later, I had an interview appointment for 5:45 a.m. the following morning with Jaybo, dispatcher, founder and managing owner of the Safety Clown Ice Cream Truck Company. "Bring your license," Jaybo half-shouted at me, voice hoarse as a carnival barker's, and hung up.

Replacing the phone, I lifted the red dry-erase marker out of its clip on the message board and made a tentative check next to item #7 on my mom's list: *Find USEFUL summer employment. Help people. Have stories to tell. Make enough to concentrate on school in the fall.* Then I sat down on the tiny lanai to watch the evening marine layer of fog roll in off the beach and fill the ravine between our condo complex and the horse-racing track down the hill.

My condo complex. I still couldn't get used to it.

My mother had scrawled her final message board list for me in the middle of the night, three hours before I drove her to the hospice to die. That had been a little over a month ago, orphaning me on the eve of my twentieth birthday. She'd left me our one-and-a-half bedroom condo, enough cash to finish my sophomore year at San Diego State without taking any new loans or other job beyond my work-study at the library, and her cactus garden. "No way even you can kill those," she'd told me, touching her fingers one final time to the tiny prickles in each individual window box. It had taken me less than four weeks to prove her wrong.

The morning of my interview, I set the alarm for 4:45 a.m. but woke a little after 3:00, prickly and unable to sleep any more. After this, the only undone item on her list would be #1: *Celebrate your birthday.* And it was a little late for that. So. No more mom lists. Nothing left to do for anyone but me. Already, I was certain I'd sell this place, maybe before September. And I'd slowly lose the memory of air-conditioners hissing in all the condos jammed up against ours. I'd forget 4:15 a.m. garbage trucks and dogs snarling through screen doors at the hot-air balloons climbing with the light to lift rich people into the sunrise.

But I probably wouldn't forget the summer afternoons playing skateboard tag with the thousand other kid residents in the alleys of our sprawling nowhere of town-home blocks, stealing each other's wish-pennies out of the fountain by the guard shack, and waiting for 3:30 p.m., when the ice cream trucks descended en masse and we engulfed them. Hours after the trucks left, the buzzing tinkle of their music stayed trapped in our ears, like the bubble of pool water you can't quite shake out.

This would be my farewell, not just fulfilment of my mother's wishes but tribute to her. To my father, too, although what I mostly remembered about him was the smell of the strawberry air-freshener he insisted my mother spray all around to hide his sick smell, even though it didn't, and the way he'd died, holding his wife's and his seven year-old son's hands in his surprisingly strong ones, croaking, "God. Damn. I can feel myself going down."

At breakfast, alone in my condo, I watched the marine layer through the open lanai door, hearing horses nickering as stable-hands led them to the beach. Right on time, I left, pointing my mother's battered blue Geo down the empty I–5 freeway. I kept the window down, and the fog buffeted my face as though I were piloting a speedboat. Jaybo's directions pointed me above 10th Street into a motionless neighbourhood of empty lots and warehouses. At that hour, even uphill and inland, mist streamed from the lampposts and chain link fences. Reaching C Street, I slowed, turned, and began creeping east, looking for a street number or sign. What I saw, mostly, were human-shaped humps curled under newspapers or garbage bags along the fencing. I was about to turn around when I spotted the hand-lettered poster board lashed by its corners to a post at the end of an otherwise deserted block:

SAFETY CLOWN

Next to the letters, someone had drawn a primitive yellow sun, with pathetic first-grade rays pointing in too many directions, so that it looked more like a beetle. I parked, walked along the fence until I located an opening, and stepped through it.

I got maybe five steps into the lot before I stopped. Strands of fog brushed against my face and hands like a spider web I'd walked through. My shoulders crept up, my hands curled in my pockets, and I stood rooted, listening. Peering to my left, I confronted the dead headlights of five hulking white vans. I looked right and found five more vans facing me in a perfect line. No movement, no lights, no people anywhere.

I was in a parking lot, after all. Discovering actual vehicles parked there rated fairly low on the discomforting revelations scale. Except for what was sprouting from them.

Clinging to them?

I took a step back, realized that put me closer to the vans behind me, and checked them, too. Sure enough, giant cockroach-shaped shadows clung vertically to each sliding passenger door from top to bottom, spindle-legs folded underneath and laced through the handles, tiny heads jutting from between knobby, jointed shoulders. It was the fog – only the fog – that made them twitch, as though preparing to lift into the air like locusts.

"Hey Jaybo," a voice called, surprisingly close behind me, and I turned again. From somewhere among the left-hand vans, a man had emerged. He had red hair, dark coveralls, a grease rag sliding around and between his fingers like a snake he was cradling.

The barker's voice I'd heard on the phone yesterday answered him. "Yep?"

"Think our lucky newbee's here."

"What's he look like?"

The guy in the coveralls flipped his grease rag into his shoulder and stared me up and down. "Kind of short. Too thin, like maybe he needs some ice cream. Good bones. I like him."

A door clicked open toward the back of the lot, and another face peered out. This one was narrow, with bulbous green eyes and a mouth that hung a little open even at rest, like an eel's. "Come on in," Jaybo said, and retreated into the lighted space.

Why did I have to be here this early, anyway?

The manager's office proved to be a silver Airstream trailer lodged against the wall of a warehouse. Making my way there, I sensed shapes drifting behind windshields, cockroach shadows shivering as the vans rocked and the fog swept over them, and with a flash of disappointment I realized that these had to be the ice-cream trucks. I'd been hoping for the milkman-style vehicles that used to service us, with their bright blue stickers of Popsicle Rockets and Igloo Pies pasted unevenly all over the sides like Garbage Pail Kid stickers on a lunchbox. I wondered if these vans even played music.

Hand extended, I stepped into the trailer. "Good morning, Mr Jaybo, I'm Max Wa—"

"Just Jaybo. You're not that short."

Instead of accepting my offered shake, he waved one arm in the air between us. The arm had no hand on the end, or at least no fingers, ending in a bulging ball of red skin. I dropped my own hand awkwardly to my side.

"Thin, though." He cocked his head. Up close, his eyes were almost yellow behind his filthy round glasses. Stubby silver hair studded his skull like pins in a cushion. "Think you're going to love all kinds of things about this job."

Except for a small stack of ledger paper and a pen cup full of cheap, chewed-on Bics, Jaybo's desk had nothing on it. On the wall behind him, he'd tacked a massive map of San Diego county, with snaky pink and blue lines criss-crossing it like veins. Other than the map and a green, steel file cabinet, the trailer's only adornment was an Al Italia calendar, two years out of date, opened to April and featuring a photograph of a woman with astonishingly long, silky brunette hair and a smooth-fitting stewardess uniform, smiling sweetly. The caption read, ROMA? PERFECT.

"You're Italian?" I asked as Jaybo settled behind the desk and dropped both hand and stump across it. There was nowhere for me to sit.

"If she is," he said, smiled with his mouth still dangling open, and wiggled the fingers he had at me. "License."

I gave mine to him. He noted the details on his ledger. Remembering this was an interview – the whole morning had felt more like sleepwalking – I straightened, smoothing my checked shirt where it disappeared into the waist of my khakis.

"Like kids, Maxwell?"

"Always. Last summer I—"

"Like making people's days better? Giving them something to look forward to?"

"Sure."

"You're hired. You'll train today with Randy. *Randy!*"

I shuffled in place. "That's it?"

Jaybo turned slightly in his chair and winked, either at me or his Al Italia woman. "I know trustworthy people when I meet them. And anyway." He grinned, thumping his stump on the desktop. "You're going to love this job."

The door of the Airstream burst open, and I turned to find the entry completely blotted out, as though some massive, magic beanstalk had sprouted there in the three minutes I'd been inside. The beanstalk bent forward, and an ordinary head popped under the top of the doorframe.

"Randy," said Jaybo. "This is Max. Make him one of us."

Randy had neatly cropped brown hair with a few shoots of grey along the temples, slitty brown eyes, and a jaw so long I half-expected him to whinny. Inviting me out by inclining his head, Randy withdrew, revealing the foggy world once more as he stood to his full height.

He wasn't that big, out in the air. My head nearly reached his shoulders, which looked square and hard under a tight green camouflage T. So maybe six-five? Six-seven? If he stood with his legs together, I thought I could probably get my arms around his calves. Maybe even his knees.

Wordlessly, he lead me around back of the trailer toward the long cement warehouse that formed the property's northernmost boundary. He whistled quietly but expertly as he did so, with little trills and grace notes. After a few seconds, the tune registered, and I started laughing.

Randy swung that epic jaw toward me. "Join in. I know you know it." His voice had an odd, strangled quality, as if his throat were too narrow for the rest of him, like the barrel of a bassoon.

I did as he'd directed. "*She'll be coming 'round the mountain when she comes*." Maybe the vans played music after all.

The warehouse door was metal and ribbed and freshly painted white. Still whistling, Randy beat on it with the heel of one huge hand, and it shuddered like a gong.

"C'mon, Monkey, open up, we got joy to spread." The jaw swung my way again like the boom of a sailboat. "Randy, by the way."

"I'm Max."

"Imax. Big Screen."

I had no idea whether that was a non-sequitur or a nickname, but it made me laugh again. Randy pummelled the door some more, and it jerked and lifted off the ground on its chain. Freezing air spilled over our feet.

"Freezer," I announced, instantly felt stupid, and so employed Mom's Law of Idiotic Comments: go one stupider. "For the ice-cream."

"Big Screen," Randy said, and thumped me on the shoulder.

Inside, I found myself facing a desk made from a slab of wood and twenty or so stacked milk crates. This desk was as empty as Jaybo's except for a sleek black Thinkpad folded open. Behind the desk on a swivel chair sat the grease-rag guy who'd greeted me, wearing gloves now. Beyond him, ceiling-high stacks of cardboard boxes with clear stretch-plastic tops fell away in rows to the back of the warehouse and out to both side walls.

"How many, Randy-man?" said the guy at the desk. His rag lolled from the pocket of his work-shirt like a friendly, panting tongue.

"Feeling good today, Monkey. Thinking Big Screen here's going to bring me luck. Let's go twenty and twenty."

Monkey shook his head and tapped the tab key on his keyboard. "Going to put us all to shame. You're learning from the best, kid. All-time champ."

Resuming his whistling, Randy marched past the desk, tousling Monkey's hair. At the first stack, Randy hunched, got his arms around the bottom box, and held there like a weightlifter preparing for a clean-and-jerk. Then he just stood up, no effort at all, and the boxes came off the ground and towered in his arms.

"God*damn*, Randy," said a new voice from the entry, and I turned to find three new people lined up by Monkey's desk. The speaker had to be over seventy, long and thinner than I was in his grey denim jacket and red Urban Outfitters cap. Next to him stood a Chinese kid about my age, and behind them a yellow-haired forty-something woman in sneakers and a sundress.

"Morning, slow pokes," Randy said, pointing toward another stack with his foot. "Big Screen, grab me another five, would you, and bring them out front?"

"Must eat half of it himself," the old guy muttered.

"He doesn't touch ice cream and you know it," said the woman in the sundress, and Randy nudged her affectionately with his elbow as he strode past.

Under cover of the patter, I approached the nearest stack of boxes, slid my arms around the top five, and gasped. They were freezing. As soon as I lifted them, the crook of my elbow began to ache, and my fingers cramped. But at least they were lighter than I was expecting. I gazed through the clear plastic of the topmost box. There they were, in their garish orange and Kool Aid-red wrappers. *We'll be bringing Popsicle Rockets when we come* . . .

"Hey, Randy," Monkey called as the big man reached the door. When Randy turned, Monkey tossed him a long white envelope, overstuffed and rubber-banded twice around. Without any sort of hitch or arm adjustment, Randy stretched out his fingers and snatched the envelope out of the air, pressing it against his tower of boxes. "Might want to count that."

The sound Randy made came as close to *pshaw* as anything I've heard an actual human attempt. He strode into the fog, and I hurried after him.

"See, Big Screen," he said without turning around, "we're all independent contractors. Great system. You pay for your product up front, in full, so the trick is buying only what you're going to sell. Jaybo gets thirty percent, Monkey gets five for keeping your van running smooth, and that's it. Rest is yours, in cash, free and clear."

Even after he mentioned the vans, I somehow forgot about the cockroach things until we were halfway back to the front of the lot. The cold and the weight from the boxes seemed to have latched onto my ribs like pincers. When I remembered and looked up, the figures were where I'd left them, just hanging against the van doors the way spiders do when you stare at them.

Randy went right on talking. "But see, the best thing about Sunshine Safety Clown, Jaybo's got the routes laid out for you. Long a route as you want, street by street, stop by stop. These are guaranteed sales, man. *Guaranteed*. You saw Jaybo's map?"

"And his girl," I murmured, boxes starting to slip, eyes still flitting between vans.

"What girl?" Randy said, lowering into a squat and settling his boxes on the asphalt next to the front-most right-hand van.

"Guess we have different priorities." I lowered my own boxes a little too fast. The bottom one thumped.

"Careful, Big Screen. You bought those, you know. Alright, I'll open her up and let's feed her."

Did I imagine him pausing for just a moment as he approached the van's side? His fingers drummed the thighs of his jeans, and his whistling ceased. Then he jammed his hand between those giant, spindly legs, twisted sideways as though tearing out a heart, and ripped open the van door.

He came back fast, whistling, and hoisted the top five boxes off his stack.

"Randy, what is that?"

"What?" he said. But he knew what I meant.

"On the side of the van."

"He's . . . a friend. Load up, and I'll show you."

For the next fifteen minutes, we arranged ice cream cases in the freezer bins that lined the inside walls of the back of the van. Around us, meanwhile, activity increased throughout the lot as more doors slid open and more ice cream disappeared into bins. Randy worked quickly. When we'd finished, he banged the bin lids shut and hopped out fast and started around front.

"Close that door, will you?" he called over his shoulder.

If there'd been a way up front from where I was, I'd have used the inside handle. But the back of the van had been sealed off, probably to help maintain coolness, and so I had no choice but to hop down and face the bug thing.

Up close, it looked wooden. The fog had left a wet residue on its slats, and I could see splotches of coloured paint all up and down them. I remembered my mother taking me to the natural history museum in Balboa Park once to see new-born moths dangling from their burst cocoons, wings drying.

Randy stuck his head out the passenger window. "Hurry up. Don't let the heat in."

With a grunt I didn't realize was coming, I reached into the nest of slats, grasped the metal handle at their centre, and yanked. The door leapt onto its runners and swung closed with a click.

"Okay. Back up," Randy said. "Further."

I could see him at the wheel, hand poised over the control panel. When he saw me looking, he nodded. "Say hello," he said, and pulled down hard.

For a second, the bug thing quivered on the pegs holding it to the van. Then it unfolded. First a leg, human-shaped, popped free of the nest and dropped earthward as though feeling for the ground. As soon as that one was fully extended, another fell. The legs had purple striping, as did the arms, which clicked open, pointing sideways. Finally, the head sprang up, tiny black eyes staring at me above a deflated balloon nose, wide red happy mouth.

Thinking that was it, I peeled myself off the neighbouring van where I'd been watching. Then the whole clown pivoted on its pegs and swung perpendicular to Randy's door. Its puffy marshmallow of a right hand pointed its little red STOP sign right at my heart.

I stepped around it to the passenger side window. "That's for cars, right? So kids can cross the street?"

Randy nodded.

I grinned. "It'd work on me."

"Me, too."

"Jaybo made those?"

Randy shook his head. "Loubob." When he saw my expression, he cocked his head in surprise. "You know Loubob?"

Memory poured through me, of my father with his determined, trembling hands on the steering wheel as he drove us to Loubobland the night before Halloween, two months before he died. The last time I'd been in a car with him.

"Yeah," I said. "I mean, I've been there. The muffler men."

"The muffler men," said Randy, and nodded. "Hop up."

I did, remembering that long, silent drive east into the farmlands of

Fallbrook, the sun pumping redness over the horizon as it sank behind us. I couldn't recall a single thing my father and I had said to each other. But I could still see Loubob's junkyard. He'd been a carnival skywheel technician, the story went, then a funhouse specialist, then a circus-truck mechanic before retiring to sell off a career's worth of accumulated spare parts and create annual Halloween displays out of rusted mufflers and scrap metal and hand-built motors. His muffler men wrapped themselves around eucalyptus tree trunks as though trying to shinny up them, shambled from behind junk piles like prowling silver skeletons, dangled from overhead branches to bump shoulders with shrieking guests. My father had loved it.

When I'd buckled myself in, Randy released the lever on the control panel, and the Safety Clown clattered back into place against the side of the van. Randy blasted the horn. An answering blast followed almost immediately from deep in the lot. Over the next sixty seconds or so, blasts erupted from all the vehicles around us. But no one honked more than once, and when I'd come back to myself enough to glance at Randy, I found him counting silently.

Eight. Nine.

Before the tenth horn blast had died to echo, he punched the gearshift into drive and moved us out of the lot. My eyes flicked to the side mirror, where I saw the clown shuddering as the wind rushed over it, and beyond that, the rest of the vans falling into line in rhythmic succession.

"You always leave all together?"

Randy shrugged. "Tradition. Team-building, you know?"

"Then shouldn't I have met the rest of the team?"

"They won't be selling your ice cream."

We were headed, I realized, for the port, and for the first time, the absurd hour made a sort of sense. The workers down here had been on all night, probably shifting huge crates inside cargo containers that trapped heat like ovens.

"So what are yours?" Randy said as we crossed the Pacific Coast Highway, angling between grunting eighteen-wheelers as we approached the docks. Between trucks and stacked crates and gantry cranes, I caught glimpses of big ships hulking in the fog, their steel siding so much more solid, somehow, than the glass-and-concrete structures perched on the land behind us.

"I'm sorry?"

"You said you guessed we have different priorities. I'm not sure I liked that. I want to know what yours are."

Startled, I turned toward his enormous frame – a super-freighter to my weekend eight-footer – and decided on caution.

"Just . . . spread a little happiness," I said. "Get some myself. Make buttloads of money so I don't have to eat Top Ramen and bologna at the end of next semester. Maybe get laid for the first time since high school."

"See?" He sounded almost defensive as he let the van glide to a stop in front of two forklifts and some more heavy machinery I had no name for. "Happiness and money. Don't know about you, but I'm thinking I haven't had my share of either, yet."

Reaching under his seat with both hands, he pulled up the first assault rifle I had ever sat beside. It was flat black and spindly except for the chamber, or whatever it was called, that ballooned off the back of the trigger area. The barrel pointed straight at me. Randy did something that made the whole thing click, swung the stock to his shoulder and sighted down into the dash, then returned the rifle to its hiding place.

"Is that an uzi?" I whispered.

"Not a Corps man, huh, Big Screen?"

"You were?"

"Six severely fucked up years. Wait here. I'll introduce you properly from your own van tomorrow."

He opened his door and hopped down, assuming point position in the phalanx of van drivers that immediately formed around him. My eyes kept wandering from the phalanx to the shadows under Randy's seat to the Safety Clown crouching in the corner of the side mirror, right above the OBJECTS MAY BE CLOSER THAN THEY APPEAR warning. My father's ghost kept floating up in front of me, too, so it didn't occur to me that we hadn't reopened the back of the van or dug into any freezer bins until Randy returned, dropping a small, square cardboard box onto my lap.

"Count those, okay?" This time, he didn't even wait for his colleagues to reach their vehicles, and he didn't wave as we u-turned and blew by them. Seconds later, we were speeding north on the freeway.

I pried the duct tape off the top of the box. "Seemed like you trusted Jaybo," I said.

"That wasn't Jaybo."

The box lid fell open, and I lifted out the topmost plastic baggie, zipped tight, packed with white powder that shifted when I pressed, like confectioner's sugar. I knew what it was, though I'd never done any. Dazed, I started counting bags, got most of the way through, and looked up.

"How many?" Randy said. I could feel his eyes on me in the mirror.

Don't react, I thought. Don't react, don't react, "*This is fucking cocaine!*"

Randy grinned. "Appreciate the appraisal. But I need a count, there, Bubba."

My brain scrambled back to the pier. I'd barely paid attention. I didn't even remember seeing anybody but Safety Clown drivers.

"Thirty-seven," I said dully.

"You're sure?"

"Thirty-eight."

"Positive?"

I nodded.

"Guess you're not going to find out what kind of gun this is yet." The note of open disappointment in his voice drew my gaze, and my gaze made him laugh. "Got ya."

The next three hours passed in a blur. The marine layer had burned away, leaving a bottomless blue emptiness overhead. We stopped at two law offices and one dental practice in Sorrento Valley. By the time we reached the dentist's, I'd started getting nauseous and rolled my window down, which is how I got to hear the receptionist with the white, winking hair yell, "Hey, Doc. Here comes the cavalry" through the open office door.

Our next stop was Ripped Racquet and Health Gym, where a pony-tailed tai chi instructor halted the class he was conducting on the circle of grass fronting the building to stop Randy. "Hey, guy, do the clown."

"You're doing him just fine," Randy answered, then gave the instructor what looked like a brotherly chuck on the shoulder of his robe as he breezed past. He was inside almost half an hour, and when he returned, he waved at me to pass him the cardboard box from the floor. He fished out three more baggies, tucking them carefully into the waistband of his jeans. "Walk-up biz," he said happily, and trotted back indoors.

From there, we cut over to the 101 and up the coast, stopping at Del Mar Plaza and the Quesadilla Shack five minutes from my condo door, where I laid myself flat on the front seat and told Randy I was known in this place. The real reason for my hiding had more to do with the number of dinners I'd eaten with my mom on the red picnic tables in the sand outside the Shack.

Randy gave me a long look, and the fear I should have been feeling all along finally prickled down my scalp. But all he did was pat my head. "You should eat, Big Screen. I get so caught up doing this, I forget half the time. Doesn't mean you should. Want a carne asada?"

Just the thought made me gag. He came back ten minutes later with a Coke for me and nothing at all for himself.

"Okay," he said. "Ready for the good stuff?"

I leaned my head against the window and kept my eyes closed, and we drove a long time. When I finally opened my eyes again, we were juddering over a dirt road just a bit narrower than the van, crushing birds-of-paradise stalks on either side as we rumbled forward. Still nauseous, increasingly nervous, I scanned the fields and saw red and orange and blue flowers nodding in the wind we made like peasants at a passing lord, but no buildings anywhere. I thought of the poppy fields of Oz, the witch's voice and her green hand caressing her crystal ball. Randy downshifted, and I sat up straight as the van coasted to a stop.

No one on this planet knew where I'd gone today. Certainly, no one other than the Safety Clown people had seen me arrive downtown. *Training*, Jaybo had called it. What if it was more of a test? And I had not accompanied Randy on a single sale.

"Get out," he said quietly, and popped the locks on both our doors.

I did, considering bolting straight into the flowers. But I had little chance of outdistancing my companion. I watched him remove his not-uzi from under his seat and step down and swing his door shut.

"Listen," I said. He was already halfway around the front of the van, using his gun machete-style to chop flowers out of his path. I'd meant to start pleading, but wound up standing still instead, gobbling up each tick of insect wing, every whisper of wind in the petals. I swear I could hear the sunlight falling.

Arriving beside me, Randy stared into the distance, dangling the rifle by the trigger-guard. For a few seconds, we stood. Above us, the blue yawned wider.

"So what do you think, Big Screen?" he finally said. "Just you and me?" In one motion, he swept the rifle butt to his shoulder and fired five quick bursts into the sky, which swallowed them. Then he grinned. "Better get that door open."

Before I'd even unlocked my knees and gulped new air into my lungs, people sprang from the flowers like rousted pheasants in a whirl of dark skin and tattered straw hats and threadbare work shirts open to the waist. Several of them chirped enthusiastic greetings at Randy in Spanish as I stumbled back against the van. He chirped right back.

"Hurry up, Big Screen," he barked, and I reached a trembling hand between clown slats and grabbed the handle and twisted. I was grateful I hadn't drunk any of the Coke from the Quesadilla Shack. If I'd had any liquid in me, I would just have pissed it all over my legs.

As soon as the door was open, Randy jumped in and threw back the nearest freezer lid. The field hands nuzzled closer to us like pups vying for suckling spots, though they avoided so much as nudging me. One, a boy of maybe twelve, met my eyes for a moment and murmured, "*Buenas dias*." Several others nodded as they edged past. I climbed up next to Randy.

"*De nada*, Hector," he was saying, handing a chocolate nut Drumstick to the nearest worker, whose spiky streak of dirt-grey goatee looked embedded in his skin like a vein of ore in rock. Hector handed Randy a dime and retreated to the back of the group, peeling eagerly at the paper wrapping.

Distribution to the whole group took less than five minutes, but Randy lingered another twenty, dangling his legs out the cabin door, talking only occasionally, smiling a lot. The workers clumped in groups of two or three, leaning on hoes and wolfing down Igloo Pies while gazing over the fields. Their dwellings, I realized, might well be hidden out here somewhere, along with any other family members who'd somehow made it this far and managed to find them. None of them spoke to me again, but every single one tipped his sombrero to Randy before melting away into the fields they tended. They left neither trash nor trace.

"This stuff sold for a dollar when I was ten," I said. "And that was ten years ago." My voice sounded strained, shaky. Randy's rifle lay seemingly forgotten between freezer bins in the van behind us. I almost made a lunge for it. But I couldn't for the life of me figure what I'd do afterward.

"Cost me a buck-twenty per," Randy said. "But see, I figure I can afford it. Starting tomorrow, you can make your own decisions. Beauty of being a Safety Clown, dude. Ain't no one going to know or care but you."

Clambering inside, he collected his rifle, hunched to avoid banging his head, and began swatting freezer lids shut. He didn't seem thoughtful enough to be deciding whether to mow me down.

"Why not just give it to them?" I asked. "The ice cream, I mean."

Randy cocked his head. The gun remained tucked under one arm against his chest. "You like insulting people, Big Screen?"

I gaped at him.

"Didn't think so. Remember, they don't know what it costs me."

He left me to slide the door shut again, and we rumbled out of the fields and returned to the coast.

Another two hours passed. We stopped at an antique shop and some accounting firms, a bowling alley and a retirement home. At the latter, I finally emerged from the van. Partially, I did so because I thought I'd better. Partially, I wanted to get away from the freon I'd been breathing virtually non-stop for the past eight hours, and which by now had given me a sledgehammer headache. But also, I'd gotten curious. The experience in the flower fields had shaken something loose in me, and I could feel it rattling around as I stepped into the mid-day heat.

Randy had already been inside fifteen minutes. I wondered if he'd received the same joyful, personal greeting there that he had everywhere else we'd gone. Edging forward, I reached the sidewalk fronting the main entrance, where my progress was blocked by a bald, pink-skinned marvel of a man whose curvature of the spine kept his head roughly level with my navel. Jabbing the legs of his metal walker into the ground like climbing pitons, the man dragged himself toward the brightly lettered sign at the edge of the parking lot that read BEACH ACCESS. Below the words on the sign was the silhouette of a longhaired bathing beauty laid out flat with her breasts poking straight up in the air. The man didn't acknowledge me as he inched past, but he did remove the cherry lollipop from his mouth, and it hovered in front of his lips like the dot at the bottom of a kicked-over question mark. I thought about lifting him, ferrying him gently to the sand.

Only then did it occur to me that the man might well have hauled himself out here for Randy. *Help people*, my mother had commanded, since the day I first started working. But help them what? Which jobs, exactly, qualified, and who got to say?

By the time Randy returned, I'd stumbled back to my seat, more confused than scared for the moment, and the question-mark man was well on his way to the bathing beauties.

"Two-thirty yet?" Randy asked, though he was the one with the watch. He checked it. "Right on."

Leaving the coast, he drove us across the freeway, over El Camino Real and into the maze of white and salmon-pink condo communities and housing developments that had all but enclosed the eastern rim of North and San Diego counties during the course of my lifetime. Any one of them could have been mine. Blood beat against my temples and massed behind my forehead. I closed my eyes, caught an imaginary glimpse of my mother bent over her potted plants at the nursery where she'd worked, better paid and sunscreened than the workers in the flower fields but nearly as invisible, and opened my eyes again to find Randy's hand hurtling toward my chest.

I twisted aside, but he didn't seem to notice, just grabbed the knob on the dash that I'd assumed was a glove box handle. Now I realized there was no glove box. Randy twisted the knob to the right.

For one blissful moment, nothing happened. Then the air shattered into winking, tinkling shards of sound. My hands rose uselessly to my ears, then dropped again. The van slowed, stopped on the curve of a cul-de-sac, and Randy shouldered his door open, nearly banging his head on the ceiling as he jumped out and rubbed his hands together.

"Watch the master, Big Screen. Learn." Striding around front, he stood with his hands on his hips, gazing into the yards like a gunslinger as the sound rained down on him. Then he bounded around the van, pulled open my door, flicked the lever on the control panel, and danced backward as the clown leapt off its stilts and started unfolding.

I staggered from the van as the first children of the entire day swept around the curve of the cul-de-sac on their skateboards and bore down on us. My ears finally filtered enough distortion for me to register the tune the van was blaring.

"*Classical Gas*?" I babbled, as Randy stepped carefully around the clown. It hung still now, STOP sign jabbed over the street.

"What about it?" Randy threw open the sliding door and began pulling up multiple bin lids.

To my amazement, I felt my lips slip upwards. "I've got a friend who claims this is the only music on earth it's impossible to make a girl have an orgasm to."

If my own smile surprised me, Randy's nearly blew me backward with its brightness. "Wish I had enough experience or knowledge to challenge that statement. Always been kind of shy, myself. And lately, I've been too busy making money. My *man*, Joel."

He stuck one huge hand past me, and the first skateboard kid to reach the van smacked it with his own. "Pop Rocket, Randy," the kid said, straightening the cargo shorts from which his watermelon-striped boxers billowed.

"Cherry, right?" Randy had already handed the kid the popsicle without waiting for an answer. "What-up, Empire?"

The reasons for that nickname never revealed themselves to me. What became immediately apparent, though, was how much this second kid liked that Randy knew it. He gave his board a kick-hop and wrapped it in his arms and stood close to the van, looking proud, as Randy gave him his ice cream. By the time that group had departed, twelve more kids, ranging in age from maybe five to no younger than me, had emerged from houses or backyards or neighbouring streets. No one seemed to mind the racket roaring out of the rooftop speaker, and a few customers even turned their bodies and faces to it, arms outstretched, eyes closed, as though accepting a cooling blast from a garden hose. Every single person knew Randy's name, and he knew most of theirs.

"You Randy's new helper?" said a soft voice so close to my ear that I thought for a second it had come from inside me.

Turning, I found myself confronting a freckle-faced girl of maybe fifteen, with a yellow drugstore whiffle bat over her bare shoulder. Self-consciously, she wound the wild strands of her strawberry-blonde hair back into her scrunchy with sweaty fingers. Her eyes, green and soft as the squares of over-watered lawn fronting the houses of this block, never left mine.

Too much time passed, and I had no answer. I wanted to borrow her bat, dare her to try to pitch a ball past me. I also wanted her to stop flirting with me because she was too young and only adding to my anxiety. I thought of my mom peering down from the Heaven she didn't believe in, and had to smother competing impulses to wave and whimper.

"You should be," the girl finally said, in that same breathy voice. "Hey, Randy." From her pocket, she withdrew a wad of bills, palmed them, and passed them into the van. Randy ducked inside and returned with a baggie, which disappeared into the girl's shorts pocket.

"Go easy, Carolina," said Randy. "Say hi to your sis."

The girl wandered away, wiggling her bat once at both or neither of us.

I sat down on the curb under the Safety Clown's arm, and the sunlight dropped on my shoulders like ballast. For the first time, I let myself ask the question. *Could I do this? Did I want to?* It'd pay for next semester, all right. And it'd certainly qualify as a story to tell. Once the statute of limitations ran out.

We were close to an hour in that one cul-de-sac, then nearly two in the fire lane of the circular parking lot of a little league complex with four grassless fields that looked stripped bare like shaved cats. Kids just kept coming. Mostly, they bought ice cream. Every now and then, one or a little group would lurk until a lull came, then dart or sidle or just stride forward and pop $75.00 or sometimes an envelope into Randy's hands.

At one point, feeling oddly jealous as yet another group of kids clustered around and jabbered at him, I asked Randy, "What happens if you're not sure?"

"What's that, Big Screen?"

"What if it's a kid you don't know? You wouldn't want to make a mistake."

"Oh." He turned to me, grinning. "I've got a system."

Not twenty minutes later, I got to see the system in action. The kid in question looked about eleven, despite the pimples peppering his forehead and leaning off the end of his nose. He hovered near the swing-set just off the parking lot, sweating and jumpy in his long-sleeved, webbed Spider-Man shirt. Finally, he came forward, eyes everywhere.

Randy glanced at me, mouthing *Watch this*. Then he stepped from the van to meet the kid, folding his arms across his cliff of a chest, and said, "Yo, friend. What's your name?"

"Zach."

"Yo, Zach. Did you need ice cream or . . . *ice cream*?"

I stared at Randy's back. He swung his head around and beamed proudly before returning full attention to his customer.

"Ice cream," the kid said, flung $75.00 into Randy's hands, and fled with his treat.

Randy employed exactly the same technique a little later with a pale, teenaged girl with black lipstick and what appeared to be at least five different henna tattoos applied one on top of another on her bare ankles under her long skirt. The resulting mess looked like hieroglyphics, or a gang tag. When Randy asked his question, her mouth unhinged, as though he'd bonked her on the head. He gave her two Drumsticks for her dollar, called it his "Welcome to Randy special," and directed me to shut down the music and reel in the clown. I did both, leaned out the window to watch the clown fold, and nearly slammed into the scowling woman's face with my own.

She wore a navy blue button-up shirt, tight blue slacks, and for a second, I thought she was a cop. She'd pulled her red hair back so tightly that the wrinkles in her forehead seemed to be splitting open. As I stared, gargling, trying to sort whether I was terrified or relieved, she banged my door with her hand, rattling the clown on its stilts. Beside me, I felt Randy settle into the driver's seat. Then his hand crossed my chest and pushed me gently back against the peeling vinyl.

"M'am. Something I can get you?" Randy asked.

"How about a brain?" the woman hissed. "How about a conscience?"

"Now, ma'am, I'm sure you have both those things."

The woman nearly spit in our faces, and my legs started shaking. Abruptly, my head jerked sideways, checking for Randy's other hand. It was on the steering wheel, not feeling around under his seat. And on his face was a smile gentler than any I'd seen all day.

"That's your natural colour, isn't it?" He didn't even turn the key in the ignition. "Beautiful. Almost maroon."

"Ever seen someone die, Mr Smarty-Arty Ice Cream Man? I have. When I was nine years old. Janitor at my school. Want to know why he died? Because some service asshole like you was parked in the fire lane and the ambulance couldn't get up the driveway."

Randy made a *pop* with his cheeks. "Right," he said. "Absolutely right. I'm sorry, and it won't happen again."

The woman blinked, hand half-raised as though she might slap the van again. Instead, she shook her head and stalked off.

"Never understand it," Randy murmured, starting the van. "Why are moral people always so angry?" Pulling out of the lot, he glanced my way, saw me ramrod straight against the seat back with my legs still trembling together. "Know many people like that, Big Screen?"

My tongue felt impossibly dry, as though it had been wrung. "Um." I put my hands on my legs, held them until they quieted. "I think I thought I was one."

"You?" Randy grinned. Then without warning he reached out and patted me on the head. "Not you, Big Screen. You don't have it in you. And you don't treat people that way. Trust your buddy Big Randy."

We stayed out four more hours. Around six, Randy began cruising family pizza restaurants, the multiplex lot just before the 7:30 p.m. shows, a twenty-four hour workout gym where he sold only ice cream (no *ice cream*) to exhausted soccer parents and desk-drones desperately stretching their bodies. Most of these people knew Randy's name, too.

Finally, a little after 9:00, on a residential street overlooking Moonlight Beach, Randy shut off the van, then turned to me. Out on the water, even the moon seemed to be burrowing a straight, white trail to his door.

"You haven't eaten a single goddamn thing, have you, Big Screen? I'm sorry about that." Almost as an afterthought, his hands slipped under the seat between his legs and came up with the rifle.

My breath caught, but by this point I was too tired to hold it. "You either," I murmured, watching his hands.

"Yeah, but . . . You'll see. Tomorrow. There's this charge people give off when you're not judging them, just giving them what they want and letting them be. It's a physical thing, man. It's in their skin, and it's more filling than any food. I'm so charged, most days, I barely even sleep. Not to mention richer."

It was true. I'd watched it happen all day. I wasn't sure anyone in my entire life had ever been as pleased to see me as Randy's customers were to see him. And he felt the same way.

The rifle slid into his lap, muzzle aimed just over my legs at the centre of the door. "You'll be back?" His voice bore no apparent threat.

Eventually, when I'd said nothing for long enough, Randy nodded. "You'll be back. You're the thoughtful sort. Like I said."

"Does it ever bother you?" I asked.

Randy stared at me, and the moon lit him. "Does what?"

Dropping the rifle back in its place, he drove us straight to the freeway and back downtown. He didn't turn on the radio or say another word. White and red reflections from the dashboard and passing cars flared in his skin like sparks.

In the lot, we found all the other vans not just parked but empty, clowns locked into cockroach position at their sides. A single low light burned in Jaybo's trailer. I wondered if he lived there, then why he would. He had to have plenty of money.

"Go home, Big Screen," Randy told me as soon as he'd backed the van into its space at the head of the right-hand row. "I've got to wipe out the bins and finish up. You get some food and sleep."

I didn't argue. My head hurt, and a loneliness less specific – and therefore all the more suffocating – than any I'd experienced before crept into my chest and filled my lungs. And yet I found myself turning to Randy, who flashed me his blinding, affect-less smile. I thought he might burst into one last chorus. *We'll all have chicken and dumplings when she comes*. But he just smiled.

The only thing I could think to say was, "Looks like we're last ones back."

"Always. Going to give me a run, Big Screen?"

Slipping from my seat, I stood blinking on the pavement while the fast-cooling air pushed my grinding teeth apart and drove some of the deadness out. My fingertips began tingling, then stinging, as though I'd just come in from sledding. I was trying to remember where I'd parked my car – could it really have been earlier today? – when the door of Jaybo's Airstream opened and his goldfish eyes peered toward me. I froze.

"Max?" Out he came. His shorts had flowers on them. Maybe all Safety Clown employees slept here. In their vans. In the freezer bins, which doubled as coffins.

"You have a good time, son? Learn a lot?"

"Tired," I managed, watching him, listening for any sign of Randy stepping out to trap me between them.

"Randy's a madman." Jaybo smiled. "No one expects you to work like that. But I thought you'd enjoy learning from the best. Like my clowns?"

I resisted the urge to look at one and shook my head.

Jaybo's smile got wider. "Got to admit they're memorable, though. Knew they'd be our logo, our signature, as soon as I saw them."

"Loubob's. Right?"

"You know Loubob's? See, I knew it, Max. No one comes to us by accident. I went there looking for belts and hoses for these babies." He waved his stump at the vans. "And there were the clowns just lying in a heap. I asked what they were, and he says, '*Project. Didn't work.*' Ever heard Loubob speak?"

I shook my head again, checked Randy's van but saw no sign of him, just the passenger door hanging ajar. Jaybo took another step closer. "Not many have. I got the whole lot for $50.00."

To his left, at the very end of the row, one of the clowns had come open, or been left that way. In the shadows, at this distance, I couldn't see its face, but it was shivering like a scarecrow in the salty ocean breeze.

"See ya," I heard myself say.

"Tomorrow. Right?"

Without answering, I turned, waiting for the rush of footsteps or flick of a rifle safety-catch, and started for the street. Just as I reached the gate I heard a thud from Randy's van, couldn't help turning, and found Randy's face filling the windshield. When he saw me looking, he pressed one gorilla-sized hand to the glass, fingers open. Waving. I got in my car and drove home.

I'd tiptoed halfway up the entry stairs before remembering it would take more than that to wake my mother. I made myself a tuna sandwich and ate a third of it, seeing Randy's last wave, his wide-open grin. The condo felt even emptier than it had for the past month, even the ghost of my father's smell drained from the walls. My mother had left no smell, ghostly or otherwise. I crawled off to bed and miraculously slept until after 4:00 a.m. before bolting awake, hyperventilating.

Flipping onto my stomach, I curled into myself like a caterpillar and managed, after ten minutes of total panic, to get myself calmed enough to start to think.

As far as I could tell, I had three choices. I could get up and join Jaybo and Randy and the gang spreading joy, ice cream, and *ice cream* throughout San Diego County, have a hundred or more people of all ages and types rush out to greet me by name whenever they saw me, and make more money in a couple months than my mom had in any one decade of her life. I could call the police, pray they found and arrested all Sunshine Safety Clown employees, and then spend the rest of my days hoping none of them got out, ever. Or I could do neither, hide here in the fog with the horses and hope Jaybo understood the absence of both me and the police as the don't-ask-don't-tell bargain I was offering.

Instead of choosing, I got sick.

For the first few hours, I figured I was faking it, or manufacturing it, anyway. Then, when the chills started, I dug around in my mother's bathroom, found a thermometer in the otherwise empty cosmetic drawer, and checked myself. I got a reading of 102, climbed back into bed, and stayed there two days.

No one called. No one knocked at the door. No one parked by the complex's sauna and played a blast of "Classical Gas". Around midnight of the second night, the phone rang, and I dragged myself out of bed. Passing my mother's doorway, I half-believed I could see her tucked into her usual corner in the king-size bed she'd once shared with my father, not moving or breathing, as though she'd snuck out of her grave to get warm.

The fever, I realized, had gone. Beneath my feet, the hardwood floor felt cool on my feet, the air gentle against my itching legs. This was just the world, after all. Big, thoroughly mapped place to sell joy or buy it, hunt company or flee it, trust yourself or your friends or your instincts, stretch the hours as much as you could, and one day vanish.

Pulling my mother's door shut, I padded into the living room and picked up the receiver just before the sixth ring, beating the answering machine. But on the other end I found only electrical hum and a distant clacking sound.

The next morning, I got up, broke eggs into a pan, and flipped on the pocket television on the counter for company. Then I stood, staring, wet yolk dripping from the end of my wooden spoon onto my mother's once-spotless hardwood floor.

Under a flashing banner that read LIVE – BREAKING NEWS, a

camera scanned a downtown parking lot. Red and blue lights flashed and reflected in the windows of ten white vans, illuminating what looked like spatters of mud all over their metal sides and grills.

"*Once again, a scene of incredible, despicable violence downtown this morning as police discover the apparent massacre and dismemberment of as many as fifteen employees of the Sunshine Safety Clown ice cream truck company. Police have long targeted the company as the key element in a major Southland drug trafficking ring, and department spokesmen confirm that this vicious mass slaying appears to be drug related. No additional specifics either about the trafficking ring or the nature and timing of the murders has been released as yet.*"

I put my hand down almost inside the frying pan, jerked back, and knocked egg everywhere. My eyes never left the screen.

"*We've had our eyes on these people for months,*" a police department spokesman was saying, as the camera prowled jerkily, restlessly behind him, capturing lights, an open van door, a helicopter overhead, body bags. More lights. "*Arrests were forthcoming. Imminent, in fact. We're disappointed and also, obviously, horrified. An attack of this ferocity is unprecedented in this county. These people are savages, and they must be rooted out of our city.*"

"Randy," I whispered, surprised that I did.

Suddenly, I was bent forward, so close to the tiny screen that it seemed I could climb into it. I waited until the camera pulled back to scan the lot again.

Then I was out the door, not even buckling my sandals until I'd driven the Geo screeching out of the condo lot to the bottom of the hill to wait for the endless, stupid light at the lip of the freeway onramp. Traffic clogged the interstate, and I was nearly an hour getting downtown, but I don't remember thinking a single thing during all that time except that I was wrong. It was ridiculous. Juvenile. Wrong.

What I should have done was go to the police. Instead, I parked as close as I could to the temporary barriers the cops had erected, edged through the block-long crowd of gawkers, got the single glimpse I needed to confirm what the cameras had already shown me, then very nearly shoved people to the ground as I forced my way back out. My breath was a barbed thing, catching in the lining of my throat and tearing it. An older Hispanic woman in a yellow shawl threw her arm around me and made comforting *shush*-ing sounds. I shook her off.

What I'd seen was blood, all right, splashed all over the vans,

coating the wheel wells and even some of the windows. I'd seen doors
flung open, some wrenched half off their hinges. What I hadn't seen
were clowns. Not a single one, anywhere. Just the wooden frames
where they'd hung like bats to sleep off the daylight.

I drove around and around downtown in a sort of crazy circle,
Hillcrest, India Street, Laurel, Broadway, South Street, the harbour,
the Gaslamp, back again. They'd been taken off, obviously. Ripped
free in the fray, or pried away by police for easier van access. This
was just another deflection, like my two-day fever, from having to
deal with my own culpability. Then I thought of muffler men peering
around trees. And I remembered the midnight phone call I'd received
last night. Sometime in the late afternoon, I stopped the car, wobbled
into a payphone booth, dialled information, paid the extra fifty cents
and let the computer connect me.

The phone in Loubobland's junkyard rang and rang. I let it,
leaning my forehead against the sun-warmed glass, sensing the ocean
scant blocks away, beating quietly underneath the boats and pilings.

Several seconds passed before I realized my call had been answered, that I was listening to silence. No one had spoken, but
someone was there.

"The clowns," I croaked.

The person on the other end grunted. "I have nothing to say."

"Just one question." I was blurting the words, trying to fit them in
before he hung up. "The project."

"What?"

"You told Jaybo the clowns were a failed project. I just want to
know what it was."

Silence. But no dial tone. I heard fumbling, for a match, maybe.
Then a long, hitching breath. "Neighbourhood watch," Loubob
said, and hung up.

That was five hours ago. Since then, I've been holed up in my
mother's condo – it will never, could never be mine – thinking mostly
about Randy. About his "Coming 'Round the Mountain" whistle
and his electric shock of joy-giving, his hand against the windshield
as he waved goodbye. I hadn't been considering joining them, I
thought. Not really. Not quite.

But I hadn't called the cops, either. Because I was scared, maybe.
But mostly because I hadn't wanted to, wasn't so sure who was doing
good, being useful, making lives easier. And I'd liked the way they
were together, the Safety Clown family. And Randy . . . I think
Randy took me for his friend. Maybe I could have been.

So I'd let them be. And the clowns had come.

I've got the blinds thrown wide, but I can't see a blessed thing out there through the fog and dark. I kept the TV off, listening instead to the air-conditioning, wondering for the thousandth time if I was supposed to have called the police, and whether that would have saved anyone. Or me.

Tomorrow, maybe the next day, if no one comes, I'm going to have to get up. Maybe I'll go to the cops, and let them laugh. I've got to find another job if I'm going to go to school, have a life. But for now I'm staying right here, in what's left of the place I grew up in, holding my knees, while my ears strain for the clacking I heard on the phone two nights ago, the clatter of footless wooden legs on stairs that will tell me once and for all if what I do matters, and whether there's really such a thing as a line, and whether I crossed it.

POPPY Z. BRITE

The Devil of Delery Street

POPPY Z. BRITE'S FIRST NOVEL, *Lost Souls*, was a punk Goth vampire fable that introduced a number of recurring characters and themes in her fiction. Winner of the British Fantasy Society's Best Newcomer Award in 1994, she followed her debut with the novels *Drawing Blood*, *Exquisite Corpse* and *The Lazarus Heart*.

Her short fiction has been collected in *Wormwood* (aka *Swamp Foetus*), *Are You Loathsome Tonight?* (a.k.a. *Self-Made Man*), *The Devil You Know*, *Wrong Things* (with Caitlín R. Kiernan) and *Triads* (with Christa Faust), while *His Mouth Will Taste of Wormwood and Other Stories* was a compilation of four stories published as part of the "Penguin 60s" series. *Guilty But Insane* is a collection of non-fiction, and she also edited two volumes of the erotic vampire anthology *Love in Vein*.

In recent years she has moved away from horror, drawing on her extensive knowledge of the New Orleans restaurant scene (she has been married to a chef for fifteen years) for a series of novels and short stories about Rickey and G-man, two young New Orleans cooks who make a name for themselves by opening a restaurant whose menu is based entirely on liquor. Brite's restaurant tales include the novels *Liquor*, *Prime* and *The Value of X*, and she is currently working on another book in the series.

" 'The Devil of Delery Street' is a blend of my old and new subject matter," the author explains, "since it is a ghost story but also a Stubbs family story (G-man, who appears as the baby Gary in this tale, is the youngest Stubbs child).

"It features my favourite New Orleans tradition, the St. Joseph's altars that are set up every March 19th by the Sicilian Catholic community as a gesture of thanks to the saint for saving Sicily from famine."

M ARY LOUISE STUBBS WAS THIRTEEN the year the family troubles began. She was called Melly because four of her younger siblings could not say her full name, or hadn't been able to when they were younger. Her fifth sibling, Gary, was only a baby and couldn't say much of anything yet. Once that strange and dreadful year was over, her mother, Mary Rose, would not allow its events to be referred to in any more specific way than "our family troubles". That was how Melly always remembered them.

Her memories seemed to date from the afternoon of her cousin Grace's funeral. Grace, the younger child of Mary Rose's sister Teresa, had been carried away by a quick and virulent form of childhood leukaemia. Now everyone was busy pretending that she had been a saint among nine-year-old girls. With the terrible un-ambiguous eye of an adolescent, Melly saw only hypocrisy in this. Grace hadn't been any saint; she was actually kind of a sneaky kid who liked to pinch smaller children when no grownups were look-ing. Melly had loved her, but didn't see the need to pretend she was now perched on the knee of the Blessed Virgin Mary.

The Stubbs family was gathered in their regular pew at St Peter and Paul, a dusty old brick church in downtown New Orleans, and Melly was having a hard time staying awake. She didn't usually sleep during regular Mass, let alone funerals, but a scratching in the wall of her bedroom had kept her up last night. She'd meant to ask her father if he would buy some rat traps, but the memory of wakefulness had left her as soon as she brushed her teeth and combed her long, coarse dark hair. She had the Sicilian colouring of her mother, a former Bonano, as did most of the other kids; only Gary was shaping up to be Irish-fair like their father.

Now, though, she began to nod off. Her brother Little Elmer, the next oldest after Melly, extended a finger and poked her in the ribs. "Father Mike ain't *that* boring," he whispered.

"Shhh," she replied. Father Mike was young, with soft dog-eyes and a thick shock of wavy hair, and Melly had a little crush on him. Not a sexy crush, it would be almost a sin to think about a priest that way, but a little warm feeling in her chest whenever she saw him.

"You the one falling asleep, not me—"

"Y'all both hush," their father murmured from Melly's other side, barely audible, and they shut up. Elmer Stubbs was a mild-tempered man, but there'd be misery later if Mary Rose caught them talking during a funeral Mass. Fortunately she was at the far end of the pew, twisting a Kleenex in her small, expressive hands. It was warm for March, and occasionally she'd reach up to blot the sweat from her brow, though she always pretended she was patting her jet-black beehive hairdo. How Melly loathed that beehive! "It's 1974, Momma," she said frequently, "time to comb it out." And Mary Rose always replied, "Nuh-uh, babe, I don't want to look like a hippie," as if a slightly more modern hairdo would transform her from a diminutive Italian housewife into a pot-smoking flower child.

Melly sat up straighter in the pew, stretched her eyes open, and hoped the rat would depart for more attractive horizons by tonight. They lived in a poor neighbourhood, the Lower Ninth Ward, but their house on Delery Street was clean. Melly knew it was, because she had to do a lot of the cleaning. Some of their neighbours' yards were full of chicken bones and crawfish shells and Melly didn't know what all else, scattered among rusty garbage cans and hulks of old cars. Surely a rat could fill his belly more easily at one of those houses.

Her wishes went unanswered for the time being; at home later, as she was changing the baby in the upstairs bedroom he shared with four-year-old Rosalie, she heard more scratching and a series of bangs behind the wall. "What you doing, Mr Rat?" she muttered. "Building you a whole 'nother house back there?"

Gary laughed and showed her the clean pink palms of his hands, as he did when anybody spoke in his presence whether they were talking to him or not. He was the sweetest-natured baby she'd ever seen, and the only one of her siblings who made her think she might want kids of her own someday. He had a little fluff of sweet-smelling curly hair on the top of his head and his eyes were the warm brown of pecan shells, not so black you couldn't tell the irises from the pupils like her own. She pinned his clean diaper shut and hoisted him onto her shoulder. "You gonna kill that old rat for me?" she asked him, and he laughed again.

Life went on as usual in the big old clapboard house, Little Elmer and Carl playing touch football after school, Henry with the other seven-year-olds in the decrepit playground down the street, Melly watching after Rosalie and the baby while Mary Rose went to Mass or fixed dinner. The house smelled of garlic and red gravy, of boys, of the sweet olive bushes that bloomed on either side of the stoop in March. They were nothing to look at the rest of the year, but every spring they turned even the poorest corners of the city luxurious with their scent.

The rat was gone for a week or two, and Melly figured her father must have put down some traps. Then suddenly it was there again, scratching behind the wall above her bed. This time the sound came deep in the night and didn't seem funny at all. She had shared her bedroom with Little Elmer until last year, when her mother said a growing girl needed her privacy and made Little Elmer bunk with the younger boys. And Melly had certainly been a growing girl: she'd gained five inches last year. She didn't like sleeping alone, though, had never done it in her life and wasn't used to the way shadows could mass around you when no one was breathing in the next bed. The creaky old house was no longer the well-known friend of her childhood, but a strange place that wanted to trap her somehow. What would happen when it caught her? Melly didn't know, but something deep in her gut seemed to liquefy when she thought of it.

She lay awake listening to the rat in the wall. Little Elmer had moved his toys into the boys' room, and Melly had put hers away in the attic, certain she would never need them again. Even Trina, the baby doll who'd been with her almost since her own babyhood, was stifling up there in a heavy garbage bag to keep out the dust. The room felt very empty. If a shadow should appear on the wall, she would know nothing was there to cast it.

The rat gnawed more loudly. Melly sat up, meaning to bang on the wall and scare it away. She did so one, two, three times. The rat banged back in perfect imitation.

She drew away, in-drawn air hissing between her teeth. No rat could have made that sound, three sharp, deliberate knocks. She extended her fist toward the wall, hesitated, then knocked once more. A mocking flurry of raps answered her, coming from the spot her knuckles had touched, then six feet above that, all the way to the right corner, to the left corner, to the ceiling, and finally under the bed. The mattress quaked. She flung herself off it, crossed the room without seeming to touch the floor, and shot into the hall screaming.

The next day was Saturday, and Mary Rose had to go to Canal Street to start looking at suits for Henry's First Communion. Carl tagged along in hopes of getting something from the bakery at D.H. Holmes. In a display of sudden, perceptive kindness typical to Stubbs males, Little Elmer volunteered to watch Rosalie and Gary. "Why don't you go shopping with Momma?" he said to Melly. "I bet she lets you get a dress or something."

"She's not gonna let me get any dress. I got all my spring school clothes already, and you know the rent's due next week."

"Well, but you like to look at stuff. Go on – I'll watch the babies."

"I ain't no baby," protested Rosalie, who was listening.

"I'll believe that when you get big enough to quit saying *ain't*." Little Elmer lifted her onto his lap. "Go on, Mel."

Full well knowing that her brother had given up a Saturday afternoon of street football in order to let her have a few hours away from the house that had frightened her so badly last night, Melly tried to enjoy herself. The life of Canal Street whirled around them, car horns, billboards, pink and gold neon signs, old ladies in their best shopping clothes, hippies in tattered regalia, a trio of lithe young black men with Afro picks embedded in their fantastic poufs of hair. Every breath was a mélange of exhaust, fried seafood, perfume, and, on the French Quarter side of the street, some mysterious tang that Melly thought might be the smell of burning marijuana. She walked beside her mother and admired the displays in the windows of the big department stores. She didn't argue when Mary Rose *tsked* at how short the skirts had gotten. The boys danced behind her making devil horns with their fingers and singing: "*Takin' care of business . . . it's a crime . . . takin' care of business and workin' overtime!*"

"They don't say *It's a crime*," said Melly, who spent just as much time listening to the radio as they did.

"Yeah?" said Carl truculently. "What they say, then?"

"*It's all mind*, I think."

"That don't make no sense!"

"*Doesn't* make *any* sense," said Mary Rose.

"But Momma, *you* say 'don't make no sense'."

It was an old family game, and all three children chorused with their mother: "Do as I say, not as I do."

As they were riding up the escalator at Maison Blanche, Melly felt safe enough to say, "Momma, what happened in my bedroom last night?"

"A bad dream," said Mary Rose firmly and without hesitation, as if she had been waiting for this question. "You just had a bad dream."

"I wasn't asleep yet, Momma. I was wide awake, and that's not any rat in my wall."

"You make an Act of Contrition tomorrow, babe. That rat ain't gonna bother you no more."

"An Act of Contrition?" Melly didn't know what she had expected her mother to say, but it wasn't that. "Why I gotta make an Act of Contrition? What'd I do wrong?"

"Nothing, Melly, nothing." They reached the top of the escalator. Mary Rose stumbled as she stepped off it, and Melly reached to steady her. "It's just to be safe."

Melly saw that her mother's eyes were frightened.

"Just to be safe," Mary Rose repeated. "It never hurts to be safe."

St Joseph's Day fell on a Tuesday that year, and Melly was allowed to miss school to join her mother on her altar-visiting rounds. They went to the altar at St Alphonsus and the one at Our Lady of Lourdes, then a tiny one belonging to a lady in their own neighbourhood, and last to the altar of Mary Rose's sister Teresa. It was generally known in the Stubbs and Bonano families that Teresa was rich; her husband Pete was whispered to make more than $10,000 a year. They lived across the parish line in Chalmette, in a one-storey brick house smaller than the Stubbs' but far newer. No one had expected Teresa to make an altar so soon after the death of her child, but Teresa said St Joseph had been helping her all these years and she wasn't going to turn her back on him now. "This year is more important than ever," she had told Mary Rose, and while Melly wasn't certain what she meant, Mary Rose seemed to take comfort in the words.

The altar was set up in the carport, three long tables groaning with roasted fish, stuffed artichokes, anise cookies, devotional candles, a big gold crucifix, and a tall statue of St Joseph holding the baby Jesus. The statue was wreathed with Christmas lights that blinked on and off, creating an intermittent halo effect. Mary Rose tucked a few dollars into the brandy snifter that had been set on the altar for donations, took a lucky bean from a cut-glass bowl full of them, and grabbed herself a plate of food. "You want some spaghetti?" she asked Melly.

"No, Momma." Melly did, but she had vowed to go on a diet for Lent. She was already planning to make the Rosy Perfection Salad she'd found on a Weight Watcher's card, even though the picture looked like a bad car wreck garnished with parsley. Instead she joined some other kids, mostly cousins and neighbours, to hear the music in the side yard.

Teresa had bragged about having a live band, but it was just an accordion player and an old man with a microphone. As was often the case at any Italian party, they were playing "Che La Luna". The kids began a circle dance as the old man sang, *"Mama dear come over here and see who's looking in my window . . . It's the baker boy and oh, he's got a cannoli in his hand . . ."* The circle parted to let Melly in. On her right was her cousin Angelina. On her left was a boy she didn't know, maybe her age, with big brown eyes and a Beatles haircut. In fact, he looked a little like Paul. She hoped her hand

wasn't sweaty as he grasped it. "*In the middle!*" cried the old man.
The kids screamed with laughter as they raised their arms and
crowded toward the middle of the circle. The music went faster
and faster, and the dance followed suit. Caught up in the moment,
she squeezed the boy's hand, and she was almost certain that he
squeezed back. A strange warm feeling welled up just under her
ribcage, like a line of electricity being drawn out of her.

She thought the shrieks of the women behind her were part of the
festivities, so she didn't know anything was wrong until something
hit her in the back. It didn't fall away, but clung there, heavy and
hard between her shoulder-blades. *A bug* was her first thought, but
reaching back, she could feel that it was bigger than even the largest
New Orleans cockroach. Something cold, with four arms and a
lumpy part in the middle. A crucifix – it felt like the big metal one that
had been on the altar. Melly couldn't understand how it was stuck to
her, and she couldn't pull it off.

"Get it off me!" she yelled. The band stopped playing with a squeal
of accordion feedback. The other children backed away. The boy
who looked like Paul wiped his hand on his pants as if cleansing
himself of her touch. She knew the gesture was probably automatic,
but that made it hurt all the worse.

"Please get it off me!"

Here came Mary Rose, pushing through the crowd of children,
spinning her daughter around and yanking hard at the crucifix. It
clung to Melly's back as if some immensely powerful magnet were
buried deep inside her, perhaps where her heart should be. "Please,
Momma," Melly sobbed, and Mary Rose yanked even harder, but
the crucifix didn't budge.

Now here was Aunt Teresa with a little pitcher that had been
sitting on the altar, a pitcher labelled HOLY WATER. She upended
the pitcher over Melly's back. A couple of the kids giggled. "Pull on it
again," said Teresa. Mary Rose did, and the image of Jesus came off
in her hand, but the cross stayed stuck to Melly. Several women in
the crowd crossed themselves and fumbled rosaries out of their
pocketbooks.

Melly pushed away from her mother, out of the circle, out of the
little fenced yard. She had never felt more alone and freakish than
she did standing there in the sun-baked street, one small person
with a big holy water stain running down her back and at least
thirty people staring at her from the other side of a fence. The
warm electric feeling abruptly left her and the cross clattered to the
asphalt.

Everybody was silent except for one old lady still praying: "Hail Mary, fulla grace, the Lord is with thee . . ."

"Grace?" Teresa whispered. "Grace?"

Melly turned her back on all the staring eyes. There was a soft collective intake of breath. Through her thin nylon blouse, it was easy to see the raw red cross-shape that had been printed in her flesh.

Melly only had disjointed flashes of the next few hours. She remembered repeating through tears, "I'm sorry, Aunt Teresa, I'm sorry" as Teresa stood holding the figure of Jesus and the denuded cross, looking from one to the other as if she couldn't quite understand how they went together. She heard people telling each other what had happened: "Did you see the way it jumped off the altar, just *flew*?" She didn't remember the ride home at all; the next thing she knew, she was in her own bed, half asleep, rocked by some strange nausea that seemed to originate in her chest instead of her stomach. Over and over she nearly drifted off; over and over the bed jerked just as she slid over the edge of consciousness, yanking her back to wakefulness. "Please let me sleep," she moaned, and a voice answered her.

"You can sleep when you're dead, Mary Louise . . ."

It was a harsh and guttural voice, a voice that might have last spoken a thousand years ago or never. The words seemed to result from an intake of breath rather than an outflow, as if the speaker were suffocating. It was the worst voice Melly had ever heard, and yet suddenly she wasn't scared so much as angry. If this thing had a voice, then it had a personality, and if it had a personality, then she could damn well tell it why it shouldn't be pounding on her walls and making holy objects stick to her back. "Who are you?" she said, sitting up.

"The Devil."

"No you're not. The Devil wouldn't waste his time scaring some poor girl from Delery Street. Who are you really?"

Silence.

"Are you Grace?"

Still nothing. She felt that she had offended it. And now she was frightened again; how had she dared to speak to such a thing, surely not the Devil but maybe some low minion? Even if it was only a ghost – she laughed at herself a little, thinking "*only* a ghost" – she oughtn't to be talking to it.

Melly sighed, got her beads out of the nightstand drawer, and started saying the rosary. She got all the way to the second decade before the beads were snatched out of her hands and scattered across the room.

Mary Rose got Father Mike to come over and bless the house. He made it clear that it wasn't an exorcism, that he wouldn't perform an exorcism if she asked, that furthermore he didn't believe the Stubbs' house was haunted; he was only doing it to put her mind at rest and maybe calm Melly down a little. Melly thought that was ridiculous. Right now she was the calmest person in the house. She found that she no longer had the warm little crush on Father Mike.

One day when her parents thought she was upstairs, she overheard the tail-end of a conversation between them. Though she knew her father was an uncommonly good man, she would never quite forgive him for asking Mary Rose, "Don't you think there's some chance she's doing all this to get attention?"

"No, I don't think so," Mary Rose had replied. "This isn't the first time crazy things happened in my family. You know that little end table my momma used to keep by her sofa?"

"I can't say I do."

"You know, Elmer, that little black table with the Italian patterns. It was hand-painted by my great-grandmother in Sicily. Lord, how that woman hated cursing and arguing – at least that's what Momma told me. Well, she passed away long before my grammaw brought the table to America, but whenever anybody in the house would start cursing or hollering at each other, the table would rise up and beat them!"

"Mary Rose, nuh-uh."

"I swear on my mother's sweet name. It happened to me a couple times, when I was real little and pitching a fit. I remember seeing that thing fly through the air toward my head – Jesus Lord! But when it hit you, it never hurt. It'd just tap you real soft, like it was saying, *You better behave.*"

"What happened to it, then?"

"The effect just wore off, I guess. Teresa's got the table now, and you know how bad her kids cut up sometimes, but that table ain't moved in thirty years. At least not that I know of."

"Well, maybe this thing with Melly will kinda taper off."

"I hope so," said Mary Rose with a long-suffering sigh. "It's hard on her, and it's hard on me too."

It was not at all hard on the younger kids. They loved it, and got to the point where they would egg it on. "Bet you can't lift me up in this chair!"

Henry would say, pulling his feet up in expectation of a ride. The spirit never gave him one, but sometimes it would tilt the chair and dump him onto the floor, reducing Rosalie and Gary to helpless giggles.

"Draw something in my book!" Rosalie would demand, leaving her scratchpad open with a crayon on top and hiding her eyes. When she looked again, often as not there would be a page full of meaningless scribbles.

"The baby done 'em," Melly said one time, trying to vacuum around them.

"He did not! He was right here by me the whole time, weren't you, Gary?"

"Lady draw," said Gary.

"Huh, you mean you can see it?" said Henry. "Aw, Melly, I wish he could tell us what it looks like! A lady, huh?"

"Shut up!" Melly told them. "Don't talk to it, don't ask it to do things, just leave it alone! You don't know how it makes me feel."

"It's not *yours*," Henry said unkindly.

"*Yes it is!*" she screamed at him. The startled look in his eyes made her feel bad, but she couldn't stop. "It is too mine! Do whatever you want, but give me . . . give me . . . oh, I don't know what I'm saying!" She ran from the room, leaving Henry to get up and turn off the vacuum.

Little Elmer and Carl did not enjoy the spirit and stayed away from home a lot that year, immersing themselves in boy-business. All in all, though, Melly thought it was amazing what people could get used to. When she heard scratching and raps in her wall, she rolled over and tried to go back to sleep. Sometimes it stopped there; sometimes things began flying around, toilet paper and jigsaw puzzles and sausages strewn around the living room, every flowerpot in the house turned upside down. Sometimes an object would hit her, but she was never hurt or (after the St Joseph's Day incident) even seriously humiliated. Once when she was sitting in the kitchen watching Mary Rose make a lasagna, there was a popping sound near the refrigerator and an egg rose into the air. Mary Rose hadn't had any eggs on the counter, so it must have come from inside the fridge. It floated lazily toward Melly, then hovered over her head. *Great*, she thought, *it's gonna smash in my hair*. Instead it tapped her lightly on the forehead, then fell and splattered gaudily against the faded old linoleum. Melly got up to fetch the dustpan, no more upset than she would have been if a dog had piddled on the floor. Once it was clear that no one was going to be hurt, the incredible had come to seem almost normal.

She wondered if this had anything to do with being Catholic, with accepting as unquestioned fact the existence of saints watching over you, helping and perhaps even hindering your enterprises; with taking for granted that the wafer in your mouth would change into flesh, the wine into blood; with praying to a ghost. She did not ponder this very deeply, because she was not a deep girl and she knew no other way to be but Catholic. When she said her prayers, she sometimes added some extra ones for the spirit in case it was a soul in purgatory.

It never spoke to her again after the night it said it was the Devil. Melly thought it might be embarrassed to have made such a claim, or possibly embarrassed to have provoked her angry response, like an overtired child who doesn't realize he's being obnoxious until he goes a step too far and his mother yells at him. She did not feel that the spirit had ever been angry with her; in retrospect, even making the crucifix stick to her back seemed little more than a desperate way of getting attention. Why it had wanted her attention so badly she didn't know, nor did she wish to ponder the question.

The nights of rapping and banging came further apart; there would be two in a week, then one, then none for two or three weeks. When they did come, the raps and flying objects seemed weaker somehow, as if the force behind them was winding down. No further scribbles appeared in Rosalie's drawing pad. Gary, though he was talking a blue streak now, said nothing more about a lady.

As Melly lay in bed one night, she felt something strange happening in her viscera. At first she thought she was bleeding, but there was no wetness, only a sensation of something warm draining from her. She put her hand on the concavity beneath her breasts, but it began to tingle unpleasantly and she took it away again. A few minutes later the sensation stopped. She felt wonderfully relaxed. It was as if she had been in pain for a long time, and had gotten so used to it that she no longer noticed the pain until it stopped.

After that night there were no more noises, no more strange happenings at all. For some time there was an undercurrent of tension in the house and among the family, as if they were bracing themselves for another assault. None came. "I miss the ghost," Henry said at the dinner table one night.

Mary Rose turned on him. "There was no ghost in this house, young man! Say anything like that again and I'll warm the seat of your pants for you!"

Henry's mouth fell open, affording everyone an unlovely view of half-chewed braciola. *Poor Henry*, Melly thought. *That was prob-*

*ably the most exciting year of his life, and Momma's never even
gonna let him talk about it.*

She didn't want to talk about it either, though. Henry would have
to sift through his memories alone.

Another year passed. Melly grew a couple more inches, but
nothing like the rapid stretch she'd experienced just before the
odd events began. Gradually she stopped fearing that she was going
to be a circus freak, the Giant Lady. She'd probably gotten some
extra height from Elmer, that was all. She joined the math club at
school, went out on a few dates, got involved with St Peter and Paul's
youth group. All she wanted in the world was to be a normal teenage
girl; she wanted that so badly that she thought she could taste
acceptance, sweet on her tongue, when other kids treated her as
just one of them. Kids who had no idea that a crucifix had once clung
to her back like it was a magnet and she was iron, kids who never
suspected that something possibly dead had once knocked on her
bedroom wall.

When the scratching started up again, so soft and sly that at first it
might have been her imagination, she thought for one black moment
of just putting a bullet in her head. Elmer didn't like guns, but crime
in the neighbourhood had begun to spiral upward, and he had one
on the high shelf of the bedroom closet. Melly knew where the bullets
were kept. But she didn't want to die, and she wasn't going to let this
stupid mindless thing tempt her into it. She rolled over and went back
to sleep.

At breakfast the next morning, the saltshaker rose off the table and
floated across the kitchen. Henry's face lit up, and he began to say
something. As Mary Rose's eye fell upon him, he shut his mouth with
a snap. Everyone else ignored it, even Gary, who at three was
exquisitely sensitive to the feelings and wants of his family. He
got along with everybody, and wouldn't dare mention the floating
saltshaker once he'd observed that the others didn't want to see it.
Melly could see that Henry still wanted to say something, but she
added her own glare to Mary Rose's, and he wilted.

There were a few more raps, a few more scratches. Then the
sounds stopped again, and for a few days there was a distinctly
injured air to the house, as if some unseen presence felt rejected. Then
there was nothing except the usual vibrant atmosphere of a house full
of children.

Melly had skipped St Joseph's Day last year, but this year Gary
and Rosalie were going to be angels in Teresa's tupa-tupa, the
ceremony in which the Holy Family entered the home and were

fed from the altar. She couldn't stand to miss that, so she squared her shoulders, steeled her spine, and accompanied the family to Teresa's house.

Cousin Angelina was playing the Blessed Virgin Mary. As soon as they got there, Melly saw her standing near the altar, slightly pudgy in a white dress, a light blue headscarf, and her usual pink-framed glasses that made her eyes look a little like a white rabbit's. She stuck out her tongue at Melly. Melly held her nose and crossed her eyes. "Who's gonna be St Joseph?" she whispered to Mary Rose.

"Well, Teresa wanted Pete to do it, but he said that'd be incestuous since he's Angelina's father. So they got some boy from the neighbourhood. I don't know his name." As she spoke, Mary Rose herded her pair of angels up the driveway toward the carport. They were dressed in white gowns with posterboard wings and tinsel haloes. Flashbulbs started going off as if they were walking the red carpet at the Academy Awards. Gary looked a little scared. Rosalie looked smug, as if she'd always known she was destined for stardom.

Drawing closer to the altar, Melly caught sight of St Joseph, a tall, slim boy wearing a rough brown robe and carrying a crooked staff. He turned, and she saw that it was the boy who had held her hand in the circle dance two years ago, the boy who looked a little like Paul McCartney. The boy who had seen her crying in the street with the shape of a crucifix embedded in her flesh.

Just as she was about to look away, he gave her a smile so sweet it made her stomach flutter. "How you doing?" he said. "I looked for you last year, but you weren't here."

"I . . . I wasn't feeling too good last year."

"Well, nice to see you. Maybe you'll dance with me later, huh?"

"Sure." Then, before she knew what was going to come out of her mouth, she said, "But I'm staying out of the circle dance!"

For a moment he looked almost shocked, and she was sorry she'd said it. Then something else dawned on his face, a mixture of surprise and admiration. He hadn't thought she would have the guts to bring it up, she guessed. From the corner of her eye she saw Angelina watching them jealously.

"Yeah," he said. "I'd do that if I were you. This year the whole altar might just rise up and bash you on the head."

"You never know."

He turned away and headed for the house. Behind her, Melly heard Mary Rose urging the angels, "Follow Mr Joe. Y'all gonna eat soon."

"I'll take 'em," said Melly. She coaxed Gary and Rosalie into the house, dropped them off with the ladies who were co-ordinating the tupa-tupa, and went into the kitchen to see if she could help with the food.

Aunt Teresa was at the stove fussing over a huge pot of red gravy. She turned and saw Melly, and for a moment fear flickered in her eyes, or maybe just sorrow. Melly wondered if she should have come after all. Then Teresa smiled, held out her arms, and drew Melly to her.

Later, as she was standing with Paul (whose real name turned out to be Tony, but she couldn't get that first impression out of her head, wasn't even particularly anxious to do so) looking at the altar, she saw the gold crucifix that had stuck to her back. She could tell it was the same one because there was a big blob of dried glue showing between the figure of Jesus and the cross. A rosary made of painted fava beans was looped over it, and there were oranges arranged around its base. Melly reached out a hand, hesitated, then gently touched the crucifix.

"Goodbye," she said under her breath, and was relieved when nothing answered her.

JAY RUSSELL

Apocalypse Now, Voyager

JAY RUSSELL IS THE pseudonym of a writer born in New York, aged in Los Angeles, and currently living in London with his wife and daughter.

Brown Harvest (a World Fantasy Award nominee for Best Novel) is a textbook guide to many of his key influences and unfortunate tendencies. The novella *Apocalypse Now, Voyager* is the latest adventure in the fantastical/comic life of reluctant supernatural detective Marty Burns, who also stars in the novels *Celestial Dogs*, *Burning Bright* and *Greed & Stuff*. Russell's other books include *Blood*, *The Twilight Zone* novelisation *Memphis/The Pool Guy*, and the short story collection *Waltzes and Whispers*.

"Marty Burns is an old friend," says Russell. "He has now appeared in three novels (including my first) and a handful of short stories, and somewhat to my surprise, I'm still not sick of him.

"'Apocalypse Now, Voyager' is one of two lengthy Marty stories I've wanted to write for several years. The impetus to finally get it on paper came by way of a request from Paul Miller of Earthling Publications for a novella he could publish as a limited edition chapbook. (God knows what it will take to drag the other one out of my head . . .)

"Once upon a time, the story was going to have a Christmas setting against which the love story would play out – Christmas in Southern California feels almost as out-of-place as the L.A. River itself – with the idea that Gordon Van Gelder would be compelled to buy it as the cover story for a holiday issue of *The Magazine of Fantasy & Science Fiction*. That never quite happened, and I still have to write Gordon a story one of these days. (Maybe if he does a Hanukkah issue . . .)

"As usual for Marty, the story is full of excruciatingly obscure references – mostly relating to Los Angeles and its bizarre history. The longer I've been away from the place, the fonder my memories of it grow. I think when I die – if I die – I'll have my ashes sprinkled over something significant there. A mini-mall? A parking lot? David Hasselhoff? Got it: a taqueria!"

I

S HE SEEMED PRETTY CHEERFUL for a woman who'd just burned off most of her pubic hair. Plunking herself down on the next bar stool, she offered up a smile.

She still wasn't wearing pants.

Or anything else for that matter.

"Buy a gal a drink?" she asked.

What the hell, I figured. How could I continue to think of myself as a stand-up guy if I didn't buy a naked lady a drink, particularly given her display of fortitude in the face of conflagration and extremis.

Besides, I've always been a sucker for women who call themselves "gals."

I waggled a finger at the bartender, who rolled his eyes heavenward, but knew her drink without having to ask. He poured three fingers of Bacardi into a highball glass then dropped in a lime wedge. She winked at him. He walked away.

"You okay?" I asked.

"Right as rain," she said. She fished out the lime and squeezed it into her rum, then tossed the rind on the bar. She delicately sipped the drink and made a yummy noise in the back of her throat.

I didn't mean to do it – even more than stand-up, I strive for sensitive – but it's tough not to let your eye wander down the fleshy curves of a naked lady when she's sitting right next to you. For all my best efforts, my gaze lingered in the vicinity of her nether regions.

She caught me ogling and another thin smile played at the corners of her mouth, as if I'd confirmed everything she ever suspected of me. I pulled a scrap of that vaunted sensitivity out of my back pocket and looked her full in the eye.

"Sorry," I said.

"Occupational hazard," she said with a shrug.

It made her tits jiggle. I failed to not look at them, too.

"Hell of an occupation," I said.

"Oooh, aren't we the judgmental one. You don't approve, I take it?"

"I didn't say that. No offence meant. Really. It's just doing that routine with the fire and the ping pong ball and all. It's impressive as all get out. But your insurance premiums must be hell."

"You kidding? I'm female, over twenty-five and I drive a Saab. Allstate loves me. It's my tuition bill that's the killer."

"Tuition?"

"You think I do this shtick 'cause I like the smell of burning bush? U.S.C. charges like money's going out of style. I'm working on a Master's in Communications."

"I never went to college," I said.

"*Quelle* surprise," she said, and finished off her rum.

"Who's judgmental now," I muttered.

She half turned to face me, leaning an elbow on the dirty bar. She rested her head in her palm and looked me up and down. I felt like *I* was the one sitting there naked. I folded my arms over my chest and crossed one leg over the other. She laughed.

"So what do *you* do then?"

"Oh, little bit of this, little bit of that," I said.

"Hmmmph. Like every other jack-off here," she mumbled.

I looked around the bar – Haw Haw's, it was called – at the drunk and doped celebrants. Bikers, mostly, in full leather regalia. Drug dealers, mules, muscle, second-story men, pimps, punks and petty thieves. A few hookers and female hangers-on liberally sprinkled among them in various states of (un)consciousness and (un)dress. A veritable convention of social deviants, moral miscreants and all-around reprobates of the worst order as far as the eye could see.

And me, of course.

"Not quite like everyone else," I said. I glanced around again and added: "Please be to god."

A wrecking ball swept across the room and hit me square between the shoulder blades. A hand big as Pittsburgh and tougher than an old bull grabbed me by the neck before I could tumble off my stool.

"The dead do walk!" the voice of doom bellowed. "Nice to see you, Marty, you good for nothing piece of shit. Where you been keeping yourself? Why don't you ever call?"

"Hi, Danny," I said. "Happy birthday."

Daniel Gabowitz, the guest of honour at this sleazy soiree, offered up a big smile. Gabbo, as he was more commonly known, was fifty-five years old that very day. In this land of the morally blind, Gabbo was truly the one-eyed king. He was three hundred plus pounds of undiluted nastiness, with a criminal record as long as his belly button-scraping grey beard. He was dressed to the nines for this most special of occasions, with shiny new leathers hugging his massive frame, stretched tight over a beer barrel belly. He caught me admiring his duds and unzipped the jacket. He revealed a black tee shirt embroidered with gold thread reading: MY MOM WENT TO LONG BEACH AND ALL I GOT WAS SLOPPY SECONDS.

"Classy," I said.

"I'll get one sent to you," he said with a wink. Gabbo knows how much I hate Long Beach.

"Hell of a wing-ding," I said, gesturing around.

"Nine inches and still growing," he roared.

I managed a chuckle in return. Hell, why not be gracious on a guy's birthday.

"And how's my little Annie?" Gabbo said. He wrapped his arms around my naked friend and mashed her breasts. "I love these big titties!"

Annie winced. I did, too. Gabbo caught my reaction, and for just a fraction of a second I saw the shame in his eyes. In *Danny's* eyes. Lord of the reprobates though he was, I knew that much of Gabbo's act was just that: an act. Gabbo was the alpha male of this particular pride of beasts, and eternal arrogance and indulgence was the price of his exalted position. But buried beneath the leather and the beer belly was a man of no small intelligence and wit. He had once been a writer and a film director of some note. Not that you'll find Gabbo doing director's commentary on any DVDs. When Hollywood turned its scabby back on him for sins real or imagined, he hacked himself a path through another jungle. I'd gotten to know both sides of the man – Gabbo and Danny – and to my surprise (and perhaps against my better judgement), I'd come to like them both.

Not much else could have dragged me down to the depths of Long Beach, a city that can only dream of someday achieving armpit-of-the-universe status.

His nanosecond of shame having passed, Gabbo bent over and buried his face between Annie's big tits and yelled "WUGGA-WUGGA-WUGGA" as he bounced his head between them. A cheer went up around us and Gabbo took a bow. Or as much of one as his massive frame allowed for.

"Catch you later, dude," he said.

"Sure thing, Danny."

And off he went.

The girl – Annie – was staring down at the bar. I could see the goose bumps that had risen down the length of her arm. I took off my jacket and slipped it over her shoulders. She looked up and offered another bright smile.

"Thanks," she said. "You're sweet."

"Gabbo's okay, really," I said. "He doesn't mean shit like that. Not entirely."

"I know," she said. "I work for him. I . . . you know. He is okay. For the business and all."

She stared back down at the bar, pulling my jacket more tightly around her. Neither of us said anything for a bit. I was about to offer to buy her another drink when she turned to me and said:

"Are you by any chance . . . Marty Burns?"

"Yeah," I said and sighed. "Only it's not by chance."

"I think you're just the man I've been looking for."

The hooker, heavily singed at the pubes, slightly long in the tooth and naked as the day she was born – except for what *had* been my freshly dry-cleaned blazer – looked up at me with an all-too-familiar mix of faint hope and tired desperation in her bloodshot eyes. Her mascara had run, too.

Welcome to my life.

II

Her name was, indeed, Annie. Annie De Beauvoir. She spelled it for me.

"But it's pronounced 'da beaver,'" she said. "As in . . ."

". . . leave it to?" I said.

"Among other things."

"You've gotta be kidding," I said.

She wasn't.

"Hell, what's in a name, anyway" I said.

She shuddered in reply. Imagine what life was like for her in high school.

We were walking down 17th Street, both fully clothed now. Annie didn't think Gabbo would appreciate her leaving the bar in the middle of his party, but I told her it would be fine. The forced hilarity of the celebration spilled out of the door behind us and echoed around the otherwise silent street. A pair of leathered up tyrannosaurs on hogs big as baby Hummers gave us the hairy eyeball as they growled past. They pulled up in front of Haw Haws and threw themselves inside to join Gabbo's birthday bash. It was going to be one hell of a game of pin the tail on the donkey. I knew that because I'd seen the real donkey they'd hauled up from Tijuana out in back. More than that, I didn't *want* to know.

"You called him Danny," she said.

"Beg pardon?"

"Gabbo. You called him Danny in the bar. You said it like you'd say anyone's name. Bob. Elvis. Osama."

"It is his name."

She snorted. "I've only ever once heard anyone call him that. It was in Haw Haw's a while back and one of the Palos Verdes Scorpions was drunk as a roast skunk. Everyone was having a real good time and all because . . . oh, I can't even remember. Some big score or something had played out. This mountain of a Scorpion picked up a keg and hoisted it over his head. 'To Dan the man,' he yelled, like he was making a toast with the keg. The whole room froze. I've never seen anything like it."

I waited for her to finish, but she didn't.

"So what happened?" I prodded.

"Gabbo shot him."

"Dead?"

Annie just shrugged. "You ever read the little sign over the front door of Haw Haws?"

"I'm waiting for the movie," I said.

She shot me a look.

"What does it say?" I asked her.

" 'Don't ask, don't tell.' It's written over a picture of Bill Clinton getting a blow job."

"Good advice."

"I heard Gabbo talk about you once."

"My ears are always burning."

"He likes you. I didn't think Gabbo liked hardly anyone, but he definitely likes you."

"What's not to like?" I said.

"He said there's something funny about you, too. Something special, he said."

"I was born under a wandering star. Or should that be *wanderin'*?"

"Gabbo's real superstitious, you know. He's funny that way."

"I didn't actually know that. But we aren't all that close, to be honest."

"What? You came to his birthday. You walked into Haw Haw's dressed . . . like that. I mean, sorry Marty, but *come on*! I don't know anyone else could do that and leave with teeth in their head."

"Gabbo . . . Danny and I have an understanding. It's a long story and the third act sucks so I won't bore you."

We'd been walking aimlessly – or so I assumed – and found ourselves at a dead end. We'd run smack dab into the concrete barrier forming the wall above the dry culvert that was laughingly known as the Los Angeles River. Annie walked up to the wall and hoisted herself on top. She stared down at the expanse of dirty concrete below. The L.A. River generally runs deeper with film crews than it does with water. Though when the water comes, look out! Seems like every year three or four people – homeless, drunks, kids messing around – get washed away because they don't realize that when the rains do come, the river actually gets wet and the water moves fast. L.A. River floods flash faster than a sitcom star's career.

Believe me, I know.

"The thing is," Annie started to say. Then she looked up over my shoulder and her eyes went wide. "Shit," she said.

"What thing is shit?" I asked.

I saw her raise up a hand.

I heard a creepy cackle behind me.

I felt a 10-ton safe drop on top of my head.

III

I'm a total sucker for medical dramas. I think it maybe goes back to my appearance on *Marcus Welby, M.D.*. I had a guest shot on it when I was a child star still riding high off the back of *Salt & Pepper*, my main and ancient claim to fame in this life. James Brolin got me sick-drunk on the last day of the week's shoot. Robert Young told us both off in no uncertain terms. We were so very ashamed.

Anyway, I can still sit and watch hospital shows all day long. And some days, I do. *St Elsewhere*, *Chicago Hope*, *ER* – you name it. I'm a sucker for having my tears jerked, you see. Possibly because of a lack of the satisfying jerking of other vital organs.

But let's not go there.

For years I've been dying to land a spot on *ER*, which is my all-time favourite doctor show. I've had my agent, Kendall, try and try to get me even a cameo role, but the producers won't bite. I think it's because Michael Crichton has it in for me; see, I had a bit part in *Looker*. I don't think Big Mike likes to be reminded of that one. (And if you want to hear me talk about Susan Dey, you'll have to get me drunk first.)

The thing about medical dramas is that if you watch enough of them – and the amount I watch is clearly more than enough – you start to think you actually know stuff about medicine. Babinksi!

Chem-7!! Type and cross-match, stat!!! My mother so much wanted for me to be a doctor. I so wanted to *play* one on TV. Regrets, I have a few . . .

The point here is that after all that medical training I feel pretty confident about making basic diagnoses. Which is how I knew I was paralysed from the waist down.

My hands were pressed up against my legs, so I knew they were still attached. But I couldn't feel a damn thing in them. I couldn't see, either, though I didn't immediately diagnose blindness. But only because I could feel the sack that had been pulled over my head. It was burlap and itchy and smelled of poultry.

I was moving, too. Or being moved. My first thought was a wheelchair, but as some semblance of clarity overtook me once more, I realized I wouldn't likely be wedged ass-over-bagged-head backwards into one. It was a rough ride, too – literally tooth-jarring as whatever-it-was I'd been jammed into rattled along a bumpy, hard surface. I could hear the echo of the wheels bouncing around above a metallic clatter. I tried to wiggle my torso and pull my arms free, but I felt something tighten around my wrists. Whatever I was in, I'd been tied to it. I was lying atop something reasonably soft, but I was still in considerable discomfort. The back of my head throbbed where I'd taken the blow that had knocked me out, but I also began to feel a twinge in my right calf, and despite the pain I was reassured by my initial misdiagnosis of paralysis. Clearly, I would have to break down and spring for those season box sets of *ER*.

"Hey," I tried yelling through the burlap. "Hey out there!"

The movement of what I was in slowed and we came to a stop. I tried to raise up my head and took another blow to the side of the noggin for the effort. I let out a squeal and collapsed back down. It was only the cushioning of the thick sack that kept it from being another knock-out shot. I felt sick to my stomach and had to work hard to fight off the nausea. If I vomited with the sack on, I was certain I would do a Jimi Hendrix. After a minute the queasiness passed.

There was a sudden lurch to the right, which threw me over to the side, pinning my arm in a painful new way. My whole body shifted and I fell off the soft bit I'd been resting on and landed on something hard that poked me in the ribs. I tried to jerk myself around, but couldn't get any purchase.

Things then came to a stop.

The burlap sack was forcefully yanked off of my head.

I panted for a lung full of the L.A. night air. I looked around.

I was in a Ralph's shopping cart, my wrists tied to the metal frame of the trolley with twisted segments of coat hanger. The thin wire had cut into my flesh and blood trailed down my arms. My legs were underneath me, the numbness a result of nothing more than painfully reduced blood flow from the awkward position and tight space.

There was indeed something soft, with hard bits, wedged under me.

It was Annie. It was the point of her bony elbow that was caught in my rib cage. Her eyes were wide open and looked up into mine.

She was unmistakably and entirely dead.

I twisted my neck around to see who was pushing the cart.

Her white hair was wild, as if charged with electricity; her eyes even wilder. She was garbed in black from neck to toes, with silver rings on every finger and a little one dangling from her nose. They caught the light from the full moon and danced in front of me like fireflies as she waved her hands wildly about. Her entire body shook with tiny convulsions.

We were down in the culvert, I realized. I was hog-tied in a shopping cart, straddling a dead women I barely knew but had seen naked, and being wheeled up the dry, concrete bed of the Los Angeles River.

The wild woman started to cackle, then looked down at me. Her lips – painted in electric pink; Ralph's must have sold-out of black lipstick – curled up, exposing crooked teeth.

"Long ways to go, Medicine Man," she said. "*Long* ways to go."

"Aww, crap," I declared.

IV

"Umm, Miss," I said. I cleared my throat.

She had her back turned to me and was staring up at the moon. She made keening noises which threatened to turn into full-fledged howls at any second. Strands of her electrified hair glowed in the moonlight as she shifted slightly from leg to leg in what looked like a kind of rain dance.

Not a cloud in the sky, thankfully.

"Hello?" I tried.

My contorted position in the shopping cart was beginning to cause a considerable degree of pain in my back and legs, and the wires digging into my wrists would have brought a big smile to Mel Gibson's face. I could feel the muscles stretched taut now and was beginning to regret the lack of paralysis, at least for the moment.

And it was just a bit disconcerting to be lying on top of a dead woman.

My captor ignored me and began gesticulating at the moon.

"*Hey lady*!" I yelled. And I felt a muscle pop in my neck from the effort.

Maybe she was a Jerry Lewis fan. In any case, she stopped her little dance routine and looked over her shoulder at me. Even with the full moon and the pervasive incandescence that is the Los Angeles night, it was dark down in the culvert. But I could still see her eyes and the mania they contained. They were like two onyx holes in the middle of her face; adits opening down into deep shafts of raw crazy.

I was fucked.

"Anybody home?" I said.

"You is disturbing me," she said.

"I think I'm a little after the fact."

She went kind of cross-eyed and I thought, not for the first nor even the thousandth time that I've got to remember life ain't a sitcom. Then she let out a cackle that more than befitted her crazed mien. The cackle turned into the previously threatened howl as she spun about, turned her face up to the sky, placed her hands around her mouth and bayed with all her might at the perfect, round circle of moon. She turned back around and smiled down at me.

"I knewed you was the one, Medicine Man. Knewed it soon as I saws you with her. Knewed you wasn't just another stiff dick."

"Why did you kill her?" I asked. "What do you want?"

That seemed to take her aback. She cocked her head, looking like nothing so much as a giant demented raven, and narrowed her eyes in puzzlement.

"Love," she said. "What does anyone want?"

"I don't understand."

"I thinks you does. I *knows* you does. Why else was you with her?"

"Annie? I don't even know her. We just met."

"But she let's them all knows her, don't she. In the biblical sense. My poor little orphan Annie."

"It wasn't like that," I tried to explain. "I'm not a . . . client. I met her at a birthday party. I bought her a drink after she burned her . . ."

How the hell was I going to explain this?

"Don't worry, Medicine Man, you *will* knows her. Deeper than any of those others."

"What others?" I asked. I didn't like the sound of that one bit.

"You'll see. We gots to get there first."

"Get where? Where are we going?"

"Upriver. We gots to get upriver before moonset. Before the water comes. Gots to make Yang-Na. Gots to find Toypurina, she of the Tongva. Then we goes see the Cat People."

The strain of holding my head up to talk finally got the better of me. It was no more comfortable, but I had to let the tension out of my neck and slumped down until my chin rested on Annie's cold shoulder.

Off to see the Cat People.

I just hoped it wasn't the remake.

V

The shopping cart must have been heavy with both me and Annie stuffed inside, but the woman in black pushed it briskly enough along the dry river floor with no discernible exertion. She'd hum to herself on and off – all Robbie Williams songs, I'm pretty sure – and emit the odd cackle, but she didn't so much as strain for breath. I tried several times to engage with her as we rolled along, to try and open up some channel of communication which might help me to get to grips with the situation, but she ignored all my entreaties. Desperate, I tried screaming out for help every time we approached an overpass, but that didn't bother her either. If there was anyone out and about up above to hear my cries, they paid them no mind. I had to admit, I'd sure as hell walk on by if I heard a distress call like mine rising up out of a Long Beach culvert after midnight.

I tried to estimate how far we'd gone. You couldn't espy any landmarks from down on the river bed, but I tried to remember my Thomas Guide geography. I wasn't sure how long I'd been out cold – I couldn't quite see my watch, either – but didn't think it had been for too long. I was judging by the position of the moon in the sky and the residual warmth that radiated from Annie's body. We'd already passed beneath one huge overpass, with so much traffic noise spilling off that it had to be the San Diego Freeway. As we came up on another big one, I made it for the Artesia Freeway overhead and reckoned that we were moving out of Long Beach and up toward Compton.

Wherever the hell we were going, we were making damn good time.

I raised my head up again when I heard the echo of a swishing noise begin to build around us. We'd rolled into a particularly narrow section of the dry river, the steeply banked walls no more than 25 feet apart here. I had to arch my back as best I could and tuck my head down into Annie's corpse to sneak a peak in front, but I could see a glow just ahead of us. I heard music, too, echoing down the culvert. I expected my captor to stop or go back, but she started walking faster. I thought sure she'd pull the sack back over my head, and prepared to scream bloody murder before she could do it.

We came around a bend in the concrete river and there were The Lost Boys.

At least, that's what it said on their tee shirts. Each of them wore an identical one: a black tee shirt emblazoned with a still from the movie – a young Kiefer Sutherland grinning evilly (it's the only way a Sutherland can grin) – and the title logo underneath.

A gang of Joel Schumacher fans: this couldn't be good.

They were all on skateboards, riding back and forth across the narrow walls of the river as though it were some colossal half-pipe. Though the river had narrowed, it was still impressive to see the kids – and none of them could have been older than thirteen – riding up and down the near vertical walls of the culvert. The speed at which they moved – the wheels of the skateboards barely seeming to hold contact with the cement as they swished along – was a wonder to behold. It was also terrifying. I once went out to dinner with a woman who worked as a nurse in the transplant unit at UCLA Medical Center. The date was a bust – she insisted on ordering liver – but I still remember her telling me how the transplant team referred to skateboards: donor cards.

"Criminy, do their parents know what they're doing?" I asked in spite of myself. "That looks awful dangerous."

"They's safe," my abductor said. "Nothing can touch 'em here. Won't allows it."

The kids spotted us and let out a series of whoops and catcalls. I thought sure they were going to attack as they sped toward us, but they all had big smiles on their faces as they skidded and swerved to a stop. I've never been big on skateboarding or snowboarding or BMX or any of that extreme sports crap that fills the cable channels in the wee hours – I don't much care for Vin Diesel, either, thank you for asking – but I had to admit the sight of the squadron of Lost Boys roaring down the river walls in formation would put Riverdance to shame (and if those last four words aren't a tautology I don't know what is).

"Vibiana!" they all cheered as they hopped off their skateboards and crowded around the shopping cart. "Vib! Vib! Vib!"

It was practically a rally – you'd think she was Jerry friggin' Springer or something. They reached out to the woman who'd bushwhacked me – was Vibiana her name? – as if her mere touch could bestow papal blessings.

"Hello, my wee ones, my graces, my wonders," she said. And she brushed her dirty fingertips against their outstretched hands. I saw sparks fly as their flesh touched.

"What have you brought us?" one of the littlest of the Lost Boys called out.

"What does you need?" she asked them.

"Magic!" they all screamed as one. They could have been in the audience of some Saturday morning kid's show cheering for prizes.

"That I always has aplenty," she laughed.

The boys all cheered again.

"Umm, hello?" I said. "A little help here, please?"

The littlest Lost Boy put his hands on the edge of the shopping cart. His nose was level with the handle. I twisted around to look him in the eye.

"Is it Annie?" he whispered. He seemed not to see me at all. "Is it, Vib? Is it Annie? *Again*?"

My captor – Vib – got all sad looking. "Aye, Zalman. It *is* Annie."

And her voice broke a little. As if *she* wasn't the one who'd killed her, cold-cocked me and dumped us both in the cart.

"Awwwww," the Lost Boys cried out around me. Many of them fell down to the ground. Some of them had real tears in their eyes.

"Can anyone hear me?" I said. "Hello, hello. Testing, one, two, three."

"Who's he?" one of the Boys asked. Another one poked me in the ribs, apparently just noticing that I was in the cart, too.

"Medicine Man," Vibiana said.

They boys all "ooooh-ed."

"He looks slam," one of the oldest looking kids said. "Kind of old school, Vib."

"Definitely slam," a fat kid in the back stood up and yelled. He quickly sat back down.

"He a Gandy?" the little kid asked. "For true?"

"I's hoping," Vibiana said. She ran her hand down the back of my head and slapped me on the back. I felt like a prize steer at a cattle auction. "The signs is all there."

"Listen, guys," I tried. "I could sure use some help here. This lady underneath me is dead. Do you understand that?"

"Well, *duh*," the older kid said. "It's *Annie*."

"I believe this woman killed her. And she's got me tied up in here."

"Would you conjure if she didn't?" the kid asked.

"I don't know what you're talking about. I'm not a conjurer . . . I'm a . . . I do a little bit of this and a . . . it's a little hard to explain actually."

"He ain't a Gandy?" the kid asked, suddenly dubious.

"Gandy's don't always know, now does they?" she said.

"Righteous true," several of the Boys called.

"Are you gonna help Vib?" the little one asked me. He touched the back of his hand to my cheek in a genuinely tender way. "You gonna help Annie? They need help, you know. Need it bad."

"I would love to help Annie. But there's not a lot I can do for her now," I said.

Vibiana howled with laughter. The Boys joined in.

"This is fucking crazy," I muttered.

"Language!" Vibiana snapped.

The littlest Lost Boy shook his head at me in a most disapproving fashion.

"You have to get me out of here," I said.

"He don't look comfortable," one of the Boys agreed.

"Vib?" the oldest one asked.

"No," she said. "Least not tills we get nearer to Yang-Na."

"Passing through the Hondo, Vib?" a Lost Boy asked.

"Aye."

"Full moon tonight," another warned.

"That's for why it's got to be. Last chance this cycle."

"Want us to go with you a ways?" the oldest one said.

"Could use the company," Vibiana said. "And the comfort."

The oldest Boy called out six names. A small squad of skateboarders got into formation around us.

"There's still time, my Annie," Vibiana whispered. "Still time for us."

The little kid was on point. "Let's roll!" he called in his prepubescent voice.

We did.

VI

The sound of wheels echoed across the culvert: the smooth ball bearings of the Lost Boys' skateboards and the squeaky clickety-clack of the wobbly shopping trolley. All else was silence except for the odd squish of the body beneath me as dead Annie's fluids shifted under my weight and gases leaked from her corpse.

It really wasn't very pleasant.

Efforts to engage the Lost Boys in conversation proved as futile as my pleas to Vibiana. The kids were obviously devoted to her, or under her spell in either a figurative or literal way. Once, when she stumbled over a Mickey's Big Mouth bottle, two of the Boys were instantly by her side, reaching out to support her before she even fell down on one knee. They touched and held her so gently that I might have thought she was their saintly grandmother. And when she righted herself, she smiled at them with the beneficence of the Madonna looking down on her little Joe. When she thanked them with a light touch of the back of her fingers to their cheeks they looked as if they would never wash their faces again.

(Then again, they were filthy little buggers who looked as if they'd never washed their faces *before*.)

"Moon's going," one of the Boys said.

Our little procession rolled to a halt. Vibiana looked up at a shroud of cloud which had come from nowhere and begun to cover the face of the moon. She stroked her chinny-chin-chin and looked worried.

"Bad omen, Vib," the eldest Boy said.

"Maybe we should go back," said the littlest one. "We got Yodels, you know, back at the Pipe. I snatched a whole carton." He pulled a mashed one out of his pocket in evidence. The foil wrapper shone like a beacon in the dark. "Yankee Doodles, too."

"A tempting offer, my pirate son," Vibiana said. "But there's Annie to thinks about. Things to be done."

"Hondo's just ahead," said a Boy. "Don't like crossing it without the moon."

"Nor me and I," Vibiana said.

The clouds thinned again and for a flash – just a trick of the moonlight, I'm sure – I saw a different Vibiana. The madness was ironed out of her expression and a glint of knowing shone in her bright eyes. Her wild hair melted into the sky and her round face seemed like a second low satellite in the darkness. I had a sudden sense that she could have been a very beautiful woman.

Then she cackled, a shrill sliver of ice that penetrated into my spine, and the illusion was shattered.

"On, my Lost Boys," she called out. "On, my warriors."

We rolled forward again.

More clouds crossed the face of the moon, and with every flicker of the night's light my weird chauffeuse seemed to take a little stumble. The Lost Boys were less sure of themselves, too, and their formation – otherwise as precise as any performed by the Blue Angels – began to break apart. They couldn't seem to restore it, either, and the Boys snarked insults at each other.

"Easy, my angels," Vib comforted.

I heard a sploshing sound and managed to peer down around the side of the cart. A thin stream of water had appeared below. The liquid looked black in the night and smelled awful. Was it sewage? It had barely rained and there shouldn't be any run-off at this time of year. At least, I hoped not. Did they dump run-off from somewhere in the wee hours of the night? I've lived in L.A. my whole life, but realized I didn't actually know the first thing about the city's river.

We came to another stop.

I contorted myself some more to get a better view of the situation. The Boys were all off their skateboards now, looking fearfully down at the murky flow that passed beneath us. Just ahead was a V in the culvert, with a section of the river branching off toward the north east. I realized, then, what the Boys had been talking about. This was L.A.'s other "river": the Rio Hondo. It's even more pathetic than the Los Angeles River. I remembered reading in the paper about a grandiose plan by the Army Corp of Engineers or some such to attempt to sink the whole thing underground, so the land above could be "properly" developed. Apparently there's a serious problem with a lack of strip malls in Los Angeles. Somewhere nearby, a desperate Angelino has to walk four whole blocks to buy a Krispy Kreme donut or a Starbucks frappucino. Can't let a situation like that linger and call ourselves civilized, now can we?

"Oh, lordy, that smell," I said. The odour was positively vile.

"Hounds is out," Vibiana whispered.

The Boys didn't like the sound of that. Me, either.

"Hondo Hounds are scary," said the littlest Boy. "They like Avril Lavigne."

"They don't know what they is," said another Boy. "And they smell."

"So what are the Hondo Hounds, exactly?" I asked. "Do they, like, chase the Cat People."

"Don't be an ass," Vibiana hissed.

Seemed like a reasonable enough question to me.

Then I heard them howl.

"Jesus fucking Christ," I said. "What is *that*?"

"Full moon," Vibiana said. She started to move forward again, but the Lost Boys hung back. She glanced over her shoulder at them, a white eyebrow arched.

"My warriors?" she asked.

The eldest looked sad, but shook his head. He pointed down at the foul smelling stream that ran in front of him. "Can't do it, Vib. Can't cross."

"Hondo Hounds are scary," the littlest one repeated. A tear rolled down his cheek.

"Aye," Vibiana said. She took a deep breath, then offered a broad smile to her knights. "Lost Boys *ruuuuule!*" she bellowed into the night. The Lost Boys yelled along with her and for a moment, the Hounds – whatever they were – fell silent. Then they bayed angrily in reply.

The Lost Boys skated briskly back downriver. Vibiana watched them go, then looked at me. "Medicine Man?" she said.

"Umm. Yeah?"

What the hell; I've been called worse. Sometimes by family.

"Can I trusts you?"

"That's a hell of a question," I said. "What with me trussed up in here with a girl you just killed and you out there pushing us up a concrete ditch to god knows where."

"That's no answer."

"What do you want me to say? What do you expect?"

"Can't pushes you past the Hounds. Can't risks it for Annie."

"Isn't it a little late to worry about that?" I said. Lying on top of a corpse didn't get any more comfortable the longer you did it.

"I cuts you free, you gots to promise you ain't gonna bolt on me. You gots to stay by my side. Take on the Hounds if it comes to it."

"Oh, well, that sounds like a deal. Is there a mail-in rebate, too?"

"Will you does it for Annie?" she asked.

"For *Annie*? Don't you get it that she's dead? That you killed her?"

Vibiana shook her head and exposed her crooked teeth.

"Ain't a quick study, is you?" she said.

"I prefer to think of myself as deliberate," I said.

"I'd prefer to think of myself as Angie Dickinson. Don't makes it so, though," she said. Okay, it dated her, but who didn't love *Police Woman*?

"What's your point?"

She looked me over again. Hard.

"You been to the Other Side, ain't you?" she asked.

"You mean Burbank?" I said.

"You knows what I mean."

And I did know, goddammit. I did. But I didn't answer right away. She reached into a pocket and pulled out a monocle she must have swiped from Werner Klemperer. She held it up to her left eye, then her right and studied me through it. Then she stuffed it back in her pocket. It had no lens.

"You been," she said. "Oh, yeah."

"I don't know what you're talking about," I lied.

She closed her eyes then, and held one hand up to her forehead. She swayed a little in the breeze, which suddenly swelled up around us. I felt the temperature drop and goose bumps broke out up and down my skin. Vibiana opened her eyes and the cold faded away.

"Lily Stein says . . ." – she furrowed her brow in concentration and the quality of her voice changed – ". . . don't be a putz all your life. *Darling*."

I went colder than the body lying beneath me. Lily Stein was a dear friend and a remarkable woman who had once saved my life, not to mention something like the soul of the world from forces of darkness. She'd also been very dead for over two years.

There was no way that Vibiana could possibly have known her. Or known that I knew her.

"Who the hell are you?" I whispered.

"Can I trusts you?" she asked me once more.

"Cut me free," I told her.

She did.

VII

We walked on as the howls in the night grew louder and giddier. Vibiana pushed the shopping cart and I trailed a half-step behind. The muscles in my back and legs throbbed and I couldn't quite turn my neck straight. Blood continued to ooze from my wrists where the coat hanger had torn the flesh. But it felt good to be out of the cart and upright.

And alive.

"How do you know Lily?" I asked.

"Don't," Vibiana replied. "Not from a hole in the dirty old ground."

"You spoke in her voice. I'd know it anywhere."

Vibiana merely shrugged. I grabbed hold of her shoulder, forcing her to stop. She growled back at me.

"What's going on here, Vibiana? You killed Annie tonight, didn't you?"

No answer.

"*Didn't you?*"

"Kilt ain't the ways to look at it."

"She's dead, isn't she?"

"Thinks of it as a transitional state," Vibiana said.

"Between what and what?"

"That's for you to helps decide."

"Me? You whomped me upside the head with . . . what *did* you whomp me with, by the way?"

"Turkey leg."

"You knocked me out with a drumstick?"

"Frozen. Past its date. They gives 'em away down the market in the Plaza, end of the day. Past their date's why. Don't tastes so good but they has their uses."

"What did you do with it?" I asked.

"Tossed it in the bin, whats you think? Told you it was past its date."

"Very tidy," I muttered.

"Your Lily friend," Vibiana said.

"What about her?"

Vibiana put her hand over her eyes again and swayed. I reached out to support her and felt how cold her skin was.

"She had a power," Vibiana said. "A strong one."

"She was a very special woman," I said.

"She vouches for you. Says you is the real Dr McCoy."

"Great, me and DeForest Kelley together again for the first time. And who vouches for you, might I ask?"

"I'm kinds of a free agent," she said and shrugged once more. "You pays your money and you takes your chances."

"Seems to me I got pickpocketed for my ante in this game."

"However you got here, you is a player."

The Hondo Hounds howled louder as if in response. We walked on.

"What in hell are they?" I said.

As we walked beneath the Imperial Highway overpass we came to the confluence of L.A.'s two dry rivers. Vibiana stopped again and gestured with a broad sweep of her hand.

"Sees for yourself."

Flaming barrels were set in a circle at the point of the Vee where the concrete rivers met. Howling figures on all fours darted between the barrels, little more than small silhouettes against the lapping orange flames. Their movements seemed choreographed and formal as they raced across the circle, occasionally butting heads or nipping each other's hind quarters. The howls were interspersed with tiny yips as one or another of the Hounds bit a little too deeply into another's flank. One of the dozen or so creatures, I noted, didn't get involved in the ritual, but sat outside the circle in the darkness, visible only by the reflected glow of the fires in its red eyes. It watched.

One of the Hounds sneezed loudly then and another – quite clearly, in a discernible English accent – said: "Bless you."

"What the . . .?" I muttered.

The Hounds were all people, I saw as we got closer and the silhouettes took on dimension in the firelight. Naked people. Naked men to be precise, running around on their hands and legs like dogs. Most of them had fur – glued on? – while they all had clearly had surgical alterations to their bodies, especially their faces. I saw a lot of extended canines and pug noses, and most had had their ears modified. Some had triangular German Shepherd ears, while a few had floppy beagle ears. Every one of them displayed a tail of one sort or another, but it wasn't bright enough to tell if these too were surgical modifications or mere decoration. As we approached them, one of the Hounds – its black patches suggested an attempt at Dalmatian, though Walt Disney would have defrosted himself before accepting the mutt as number 102 – suddenly started chasing his tail. I looked away as he futilely attempted to lick his own dangling balls.

"Oh, lord," I said, "I bet you don't see stuff like this on the Mississippi."

The Hounds had spotted us now and formed themselves into a loose pack. The one beast still sat outside the circle of flames, eyes flashing in the darkness. The others were inching up on us, snarling and growling and pawing the ground. It should have been impossible to take this bunch of naked jerks seriously, but suddenly they looked like what they were pretending to be: a pack of feral dogs. I could sense Vibiana's fear as she froze in position, her hands clutching the handle of the shopping cart. The Hounds had very quickly and slickly cut us off from any avenue of retreat.

"Better gets ready and does what you need to do," Vibiana whispered to me. "Them teeths is sharp."

"I don't suppose you've got any more turkey legs on you?" I asked. It was a purely rhetorical question.

The snarling of the Hounds ceased and I saw one of the German Shepherd guys get ready to spring. He'd had his nose extended into a kind of hairy snout. What self-respecting plastic surgeon would do such work? (But then, who would do what had been done to Joan

Rivers?) The Hound was sculpted muscle beneath his fake fur and those sharpened teeth looked like they could tear your throat out. I desperately looked around for a way to defend myself and saw nothing.

This was not how I ever expected to check out.

I saw the Hound's tensed muscles flex, readied myself to bring an elbow around at the last minute to drive into that false snout and hope for the best when a gravelly voice called out.

"Marty? Marty Burns?"

It would be an understatement to suggest that I was taken by surprise. But then, so were the other pooches. They turned and looked back at an especially beagle-ish Hound ambling up from the rear of the pack. He came right up to me and sniffed at my leg, then buried his nose in my crotch and took another deep whiff.

"It *is* you!" he growled.

He sat back on his haunches and offered up a paw. I mean hand, of course. His tongue was lolling out of his mouth in a big dopey grin, but after a few seconds of study of his considerably augmented face, I recognized the man underneath all the body modification.

"Guy?" I tried. "Guy Bradley?"

"Woof," he barked.

We shook. Then he licked the back of my hand and wagged his tail.

The rest of the Hounds returned to the circle and went on with their ritual.

"I knews you was the right choice," Vibiana said and slapped me on the back. Then she grinned up at the moon and whispered to the ancient satellite: "Thank ye, old gal."

"So," I said to the Hound, "how's tricks?"

VIII

You remember Guy Bradley. Really. Even if you don't recognize his name.

Guy probably wore more polyester suits and wide ties than any man in the history of television. For a period of about five years, Guy was the bad guy at least once in every detective show on the air. He had puffed-up Seventies hair, a thick black Village People moustache and an oversized pinky ring. Or tinted aviator glasses. Or both. And always one of those awful suits and ties. (I think those ties were made illegal in 1981.) Guy was never a regular on any of those shows, but was buds with a couple of big network casting directors (one was his sister-in-law) and so he always had work. *Banacek*, *Madigan*, *Banyon*, *Quincy* – they all nailed Guy, some of them more than once. And usually at the end of a chase scene involving one of those boxy American cars that eventually slammed into a telephone pole. The dazed dude in the shiny suit who staggered out the door and into the handcuffs? That was Guy. At least, when it wasn't Bradford Dillman.

NBC even gave him a shot at his own series back in 1978. They shot a pilot called *Brannigan, Again*. I don't know what it was supposed to mean, either, or why the hell that comma was in the title, but I was in it, too. That's how we met. We were both on the sauce at the time and made some merry hell together. We had a great time on the shoot and palled around pretty close for a few months after.

The pilot never so much as made it to air.

Our friendship waned – it was purely a relationship born of fermentation – and I'd seen Guy around town a few times in the intervening years, even on the tube twice or thrice, but probably not for a decade that I could recall. That's a lot of water down the L.A. River.

"So, uh, how you been, Guy?" I asked.

He cocked his head and howled up at the moon. Vibiana nodded approvingly.

"Grrr-r-r-reat," he said.

"That's good. That's nice."

"I'm a Hound now," he told me.

"Yes, so I see. How's that working out for you, then?"

"You haven't met a Hound before, have you?"

"No, I can't say that I have." I glanced at the dead girl in the cart and crazed Vibiana standing over her. "But then this is turning out to be a cherry-popper of a night for me. A kindergarten to Ph.D. learning experience."

"We're trans-specied," he said. Then he lolled his tongue out and panted.

"Ahhh, no kidding?"

"It's being acknowledged more and more. Why should the trans-gendered and intersexed get acknowledged and not us? I mean, is that fair?"

"Not fair at all." *Intersexed?*

"It's the greatest goddamn thing in the world, Marty. It's the best thing that ever happened to me. Kicks Scientology in the fucking ass. It's a whole new life."

"A dog's life," I said.

"Don't knock it, Marty, not till you've tried it. What's so bad about a dog's life, huh? You eat what you want, when you want. You sleep when you feel like it and you piss and shit where you please. No agents, no casting directors, no ex-wives or bankruptcy lawyers or bailiffs. No television fucking producers. Grrrrr."

"A little light on the creature comforts, though, isn't?" I asked. Then added: "You should pardon the expression."

"There's more to life than designer shoes and fast cars, Marty."

Guy gave a little flick of his head to indicate that I should bend down so he could whisper in my ear. I squatted down beside him and he pressed his muzzle against the side of my head. His nose was cold. I think that's a good sign.

"The sex is unbelievable," he told me.

"You don't say."

"Arf, baby. I mean, I always had a yen for doggy-style, but you ain't lived until you've had a bitch in heat with your pack. That's what tonight is all about."

"You're not going to hump my leg or anything are you, Guy?"

He shook his head like he had a rag between his teeth. "She's over there," he whispered.

I looked back to where he was pointing, at the figure still outside the main circle of barrels. I could see now that it was a woman who was curled up there. She looked furry, too, and as naked as the other Hounds. She briefly padded out into the circle and turned around, displaying her hairy rear. The Hounds went wild.

"This is all for her," Guy told me. "The males play the challenge to see who gets first rights on the bitch. But . . ." he raised his head and sniffed at the air in the direction of the woman ". . . she's so hot tonight, we'll all get our chance. Can't you smell her?"

And he howled again.

"Guy?" I whispered.

"Huh?"

"This woman I'm with: Vibiana. Do you know her?"

He growled slightly. "She's not a Hound."

"Yeah, I guessed that. What do you know about her?"

"She and the other one come through here every month."

"The other one?" I asked.

"In the cart. The dead one."

"Annie?"

"I don't know her name. She's always dead when they pass this way. We're not so crazy about them, tell you the truth."

"What do mean she's always dead? When was the last time you saw her?"

"I told you: last month. Always round the full moon. It's the time of the heat, so I remember."

"That can't be," I said. "She was alive just a few hours ago. I. . . ."

I realized that everything had gone quiet around us and looked up. The Hounds had assembled in two lines and the bitch was walking on all fours between them. She had long red hair, like a setter's, that covered most of her body. She moved with an easy grace and as she looked toward me I saw that the glint in her eyes wasn't natural: she wore – or had implanted – spooky contact lenses. The breeze kicked up behind her as she sidled toward us and for a moment I swore I *could* smell her heat. Vibiana muttered behind me.

"You were not to pass this way again," the female Hound hissed at Vibiana. "You were warned."

"I does as I must," Vibiana replied. She pointed at me. "I comes with him." She gestured at Annie in the cart. "I does it for her."

The bitch growled from deep in her chest and the other Hounds echoed the menacing cry. Then she came up beside Guy and rubbed flanks with him. I saw him . . . stir. He instinctively began to move behind her and wrap his arms around her, but she turned her neck and nipped at him and with a yowl he bounded away. More cautiously he padded back over beside me and sat on his haunches. I could still see his tumescent doghood dangling.

"Marty," he growled, "this is Lucky. Lucky, my old pal Marty Burns."

Lucky the bitch slunk up to me and sniffed. I held my hand out, palm up. She rested her chin on it and I gave her a little scratch behind the ear. A couple of the Hounds snarled in the night, but I stood my ground. Not only did Lucky have body length red hair flowing from her scalp, she was covered in wine red fur. I don't know if it was a costume or what, but it looked real. Her exposed breasts were furry too, expect for the nipples, big and hard in the night breeze.

"How *you* doing?" I said.

She rolled onto her back and raised her arms and legs in the air.

"She likes to have her stomach scratched," Guy whispered.

When in Rome . . .

Her right leg started to twitch as I ran my fingers up and down the soft fur of her belly, and her leg spasmed faster the harder I scratched. I carefully avoided getting too close to any conceivable erogenous zone, though under the circumstances I couldn't be sure what that might mean. I don't know what the deal with this bitch was, but her fur sure felt real to me. Kind of nice, too.

All of a sudden, Lucky rolled over and bolted to her feet. She shook herself from head to tail – it was long, red and bushy – as if she'd just jumped out of a bath or a lake. Then she ran back into the middle of the circle of baying Hounds. They were all visibly . . . excited. Lucky stretched languorously, displaying herself for all the pack to see. A guy working on some kind of Jack Russell thing clearly couldn't wait another second and tried to mount her from behind. She kicked out at him and caught him square in the Snoopies. He yipped his way back into the pack. Then Lucky stood up on her hind legs . . . I mean, stood up and pointed at us.

"You may pass this moon, Vibiana of Los Angeles. You may pass because he is with you."

She meant me.

"But do not cross the Hondo again. Next moon will not find me so forgiving."

"Next moon, Goddess willing, I won't has to pass this way. I'm counting on him, too. For an end to the journeys."

"That is not my concern. The heat is upon me and the night is too short."

The pack drew in toward Lucky. I didn't particularly care to watch what was going to happen next as Lucky dropped back down to all fours. She stood up again, though, and gestured at Guy.

"You will accompany them, Boner," she said. "See to their safe passage."

"Awwww, hell," Guy moaned. He rapidly (and thankfully from my point of view) de-tumesced. I suppose I could understand his disappointment what with the full moon only coming once a month. Still, my average isn't always that good.

"Let's get the hell out of here," I whispered to Vibiana.

"I concurs," she said.

"Awroof," Guy said. A little unenthusiastically, I thought.

Vibiana pushed the trolley and Guy and I followed. I didn't look back when the furious sounds of yowls and squeals (and one high-pitched "Yes, yes, yes!") commenced, but Guy wistfully craned his head and whimpered over what he was leaving behind.

"*Boner*?" I asked.

"It's a long story," was all he would say on the matter.

We journeyed on upstream.

IX

By my reckoning, we passed through Cudahy and Bell Gardens and most of Vernon uneventfully. Vibiana continued to lead the way, pushing the cart in front of her. Guy – I couldn't quite bring myself to call him Boner – trotted along beside me, occasionally dashing off to lift his leg against one of the concrete walls. I thought he might give up the routine once he was out of sight of his fellow . . . mongrels, but he insisted on running on all fours, sniffing the ground and doing the kinds of things that dogs are wont to do. The truth is that after a while, I started thinking of him as a real dog and at one point, after he chased away a nasty looking coon cat which hissed at us from the ruins of a packing crate on the dry river bed, I actually patted him on top of the head and offered up a "good boy."

Vibiana laughed.

We started to see more people navigating the river as we neared downtown. There were homeless men and women curled up in their boxes under the bridges, and winos drinking their T-bird and Night Train, and kids, some in gang colours – and in skin of all colours – fucking with or just plain fucking each other as a way to pass the dark, lonely hours of the night. We ignored all of them, and they ignored us.

A thin trickle of water, no wider than my hand, could be seen running down the very centre of the river as we neared the 1st Street overpass. Guy ran over to it and sniffed the water, then flicked at it tentatively with his tongue. He yelped his dismay at the taste and ran around in circles. Vibiana crouched down and kept scrambling around as well. I couldn't figure out what she was doing, until I saw that she was searching for a position from which she could see the full moon's reflection in the tiny stream. She passed her hands over the water several times and muttered under her breath. Then she pulled a straight razor from her shoe and sliced the tip of her finger with its edge. That brought another loud yip from Guy who ran and hid behind my legs. I patted the back of his head to calm him down while Vibiana squeezed drops of her blood into the water and studied the patterns they made in the image of the moon's face. She nodded her head approvingly and stood up.

"Good omens, Medicine Man," she said. She ignored the blood that continued to drip from her finger. "Our girl is definitely abouts tonight."

"Which girl is that?" I said.

"Toypurina, fool!" she said. "We gots to get off the river, though."

Guy shook his head furiously. "Never get out of the fucking boat," he barked.

"Stairs up that way," she said, pointing. "Takes us where we wants to get."

I looked over at the steep set of zig-zagging steps cut into the side of the culvert. The river bed was set very deep in this part of downtown L.A. and it was a long walk up. I glanced at the cart with the dead girl in it, then back at the steps.

"What do we do about Annie?" I asked.

Vibiana flashed her broken teeth at me. A tiny red gem had been inset into a back molar and it shone like a weird evil eye in the moonlight. A prescient shiver ran through me.

"Heads or feets?" she asked, cackling.

I chose feet. (Wouldn't you?)

Vibiana must have been remarkably strong, because she was stuck with the harder job of walking backward up the stairs carrying the bulk of Annie's literally dead weight. Guy was no help at all, particularly because he insisted on stopping to pee a drop or two on what seemed like every fifth step. I would have been deeply annoyed but for marvelling at his bladder control.

A glow emanated from a ten-foot landing set into the wall about halfway up the climb and as we approached it I braced myself for trouble when I saw half-a-dozen Chicano teens in gang colours crouched in a circle on the concrete. They watched us carefully as we squeezed past them, but none of them so much as made a move for the guns they all had tucked into their waistbands idiot-style. As we climbed up the next flight of steps, I glanced back and saw that what I assumed to be a drug-deal or gang rape in process was actually an intense-looking game of Risk.

Go figure kids today.

I was panting more furiously than Guy by the time we made it up to street level, but Vibiana hadn't so much as broken a sweat.

"I wouldn't have made you for a fitness freak," I said to her, letting go of Annie's cold ankles and collapsing onto a concrete bench along the river wall.

Vibiana gently lowered Annie's top half to the ground. She kissed her palm then pressed it to Annie's forehead as she laid her on the dirty sidewalk.

"It's all up here," she said, touching her fingers to her temple. "Everything's mental. In the head, don't you know."

"Woof, baby," Guy agreed.

I was too tired to do more than nod.

"Now what?" I asked.

Vibiana stood up as tall as she could. She started to turn in slow circles again, looking straight up at the moon. I heard her take an enormous breath and saw her hand briefly pass in front of her mouth. Then she exhaled with a leonine roar, and spittle – or something – exploded out from between her lips and geysered up into the air above her. A form took shape overhead, something like the foamy crest of a wave glowing argent. The wave rocked back and forth, tiny Hokusai fractals spilling off it and rising into the sky like sparks off a Jacob's Ladder. Then it crashed out in the direction of Union Station and faded away.

Vibiana offered me the hint of a smile and gestured in the direction indicated by the wave. Wearily, I stood up.

"I know, I know," I muttered, "heads or feets."

In fact, Guy sniffed out a small hand truck abandoned in an alley no more than half a block from the river. It wasn't easy or elegant, but we managed to balance Annie on the apron of it without dragging any of her on the ground. Vibiana pulled her along behind like a happy little kid tugging a red Radio Flyer.

Well, a happy little psychopathic kid.

The streets were deserted – not too surprising given the neighbourhood and the hour – but the silence and stillness that had set in since leaving the river was spookier than the run of the mill menace of the empty city at night. Under normal circumstances (a place as far removed from my life, it too often seems to me, as over the rainbow), I wouldn't be caught dead walking alone through such a part of town – and as a typically uptight, Westside gringo, I always imagined that dead is precisely how I would end up if caught here. But none of that usual paranoia bothered me. Though I recognized the familiarity of the street signs and the architecture, it felt as if the trip upriver had taken us into some separate Los Angeles. If not for a pink day-glo poster of Angelyne fly-posted over the rusty steel shutters of a carneceria, I might well have believed we had stumbled into a parallel universe.

There can't be *two* universes with Angelyne in them. Surely.

As we headed up an alley behind Vignes Street, a peculiar odour became noticeable. I suppose it was a genuine L.A. moment in that it took me a few seconds to identify the scent as burning tobacco – who the hell smokes these days? It wasn't the usual foul stench of cigarettes or cigars, though, but an altogether earthier, sweeter smell. I've never been a smoker – other than pachinko, it's the only serious vice I've not succumbed to – but if tobacco had smelled as rich and tasty as this, I'd have come up to the Kool taste long ago and happily punched my ticket on the emphysema express. Guy took a whiff and sneezed explosively. Vibiana sniffed at the air and changed direction to follow her nose and the smell.

I hurried along behind them.

We were approaching the fringes of the railroad yards and spurs that mark the turf of Union Station. Wagging his tail, Guy led us through a crudely cut gap in some cyclone fencing and into an overgrown field littered with rusted out freight cars and the detritus of countless fly-tippers. I suspected that the rent in the fence had been made by the illegal dumpers. There were old fridges and stoves and washing machines galore, and a small mountain of cracked computer monitors and CPUs: it appeared that this was where old Dells came to die.

There was also a rickety storage shed, made of tin with a tarpaper roof that looked as though it had been blown in by a tornado from somewhere in the Mississippi Delta. Light spilled out of the sole empty window and I half expected to hear the twang of a blues guitar or a heartbreak harmonica filling the night.

The only sound was the breeze blowing through the appliance carcasses and Guy's rhythmic panting.

"Never get out of the fucking boat," I repeated. Guy whimpered. On we went.

On either side of the shack's front door – it was more like a crude slash in the sheet of tin, just wide enough to squeeze through if you were on Atkins – stood intricately carved wooden Indians, one female and one male. The woman – and I know this sounds goofy given that it was just a hunk of wood – had this incredibly provocative come-hither look etched into her dark face. It was in the slight parting of the delicate lips and the askance look of her almond shaped eyes.

Then I noticed that her throat had been slit and her hands were raised up not in a gesture of welcome but one of supplication.

The male had nothing come-hither about him. His lips were drawn back in a snarl, his eyes wide and wild, looking every bit like John Wayne's worst prairie nightmare. One arm was raised above his head and the hand clutched a cruel-looking blade – the same one which had slit his companion's throat? The other hand was cupped at his side. It held a fistful of big, black cigars. The earthy tobacco scent had its origin inside the shack

"Do we knock?" I asked.

"She knows we's here," Vibiana said. She bent down and picked up Annie's body as if cradling a baby. She stood up with hardly an effort – I couldn't have done it – and gracefully slipped through the narrow entryway, careful not to so much as scrape Annie's dead skin on the jagged edges of the door. Guy looked up at me then followed her through with a tentative yip. I started to go in, then on a whim stopped and took a cigar from the Indian's hand.

It wasn't exactly a palace inside.

There was no floor as such, just the dirt of the field that surrounded the shack, with a few bold weeds springing up where they could. A filthy blanket lay across the centre and a cast-iron basin filled with dark liquid stood in the corner. The light was supplied by a flickering lantern suspended from a metal support beam propping the roof up.

Sitting atop the blanket, legs folded beneath her, was a fabulously pregnant Native American woman of perhaps eighteen or nineteen. She had honey skin which shimmered in the flickering light of the lantern flame and long black hair down to the floor which shone like Catholic school shoes. Because she was so incredibly pregnant – gravid, I think the right word is – her face and extremities so plump with life, her breasts swollen with milk, that I didn't at first realize that she must have been the model for the carved female figure out in front.

Her throat was intact, though. And she was smoking one of the black cigars. It was evidently the source of the sweet odour we'd sniffed from so far away.

"Don't believe the Surgeon General, huh?" I said, eyeing her massive belly.

She took a deep puff and blew the smoke straight at me. It hung together in the air, taking on the shape of a butterfly that flew straight at me and burst like a soap bubble on the tip of my nose.

There is no polite way to say this: the burst of smoke smelled like pussy. Or how pussy might smell if it had been used to smoke a cigar.

Or so I imagine, not being Bill Clinton.

"Huh," I said.

"Who's the square?" the woman on the blanket asked. She was speaking to Vibiana, but pointing to me.

"Medicine Man," Vibiana said. She was still cradling Annie's body.

The Native American woman narrowed her eyes at me and rubbed her tummy with the hand holding the cigar. She studied me like she was wearing X-ray Spex and wanted a peep at the package I kept in my skivvies.

"Maybe," she said, after a while.

"Toypurina," Vibiana intoned rather formally. "I beseeches thee."

"Again," the woman said, a little bit sadly.

Vibiana gently laid Annie's body down on the blanket in front of

Toypurina. She gave Annie a tiny kiss on the forehead. Then she got down on one knee and said:

"I comes here to Yang-Na, City Beneaths the City, with tribute and entreaty for you, brave Tongva lady. I brings my beloved for you to breathes life into once more. And make her mine as is meant to be."

"And what do you bring me, Vibiana of the City Above?"

Vibiana raised an eyebrow in a what-you-talking-'bout-Willis expression.

"I brings *him*," she said, pointing a thumb my way.

"Excuse me," I interrupted. "I don't mean to piss on anyone's Manolo Blahniks here," – actually, Toypurina was barefoot and Vibiana wore a pair of beat-up, bargain store sneakers of the type known as "skips" when I was a kid – "but I ain't the door prize in whatever game of tag you two crazy ladies are playing. I've come this far because . . ."

Why the hell *had* I come this far? It wasn't an easy thing to explain.

Toypurina roared with laughter. She sounded exactly like Roseanne Barr.

"Well brought, Vibiana. I accept your tribute. I will honor your entreaty."

"I thanks ye," Vibiana said and bowed down low. She winked at me.

"Listen," I started to say.

But Toypurina held up her hand to silence me. With no small effort, she waddled her way to her knees and then got to her feet. She gingerly stepped over Annie's body and stood in front of me. She took another big hit off her cigar, leaned forward and pressed her lips to mine. She blew the pungent smoke into my mouth until it filled my lungs.

I fell backwards into a mine shaft.

The darkness was so solid, I thought I might bang my head on it. After a while the sense of free-fall eased, but was replaced by a feeling of sideways motion. Direction, really, ceased to have any meaning. I just knew I was travelling someplace very far and hard to reach and there wouldn't be any rest stops along the way.

Than I felt a hand holding onto mine. Ribbons of coloured light forced cracks in the darkness. I stood atop a rocky bluff looking out on a blood red sea. Toypurina was beside me, no longer pregnant. Even in this strange place, in these baffling circumstances, her beauty was a thing to behold. She held onto my left hand with her right. She held another hand in her left: it belonged to a boy of three or four, naked and playing with himself in the unselfconscious way that children can and do.

"Where are we?" I asked.

"You already know," Toypurina said.

And I did. This was . . . The Other Side. I'd been here once before, though it had looked nothing like where we now stood. Different coasts, same undiscovered country.

"We shouldn't be here," I said. I knew we couldn't stay for long.

"No," Toypurina agreed.

"We're here for Annie."

"Yes."

"Who's the kid?" I asked. But I already knew. The boy had lost interest in his penis and was now picking his nose, but certain beauty is genetic. He most definitely had his mother's eyes. He flicked a particularly slick booger off his thumb and into the sea. Then he pointed toward the surf.

A dark ball bobbed up an down on the pink foam of the wave crests. It was a head. It was attached to a body. It rose up and down with the waves, but betrayed no independent movement. Silver fish or perhaps rays leapt up out of the red surf all around the body. They crackled and flashed like tiny bolts of lightning when they re-entered the water.

"There isn't much time," Toypurina said. "They will devour her."

"What do we do?" I asked.

Toypurina smiled. She gestured at the roiling sea below as if to say "last one in is a rotten egg."

I hesitated; I don't mind rotten eggs. I glanced down at the distant surf, the circling fish which, I saw, had long sharp teeth. A big wave crashed through, tossing the body up and flipping it over. It was enough for me to be able to recognize Annie's face. I knew what I was supposed to do, but couldn't quite bring myself to take the plunge. I glanced back at Toypurina who studied me expectantly. I looked for her son, who was no longer standing beside her.

He was behind me.

He pushed.

I fell.

The little bastard.

X

The tide tasted coppery like blood, but was as thin as Hawaiian Punch. The waves roared big and rough occasionally dunking me under, but the water was unexpectedly warm – like a bath. It was intense, but not entirely unpleasant – like the hot tub at any George Clooney party.

Then the silver fish started biting.

At first, the nips just felt like paper cuts. But the little buggers were persistent and some of them didn't just bite, they hung on. At first I could kick them off, but as more and more of them latched on to me, it became a struggle to shake them off and stay afloat in the rough red surf. And at the same time I was trying to grab hold of Annie in order to try and drag her to shore, though she seemed just as dead here as she had in the shopping cart on the L.A. River. Every time I'd manage to fasten an arm around her, another group of silver fish would come at me. Quite a few had latched on to her, too, and having affixed themselves to her, chewed deeply into her flesh. I caught a mouthful of pink foam – it felt like cotton in my mouth but tasted like meringue – and lost hold of her once more. I slipped under the water (or whatever it was) and felt another half dozen of the biting fish close their mouths on my arms and legs.

Annie was being devoured now by swarms of the silver nasties and I was finding it harder just to swat the creatures away. I started to gag on the thick foam as I got swept under once more. None of the fish was much bigger than my thumb, but they were ferocious and the sheer volume of them overwhelmed me. I could feel them not just biting into me, but grabbing hold and working together to keep me under. I used one foot to scrape ten of them off the other leg, but a dozen more soon took their place. Tendrils of black began to invade the red which filled my eyes and I felt desperation take hold of me as sure as the fish and knew I couldn't struggle against them for much longer. I managed one final lunge up through the red water and gulped a quick mouthful of air before being pulled down again. Just before I went back under, I thought I heard a splash, but then the fish were on me and I didn't have time to think about it.

A dark shape – a much bigger fish – swished past me. It moved fast and unsettled the silver nibblers. It flitted past again, dislodging a good half of them from my upper body. It was enough to allow me back to the surface for some much-needed oxygen. Gasping as I broke through the water, I kicked another bunch of the fish free from my feet and legs. The black shape shot up through the water next to me.

It was the kid. The willy-wagger and nose picker. Toypurina's boy. He flashed me a demonesque smile and plunged back under the water.

The silver fish went flying.

The kid was half-shark as he tore through the silver shoal. As he snaked among them, he opened his little boy mouth and snapped at the tiny fish, biting in half as many as he could reach. He had huge teeth. Some of the fish he spat out, most of them he simply devoured. The silver fish began to scatter – clearly, the kid scared the piss out of them.

Me, too.

But hey: never let it be said that Marty Burns looks a gift piranha in the mouth.

While the silver fish were flailing about in terror of the little boy with the big gnashers, I fought my way through the waves and back to where Annie bobbed. I swatted a few silver stragglers off of her and began to pull her toward the shore. The silver fish were regrouping now and Toypurina's kid was starting to look a little tired. Still swallowing tufts of the thick foam I redoubled my efforts until I could feel solid ground under my feet. I stumbled and went under, getting a lung full of the disgusting red liquid, but I held onto Annie. On my knees I managed to drag us both to the water's edge and up onto the sand.

Except it wasn't sand. Or rocks, or mud or any of what you might expect along a normal seashore.

The beach was made of breakfast cereal. Thousands upon millions of individual rice pops, corn flakes, puffed wheat, Fruit Loops, Trix . . . the last thing I remembered as I passed out on the crunchy shore, Annie beside me, was the distant sound of Roseanne's laughter ringing in my ears and the unnaturally sweet taste of Cap'n Crunch in my mouth.

With Crunchberries.

I opened my eyes and looked up at Guy's tongue. It was happily lolling out of his mouth. He gave me a big lick on the chin and then bounded back to the corner of the shack.

I sat up.

Toypurina was again perched cross-legged – I'm not a politically correct kind of guy, but under the circumstances I don't think I can bring myself to refer to how she sat as Indian-style – on her blanket. Still pregnant as a mama elephant. Still puffing away on her sweet-smelling stogie. She smiled at me and I felt like I'd just won *American Idol*. I nodded back and she flicked her eyes toward the other corner of the shack. I followed her gaze.

Vibiana was hunched in the corner, back against the wall. She was cradling Annie in her arms and stroking her hair. I looked back at Toypurina, but her attention was fixed on the pair. I had just got up on my haunches, feeling all pins and needles in my legs, when Annie's eyes opened wide. Then her mouth.

She screamed.

She screamed so loud, I went over backward on my ass. So loud, and so painful was the cry that escaped her, that I clamped my hands over my ears.

Still she screamed.

Guy whined and bounded out of the door. Toypurina rubbed at the planet of her belly and took a series of quick puffs on her cigar, blowing the smoke toward the corner.

Vibiana held tighter onto Annie. She wrapped her arms around her head and pressed the girl tightly into her bosom.

The screaming stopped.

I took my hands away from my head and saw Toypurina nod. Vibiana loosened her grip and let Annie sink down into her lap, still stroking her hair, but smiling at the no-longer dead girl. She looked up and grinned broadly at me, nodding all the while.

"I knowed you was the right one, Medicine Man," she said. She looked like she wanted to kiss me. It's not a look I see that often.

Toypurina laughed. Roseanne again.

And then something like awareness took hold of Annie's face. I could see it in her eyes and the way she licked her lips. She tried to sit up – I heard something crack and thought about rigor mortis – and Vibiana helped her. She started to tumble over and Vibiana caught her, supporting her back and neck as you would an infant. Annie turned her head and her neck creaked. She looked all around – at the shack, at Toypurina, at me; even Guy had stuck his snout back inside the door – and tears welled in her eyes.

"Not again," she cried out. "Oh, god, not again."

XI

We were heading back toward the river. Incredibly, Annie was able to walk under her own power, though she stumbled every so often, like an old woman who'd gone out without her cane. One of us was always there to catch her – Vibiana on her left, me on her right. Guy went on ahead of us sniffing at the trees and curbs. We proceeded largely in silence, broken only by the occasional tinkle of Guy marking his territory.

"Will you seek the Cat People, too?" Toypurina had asked back in the shack. I assumed she was talking to Vibiana, but saw she was looking at me.

"Beats me," I said. "I am in way over my head here. Again."

"You did very well. Truly you could be a shaman."

"If tractor-trailer school doesn't pan out, I'll think about it," I said. Then asked: "What were those things?"

My arms were covered with tiny red welts where the fish had sicced onto me. I rolled up my trousers and saw marks on my legs as well.

"Soul fish," Toypurina said.

"I've eaten a lot of flounder in my time," I said, "and even allowing for the pan, they never looked like that."

She had to spell it for me before I caught on.

"I tolds you he was Medicine Man," Vibiana practically shouted. She beamed at me like the proud mama at a bar mitzvah.

Toypurina offered a half-nod, half-shake of her head. And puffed on her cigar.

"The boy?" I said. I wasn't sure how to ask her about him.

"My son," Toypurina flatly stated. "His name will be . . ." – she paused as if translating something in her head – ". . . Light-in-the-Dark-Heart."

"Nicer than Howie," I said. Then I pointed at her impossibly swollen abdomen. "So, uh, how far along are you?"

Toypurina again looked up into the air, performing some mental calculation.

"A little over three hundred years," she said.

Ask a stupid question . . .

"The Cat People await," Toypurina said.

We took the hint.

Vibiana bowed to the shamaness and sputtered her thanks, but Toypurina interrupted her. "This shall be the last time, Vibiana of Above. You won't find me here again."

"Hopefully, we won't has to look," Vibiana told her.

"You," Toypurina said, pointing her cigar at Guy. He had been nibbling at his fur in the corner, anxious to get a move on. He looked up at her and she told him blankly: "You are not a dog."

Guy started to whine.

"You may return when you want to know your spirit self truly," she told him.

He ran out the door as if she'd announced it was bath time.

"And you," she said to me. "You may know now if you choose."

I thought about it for a minute, wondered what insight she might be able to impart to me, if there was some vital piece of information about the essence of my spirit or soul she could give me which might lead to knowing, enlightenment, self-contentment.

I scratched the back of my head, thought about the situation. "I'm cool," I said.

She gave me a big thumb's up in reply. Then she turned to Annie and said: "It is your choice, too, you know. It always has been and it still is."

Annie, still ashen and shaky – as you would be just coming back from the dead and all – looked up tearfully at Toypurina. "I know," she croaked. "Don't you think I know?"

More clouds were drifting across the early morning sky as we approached the edge of the dry river up near Spring Street. There was no one else around, on the concrete banks or down in the dirty culvert. The breeze had kicked up to approximate a proper wind and there was just a hint of something wet in the air. The moon, I thought, was beginning its slow surrender to the day. Hurry sun-up, thought I.

We walked down another set of zig-zagging stairs, returning to the floor of the river. There wasn't a whole lot to see in either direction.

"Now what?" I asked.

"Gots to still go upriver," Vibiana said, looking up at the sky. She must have been thinking as I had. She took a longing glance at Annie, then at the stretch of river snaking off to the north and west, through Chavez Ravine and the hills beyond. "I'll be backs in a tick."

She ran off into the darkness.

I turned to Annie, who'd been quiet since emerging from Toypurina's shack. Not to mention wherever else she'd been. She stood staring down at the damp river floor, shivering in the wind's chill. For the second time that night, I took off my jacket and placed it around her shoulders.

"Hey," I said. "You there?"

"Yeah," she coughed. She almost managed a smile back at me.

"Quite a night," I said.

"Vibiana definitely takes me places. Oh, yeah."

"Couldn't she just book a weekend in Santa Barbara like everyone else?"

Annie shook her head. Shivered some more.

"What is this all about, Annie? What is Vibiana to you? What is she, period?"

"She's my lover, Marty," Annie said deadly. "She's my lover and my killer."

"You know, I'm a pretty open-minded type," I said, "but I'm having a little trouble with all this."

She looked up at the moon, then over at Guy sniffing an old bicycle seat. "Get in line," she said.

"When you . . . came to, in the shack. The first words you said were 'not again.' Or something like that. What did you mean?"

"I've been here before. We've been here before, Vib and me. Here and . . . *there*."

"Where I found you. In the red water with the soul fish?"

"Yeah. Thanks, by the way. For bringing me back. I understand why Gabbo lets you call him Danny."

She said all this the way you might read out the phone number of a dry cleaner from the yellow pages. I wondered exactly how much of her had come back with me from that strange place.

"I've been married three times, Annie. Four depending on the strictness of your definitions and the lawyers involved. I've seen a lot and been a lot of places. The one thing I've learned in all the years is never judge or think you can figure out what goes on between two people who think they're in love. There's nothing too normal or too weird between people. Because it can only ever be between them and for them to understand. But I've got to say this to you, Annie, and I think I've maybe earned the right tonight: what the hell are you doing with her?"

Annie laughed then and it should have been nice to know she could still do it. But it was a hollow and bitter thing that passed through and twisted her lips. Guy retreated at the sound of it. I'd have liked to do the same. But I wanted to hear the answer.

"She saved me, once. Saved me from a very terrible thing. I loved her for it. I still do."

"So that gives her the right to . . . do what it is she's doing to you? What is she doing to you? What could she have saved you from more terrible than this?"

Annie peeked up at the waning moon and stuck out her tongue.

"She's remaking me," she said.

"Into what?"

"Something . . ." – she stifled a chuckle – ". . . some*one* who can still love her. Who she can still love. Love dies hard, you know. Harder than the monsters in those stupid horror movies. Freddy. Jason. Love."

I heard a squeaking noise coming at us from the dark in the direction Vibiana had disappeared. I had a feeling we didn't have much longer to talk in private.

"But why do *you* do it, Annie? Why are you putting yourself through this? That's what I don't understand."

She did smile at me now, and it was for real.

"Somewhere, inside, buried deep maybe, I still love her, too," she said.

"Jesus," I muttered. I saw something coming toward us now, some peculiar vehicle squeaking its way down the river. Someone, it had to be Vibiana, was flapping away on top of it.

"How many times?" I asked hurriedly. "How many times have you been through this?"

Annie looked up at the sky again. "Every moon. Every goddamn moon."

"So why not stop it. Right now, right this minute. Just stop and let's go. Not back to Long Beach, either."

"I can't," she whispered.

"You can if you want to," I said.

"I can't."

And she turned so that the fullness of the moon lit up her face and she pulled down on the collar of her shirt.

There was a gaping hole in her chest where her heart should be. Just a big wet hole, glistening in the moonlight.

"I *really* can't," she said. "The Cat People will complete me. Complete us."

I felt my gorge rise and had to fight off being sick. Before I could say any more – or go mad over the impossibility of it all – Vibiana came screeching in on her new set of wheels. I'd never seen anything like it. Or rather, the last time I'd seen anything like it was an episode of *Green Acres*. It was a railroad handcar. The kind with the big handle that you pump up and down to move along the tracks. But this one had fat rubber wheels for transit along the river bed.

"Criminy," I said. "Where did you find that?"

Vibiana cackled. "The moon provides. Climbs aboard, my special ones."

I tendered a long look at Annie. Vibiana hissed.

"You know," she said, eyeing me angrily again.

I nodded. I thought about decking her, couldn't think how that would help. I just stood there.

"Let's us all finish the journey, then. One big happy family."

Annie and Guy sat down on the middle of the car. Vibiana and I each took one side of the handle. We began to pump.

Upriver we went.

XII

We moved at a surprisingly fast pace up the concrete river bed, even through the thin stream of running water that dribbled beneath us as we made our way into the Valley. Annie stared silently into the night and Guy looked troubled, but I was panting like the proverbial dog from pumping the handcar. Vibiana wore a sheen of sweat – it somehow made her look even crazier; you'd have thought there'd be a limit – but otherwise appeared untroubled by the effort of moving us up the now slick river bed. Every so often, usually when a passing cloud obscured the moon, she would cast a worried look skyward. There was moisture in the air up here and the first scent of morning, too. Perhaps they were the same thing.

I had a feeling we didn't have far to go.

"What do you think love is?" I said, between gasps.

Guy and Annie both looked at me, but my eyes were locked on Vibiana's. She showed me her crooked teeth.

"It's most specials," she said.

"That's not an answer," I said. "That's a Valentine's Day card."

"You tells me then," she said.

"But I'm asking you. It's your show. I mean, love is what this is all about, isn't it? Wouldn't you say?"

"I hasn't said nothing," Vibiana growled. I'd clearly touched a nerve.

"No you hasn't. Most curious, I thinks."

"You making fun of me?"

"Probably. It's a cheap shot. Sorry."

She grunted.

"But about love," I continued.

"What?"

"I've been around Hollywood a lot of years. Everybody says they love each other all the time. No one ever means it, so the word is useless. *I love ya, babe. I'd love to have lunch with you. I love my agent. I'd love to suck your cock.* It's all the same, all said the same."

"Trash mouth!" Vibiana yelled.

"But it's not just words, is it? And not just sex. If it was, Annie here would be bursting with love. It would be dribbling down her thighs and chin every night and she could collect it in buckets and sell it on a street corner stand like lemonade."

I forced myself not to look at Annie, but even in peripheral vision, in the dark, I saw tears on her cheeks. Guy began to whine.

"So what is love then?" I asked again.

"It's together forever," Vibiana yelled at me. "It's giving to the other. It's making you happy and making two into one."

"Okay," I said. "That's a little bit better. I can maybe buy into some of that. Though it still reeks a little bit of Hallmark to these ears."

"Speaks then, Medicine Man. You tells me."

"I live alone, so what do I know? Or maybe, I live alone because I do know. I think love is about courage. I think love is about lack of fear. Love is being brave enough to give to someone else the bit of you that you most want to keep for yourself. That's why love is about the heart, because the heart is always the centre of a thing. And love is about not being afraid to know yourself. How else can you ever hope to know another person? And there is nothing more scary than knowing yourself. People spasmodically say that the opposite of love is hate, because that's the simple and easy way we all like to skip through our lives. But the opposite of love – the enemy of love – is fear. And that's why love is always so Valentine's Day special and genuinely magical when it's real: because it means, even if only for hours or seconds at a time, the banishment of fear. And ain't that a thing?"

Vibiana didn't reply; she was looking past me at something in the distance.

"Annie, here, seems like someone who has a lot to fear, yet she seethes with courage. How else could she endure what she does? For you, Vibiana."

"She loves me," Vibiana whispered.

"I do believe that," I said. "But do you love her? Really?"

"Medicine Man . . ." she warned.

"Or are you just too afraid? It can't be both."

Vibiana unexpectedly let go of the pump handle and I nearly went flying off the edge of the car. We had arrived at a huge bend in the river. The concrete bed had given way to sand and gravel here and what had been a trickle of water along the floor was now deep enough to slosh around in. Set into the walls of the curved bank – it formed a kind of semi-circle or natural amphitheatre – were a series of drainage pipes with steel covers at least 6 feet across. On each of the massive covers was painted the face of a cat. Some were cute and cartoony, others dark and menacing. They appeared to have been painted by different hands in different styles at different times, from '60s psychedelia to '90s gangbanger. They all had pointy ears and big eyes that seemed, uncannily, to follow you. All but one – so vicious in rendering that it must have scared off even the most vandalic of taggers – had been defaced to greater or lesser degrees with graffiti. Of course, to the Department of Water and Power, the cats themselves were probably no more than graffiti. I thought they were beautiful.

These had to be the Cat People.

Vibiana must have read my mind. "We is arrivened," she announced.

XIII

We all hopped off the handcar. Vibiana gave it a shove and it rolled toward the far side of the river, coming to a lurching stop when one wheel tumbled into a waist-deep pothole. Guy most definitely did not like the look of the cats, though there was something distinctly less canine about him since the encounter with Toypurina. He was standing upright on his hind legs . . . his legs, for one thing. And he was starting to look more sheepish than mutt-like about his nakedness. A little bit chilly, too, judging from the key shrinkage. He still sniffed at the air and whined a bit in the back of his throat, but there was a lack of conviction to it. Trans-specied, my ass!

Vibiana had a broad grin on her face, arms raised high, as she danced slow circles in front of the cats. She curtsied to each one as she whirled by and the wind kicked up behind her as she went round and round. She was speaking or singing, but it might as well have been in tongues for all I was able to understand.

She was entirely mad.

Annie stood beside me, shoulders hunched, hands pressed against the hole in her chest where her heart should be. She stared down at the river-bed, the water deep enough in this semi-circular enclosure to lap over her exposed toes. I reached out a hand to touch her shoulder, but she shrugged me off.

"You might not want to watch this," she said. She took off my jacket and returned it to me. Then she walked over to Vibiana and laid herself down in the water.

Vibiana froze mid-step in her mad dervish. She leaned over Annie and her face lit up with glee, like a kid descending on a pile of presents under the tree on Christmas morning. She reached out and tore off Annie's shirt, exposing her hollowed chest. I felt sick again at the sight of the wet hole, but found I couldn't look away. I bet old Gabbo wouldn't Wugga-Wugga her just now. I heard the wet sploshes of Guy running off behind me, but didn't so much as blink.

Vibiana raised up her arms and beseeched the moon, still playing hide and seek with the clouds. Seemingly at her imploring its light burst through again and she shrieked in ecstasy. She tore off her own black top and the undergarments beneath. She had a broad stomach that obscured the existence of hips, and flabby, lozenge-shaped breasts that nearly touched her navel. She reached into the water and lifted Annie up like a baby, pressing her beloved's face to her massive chest and forcing a plum coloured nipple into her mouth.

Annie suckled.

The wind blew fiercer and the cats on the walls appeared to move. I felt a rumbling in the ground beneath me and saw that the water level had risen above the tops of my shoes. I could feel the air pressure drop around me and smelled ozone in the air. Clouds thickened in the sky, but the light of the moon continued to shine down on us for the moment. Vibiana screeched once more at the sky, then laid Annie back down in the water. She swung a leg around and straddled Annie. She bent over and kissed Annie fiercely on the mouth.

Somewhere there was a lightning strike. A few seconds later came the giant's belly-rumble of thunder. I felt a fat raindrop strike the middle of my bald spot.

Vibiana raised up her head to again study the clouds and a wave of panic washed across her face. She froze like that until the moon returned through another break in the quickly forming storm. When the moonlight returned, she acted.

She raised up her right hand and closed her eyes.

Vibiana plunged her fingers between her breasts and right on through the skin until her arm was buried wrist deep inside her chest. She screamed, as if in childbirth, her face contorted in jagged curves of pain, as she rooted around inside herself. She howled and screeched and shrieked into the night until her fingers found the treasure they sought and her hand emerged with a pumping red blob. Quicker than I could follow, and as the moon again vanished, she took her heart and thrust it inside the hole in Annie's chest. Annie's eyes shot open and she bolted upright, kept from a pain-driven levitation into the sky only by Vibiana's considerable weight. She plunged her own right hand inside Vibiana's chest and they drew themselves together.

The pair of them made the sound of Hell's rusty gates opening for Ol' Nick himself. I clasped my hands over my ears and had to look away as the moon disappeared entirely behind the clouds.

Then the deluge hit.

The earth shook beneath me and I thought it must be an earth-quake. I opened my eyes and saw the Cat People quivering. Then I realized what it was: the drainage covers were opening before the force of water being expelled. The bobbing covers flew open, smashing the faces of the cats against the concrete wall above and torrents of water came flooding through.

"Annie!" I screamed.

I took a step toward the pair of lovers still clutching each other on the river bed. The roar of the water geysering out of the pipes drowned even their awful screams. I saw Vibiana turn her head towards the vanished cats – the foamy water was the Cheshire rivercat's grin – then they were both knocked over and dragged under by the force of the tide. It hit me, too, and I went ass over crown as the water took out my legs. I went sprawling along the gravely river bed on my back, felt the rocks and stones tear through my clothes and open up my skin as the raw force of the unleashed and suddenly extant river carried me away. I tried to gain some purchase in the loose river bottom, but merely felt the nails get ripped off my fingers for the effort. I tried to turn myself over in the stream, thinking I could swim with the tide and avoid smashing my skull, but the water pouring out of the circle of drains formed spiralling cross-currents and I couldn't get my balance. An extra strong vomit of water from the mouth of one of the cats sent me hurtling straight toward a concrete channel along the edge of the culvert. I prepared myself for the inevitable cantaloupe squelch of skull on stone – had time to think: what a headline this is going to make on page 64 of *Variety* – when something grabbed my leg and spun me around and out of harm's way.

It was Guy. He had my trouser leg between his teeth and was dog-paddling for the high ground like the unholy offspring of Lassie and Rin-Tin-Tin.

"Good boy!" I yelled.

Out of the worst of the spilling torrent, Guy reached over and grabbed me around the chest. Together we were able to kick our way to the rim of the culvert and a concrete walkway above the still-rising water.

"Thanks," I managed, catching my breath. "You're a hell of a swimmer."

"I did two seasons of *Baywatch*," he explained.

"It must have been raining all night up north for them to dump this much water," I said. I scoured the swirling river for some sign of Annie and Vibiana. Without the moon it was hard to make much out in the foam. "Can you see them?" I asked.

Guy started running – on two legs – down the walkway. The water was lapping over the edge now, and he slipped once but managed not to fall in. He was sniffing at the air.

"There!" he said and pointed.

I saw two intertwined forms rolling downstream past us. They were still locked in embrace and I couldn't tell if they were all right. Of course, given what I had witnessed before the flood broke, I didn't know what that might mean in the best of circumstances.

"If we lose them around the bend, we'll never catch up," I said. But I couldn't see how to reach them.

"There," Guy said.

A dozen yards down the walkway, someone had dumped a stack of old mattresses. We ran over to them. Serta Perfect Sleepers. God bless Joey Heatherton, wherever she is today.

"Will they float?" I said.

"He who dares, wins" Guy said.

I raised an eyebrow at him.

"Hounds' code," he told me.

We jumped on a mattress and pushed out into the river. I thought we were going to capsize on the first wave, but Guy rolled to one side and I went to the other and we managed to keep our balance. We each dangled an arm and a leg over the side and after a little to-ing and fro-ing found we could roughly steer the mattress in the direction we wanted to go. The ride was rough and our vessel was taking on water fast, but it somehow stayed afloat. The worst thing, actually, were the stains on the top. I didn't like to think too much about the big brown ones. Guy sniffed at them and yelped.

Annie and Vibiana were still visible not too far in front of us, though it hadn't appeared that either had so much as lifted her head to breathe. I feared the worst and paddled harder. The pair of them were being pushed by a sudden surge in the current toward the hard wall of the river. Guy pointed but I saw it at the same time. Just beyond where they were bound to hit was a set of those zig-zag stairs leading up to ground level. If we could manage to ride the current just right we could swing around, head them off and jump the river and onto the steps.

We fought the water for all we were worth.

Guy yowled and I screamed when we saw the entwined lovers bounce hard off the culvert's concrete barrier. I could see Annie's face, but her eyes were closed and I couldn't detect any sign of life. Still, the contact slowed them up and gave us the chance we needed to come around past them. A steel banister ran the length of the zig-zag stairs and as I steered and kicked us close, Guy reached out and grabbed hold of it. He must have been stronger than he looked, because the force of the current whipped us around and slammed the mattress into the stairs, but Guy held on tight. With him holding onto the pole and the mattress, and me dangling off the other end, I managed to scissor Annie and Vibiana between my legs as the water tried to sweep them past. I almost lost my grip on the mattress, but dug my fingers through the cover and grabbed hold of the springs. The rusty metal inside cut into my palms, but I was not about to let go. Guy pulled the edge of the mattress up onto a wide step and then reached out for me. He pulled me up and I dragged Annie and Vibiana along with my legs. Just when I thought I couldn't hold them another second, they were close enough for Guy to stretch out and take hold of Annie. Between us we got them up onto a step as a fresh burst of current tore the mattress away. It submerged as it quickly disappeared downstream.

We pulled the two women apart, but the water was still rising and we had to hurry to drag them higher up the stairs. We reached a platform more than halfway up the wall which seemed safe enough. I turned Annie onto her back and bent down to put my ear to her chest.

It was only then that I realized she had a chest again. The wet hole where her heart had gone missing was healed over without so much as a scar. I looked over at Vibiana and saw that her massive chest was similarly restored and whole. I shook my head.

They both opened their eyes.

They turned toward each other and embraced.

"Woof-woof," Guy said. I nodded my agreement.

I knew exactly what he meant.

Annie wore my wet shirt. Vib was bare tits to the world. The moon had sunk and the sun was rising and things would be dry soon enough. The two of them sat along the concrete barrier marking the edge of the Los Angeles River. They talked, holding each other's faces in their hands. I have no idea what they said; didn't want or need to know.

What did anyone else's opinion about two lovers matter, anyway?

Guy was standing beside me, shivering. He was on his legs now and pulling uncomfortably at his ears. I think he was facing a bit of an identity crisis.

"So, uh, got a good agent these days, Marty?" he asked.

"I *love* my agent," I told him. It was even true. "I'll give you her number."

"Thanks," he barked.

I think we both felt a little self-conscious watching Annie and Vibiana, but neither of us could look away. Not even when they pressed their mouths together in a passionate and enduring kiss.

"They're fucking crazy, man," Guy said.

I looked at him standing there, naked, with his surgically modified ears and snout, a fake tail (wagging) grafted over his ass, and plugs of doggy fur transplanted all over his body. He was shaking his head in wonderment, befuddlement, even a touch of glee.

"Maybe," I said.

I reached into my pocket and found the cigar I'd swiped from Toypurina. Magically – courtesy of the Tongva shamaness, I reckon – it was bone dry and I was able to light it with my Zippo. I took a puff and found it tasted like heaven.

"But ain't that just love?" I added.

KELLY LINK

Stone Animals

KELLY LINK LIVES in Northampton, Massachusetts with her husband, Gavin J. Grant. They publish the twice-yearly magazine *Lady Churchill's Rosebud Wristlet* and, with Ellen Datlow, they now co-edit *The Year's Best Fantasy and Horror* anthology series.

Link is the author of the collections *Stranger Things Happen* and *Magic for Beginners*, and her fiction has won a Nebula Award, a World Fantasy Award and the James Tiptree, Jr Award.

Short stories have recently appeared in *McSweeney's Mammoth Treasury of Thrilling Tales*, *Conjunctions*, *The Year's Best Science Fiction and Fantasy for Teens: First Annual Collection* and *Best American Short Stories*. She is not working on a novel.

"I've always been fascinated by paint strips and by how people name things like children, and colours," admits Link. "Where the rabbits come from, I don't know, but Jeffrey Ford has pointed out to me that they are associated with pregnant women and with insanity.

"When I was writing this story, I couldn't figure out if the ending was terrifying or profoundly silly, but hopefully it's both of those things."

H ENRY ASKED A QUESTION. He was joking.

"As a matter of fact," the real estate agent snapped, "it is."

It was not a question she had expected to be asked. She gave Henry a goofy, appeasing smile and yanked at the hem of the skirt of her pink linen suit, which seemed as if it might, at any moment, go rolling up her knees like a window shade. She was younger than Henry, and sold houses that she couldn't afford to buy.

"It's reflected in the asking price, of course," she said. "Like you said."

Henry stared at her. She blushed.

"I've never seen anything," she said. "But there are stories. Not stories that I know. I just know there are stories. If you believe that sort of thing."

"I don't," Henry said. When he looked over to see if Catherine had heard, she had her head up the tiled fireplace, as if she were trying it on, to see whether it fit. Catherine was six months pregnant. Nothing fit her except for Henry's baseball caps, his sweatpants, his T-shirts. But she liked the fireplace.

Carleton was running up and down the staircase, slapping his heels down hard, keeping his head down and his hands folded around the banister. Carleton was serious about how he played. Tilly sat on the landing, reading a book, legs poking out through the railings. Whenever Carleton ran past, he thumped her on the head, but Tilly never said a word. Carleton would be sorry later, and never even know why.

Catherine took her head out of the fireplace. "Guys," she said. "Carleton, Tilly. Slow down a minute and tell me what you think. Think King Spanky will be okay out here?"

"King Spanky is a cat, Mom," Tilly said. "Maybe we should get a dog, you know, to help protect us." She could tell by looking at her mother that they were going to move. She didn't know how she felt about this, except she had plans for the yard. A yard like that needed a dog.

"I don't like big dogs," said Carleton, six years old and small for his age. "I don't like this staircase. It's too big."

"Carleton," Henry said. "Come here. I need a hug."

Carleton came down the stairs. He lay down on his stomach on the floor and rolled, noisily, floppily, slowly, over to where Henry stood with the real estate agent. He curled like a dead snake around Henry's ankles. "I don't like those dogs outside," he said.

"I know it looks like we're out in the middle of nothing, but if you go down through the backyard, cut through that stand of trees, there's this little path. It takes you straight down to the train station. Ten minute bike ride," the agent said. Nobody ever remembered her name, which was why she had to wear too-tight skirts. She was, as it happened, writing a romance novel, and she spent a lot of time making up pseudonyms, just in case she ever finished it. Ophelia Pink. Matilde Hightower. LaLa Treeble. Or maybe she'd write Gothics. Ghost stories. But not about people like these. "Another ten minutes on that path and you're in town."

"What dogs, Carleton?" Henry said.

"I think they're lions, Carleton," said Catherine. "You mean the stone ones beside the door? Just like the lions at the library. You love those lions, Carleton. Patience and Fortitude?"

"I've always thought they were rabbits," the real estate agent said. "You know, because of the ears. They have big ears." She flopped her hands and then tugged at her skirt which would not stay down. "I think they're pretty valuable. The guy who built the house had a gallery in New York. He knew a lot of sculptors."

Henry was struck by that. He didn't think he knew a single sculptor.

"I don't like the rabbits," Carleton said. "I don't like the staircase. I don't like this room. It's too big. I don't like *her*."

"Carleton," Henry said. He smiled at the real estate agent.

"I don't like the house," Carleton said, clinging to Henry's ankles. "I don't like houses. I don't want to live in a house."

"Then we'll build you a tepee out on the lawn," Catherine said. She sat on the stairs beside Tilly, who shifted her weight, almost imperceptibly, towards Catherine. Catherine sat as still as possible. Tilly was in Fourth Grade and difficult in a way that girls weren't supposed to be. Mostly she refused to be cuddled or babied. But she sat there, leaning on Catherine's arm, emanating saintly fragrances: peacefulness, placidness, goodness. *I want this house*, Catherine said, moving her lips like a silent movie heroine, to Henry, so that neither Carleton nor the agent, who had bent over to inspect a piece of dust on the floor, could see. "You can live in your tepee, and we'll invite you to come over for lunch. You like lunch, don't you? Peanut butter sandwiches?"

"I don't," Carleton said and sobbed once.

But they bought the house anyway. The real estate agent got her commission. Tilly rubbed the waxy, stone ears of the rabbits on the way out, pretending that they already belonged to her. They were as tall as she was, but that wouldn't always be true. Carleton had a peanut butter sandwich.

The rabbits sat on either side of the front door. Two stone animals sitting on cracked, mossy haunches. They were shapeless, lumpish, patient in a way that seemed not worn down, but perhaps never really finished in the first place. There was something about them that reminded Henry of Stonehenge. Catherine thought of topiary shapes; *The Velveteen Rabbit*; soldiers who stand guard in front of palaces and never even twitch their noses. Maybe they could be donated to a museum. Or broken up with jackhammers. They didn't suit the house at all.

"So what's the house like?" said Henry's boss. She was carefully stretching rubber bands around her rubber band ball. By now the rubber band ball was so big, she had to get special extra-large rubber bands from the art department. She claimed it helped her think. She had tried knitting for a while, but it turned out that knitting was too utilitarian, too feminine. Making an enormous ball out of rubber bands struck the right note. It was something a man might do.

It took up half of her desk. Under the fluorescent office lights it had a peeled red liveliness. You almost expected it to shoot forwards and out the door. The larger it got, the more it looked like some kind of eyeless, hairless, legless animal. Maybe a dog. A Carleton-sized dog, Henry thought, although not a Carleton-sized rubber band ball.

Catherine joked sometimes about using Carleton as a measure of unit.

"Big," Henry said. "Haunted."

"Really?" his boss said. "So's this rubber band." She aimed a rubber band at Henry and shot him in the elbow. This was meant to suggest that she and Henry were good friends, and just goofing around, the way good friends did. But what it really meant was that she was angry at him. "Don't leave me," she said.

"I'm only two hours away." Henry put up his hand to ward off rubber bands. "Quit it. We talk on the phone, we use e-mail. I come back to town when you need me in the office."

"You're sure this is a good idea?" his boss said. She fixed her reptilian, watery gaze on him. She had problematical tear ducts. Though she could have had a minor surgical procedure to fix this, she'd chosen not to. It was a tactical advantage, the way it spooked people.

It didn't really matter that Henry remained immune to rubber bands and crocodile tears. She had backup strategies. She thought about which would be most effective while Henry pitched his stupid idea all over again.

Henry had the movers' phone number in his pocket, like a talisman. He wanted to take it out, wave it at The Crocodile, say look at this! Instead he said, "For nine years, we've lived in an apartment next door to a building that smells like urine. Like someone built an entire building out of bricks made of compressed, red pee. Someone spit on Catherine in the street last week. This old Russian lady in a fur coat. A kid rang our doorbell the other day, and tried to sell us gas masks. Door-to-door gas mask salesmen. Catherine bought one. When she told me about it she burst into tears. She said she couldn't figure out if she was feeling guilty because she'd bought a gas mask, or if it was because she hadn't bought enough for everyone."

"Good Chinese food," his boss said. "Good movies. Good book-stores. Good dry cleaners. Good conversation."

"Treehouses," Henry said. "I had a treehouse when I was a kid."

"You were never a kid," his boss said.

"Three bathrooms. Crown mouldings. We can't even see our nearest neighbour's house. I get up in the morning, have coffee, put Carleton and Tilly on the bus, and go to work in my pyjamas."

"What about Catherine?" The Crocodile put her head down on her rubber band ball. Possibly this was a gesture of defeat.

"There was that thing. Catherine's whole department is leaving. Like rats deserting a sinking ship. Anyway, Catherine needs a change. And so do I," Henry said. "We've got another kid on the way. We're going to garden. Catherine'll teach ESL, find a book group, write her book. Teach the kids how to play bridge. You've got to start them early."

He picked a rubber band off the floor and offered it to his boss. "You should come out and visit some weekend."

"I never go upstate," the Crocodile said. She held onto her rubber band ball. "Too many ghosts."

"Are you going to miss this? Living here?" Catherine said. She couldn't stand the way her stomach poked out. She couldn't see past it. She held up her left foot to make sure it was still there, and pulled the sheet off Henry.

"I love the house," Henry said.

"Me too," Catherine said. She was biting her fingernails. Henry could hear her teeth going *click, click*. Now she had both feet up in the air. She wiggled them around. Hello, feet.

"What are you doing?"

She put them down again. On the street outside, cars came and went, pushing smears of light along the ceiling, slow and fast at the same time. The baby was wriggling around inside her, kicking out with both feet like it was swimming across the English Channel, the Pacific. Kicking all the way to China. "Did you buy that story about the former owners moving to France?"

"I don't believe in France," Henry said. "*Je ne crois pas en France.*"

"Neither do I," Catherine said. "Henry?"

"What?"

"Do you love the house?"

"I love the house."

"I love it more than you do," Catherine said, although Henry hated it when she said things like that. "What do you love best?"

"That room in the front," Henry said. "With the windows. Our bedroom. Those weird rabbit statues."

"Me too," Catherine said, although she didn't. "I love those rabbits."

Then she said, "Do you ever worry about Carleton and Tilly?"

"What do you mean?" Henry said. He looked at the alarm clock: it was 4:00 a.m. "Why are we awake right now?"

"Sometimes I worry that I love one of them better," Catherine said. "Like I might love Tilly better. Because she used to wet the bed. Because she's always so angry. Or Carleton, because he was so sick when he was little."

"I love them both the same," Henry said.

He didn't even know he was lying. Catherine knew, though. She knew he was lying, and she knew he didn't even know it. Most of the time she thought that it was okay. As long as he thought he loved them both the same, and acted as if he did, that was good enough.

"Well, do you ever worry that you love them more than me?" she said. "Or that I love them more than I love you?"

"Do you?" Henry said.

"Of course," Catherine said. "I have to. It's my job."

She found the gas mask in a box of wineglasses, and also six recent issues of the *New Yorker*, which she still might get a chance to read someday. She put the gas mask under the sink and the *New Yorkers* in the sink. Why not? It was her sink. She could put anything she wanted into it. She took the magazines out again and put them into the refrigerator, just for fun.

Henry came into the kitchen, holding silver candlesticks and a stuffed armadillo, which someone had made into a purse. It had a shoulder strap made out of its own skin. You opened its mouth and put things inside it, lipstick and subway tokens. It had pink gimlet eyes and smelled strongly of vinegar. It belonged to Tilly, although how it had come into her possession was unclear. Tilly claimed she'd won it at school in a contest involving donuts. Catherine thought it more likely Tilly had either stolen it or (slightly preferable) found it in someone's trash. Now Tilly kept her most valuable belongings inside the purse, to keep them safe from Carleton who was covetous of the precious things—

– because they were small, and because they belonged to Tilly – but afraid of the armadillo.

"I've already told her she can't take it to school for at least the first two weeks. Then we'll see." She took the purse from Henry and put it under the sink with the gas mask.

"What are they doing?" Henry said. Framed in the kitchen window, Carleton and Tilly hunched over the lawn. They had a pair of scissors and a notebook and a stapler.

"They're collecting grass," Catherine took dishes out of a box, put the bubble wrap aside for Tilly to stomp, and stowed the dishes in a cabinet. The baby kicked like it knew all about bubble wrap. "Woah, fireplace," she said. "We don't have a dancing license in there."

Henry put out his hand, rapped on Catherine's stomach. *Knock, knock.* It was Tilly's joke. Catherine would say, "Who's there?" and Tilly would say, "Candlestick's here. Fat Man's here. Box. Hammer. Milkshake. Clarinet. Mousetrap. Fiddlestick." Tilly had a whole list of names for the baby. The real estate agent would have approved.

"Where's King Spanky?" Henry said.

"Under our bed," Catherine said. "He's up in the box frame."

"Have we unpacked the alarm clock?" Henry said.

"Poor King Spanky," Catherine said. "Nobody to love except an alarm clock. Come upstairs and let's see if we can shake him out of the bed. I've got a present for you."

The present was in a U-Haul box exactly like all the other boxes in the bedroom, except that Catherine had written HENRY'S PRESENT on it instead of LARGE FRONT BEDROOM. Inside the box were Styrofoam peanuts and then a smaller box from Takashimaya. The Takashimaya box was fastened with a silver ribbon. The tissue paper inside was dull gold, and inside the tissue paper was a green silk robe with orange sleeves and heraldic animals in orange and gold thread. "Lions," Henry said.

"Rabbits," Catherine said.

"I didn't get you anything," Henry said.

Catherine smiled nobly. She liked giving presents better than getting presents. She'd never told Henry, because it seemed to her that it must be selfish in some way she'd never bothered to figure out. Catherine was grateful to be married to Henry, who accepted all presents as his due; who looked good in the clothes that she bought him; who was vain, in an easygoing way, about his good looks. Buying clothes for Henry was especially satisfying now, while she was pregnant and couldn't buy them for herself.

She said, "If you don't like it, then I'll keep it. Look at you, look at those sleeves. You look like the emperor of Japan."

They had already colonized the bedroom, making it full of things that belonged to them. There was Catherine's mirror on the wall, and their mahogany wardrobe, their first real piece of furniture, a wedding present from Catherine's great aunt. There was their serviceable, queen-size bed with King Spanky lodged up inside it, and there was Henry, spinning his arms in the wide orange sleeves, like an embroidered windmill. Henry could see all of these things in the mirror, and behind him, their lawn and Tilly and Carleton, stapling grass into their notebook. He saw all of these things and he found them good. But he couldn't see Catherine. When he turned around, she stood in the doorway, frowning at him. She had the alarm clock in her hand.

"Look at you," she said again. It worried her, the way something, someone, *Henry*, could suddenly look like a place she'd never been before. The alarm began to ring and King Spanky came out from under the bed, trotting over to Catherine. She bent over, awkwardly – ungraceful, ungainly, so clumsy, so fucking awkward, being pregnant was like wearing a fucking suitcase strapped across your middle – put the alarm clock down on the ground, and King Spanky hunkered down in front of it, his nose against the ringing glass face.

And that made her laugh again. Henry loved Catherine's laugh. Downstairs, their children slammed a door open, ran through the house, carrying scissors, both Catherine and Henry knew, and slammed another door open and were outside again, leaving behind the smell of grass. There was a store in New York where you could buy a perfume that smelled like that.

Catherine, Carleton and Tilly came back from the grocery store with a tire, a rope to hang it from, and a box of pancake mix for dinner. Henry was online, looking at a jpeg of a rubber band ball. There was a message too. The Crocodile needed him to come into the office. It would be just a few days. Someone was setting fires and there was no one smart enough to see how to put them out except for him. They were his accounts. He had to come in and save them. She knew Catherine and Henry's apartment hadn't sold; she'd checked with their listing agent. So surely it wouldn't be impossible, not impossible, only inconvenient.

He went downstairs to tell Catherine. "That *witch*," she said, and then bit her lip. "She called the listing agent? I'm sorry. We talked about this. Never mind. Just give me a moment."

Catherine inhaled. Exhaled. Inhaled. If she were Carleton she would hold her breath until her face turned red and Henry agreed to stay home, but then again, it never worked for Carleton. "We ran into our new neighbours in the grocery store. She's about the same age as me. Liz and Marcus. One kid, older, a girl, um, I think her name was Alison, maybe from a first marriage – potential babysitter, which is really good news. Liz is a lawyer. Gorgeous. Reads Oprah books. He likes to cook."

"So do I," Henry said.

"You're better looking," Catherine said. "So do you have to go back tonight, or can you take the train in the morning?"

"The morning is fine," Henry said, wanting to seem agreeable.

Carleton appeared in the kitchen, his arms pinned around King Spanky's middle. The cat's front legs stuck straight out, as if Carleton were dowsing. King Spanky's eyes were closed. Its whiskers twitched Morse code. "What are you wearing?" Carleton said.

"My new uniform," Henry said. "I wear it to work."

"Where do you work?" Carleton said, testing.

"I work at home," Henry said. Catherine snorted.

"He looks like the king of rabbits, doesn't he? The emperor of Rabbitaly," she said, no longer sounding particularly pleased about this.

"He looks like a princess," Carleton said, now pointing King Spanky at Henry like a gun.

"Where's your grass collection?" Henry said. "Can I see it?"

"No," Carleton said. He put King Spanky on the floor, and the cat slunk out of the kitchen, heading for the staircase, the bedroom, the safety of the bedsprings, the beloved alarm clock, the beloved. The beloved may be treacherous, greasy-headed and given to evil habits, or else it can be a man in his late forties who works too much, or it can be an alarm clock.

"After dinner," Henry said, trying again, "we could go out and find a tree for your tire swing."

"No," Carleton said, regretfully. He lingered in the kitchen, hoping to be asked a question to which he could say yes.

"Where's your sister?" Henry said.

"Watching television," Carleton said. "I don't like the television here."

"It's too big," Henry said, but Catherine didn't laugh.

Henry dreams he is the king of the real estate agents. Henry loves his job. He tries to sell a house to a young couple with twitchy noses and big dark eyes. Why does he always dream that he's trying to sell things?

The couple stare at him nervously. He leans towards them as if he's going to whisper something in their silly, expectant ears. It's a secret he's never told anyone before. It's a secret he didn't even know that he knew. "Let's stop fooling," he says. "You can't afford to buy this house. You don't have any money. You're rabbits."

"Where do you work?" Carleton said, in the morning, when Henry called from Grand Central.

"I work at home," Henry said. "Home where we live now, where you are. Eventually. Just not today. Are you getting ready for school?"

Carleton put the phone down. Henry could hear him saying something to Catherine. "He says he's not nervous about school," she said. "He's a brave kid."

"I kissed you this morning," Henry said, "but you didn't wake up. There were all these rabbits on the lawn. They were huge. King Spanky-sized. They were just sitting there like they were waiting for the sun to come up. It was funny, like some kind of art installation. But it was kind of creepy too. Think they'd been there all night?"

"Rabbits? Can they have rabies? I saw them this morning when I got up," Catherine said. "Carleton didn't want to brush his teeth this morning. He says something's wrong with his toothbrush."

"Maybe he dropped it in the toilet, and he doesn't want to tell you," Henry said.

"Maybe you could buy a new toothbrush and bring it home," Catherine said. "He doesn't want one from the drugstore here. He wants one from New York."

"Where's Tilly?" Henry said.

"She says she's trying to figure out what's wrong with Carleton's toothbrush. She's still in the bathroom." Catherine said.

"Can I talk to her for a second?" Henry said.

"Tell her she needs to get dressed and eat her Cheerios," Catherine said. "After I drive them to school, Liz is coming over for coffee. Then we're going to go out for lunch. I'm not unpacking another box until you get home. Here's Tilly."

"Hi," Tilly said. She sounded as if she were asking a question.

Tilly never liked talking to people on the telephone. How were you supposed to know if they were really who they said they were? And even if they were who they claimed to be, they didn't know whether you were who you said you were. You could be someone else. They might give away information about you, and not even know it. There were no protocols. No precautions.

She said, "Did you brush your teeth this morning?"

"Good morning, Tilly," her father (if it was her father) said. "My toothbrush was fine. Perfectly normal."

"That's good," Tilly said. "I let Carleton use mine."

"That was very generous," Henry said.

"No problem," Tilly said. Sharing things with Carleton wasn't like having to share things with other people. It wasn't really like sharing things at all. Carleton belonged to her, like the toothbrush. "Mom says that when we get home today, we can draw on the walls in our rooms if we want to, while we decide what colour we want to paint them."

"Sounds like fun," Henry said. "Can I draw on them too?"

"Maybe," Tilly said. She had already said too much. "Gotta go. Gotta eat breakfast."

"Don't be worried about school," Henry said.

"I'm not worried about school," Tilly said.

"I love you," Henry said.

"I'm real concerned about this toothbrush," Tilly said.

He only closed his eyes for a minute. Just for a minute. When he woke up, it was dark and he didn't know where he was. He stood up and went over to the door, almost tripping over something. It sailed away from him in an exuberant, rollicking sweep. According to the clock on his desk, it was 4:00 a.m. Why was it always 4:00 a.m.? There were four messages on his cell phone, all from Catherine.

He went online and checked train schedules. Then he sent Catherine a fast e-mail:

Fell asleep @ midnight? Mssed trains. Awake now, going to keep on working. Pttng out fires. Take the train home early afternoon? Still lv me?

Before he went back to work, he kicked the rubber band ball back down the hall toward the Crocodile's door.

Catherine called him at 8:45.

"I'm sorry," Henry said.

"I bet you are," Catherine said.

"I can't find my razor. I think the Crocodile had some kind of tantrum and tossed my stuff."

"Carleton will love that," Catherine said. "Maybe you should sneak in the house and shave before dinner. He had a hard day at school yesterday."

"Maybe I should grow a beard," Henry said. "He can't be afraid of everything, all the time. Tell me about the first day of school."

"We'll talk about it later," Catherine said. "Liz just drove up. I'm going to be her guest at the gym. Just make it home for dinner."

At 6:00 p.m. Henry e-mailed Catherine again. "Srry. Accidentally startd avalanche while puttng out fires. Wait up for me? How ws 2nd day of school?" She didn't write him back. He called and no one picked up the phone. She didn't call.

He took the last train home. By the time it reached the station, he was the only one left in his car. He unchained his bicycle and rode it home in the dark. Rabbits pelted across the footpath in front of his bike. There were rabbits foraging on his lawn. They froze as he dismounted and pushed the bicycle across the grass. The lawn was rumpled; the bike went up and down over invisible depressions that he supposed were rabbit holes. There were two short, fat men standing in the dark on either side of the front door, waiting for him, but when he came closer, he remembered that they were stone rabbits. "Knock, knock," he said.

The real rabbits on the lawn tipped their ears at him. The stone rabbits waited for the punch line, but they were just stone rabbits. They had nothing better to do.

The front door wasn't locked. He walked through the downstairs rooms, putting his hands on the backs and tops of furniture. In the kitchen, cut-down boxes leaned in stacks against the wall, waiting to be recycled or remade into cardboard houses and spaceships and tunnels for Carleton and Tilly.

Catherine had unpacked Carleton's room. Night-lights in the shape of bears and geese and cats were plugged into every floor outlet. There were little low-watt table lamps as well – hippo, robot, gorilla, pirate ship. Everything was soaked in a tender, peaceable light, translating Carleton's room into something more than a bedroom: something luminous, numinous, a cartoony midnight church of sleep.

Tilly was sleeping in the other bed.

Tilly would never admit that she sleepwalked, the same way that she would never admit that she sometimes still wet the bed. But she refused to make friends. Making friends would have meant spending the night in strange houses. Tomorrow morning she would insist that

Henry or Catherine must have carried her from her room, put her to bed in Carleton's room for reasons of their own.

Henry knelt down between the two beds and kissed Carleton on the forehead. He kissed Tilly, smoothed her hair. How could he not love Tilly better? He'd known her longer. She was so brave, so angry.

On the walls of Carleton's bedroom, Henry's children had drawn a house. A cat nearly as big as the house. There was a crown on the cat's head. Trees or flowers with pairs of leaves that pointed straight up, still bigger, and a stick figure on a stick bicycle, riding past the trees. When he looked closer, he thought that maybe the trees were actually rabbits. The wall smelled like Fruit Loops. Someone had written HENRY IS A RAT FINK! HA HA! He recognized his wife's handwriting.

"Scented markers," Catherine said. She stood in the door, holding a pillow against her stomach. "I was sleeping downstairs on the sofa. You walked right past and didn't see me."

"The front door was unlocked," Henry said.

"Liz says nobody ever locks their doors out here," Catherine said. "Are you coming to bed, or were you just stopping by to see how we were?"

"I have to go back in tomorrow." Henry said. He pulled a toothbrush out of his pocket and showed it to her. "There's a box of Krispy Kreme donuts on the kitchen counter."

"Delete the donuts," Catherine said. "I'm not that easy." She took a step towards him and accidentally kicked King Spanky. The cat yowled. Carleton woke up. He said, "Who's there? Who's there?"

"It's me," Henry said. He knelt beside Carleton's bed in the light of the Winnie the Pooh lamp. "I brought you a new toothbrush."

Carleton whimpered.

"What's wrong, spaceman?" Henry said. "It's just a toothbrush." He leaned towards Carleton and Carleton scooted back. He began to scream.

In the other bed, Tilly was dreaming about rabbits. When she'd come home from school, she and Carleton had seen rabbits, sitting on the lawn as if they had kept watch over the house all the time that Tilly had been gone. In her dream they were still there. She dreamed she was creeping up on them. They opened their mouths, wide enough to reach inside like she was some kind of rabbit dentist, and so she did. She put her hand around something small and cold and hard. Maybe it was a ring, a diamond ring. Or a. Or. It was a. She couldn't wait to show Carleton. Her arm was inside the rabbit all the way to her shoulder. Someone put their hand around her wrist and yanked. Somewhere her mother was talking. She said—

"It's the beard."

Catherine couldn't decide whether to laugh or cry or scream like Carleton. That would surprise Carleton, if she started screaming, too. "Shoo! Shoo, Henry – go shave and come back as quick as you can, or else he'll never go back to sleep."

"Carleton, honey," she was saying as Henry left the room. "It's your dad. It's not Santa Claus. It's not the big bad wolf. It's your dad. Your dad just forgot. Why don't you tell me a story? Or do you want to go watch your daddy shave?"

Catherine's hot water bottle was draped over the tub. Towels were heaped on the floor. Henry's things had been put away behind the mirror. It made him feel tired, thinking of all the other things that still had to be put away. He washed his hands, then looked at the bar of soap. It didn't feel right. He put it back on the sink, bent over and sniffed it and then tore off a piece of toilet paper, used the toilet paper to pick up the soap. He threw it in the trash and unwrapped a new bar of soap. There was nothing wrong with the new soap. There was nothing wrong with the old soap either. He was just tired. He washed his hands and lathered up his face, shaved off his beard and watched the little bristles of hair wash down the sink. When he went to show Carleton his brand new face, Catherine was curled up in bed beside Carleton. They were both asleep. They were still asleep when he left the house at 5:30 the next morning.

"Where are you?" Catherine said.

"I'm on my way home. I'm on the train." The train was still in the station. They would be leaving any minute. They had been leaving any minute for the last hour or so, and before that, they had had to get off the train twice, and then back on again. They had been assured there was nothing to worry about. There was no bomb threat. There was no bomb. The delay was only temporary. The people on the train looked at each other, trying to seem as if they were not looking. Everyone had their cell phones out.

"The rabbits are out on the lawn again," Catherine said. "There must be at least fifty or sixty. I've never counted rabbits before. Tilly keeps trying to go outside to make friends with them, but as soon as she's outside, they all go bouncing away like beach balls. I talked to a lawn specialist today. He says we need to do something about it, which is what Liz was saying. Rabbits can be a big problem out here. They've probably got tunnels and warrens all through the yard. It could be a problem. Like living on top of a sinkhole. But Tilly is never going to forgive us. She knows something's up. She says she doesn't want a dog anymore. It would scare away the rabbits. Do you think we should get a dog?"

"So what do they do? Put out poison? Dig up the yard?" Henry said. The man in the seat in front of him got up. He took his bags out of the luggage rack and left the train. Everyone watched him go, pretending they were not.

"He was telling me they have these devices, kind of like ultrasound equipment. They plot out the tunnels, close them up, and then gas the rabbits. It sounds gruesome," Catherine said. "And this kid, this baby has been kicking the daylights out of me. All day long it's kick, kick, jump, kick, like some kind of martial artist. He's going to be an angry kid, Henry. Just like his sister. Her sister. Or maybe I'm going to give birth to rabbits."

"As long as they have your eyes and my chin," Henry said.

"I've gotta go," Catherine said. "I have to pee again. All day long it's the kid jumping, me peeing, Tilly getting her heart broken because she can't make friends with the rabbits, me worrying because she doesn't want to make friends with other kids, just with rabbits, Carleton asking if today he has to go to school, does he have to go to school tomorrow, why am I making him go to school when everybody there is bigger than him, why is my stomach so big and fat, why does his teacher tell him to act like a big boy? Henry, why are we doing this again? Why am I pregnant? And where are you? Why aren't you here? What about our deal? Don't you want to be here?"

"I'm sorry," Henry said. "I'll talk to The Crocodile. We'll work something out."

"I thought you wanted this too, Henry. Don't you?"

"Of course," Henry said. "Of course I want this."

"I've gotta go," Catherine said again. "Liz is bringing some women over. We're finally starting that book club. We're going to read *Fight Club*. Her stepdaughter Alison is going to look after Tilly and Carleton for me. I've already talked to Tilly. She promises she won't bite or hit or make Alison cry."

"What's the trade? A few hours of bonus TV?"

"No," Catherine said. "Something's up with the TV."

"What's wrong with the TV?"

"I don't know," Catherine said. "It's working fine. But the kids won't go near it. Isn't that great? It's the same thing as the toothbrush. You'll see when you get home. I mean, it's not just the kids. I was watching the news earlier, and then I had to turn it off. It wasn't the news. It was the TV."

"So it's the downstairs bathroom and the coffee maker and Carleton's toothbrush and now the TV?"

"There's some other stuff as well, since this morning. Your office, apparently. Everything in it – your desk, your bookshelves, your chair, even the paper clips."

"That's probably a good thing, right? I mean, that way they'll stay out of there."

"I guess," Catherine said. "The thing is, I went and stood in there for a while and it gave me the creeps, too. So now I can't pick up e-mail. And I had to throw out more soap. And King Spanky doesn't love the alarm clock anymore. He won't come out from under the bed when I set it off."

"The alarm clock too?"

"It does sound different," Catherine said. "Just a little bit different. Or maybe I'm insane. This morning, Carleton told me that he knew where our house was. He said we were living in a secret part of Central Park. He said he recognizes the trees. He thinks that if he walks down that little path, he'll get mugged. I've really got to go, Henry, or I'm going to wet my pants, and I don't have time to change again before everyone gets here."

"I love you," Henry said.

"Then why aren't you here?" Catherine said victoriously. She hung up and ran down the hallway towards the downstairs bathroom. But when she got there, she turned around. She went racing up the stairs, pulling down her pants as she went, and barely got to the master bedroom bathroom in time. All day long she'd gone up and down the stairs, feeling extremely silly. There was nothing wrong with the downstairs bathroom. It's just the fixtures. When you flush the toilet or run water in the sink. She doesn't like the sound the water makes.

Several times now, Henry had come home and found Catherine painting rooms, which was a problem. The problem was that Henry kept going away. If he didn't keep going away, he wouldn't have to keep coming home. That was Catherine's point. Henry's point was that Catherine wasn't supposed to be painting rooms while she was pregnant. Pregnant women were supposed to stay away from paint fumes.

Catherine solved this problem by wearing the gas mask while she painted. She had known the gas mask would come in handy. She told Henry she promised to stop painting as soon as he started working at home, which was the plan. Meanwhile, she couldn't decide on colours. She and Carleton and Tilly spent hours looking at paint strips with colours that had names like Sangria, Peat Bog, Tulip, Tantrum, Planetarium, Galactica, Tea Leaf, Egg Yolk, Tinker Toy, Gauguin, Susan, Envy, Aztec, Utopia, Wax Apple, Rice Bowl, Cry Baby, Fat Lip, Green Banana, Trampoline, Finger Nail. It was a wonderful way to spend time. They went off to school, and when they got home, the living room would be Harp Seal instead of Full Moon. They'd spend some time with that colour, getting to know it, ignoring the television, which was haunted (haunted wasn't the right word, of course, but Catherine couldn't think what the right word was) and then a couple of days later, Catherine would go buy some more primer and start again. Carleton and Tilly loved this. They begged her to repaint their bedrooms. She did.

She wished she could eat paint. Whenever she opened a can of paint, her mouth filled with saliva. When she'd been pregnant with Carleton, she hadn't been able to eat anything except for olives and hearts of palm and dry toast. When she'd been pregnant with Tilly, she'd eaten dirt, once, in Central Park. Tilly thought they should name the baby after a paint colour, Chalk, or Dilly Dilly, or Keel-hauled. Lapis Lazulily. Knock, knock.

Catherine kept meaning to ask Henry to take the television and put it in the garage. Nobody ever watched it now. They'd had to stop using the microwave as well, and a colander, some of the flatware, and she was keeping an eye on the toaster. She had a premonition, or an intuition. It didn't feel wrong, not yet, but she had a feeling about it. There was a gorgeous pair of earrings that Henry had given her – how was it possible to be spooked by a pair of diamond earrings? – and yet. Carleton wouldn't play with his Lincoln Logs, and so they were going to the Salvation Army, and Tilly's armadillo purse had disappeared. Tilly hadn't said anything about it, and Catherine hadn't wanted to ask.

Sometimes, if Henry wasn't coming home, Catherine painted after Carleton and Tilly went to bed. Sometimes Tilly would walk into the room where Catherine was working, Tilly's eyes closed, her mouth open, a tourist-somnambulist. She'd stand there, with her head cocked towards Catherine. If Catherine spoke to her, she never answered, and if Catherine took her hand, she would follow Catherine back to her own bed and lie down again. But sometimes Catherine let Tilly stand there and keep her company. Tilly was never so attentive, so *present*, when she was awake. Eventually she would turn and leave the room and Catherine would listen to her climb back up the stairs. Then she would be alone again.

* * *

Catherine dreams about colours. It turns out her marriage was the same colour she had just painted the foyer. Velveteen Fade. Leonard Felter, who had had an ongoing affair with two of his graduate students, several adjuncts, two tenured faculty members, brought down Catherine's entire department, and saved Catherine's marriage, would make a good lipstick or nail polish. Peach Nooky. There's The Crocodile, a particularly bilious Eau De Vil, a colour that tastes bad when you say it. Her mother, who had always been disappointed by Catherine's choices, turned out to have been a beautiful, rich, deep chocolate. Why hadn't Catherine ever seen that before? Too late, too late. It made her want to cry.

Liz and she are drinking paint, thick and pale as cream. "Have some more paint," Catherine says. "Do you want sugar?"

"Yes, lots," Liz says. "What colour are you going to paint the rabbits?"

Catherine passes her the sugar. She hasn't even thought about the rabbits, except which rabbits does Liz mean, the stone rabbits or the real rabbits? How do you make them hold still?

"I got something for you," Liz says. She's got Tilly's armadillo purse. It's full of paint strips. Catherine's mouth fills with water.

Henry dreams he has an appointment with the exterminator. "You've got to take care of this," he says. "We have two small children. These things could be rabid. They might carry plague."

"See what I can do," the exterminator says, sounding glum. He stands next to Henry. He's an odd-looking, twitchy guy. He has big ears. They contemplate the skyscrapers that poke out of the grass like obelisks. The lawn is teeming with skyscrapers. "Never seen anything like this before. Never wanted to see anything like this. But if you want my opinion, it's the house that's the real problem—"

"Never mind about my wife," Henry says. He squats down beside a knee-high art deco skyscraper, and peers into a window. A little man looks back at him and shakes his fists, screaming something obscene. Henry flicks a finger at the window, almost hard enough to break it. He feels hot all over. He's never felt this angry before in his life, not even when Catherine told him that she'd accidentally slept with Leonard Felter. The little bastard is going to regret what he just said, whatever it was. He lifts his foot.

The exterminator says, "I wouldn't do that if I were you. You have to dig them up, get the roots. Otherwise, they just grow back. Like your house. Which is really just the tip of the iceberg lettuce, so to speak. You've probably got seventy, eighty stories underground.

You gone down on the elevator yet? Talked to the people living down there? It's your house, and you're just going to let them live there rent-free? Mess with your things like that?"

"What?" Henry says, and then he hears helicopters, fighter planes the size of hummingbirds. "Is this really necessary?" he says to the exterminator.

The exterminator nods. "You have to catch them off guard."

"Maybe we're being hasty," Henry says. He has to yell to be heard above the noise of the tiny, tinny, furious planes. "Maybe we can settle this peacefully."

"Hemree," the interrogator says, shaking his head. "You called me in, because I'm the expert, and you knew you needed help."

Henry wants to say "You're saying my name wrong." But he doesn't want to hurt the undertaker's feelings.

The alligator keeps on talking. "Listen up, Hemreeee, and shut up about negotiations and such, because if we don't take care of this right away, it may be too late. This isn't about homeownership, or lawn care, Hemreeeeee, this is war. The lives of your children are at stake. The happiness of your family. Be brave. Be strong. Just hang on to your rabbit and fire when you see delight in their eyes."

He woke up. "Catherine," he whispered. "Are you awake? I was having this dream."

Catherine laughed. "That's the phone, Liz," she said. "It's probably Henry, saying he'll be late."

"Catherine," Henry said. "Who are you talking to?"

"Are you mad at me, Henry?" Catherine said. "Is that why you won't come home?"

"I'm right here," Henry said.

"You take your rabbits and your crocodiles and get out of here," Catherine said. "And then come straight home again."

She sat up in bed and pointed her finger. "I am sick and tired of being spied on by rabbits!"

When Henry looked, something stood beside the bed, rocking back and forth on its heels. He fumbled for the light, got it on, and saw Tilly, her mouth open, her eyes closed. She looked larger than she ever did when she was awake. "It's just Tilly," he said to Catherine, but Catherine lay back down again. She put her pillow over her head. When he picked Tilly up, to carry her back to bed, she was warm and sweaty, her heart racing as if she had been running through all the rooms of the house.

He walked through the house. He rapped on walls, testing. He put his ear against the floor. No elevator. No secret rooms, no hidden passageways. There isn't even a basement.

Tilly has divided the yard in half. Carleton is not allowed in her half, unless she gives permission.

From the bottom of her half of the yard, where the trees run beside the driveway, Tilly can barely see the house. She's decided to name the yard Matilda's Rabbit Kingdom. Tilly loves naming things. When the new baby is born, her mother has promised that she can help pick out the real names, although there will only be two real names, a first one and a middle. Tilly doesn't understand why there can only be two. Oishi means delicious in Japanese. That would make a good name, either for the baby or for the yard, because of the grass. She knows the yard isn't as big as Central Park, but it's just as good, even if there aren't any pagodas or castles or carriages or people on roller skates.

There's plenty of grass. There are hundreds of rabbits. They live in an enormous underground city, maybe a city just like New York. Maybe her dad can stop working in New York, and come work under the lawn instead. She could help him, go to work with him. She could be a biologist, like Jane Goodall, and go and live underground with the rabbits. Last year her ambition had been to go and live secretly in the Metropolitan Museum of Art, but someone has already done that, even if it's only in a book. Tilly feels sorry for Carleton. Everything he ever does, she'll have already been there. She'll already have done that.

Tilly has left her armadillo purse sticking out of a rabbit hole. First she made the hole bigger, then she packed the dirt back in around the armadillo so that only the shiny, peeled snout poked out. Carleton digs it out again with his stick. Maybe Tilly meant him to find it. Maybe it was a present for the rabbits, except what is it doing here, in his half of the yard? When he lived in the apartment, he was afraid of the armadillo purse, but there are better things to be afraid of out here. But be careful, Carleton. Might as well be careful. The armadillo purse says don't touch me. So he doesn't. He uses his stick to pry open the snap-mouth, dumps out Tilly's most valuable things, and with his stick pushes them one by one down the hole. Then he puts his ear to the rabbit hole so that he can hear the rabbits say thank you. Saying thank you is polite. But the rabbits say nothing. They're holding their breath, waiting for him to go away. Carleton waits too. Tilly's armadillo, empty and smelly and haunted, makes his eyes water.

Someone comes up and stands behind him. "I didn't do it," he says, "They fell."

But when he turns around, it's the girl who lives next door. Alison. The sun is behind her and makes her shine. He squints. "You can come over to my house if you want to," she says. "Your mom says. She's going to pay me fifteen bucks an hour, which is way too much. Are your parents really rich or something? What's that?"

"It's Tilly's," he says. "But I don't think she wants it any more."

She picks up Tilly's armadillo. "Pretty cool," she says. "Maybe I'll keep it for her."

Deep underground, the rabbits stamp their feet in rage.

Catherine loves the house. She loves her new life. She's never understood people who get stuck, become unhappy, can't change, adapt. So she's out of a job. So what? She'll find something else to do. So Henry can't leave his job yet, won't leave his job yet. So the house is haunted. That's okay. They'll work through it. She buys some books on gardening. She plants a rose bush and a climbing vine in a pot. Tilly helps. The rabbits eat off all the leaves. They bite through the vine.

"Shit," Catherine says, when she sees what they've done. She shakes her fists at the rabbits on the lawn. The rabbits flick their ears at her. They're laughing, she knows it. She's too big to chase after them.

"Henry, wake up. Wake up."

"I'm awake," he said, and then he was. Catherine was crying. noisy, wet, ugly sobs. He put his hand out and touched her face. Her nose was running.

"Stop crying," he said. "I'm awake. Why are you crying?"

"Because you weren't here," she said. "And then I woke up and you were here, but when I wake up tomorrow morning you'll be gone again. I miss you. Don't you miss me?"

"I'm sorry," he said. "I'm sorry I'm not here. I'm here now. Come here."

"No," she said. She stopped crying, but her nose still leaked. "And now the dishwasher is haunted. We have to get a new dishwasher before I have this baby. You can't have a baby and not have a dishwasher. And you have to live here with us. Because I'm going to need some help this time. Remember Carleton, how fucking hard that was."

"He was one cranky baby," Henry said. When Carleton was three months old, Henry had realized that they'd misunderstood something. Babies weren't babies, they were land mines, bear traps, wasp nests. They were a noise, which was sometimes even not a noise, but merely a listening for a noise; they were a damp, chalky smell; they were the heaving, jerky, sticky manifestation of not-sleep. Once Henry had stood and watched Carleton in his crib, sleeping peacefully. He had not done what he wanted to do. He had not bent over and yelled in Carleton's ear. Henry still hadn't forgiven Carleton, not yet, not entirely, not for making him feel that way.

"Why do you have to love your job so much?" Catherine said.

"I don't know," Henry said. "I don't love it."

"Don't lie to me," Catherine said.

"I love you better," Henry said. He does, he does, he does loves Catherine better. He's already made that decision. But she isn't even listening.

"Remember when Carleton was little and you would get up in the morning and go to work and leave me all alone with them?" Catherine poked him in the side. "I used to hate you. You'd come home with takeout, and I'd forget I hated you, but then I'd remember again, and I'd hate you even more because it was so easy for you to trick me, to make things okay again, just because for an hour I could sit in the bathtub and eat Chinese food and wash my hair."

"You used to carry an extra shirt with you, when you went out," Henry said. He put his hand down inside her T-shirt, on her fat, full breast. "In case you leaked."

"You can't touch that breast," Catherine said. "It's haunted." She blew her nose on the sheets.

Catherine's friend Lucy owns an online boutique, Nice Clothes for Fat People. There's a woman in Tarrytown who knits stretchy, sexy argyle sweaters exclusively for NCFP, and Lucy has an appointment with her. She wants to stop off and see Catherine afterwards, before she has to drive back to the city again. Catherine gives her directions, and then begins to clean house, feeling out of sorts. She's not sure she wants to see Lucy right now. Carleton has always been afraid of Lucy, which is embarrassing. And Catherine doesn't want to talk about Henry. She doesn't want to explain about the downstairs bathroom. She had planned to spend the day painting the wood trim in the dining room, but now she'll have to wait.

The doorbell rings, but when Catherine goes to answer it, no one is there. Later on, after Tilly and Carleton have come home, it rings again, but no one is there. It rings and rings, as if Lucy is standing outside, pressing the bell over and over again. Finally Catherine pulls out the wire. She tries calling Lucy's cell phone, but can't get through. Then Henry calls. He says that he's going to be late.

Liz opens the front door, yells, "Hello, anyone home! You've got to see your rabbits, there must be thousands of them. Catherine, is something wrong with your doorbell?"

Henry's bike, so far, was okay. He wondered what they'd do if the Toyota suddenly became haunted. Would Catherine want to sell it? Would resale value be affected? The car and Catherine and the kids were gone when he got home, so he put on a pair of work gloves and went through the house with a cardboard box, collecting all the things that felt haunted. A hairbrush in Tilly's room, an old pair of Catherine's tennis shoes. A pair of Catherine's underwear that he finds at the foot of the bed. When he picked them up he felt a sudden shock of longing for Catherine, like he'd been hit by some kind of spooky lightning. It hit him in the pit of the stomach, like a cramp. He dropped the underwear in the box.

The silk kimono from Takashimaya. Two of Carleton's night-lights. He opened the door to his office, put the box inside. All the hair on his arms stood up. He closed the door.

Then he went downstairs and cleaned paintbrushes. If the paint-brushes were becoming haunted, if Catherine was throwing them out and buying new ones, she wasn't saying. Maybe he should check the Visa bill. How much were they spending on paint anyway?

Catherine came into the kitchen and gave him a hug. "I'm glad you're home," she said. He pressed his nose into her neck and inhaled. "I left the car running – I've got to pee. Would you go pick up the kids for me?"

"Where are they?" Henry said.

"They're over at Liz's. Alison is babysitting them. Do you have money on you?"

"You mean I'll meet some neighbours?"

"Wow, sure," Catherine said. "If you think you're ready. Are you ready? Do you know where they live?"

"They're our neighbours, right?"

"Take a left out of the driveway, go about a quarter of a mile, and they're the red house with all the trees in front."

But when he drove up to the red house and went and rang the doorbell, no one answered. He heard a child come running down a flight of stairs and then stop and stand in front of the door.

"Carleton? Alison?" he said. "Excuse me, this is Catherine's husband, Henry. Carleton and Tilly's dad." The whispering stopped. He
waited for a bit. When he crouched down and lifted the mail slot, he
thought he saw someone's feet, the hem of a coat, something furry? A
dog? Someone standing very still, just to the right of the door?
Carleton, playing games. "I see you," he said, and wiggled his fingers
through the mail slot. Then he thought maybe it wasn't Carleton
after all. He got up quickly and went back to the car. He drove into
town and bought more soap.

Tilly was standing in the driveway when he got home, her hands
on her hips. "Hi Dad," she said. "I'm looking for King Spanky. He
got outside. Look what Alison found."

She held out a tiny toy bow strung with what looked like dental
floss, an arrow the size of a needle.

"Be careful with that," Henry said. "It looks sharp. Archery
Barbie, right? So did you guys have a good time with Alison?"

"Alison's okay," Tilly said. She belched. " 'Scuse me. I don't feel
very good."

"What's wrong?" Henry said.

"My stomach is funny," Tilly said. She looked up at him, frowned,
and then vomited all over his shirt, his pants.

"Tilly!" he said. He yanked off his shirt, used a sleeve to wipe her
mouth. The vomit was foamy and green.

"It tastes horrible," she said. She sounded surprised. "Why does it
always taste so bad when you throw up?"

"So that you won't go around doing it for fun," he said. "Are you
going to do it again?"

"I don't think so," she said, making a face.

"Then I'm going to go wash up and change clothes. What were
you eating, anyway?"

"Grass," Tilly said.

"Well, no wonder," Henry said. "I thought you were smarter than
that, Tilly. Don't do that anymore."

"I wasn't planning to," Tilly said. She spit in the grass.

When Henry opened the front door, he could hear Catherine
talking in the kitchen. "The funny thing is," she said. "none of it was
true. It was just made up, just like something Carleton would do. Just
to get attention."

"Dad," Carleton said. He was jumping up and down on one foot.
"Want to hear a song?"

"I was looking for you," Henry said. "Did Alison bring you home?
Do you need to go to the bathroom?"

"Why aren't you wearing any clothes?" Carleton said.

Someone in the kitchen laughed, as if they had heard this.

"I had an accident," Henry said, whispering. "But you're right, Carleton, I should go change." He took a shower, rinsed and wrung out his shirt, put on clean clothes, but by the time he got downstairs, Catherine and Carleton and Tilly were eating Cheerios for dinner. They were using paper bowls, plastic spoons, as if it were a picnic. "Liz was here, and Alison, but they were going to a movie," she said. "They said they'd meet you some other day. It was awful – when they came in the door, King Spanky went rushing outside. He's been watching the rabbits all day. If he catches one, Tilly is going to be so upset."

"Tilly's been eating grass," Henry said.

Tilly blinked. As if.

"Not again!" Catherine said. "Tilly, real people don't eat grass. Oh, look, fantastic, there's King Spanky. Who let him in? What's he got in his mouth?"

King Spanky sits with his back to them. He coughs and something drops to the floor, maybe a frog, or a baby rabbit. It goes scrabbling across the floor, half-leaping, dragging one leg. King Spanky just sits there, watching as it disappears under the sofa. Carleton freaks out. Tilly is shouting "Bad King Spanky! Bad cat!" When Henry and Catherine push the sofa back, it's too late, there's just King Spanky and a little blob of sticky blood on the floor.

Catherine would like to write a novel. She'd like to write a novel with no children in it. The problem with novels with children in them is that bad things will happen either to the children or else to the parents. She wants to write something funny, something romantic.

It isn't very comfortable to sit down now that she's so big. She's started writing on the walls. She writes in pencil. She names her characters after paint colours. She imagines them leading beautiful, happy, useful lives. No haunted toasters. No mothers no children no crocodiles no photocopy machines no Leonard Felters. She writes for two or three hours, and then she paints the walls again before anyone gets home. That's always the best part.

"I need you next weekend," the Crocodile said. Her rubber band ball sat on the floor beside her desk. She had her feet up on it, in an attempt to show it who was boss. The rubber band ball was getting too big for its britches. Someone was going to have to teach it a lesson, send it a memo.

She looked tired. Henry said, "You don't need me."

"I do," the Crocodile said, yawning. "I *do*. The clients want to take you out to dinner at Lutece when they come in to town. They want to go see musicals with you. *Rent. Phantom of the Cabaret Lion*. They want to go to Coney Island with you and eat hot dogs. They want to go out to trendy bars and clubs and pick up strippers and publicists and performance artists. They want to talk about poetry, philosophy, sports, politics, their lousy relationships with their fathers. They want to ask you for advice about their love lives. They want you to come to the weddings of their children and make toasts. You're indispensable, honey. I hope you know that."

"Catherine and I are having some problems with rabbits," Henry said. The rabbits were easier to explain than the other thing. "They've taken over the yard. Things are a little crazy."

"I don't know anything about rabbits," the Crocodile said, digging her pointy heels into the flesh of the rubber band ball until she could feel the red rubber blood come running out. She pinned Henry with her beautiful, watery eyes.

"Henry." She said his name so quietly that he had to lean forward to hear what she was saying.

She said, "You have the best of both worlds. A wife and children who adore you, a beautiful house in the country, a secure job at a company that depends on you, a boss who appreciates your talents, clients who think you're the shit. You *are* the shit, Henry, and the thing is, you're probably thinking that no one deserves to have all this. You think you have to make a choice. You think you have to give up something. But you don't have to give up anything, Henry, and anyone who tells you otherwise is a fucking rabbit. Don't listen to them. You can have it all. You *deserve* to have it all. You love your job. Do you love your job?"

"I love my job," Henry says. The Crocodile smiles at him tearily. It's true. He loves his job.

When Henry came home, it must have been after midnight, because he never got home before midnight. He found Catherine standing on a ladder in the kitchen, one foot resting on the sink. She was wearing her gas mask, a black cotton sports bra, and a pair of black sweatpants rolled down so far that he could see she wasn't wearing any underwear. Her stomach stuck out so far she had to hold her arms at a funny angle to run the roller up and down the wall in front of her. Up and down in a "V". Then fill the "V" in. She had painted the kitchen ceiling a shade of purple so dark it almost looked black. Midnight Eggplant.

Catherine had recently begun buying paints from a speciality catalogue. All the colours are named after famous books, *Madame Bovary*, *Forever Amber*, *Fahrenheit 451*, *Tin Drum*, *A Curtain of Green*, *Twenty Thousand Leagues Under the Sea*. She was painting the walls *Catch-22*, a novel she'd taught over and over again to undergraduates. It had gone over pretty well. The paint colour was nice too. She couldn't decide if she missed teaching. The thing about teaching and having children is that you always ended up treating your children like undergraduates, and your undergraduates like children. There was a particular tone of voice. She'd even used it on Henry a few times, just to see if it worked.

All the cabinets were fenced around with masking tape, like a crime scene. The room stank of new paint.

Catherine took off the gas mask and said, "Tilly picked it out. What do you think?" Her hands were on her hips. Her stomach poked out at Henry. The gas mask had left a ring of white and red around her eyes and chin.

Henry said, "How was the dinner party?"

"We had fettuccine. Liz and Marcus stayed and helped me do the dishes."

("Is something wrong with your dishwasher?" "No. I mean, yes. We're getting a new one.")

She had had a feeling. It had been a feeling like *déjà vu*, or being drunk, or falling in love. Like teaching. She had imagined an audience of rabbits out on the lawn, watching her dinner party. A classroom of rabbits, watching a documentary. Rabbit television. Her skin had felt electric.

"So she's a lawyer?" Henry said.

"You haven't even met them yet," Catherine said, suddenly feeling possessive. "But I like them. I really, really like them. They wanted to know all about us. You. I think they think that either we're having marriage problems or that you're imaginary. Finally I took Liz upstairs and showed her your stuff in the closet. I pulled out the wedding album and showed them photos."

"Maybe we could invite them over on Sunday? For a cookout?" Henry said.

"They're away next weekend," Catherine said. "They're going up to the mountains on Friday. They have a house up there. They've invited us. To come along."

"I can't," Henry said. "I have to take care of some clients next weekend. Some big shots. We're having some cash flow problems. Besides, are you allowed to go away? Did you check with your doctor, what's his name again, Dr Marks?"

"You mean, did I get my permission slip signed?" Catherine said. Henry put his hand on her leg and held on. "Dr Marks said I'm ship-shape. Those were his exact words. Or maybe he said tip-top. It was something alliterative."

"Well, I guess you ought to go, then," Henry said. He rested his head against her stomach. She let him. He looked so tired. "Before Golf Cart shows up. Or what is Tilly calling the baby now?"

"She's around here somewhere," Catherine said. "I keep putting her back in her bed and she keeps getting out again. Maybe she's looking for you."

"Did you get my e-mail?" Henry said. He was listening to Catherine's stomach. He wasn't going to stop touching her unless she told him to.

"You know I can't check e-mail on your computer anymore," Catherine said.

"This is so stupid," Henry said. "This house isn't haunted. There isn't any such thing as a haunted house."

"It isn't the house," Catherine said. "It's the stuff we brought with us. Except for the downstairs bathroom, and that might just be a draft, or an electrical problem. The house is fine. I love the house."

"Our stuff is fine," Henry said. "I love our stuff."

"If you really think our stuff is fine," Catherine said, "then why did you buy a new alarm clock? Why do you keep throwing out the soap?"

"It's the move," Henry said. "It's was a hard move."

"King Spanky hasn't eaten his food in three days," Catherine said. "At first I thought it was the food, and I bought new food and he came down and ate it and I realized it wasn't the food, it was King Spanky. I couldn't sleep all night, knowing he was up under the bed. Poor spooky guy. I don't know what to do. Take him to the vet? What do I say? Excuse me, but I think my cat is haunted? Anyway, I can't get him out of the bed. Not even with the old alarm clock, the haunted one."

"I'll try," Henry said. "Let me try and see if I can get him out." But he didn't move. Catherine tugged at a piece of his hair and he put up his hand. She gave him her roller. He popped off the cylinder and bagged it and put it in the freezer, which was full of paintbrushes and other rollers. He helped Catherine down from the ladder. "I wish you would stop painting."

"I can't," she said. "It has to be perfect. If I can just get it right, then everything will go back to normal and stop being haunted and the rabbits won't tunnel under the house and make it fall down, and you'll come home and stay home, and our neighbours will finally get to meet you and they'll like you and you'll like them, and Carleton will stop being afraid of everything, and Tilly will fall asleep in her own bed, and stay there, and—"

"Hey," Henry said. "It's all going to work out. It's all good. I really like this colour."

"I don't know," Catherine said. She yawned. "You don't think it looks too old-fashioned?"

They went upstairs and Catherine took a bath while Henry tried to coax King Spanky out of the bed. But King Spanky wouldn't come out. When Henry got down on his hands and knees, and stuck the flashlight under the bed, he could see King Spanky's eyes, his tail hanging down from the box frame.

Out on the lawn the rabbits were perfectly still. Then they sprang up in the air, turning and dropping and landing and then freezing again. Catherine stood at the window of the bathroom, towelling her hair. She turned the bathroom light off, so that she could see them better. The moonlight picked out their shining eyes, the moon-coloured fur, each hair tipped in paint. They were playing some rabbit game like leapfrog. Or they were dancing the quadrille. Fighting a rabbit war. Did rabbits fight wars? Catherine didn't know. They ran at each other and then turned and darted back, jumping and crouching and rising up on their back legs. A pair of rabbits took off in tandem, like racehorses, sailing through the air and over a long curled shape in the grass. Then back over again. She put her face against the window. It was Tilly, stretched out against the grass, Tilly's legs and feet bare and white.

"Tilly," she said, and ran out of the bathroom, wearing only the towel around her hair.

"What is it?" Henry said, as Catherine darted past him, and down the stairs. He ran after her, and by the time she had opened the front door, was kneeling beside Tilly, the wet grass tickling her thighs and her belly, Henry was there too and he picked up Tilly and carried her back into the house. They wrapped her in a blanket and put her in her bed and because neither of them wanted to sleep in the bed where King Spanky was hiding, they lay down on the sofa in the family room, curled up against each other. When they woke up in the morning, Tilly was asleep in a ball at their feet.

*   *   *

For a minute or two, last year, Catherine thought she had it figured out. She was married to a man whose speciality was solving problems, salvaging bad situations. If she did something dramatic enough, if she fucked up badly enough, it would save her marriage. And it did, except that once the problem was solved and the marriage was saved and the baby was conceived and the house was bought, then Henry went back to work.

She stands at the window in the bedroom and looks out at all the trees. For a minute she imagines that Carleton is right, and they are living in Central Park and 5th Avenue is just right over there. Henry's office is just a few blocks away. All those rabbits are just tourists.

Henry wakes up in the middle of the night. There are people downstairs. He can hear women talking, laughing and he realizes Catherine's book club must have come over. He gets out of bed. It's dark. What time is it anyway? But the alarm clock is haunted again. He unplugs it. As he comes down the stairs, a voice says, "Well, will you look at that!" and then, "Right under his nose the whole time!"

Henry walks through the house, turning on lights. Tilly stands in the middle of the kitchen. "May I ask who's calling?" she says. She's got Henry's cell phone tucked between her shoulder and her face. She's holding it upside down. Her eyes are open, but she's asleep.

"Who are you talking to?" Henry says.

"The rabbits," Tilly says. She tilts her head, listening. Then she laughs. "Call back later," she says. "He doesn't want to talk to you. Yeah. Okay." She hands Henry his phone. "They said it's no one you know."

"Are you awake?" Henry says.

"Yes," Tilly says, still asleep. He carries her back upstairs. He makes a bed out of pillows in the hall closet and lays her down across them. He tucks a blanket around her. If she refuses to wake up in the same bed that she goes to sleep in, then maybe they should make it a game. If you can't beat them, join them.

Catherine hadn't had an affair with Leonard Felter. She hadn't even slept with him. She had just said she had, because she was so mad at Henry. She could have slept with Leonard Felter. The opportunity had been there. And he had been magical, somehow: the only member of the department who could make the photocopier make copies, and he was nice to all of the secretaries. Too nice, as it turned out. And then, when it turned out that Leonard Felter had been fucking everyone, Catherine had felt she couldn't take it back. So she and Henry had gone to therapy together. Henry had taken some time off work. They'd taken the kids to Disney World. They'd gotten pregnant. She'd been remorseful for something she hadn't done. Henry had forgiven her. Really, she'd saved their marriage. But it had been the sort of thing you could only do once.

If someone had to save the marriage a second time, it would have to be Henry.

Henry went looking for King Spanky. They were going to see the vet: he had the cat cage in the car, but no King Spanky. It was early afternoon, and the rabbits were out on the lawn. Up above, a bird hung, motionless, on a hook of air. Henry craned his head, looking up. It was a big bird, a hawk maybe? It circled, once, twice, again, and then dropped like a stone, towards the rabbits. The rabbits didn't move. There was something about the way they waited, as if this was all a game. The bird cut through the air, folded like a knife, and then it jerked, tumbled, fell. The wings loose. The bird smashed into the grass and feathers flew up. The rabbits moved closer, as if investigating.

Henry went to see for himself. The rabbits scattered, and the lawn was empty. No rabbits, no bird. But there, down in the trees, beside the bike path, Henry saw something move. King Spanky swung his tail angrily, slunk into the woods.

When Henry came out of the woods, the rabbits were back guarding the lawn again and Catherine was calling his name. "Where were you?" she said. She was wearing her gas mask around her neck, and there was a smear of paint on her arm. Whiskey Horse. She'd been painting the linen closet.

"King Spanky took off," Henry said. "I couldn't catch him. I saw the weirdest thing – this bird was going after the rabbits, and then it fell—"

"Marcus came by," Catherine said. Her cheeks were flushed. He knew that if he touched her, her skin would be hot. "He stopped by to see if you wanted to go play golf."

"Who wants to play golf?" Henry said. "I want to go upstairs with you. Where are the kids?"

"Alison took them into town, to see a movie," Catherine said. "I'm going to pick them up at three."

Henry lifted the gas mask off her neck, fitted it around her face. He unbuttoned her shirt, undid the clasp of her bra. "Better take this off," he said. "Better take all your clothes off. I think they're haunted."

"You know what would make a great paint colour? Can't believe no one has done this yet. Yellow Sticky. What about King Spanky?" Catherine said. She sounded like Darth Vader, maybe on purpose, and Henry thought it was sexy: Darth Vader, pregnant, with his child. She put her hand against his chest and shoved. Not too hard, but harder than she meant to. It turned out that painting had given her some serious muscle. That will be a good thing when she has another kid to haul around.

"Yellow Sticky. That's great. Forget King Spanky," Henry said. "He's great."

Catherine was painting Tilly's room Lavender Fist. It was going to be a surprise. But when Tilly saw it, she burst into tears. "Why can't you just leave it alone?" she said. "I liked it the way it was."

"I thought you liked purple," Catherine said, astounded. She took off her gas mask.

"I hate purple," Tilly said. "And I hate you. You're so fat. Even Carleton thinks so."

"Tilly!" Catherine said. She laughed. "I'm pregnant, remember?"

"That's what you think," Tilly said. She ran out of the room and across the hall. There were crashing noises, the sounds of things breaking.

"Tilly!" Catherine said.

Tilly stood in the middle of Carleton's room. All around her lay broken night-lights, lamps, broken light bulbs. The carpet was dusted in glass. Tilly's feet were bare and Catherine looked down, realized that she wasn't wearing shoes either. "Don't move, Tilly," she said.

"They were haunted," Tilly said and began to cry.

"So how come your dad's never home?" Alison said.

"I don't know," Carleton said. "Guess what? Tilly broke all my night-lights?"

"Yeah," Alison said. "You must be pretty mad."

"No, it's good that she did," Carleton said, explaining. "They were haunted. Tilly didn't want me to be afraid."

"But aren't you afraid of the dark?" Alison said.

"Tilly said I shouldn't be," Carleton said. "She said the rabbits stay awake all night, that they make sure everything is okay, even when it's dark. Tilly slept outside once, and the rabbits protected her."

"So you're going to stay with us this weekend," Alison said.

"Yes," Carleton said.

"But your dad isn't coming," Alison said.

"No," Carleton said. "I don't know."

"Want to go higher?" Alison said. She pushed the swing and sent him soaring.

When Henry puts his hand against the wall in the living room, it gives a little, as if the wall is pregnant. The paint under the paint is wet. He walks around the house, running his hands along the walls. Catherine has been painting a mural in the foyer. She's painted trees and trees and trees. Golden trees with brown leaves and green leaves and red leaves, and reddish trees with purple leaves and yellow leaves and pink leaves. She's even painted some leaves on the wooden floor, as if the trees are dropping them. "Catherine," he says. "You have got to stop painting the damn walls. The rooms are getting smaller."

Nobody says anything back. Catherine and Tilly and Carleton aren't home. It's the first time Henry has spent the night alone in his house. He can't sleep. There's no television to watch. Henry throws out all of Catherine's paintbrushes. But when Catherine gets home, she'll just buy new ones.

He sleeps on the couch, and during the night someone comes and stands and watches him sleep. Tilly. Then he wakes up and remembers that Tilly isn't there.

The rabbits watch the house all night long. It's their job.

Tilly is talking to the rabbits. It's cold outside, and she's lost her gloves. "What's your name?" she says. "Oh, you beauty. You beauty." She's on her hands and knees. Carleton watches from his side of the yard.

"Can I come over?" he says. "Can I please come over?"

Tilly ignores him. She gets down on her hands and knees, moving even closer to the rabbits. There are three rabbits, one of them almost close enough to touch. If she moved her hand, slowly, maybe she could grab one by the ears. Maybe she can catch one and train it to live inside. They need a pet rabbit. King Spanky is haunted. He spends most of his time outside. Her parents keep their bedroom door shut so that King Spanky can't get in.

"Good rabbit," Tilly says. "Just stay still. Stay still."

The rabbits flick their ears. Carleton begins to sing a song Alison has taught them, a skipping song. Carleton is such a girl. Tilly puts out her hand. There's something tangled around the rabbit's neck, like a piece of string or a leash. She wiggles closer, holding out her hand. She stares and stares and can hardly believe her eyes. There's a person, a little man sitting behind the rabbit's ears, holding on to the rabbit's fur and the piece of knotted string, with one hand. His other hand is cocked back, like he's going to throw something. He's looking right at her – his hand flies forward and something hits her hand. She pulls her hand back, astounded. "Hey!" she says, and she falls over on her side and watches the rabbits go springing away. "Hey, you! Come back!"

"What?" Carleton yells. He's frantic. "What are you doing? Why won't you let me come over?"

She closes her eyes, just for a second. Shut up, Carleton. Just shut up. Her hand is throbbing and she lies down, holds her hand up to her face. Shut. Up.

Wake up. Wake *up*. When she wakes up, Carleton is sitting beside her. "What are you doing on my side?" she says and he shrugs.

"What are you doing?" he says. He rocks back and forth on his knees. "Why did you fall over?"

"None of your business," she says. She can't remember what she was doing. Everything looks funny. Especially Carleton. "What's wrong with you?"

"Nothing's wrong with me," Carleton says, but something is wrong. She studies his face and begins to feel sick, as if she's been eating grass. Those sneaky rabbits! They've been distracting her, and now, while she wasn't paying attention, Carleton's become haunted.

"Oh yes it is," Tilly says, forgetting to be afraid, forgetting her hand hurts, getting angry instead. She's not the one to blame. This is her mother's fault, her father's fault, and it's Carleton's fault, too. How could he have let this happen? "You just don't know it's wrong. I'm going to tell Mom."

Haunted Carleton is still a Carleton who can be bossed around. "Don't tell," he begs.

Tilly pretends to think about this, although she's already made up her mind. Because what can she say? Either her mother will notice that something's wrong or else she won't. Better to wait and see. "Just stay away from me," she tells Carleton. "You give me the creeps."

Carleton begins to cry, but Tilly is firm. He turns around, walks slowly back to his half of the yard, still crying. For the rest of the afternoon, he sits beneath the azalea bush at the edge of his side of the yard, and cries. It gives Tilly the creeps. Her hand throbs where something has stung it. The rabbits are all hiding underground. King Spanky has gone hunting.

*   *   *

"What's up with Carleton?" Henry said, coming downstairs. He couldn't stop yawning. It wasn't that he was tired, although he was tired. He hadn't given Carleton a goodnight kiss, just in case it turned out he was coming down with a cold. He didn't want Carleton to catch it. But it looked like Carleton, too, was already coming down with something.

Catherine shrugged. Paint samples were balanced across her stomach like she'd been playing solitaire. All weekend long, away from the house, she'd thought about repainting Henry's office. She'd never painted a haunted room before. Maybe if you mixed the paint with a little bit of holy water? She wasn't sure: What was holy water, anyway? Could you buy it? "Tilly's being mean to him," she said. "I wish they would make some friends out here. He keeps talking about the new baby, about how he'll take care of it. He says it can sleep in his room. I've been trying to explain babies to him, about how all they do is sleep and eat and cry."

"And get bigger," Henry said.

"That too," Catherine said. "So did he go to sleep okay?"

"Eventually," Henry said. "He's just acting really weird."

"How is that different from usual?" Catherine said. She yawned. "Is Tilly finished with her homework?"

"I don't know," Henry said. "You know, just weird. Different weird. Maybe he's going through a weird spell. Tilly wanted me to help her with her math, but I couldn't get it to come out right. So what's up with my office?"

"I cleared it out," Catherine said. "Alison and Liz came over and helped. I told them we were going to redecorate. Why is it that we're the only ones who notice everything is fucking haunted around here?"

"So where'd you put my stuff?" Henry said. "What's up?"

"You're not working here now," Catherine pointed out. She didn't sound angry, just tired. "Besides, it's all haunted, right? So I took your computer into the shop, so they could have a look at it. I don't know, maybe they can unhaunt it."

"Well," Henry said. "Okay. Is that what you told them? It's haunted?"

"Don't be ridiculous," Catherine said. She discarded a paint strip. Too lemony. "So I heard about the bomb scare on the radio."

"Yeah," Henry said. "The subways were full of kids with crew cuts and machine guns. And they evacuated our building for about an hour. We all went and stood outside, holding onto our laptops like idiots, just in case. The Crocodile carried out her rubber band

ball, which must weigh about thirty pounds. It kind of freaked
people out, even the firemen. I thought the bomb squad was going
to blow it up. So tell me about your weekend."

"Tell me about yours," Catherine said.

"You know," Henry said. "Those clients are assholes. But they
don't know they're assholes, so it's kind of okay. You just have to
feel sorry for them. They don't get it. You have to explain how to
have fun, and then they get anxious, so they drink a lot and so you
have to drink too. Even The Crocodile got drunk. She did this weird
wriggly dance to a Pete Seeger song. So what's their place like?"

"It's nice," Catherine said. "You know, really nice."

"So you had a good weekend? Carleton and Tilly had a good
time?"

"It was really nice," Catherine said. "No, really, it was great. I had
a fucking great time. So you're sure you can make it home for dinner
on Thursday."

It wasn't a question.

"Carleton looks like he might be coming down with something,"
Henry said. "Here. Do you think I feel hot? Or is it cold in here?"

Catherine said, "You're fine. It's going to be Liz and Marcus and
some of the women from the book group and their husbands, and
what's her name, the real estate agent. I invited her too. Did you
know she's written a book? I was going to do that! I'm getting the
new dishwasher tomorrow. No more paper plates. And the lawn care
specialist is coming on Monday to take care of the rabbits. I thought
I'd drop off King Spanky at the vet, take Tilly and Carleton back to
the city, stay with Lucy for two or three days – did you know she
tried to find this place and got lost? She's supposed to come up for
dinner too – just in case the poison doesn't go away right away, you
know, or in case we end up with piles of dead rabbits on the lawn.
Your job is to make sure there are no dead rabbits when I bring Tilly
and Carleton back."

"I guess I can do that," Henry said.

"You'd better," Catherine said. She stood up, with some difficulty,
and came and leaned over his chair. Her stomach bumped into his
shoulder. Her breath was hot. Her hands were full of strips of colour.
"Sometimes I wish that instead of working for the Crocodile, you
were having an affair with her. I mean, that way you'd come home
when you're supposed to. You wouldn't want me to be suspicious."

"I don't have any time to have affairs," Henry said. He sounded
put out. Maybe he was thinking about Leonard Felter. Or maybe he
was picturing the Crocodile naked. The Crocodile wearing stretchy

red rubber sex gear. Catherine imagined telling Henry the truth about Leonard Felter. I didn't have an affair. Did not. Is that a problem?

"That's exactly what I mean," Catherine said. "You'd better be here for dinner. You live here, Henry. You're my husband. I want you to meet our friends. I want you to be here when I have this baby. I want you to fix what's wrong with the downstairs bathroom. I want you to talk to Tilly. She's having a rough time. She won't talk to me about it."

"Tilly's fine," Henry said. "We had a long talk tonight. She said she's sorry she broke all of Carleton's night-lights. I like the trees, by the way. You're not going to paint over them, are you?"

"I had all this leftover paint," Catherine said. "I was getting tired of just painting with the rollers. I wanted to do something fancier."

"You could paint some trees in my office, when you paint my office."

"Maybe," Catherine said. "Ooof, this baby won't stop kicking me." She lay down on the floor in front of Henry, and lifted her feet into his lap. "Rub my feet. I've still got so much fucking paint. But once your office is done, I'm done with the painting. Tilly told me to stop it or else. She keeps hiding my gas mask. Will you be here for dinner?"

"I'll be here for dinner," Henry said, rubbing her feet. He really meant it. He was thinking about the exterminator, about rabbit corpses scattered all across the lawn, like a war zone. Poor rabbits. What a mess.

After they went to see the therapist, after they went to Disney World and came home again, Henry said to Catherine, "I don't want to talk about it any more. I don't want to talk about it ever again. Can we not talk about it?"

"Talk about what?" Catherine said. But she had almost been sorry. It had been so much work. She'd had to invent so many details that eventually it began to seem as if she hadn't made it up after all. It was too strange, too confusing, to pretend it had never happened, when, after all, it *had* never happened.

Catherine is dressing for dinner. When she looks in the mirror, she's as big as a cruise ship. A water tower. She doesn't look like herself at all. The baby kicks her right under the ribs.

"Stop that," she says. She's sure the baby is going to be a girl. Tilly won't be pleased. Tilly has been extra good all day. She helped make the salad. She set the table. She put on a nice dress.

Tilly is hiding from Carleton under a table in the foyer. If Carleton finds her, Tilly will scream. Carleton is haunted, and nobody has noticed. Nobody cares except Tilly. Tilly says names for the baby, under her breath. Dollop. Shampool. Custard. Knock, knock. The rabbits are out on the lawn, and King Spanky has gotten into the bed again, and he won't come out, not for a million haunted alarm clocks.

Her mother has painted trees all along the wall under the staircase. They don't look like real trees. They aren't real colours. It doesn't look like Central Park at all. In among the trees, her mother has painted a little door. It isn't a real door, except that when Tilly goes over to look at it, it is real. There's a doorknob, and when Tilly turns it, the door opens. Underneath the stairs, there's another set of stairs, little dirt stairs, going down. On the third stair, there's a rabbit sitting there, looking up at Tilly. It hops down, one step, and then another. Then another.

"Rumpled Stiltskin!" Tilly says to the rabbit. "Lipstick!"

Catherine goes to the closet to get out Henry's pink shirt. What's the name of that real estate agent? Why can't she ever remember? She lays the shirt on the bed and then stands there for a moment, stunned. It's too much. The pink shirt is haunted. She pulls out all of Henry's suits, his shirts, his ties. All haunted. Every fucking thing is haunted. Even the fucking shoes. When she pulls out the drawers, socks, underwear, handkerchiefs, everything, it's all spoiled. All haunted. Henry doesn't have a thing to wear. She goes downstairs, gets trash bags, and goes back upstairs again. She begins to dump clothes into the trash bags.

She can see Carleton framed in the bedroom window. He's chasing the rabbits with a stick. She hoists open the window, leans out, yells, "Stay away from those fucking rabbits, Carleton! Do you hear me?"

She doesn't recognize her own voice.

Tilly is running around downstairs somewhere. She's yelling too, but her voice gets farther and farther away, fainter and fainter. She's yelling, "Hairbrush! Zeppelin! Torpedo! Marmalade!"

The doorbell rings.

The Crocodile started laughing. "Okay, Henry. Calm down."

He fired off another rubber band. "I mean it," he said. "I'm late. I'll be late. She's going to kill me."

"Tell her it's my fault," The Crocodile said. "So they started dinner without you. Big deal."

"I tried calling," Henry said. "Nobody answered." He had an idea that the phone was haunted now. That's why Catherine wasn't answering. They'd have to get a new phone. Maybe the lawn specialist would know a house specialist. Maybe somebody could do something about this. "I should go home," he said. "I should go home right now." But he didn't get up. "I think we've gotten ourselves into a mess, me and Catherine. I don't think things are good right now."

"Tell someone who cares," The Crocodile suggested. She wiped at her eyes. "Get out of here. Go catch your train. Have a great weekend. See you on Monday."

So Henry goes home, he has to go home, but of course he's late, it's too late. The train is haunted. The closer they get to his station, the more haunted the train gets. None of the other passengers seem to notice. It makes Henry sick to his stomach. And of course, his bike turns out to be haunted, too. It's too much. He can't ride it home. He leaves it at the station and he walks home in the dark, down the bike path. Something follows him home. Maybe it's King Spanky.

Here's the yard, and here's his house. He loves his house, how it's all lit up. You can see right through the windows, you can see the living room, which Catherine has painted Ghost Crab. The trim is Rat Fink. Catherine has worked so hard. The driveway is full of cars, and inside, people are eating dinner. They're admiring Catherine's trees. They haven't waited for him, and that's fine. His neighbours: he loves his neighbours. He's going to love them as soon as he meets them. His wife is going to have a baby any day now. His daughter will stop walking in her sleep. His son isn't haunted. The moon shines down and paints the world a colour he's never seen before. Oh, Catherine, wait till you see this. Shining lawn, shining rabbits, shining world. The rabbits are out on the lawn. They've been waiting for him, all this time, they've been waiting. Here's his rabbit, his very own rabbit. Who needs a bike? He sits on his rabbit, legs pressed against the warm, silky, shining flanks, one hand holding on to the rabbit's fur, the knotted string around its neck. He has something in his other hand, and when he looks, he sees it's a spear. All around him, the others are sitting on their rabbits, waiting patiently, quietly. They've been waiting for a long time, but the waiting is almost over. In a little while, the dinner party will be over and the war will begin.

KIM NEWMAN

Soho Golem

KIM NEWMAN HAS WON the Bram Stoker Award, the British Fantasy Award, the British Science Fiction Award, the Children of the Night Award, the Fiction Award of the Lord Ruthven Assembly and the International Horror Critics Guild Award.

Author, reviewer and broadcaster, his novels include *The Night Mayor*, *Bad Dreams*, *Jago*, *The Quorum*, *Back in the USSR* (with Eugene Byrne), *Life's Lottery* and the acclaimed *Anno Dracula* sequence – comprising the title novel, plus *The Bloody Red Baron* and *Judgment of Tears* (aka *Dracula Cha Cha Cha*).

Newman's short fiction, which is often linked by recurring themes and characters, has been collected in *The Original Dr Shade and Other Stories*, *Famous Monsters*, *Seven Stars*, *Unforgivable Stories*, *Where the Bodies Are Buried* and *Dead Travel Fast*. *Time and Relative* is a prequel to the BBC-TV series in Telos Publishing's "Doctor Who Novellas" series, and his non-fiction study *TV Classics: Doctor Who* is published by the British Film Institute.

Forthcoming are *Horror: Another 100 Best Books* (with Stephen Jones) from Carroll & Graf, and a collection of stories for MonkeyBrain Books with the probable title *The Man from the Diogenes Club*.

"'Soho Golem' is another in the series of 1970s-set barbed pulp-nostalgia stories," explains Newman. "I'd just written the substantial 'Swellhead' (in *Night Visions 11*), which brings the character of Jeperson into the present day, and wanted to get back to his 1970s heyday.

"Here, I wanted to get into the history of the British sex industry (traditionally associated with Soho), especially in its faintly embarrassing 1970s period but with roots in things like the nude volleyball films of the late 1950s and the saucy Soho of early 1960s films like *Beat Girl* and *Too Hot to Handle* (from which I poached a character).

"Looking at artefacts like the *Confessions* series of books and films, it's impossible to imagine they were ever considered a) hot stuff, b) funny or c) profitable – but they displaced some considerable cultural water at the time. Now, there are a few good books about British sex films or the life and works of Mary Millington, but when these things were going on, it was under everyone's radar.

"I remember wandering through Soho with my friend Dean Skilton some time in the 1970s, looking into shops that sold 8mm cut-downs of Laurel & Hardy or Universal horror films out front with doubtless more dubious business in the backroom, and some wideboy type scared us away by offering a good deal on a dozen reels of Nazi concentration camp atrocity footage.

"There are some proper bits of history here, especially about police corruption and the seedier side of the entertainment industry – but mostly the story's for fun."

"Of all quarters in the queer adventurous amalgam called London, Soho is perhaps least suited to the Forsyte spirit . . . Untidy, full of Greeks, Ishmaelites, cats, Italians, tomatoes, restaurants, organs, coloured stuffs, queer names, people looking out of upper windows, it dwells remote from the British Body Politic."

—John Galsworthy

I Spoiling the Barrel

ON A FINE MAY DAY in 197–, Fred Regent and Richard Jeperson stood in Old Compton Street, London W1. The pavement underfoot was warm and slightly tacky, as if it might retain the prints of Fred's scruffy but sturdy Doc Martens and Richard's elastic-sided claret-coloured thigh-high boots.

Slightly to the North of but parallel with the theatrical parade of Shaftesbury Avenue, Old Compton Street was among Soho's main thoroughfares. Blitzed in the War, the square mile patch had regenerated patchwork fashion to satisfy or exploit the desires of a constant flux of passers-through. People came here for every kind of "lift". Italian coffee-houses had opened on this street a century ago; now, you could buy a thousand varieties of frothy heart-attack in a cup. This was where waves of "dangerous" music broke, from bebop to glitter rock. Within sight, careers had begun and ended: Tommy Steele strumming in an espresso skiffle trio, Jimi Hendrix choking in an alley beside The Intrepid Fox.

Also, famously and blatantly, Soho was a red-light district, home to the city's vice rackets for two hundred years. Above window displays were neon and plastic come-ons: GIRLS GIRLS GIRLS – LIVE NUDE BED REVUE – GOLDILOXXX AND THE THREE BARES. Above doorbells were hand-printed cards: FRENCH MODEL ONE FLIGHT UP, BUSTY BRUNETTE, BELL TWO, HOUSE OF THWACKS: DISCIPLINE ENFORCED.

Fred checked the address against his scribbled note. "The scene of the crime," he told Richard.

Richard took off and folded his slim, side-panelled sunglasses. They slid into a tube that clipped to his top pocket like a thick fountain-pen. "Just the one crime?" he said.

"Couldn't say, guv," replied Fred. "One big one, so far this week."

Richard shrugged – which, in today's peacock-pattern watered silk safari jacket, was dangerously close to flouncing. Even in the cosmopolitan freak show of Soho, Richard's Carnabethan ensemble attracted attention from all sexes. Currently, he wore scarlet buccaneer britches fit tighter than a surgical glove, a black-and-white spiral-pattern beret pinned to his frizzy length of coal-black hair, a frill-fronted mauve shirt with collar-points wider than his shoulders, and a filmy ascot whose colours shifted with the light.

"I certainly *feel* a measure of recent turmoil," said Richard, who called himself 'sensitive' rather than 'spooky'. He flexed long fingers, as if taking a Braille reading from the air. "It certainly could be a death unnatural and occult. Still, in this parish, it'd be unusual *not* to find a soupçon of eldritch atmos., eh? This is East of Piccadilly, *mon ami*. Vibes swirl like a walnut whip. If London has a psychic storm centre, it's on this page of the *A to Z*. Look about, pal – most punters here are dowsing with their dickybirds. It's not hard to find water."

A skinny blonde in hot-pants, platforms and a paisley halter-top sidled out of Crawford Street. She cast a lazy look at them, eyes hoisting pennyweights of pancake and false lash. Richard bowed to her with a cavalier flourish, smile lifting his Fu Manchu. The girl's own psychic powers cut in.

"Fuzz," she sniffed, and scarpered.

"Everyone's a detective," Richard observed, straightening.

"Or a tart," said Fred.

The girl fled. Heart-shaped windows cut out of the seat of her shorts showed pale skin and a silver of marks-and-sparks knicker. Four-inch stack-soles made for a tottering, *Thunderbirds*-puppet gait which was funnier than sexy.

"That said, shouldn't this place be veritably *swarming* with the filth?" commented Richard. "One of their own down, and all that. Uniforms, sirens, yellow tape across the door, Black Mariahs hauling in the usual susses, grasses shaken down? All holidays cancelled, whole shift working overtime to nick the toerag who snuffed a copper while he was about his duty? And where's the wreath? There should be one on the street, with some junior Hawkshaw posted in that alcove there, in case the crim revisits the scene to gloat and lingers long enough to get nabbed."

Richard had put his finger on something which had bothered Fred. One of the man's talents was noticing things unusual by their absence. The proverbial dog that didn't bark in the night.

"This isn't Dock Green, Richard. And DI Brian 'Boot Boy' Booth isn't – *wasn't* – George Dixon."

Now he thought about it, Fred wondered if Busy had even told the Yard about Booth. He might have thought giving Fred the shout was all duty, and a sense of self-preservation, required. In which case, there would be a load of forms to fill in before bed-time.

Usually, Fred got involved in cases by Richard. They were both assets of the Diogenes Club, an institution that quietly existed to cope with matters beyond the purview of regular police and intelligence services. Last month, it had been flower children plucked from Glastonbury Tor by "bright lights in the sky" which the boffins reckoned were extra-dimensional rather than extra-terrestrial; before that, a Brixton *papa loa* whose racket was giving out teterodotoxin-cut ganja at a street festival and enslaving a cadre of *zombis* through the voodoo beat of a reggae number Fred still couldn't get out of his head.

This time, the call came directly to Fred from Harry "Busy" Boddey. Fred's secondment to work with Richard had been extended so long he sometimes forgot he was still a sergeant in the Metropolitan Police, with space in the boot-rack at New Scotland Yard. He hadn't seen Busy since Hendon College, which was deliberate. DC Boddey was a trimmer, a taker-of-shortcuts; the cheery cheeky chappie chatter and carved-into-his-cheeks smirk didn't distract from ice-chips in his eyes. Through rozzer gossip, Fred heard Busy had landed his dream job.

On the phone, Busy hadn't sounded as if he were still smirking. "It's my guv'nor, Freddo," he had explained. "DI Booth is dead.

Killed. It's one of yours, pal. One of the *weird ones*, y'know. Off the books. So far off the books it's not even on the bloody shelf. The horror shows that bring out that long-haired *pouffe* with the 'tache and the clothes. Booth was *smashed*. While sittin' in his office. Looks like he was hit by a bleedin' express train. Five blokes with sledge-hammers couldn't do that much damage."

Fred's first reaction was to assume five blokes with sledge-hammers had outdone themselves and the regular plods could track them easily by the blood-drip trail. Gruesome, admittedly, but hardly in the same docket as time-warping Nazi demons, extra-dimensional hippie harvesting, spirits of ancient Egypt, dread-locked rasta zombies or brain-bending seminars in Sussex. Still, the Diogenes Club had nothing on at the moment and it was sunny out. No point lazing around the flat on an inflatable chair with a slow leak, with the snooker commentator on the BBC continually rubbing it in that he hadn't sprung for a colour telly ("for those of you watching in black and white, Reardon's coming up on the pink.") Once Busy was off the line, Fred had given Richard a bell and arranged to meet him here, outside Booth's Soho HQ.

Richard arched an elegant eyebrow. " 'Skinderella's'?"

The name was up in glittery purple letters, surrounded by silver-paper suns whose points curled like two-days-dead starfish. The light of this constellation was reaching Earth well after the stars had burned out. In the star-hearts were photographs of female faces, with hairstyles and smiles from ten years before. Once colour, the snaps were bleached to a peculiar aquamarine that made the girls look drowned. The door was wedged open, but glittery streamers curtained the way in.

Somewhere, tinny music played through maladjusted speakers. It could have been Melanie's "I've Got a Brand New Pair of Roller-Skates (You've Got a Brand New Key)" or John Fred and His Playboy Band's "Judy in Disguise (With Glasses)" or anything with that rinky-dink, teeth-scraping rhythm.

Fred checked his note again. He guessed why Busy had given him a street address rather than just named the place.

A board propped on an easel on the street promised TONITE'S TASTIES – HELENA TROIS, THE MYSTERIOUS ZARANA AND FREAK-OUT FRANKIE. Black and white head-shots were pinned around the names, all of women looking back over naked shoulders. In the window stood life-size cardboard cut-outs of girls who wore only sparkly G-strings and high-heels, leaning in unnatural and/or uncomfortable positions. As a token of respect to the Indecent

Displays Act, coloured paper circles were stuck like grocer's price-tags over nipples. One or two had fallen off, leaving the girls stuck with blobby glue-pasties.

A book-rack, just like the ones in a newsagent's or bus station, was chained to a Victorian boot-scraper to prevent theft. Paperback shapes in the wire-slots were wrapped in brown paper like a surrealist installation. The wrapping was partially torn off one, disclosing a title which caught Fred's eye, *Confessions of a Psychic Investigator*. He plucked the book, skinned it and looked at the cover. A thirty-ish blonde in a school-cap and navy-blue knickers, braids conveniently arranged over her breasts, did a shocked comedy double-take as a 'ghost' in a long sheet ripped off her gymslip with warty rubber horror-hands. The author was a Lesley Behan.

"Nice to see the field getting serious attention," drawled Richard. "You should buy that. I'm not aware of Miss Behan's contribution to the literature of the occult."

Also on offer were FILMS – CONTINUOUS, at a ticket price well above that charged by self-respecting Odeons or Classics; this after-noon's 'XXX' triple-bill was *Sixth Form Girls in Chains*, *Chocolate Sandwich* and *Sexier Than Sex*.

"Now, that's just ridiculous," exclaimed Fred. "How can anything be, well, *sexier* than sex? It's like saying wetter than water."

"Perhaps a philosophical point is intended. After all, is not reality sometimes a disappointment, set against its imagined or anticipated version?"

"One thing I guarantee is that what won't be *sexier than sex* will be these films."

"You sound like a connoisseur."

"I once spent two weeks in the back row of one of these pokey little cinemas on an undercover job. We were after some nutter who liked to throw ammonia in the faces of the usherettes. In the end, they nabbed him somewhere else. All I got out of it was eyestrain. I didn't even want to think about chatting up a bird for six months. I've actually seen *Chocolate Sandwich*. It's about this West Indian bloke, a plumber, and these housewives . . ."

Richard made a face, indicating he didn't want to know any more.

Locating a panel of buttons by the streamers, Richard pressed one. A buzzer sounded inside.

"Frederick," Richard began, "this might seem naïve to someone *au fait* with the ins and outs of policing the capital, but isn't it something of a *conflict of interests* that the policeman in charge of the Obscene

Publications Squad should work above – not to put too fine a point on it – a strip club?"

Fred coughed a little. The OPS was one of those embarrassments the average copper tried not to bring up if he had any intention of becoming an above-average copper.

"Don't hem and haw, man," snapped Richard.

"Have you ever heard the expression 'one bad apple'?"

" 'Spoils the barrel'? Indeed."

Fred found himself whispering. "You know we don't have police corruption in this country?"

"That's the impression given by the patriotic press."

"Well, it might not be 100-per-cent true."

Before he could further disenchant Richard, the streamers parted. White, beringed hands reached out and fastened on Fred's shoulders. He was pulled into warm, fragrant darkness.

II Queen of the Nile

When his eyes got used to the gloom, Fred found he was being held close by a tiny woman in a Cleopatra outfit. She had Egyptian eye make-up and a sprinkling of glitter on her bare shoulders. A rearing tin cobra stuck to the front of her stiff black wig prodded his chin.

"Steady on, luv," he said.

"You've made a conquest, Fred," commented Richard, slyly.

Fred took the girl's fingers off his shoulders and gave them back to her. She waved them about in the region of her brass bra, then put them behind her. He had an idea she was a bit embarrassed by her hands, which were large for her size.

"You're the ghost-exterminators," she said, in broad Sarf Lahn-dahn tones. "Thank Gawd you're here."

Richard reached behind her, took one of her hands, turned it over and kissed her palm dead-centre.

"And you must be the Mysterious Zarana, Queen of the Nile."

Her eyes widened, cracking a black bar of eyeshadow. "Lumme, you really are psychic."

Richard smiled. "Your picture is outside," he said.

She was a bit disappointed. "It's Zarana Roberts, really. Dad was out in Egypt during the War."

"Pleased to meet you. I'm Richard Jeperson, and the fellow you've enraptured is Fred Regent."

Fred wondered if he was blushing. It'd be too dim in here to tell.

Zarana did something like a curtsey, with a little eyelash-fluttering smile like the one in her mug-shot.

Then she was serious. "Busy Boddey's goin' spare," she said. "Ever since the *thing* happened. He's been on the blower to half the town . . ."

Which meant there *should* be more police here.

"Now he's up outside Boot Boy's office, keepin' guard. None of the girls wanted to go up there. Not even before the *thing*. I mean, taking your knickers off in public for a livin' is one thing, but Boot Boy Booth is another, if you know what I mean."

Fred had heard a few things about DI Booth. "We should take a look-see," said Fred, trying to sound more casual than he felt.

"Rather you than me, ducks," said Zarana. "Fancy a cuppa? Ty-Phoo's two pound to the customers, but I can get you sorted compliments of the management."

"That would be most welcome, Miss Roberts," said Richard.

"Zarana, please. No need to be formal."

"Thank you, *Zarana*."

"You too, Freddy Friday," she said, prodding him in the ribs with a knuckle-ring, finding a soft spot close to his heart and grinding it. "Come on."

"Zarana," he said.

"Not so difficult, is it?"

It wasn't, but he thought she'd left her mark on him.

She bustled off, "backstage" – which might have been called a cupboard anywhere else. The walls, floor and ceiling were covered with brown shag-pile. At the end of the corridor was a bar-theatre space, where a Chinese girl, spot-lit on a dais, peeled a *cheongsam* off her shoulders. A sparse audience kept to their shadows. Fred wondered who these folk were – it was half past three in the afternoon, didn't they have jobs to go to? Mechanical moaning and oom-pah musak seeped from an alcove under the stairs. The basement screening room was probably a fire-trap. Booth should at least have made sure the place was up to public safety specifications.

A proper staircase led upwards. Serried beside it were framed posters of strippers.

"There's your ghosts," said Zarana, returning with tea-bag teas in an I'M BACKING BRITAIN mug and a breast-shaped tankard. She gave Richard the union jack and Fred the pewter tit.

The posters were in different styles, going back through the years – Sunday supplement full-colour and psychedelic design giving way to black and white and blocky red lettering. It was like a reverse strip:

the older the picture, the more clothed the girls. Over the years, standards had changed – at least insofar as what could be shown on the street.

"Tiger Sharkey, also known as Theresa D'Arbanvilliers-Holmes," said Zarana, in gossipy museum guide tones, indicating a wild-haired blonde in a Jungle Jillian leather bikini. "Married a Tory MP, she did, and pays Boot Boy a fair slice of cake every month not to have the 'glamour films' she used to make sent to the *News of the World*. I hope you don't count that as a motive, since she's a love, honestly. Felicity Mane, the Flickering Flayme. On the game in Huddersfield, poor dear. Trixie Truelove. Her proper name's Mavis Jones and she's still here, doin' make-up and costumes. She knitted my snake-wig. Put on a bit of weight since that photo was taken."

Zarana had accompanied them to a landing, where she paused.

"And here's our founder, bleedin' Royalty with tassels. If I'd half a crown for every cove who comes in here and says birds today ain't fit to tie her G-string, I'd have a villa on Capri and be payin' muscle boys to shake their bums at me."

The poster showed a slim-hipped blonde posing coyly, Venus-style. Even in faded black and white, she was a startler. A platinum rope of hair wound around her neck, across her breasts, about her waist and fanned out to serve as a loincloth. She had huge, sad eyes and a dimple in one cheek.

"Pony-Tail," said Zarana.

Fred knew. Trev Bailey, who sat two desks along from him at school, once had a "photography" magazine with Pony-Tail's picture on the cover confiscated by a maths master. Later, the offending article was found in the rubbish bin by the bike sheds, crumpled and suspiciously stained. The teacher was called 'Wanker' Lewis for the rest of his career.

Zarana considered the poster. "You'd think she invented nudity from the way they rabbit on about her."

During that two-week stint in a porn cinema, the only film that had jolted Fred awake – and even slightly stirred his interest – was *Views of Nudes*. A scratchy black and white 1950s antique about well-spoken naked persons playing volleyball at a Torquay naturist camp, with strategically placed shrubs to save their embarrassment. It was out of place amid the bloodily-colourful socks-on couplings of randily joyless Scandinavians as Glenn Miller at the Frug a-Go-Go. *Views of Nudes* was booed by raincoats, until they were stunned to a hush by Pony-Tail. In a blatantly spliced-in, gloriously faded-to-pink colour sequence, she stripped in a stable, getting out of riding habit and jodhpurs (editing tricks were necessary to manage the boots) and whipping her hair about. She frightened the horses but excited the audience; the tally-ho soundtrack was soon augmented by the chink of spare change in active pockets. Fred had to admit Pony-Tail, who could look young as twelve or old as sin, had *something*.

"Where is *she* now?" asked Richard.

Zarana made mystic gestures. "That's the ghosty part. Nobody knows. Or is saying, if they do. She vanished. She could write her own paycheques if she came out of retirement. Of course, she'll be a crone now. Bleedin' Pony-Tail. I bet it wasn't even her own hair. Nice mince pies, though. I heard she might have been got out of the way, so she could really be a ghost. I think that's why you're here. It's what Busy Boddey's afraid of."

They looked upwards, where the stairway narrowed. Bulbs were burned out or broken. The next landing was in deep shadow.

"I'll stay here, if you don't mind," said Zarana.

"Come on, Fred, let's get on with it," said Richard.

Zarana's fingers touched the lapel of his crombie jacket, felt the fabric and let him go. "Careful, Freddy," she said.

"Certainly will, Queenie."

Richard was halfway up, into the dark. Fred left the girl and followed.

III Mr Sludge

Fred saw DC Harry "Busy" Boddey was in a right state. When Fred and Richard entered the ante-chamber with him, Busy jumped off his stool.

The inner door was smashed off its hinges.

The "five blokes with sledge-hammers" theory looked better and better.

Neither Fred nor Richard had so much as sipped their tea, but the stench made them raise cups to their mouths, not so much for the swallow but the strong smell.

"See," said Boddey, nodding at the empty doorway.

Fred got a look into the office beyond. Something limp sat at and over a broken desk. Red splashes Jackson Pollocked over strewn papers, abused glossies, demolished furniture and pulled-down posters.

"Stone the crows," said Fred.

Busy whimpered. Fred would have marked him down as one of those joke-over-dismembered-body-parts coppers, but this took things to extremes.

Richard had his feelers out – he called them "mentacles". He stood straight and calm, eyes fluttered shut, nose raised like a wine-taster doing a blind test, fingers waving like fronds.

"What's the looney up to?" asked Busy, bitterly.

Fred slapped him. "Trying to help," he told the shocked policeman. "Now shut up, Busy Lizzie!"

Richard snapped out of it. "No need for additional ultra-violence," he said. "There's been quite enough of that. You, Constable Boddey, give me the court report."

Busy looked up at Richard. Fred nodded at him.

"This morning, something came here and did . . . *that* . . . to Booth."

"Very concise. Did you find the *corpus*?"

Busy shook his head. "No, it was Brie. One of the girls. Massive knockers. Does secretarial stuff too. She's scarpered. You won't see her Bristols round here again in a hurry."

"Was anything seen of the assailant or assailants?"

Busy shut up.

"Now now, come come . . . you called Fred for a reason. The Diogenes Club has a reputation. We don't involve ourselves in gangland feuds or routine police-work. We're here for more arcane matters."

Busy tried hard to stop shaking. "I saw *it*," he said.

"The murder?" prompted Richard.

"The murderer."

"It?"

"He, I suppose. When Brie screamed, I came upstairs. It was still here, standing in that doorway. It had done its business, just like that, in seconds I reckon. Thump thump thump and the show's over, folks, haven't you got homes to go to? It had a big coat, like a flasher, a dirty mac, and a hat, old-fashioned . . ."

"Tricorn, shako, topper . . ."

"No, one of those movie gangster jobs. Trilby."

"So, we have his clothes described. What about the rest? Size?"

Busy held his hands apart, like a fisherman telling a whopper.

"Huge, giant, wide, thick . . ."

"Face?"

"No."

"No, you can't bear to remember? Or no, no face?"

Busy shook his head.

"What you said second. Just greyey white, sludge-features. With eyes, though. Like poached eggs."

"A mask," suggested Fred.

"Don't think so. Masks can't change expressions. Can't *smile*. It did. It saw me and Brie, and it *smiled*. How can something with no mouth to speak of smile? Well, it was bloody managing, that's all I can say. God, that *smile*!"

Busy covered his face again.

Richard looked about the ante-chamber. Spots of blood and something like mud dotted about the doorway, but this room was clean. Floor-to-ceiling shelves held box-files with faded ink dates on their spines. A coffee-table by Busy's stool had a neatly-arranged fan of girlie magazines – *Knight*, *Whoops!*, *Big and Bouncy*, *Strict*, *Cherry*, *Exclusive*. An undisturbed coat-tree bore a mohair topcoat, a bowler hat and an umbrella. Savile Row, definitely. Better quality than anyone on a Scotland Yard wage could afford without going into debt.

There was a clear demarcation line. The devastation was confined to the inner office.

"Your Mr Sludge made quite an entrance," said Richard. "Splashy, in fact. But the exit was more discreet."

Busy nodded.

Fred took the constable's chin and forced him to look at Richard. Busy swallowed.

"It *emptied out* somehow," he said, making a swirling gesture, "as if going down a plug-hole, then it was just gone, coat and hat and all."

"Intriguing." Richard took another gulp of tea, and put his mug down on the cover of *Knight*, blotting the chest of a girl wearing parts of a suit of armour. "So we have something here substantial enough to wreak considerable damage but capable of, as it were, *evaporating*. You were quite right to call us, Constable Boddey. If there's a phantasm, golem or *affrit* in the case, it falls under our purview."

Fred let Busy go.

He was surprised to find he felt a sympathy twinge for Busy. He wasn't a chancer anymore, just a shell-shocked survivor who'd have to live with bad dreams.

Richard produced a scraper from a flapped side-pocket. He ventured gingerly into the office, careful not to brush against anything dripping. He took a sample of something congealed and sticky.

"Sludge, indeed," he said. "Plasm of some specie. Ecto-, perhaps. Or psycho-, eroto- or haemo-. Then again, it could just be *gunk*."

He scraped it back onto the door-jamb.

"I just need to know one more thing," said Richard, addressing Busy. "Who else have you told?"

Busy looked up, a sparkle of the old cunning reminding Fred he *was* still the same flash git he'd known at Hendon.

"Um," began Busy.

There was a commotion downstairs. People arriving.

"Not the police," Richard observed, instantly.

His hawkish brows narrowed. Busy shrank, trying to slip back into shivering wreck status to avoid answering for his actions.

A yelping and ouching indicated someone was being dragged upstairs.

Zarana was pushed into the room. This time Fred caught hold of her. She put her face to his chest so as not to look into Booth's office.

A beef-faced, big-bellied man in a dark suit that had fit him better in 1965 was at the top of the stairs, wheezing. Charging up two flights was something he hadn't done in a while. Someone (almost certainly a young woman) had persuaded him that a paisley scarf worn under an open violet shirt would make him look less behind-the-times – the sweaty *foulard* flopped on his sternum like a dead (but with-it) herring.

A pair of heavy lads backed him up.

The newcomer was so used to being a hard man he hadn't bothered to keep in shape. People were still afraid of him for things he'd done years ago. If half what Fred had heard about Mickey "Burly" Gates were true, people were right. Gates had apprenticed as a meat-cutter at Smithfield's before joining the firm. Throughout his career, Gates had been in meat of one sort or another.

Allegedly, he kept his hand in with his old chopper.

Gates took in Richard, from pointed boot-toes to tumble of long hair.

"Who the bloody hell are you?" he demanded, "and what the bleeding hell do you think you look like?"

Richard shrugged his eyebrows and commented, "Charming."

Then the meat-cutter saw Boot Boy Booth. "Jesus wept!" Gates said, involuntarily crossing himself.

"Friend of yours?" asked Richard, casually.

Gates tore his gaze away from the red ruin in the inner office and looked again at Richard, squinting.

"This is them, Mickey," said Busy Boddey – it didn't surprise Fred that a DC in the OPS was on first-name terms with Burly Gates. "Specialists in ghosties and ghoulies. The Odd Squad."

Richard cocked an eyebrow. "I haven't heard that one before. Not so sure I care for it."

"I understand about specialists," said Gates, making an effort to calm down. "I use them a lot. Like plumbers. If they do a diamond job, I'm a happy chappie and the packet of notes is nice and thick. If they don't . . . well, they forfeit my custom and, as it happens, tend to retire early. Clear?"

"Crystalline," drawled Richard, not really listening.

A framed photograph had caught his attention. Pony-Tail, again – in St Trinian's uniform, with hockey-stick and straw boater. Ten years gone, and the girl was still all over Soho.

"Diamond," said Gates. "So, get on and specialize. I don't really care what happened, just so long as it don't happen again on my patch. Track down who . . ."

"*What*, most likely."

". . . or *what* did this, and make sure they get put out of business."

Richard looked at Gates and did something shocking. He giggled.

Gates' red face shaded towards crimson. Sweat steamed off his forehead.

Richard's giggle became a full-throated King Laugh. He made gun-fingers and shot off all twelve chambers at Gates. Fred had to swallow a smirk.

Gates searched his waistband for a chopper. Mercifully, he had left it at home.

Richard shut off his laugh. "You've made a fundamental error in assessing this situation," he told Gates. "I am not a plumber or a cabbie. I am, as it were, not for hire. I cannot be suborned into serving your interests – or, indeed, any but my own. Call me a dilettante if you wish, but there it is. I am here as a favour to my good friend, Sergeant Regent, and because the matter has features of uncommon interest."

Gates goggled in amazement.

"You evidently consider yourself a *power* in this district," observed Richard.

"I could have Eric and Colin snap you like a twig, sunshine."

Gates' heavy lads pricked up their ears. They cracked hairy knuckles.

"You could have them try," said Richard, amused. "It wouldn't advance your cause one whit, but if you feel the need, go ahead. Powerlessness must be a new, disorienting condition for you. I understand your need to attempt to reaffirm yourself. However, if upon second thought you'd rather not annoy me further and leave me to continue my investigations, kindly quit my crime scene. This isn't your fiefdom any more. This is where the wild things are. Is that, ah, *diamond*?"

Gates' mouth opened and closed like a beached fish's.

He grunted and left. Eric and Colin directed the full frighteners at the room, but only Busy cringed. Richard waved at them, a flutter of farewell and dismissal.

"Toodle-oo, fellows."

Eric and Colin vanished.

Fred breathed again. He hoped Zarana hadn't noticed him trembling.

IV Local History

"Let's see if I have this straight," began Richard, setting his thimble-cup down on the red Formica table, " 'Skinderella's' is *owned* by that irritable gent Gates, but was *managed* by a serving police officer? Setting aside that puzzle, I understand that Mr Gates is a big fellow around these parts?"

Zarana nodded. "He has a ton of clubs. Chi-Chi's, the Hot-Lite in Dean Street, Dirty Gertie's (at Number Thirty), the Prefects' Hut, the National Girlery . . ."

She had taken off her *Carry On Cleo* gear (on stage, not that Fred had caught her turn), and now wore a lime-green mini with matching knit waistcoat, Donovan hat and shaggy boots. She had nondescript, shortish brown hair – pinned so she could get the wig back on quickly for her 5:30.

They sat in Froff, a Greek Street café. Gleaming, steam-puffing espresso machinery was held over from when it was called Mama Guglielmi's. A new vibe was signalled by deep purple tactile wall-paper, paper flowers stuck to mirrors and sitar musak. Waiters wore tie-dye T-shirts and multi-coloured jeans wider at the ankles than Fred's sta-presses were at the waist. The staff were wary of Fred. His just-growing-out skinhead haircut (a 'suedehead') made him look like the natural enemy of all things hippie, but he sussed that they had Soho antennae that twitched if there was a non-bent policeman about. He had pointedly been asked if he'd like a bacon sarnie. As it happens, the one which turned up was excellent, even if he had to make a conscious effort to blank out the memory of Boot Boy Booth's death-site to face his nosh.

Two tables over, a rat-faced herbert in a fringed Shane jacket two sizes too big for his thin shoulders sold silver-foil slivers to fresh-from-the-country kids who were going to be disappointed when they tried to smoke the contents.

"Mr Gates strikes me as somewhat *traditional* for these environs," said Richard.

Zarana drew four corners in the air and sniggered.

"Indeed," said Richard. "The original Soho Square."

"Burly Gates started out as meat-cutter," said Fred. "Then as a bouncer, for Schluderpacheru."

"Yeah, Popeye," said Zarana. "Now there's a *real* creep."

"Fred, you are familiar with this foreign-sounding person?"

"Konstantin Schluderpacheru. Vice Lord back when we had rationing. Soho was overrun by demobbed blokes with money in their pockets and bad habits picked up in the War. No one's sure where he comes from, but he claims to be Czech. Besides the striptease places, he was – probably still *is* – landlord for a lot of first- and second-floor properties with single female tenants."

"Knockin' shops," said Zarana, with distaste. "Don't gawp, Freddy. I show it, I don't sell it."

Richard patted a hand over Zarana's large fist.

"I'm amazed you have such a command of local history," Richard told Fred.

"It's what Every Young Copper Should Know. Faces and statistics. At the Yard, they print them on cigarette cards."

Fred was pleased that for once he was filling in Richard on arcana. Usually, it was the other way around.

"Pray continue, Frederick."

"Come the late '50s, Mickey Gates is a jumped-up teddy boy rousting drunks at Schluderpacheru's places. He was a double act with a cove by the name of Grek Cohen, who used to be a wrestler. One of those man-mountain types. The story went that you could stick a flick-knife into him over and over for five minutes and he wouldn't even notice. Burly and Grek worked up a nice little protection racket, originally targeting Schluderpacheru's competition. Also, they started smut-peddling – brown-paper-wrapped little mags and pics. Gates calls himself a 'publisher' now, which means the same stuff on glossier paper. You saw his stuff in Booth's reception area. *Knight*, *Whoops!*, *Cherry*. Those are the 'respectable' ones."

"You're well up on this."

"Where do you think all the stuff confiscated in raids winds up? Night shifts at police stations get very boring."

"I was in *Knight* once," said Zarana. "A Roarin' Twenties set, shimmerin' fringes, long beads."

"Schluderpacheru thought porn was peanuts, and let Burly and Grek scurry around picking up grubby pennies. Big mistake. Pennies add up to a grubby pile. They acquired leases to half the district. They were the new Vice Lords."

"How did their erstwhile employer take that?" asked Richard.

"That's the funny part. Schluderpacheru was in the Variety Club of Great Britain by then. He got into the film business, as an agent and then a producer. He leased his 'talent' to quota quickies. Pony-Tail played the victim in a murder mystery, *Soho Girl*. After she got killed and before Zachary Scott found out Sid James did it, audiences lost interest. But when she was on the screen, they sat up to attention. Schluderpacheru reckoned he had the next Diana Dors under exclusive contract. Well, maybe the next Shirley Anne Field. Blonde and British, you know. This made him feel like the unpronounceable answer to Lew Grade. He planned to build a whole film around her . . ."

"*Brighton Belle*," said Zarana. "Mavis was goin' to be in it."

"He was going to give her a proper name. Gladys Glamour, or something. But it didn't happen. Schluderpacheru became a producer, but not with Pony-Tail as his star. She disappeared about that time – presumably wriggling out of the lifetime contract, and making things easier for Shirley Anne Field. Burly and Grek were taking over the clubs and Schluderpacheru had to put up some sort of fight or lose face. If people weren't respectful, which is to say terrified, of him, his empire would tumble. But he also knew he needed to ditch girlie shows if he wanted to be invited to the Royal Film Performance. So, in 1963 or thereabouts, Soho had a not very convincing gang war. In the end, Schluderpacheru divested himself of the clubs – retaining enough of an interest to claim a stipend from Gates."

"And Grek Cohen?"

"When the dust settled, Grek was nowhere to be seen. His missing persons file at the Yard is still open. In order to make friends again, Schluderpacheru and Gates had to agree neither were to blame for their disagreement. But someone had to be, to satisfy pimps' honour or whatever. Grek was handy, stupid and expendable. That said, God knows how they got rid of him. Not with a flick-knife, obviously."

"Mavis says it was *her*," blurted Zarana.

Richard and Fred looked at the girl. There was a long pause.

"I'm not goin' to be a grass," she said. "Life expectancy is short enough in this place."

"I'm not a policeman," said Richard. "And Fred barely counts as a plod. Look at the crimes he's ignoring just by sitting here."

The rat-faced bogus dealer pricked up his ears, took a good look at Fred and headed for the hills.

"This is all gossip. Mavis tells it different every time. She gets it mixed up with Samson and Delilah. The big thing is that Grek Cohen was besotted with Pony-Tail, devoted like a kid to a kitten, the whole *King Kong* scene."

" 'It wasn't the airplanes,' " quoted Richard, " 't'was Beauty killed the Beast.' "

Zarana nodded. "How else could Popeye and Gates get to Grek? They took Pony-Tail away, threatened to carve her face up unless Grek turned himself over to them, lay down for whatever was comin' – an express train, most likely. Then, the bastards probably did her in anyway, no matter what they say about her now."

"So, at the bottom of it all, there's an unwilling *femme fatale*, a lure and a sacrifice."

"It makes sense," said Fred, "two mystery disappearances about the same time. Bound to be a connection."

Richard clicked a spoon against his teeth. "It seems singular to me that this Pony-Tail person is so frequently mentioned. As if she were a presiding spirit, patron saint of stripteaserie, the Florence Nightingale of ecdysiasts."

Fred remembered the girl in the stables. He slowed the film down in memory. Pony-Tail was looking beyond the camera, fixing her eye on one face in the darkness, undressing just for him.

"She can't have been *that* good," said Zarana. "She just took her clobber off to music. It's not astro-physics."

Richard and Fred still thought about her.

"Men," said Zarana. "What a shower!"

Something exploded against the window like a catapulted octopus, splattering black tentacles across the glass.

"Interesting," said Richard.

V The Festival

The girl Fred had scared earlier staggered into Froff, one heel broken, halter torn, hair dripping. Tarry black stuff streaked her face and arms.

Outside the star-splattered window, a black-uniformed army marched down Greek Street, lobbing paint-grenades. Advance scouts whirled plastic bull-roarers. Voiceless screaming and sticky missiles generally cleared the way.

A waiter tried to shove the tom back onto the street, but she wasn't shifting. A runnel of blood mixed in with black on her face.

"Assault with a deadly weapon, miss," said Fred, raising his voice. "Could you identify the culprit?"

She shook her lopsided head, and said "I don't want to get involved. It's not healthy."

"Nothing you do seems healthy. Have you considered going home to mum?"

"Who do you think put me out in the first place, PC Plod?"

She sat down at a table and asked for tea, spilling odd coins from a tiny, long-handled purse to prove she could pay for it. She fished out some safety-pins and made emergency repairs to her top. Then, she picked at her hair. The drying, setting goo made unusual spikes. If she kept at it, she might set a new fashion.

A second wave of marchers passed, waving banners. It was less like a parade of protest than a show of force.

"They do this once a bleedin' week," groaned Zarana.

Fred saw slogans – DOWN WITH SIN!, HEED THE WRATH, HARLOTS OUT, SMITE THE FLESH-PEDDLERS.

"Booth went spare about that little lot," said Zarana.

"The late, lamented?" prompted Richard.

"Someone must lament, though you'd be hard-pressed to find anyone to own up to it."

"We never did establish why the Obscene Publications Squad was head-quartered in 'Skinderella's'. If you remember, I did ask."

Zarana looked to Fred for the nod. He gave it.

"It was a payoff to Boot Boy from Mickey Gates. Booth took a fat profit out of the place. In Soho, the coppers are full partners in the smut rackets. They get all the perks. Law's in the way of folk who want to sell and other folk who want to buy, so who's to complain if the law ducks aside? Then sticks out its greedy hand?"

Richard looked disappointed. His battles took place beyond the ken of the rest of the world, and he hadn't kept up on tediously everyday crime.

"She's right, guv'nor," said Fred. "It's an open secret. Every new broom at the Yard promises to sweep clean, then lifts the rock in Soho, takes a look at what's squirming, and decides to do something else. More parking meters."

"You're telling me that the squad charged with *regulating* obscenity is actually responsible for *disseminating* it?"

"More or less."

"Good grief," said Richard. "I assume our friends in black take objection to this *laissez-faire* situation?"

Zarana nodded. "When this mob showed up, Gates bent Booth's ear off. He *was* payin' for protection, so he thought he was entitled to it."

The marchers wore plain unisex boiler-suits, and wound black scarves around their heads and lower faces. It must get steamy in those outfits on a hot day, but they were also indistinguishable from each other come an identity parade. They were well-drilled – placard-wavers, bull-roarers and paint grenadiers all in place and working with brisk, brutal efficiency.

"You can't buy them off," said Zarana. "Booth tried that straight away. They're god-bothered loonies."

"There's no explicit mention of God in their various slogans," mused Richard.

"They call themselves The Festival of Morality," said Zarana.

Richard looked at the protesters. He steepled his fingers and closed his eyes, reaching out to get a deeper impression of them. Then he snapped to.

"Frederick, are you up to date on this movement?"

"Only what I read in the papers. You can imagine why they're here – to take a stand against immorality and licentiousness. They're a reaction to the 'permissive society'. When blokes like Booth get too blatant, and stop keeping seamy stuff out of sight, someone else will step in and call for a Bonfire of the Bleedin' Vanities."

"Lord Leaves," said Zarana.

"Of course," said Richard. "Algernon Arbuthnot Leaves, Lord Leaves of Leng. Him, I know of."

"That's the bloke," she said, pointing. "High Lord Muckety-Muck of Killjoy."

An open-top black limousine decorated with white symbols crawled along at the centre of the procession. Sat on a raised throne-like affair in the back was an old, old man in long black robes and an ear-flapped skullcap. It struck Fred that he really had copied his look from Savonarola. His hands were liver-spotted and gnarled, but he could hold up a megaphone and bellow with the best of them.

"Is he *singing*?" asked Fred.

"Not exactly Gilbert O'Sullivan, is he?' sniped Zarana.

"You have to applaud the effort," said Richard. "He's not afraid of seeming ridiculous."

Zarana, who obviously took the Festival personally, kept quiet.

Lord Leaves continued to give vent. In the front passenger seat, next to a uniformed chauffeur, sat a twelve-year-old blond boy with a black blindfold around his eyes – presumably to save him from sights that might warp his little mind. The lad strummed an amplified acoustic guitar, accompanying the Father of the Festival. Looking up beside His Lordship was an adoring young woman dressed like some sort of nun, hair completely covered by a wimple, blue eyes blazing with groupie-like adoration.

Fred made out the words:

"Sin and sodomy, lust and lechery . . . bring about man's fall,
Filth and blasphemy, porn and obloquy . . . I despise them all!"

The woman rattled a black tambourine. It struck Fred that she was the most genuinely *aroused* person he'd seen all day – certainly more turned on than the tarts and punters on the streets.

The insight gave him a weird thrill, which Zarana noticed. She tugged his sleeve, drawing attention to herself with a cattish little frown.

"Not often one hears the word 'obloquy' used in a lyric," said Richard. "I shall consider writing a letter to *The Times*."

The tambourine woman's electric gaze passed over the street, as if scouting (quite sensibly) for assassins, and hit on Froff. Fred thought for a moment she was looking exciting hatred directly into his bowels, but then sensed the attention was for Zarana.

He put an arm round her (again). "Don't let them bother you, luv," he said.

"Easy for you to say," she sniffed. "It takes a week to get that gunk off, and you can't work. In my line, there ain't exactly paid sick days or invalidity benefits."

"Is that Leaves' granddaughter looking daggers?" Fred asked Zarana. "High Priestess in charge of ripping out hearts."

"You should glance at the society pages when flipping through the paper to the racing results," said Richard. "That is Lady Celia Asquith-Leaves. His Lordship's wife."

"Dirty old sod," breathed Zarana.

"One mustn't rush to judgement," said Richard, which was quite comical in the circumstances.

An image of His Lordship's wedding night sprung up in Fred's mind. He did his best to try to expunge it completely.

"I bet they *read* the magazines before throwin' them into the fire," said Zarana, not helping at all. "Then get worked up into a lather and . . ."

"You're making our Fred uncomfortable, Queen of the Nile," said Richard.

"Sorry, I'm sure," said Zarana, wriggling close to him.

Fred wished he were somewhere else. Say, sinking knee-deep into freezing mire on Dartmoor with hooded slime-cultists puffing poison thorns at him through blowpipes and ichorous elderly things summoned from the bog-bottom padding after him on yard-long, mossy feet.

The parade came to a halt. Uniformed police constables moved in. Their path was blocked by serried ranks of bull-roarers and placard-wavers. The Festival had a solid grasp of demo tactics.

Lord Leaves finished his song and tossed his megaphone to a minion.

He flung back his robes like the Man With No Name tossing his poncho over his shoulder. He wore what looked like a black body stocking, circled with the white symbols that were also marked on his car. He picked up something that looked a lot like a sten gun fed by a thick hosepipe.

Zarana darted under the table.

Fred realized the girl knew more than he did and was probably being sensible, but couldn't resist the street theatre.

Soho residents – 'denizens', really – mounted some sort of counter-attack, ponces linking arms with toms, bruisers emerging from sex shops and strip clubs to put up a stout defence. They jostled the foot-soldiers of the Festival.

Lord Leaves of Leng twisted a nozzle on his gun.

A high-pressure stream of black liquid squirted in an arc, splashing down on the counter-protesters – who scattered.

A disciplined, scripted cheer rose from the black-clad ranks.

"I defy," yelled His Lordship, unamplified but booming. "I shall smite."

He played the jet-spray against windows and hoardings.

Wheeling around, back and forth, Lord Leaves scrawled thick, dripping lines across signage and come-on posters, upping the flow whenever an image of an unclad woman got in the way. The black liquid was thinner than paint but lumpy and staining. Neon tubes fizzed and burst. He aimed his jet at a porn-broker's window, pushing in the glass and smashing down racks of 8mm film loops, Swedish magazines, plastic novelties and brown-paper-bagged glossies. An angry manager lost his footing as he tried to protect his merchandise. He scrabbled around in the wet mess, falling heavily.

The cheers became more genuine. Harsh, mocking laughter.

Zarana peeped up again. "Tell me when it's over," she said.

"His Lordship enjoys taking the fight to the fallen," observed Richard. "He is something of a showman."

"You know what these Jesus freaks are like, guv'nor."

"Those white symbols on his suit and car have nothing to do with Christianity, Frederick. Which is interesting, don't you think. Lord Leaves is a man of great faith, evidently. An inspiration to followers. A black beacon of morality in an age he might deem is going to the dogs. Yet his faith isn't one hitherto associated with *morality* in the limited sense expressed here. The only thing I've seen in Soho that really goes with those symbols was your dead policemen. Lord Leaves is a great one for *smiting* and the late DI Booth was certainly *smitten*."

Fred looked again at Lord Leaves, exulting as liquid filth poured down upon harlots and whore-mongers. He considered the blue-eyed priestess, the blindfolded minstrel, the well-drilled troops. The Nazis had been against decadence, too.

"That, my dears," said Richard, pointing at Lord Leaves of Leng, "is a Suspect."

VI Repeat Offender

By nightfall, the street looked as if the Luftwaffe were blitzing again. Lights came on by fits and starts, many broken or sparking. The pavement was shiny, as black goo congealed into plasticky, pungent shellac.

Fred tried to avoid getting any on his Docs.

The march turned into a torchlight rally in Soho Square. Lord Leaves sang more songs – "Cast the First Stone" was surprisingly catchy – between other "turns". "Concerned parents" made halting speeches, and "fallen souls" recanted previous harlotry at great length and in explicit detail.

Zarana had popped back to "Skindy's", to see if she needed to go on again. The management might dim the lights this evening, if not in tribute to the late DI Booth then to avoid attracting an angry mob of torch-wielding zealots. She had invited Fred to come watch her Queen of the Nile routine some time when all hell wasn't breaking loose. A snake was involved, apparently.

Richard pottered around ruins, trying to pick up "impressions". Fred gathered it wasn't easy. At the calmest of times, Soho was awash with emotional discharge. Now, it was a maelstrom of mixed feelings. If all this energy could be piped to power stations, the United Kingdom wouldn't need North Sea oil.

Fred showed his warrant card to a stray constable and asked for a report. The copper had a splurge of black across his uniform and was looking for his lost helmet. He was in a state of high pissed-offness.

"If this had been a student demo at the Yank Embassy," complained the constable, "the Special Patrol Group would be out in body-armour, with CS gas and riot-shields. A hundred arrests before supper-time, commendations all round. Because it's bloody prudes, it was just me and poor old Baxter trying 'move along nicely now' on an army of roaring dervishes. Bastards said they'd march tomorrow, then switched schedules. That Lord Leaves is a menace. I'd rather have Hell's Angels any day."

Fred remembered he still hadn't called New Scotland Yard to share the sad news about DI Booth. At this rate, they would read about it in the morning papers. Richard said a forensics team would only get in the way. It was nice having such pull in high places that he could conduct his own private murder investigation.

Among those who came out to peep at the mess was Mickey Gates.

Through the rolled-down window of an I've-got-money Rolls Royce, Gates watched, a hard-faced dolly bird in each armpit, foot-long cigar in his gob. Eric and Colin, his monkeys, supervised damage control at a couple of Gates enterprises – a private cinema club and a "sex arcade". They chased off scavengers.

"Mr Gates is having a bad day," said Fred.

The PC cheered up a bit.

"Isn't his Roller illegally parked?" said Fred. "See if you can rustle up a traffic warden. Get him ticketed."

The constable laughed. "Wouldn't I like to see that."

Gates caught sight of Richard and frowned, even more furiously. He was on the point of shouting something.

Suddenly, with an almighty *whump!*, a giant invisible boot came down on the Rolls. The roof caved and windows burst. Side-doors buckled, ejecting the matched set of dollies. They crab-walked away, awkward in hot-pants and fishnets, scraping knees and elbows, hairdos loose. At least, they were well out of it.

Fred saw Mickey bite off a chunk of cigar and swallow it.

Then metal folded around him. The car lifted off the street, and *bent*. Metal crumpled with dinosaur screams. Dents appeared in the bodywork. The boot ruptured, vomiting a stream of bright, shiny paper – torn girlie magazines.

Richard was nearer than Fred. He considered the sight, with cool interest. Sometimes, the guv'nor just plain forgot to be sensibly scared – that was one of the talents Fred brought to the team.

Eric and Colin just stood and gaped, like dozens of others. None of them tried to get too close.

Whatever was crushing the Roller wasn't quite invisible.

Greyish stuff swirled up, from the street and the rubble, lacing out of thin air, forming a giant, squat man-shape. Mr Sludge had a domed lump of head but no neck. The bubble body, thick and smeary, distorted light. Power flexed in trunk-like limbs.

Red dripped from the car, which buckled and compacted as if in a press at a wrecking yard. As the Rolls was abused, the giant became more solid. Fred had no doubt this was the phantasm, golem or *affrit* that had killed Booth. The M.O. was unmistakable. Mr Sludge glistened, glowing almost. Blood-squirts shot into its body, lighting up a nerve-network of red traces. Girlie pictures clung to its torso, plastered like papier-mâché layers, smoothing over an enormous musculature. Bright smiles and air-brushed curves, pink tits and bums, faded to grey leatheriness. Dozens of nipples stood out like scabs for a few seconds, then healed.

Like a Herculean weight-lifter, Mr Sludge hoisted high a rough cube that had been a car and its occupant.

Richard tried gestures and incantations, which got the thing's attention but little else.

The grey giant looked down at the Man From the Diogenes Club.

Fred remembered what Busy Boddey had said about its mouthless smile. Here it was again. Eyelights shone.

The car-lump was bowled at Richard.

Fred ran and jumped, shoving his guv'nor out of the way. They sprawled on the pavement as the heavy cube tore into the road. The Spirit of Ecstasy bonnet-ornament stuck up from the mess, undamaged, wings shining. Solid workmanship, that. Gates had known enough to buy British.

Mr Sludge bellowed triumph, an unearthly sound produced by leather lungs and aolean harp vocal cords. The roar rose into the skies. Fred's eardrums hurt, and the noise invaded his skull, sprouting pain-blossoms behind his eyes. The giant's *substance* flowed into *sound*, and departed with the dying echo. The killer flew up up and away, passing from this plane of existence. Detritus showered from the space it had occupied. Stiff, faded fold-outs fell like autumn leaves.

Richard sat up, fastidiously flicking bits of filth from his clothes. "So, it's a repeat offender," he said. "Naughty naughty."

VII Go-Go Golem

"What *was* that?" Fred asked.

"As I said, a phantasm, golem, *affrit*, revenant, whatever. An energy presence."

"It came out of *nothing*."

Richard raised a finger. "No, Frederick, not *nothing*. It accumulated matter, *stuff*. It displaced air. It had a physical effect on this world."

Fred looked at the metal lump in the road. Workmen with acetylene-torches were trying to crack it open.

"I'll say it was physical."

An ambulance was on the scene. No one had hopes for the "patient". Ordinary police took witness statements, then quietly tore pages from their note-books. Reports of the day's business had been made to Euan Price, Fred's contact at New Scotland Yard, and the Ruling Cabal of the Diogenes Club, Richard's notional superiors. Assistance had been grudgingly offered, but there was a sense that since Fred and Richard got into the case by themselves – thank you very much, Busy Boddey! – it would be as well if they did the heavy lifting and got it tidied away as quietly as possible.

"It came from nothing, though," said Fred. "Empty air."

"There's no such thing as *nothing*," said Richard. "All sort of stuff washes about. And it can change form, just as water solidifies into ice. Our Mr Sludge gets punching weight from what comes to hand. Very neat and efficient. It's probably tethered to the district. You heard Lord Leaves, 'sin and sodomy, lust and lechery'. Potent stuff, that. Especially if you stir in the *frustration*. Tantalising come-ons whip up the imagination. Then, there's the let-down of finding out that what's on offer can't match what was hoped for. That's what's really wrong with porn, by the way – not that it's against morality, but that it always delivers short measure."

Fred wasn't so sure. Richard had never seen Pony-Tail.

He thought of Zarana's snake dance – and had an inkling that her reality might live up to what he could imagine. At least he had something to look forward to.

"There's so much surplus emotion around here," said Richard, "strewn like used paper tissues. It's a wonder these things don't spontaneously generate all the time."

The cube cracked. Someone swore.

"It'll be closed casket," said Fred.

Dark, silent figures joined the crowds, members of the Festival.

They watched the cutting-crew extricate the former meat-man from his car. The rally in Soho Square was over. To the faithful, it must seem as if Lord Leaves' prayers produced impressive instant results.

A banner unfurled, proclaiming the wages of sin as death.

"The most interesting thing about our go-go golem," said Richard, "is that there's *someone* inside."

"A dog-handler, setting the beast on its prey?"

"There is such a person, undoubtedly. A *summoner*. We'll get to him or her later. But what interests me just now is that some *personality* persists inside our Mr Sludge. An earthbound spirit, doing the summoner's bidding. It's not easy to get a ghost to follow orders. There has to be some sort of shared purpose. You can't just invoke, say, Henry the Fifth, dress him in ectoplasmic armour, and send him out to murder the Bay City Rollers for offences against humanity."

"But you could get him to fight the French?"

"Precisely. You're learning."

"It rubs off after a while. So, you've got His Bloody Lordship, who hates the porn barons . . ."

"And dresses like a high initiate in the sort of religion with a solid track record in revenant-raising."

Fred remembered Lord Leaves' stern, aged features as he sang or hosed. And his wife's ecstatic excitement. These people loved smiting more than they hated sin.

"So who's he raised up? Some old-time Puritan book-burner?"

"That's a thought. Mrs Grundy or Dr Bowdler? I think not, though. No point going to all the trouble of ensouling an amorphous mass of power if all it's going to do is sing hymns or write complaining letters."

Fred thought about the crimes. He set aside the method – the *weird* stuff – and tried to concentrate on the motive. Maybe thinking of the golem as a plain old crim would help.

"What about a nutter? Someone 'down on whores' like that nutcase who threw ammonia in porn cinemas. He hated it that the films turned him on, but couldn't stop himself being in the front row every night. He was looking to blame someone else for his own 'urges'."

They were outside the Dog and Duck pub now. There was a buzz about an "accident" in Greek Street earlier, and a grumbling persisted regarding the Festival's hosepipe habits. But things were getting back to Soho normal – shrill laughs, loud music (Mott the Hoople's "All the Way From Memphis" from the Dog versus Roxy

Music's "Virginia Plain" from the Crown and Two Chairmen up the road), busy fillies getting close to sozzled blokes, shills from the strip-joints inviting passersby, plods looking the other way.

Richard considered Fred's Ripper theory and decided it wouldn't do. "Our victims have both been *men*. The higher-ups. The inadequates you're talking about go after women – strippers, models, prostitutes, usherettes. Our killer has been precise about who gets hurt. The girls in Gates' car got away with damage only to their dignity."

"So, we're scouting the afterlife for someone who hates bent coppers and cockney ponces?"

Richard spread his hands.

"Neither of the dead men had fan clubs, mate," said Fred.

"I can think of two Soho disappearees who might have motive for doing away with Mickey Gates. We can rule out Pony-Tail, the patron saint of strip-tease. Our golem is definitely a feller. Shaped like a former wrestler, bouncer and strong-arm man. 'One of those man-mountain types', you said. Droppeth the penny?"

"Grek Cohen?"

Richard snapped his fingers. "Of course, it would be peachier if Cohen had some grudge against Booth."

Fred bit his lip. "Very sharp," he said. "In '63, Booth was a rising DC, already knee-deep in Soho rackets. They say he brokered the deal between Schluderpacheru and Gates. It's what set him up for . . . well, for life. I wouldn't be surprised if he was the one who snatched the girl, to lure Grek. Then, afterwards, he . . . *thwick*!" He cut his throat with a thumb.

Richard's brows narrowed. "It occurs to me that Mr Schluderpacheru might, at present, be a worried man."

"Couldn't happen to a nicer bloke."

"Come come, now now. We frown on killing people with the Dark Arts, no matter their character defects. There are often unhappy consequences. It's proverbially difficult to get the genie back in the bottle."

That was not a comforting thought.

VIII Lord Soho

Back at Skinderella's, Fred learned Zarana had done her snake dance to an audience of precisely two paying punters, plus malingerers from a clean-up crew the Yard sent round to remove Booth's body and seal his files. The ghost at the feast was Inspector Roger "No

Mates" Macendale, who had annoyed someone once and been cursed with the job of investigating police corruption cases. Macendale had avoided the OPS mess for years; now, in Booth's office, he was literally treading in it.

Boddey was trying to make himself helpful, hopping from one foot to the other like a playground semi-outcast trying to get in cosy with bullies by directing their attention to even more marginalized kids. Busy hoped to cast himself as a heroic whistle-blower, soldiering on in an impossible job, never taking so much as a penny from the Vice Lords who'd suborned his guv'nor. It was going to be hard to explain away the Jaguar in the garage of his family villa in Surbiton, and the equally high-maintenance, luxury model girlfriends in rented flats from Belgravia to Hampstead.

With the corpse removed from the premises, Richard had commandeered the phone and was making calls. The Ruling Cabal had pull from the House of Lords to the councils of gangland. Richard used it to solicit backstory on the Festival of Morality, the Big Soho Carve-Up of 1963, the box-office records of Imperial Anglo-British/John Bull Films, Ltd (Graf Konstantin Hermann Rezetsky Bolakov ze Schluderpacheru, prop.), golem-raising rituals, the presumably late Immanuel Cohen ("Grek" was from his wrestling style, "Graeco-Roman") and the legal tangle of the Obscene Displays act.

Fred sat in the bar, skim-reading *Confessions of a Psychic Investigator*. He had slipped the book into his pocket earlier and, what with the excitement, forgotten it until now. Chapter One, "The Ghost Gets Laid", introduced medallion-wearing open-frilly-shirt magician "Robert Jasperson" and his cheeky cockney wide-boy sidekick "Bert Royale", who ran a cleaning service to get rid of unwanted spooks. Their first big case was a summons to a posh school where a succubus was molesting older girls and younger teachers with "midnight gropings and tonguings". Fred was miffed to discover that the gormless Bert spent all his time peeping through keyholes, getting "hot and bothered" as the apparently irresistible Jasperson enjoyed "rampaging rumpy-pumpy" with the French and Biology mistresses, the girls' netball team, his "tantric sex magickian" assistant Clitoria, and a passing district nurse. At the climax, the randy git solved the case by converting the "heavily-knockered" ghost girlie (a nun walled up centuries earlier for instructing the novitiates in "Mysteries of the Orgasm") to "proper hetero shaggery" with vigorous application of his "mighty shaft". Lesley Behan (which Fred suspected wasn't her birth name) made Jasperson out to be the sort of psychic detective who couldn't so much as take out an anemometer to read a cold spot in a haunted house without being pounced upon by suburban housewives, high society nymphomaniacs, teenage virgins, Dutch au pair girls, or two-way bike chicks.

"Losin' yourself in a good book?"

Fred looked up from a scene involving an "Orgy of Bubastis" and saw Zarana, in her civvies.

"Not exactly," he said, folding the book and hiding it in his back pocket. "You heard about Gates?"

Zarana cringed. "Some of the girls from Dirty Gertie's were in after it happened. We're all worried about bein' out of jobs. A lot of us are considerin' other lines of work. Actin', mostly."

"Including you?"

She looked glum. "John Bull Films has a company to compete with Hammer, Gruesome Pictures. I've done three-day bits for them – wenches chewed by werewolves, maids bitten on the nipple by vampire queens, dollymops gutted by Reg the Ripper. They couldn't afford Jack, apparently. I don't much fancy gettin' killed over and over again. And those are Popeye's 'respectable' pictures. He also makes the *Sexploits* films . . . you know, *Sexploits of a Long-Distance Lorry Driver*, *Sexploits of a Merseyside Meter Maid*, *Sexploits of a Quantity Surveyor*. You don't get in those unless you turn up at his palace for bun-fights they call 'trade shows' and go upstairs with fat, baldin' men who own provincial cinemas and stink of stale Kia-Ora. I'd rather work in a biscuit factory in Barnet."

"There are other film companies."

"Not if you've got a John Bull brand on your bum. Popeye can get you blacklisted. So I ain't goin' to be a Bond girl or a wife of Henry VIII. It'll be back to modellin'." Zarana held up her hands, made gestures in the air, turned her wrists.

"Glamour modelling?"

"Hand modellin'. Close-ups of washin'-up liquid bottles bein' squeezed. Fingers brushin' a freshly-shaved manly chin."

She brushed his chin, reminding him that he wasn't freshly-shaved. "Don't you think I have delectable digits?"

"Absolutely, Queenie."

"You're a love, Freddy Friday. The mitts are too big for the rest of me, but in close-up no one notices." She stuck a kiss on the side of his head, tiny tongue slipping into his ear.

Fred realized he was doing better on this case than poor old Bert Royale. Still, Zarana wasn't like the paper cut-out birds in the book. And, after two appalling crime scenes in one day, he doubted whether he'd be able to raise the enthusiasm for "rampaging rumpy-pumpy".

"I'll get by," said Zarana. "I'm gettin' too old and tired for strippin'. It's murder on the plates."

Fred thought she might be about twenty-four.

Richard slid out of the darkness and took a stool next to them, squeezing Zarana's hand in greeting. Fred, for once, was sensitive – Zarana liked Richard, but fancied Fred. One in the eye for Robert Jasperson, Mighty Shaftsman.

"Here's a funny thing," said Richard. "Where do you think Lord Leaves of Leng hangs his hat?"

"Some Georgian pile with half Hampshire around it?" ventured Fred.

"And a dinky *pied-a-terre* in Kinghtsbridge," added Zarana, "handy for Harrod's so his wife can shop her little heart out?"

Richard smiled in triumph. "That's what I thought, but – no – Algernon Arbuthnot Leaves resides right here, in Soho. It's a Georgian, all right. A town house in Golden Square, about five minutes away from this fleshpot. You notice he didn't have his rally outside his own front door and tick off the neighbours. Konstantin Schluderpacheru is one of those, two doors down. According to *Screen International*, John Bull Films have a more or less permanent party going on there. Top folk from showbiz getting zonked, dollies draped around the furniture, hospitality free-flowing, cut-throat deals signed in blood in the bathrooms."

Fred noticed Zarana shuddered. He remembered what she'd said about "trade shows".

"Gates lived on three floors above the Hot-Lite, in Dean Street. DI Booth had a split-level mews flat off D'Arblay Street for which he didn't pay rent. Fred's old classmate Harry Boddey makes do with five spacious rooms and a rooftop garden in Ramillies Street. Soho is the place to live, it seems."

"I share with two other girls in Falconburg Court, off Soho Square," said Zarana, unashamed. "Handy for the clubs."

"Undoubtedly. But it's His Lordship who stands out, as it were."

"That explains why he's so worked up about smut," said Fred. "What with him being local. Probably worried about his wife getting a shock every time she pops out for a pinta. The place fills up with blokes out looking for . . . well, you know. A decent woman isn't safe."

"I doubt Lady Celia does her own popping, Frederick. Folk like the Leaves have people to do that for them."

Fred felt a full-bore glare aimed at him. Zarana was furious. He hadn't thought through that 'decent woman' remark and dug a hole it would take a lot of fancy footwork to get out of.

"No woman is safe," he amended, which actually didn't make things better.

Those model's hands made knuckly fists.

"You know what I mean," he said exasperated, fending her off. "You must get as much unwanted aggro out there as anyone."

Zarana cooled and decided to let him off with a vicious pinch. "Fair point. When I walk home, if I can't get a bouncer to see me to my door, I wrap up in an old coat that makes me look like someone's grandmother. Even then, idiots give me stick. They see you naked and think they know about you."

"Besides, there's something weird about Leaves' wife," said Fred. "Did you see her face? She might be against filth and fun, but she's charged-up about *something*."

"Yeah, I know," admitted Zarana. "Among his other earners, Gates puts out – used to put out – a spankin' mag. You know, 'it's six of the best 'pon your quiverin' buttocks, Fiona!' Lady Leaves looks like a *Strict* model. One of the thrashers."

Fred liked the idea of Lord Leaves flicking through a porn mag before writing his next morality song and seeing wifey's bright little eyes staring up from a fladge lay-out. Under her wimple and robe, Lady Celia could easily be wearing black leather and straps. He tried to stop thinking of that. It was all Lesley Behan's fault, for warping his mind.

"I've looked over some of Lord Leaves' recent speeches," said Richard. "He continually harps on the theme of himself as the last moral man in Soho, surrounded by a rising tide of obscenity, crying halt! to the advance of corruption. He sounds like someone who wants something *back*. This whole square mile."

IX Private Files

Boddey was in handcuffs, being eased firmly towards the door and a waiting Black Mariah. About time too, thought Fred.

"What are you doing him for, sir?" he asked DI Macendale.

"Tampering with evidence, for a start."

"Freddo, it weren't me," pleaded Busy.

"Files upstairs have been filleted," said Macendale. "We've got enough to hang Booth and a whole lot more, but choice items have been spirited away . . ."

KIM NEWMAN

Richard was interested. "What, specifically, is missing?"

Macendale looked glum. "Hard to say. But gaps are obvious."

"Constable Boddey," said Richard, "have you any ideas what ought to be there but isn't?"

"I didn't touch it!"

"I didn't say you did," said Richard. "I asked you if you knew what *it* was."

"Will it help me?" Busy asked, tiny spark of cunning twitching the corners of his mouth. It was the ghost of his smirk.

"It will help *us*," said Richard, gesturing to keep Busy's attention.

Macendale shook his head. He wanted to get home to his cocoa and be up early tomorrow to swoop on high-ranking bent coppers. He would already have Busy down as grass-in-training, and ready to cut a deal to get the higher-ups named. The people who'd let Booth get away with it all these years.

Busy swallowed. He had got more tear-streaked throughout the day.

"I'd have to look."

"Under no circumstances . . ." began Macendale.

Richard unfolded a document and presented it to the inspector. Macendale's lips moved and his eyes swivelled from side to side as he read. Richard kindly pointed out official seals and signatures.

"Uh, carry on, Mr Jeperson," said Macendale, fuming.

Richard took back the precious document, and slipped it into an inside pocket.

"Let's take Constable Boddey upstairs," he said.

Busy shrank with terror. Macendale at least got enjoyment from that, and manhandled his prisoner up to Booth's office.

A door that looked like a broom cupboard led to a tiny space lined with metal filing cabinets. Locks were smashed. Richard took an interest in the damage, which could have been done with a sledge-hammer. He scraped dried scum from a shiny dent in the dull metal and showed it to Fred.

Only two people at a time could get in the room, and they found it cramped if any drawers were pulled out. Richard withdrew and let Macendale supervise Busy as he went through the files. The inspector kept a close eye on the miscreant – as if expecting him to grab and swallow something incriminating. At that, Fred wouldn't have put it past him.

Richard took Fred aside. "Our Mr Sludge has subtler habits than we thought," he said. "Smash-kill-grind-crunch is one thing, but filching evidence from locked cabinets in a hidden room suggests a lighter touch. That's where our summoner comes in."

"Still think it's Leaves?"

Richard considered. "Booth's files would interest a moral crusader. In addition to protesting against the mere existence of licentiousness, I assume Lord Leaves agitates against folk who profit from immorality, encouraging their prosecution on criminal grounds. I imagine that's why Booth was first on the to-kill list – it should have been his job to pursue Gates and the like for what I assume were many, many infractions of the letter of the law."

"Campaigners have tried private prosecutions," admitted Fred. "Stooges fronting the sex shops or porn cinemas get slapped with huge fines, which are paid promptly in big bundles of cash. Confiscated stock is replaced by closing time, and some new face is behind the counter the next day. Burly Gates rarely even gets mentioned in court."

Macendale brought Busy out of the file-room.

"So?" asked Richard.

"He's shamming," said Macendale.

"I'm *not*," whined Busy. "Honest. All that's missing is old stuff. Records from the '60s. Memorabilia."

"Memorabilia?" asked Richard, intrigued.

"Publicity eight-by-tens, brochures, mags. Too tame for today's market, but nostalgia is booming. Private collectors pay high prices for vintage smut. Anything with Pony-Tail is worth a packet."

Fred and Richard exchanged a look. Pony-Tail, again. Was Grek still trying to rescue his tasselled princess?

"Booth had it salted away. Came with the place. Called it his school fee fund. He had kids."

"That's all that's gone?" asked Richard.

Busy wriggled, which was what a shrug looked like with handcuffs.

"There's something else," said Richard.

Busy couldn't look away from Richard's eyes. "It's other . . . investments," admitted Busy. "Eight millimetre films of tarts who've got new lives and want to keep old ones forgotten. Explicit photos of girls, and some lads as well, with prominent people – film and TV stars, business magnates, politicians, *policemen*, judges, pop singers. You can imagine the kinkiness, and how eager they are to keep it hush-hush. Some were paying off like rigged slot-machines."

"Blackmail," said Richard.

Busy wriggled again. "That's it. That's all of it."

Fred remembered Zarana had mentioned Booth was milking a former stripper to keep her stag films out of the Sunday papers.

Evidently, it was a cottage industry. That bulked out the suspect list, though – with the goods flown – it'd be hard to add actual names.

"It's no surprise Booth and Gates were in the blackmail racket," said Fred.

"Not Gates," said Busy, surprised. "The other one, Schluder-pacheru."

X The Party Scene

Golden Square, London W1. Handy for Wardour Street, where all the film companies – major and (very) minor – keep offices. A semi-secluded haven of dignified mansions off Brewer Street, the (even) sleazier continuation of Old Compton Street.

A hop south was the Windmill Theatre, where nude girls had been appearing nightly since the War. The Windmill boasted WE NEVER CLOSED, despite air raids and police sweeps, working within the law of the day by presenting bare lovelies in posed tableaux. Vice squad officers kept reserved seats, allegedly prepared to haul the curtain down if a gooseflesh girl so much as blinked. Fred assumed the predecessors of Boot Boy Booth just enjoyed the ogling oppor-tunities, and the thick envelopes of ten-bob notes mysteriously slipped into their programmes. The Windmill was now a Dad's idea of naughty – patriotic songs and patter comedians, and mere glimpses of skin. It was rendered outmoded by flickering "X"-certificate fare on offer in Piccadilly Circus at the Moulin and Eros sex cinemas (the latter opposite the statue of Eros), let alone the clubs, "reviews" and in-all-but-name brothels clustered at the lower end of Berwick Street. Plus *Oh, Calcutta!*, settled in for a long run at the Royalty Theatre: a Windmill show with sarky sketches and nudes that moved, suitable for trendy poseur and carriage trade alike.

Konstantin Schluderpacheru's town house might as well have sported a huge neon sign with BAD SCENE written on it. The windows were open but curtained. Shifting, multi-coloured lights gave the building a flashy, disco come-on look. Live music poured out, heavy on the bongos and the fuzz-pedal. Glittery people came and went, in states of disrepair. A Eurovision Song Contest runner-up clung to the square's railings, bird-thin shoulders exposed by her backless dress, heaving liquid vomit into the bushes. A working-class novelist swigged from a pint-mug of vodka, and berated the pop princess. He blamed her for his inability to write anything worth-while since moving from Liverpool to Hampstead and Ibiza.

"No wonder Lord Leaves hates these people," said Richard.

Two doors down, His Lordship's house was dark and shut up tight. At 10:30 in the evening, all good moral crusaders should be tucked into their twin beds, eyes screwed shut, ears plugged against the seepage of party noise. Or else peering with night-vision scopes at the comings and goings two doors away, keeping careful note of the names and faces.

Schluderpacheru might be the King of Blackmail, but Fred had no doubt that the Festival would use the same tactics. Lord Leaves needed a flock of politicians and newspaper people in his pocket. No one made a better, more vocal supporter of decency than a dignitary with something to hide.

As expected, Schluderpacheru's front door was guarded like a *führerbunker*. With the soaring death rate among the host's known associates, extra muscle was packed in. Skin-headed ex-boxers in tuxedos stood by. Fred spotted a couple of off-duty plods stationed about the square, moonlighting to cover their hire purchase payments.

"Come on, lads," said Zarana, linking arms with Fred and Richard, and steering them towards the door. "Teeth and smiles."

There were flashbulb photographers in wait.

After Richard had theorized that it would be difficult to secure an entrée into the Schluderpacheru house, Zarana pointed out that it was one of the many places in London to which entrance was impossible unless you were, or were with, a stunningly beautiful girl. She then dug out her standing invitation, initialled K.S. in green ink. When not working her Queen of the Nile routine, Zarana did a high society act as "Contessa de Undressa". With different make-up and costume, she looked like a different person. In full Contessa drag, she wore a floor-length red silk evening dress secured by four tiny-but-sturdy clasps, an upswept blonde wig (complete with tiara) and a box full of impressive paste jewels. Thanks to spike-heels and the towering wig, she was a foot taller. She looked down her patrician nose like someone who would snub the Royal Family as middle-class German parvenus. If she kept her mahf shut, the illusion was perfect.

To Richard, this was a stroke of luck. He had no qualms about letting an "s.b.g." join the fun. A semi-official amateur himself, he would take help from whoever offered, assuming they were capable of taking care of themselves. Even with multiple deaths and supernatural maniacs in the case, Richard saw it as a bit of a lark that would be jollier with a pretty face along. Fred was less cavalier: from their earlier chat, he knew Zarana would put herself in an uncomfortable position by taking up the green-initialled invitation. She assured him that Schluderpacheru's guests could hardly be a bigger shower than the Skindy's clientele and besides she could rely on him to protect her. That was a joke, but he took it seriously. She covered doubt well – she was a skilled performer, after all – but Fred picked it up. Again, it struck Fred funny that where Zarana was concerned, he was more in tune with the vibes than the supposed "sensitive".

Zarana presented the invitation to a squat, thick man who wore sunglasses after dark and turned on a full-wattage smile.

"This is Happenin' Herbert, the pop artist," she said, indicating Richard, who flashed the peace sign. "And this is the famous Fred, who you must have read about in the Sunday supplements."

The goon clocked the "K.S.", returned the gilt-edged card to Zarana, and stood aside. The door opened.

The mirror-lined reception hall multiplied their images to infinity. Fred wore a white dinner jacket appropriated from the Skinderella's costume store (what act was it part of?) and now saw it didn't really go with his jeans and docs. He tried to be the sort of Fred who made sure he got written up as fashionable, then wore something else equally stupid when people copied him.

One of the mirrors had a tell-tale grey-veil tint. There would be two-way glass all over the house, especially in the upstairs bedrooms, and cine-cameras grinding away, adding to the Blackmail King's investment portfolio. Fred resolved not to use the toilet while he was here.

Zarana made a kiss-mouth at the mirror.

They proceeded into a large, half-sunken room full of chattery people and flashing lights. On a stage, a combo performed "She's Not There", trying not to mind that nobody was paying attention. In the centre of the ballroom was a bath of light – a swimming pool the size of a family plot, with a lighting array inset into the walls. A very drunk, very white girl wearing only a bikini bottom sat on the edge, splashing with her little legs, making waves that broke against the chest of a fully-dressed, white-haired man who floated with a dreamy smile stuck on his face, puffing happily on a pipe of tobacco and hash, the wings of his Ganex raincoat spread out like lily-pads.

"That's . . ." began Fred.

"Yes," said Richard.

"And with him is . . ."

"Yes, her. She's in all the *Sexploits* films, and *Stow It, Sandra*. Not much of an actress, but she does this trick with her mouth and two golf balls that turns strong men to custard. I worked with her once. She's a right cow."

"Blimey," said Fred. "You wouldn't have thought it. I'd have expected him to be with Lord Leaves' crowd, protesting. He couldn't exactly show up at his party conference with her on his arm and expect to get re-elected."

"Don't be so sure, Freddy," said Zarana.

"I'd say something about 'strange bedfellows'," said Richard, "but I suspect that the beds here have seen a lot stranger."

A small, round man in a skin-tight moiré kaftan approached Zarana, pupils contracted to pinpricks, sweating profusely. He stuck out his tongue, which had a half-dissolved pill balanced on its end, and reached for Zarana with chubby, wriggly hands. Fred slapped him away and wagged a finger. He looked as if he was about to cry, then latched onto a passing black girl with a silver wig and matching lipstick and paddled along in her wake.

"Business as bleedin' usual," she said.

"*Ou se trouve* mine host?" asked Richard.

She scanned the room. "Not here. There's a room upstairs, for his inner circle. Wood panels, ghastly pictures of satyrs and fat bints, hundred-year-old brandy, private screenin' room. Popeye holds court there. Though most of his cronies are here. You can tell them because they look bloody worried."

Dotted throughout the senseless crowd were furrowed faces.

Richard hummed. "The oases of desperation do stand out somewhat. Or, at least, sobriety."

"Did you see that Vincent Price film about the fancy-dress ball?"

Fred knew what Zarana meant. "*Masque of the Red Death*?"

"This is that, isn't it? Rich people makin' animals of themselves tryin' to have a good time, with the plague outside, ravagin' the countryside."

"And the Red Death approaches the castle doors," said Richard.

"It's time Death knocked here like bleedin' Avon callin'," said Zarana.

"Let's slide upstairs and try to see Prince Prospero," said Richard.

Fred turned to Zarana to tell her to find a loitering spot in the crowd and wait for them.

"No fear, Freddy," she said. "You're not leavin' me behind. It's not safe here . . ."

A couple of football players with enormous bouffant perms and mutton chops shaped like Roman helmet cheek-pieces caught sight of Zarana and began dribbling towards the goal area. They wore suits that flapped like flags.

"Point taken," said Fred.

XI Coming in at the End

Without Zarana, they would never have found the inner sanctum. Schluderpacheru's house was like a funfair maze: zigzag corridors that cheated perspective, flock wallpaper with an optical illusion theme, floor-to-ceiling joke paintings of doors, set decoration left over from Gruesome Pictures, actual doors chameleoned into walls, burning bowls of heady incense. There were chalk-marks on the floor, recently scrawled runes.

"Schluderpacheru has taken precautions," said Richard, toeing a symbol. "I suppose he learned in the old country."

Zarana led them round a corner and they found themselves looking up at a 9-foot-tall man, with a distinguished rising wave of grey hair and a superbly-cut, wide-lapelled suit. He was sleek, with shining, somehow wicked eyes, and wore a mediaeval armoured glove.

It was a lifelike portrait, painted directly onto a wood panel.

"That's Popeye," said Zarana. "Larger than life and twice as creepy."

One of his eyes was brown and lazy-lidded, the other green and staring.

Voices came from behind the picture, raised but indistinct, arguing in a language Fred didn't recognize.

"There's a trick to this," said Zarana, patting the portrait. She found studs on the metal glove, and twiddled them. "Boys and their bleedin' toys."

With a click and a whoosh, the painting split diagonally and disappeared into recesses.

Beyond was a room illuminated by a blazing fire in an open grate – in contravention of the Clean Air Act, Fred noted – and burning oil-lamps. Two men were outlined by flame-light, both wearing symbol-marked dressing gowns, locked in struggle, argument turned phy-sical. One was Schluderpacheru, under-sized in person, hair awry. Half his face wrinkled with effort, but the left side was plastic surgery-smooth, with the fixed, glaring green eye. He had the upper hand, but Lord Leaves – for all his years – fought fiercely; his fingers sank deep into Schluderpacheru's windpipe, incantations rattled in the back of his throat. In one corner shrank Lady Celia, holding a fold of habit over her face like an Arab wife, eyes startlingly bright and excited.

Swirling in the air before the fire were scraps of matter in the shape of a big man, struggling to cohere but tearing apart as much as it came together. Mr Sludge – Grek Cohen – had an invitation to the party, but wasn't here yet.

Everyone froze to look at them. Even the phantasm.

"We seem to have come in at the end of the story," said Richard.

Schluderpacheru and Lord Leaves spared them barely a glance, then got back to their grappling. The artificial side of the host's face bulged. His eyeball popped, escaping its wet red socket. The egg-sized glass eye fell heavily, thumping Lord Leaves on the forehead. His Lordship, stunned, lost his grip and Schluderpacheru – who presumably couldn't pull that trick twice – dropped him. The King of Blackmail passed a hand over his hair, prissily fixing its dove-grey wave in place, but didn't seem concerned about his empty eye-socket.

"I know who you are, magician," Schluderpacheru told Richard. "And I don't need help. This war of witchery is about to end. To my satisfaction."

He took a metal triangle from a stand, holding it like a trowel. It gleamed, two sides sharpened to razor-edges. Schluderpacheru dropped to one knee, raising the triangle high, then brought the killing point down heavily. Lord Leaves' breast-bone snapped.

Lady Celia yelped, but her husband said nothing.

The wedge-knife was embedded in His Lordship's chest. He kicked, leaked a little, and was still.

"There," said Schluderpacheru. "That's done. No more Festival. No more bother."

Smug and suave, he considered the man-shaped cloud.

"Go away, Grek," he said. "Your summoner's dead. You've no place here, no toehold in this world. You should have stayed where you were."

Matter swarmed thickly, lacing together. Embers from the fire were sucked up and clustered into a burning heart. Stuff came from somewhere, from all around, and knitted. Greyish liquid seeped out of the air, running into and around the big shape, slicking over. A big-browed face formed out of the darkness. It looked down on the one-eyed man.

For a moment, Schluderpacheru was puzzled. He glanced at Lord Leaves, to make sure he was dead, then – panic sparking in his remaining eye – around the room, fixing on each face in turn.

"You—" he blurted.

Grek Cohen was solid now, a colossal statue of sludge, boiling with ghost-life. He gave off a spent-match stink.

Huge hands clapped, catching Schluderpacheru's head. The top of his skull popped and his one eye leaked blood as his face was ground to paste between rough, new-made palms.

Zarana shoved her face into Fred's jacket, again. Richard whistled. Cohen lifted Schluderpacheru – his arms and legs flopped limp, his shoes dangled inches above the carpet. Cohen tossed the corpse into the fireplace. The robe flared at once, then fire began to eat into the flesh. Foul cooking smell filled the room.

"That's the last of them," Richard addressed the colossus. "The three who betrayed you, Mr Cohen. The three who did away with the girl you died for. And Lord Leaves, too. You have no master here. Your purpose is achieved. Yet you remain. Why, I wonder?"

Richard walked up to the golem, and examined it as if he were thinking of buying. Grue dripped from its spade-sized hands. Fred held Zarana, and looked around the room.

Lady Celia was mad, poor love, tearing at her habits.

Richard made some experimental gestures. Cohen stood solid.

"Hmmn, interesting. By all rights, you should evaporate. This is a rum do."

Lady Celia's wimple came apart, leaving her pale face framed by an alice band. Her unconfined hair poured out – impossible lengths of it, blinding white-blonde, shining in firelight.

In a flash, Fred put it together. It was dizzying, sickening.

"Pony-Tail," he said.

Zarana dared to peep. "So it bleedin' is," she exclaimed. "Wonders never cease!"

Richard also directed his attention to Lord Leaves' young widow.

Lady Celia stood up, shedding the remains of her habit as elegantly as she had ever undressed, slipping the band off her crown, shaking out her hair.

"Now I see what they were talking about," said Richard.

The woman was nude, Godiva-curtained by her hair. It seemed alive, like Medusa-tendrils. She gathered the mane in her hands, and held it at the back of her neck, winding her band about it. She had her pony-tail again.

She couldn't have been thirty yet; how young had she been when she was a striptease star? She hadn't been legal, for certain.

"Grek Cohen had no master, just a mistress."

Lady Celia nodded to Richard. She formed a sly smile.

Fred felt it again, the warmth this woman projected. An icy warmth to be sure, but persuasive. He saw the guile working on Richard too, on the thing that had been Grek Cohen. This was a woman a man wanted to shield – he would put himself between her and any horror, and think the prick of a blade-point in his spine was the first touch of a caress.

Pony-Tail stood over Lord Leaves. "Goodbye, Daddy," she said. She had a finishing school accent, clear and sharp as crystal. She raised her bare foot to his face, stroked his slack cheek with her toes, then deftly scraped his eyes shut. "You were always my first."

"Clouds of mystery part," said Richard.

Pony-Tail giggled, and looked fifteen again. "Have I been naughty?"

"Does *he* know what you did?" Fred asked.

She looked at him, teasing and quizzical. Fred indicated Cohen.

"Does he know it was you? Booth, Schluderpacheru and Gates didn't kidnap you in 1963. I'll bet it was your idea. His original body is under a foundation stone somewhere, isn't it? Did you do it yourself, or just watch? Was he happy anyway, just that you smiled at him as the concrete poured in? What a mug! Ten years on, and he's still your pet, isn't he? This has all been cleaning house. Had they started blackmailing you – those idiots! – threatening to expose Lady Celia Leaves as the notorious Pony-Tail? That would be one for the *News of the World*. Scupper His Lordship's Festival of Morality once and for all. Or was it just money they wanted?"

She smiled, enigmatically. "You know what they *really* wanted?" she said, tilting her head to one side. "More than money, more than business as usual, more than power? They wanted *me*. They wanted me *back*."

She did a few steps, hair alive around her shoulders.

"Pony-Tail . . . returns," she said, presenting herself. "Pony-Tail . . . rides again!"

Fred fancied Cohen was smiling, appreciating her act. He had never really been fooled, but her act was just so damned *good* that it was impossible not to play along. Fred guessed Lord Leaves had been the same, opening his big book of spells just for a wink and a smile and a peek.

"I suppose this is your final performance," said Richard.

"Maybe not. What with everything, I'm Queen of Soho. No one in the way. The Festival will follow my lead. Can you imagine what I can make them do? It'll be a twenty-four-hour riot. And I can buy or run everything else in sight. Maybe I will come back, do the shows and the films and the telly. Only this time, I'll do it for me, not *them*, not men, not you."

She laid her head against Cohen's pebbled side, a girl petting her horse.

"It's the dancing, isn't it?" asked Richard, fascinated.

"Very clever, Mr Magician," she said. She bent over double from a full-stand and touched her toes, then sprung back upright, hands on hips, perfectly balanced, perfectly supple. "Yes, it's the dancing. Daddy started me off. He brought me up to be an initiate of Erzuli, Baphomet and Nyarlathotep. Ritual dance, steps along the paths of power. I had to go out into the world, break away from the Festival, find my own dance. Then I had to go back, for a while. It was part of the pattern. Now, I have new steps, new paths, new dances. I don't need any of them any more."

She was always in motion, dancing to the rhythm of her heartbeat. She was a white flame, endlessly mesmerizing, lovely but deadly.

"What about him?" asked Fred.

Pony-Tail looked up at Cohen's caricature of a face, almost fondly. "He's my masterpiece," she said. "How many other strippers really can dance to raise the dead?"

"You know a lot of dead people," Richard observed.

"I'm afraid I shall know some more, soon."

Zarana flashed anger at the woman. "You ain't that special, you know."

"My friend would argue with you," said Pony-Tail, concentrating.

Cohen reacted to her change of mood, swelling into a more menacing aspect.

Richard muttered magics, which the dancing priestess dispelled with blown kisses.

"She's not your friend, Grekko," said Zarana. "She killed you, for a start."

"He knows, he doesn't care. None of them would care. Because it was *me*. Next to me, you're nothing, missy."

Zarana faced up to Pony-Tail.

Cohen's arm rose, ratcheting like a guillotine blade. Fred stepped forward, to pull Zarana out of the way.

The girl eluded him and bore down on Lady Celia. The Queen of the Nile versus the Queen of Soho. Pony-Tail meets Contessa de Undressa. No holds barred. One fatal fall for the crown.

Zarana punched Pony-Tail in the stomach. Cohen roared.

Lady Celia doubled, hair tenting around her, then recovered in an instant and flicked out with contemptuous fingers. She twisted a clasp off Zarana's shoulder, and the dress came apart. Zarana held the scraps to her body, hobbled.

"I can't believe that rag is still kicking around. It was made for me."

Fred helped Zarana stay on her feet. He looked from the cockney Egyptian, awkward in the too-loose gown, to the white goddess, sinuous and unashamed in the firelight. Like everyone else, he dreamed of Pony-Tail; the difference was he knew she wasn't real.

"After this, I suppose the big fella's finished," said Fred. "All work done."

Pony-Tail cocked her head, considering. "I might bring him out for special occasions. Summoning is an effort, but he's worth it, don't you think?"

"You hear that, Immanuel?" said Fred. "After this, you're going back in the attic."

Cohen was a statue, arm up.

"Good work, Frederick," said Richard. "Keep at it."

"You did all this to be with her, and she's shafted you. Again. Are you really as dim as they say? The cleverclogs. Burly Gates, Boot Boy Booth, Popeye Schluderpacheru. They all *laughed* at you, Grek. Know what I mean? The big ape doolally over the princess. Like King Sodding Kong, they said. When they decided to dump you, she leaped at the chance to help. It was how she bought her way out, got back into His Lordship's house. Couldn't get into the Royal Enclosure with a lovesick gorilla mooning about, could she?"

"None of this matters," said Pony-Tail, bored. "Really."

"And now you've done for them all, and you *still* don't get the girl! Mate, you have been fitted up for a proper set of cap and bells. You must be the biggest mug punter in Soho."

The huge arm came down. The hand closed, on Pony-Tail's rope of hair.

"Ouch," she said, irritated.

Cohen held her by a leash.

Fred saw a glint of annoyance in her eye, an unattractive, petty expression. Then a sense of what was suddenly lost, a bulb of panic sprouting.

Thick arms hoisted Lady Celia Asquith-Leaves, the incomparable Pony-Tail, off the floor and hugged to Cohen's chest, her struggling body shoved into the muck and mud of its trunk. Her arms and feet stuck out, flapping and kicking. Her face sank under the surface. Grey mass surged around the screaming "O" of her mouth, then filled it, staunching her noise.

"Finally," said Richard.

Now Grek Cohen had Pony-Tail, rather than the other way round, Richard's gestures and incantations had an effect. The colossus, growing insubstantial, rose like a hot-air balloon, bumping the ceiling. On its excuse for a face was a last smile.

"I think a withdrawal is in order," said Richard.

Fred and Zarana backed out of the inner sanctum. Richard followed, keeping up a stream of reverse conjurations.

"Where's his wand?" asked Zarana.

"It's in the fingers," said Richard.

"Magic."

The colossus shrank to the size of a floating man, Grek Cohen superimposed upon Pony-Tail, her limbs encased in his, her face shrieking soundlessly through his battered mask, her electric eyes staring madness through his dull, dead lamps.

The carpet pulled up and spiralled around the phantasm, spilling flaming oil and rolling Leaves away. Cohen contracted to a dozen flaming points and whooshed into darkness.

The girl was gone with him, leaving only her hair. It drifted to the floor, strands crackling as they brushed flame. Swathes fell about like cast-off string.

The gorilla got the girl, which should count as a happy ending. Fred hoped never to see either again.

"The socially conscious thing would be to put out that fire," said Richard, "before the house burns down around the guests."

Zarana shifted a vase and disclosed a fire-extinguisher.

"Just the ticket."

As she tossed the extinguisher to Richard, her dress finally fell off. Fred couldn't look away. She noticed.

"That's better," she said. "I was worried. I thought that cow had you under her bloody spell, like she had all the other idiots."

After long, brazen seconds, she gathered up the gown and fastened it.

Weirdly, the little fiddle she did to reassemble her costume and cover herself struck Fred as sexier than Pony-Tail getting her kit off.

"There's no comparison, luv," said Fred.

Richard unloosed a surge of white foam at the flames.

XII Sexploits of a Psychic Investigator's Assistant

Near dawn, in the big bed in her tiny room in Falconburg Court, Fred finally drifted towards sleep.

As far as he was concerned, Zarana was the real Queen of the Nile.

A warm, dry, intimate touch slid across his belly.

"Luv, I'm not sure I could manage again . . ."

She pressed fingers to his face and he realized he had spoken too soon. She planted a tongue-twisting kiss on him. He pulled her closer, as they negotiated the tangle of sheets.

The sliding touch across his stomach was still there.

Zarana broke the kiss and stroked his chest, fingertips moving towards the slithering touch.

"Freddy, meet Ramsbottom."

He was fully awake now, and – as Lesley Behan might have it – "raring for rumpy-pumpy". But there was a new player in the game.

"*Ramsbottom*?" he demanded.

"The other bloke in my life," said Zarana.

In the pre-dawn light, Fred discovered he and Zarana were wound together in the coils of a contented snake.

"Love me, love my python," said Zarana.

"Fair enough," said Fred.

DALE BAILEY

Spells for Halloween: An Acrostic

DALE BAILEY IS THE author of the novels, *House of Bones*, *The Fallen* and *Sleeping Policemen* (written in collaboration with Jack Slay, Jr.). The latter is hardboiled *noir* in the tradition of Jim Thompson and James M. Cain, although his editor calls it horror. It is due to appear from Golden Gryphon Press, who also published Bailey's short fiction collection, *The Resurrection Man's Legacy and Other Stories*.

As the author explains: " 'Spells for Halloween: An Acrostic' was commissioned by the editors of the *Charlotte Observer* and serialized in the *Catawba Valley Neighbors* section of the newspaper – one letter at a time – as a Halloween feature.

"I took the assignment as a lark and quickly found myself in deeper waters than I had anticipated. The first challenge was coming up with an idea for each letter that was both sufficiently Halloween-ish and surprising enough to be interesting – 'W is for Witch' simply wouldn't do.

"The second challenge was telling each of the nine stories in such a limited space. The longest is just 154 words – a useful discipline in making every word count for any writer."

H IS FOR HECATE. The moon is changeable and strange, and exerts powerful influences. Tides answer her call. Lunatics are said to respond as she waxes and wanes. The moon has two faces, a light one and a dark. In her bright aspect rules Diana, the virgin of the hunt. But in her darker face there reigns another god, unseen by sublunary eyes: Hecate, Queen of Crossroads, said by legend to reign also in Hell. Darkness falls. The harvest moon climbs the ladder of the sky, and the old year withers. We too have dual faces. We too stand at a crossroads. Good and evil. Darkness and light. There is a goddess in the moon. Pray she doesn't see you.

A is for Abaddon, the Kingdom of the Dead. Madness comes to men too long stranded on the ice. In 1912, Captain Robert Falcon Scott perished following an assault on the South Pole. His journal survives. An unpublished entry preserved in the Rare Book Room of the British Library describes a strange experience. Three days from their final campsite, Scott and his remaining men found a stairway hacked into the ice. Down and down and down it wound, into a bottomless abyss, but no one among them dared descend. A stench of brimstone rose up from the sundered earth, the sound of distant screams. No later expedition has confirmed Captain Scott's experience. Of one fact, however, all who brave the frozen continent are certain: Hell is cold.

L is for Lillith, the Queen of Demons. There are those who believe that Adam had another spouse, summoned out of earth in Eden to be his helpmate. Lillith was wise and lovely to behold, but she was proud as well, and loathe to submit to another's will. Above all things she longed to rule in Eden as her husband's equal. And so she was dismissed from Paradise, condemned to wander alone through the wilderness of a yet-unfinished world. In Eve, Adam found a more suitable mate, and so enjoyed his happiness for yet awhile. But Lillith, pining for solace and companionship in her turn, entertained demons, and brought forth a race of witches. In outer darkness, she suckles them still, and waits for her revenge.

L is for Lycanthrope. Beware the generosity of strangers. Once upon a time a poor man named Peter, walking in the woods at night, met a stranger on the path. The stranger's eyes were yellow, but his voice was sweet and Peter had from him a kingly gift: a cloak of fine grey fur. On autumn nights it warmed him. But when the moon grew full thereafter, unholy appetites seized him and he could not abide to be indoors. Livestock disappeared, then children. Peter alone, of all the villagers, dared walk in darkness. It is said that Red Riding Hood met him once, in the depths of the haunted wood. These are merely children's tales, of course. But a bloated yellow moon looms in the October sky, and the scent of change is in the air. Wolves walk among us always. The worst among them wear their fur on the inside of their skin.

O is for Ouroboros, the great serpent who encircles the world. The ancient Norsemen knew him as Jörmungandr, the Hindu as Sesa. Under earth he lies and under sea, in a cold abyss of stone where no human foot has fallen, in trenches fathoms deep beneath the waves, where no outer light can pierce. Vast fish ply the icy currents, blind behemoths, cyclopean shapes unseen by human eye. Ouroboros dwarfs them. A time draws near when he will awaken and ungirdle the planet at last. Cities will crumble in the deluge. Continents will sink. The earth trembles beneath an October sky. Already Ouroboros stirs.

W is for Wendigo. There are voices in the wind. The Indians knew them long ago. When polar gales swept down over plains three centuries gone, the Algonquin trembled in their lodges and whispered of the Wendigo – of families slaughtered in their beds, of betrayal and bloodstained hands, of hungry spirits in the wind that drove men to murder the ones they loved the most. The Algonquin have dwindled now. But the Wendigo is with us still. Have a care when the wind picks up on a chill October night. Lock the doors. Latch the windows. Pull the covers tight. Pray for your loved ones, sleeping in the rooms around you. Try not to think about the knives in the kitchen, or the axe in the garage. There are voices in the wind. Whatever you do, don't listen.

E is for Eunuchs, the sexless ones. The mushroom people are not born, they grow. Deep in the sewers underneath our cities, far down in the bowels of the planet, they stir themselves to life. Who can say how they came to be, what spore of cast-off intelligence took root and flourished there, in that black and foetid muck? But they exist. In their secret cities underneath our feet, they batten on human waste and nurse their hatred of the sunlit regions of the world. Their strength and courage grows. Their plans ripen. Already they creep up into our moonlit streets to snatch unwary late-night walkers and sate more sanguinary hungers. Beware the shadow under the grate. Beware the pad of distant footsteps. The assault draws near.

E is for Empyrean, the farthest reach of heaven. Lucifer fell there, bearer of God's brightest light. For years unmeasurable by any merely human scale, he nursed in silence his cold resentments.

And then, taking courage, he laid his plans, gathered to him allies among the host of seraphim, and rose up against the Lord. The Empyrean ran with the blood of angels, and on the field of combat, he fell. Divested of his name and rank among the angels, his light extinguished, he plunged into darkness. With all his bright company he fell, nine days and nine nights, into the abyss, where he took a new name and clothed himself in the likeness of the serpent. In heaven, the Empyrean was restored. But Satan too has his realm, and rules there, consort of the Queen of Hell.

N is for *Necronomicon*. Some books should not be read. A century ago, they exhumed it from the dust of a Fourth Dynasty Egyptian tomb. The archaeologist who discovered it perished soon afterwards. The courier who smuggled it to America was murdered mere hours after surrendering his unlawful charge. It rests now, under lock and key, in the Manuscript Archive of Miskatonic University. The *Necronomicon*, the Book of the Dead: 4,000 years forbidden, bound in human flesh, and inked in blood. There are those who long to read the secrets in its pages – who crave to chant its ancient incantations, and summon back to rule among us vile gods long banished to the outer dark. In secret, they plot to possess it. Some books should not be read – but will be.

LISA TUTTLE

My Death

LISA TUTTLE WAS BORN in Houston, Texas, but has lived in Britain since 1980. She sold her first story in 1971 and won the John W. Campbell Award in 1974 for best new science fiction writer.

Her first book, *Windhaven* (1981) was a collaboration with George R.R. Martin, since when she has written such novels as *Familiar Spirit, Gabriel: A Novel of Reincarnation, Lost Futures, The Pillow Friend* and *The Mysteries*.

Her short fiction has been collected in *A Nest of Nightmares, A Spaceship Built of Stone and Other Stories, Memories of the Body: Tales of Desire and Transformation* and *Ghosts & Other Lovers*. The latter volume, plus another collection entitled *My Pathology*, have been released as e-books.

Tuttle's other works include the Young Adult novels *Snake Inside, Panther in Argyll* and *Love On-Line*. She is also the author of the non-fiction guides *Encyclopedia of Feminism, Heroines: Women Inspired by Women* and *Mike Harrison's Dreamlands*, the erotic fantasy *Angela's Rainbow*, and she has edited the acclaimed horror anthology by women, *Skin of the Soul*, and the anthology of erotic ambiguity, *Crossing the Border*.

"This is the second story I've written about the White Goddess," the author reveals. "The first ('The Other Mother') was inspired by Robert Graves' famous book, whereas this one grew out of my long fascination with Laura Riding, the American poet whom Graves at one time believed to be the living incarnation of the Goddess.

"I read the first biography of Laura Riding – *In Extremis* by Deborah Baker – when it was published in 1994, and was deeply struck by the description of how Riding's first sighting of the island of Majorca caused her to exclaim, 'I've seen my death!'. I remember it vividly, because it felt like the seed of a story, possibly connected to another idea I'd had about locating Circe's magical isle in the Scottish Hebrides.

"Yet when I finally began to write 'My Death', I went back to the Baker biography, intending to use that great quote – and couldn't find it anywhere. Or anything at all like it. Had I imagined it? Did I make the whole thing up?

"I'm still not sure."

> "why must I write?
> you would not care for this,
> but She draws the veil aside,
>
> unbinds my eyes,
> commands,
> write, write or die"
> —H.D., from *Hermetic Definition*

> ". . . a typical death island where the familiar
> Death-goddess sings as she spins."
> —Robert Graves, from *The Greek Myths*

I

AS I TRAVELLED, I watched the landscape – lochs and hillsides, the trees still winter-bare, etched against a soft, grey sky – and all the time my empty hand moved on my lap, tracing the pattern the branches made, smoothing the lines of the hills.

That drawing could be a way of not thinking and a barrier against feeling I didn't need a psychotherapist to tell me. Once upon a time I would have whiled away the journey by making up stories but since Allan's death this escape had failed me.

I had been a writer all my life – professionally, thirty years, but the urge to make up stories went back even further. Whether they were for my own private entertainment, or printed out and hand-bound as presents for family, whether they appeared in fanzines or between hardcovers, one thousand words long or one hundred thousand, sold barely two hundred copies or hovered at the bottom of (one) bestseller list, whether they won glowing reviews or were uniformly ignored, my stories were me, they were what I did. Publishers might fail me, readers lose interest, but that a story itself might let me down was something that had never occurred before.

Strange that I could still take pleasure in sketching, because that was so completely associated with my life with Allan that the reminder ought to have been too painful. He had been a keen amateur artist, a weekend water-colourist, and, following his relaxed example, I'd tried my hand on our first holiday together, and liked the results. It became something we could do together, another shared interest. I had not painted or sketched since childhood, having decided very early in life that I must devote myself to the one thing I was good at in order to succeed. Anything else seemed like a waste of time.

Allan had never seen life in those terms; he came from a different world. He was English, middle-class, ten years older than me. My parents were self-made, first generation Americans who knew and thought very little about what their parents had left behind, whereas his could trace their ancestry back to the Middle Ages, and while they were nothing so vulgar as rich, they had never had to worry about money. Allan had gone to a "progressive" school where the importance of being well-rounded was emphasized, and little attention was given to the practicalities of earning a living. And so he was athletic – he could play cricket and football, swim, shoot and sail – and musical, and artistic, and handy – a good plain cook, he could put up a garden shed or any large item of flat-packed furniture by himself – and prodigiously well-read. But, as he sometimes said with a sigh, his skills were many, useful and entertaining, but not the sort to attract financial reward.

We'd been living modestly but comfortably mainly on his investments, augmented by my erratic writing income, until the collapse of the stock market. Before we'd done more than consider ways we might live even more modestly, Allan had died from a massive heart attack.

I had no debts – even the mortgage was paid off – but my writing income had dried to the merest trickle, and the past year and a half had eaten away at my savings. Something had to change – which was why I was on my way to Edinburgh to meet my agent.

I hadn't seen Selwyn in several years. At least, not on business – he had come up to Scotland for Allan's funeral. When he'd sent me an e-mail to say he would be in Edinburgh on business, and was it possible I'd be free for lunch, I'd known it was an opportunity I had to take. I'd written nothing to speak of since Allan's death, one year and five months ago. I still didn't know if I would ever want to write again, but I had to make some money, and I wasn't trained or qualified to do anything else. The prospect of embarking, in my fifties, on a new, low-paid career as a cleaner or carer was too grim to contemplate.

I'd hoped having a deadline would focus my mind, but by the time I arrived at Waverley Station the only thing I felt sure of was that, as stories had failed me, my next book would have to be non-fiction.

I arrived with time to spare and, as it wasn't raining, and was, for February, remarkably mild, I took a stroll up to the National Gallery. Access to art was one thing I really missed in my remote country home. I had lots of books, but reproductions just weren't the same as being able to wander around a spacious gallery staring at the original paintings.

It was hard to relax and concentrate on the pictures that day; my mind was jittering around, desperate for an idea. And then all of a sudden, there *she* was.

There she stood, an imposing female figure in a dark purple robe, crowned with a gold filigreed tiara in her reddish-gold hair, one slim white arm held up commandingly, her pale face stern and angular, not entirely beautiful, but unique, arresting, and as intimately familiar to me as were the fleshy, naked-looking pink and grey swine who scattered and bolted in terror before her. I also knew the pile of stones behind her, and the grove of trees, and, in the middle distance, the sly, crouching figure of her nemesis hiding behind a rock as he watched and waited.

"Circe", 1928, by W.E. Logan.

It was like coming across an old friend in an unfamiliar place. As a college student, I'd had a poster-print of this same painting hanging on the wall of my dormitory room. Later, it had accompanied me to adorn various apartments in New York, Seattle, New Orleans and Austin, but, despite my affection for it, I'd never bothered to have it framed, and by the time I left for London it was too frayed and torn and stained to move again.

For ten eventful, formative years this picture had been part of my life. I had gazed up at her and Circe had looked down on me through times of heartbreak and exultation, in boredom and in ecstasy. I much preferred the powerful enchantress who would turn men into pigs to the dreamier, more passive maidens beloved of my contemporaries. The walls of my friends' rooms featured reproductions of Pre-Raphaelite beauties: poor, drowned Ophelia, Mariana waiting patiently at her window, Isabella moping over her pot of basil. I preferred Circe's more angular and determined features, her lively, impatient stare: *Cast out that swine!* she advised. *All men are pigs. You don't need them. Live alone, like me, and make magic.*

I gazed with wonder at the original painting. It was so much more vivid and alive than the rather dull tones of the reproduction. Although I'd visited the National Gallery of Scotland many times before, I could not remember having seen it here before. Now I noticed details in it that I didn't recall from the reproduction: the distinct shape of oak-leaf, and a scattering of acorns on the ground; a line of alders in the distance – alders, the tree of resurrection and concealment – and above, in a patch of blue sky, hovered a tiny bird, Circe's namesake, the female falcon.

My fascination with this painting when I was younger was mostly to do with the subject matter: I liked pictures that told a story, and the stories I liked best were from ancient mythology. I had been sadly disappointed by all the other paintings by W.E. Logan which I had managed to track down: they were either landscapes (mostly of the South of France) or dull portraits of middle-class Glaswegians.

"Circe", which marked a total departure in style and approach, had also been W.E. Logan's last completed painting. His model was a young art student called Helen Elizabeth Ralston – an American who had gone to Glasgow to study art. Shortly after Logan completed his study of her as the enchantress, she had fallen – or leaped – from the high window of a flat in the west-end of Glasgow. Although badly injured, she survived. Logan had left his wife and children to devote himself to Helen. He paid for her operations and the medical care she needed, and during the long hours he spent sitting at her bedside, he'd made up a story about a little girl who had walked out of a high window and discovered a world of adventure in the clouds high above the city. As he talked, he sketched, creating a sharp-nosed determined little girl menaced and befriended by weird, amorphous cloud-shapes, and then he put the pictures in order, and wrote up the text to create *Hermine in Cloud-Land*, his first book, and a popular seller in Britain throughout the 1930s.

The real Helen Ralston was not only Logan's muse and inspiration, but went on to become a successful writer herself. She'd written the cult classic *In Troy*, that amazing, poetic cry of a book, which throughout my twenties had been practically my bible.

And yet I'd had no idea, when I'd huddled on my bed and lost myself in the mythic story and compelling, almost ritualistic phrases of *In Troy*, that its author was staring down at me from the wall. I'd only discovered that in the early 1980s, when I was living in London and *In Troy* was reprinted as one of those green-backed Virago

Classics, with a detail from W.E. Logan's "Circe" on the cover. Angela Carter had written the appreciative introduction to the reprint, and it was there that I had learned of Helen Elizabeth Ralston's relationship with W.E. (Willy) Logan.

Feeling suddenly much livelier, I left the gallery and went down Princes Street to the big bookshop there. I couldn't find *In Troy* or anything else by Helen Ralston in the fiction section. Browsing through the essays and criticism I eventually found a book called *A Late Flowering* by some American academic which devoted a whole chapter to the books of Helen Ralston. Willy Logan was better represented. Under "L" in the fiction section was a whole row of his novels, the uniform edition from Canongate. The only book I'd read of his was one based on Celtic mythology which had been published, with an amazing George Barr cover, in the Ballantine Adult Fantasy line around about 1968. I remembered nothing at all about it now, not even the title.

After a little hesitation I decided to try *In Circe's Snare* for its suggestive title, and I also bought *Second Chance at Life* by Brian Ross, a big fat biography of Logan, recently published. And then I noticed the time, and knew I had to run.

II

Selwyn was waiting for me at the restaurant. He stood up, beaming, and came over to give me a close, warm hug.

"My dear. You're looking very well."

I'd been feeling flushed and sweaty, but his appreciative gaze made me feel better. He'd always had the knack of that. Selwyn was an attractive man, even if these days he had to rely on expensive, well-cut clothes to disguise his expanding middle. His hair, no longer long and shaggy, nevertheless was still thick and only slightly sprinkled with grey. When young, he'd worn little round Lennon-type glasses; now, contact lenses made his brown eyes even more liquid, and his eyelashes were as enviably thick and black as I remembered.

"Let's order quickly, and then we can talk," he said after I was settled. "I've already ordered wine, if white's all right with you; if not—"

"It's fine. What do you recommend?"

"Everything is good here; the crab cakes are sensational."

"That sounds good." I was relieved not to have to bother with the menu, being a little out of practice with restaurants. "Crab cakes with a green salad."

Smoothly he summoned the waiter and swiftly sent him away again, and then those brown eyes, gentle yet disconcertingly sharp, were focused on me again. "So. How *are* you? Really."

"Fine. I'm fine. I mean – I'm not, not really, but, you know, life goes on. I'm okay."

"Writing again?"

I took a deep breath and shook my head.

His eyebrows went up. "But – your novel. You were writing a novel."

He meant a year and a half ago.

"It wasn't any good."

"Please. You're much too close to it. You need another perspective. Send it to me, whatever you've got, and I'll give you my thoughts on it. I'll be honest, I promise."

I trusted Selwyn's opinion more than most, but I'd never liked anyone reading my rough drafts – sometimes I could scarcely bear to read them through myself. This one was permeated by Allan, and the happy, hopeful person who had written it was gone.

"There's no point," I said. "I'm not going to finish it. Even if you liked it, even if there's something good in it – too much has changed. I can't get back into that frame of mind; I don't even want to try. I need to get on and write the *next* book."

"All right. That sounds good to me. So what might the next book be?"

To my relief, the waiter arrived then with our drinks. When the wine had been poured I raised my glass to his and said, "To the next book!"

"To the next book," he agreed. We clinked glasses and sipped, and then he waited for me to explain.

Finally I said, "It's going to be non-fiction."

My last non-fiction book had been published nearly fifteen years ago, and had been neither a howling success nor a disaster. There had been good reviews, and the first printing had sold out. Unfortunately for me, there was never a second printing, nor the expected paperback sale. The publisher was taken over in mid-process, and my editor was among the many staff members to be "rationalized" and let go. My book got lost in the shuffle, and by the time I'd come up with an idea for another, the fashion had changed, no one was really interested, and my brave new career as an author of popular non-fiction had fizzled out. All that was a very long time ago: I didn't see why I shouldn't be allowed to start again.

Selwyn nodded. When he spoke, I could tell that his thoughts had been following the same track as mine. "It was the publisher's fault that you didn't do a lot better last time. That was a good book, and it always had the potential to be a steady seller on the backlist. I don't know why they didn't stick with it, but it was nothing to do with you – you did a great job with it, and it could have, *should* have, launched a whole new career for you." He paused to take a drink of wine and then looked at me inquiringly. "What sort of non-fiction?"

"Biography?"

"Perfect. With your understanding of characters, your ability to bring them to life in fiction – yes, you'd do very well, writing a life."

Even though I knew it was his job to build me up and promote me, I couldn't help feeling pleased. I responded to his praise like a parched plant to water.

"Really?"

"Absolutely." He beamed. "There's always a demand for good biographies, so selling it shouldn't be tough. I don't know how much I could get you up-front, that would depend – they can be expensive projects, you know, take a long time to write, and there's travel, research . . . of course, there are grants, too –" he broke off suddenly and cocked his head at me. "Now, tell me, do you have a particular subject in mind? Because *who* it is could make a big difference."

"Helen Ralston." Until I spoke, I hadn't really known.

Plenty of well-read people would have responded, quite reasonably, with a blank stare or a puzzled shake of the head. Helen Ralston was hardly a household name, now or ever. Her fame, such as it was, rested entirely on one book. *In Troy* had been published by a small press in the 1930s and developed a kind of underground reputation, read by few but admired by those discerning readers who made the effort. In the 1960s it was published again – in America for the first time – and there was even a mass-market paperback, which is what I'd read in college. It was revived from obscurity once again by Virago in the 1980s, but, from the results of my bookstore visit before lunch, I was pretty sure it was out of print again.

Selwyn knew all this as well as I did. Not only was he a voracious reader, but before becoming an agent he'd been a book-dealer, twentieth-century first editions his speciality.

"I sold my first edition of *In Troy* to Carmen Callil," he said.

I was horrified. "Not to set from?" Reprints like the Virago Classics are photo-offset from other editions, a process that destroys the original book.

He shook his head. "No. She already had a copy of the 1964 Peter Owen edition. She wanted the first for herself. I let her have it for sixty quid. These days, I doubt you could get a first edition for under three hundred."

It always amazed me that people could remember how much they'd paid for things in the past. Such specifics eluded me. I could only remember emotionally, comparatively: something had cost *a lot* or *not much*.

"I should talk to Carmen," I said. "She probably met Helen Ralston when she decided to publish her."

"Probably." He had a thoughtful look on his face. "Didn't we talk about *In Troy* once before? When I was selling *Isis*. *In Troy* had some influence on your book, didn't it?"

I ducked my head in agreement, slightly embarrassed. *Isis* was either my first or my second novel, depending on whether you judged by date of composition or actual publication. Either way, I'd written it a lifetime ago. I could hardly recall the young woman I had been when I'd started it, and by now my attitude towards that novel – once so important to me – was clear-eyed, critical, fond but distant. "Yes, it was my model. Almost too much influence, it had – I didn't realize how deeply I'd absorbed *In Troy* until my second or third revision of *Isis*. Then I had to cut out great tranches of poetic prose because it was too much like hers, and wasn't really *me* at all."

I recalled how I'd been pierced, at the age of nineteen, by the insights and language of *In Troy*. It felt at times like I was reading my own story, only written so much better than I could ever hope to match. It was such an amazingly personal book, I felt it had been written for me alone. If Helen of Troy was Helen Ralston's mythic equivalent for the purposes of her novel, then she was mine. Somehow, the author's affair with her teacher in Scotland was exactly the same as mine, fifty years later in upstate New York. Details of time, space, location and even personal identity were insignificant set in the balance with the eternal truths, the great rhythms of birth and death and change.

I had a genuine, Proustian rush then, the undeniable certainty that time could be conquered. All at once, sitting at a table in an Edinburgh restaurant, the taste of wine sharp and fresh on my tongue, I felt myself still curled in the basket chair in that long-ago dorm room in upstate New York, the smell of a joss-stick from my room-mate's side of the room competing with the clove, orange and cinnamon scent of the cup of Constant Comment tea I sipped while I read, the sound of Joni Mitchell on the stereo as Helen Ralston's words blazed up at me, changing me and my world forever with the universe-destroying, universe-creating revelation that time is an illusion.

"I was *meant* to write this book," I said to my agent, with all the passion and conviction of the teenager I had been thirty-two years ago.

He didn't grin, but I caught the spark of amusement in his eyes, and it made me scowl with self-doubt. "You think I'm crazy?"

"No. No." He leaned across the table and put his hand firmly on mine. "I think you sound like your old self again."

Our food arrived and we talked about other things.

The crab cakes were, indeed, superb. They were served with a crunchy potato gallette and a delicious mixture of seared red peppers and Spanish onion. My salad included rocket, watercress, baby spinach, and some other tasty and exotic leaves I couldn't identify, all tossed in a subtle, herby balsamic dressing. When I exclaimed at it, Selewyn grinned and shook his head.

"You should get out more. That's a standard restaurant salad."

My nearest restaurant was a 20-mile drive away, and didn't suit my budget.

"I don't get out much, but I'd make this for myself, if I could get rocket in the Co-Op."

"The Co-Op?" His delivery brought to mind Dame Edith Evans uttering the immortal question – "A hand bag?" – in *The Importance of Being Earnest*.

"Does the Co-Op still exist? And you *shop* there?"

"When I must."

"Oh, my dear. When *are* you moving back to civilization?"

"I don't consider that civilization resides in consumer convenience, actually."

"No." He sounded unconvinced. "But what do you *do* out in the country? I mean, what's the great appeal?" Selwyn was such a complete urbanite, he couldn't imagine any use for countryside except to provide a quiet chill-out zone at the weekend.

"I do the same things I'd do anywhere else."

"You'd shop at the Co-Op?"

I laughed. "Well, no. But I can write anywhere."

"Of course you can. And when you're not writing, in the city, there's art galleries, theatres, bookstores . . . what is it you like about the country?"

"The hills, the sea, peace and quiet, going for walks, going sailing . . ."

He was nodding. "I remember, I remember. I grilled you on this before, when you told me you were going to marry your former editor and leave London. I couldn't understand it. *Not* the part about marrying Allan – who was a better man than the publishing world deserved – but why leave London?"

I sighed a little. "We'd decided to down-shift. Allan hated his job; I was fed up in general . . . we figured out we could sell our flats, and buy a boat, spend more time together, and have a better quality of life on less money there."

"It still suits you?"

I pushed a strip of red pepper around on my plate. That life had been planned for, and suited, two people. After Allan's death I'd taken the advice of my closest friends not to rush into anything or do anything too drastic, so I hadn't moved, or made any major changes to my life. What was the point, anyway? Nothing I could do would change the only thing that really mattered.

"I couldn't afford to move back to London."

"There are other places. Don't tell the folks down south I said so, but I actually prefer Edinburgh. Or Glasgow."

"I guess you haven't checked out property prices since devolution."

"But surely if you sold your farm—"

"It's not a farm, Selwyn, it's a farm *cottage*. A dinky toy. Somebody else owns the farm and the nice big farmhouse and all the land and lets us share the farm track."

"Still, it must be worth something. Think about it. Once you start writing this book you won't want to have the hassle of moving, but you will want to be near a good library."

I thought of myself in a library, surrounded by stacks of books. The idea of having a project, things to look up, real work to do again, was incredibly seductive.

"The first thing is to put together a proposal, something I can show around. Just a few basic facts, the reason Helen Ralston is of interest, the stance you're going to take, why she's well overdue for a biography—" he broke off. "There hasn't already been one, has there?"

"Not that I know of."

"Mmm. Better check the more obscure university press catalogues . . . you can do that on-line. And ask around, just in case somebody is already working on her. It would be good to know."

My heart gave a jolt. "If there was . . . couldn't I still write mine?"

"The trouble is, publishers are always ready to commission a new life of Dickens or Churchill, but nobody wants to publish two 'first' biographies in the same year – probably not even in the same decade."

Until a couple of hours ago, I hadn't given Helen Ralston more than a passing thought in years. I'd had no notion of writing her biography before lunch, and yet now it was the one thing I most wanted to do. I couldn't bear the idea of giving it up.

"How will I find out if somebody else is already doing one?"

"Don't look so tragic! If someone *has* got a commission, it may be some boring old academic who's going to take ten years, and you could get yours out first. Anyway, don't worry about it. Just have a scout around. If there's going to be a biography coming out next year, well, much better to find out now, before you've invested a lot of time and energy in it."

Forewarned wasn't necessarily forearmed, I thought. I didn't put much stock in the theory of minimizing pain that way. If I'd known in advance that Allan would die of a heart attack at the age of sixty it wouldn't have hurt any less when it happened, and it wouldn't have stopped me loving him. I did know, when I married him, that his father had died of a heart attack at sixty, and even without that genetic factor, the statistical chances were that I'd outlive him by a couple of decades. I came of sturdy peasant stock, and the women in my family were long-lived.

"How do I scout around? I mean, who do I talk to?"

"You could start with her."

"Her? You mean Helen Ralston?"

He was surprised by my surprise. "She is still alive?"

"Is she? She'd be awfully old."

"Ninety-six or ninety-seven. Not impossible. I don't remember seeing an obituary of her in the last few years."

"Me either. I'm sure I would have noticed. Well. I guess they might still have an address for her at Virago. And there's a biography of Willy Logan, quite new, that should have something." I patted the heavy square shape of it in the bag slung across the side of my chair.

"Dessert? No? Coffee?" He summoned the waiter and, when he'd gone away again, turned back to me. "By the way, I know someone who owns one of Helen Ralston's paintings."

" 'By the way'?"

He smiled. "Really, I just remembered. And he lives here in Edinburgh. An old friend. I should probably call in on him while I'm here – are you free for the rest of this afternoon, or do you have to rush off?"

"I'm free. Do you mean it? I'd love to see it!"

I felt a little stunned by this sudden unexpected bonus. While Selwyn got out his phone and made the call I tried to imagine what a

Helen Ralston painting would look like. Although I knew she'd been an art student, I thought of her always as a writer, and I'd never seen so much as a description of one of her paintings. That it should have fallen into my lap like this, before I'd even started work, did not strike me as odd or unusual. Everyone who writes or researches knows that this sort of serendipity – the chance discovery, the perfectly timed meeting, the amazing coincidence – is far from rare. The fact that this first one had come along so soon, before I was definitely committed to the project, just confirmed my feeling: I was *meant* to write this book.

III

Selwyn's friend lived a short cab ride away in an area known as The Colonies. This was a collection of quaint, tidy little cottages set in eleven parallel terraces, built, he told me, in 1861 to provide affordable housing for respectable artisans and their families, and now much in demand among singles and young professional couples for their central location and old-fashioned charm.

The sight of these neat little houses set out like a model village in narrow, cobbled streets roused the long-dormant American tourist in me, and before I could crush her down again I was gushing, "Ooh, they're so *cute!*"

The big black cab had to stop on the corner to let us out, as it clearly would not be able to turn around if it went any further.

"They're just adorable!" I became more excited as I noticed the window boxes and trim green lawns. In its day, this had been inexpensive housing, but that hadn't translated into an ugly utilitarianism. The houses were small – I couldn't imagine how they'd ever been thought suitable for the large families people had in the old days – but their proportions were appealing to the eye and they didn't look cramped. "What a great place to live – so quiet and pretty, like a village, but right in the middle of the city. You could walk everywhere from here, or bike, you wouldn't even need a car."

Selwyn was looking amused. "I'll get Alistair to let you know as soon as one comes on the market. They're very much in demand, but with advance notice maybe you could put in a pre-emptive bid."

"I didn't mean *I* wanted to live here—" but as I spoke, I thought again. Why shouldn't it be me living the life I'd suddenly glimpsed, in a small, neat, pretty house or a flat within an ancient city? I still loved the country, but after all, there were trains and buses for whenever I wanted a day out, and these days I was feeling distinctly more starved of culture than I was of fresh air and wide open spaces.

"Well," I said, changing tack, "If you can re-launch my career, I will definitely think about re-launching my life."

He draped an arm loosely about my shoulders and led me gently down the street. "*We* – the operative word is *we* – are going to re-launch your career, big-time. Turn in at the green gate."

The house where Selwyn's friend lived was divided into two residences, top and bottom. His was upstairs, the front door reached by a rather elegant sweeping curve of stairs.

A thin, neat, very clean-looking old man opened the door to us. This was Alistair Reid. He had a long nose and slightly protuberant bright blue eyes in a reddish, taut-skinned face. His cheeks were as shiny as apples – I imagined him buffing them every morning – and his sleeked back hair was cream-coloured.

"I've just put the kettle on," he said, leading us into his sitting room. "Indian, or China?"

He was looking at me. I looked at Selwyn.

"China, if you've got it."

"I should hardly make the offer if I hadn't got it," the old man said reprovingly. But despite his tone there was a twinkle in his eye so I guessed it was meant to be a joke. "Please, make yourselves at home. I'll not be long," he said as he left us.

I looked around the room, which was light and airy and beautifully furnished. It was clear even to my untutored eye that the delicate writing table beside the window, the glass-fronted bookcase in the corner, and the dark chest beside the door were all very old, finely made, unique pieces which were undoubtedly very expensive. Even the couch where Selwyn and I perched had a solidity and individuality about it which suggested it had not been mass-produced.

The pale walls were hung with paintings. I got up and went to look at them. One wall displayed a series of watercolour landscapes, the usual Scottish scenes of mountains, water, cloud-streaked skies and island-dotted seas. They were attractive enough, yet rather bland; more accomplished than my own attempts, but nothing special.

Beside the bookcase were two still-lifes in oils: one, very realistic and very dark, looked old; I guessed it could be two or three hundred years old. It depicted a large, dead fish lying on a marble slab with a bundle of herbs and, incongruously, a single yellow flower. The other painting was much more modern in style, an arrangement of a blue bowl, dull silver spoon and bright yellow lemon on a surface in front of a window, partly visible behind a blue and white striped curtain.

The largest painting in the room had a whole wall to itself. It was the portrait of a young woman. She had smartly bobbed hair and wore a long single strand of pearls against a dark green tunic. I stared at this picture for some time before noticing that it was signed in the lower left-hand corner with the initials W.E.L.

Alistair Reid came in with a tray which he set down on a small table near the couch. I went back to take a seat and saw, with some dismay, that besides the tea he'd brought a plate of thinly sliced, liberally buttered white bread, and another plate piled high with small, iced cakes.

"Store-bought, I'm afraid," he said in his soft, lilting voice. "But I can recommend them. They're really rather nice. Or would you rather have sandwiches? I wasn't sure. It won't take me a moment to make them if you'd like. Ham, or cheese, or anchovy paste, or tomato."

"Thank you, Alistair, you're more than kind, but we've just had lunch," Selwyn said. He turned to me. "You know the old joke, that in Glasgow, unexpected afternoon visitors are greeted with the cry of 'You'll be wanting your tea, then' whereas in Edinburgh, no matter the time, it's always, 'You'll have had your tea then.'" He shot a grin in the old man's direction. "Well, I should have warned you, but Alistair has devoted his *life* to disproving that calumny on the hospitable souls of native Edinburghers."

"Oh, go on, I know you've a sweet tooth," Alistair said, not quite smiling.

"Well, I think I might just manage a fancy or two," said Selwyn.

I took a slice of bread and butter and eventually allowed a cake to be pressed upon me, feeling glad that we'd skipped dessert. The tea was light and delicate, flavoured with jasmine blossoms.

Alistair leaned towards me. "I believe when I came in I saw you admiring the portrait of my mother?"

"That was your mother? Painted by W.E. Logan?"

He nodded, eyelids drooping a little. "Long before I was born, of course. Her father commissioned it in 1926. It was quite possibly the last portrait W.E. Logan ever painted, apart from some studies of Helen Ralston, of course." He gestured towards the watercolour landscapes. "And those are my mother's."

"Your mother was an artist, too?"

He shook his head. "Oh, no. My mother painted purely for her own enjoyment. I have them on display because they remind me of her, and because of where they were painted. It's where we always took our summer holidays, on the west coast, in Argyll."

"That's where I'm from!"

"Really? I'd have guessed you're from much further west." A teasing smile flickered about his thin lips.

I felt a little weary and tried not to show it. No matter how long I lived in Britain – and it was now nearly a quarter of a century – I could never pass for native. As soon as I opened my mouth I was a foreigner, always required to account for my past. Yet I didn't want to be unkind or rude, and it wasn't fair to take offence where none was intended. Scots, unlike some other Europeans, were generally fond of Americans.

"I was born in Texas," I said. "Later I lived in New York, and then London. I've been living in Argyll for just over ten years. It's a tiny little place called Mealdarroch, not far from—"

"But that's exactly where we stayed!" he exclaimed. "It was always Mealdarroch, or Ardfern." Looking delighted, he turned to Selwyn. "My dear, how marvellous! You never said you were bringing someone from Mealdarroch! My favourite spot in the universe!" He turned back to me. "You sail, of course."

"We – I – have a boat. My husband loved to sail. Since he died, I haven't felt like taking her out on my own."

"Oh, my dear, I am so sorry." His sharp blue eyes were suddenly gentle.

I looked down at my teacup, into the light gold liquid, and thought of how one might recreate that colour in a watercolour wash. After a moment I could face him again, quite calm.

"I was looking at your pictures trying to guess which one was by Helen Ralston. But if the watercolours are your mother's, and the portrait by Logan—"

His eyes widened. "Oh, that's not hanging in here! I could hardly have it on display to all and sundry – far too risky!"

I thought at first he was speaking of *risk* before I realized he meant the painting itself was *risqué* – did he mean it was a nude figure? But nudes had been common currency in fine art for a long time and surely were acceptable even in buttoned-down Calvinist Scotland?

Alistair turned to Selwyn. "Didn't you explain?"

"I thought she'd better see for herself."

I tried to imagine it. Had Helen Ralston turned the tables on the male-dominated art world and depicted her lover in the altogether? Willy Logan and his little willy? And if it wasn't so little, or dangling . . .? The erect penis was taboo even today.

"May I see it?"

"But of course. Drink up your tea. Sure you won't have another fancy cake? No? Selwyn? Oh, go on, dear boy, no one cares about your figure now!"

We went out by the door we had come in, back into the tiny entrance-way, where a steep, narrow staircase rose to the left.

"Go halfway up the stair," Alistair instructed. "It's too narrow for more than one person at a time. You'll see it hanging on the wall just at the turn of the stair."

It certainly was narrow, and steep. Maybe that was the reason for the inclusion of the little half-landing, to give the intrepid climber a space to pause and make a 90° turn before mounting to the floor above.

The picture hung on the wall that faced the second flight of stairs. It was about 8″ × 10″, or the size of a standard sheet of paper torn from an artist's pad. I saw a watercolour landscape, not so very different from the pictures hanging in the room downstairs.

Then there was a click from the hall below, and the shaded bulb above my head blazed, illuminating the picture.

I gazed at the painted image of an island, a rocky island rendered loosely in shades of brown and green and grey and greyish pink. I remained unimpressed, and baffled by Alistair's attitude towards this uninspired daub. *Risky?*

And then, all at once, as if another light had been switched on, I saw the hidden picture. Within the contours of the island was a woman. A woman, naked, on her back, her knees up and legs splayed open, her face hidden by a forearm flung across it and by the long hair – greenish, greyish – that flowed around her like the sea.

The centre of the painting, what drew the eye and commanded the attention, was the woman's vulva: all the life of the painting was concentrated there. A slash of pink, startling against the mossy greens and browns, seemed to touch a nerve in my own groin.

One immediate, furious thought rose in my mind: *How could she expose herself like that?*

Somehow I knew this was a self-portrait, that the artist would not have exploited another woman in this way. Yet she had not flinched from depicting *herself* as naked, passive, open, sexually receptive – no, sexually voracious, demanding to be looked at, to be taken, explored, used, filled . . .

Well, why not? I was all in favour of female autonomy, in the freedom of women to act out of their own desires, whatever they were. After all, I still called myself a feminist, and I had come of age during the '60s, a member of the post-Pill, pre-AIDS, sexually liberated generation who believed in letting it all hang out, and a woman's right to choose.

And yet – and yet—

Whatever theory I held, the sight of this picture made me cringe away in revulsion, even fear. As if this was something I should not have seen, something which should not have been revealed. It was deeper than reason; I simply felt there was something wrong and *dangerous* in this painting.

Then, like a cloud passing across the sun, the atmosphere changed again. Outlines blurred, colours became drab, and abruptly the painting was only the depiction of an island in the sea.

But I knew now what was hidden in those rocky outlines, and I didn't trust it to stay hidden. I turned away immediately and saw the two men who stood at the bottom of the stairs, looking up at me.

There was a sudden rush of blood to my head: my cheeks burned. They knew what I'd been looking at; they'd seen it, too. And then, far worse than the embarrassment, came a clutch of fear, because I was a woman, and my only way out was blocked by two men.

The moment passed. The old man went back into the other room, and I was looking down at Selwyn, whom I'd known for twenty years.

I hated the fact that I was blushing, but I'd look even more of a fool if I hovered there on the landing waiting for the red to fade, so I went down. Unostentatiously polite as ever, he turned away, allowing me to follow him into the sitting room where Alistair waited for us.

Selwyn cleared his throat. "Well—"

"Sit down," said the old man. "You'll want to hear the story. First, let me fetch down the picture. There's something written on the back that you should see."

In uneasy silence, we sat down. The silence was uneasy on my part, anyway, as I struggled to understand my own reaction. I was not a prude, and although hardcore porn made me uncomfortable, mere nudity didn't. I had no problem, usually, with images of healthy female bodies and I'd seen beaver shots before, far more graphic than Helen Ralston's *trompe-l'œil* depiction.

In the nineteenth century Gustave Courbet had painted a detailed, close-up, highly realistic view of a woman's pubic area, calling it "The Origin of the World". At the time, this was a deeply shocking thing to have done, and although Courbet was a well-respected artist, the painting could not be shown. Now, of course, it could be seen by anyone who cared to call up a reproduction on the internet, purchased in museum shops all over the world as a postcard or poster, and for all I knew it was available on T-shirts and mouse-mats, too.

Courbet's realistic depiction was far more graphic than Ralston's impressionistic watercolour, and it might be argued that, as a male artist, he was objectifying women, serving her sexual parts up on canvas for the viewing pleasure of his fellow men, whereas Ralston had been exploring her own feelings about herself with, possibly, no intention of ever having it on public display. The question I should be asking myself was why, when Courbet's picture did not disturb me, hers *did*.

Alistair returned, carrying the picture. He handed it to me, face down, and I took it, gingerly, awkwardly, into my lap.

"I had it mounted with a bit cut away at the back so you can still see what she wrote," he explained.

I looked down and had my first sight of Helen Ralston's bold, clear handwriting:

My Death
14 April, 1929
This, like all I own or produce, is for
My Beloved Willy
HER

I shivered and made to pass it to Selwyn, but he demurred: he'd seen it before. So I went on holding it in my lap, feeling it slowly burning a hole in me, and looked at Alistair.

"Why 'My Death'? Did she mean . . . sexuality equates with death?"

He spread his hands. "Much more than that, I'm sure. The two of them used certain words almost as if they were a special code, and capital-D Death was one of them. And consider the painting: the woman is also an island. A particular island, from your part of the world," he added with a nod at me. "In fact, I must have sailed past it many times myself on our family holidays, although I don't think we ever landed there. According to Willy Logan in his memoirs, the moment she set eyes upon the island she declared, 'I've seen my death.' Whether 'my death' meant the same as capital-D Death to them, I couldn't say, but clearly it wasn't perceived as a threat or I'm sure they would have sailed away, rather than dropping anchor and going ashore, full of excitement, to explore."

I knew that in the Tarot the Death card did not signify physical demise, but rather meant a sudden, dramatic change of fortune. And sometimes people had to dare death in order to regain their lives. I wondered if Helen Ralston had been a precursor of Sylvia Plath, if she was another Lady Lazarus, making death her life's art. First, out of a window into the air; the second time, on a rocky island . . .

"What happened? Did something happen there?"

"Logan went blind," Selwyn told me.

I had known, of course, that Logan had lost his sight – the transformation of a rather dull, society painter into the blind poetic visionary was the most famous thing about him. But I didn't know how it had happened. "On the island? Some sort of accident?"

"No accident," said Alistair crisply. "Haven't you read *Touched by the Goddess*? You must read Logan's memoirs. His explanation . . . well, it's hardly satisfactory, but it's all we have. No one will ever know what *really* happened."

Had Logan intervened somehow, I wondered. Had the Death waiting for Helen been made to give her up, but taken Logan's sight in exchange? It was clear that Alistair wasn't going to tell – if he knew.

"How did you come to have the painting?" Selwyn asked.

"You know I was an art and antiques dealer back in the 1970s and '80s. Torquil Logan – Willy's youngest son – was on the fringe of the trade himself, and that was how we knew each other. When the old man died, although his literary agent was the executor of his estate, it was the sons and daughters who did all the donkey work of clearing out his things, and deciding what should be sold, or given away, shipped to the library which was to have the official collection, or whatever. Torquil got in touch with me when he came across 'My Death' – it was in an envelope at the back of a file of old letters, and probably had not been seen in fifty years.

"He knew what it was, straight away. Well, of course: it was described in *Touched by the Goddess* right down to the inscription on the back, and invested with huge significance as the last work of art he ever looked at, the final gift from his mistress/muse, and even as a sort of premonition of what was about to happen to him, his blinding by the goddess.

"And Torquil didn't know what to do with it. *He* didn't want it; in fact, he told me, he felt a sort of revulsion about the very thought of having it in his house. He couldn't ask his mother – she was in poor health, and quite devastated by the loss of her husband; he didn't want to take any risks by even reminding her in any way of the existence of Helen Ralston. He'd considered leaving it in the envelope and slipping it into one of the boxes destined for the library – it would be safe enough in a university collection, he thought, and yet the idea of students looking at it, and writing about it in their theses made him feel queasy, just as did the thought of it going into a public auction, to be numbered and listed and described in a catalogue."

Alistair paused and took a deep breath. Then he went on. "I offered to take care of it for him. I promised there'd be no publicity. In fact, I said, if the price was right, I'd be happy to buy it for myself, not to sell on. Torq knew, because we'd talked about it, just how important Willy Logan's books had been to me. Especially as a young man. That mystical strand of his, the idea that the old gods are still alive in the land and can be brought back to life through us, *in* us – I can't quite explain how deeply that affected me, but the idea of owning something which had belonged to him, which had been so deeply, personally meaningful, was irresistible.

"And Torquil said I could have it. In fact, he said he would like to *give* it to me. He didn't want payment; it didn't seem right to sell it. I protested, but he wouldn't hear of it. In fact, he mailed it to me that same day, by ordinary post, in a padded envelope, but otherwise unprotected – when I think how easily it could have been lost or damaged . . ."

We all stared at the thing in my lap. Unable to bear it any longer, I lifted the framed painting like a tray and held it out to Alistair. When he didn't respond, I glared at him, but still he made no move to take it away.

"I could never sell it," he said quietly. "I've respected Torquil's feelings about that. And yet, I've never felt right about owning it. It came to me by chance." He paused. I saw his tongue appear at the corner of his mouth and run quickly around his lips. "I'd like you to have it."

"Me!" I felt the same unexpectedly sexual shock I'd had on first recognizing the hidden meaning of the picture I now held. "Oh, no, I couldn't. It's not right."

"Selwyn tells me you're writing a biography of Helen Ralston. I've felt for some time that the painting should go back to her, but I didn't know how to approach her. It seemed too difficult, and potentially too disturbing. How would she feel to learn that a male stranger had this very personal thing? Yet she might want it back. And it *is* hers, by rights, since Willy's death. It might come more easily from another woman, and, as her biographer, you'll be in on lots of intimate secrets; she'll have to accept that . . ."

"I don't know that she'll even accept me as her biographer. I can't. I don't even know if she's still alive." I couldn't seem to stop shaking my head.

"Of course she will. Of course she is. And if she doesn't want it, or you can't find her, and you don't feel you can keep it yourself, well, you could always mail it back to me in a plain brown envelope. Please."

And although I really didn't want to do it, in the end I found it impossible not to agree.

I'd booked a room for the night at Jury's hotel, which was located just behind the train station. I'd planned, when I'd booked, to take myself out for a nice dinner and to see a movie, but by the time I'd parted from Selwyn, very late in the afternoon, the only thing I wanted was to find out more about Helen Ralston.

I hit another bookshop, where I determined that *In Troy* was definitely out of print, and so was that old-fashioned children's classic *Hermine in Cloud-Land*. "But you can find loads of second-hand copies on the Internet," a helpful clerk assured me.

"Thanks, I'll do that when I get home," I said, and paid for a copy of *Touched by the Goddess*. I bought a selection of interesting-looking gourmet salads from Marks and Spencer – ah, the luxuries of city life! – and settled into my hotel room to read everything in the big fat biography of Willy Logan which had anything to do with Helen Ralston.

IV

She was the girl from faraway, the girl from another land, and she swept into the dreich damp grey streets of Glasgow like a warm wind, smelling of exotic spices and a hint of dangerous mystery. She claimed to be half-Greek and half-Irish, with a mother who told fortunes and a father possessed of the second sight. She herself, according to at least one bewildered classmate, was subject to 'fits' when she would go rigid and begin to prophesy in a voice manifestly not her own – afterwards, she appeared exhausted, and claimed to remember nothing.

In appearance, she made a most unlikely *femme fatale*. She was small and skinny, with sharp features, including a prominent nose, and her eyes, although large and lustrous, were disturbingly deep-set. Logan's portrait glamorized her; the few photographs taken of Helen Ralston in the late 1920s reveal an odd shrunken figure who appeared prematurely old.

Helen Elizabeth Ralston was a new student on the rolls of The Glasgow School of Art in September 1927; prior to that she had studied at Syracuse University, New York. Her reasons for departing

New York for Glasgow are unknown. She had no Scottish connections whatsoever, and was far from wealthy. Although her tuition fees were paid in advance, she clearly found it a struggle to pay for supplies and other necessities of life. A fellow student, Mabel Scott Smith, recalls buying her dinner more than once, and made it a practice to bring along an extra bun for Helen at tea time: "She would pretend she'd forgotten, or that she wasn't hungry, but the truth was, she didn't have a penny to spare. Everybody knew she was broke, even though you thought Americans must all be rich. She went around with a portfolio of drawings, trying to sell to the papers, but she never had a hope. She was good, but so were plenty others, and times were hard. It was even worse in Glasgow than in other places; you couldn't make money from pretty pictures there, not then."

The budding friendship between Mabel and Helen came to an abrupt end when the American student moved out of her shared lodgings and into a west end flat paid for by W.E. Logan. Mabel Smith: "It wasn't the sex – we art school girls had quite a liberal attitude towards that! – but that she would let herself be *kept* and by a married man! I lost my respect for Mr Logan, too."

Logan noticed the "young-old" quality of Helen Ralston's face during his first class with her, and invited her to sit for him on Saturday afternoon. He singled out several students like this every year; there was nothing unusual, or improper, in his attentions. But from her first sitting it was clear that Helen would be different. Fixing her large, hypnotic eyes upon him, she began to speak, and immediately held him spellbound by her stories.

These were probably mostly a retelling of myths and legends from many different cultures, Russian fairy-tales mingled with Greek myths, and Celtic motifs interwoven with material stolen from the Arabian Nights. To Logan they were pure magic, and ignited in him the passion for myth which would dominate his life.

In his autobiography Logan writes of certain "magical" moments in his early childhood. Apart from that, however, there is no evidence that he experienced any significant mystical or spiritual leanings before meeting Helen Ralston.

Despite the stories she told him about her background, Helen Elizabeth Ralston had neither Greek nor Irish blood. Her parents, Ben and Sadie Rudinski, were Polish Jews who arrived in New York around 1890. By the time their last child, Helen, was born, in Brooklyn in 1907, the family fortunes were thriving. Helen's artistic ambitions were encouraged, and she was both educated and indulged. As America prepared to go to war in 1917, the Rudinskis changed their name to Ralston – around this time, Helen adopted Elizabeth as a middle name and began signing her drawings with the initials HER.

Helen did well at school, and was accepted into the undergraduate liberal arts programme at Syracuse University. Her grades from her freshman year were good, and she participated in the drama society (painting sets and making costumes rather than acting) and contributed to the student newspaper, and seemed in general to have settled. But instead of returning as expected for a second year, Helen Elizabeth Ralston applied to the Glasgow School of Art, and embarked on a new life in Great Britain.

Logan wrote later that she made this great change in her life on the prompting of a dream. He also believed that her parents were dead, that she was an only child, and that she had been self-supporting since the age of thirteen. It is impossible to know for certain when the relationship between them altered and they became lovers, as Logan is uncharacteristically reticent about this in his memoirs. But by January 1928 he had begun to paint "Circe", and by March she was living in the flat for which he paid the rent, and to which he was a frequent visitor.

After January, although she did not formally withdraw from the School, Helen attended fewer and fewer classes, until, by March, the other students scarcely saw her at all, unless she was in Logan's company. Their relationship was certainly gossiped about, but Logan's reputation was such that some thought him above suspicion. He was a respectable family man, with several children and a beautiful, gentle wife from a well-to-do Edinburgh background. The American student was such an odd creature it was hard to credit that the great W.E. Logan was seriously attracted to her.

He had often taken a paternal interest in his students, male and female, and had even been known to make small financial contributions to help support those who were talented but poor. Helen Ralston clearly fell into that category. Brian Ross, Logan's biographer, suggested that Logan's natural innocence combined with generosity and good intentions might have got him into trouble. He thought that Helen had fallen in love with the great man, who had been interested in her only as a model. When "Circe" was finished, and it became clear that he would no longer be spending so much time alone in the studio with her, she had thrown herself out of the window in despair, and only then had he become aware of her true feelings for him.

I shut Ross's book in disgust. In the whole history of human relationships, how many men had ever rented an expensive flat for an unrelated female without expecting sexual favours in return? If she'd been one-sidedly in love with him, her suicide attempt would have been his signal to run like hell, not to abandon wife and children to nurse her back to health. Logan's sacrifice only made sense if he was deeply in love with her, and her leap had shocked him into recognizing his responsibilities.

I was willing to believe that it had been one-sided – on *his* part. She might have stopped going to art school to avoid him, even though her poverty had forced her into accepting his financial support, and she might have hoped that, once he no longer needed her to model for "Circe" she would have nothing more to do with him. Only he wouldn't let her go – maybe he'd turned up that August day not to say goodbye, but to tell her he was going to leave his wife and children to live with her. I imagined her backing away from him, evading his hands, his lips, his unwanted declarations of undying devotion until finally, in a final, desperate squirm out of his arms, she'd fallen out of the window.

I frowned as I considered this. What sort of window was it? How did a conscious, healthy adult fall out of a window? I found it hard to visualize from Ross's description – he said she was "sitting on the window ledge". Sideways, or with her back to the air? It was August, and hot, so naturally enough the windows were open. Did she lean too far back and lose her balance, or did she deliberately swivel around and jump?

I picked up *Touched by the Goddess* and paged through it looking for references to Hermine, which was his name for Helen. There was no index. One reference leaped out at me:

Truth then flying out the window, Hermine went after it. She caught it, although she nearly died in the attempt, and so restored me to the way of truth, and life.

Well, that was a lot of help. Logan was concerned with myth, as he saw it, a deeper truth than mere facts could provide.

I turned back to Ross again. It seemed that, however briefly, an attempted murder charge had been considered, on the grounds of Logan's distraught "confession" to a policeman at the hospital to which Helen had been taken. Undoubtedly, he'd been filled with feelings of guilt, but was it the guilt of a violent seducer, or that of a man who felt torn between two women, or simply what anyone close to an attempted suicide might feel? Even his actual words at the time were unclear. And, as Ross pointed out, suicide was a crime, so

Logan might have been trying to save Helen from prosecution and/or deportation for attempted self-murder by suggesting it was really his fault.

More than one story could be told about what had happened in that room in Glasgow, a room with an open window, four storeys up, on a warm August day in 1928. There had been only two witnesses, who were also the protagonists, or the protagonist and the antagonist, the two people in the room, Willy Logan and Helen Ralston.

Ross wrote far more clearly and simply than Logan in his attempt to establish the truth, but, as far as I could see, he was no less biased, and no more reliable, because there was only one story he wanted to tell, and that was Willy Logan's. Helen's experience, her interpretation, her story, was nowhere in his book.

I went back to the beginning and made my way carefully through the acknowledgements. This ran to over two pages of names of all the people who had helped him in some way, and Helen Ralston's name was not included. If she was dead, I thought, he might have quoted from one of her books, or letters – surely she had written about her relationship with Logan at some point, to someone? Some of the passages from *In Troy* could well have been pertinent. His restraint made me think he must have been refused permission to quote, with possibly the threat of legal action if he said anything about her which could be deemed offensive . . . the libel laws in Britain were pretty fierce, and if the old lady had a taste for litigation that would have tied his hands.

I read swiftly through the pages that dealt with Logan's desertion of his family, his devoted vigils beside Helen's hospital bed, the loss of his job scarcely registering on him, her surgery, the creation of little Hermine and her adventures, then Helen's convalescence in the west end flat, now *their* home, until, in the spring of 1929, although she still had to walk with a cane, Helen was deemed well enough to travel, and Logan took her on a sailing holiday up the west coast. In the fresh air away from the city they would rest and sketch and grow strong, Willy wrote in a letter to his son Torquil, adding:

I hope you know how much I love you, darling boy, and that I don't stay away out of crossness or dislike or any wrong reason, but only because Helen needs me so much more than the rest of you do. She has been very ill, you know, but finally is getting better. I hope soon she will be well enough to meet you. I have written and drawn a funny little story for her which I think you

will like, too. It is to be published as a book in September, and I
have told the publishers to be sure to send you your very own
copy . . .

On their first day out, they spotted a small island which caught
Helen's attention. In Logan's description, Helen went 'rigid', her face
paled, and her large, shiny eyes seemed to become even larger, a trio
of symptoms which had always heralded her prophesying fits. This
time all she said was, "I've seen my death. My death is there."

Logan never explained why, in that case, he didn't just sail as far
away from the island as he could. To him, it was self-evidently
necessary to go where Helen had foreseen her own death. In his novel
In Circe's Snare (1948) Logan has Odysseus declare, "Every man
must seek his own death."

"And every woman, too," Circe chimed in quickly. "If, that is, she
wishes to be more than just a woman."

On the charts the island bears the name of *Eilean nan Achlan.* At
the time, this probably meant nothing to Logan, but later, when he
began his study of Gaelic, he would have found that it bears the
meaning "the isle of lamentation".

Modern archaeologists believe that Achlan was an important
funerary site in pre-Christian Scotland. Not only the name points
to this conclusion, but the many cairns, including one large cham-
bered tomb, still awaiting serious excavation today, believed to have
been in use for a period of several hundred years. There was a
tradition for a long time on the west coast of interring the dead on
uninhabited islands reserved for that purpose. More often these
islands were located in lakes or inland lochs, but Achlan's position
in the straits of Jura, relatively near to the mainland shore, would
have made it equally accessible and therefore suitable for this
purpose.

Because it was late in the day, they did not attempt to land just then,
but dropped anchor and spent the night on board in view of the little
island. While the light was good they both made watercolour sketches
of it. What Logan thought of his own painting – the last he would ever
produce – or what became of it is not recorded. But, as Logan recalled
in *Touched by the Goddess*, Helen's swiftly rendered landscape was
"technically remarkably assured, and quite surprising; the most remarkable piece of work I ever saw her produce." He expressed his
belief that already "The Goddess was working through her." On the
back of the little sketch she wrote the title "My Death", the date – 14
April 1929 – and and a dedication to her lover.

Reading this, I was quite certain that Brian Ross had never set eyes on the painting he seemed to describe. The passage was footnoted; I looked it up and read, "The current whereabouts of this painting is unknown. Personal correspondence with Torquil Logan."

I looked across the room where the painting now lay in a plain brown envelope. Alistair would have been happy to give me the frame, but I thought it would be too much to cart around. After all, I didn't intend to hang it, but just return it to the woman who had painted it.

The morning of 15 April 1929 dawned calm and fine. The sun was shining, the air warm for April, and quite still: perfect weather for exploring the island. Helen stripped off her clothes, wrapped them in a Sou'wester to make a waterproof bundle she could carry on top of her head, and had slipped over the side of the boat while Willy was still blinking sleep from his eyes. She gave a sudden sharp hiss as the salt water hit her scarred back and legs: the sight of those raw, red wounds against her pale flesh seemed to reproach Willy, and although the water was not very deep he felt obliged to follow her lead and strip completely rather than just removing shoes and trousers as he would have preferred.

Naked as Adam and Eve they emerged from the sea to set foot on their new Eden. As they travelled inland, the two noticed signs of ancient human activity everywhere: burial mounds, standing stones, and slabs covered with the obsessively repeated cup and ring markings which appear throughout the west of Scotland and Ireland, their ancient significance long forgotten. Eventually they came upon the ruins of some old building, and a well. Although it was more likely to have been either an enclosure for sheep, or an early Christian hermit's cell, Logan decided their find was a "shrine" or "temple", and proclaimed this the *omphalos* of the island where they would rest, and drink the good fresh water, and give thanks to the Goddess.

In later years, Willy Logan would connect the Gaelic *Achlan* with the ancient Greek *Aeaea* "wailing", the name of the "typical death island" which was the home of the enchantress Circe.

After their pagan prayers, they made love within the boundaries of the shrine. According to his much later account, this act was at Helen's urging, and was the first sexual intercourse they'd had since her fall. Yet all did not go as planned. Reading between the lines, it appears that Willy was unable to sustain an erection. Determined to please his mistress, he had to use "other means". Oral sex is fairly obviously implied. He brought his lover to orgasm – his surprise suggests that this, too, may have been a first – and almost immediately after that, darkness fell. His lover's transformed, contorted face was the last thing he ever saw.

An annihilating blow, for an artist to lose his sight, and this event became the centre of the myth which Willy Logan was to create of his life. Although it was a moment of terror, in his writing he would describe it in terms more of awe than of fear, and of discovery and re-birth rather than of death and loss.

"The Goddess is come!" he cried (or so he claims, in his auto-biography). "Oh, how she dazzles!" Then: "Where is She? Where is the sun? Is it night?" So suddenly, orgasmically, W.E. Logan had been plunged into perpetual night, yet, spiritually, he might have said "I was blind, but now can see."

With *Touched by the Goddess* open beside *Second Chance at Life* it was easy to see how closely Ross followed Logan's own account. Yet although he did not accept every detail uncritically, he did no more than provide a slightly ironic commentary as counterpoint to Logan's "facts". No matter how I struggled and searched, I could find no other voice, no other view, but Logan's. Helen's absence was glaring. In Logan's own autobiography, Helen was less an individual than an idea, and in Ross's book she was scarcely even that.

Yet she had certainly been there on the island; and if Logan wanted to blame her for his blindness (I was shocked by his choosing to quote, without irony, a sixteenth century Arabian scholar who declared that any man who looked into a woman's vagina would go blind) he had also to recognize that she had saved him.

While Willy wept and raved about the Goddess, Helen had managed to get him back onto the boat, which she then sailed, single-handed, into Crinan Harbour. (And where, I wondered, had the girl from New York learned to sail?)

Fortunately for them, a doctor from Glasgow was staying with his wife in the Crinan Hotel – and the wife turned out to be some sort of second-cousin to Logan's mother. They immediately offered to cut short their holiday and drive Logan and Helen to Glasgow, where he could be seen by specialists.

By the time they reached Glasgow, Logan was almost super-naturally calm. He had accepted his blindness, he was convinced it was permanent and that nothing could be done about it. But his wish to go home with Helen was over-ruled. A bed was found for him at the Western Infirmary, and arrangements were made for a battery of tests and examinations by a variety of specialists as soon as possible.

In the meantime, all were agreed, he must rest. Once she'd seen him settled in, Helen Ralston went to the nearest post office to despatch a telegram to Mrs William Logan, whom she knew to be staying with the children and her parents in Edinburgh.

WILLY BLIND PLEASE COME AT ONCE GLASGOW WESTERN INFIRMARY

She did not sign the telegram. As soon as it was sent, she went to the flat she'd shared with Willy and packed her bags. She left Glasgow that night, on a train bound for London, and never saw, or directly communicated with, Willy Logan again.

What would make someone who had painted a sexually explicit portrait of herself, dedicating it to her beloved, abandon that same man, blind and helpless, only twenty-four hours later? Brian Ross did not speculate or comment. I wondered who she went to in London.

I checked the index for further references to Helen Ralston. There were only a few, and every one of them concerned something Logan had written later about their brief time together (most of them were clustered in the chapter about the writing of *Touched by the Goddess* in 1956.) You'd never know from this book that Helen Ralston had ever done or been anything of the slightest importance in the world except to be, for a little while, Logan's chief muse and model. None of her books were listed in the "Selected Bibliography" at the end, not even *In Troy*.

I became all the more determined to tell Helen Ralston's story.

V

I didn't sleep well that night – I rarely do, away from home. I had brief, disturbing dreams. The one that frightened me most, making me wake with a gasp and a pounding heart, was about "My Death". I dreamed that when I got home and took the picture out to look at it, I found it was just an ordinary watercolour sketch of island, sea and sky, no more unusual or accomplished than one of my own.

I don't know why that should have been so terrifying – especially considering how upsetting I'd found the hidden picture – but when I woke, heart pounding like a drum, it was impossible to put it out of my mind. I had to get up and look at the picture again to be sure I hadn't imagined the whole thing.

At first sight it was an island, but as I waited, staring through sleep-blurred eyes, the outlines underwent the same, subtle shift I'd seen before, and I was looking down at a woman lying with her legs splayed open. This time, the sight was not so disturbing, maybe because I'd been expecting it, maybe because this time I was alone, half-asleep, naked myself, and feeling a certain amount of indignant sisterly support for a fellow writer who'd practically been written out of history.

I put the picture away, oddly comforted, and went back to bed, reflecting on the oddness of dreams.

In the jumbled, fragmented memories I carry from my childhood there are probably nearly as many dreams as images from waking life. I thought of one which might have been my earliest remembered nightmare. I was probably about four years old – I don't think I'd started school yet – when I woke up screaming. The image I retained of the dream, the thing which had frightened me so, was an ugly, clown-like doll made of soft red and cream-coloured rubber. When you squeezed it, bulbous eyes popped out on stalks and the mouth opened in a gaping scream. As I recall it now, it was disturbingly ugly, not really an appropriate toy for a very young child, but it had been mine when I was younger, at least until I'd bitten its nose off, at which point it had been taken away from me. At the time when I had the dream I hadn't seen it for a year or more – I don't think I consciously remembered it until its sudden looming appearance in a dream had frightened me awake.

When I told my mother about the dream, she was puzzled.

"But what's scary about that? You were never scared of that doll."

I shook my head, meaning that the doll I'd owned – and barely remembered – had never scared me. "But it was very scary," I said, meaning that the reappearance of it in my dream had been terrifying.

My mother looked at me, baffled. "But it's *not* scary," she said gently. I'm sure she was trying to make me feel better, and thought this reasonable statement would help. She was absolutely amazed when it had the opposite result, and I burst into tears.

Of course she had no idea why, and of course I couldn't explain. Now I think – and of course I could be wrong – that what upset me was that I'd just realized that my mother and I were separate people. We didn't share the same dreams or nightmares. I was alone in the universe, like everybody else. In some confused way, *that* was what the doll had been telling me. Once it had loved me enough to let me eat its nose; now it would make me wake up screaming.

VI

As soon as I was home and through the back door, sorrow was on me like an untrained, wet and smelly dog.

My kitchen smelled of untreated damp and ancient cooking – an unappetizing combination of mould, old vegetables and fried onions. The creeping patch of black mould had returned to the ceiling in the corner nearest the back door, and the pile of newspapers meant for recycling was weeks old. There were crumbs on the table along with a pile of unanswered mail and three dirty cups; a bath-towel draped across one of the chairs, and an odd sock on the floor. When I'd left, the general dirt and untidiness had been invisibly familiar, but now I saw it as a stranger might, and was dismayed. The very thought of all that needed to be done made me tired.

I couldn't cope with it now. Without even pausing to make a cup of tea, I dumped my bag in the bedroom and escaped upstairs to the loft-conversion which was my office. There it was untidy, but not noticeably unclean, and the air was filled with the friendly familiar smell of old books. I picked my way through the stacks on the floor to my desk, where I switched on the computer and went straight to my e-mail inbox.

Selwyn, bless him, was already on the case, but along with the rousing words of his faith in my ability to write a "splendid, uniquely insightful biography" of Helen Ralston, his e-mail carried disquieting news. He'd found an article – 'Masks and Identity in Three American Novels' – published three years earlier in an academic journal. The author, Lilith Fischler, Tulane University, was said to be working on a book about Helen Elizabeth Ralston.

This should certainly be taken with a grain of salt (he wrote) – *academics are required to be always working on some project or other, and very few of these putative books ever appear in print. And if it does exist it is more likely to be a critical study than a biography. But why don't you ask her and find out?*

The prospect scared me right out of the office and back downstairs, where I began to clean the kitchen. As I scrubbed and washed and tidied, I brooded about what to do.

I must write to her, of course. But what should I say? How much should I tell her? How could I get her on my side?

My usual inclination when writing to strangers is to keep the letter short and formal, but I knew that this could backfire. I could come across as cold when I only meant to be unobtrusive, and, in an e-mail, particularly, it was treacherously easy to be misunderstood. What if Lilith Fischler read my formality as arrogance? I didn't want to alienate her; with a little effort maybe she'd be glad to help. Writing this letter required almost as much care as composing a book proposal to send to an unknown editor.

I considered my approach very carefully, balancing and polishing phrases as I scrubbed the kitchen surfaces. By the time I had the room spruced up, the letter was ready in my head. I ate a sandwich, and went upstairs to write to the address Selwyn had provided.

Next I went looking for my copy of *In Troy*. It wasn't on the shelf where I'd remembered it, so I searched all the bookcases, and then, very carefully, investigated every stack and corner of my office. I didn't remember lending it to anyone, so it was probably in one of the boxes in the loft, where the only way to find a particular book was to crouch down with a flashlight in the dark, and dig.

Instead, I went on line to see what I could find out about Helen Ralston.

My first trawl didn't net me much, but I was able to find copies of her second and fifth novels, as well as one of the many reprints of *Hermine in Cloud-Land* available to order. Two first editions of *In Troy* were listed: the dealer in London was asking $452.82 while one in San Francisco offered a lovingly-described "very fine" copy for a mere $320.00. There were also lots of the Virago edition about, with the cheapest offered at $2.00. On a whim, I added that to my order.

Before I logged off I checked my e-mail again and found that Lilith Fischler had already replied.

My efforts had paid off. Her reply was as transparently open and friendly as I had struggled to make mine seem, and she told me exactly what I had been hoping to hear. She was *not* writing a biography, only a critical study of *In Troy*. Her essay would be appearing in an anthology to be published by Weslayan University Press next year – she'd be happy to send me a copy as a file attachment. More importantly, she knew how to get in touch with Helen Ralston:

> She was happy to talk about her writing, but not so much about her early life, and especially not about the relationship with W.E. Logan. But she sent very clear and interesting answers to every-thing else. I don't know if she will be quite as energetic and coherent now, since she had a stroke last year. Her daughter, Clarissa Breen, wrote to me that she was recovering well, but couldn't live on her own any more. They sold the flat in London, and Helen is now living with Clarissa in Glasgow. I'm sure she wouldn't mind me giving you the phone number . . .

At nine o'clock the next morning, I rang the number Lilith Fischler had given me, and asked the woman who answered if I could speak to Helen Ralston.

"May I ask who's calling?"

I gave my name, adding quickly, "She doesn't know me; I'm a writer. I wanted to talk to her about her work."

"Hold on a minute, I'll just get her."

Much more than a minute passed before the phone was picked up again, and I heard the same woman's voice saying, "I'm sorry, she doesn't want to speak on the phone; can you come here?"

I was so startled I could hardly speak at first. I'd assumed that this invitation would come much later, if at all. I finally managed to say, "Of course. If you'll give me directions. But I'm quite a distance away – in Argyll, on the west coast. It'll take me a couple of hours to drive to Glasgow."

"Ah. Well, tomorrow would be better, then. She's at her best in the mornings; she flags a bit around mid-day."

"I could come tomorrow. Whatever time suits you."

"Nine o'clock?"

"I'll be there."

"Thank you," she said warmly, surprising me. "I know mother is looking forward to meeting you. She doesn't have much excitement in her life these days – it was a real blow to her to have to leave London. The mention of your name perked her right up."

"That's nice," I said, surprised that my name should mean anything to Helen Ralston. "Can you tell me how to get to your house?"

"Do you know Glasgow at all? Well, it's not difficult, if you come in on the Great Western Road . . ."

VII

Helen Ralston lived with her daughter in an ordinary two-storey, semi-detached house in a quiet neighbourhood on the north-western edge of the city. The drive through Argyll, along the narrow, loch-hugging road, switching back upon itself again and again as it crossed a land divided and defined by water, up into the mountains and then down again, went more swiftly than I'd dared to hope, without any of the delays that could be caused by log-lorries, farm vehicles and road works, and I was parking on the street in front of the house at five minutes after nine o'clock the following morning. I got out of the car stiffly, feeling numb and a little dazed by the speed of it all – that so soon after deciding I wanted to write about Helen Ralston I should be meeting her seemed little short of miraculous.

Her picture "My Death" was in the boot of the car, well-wrapped, ready to be handed back to its rightful owner, yet now that I was here in front of her house, I hesitated. Remembering my own initial strong, visceral reaction to it, I could not expect that the artist's reaction would be the ordinary one of someone to whom a piece of lost property has been returned. What if she was angry that I'd seen it? I decided to wait and see, try to find out her likely response before admitting that I had it.

That settled, I opened the side door to take out my bag, and hesitated again at the sight of my new tape recorder, bought yesterday in the Woolworths in Oban.

I was unprepared for this interview in more ways than one.

Yesterday, I had discovered that the cassette recorder which had seen me through more than ten years of occasional interviewing was no longer working. I'd driven off to Oban immediately to buy one, only to find that the electronics shop I'd remembered had closed down – driven out of business, I guessed, by the stacks of cut-price VCRs, DVD players, printers, personal stereos and telephones on sale in the aisles of Tesco. Alas for me, Tesco did not sell cassette recorders – players, yes, but nothing with a recording function. The closest equivalent I'd been able to find after searching every store in town was a toy for young children. It was the size of a school lunch-box and made of bright red and yellow plastic, with a bright blue microphone attached to it by a curly yellow cord. But it worked, and so I'd bought it.

Now, though, I knew I couldn't possibly arrive for my first meeting with Helen Elizabeth Ralston clutching this children's toy. In any case, she hadn't agreed to an interview; I hadn't even spoken to her yet. I couldn't remember if I'd told her daughter that I was planning to write a biography, but I was pretty sure I'd said only that I admired her mother's work and wanted to talk to her about it. Best if this first meeting should be informal, relaxed, a friendly conversation. Questions "for the record" could come later.

With some relief, I left the childish machine in the car and locked the door behind me. Now my dissatisfaction with the few questions I'd been able to formulate no longer mattered, no more than the fact that I could barely remember anything about *In Troy* (I'd spent a fruitless hour searching the loft for it) and hadn't yet even seen any of her other books. We were just going to talk.

From the first moment I saw her, I knew I would like Clarissa Breen. Sometimes it happens like that: you seem to recognize someone you've never set eyes on before, and feel drawn to them, as if you're both members of the same, far-flung family. I don't know why it should be, but those instantaneous feelings are nearly always right.

I smiled at her, and she smiled back, and from the warmth and interest in her grey eyes I knew she felt the same about me.

She was a slight, trim woman who appeared to be about my own age, her light brown hair in a short, feathery cut. The only faintly whispered echo of Circe's features were in her deep-set, luminous eyes; her own face was softer, wider, friendlier, her chin and nose less prominent, and she had a lovely, long smiling mouth.

As I liked her, so I also felt immediately at home in her house. I liked the dramatic mauve colour of the entrance hall, the atmospheric black and white photographs hanging on the wall opposite the stairs, the scent of fresh coffee and something baking that wafted through from the back of the house.

The room to which she led me was a combination of kitchen and living room. At one end, a wicker couch was set into a window recess, grouped together with a glass-topped table and a couple of arm chairs. My eyes were briefly distracted by the green of the garden beyond the window, where birds hopped and hovered around a bird-table, and then I caught sight of the shrivelled, white-haired figure hunched in a chair, and my heart gave a great, frightened leap.

"Mum, here's someone come to see you."

Feeling horribly self-conscious, more awkward than I had since the first few interviews I'd done for a student newspaper, I went forward on legs that felt like sticks of wood. Bending down to her, speaking in a voice that struck my own ears as harsh and unnatural, I introduced myself and began to explain my interest. I hadn't got very far before she interrupted.

"I know who you are," she said sharply, blinking watery blue eyes. "I was wondering when you'd finally get here."

Although I felt intimidated, I said, "I left home before seven. I think I made pretty good time."

The old lady made an impatient, huffing sound and stretched out an arm. "That's not what I meant. Never mind. I suppose we should say how do you do."

Awkward still, and wishing that my heart would stop racing, I took her skinny, age-spotted hand gently in mine. "I'm very pleased to meet you. Thank you so much for letting me come."

"You're younger than I thought you'd be. I suppose you think you're old."

I smiled uncertainly. "I think I'm middle-aged, although that's right only if I live to a hundred."

She made a little sound, half sniff, half grunt. "Well, sit down," she said. "I suppose you'll want to ask me questions about my life?"

Clarissa came over with a tray. "Coffee all right for you? Mum, do you want anything else?" She turned to me. "I'll be in my office, down the hall, first door on the right – just come and knock if you need anything, but I'm sure Mum will look after you."

I felt sorry to see her go.

"Like her?"

Helen's question startled me. "She seems very nice."

"She is. She's a wonderful daughter, but, more than that, I think we'd be friends even if we weren't related."

"That must be nice, to feel like that. To have that sort of relationship." I waited tensely for the inevitable next question, but it didn't come.

"Yes. It is."

I took a sip of coffee, then put the cup down and rummaged in my bag for notepad and pen. "I thought . . . do you mind if I take a few notes? Or, or would you rather we just talked, and I could record a more formal interview later?"

"It's up to you. Why ask me? Surely you've done this sort of thing before." She sounded disapproving, and I didn't blame her. I didn't understand myself what had thrown me into such a flutter, as if I were a kid again, the novice reporter speechless before her first visiting celebrity. I'd interviewed more than a hundred people, most of them more famous than Helen Elizabeth Ralston. But this was different, not only because this wasn't an assignment – there was no newspaper behind me, I didn't even have a contract for a book – but because it was *her*. She mattered so much; I wanted her to like me; I wanted to be friends with the author of *In Troy*.

And I knew that if I wanted to prove myself to her, I was going about it in exactly the wrong way.

"I want you to be comfortable," I said, as firmly as I could. "I did think that we might start by chatting – I'll bring a recorder next time – and if there's anything you don't want to talk about . . ."

"I'll let you know."

"Okay, then." I took a deep breath and took the plunge. "What made you, an American, decide to come to Glasgow to study art?"

She peered at me. "Right to the heart of it? All right, let's get this over with. It was for W.E. Logan."

"You knew his work?"

"I had seen one painting, a landscape. One of my teachers, the head of the art department at Syracuse, owned it. He had met Logan and some other Scottish painters on a visit to the South of France a few years earlier, and been very impressed by his work . . . although not, I think, quite as greatly impressed by it as I was. I don't know, young people, they're so wild, so ready to fly off at the slightest encouragement, don't you think?" She shot me a little, conspiratorial smile. "Well, I was, anyway. I must have been searching for a mentor, as young people often do. At any rate, soon after seeing this picture, which I convinced myself was a masterpiece, I wrote off to the artist, Mr Logan, in far-away Scotland, and I sent him some of my sketches, and I asked for his comments and advice.

"And his advice – now, you may find this hard to believe, but I still have the letter; I've kept it all these years, and I'll let you see it later – his response was to praise my work to the skies and tell me that the next step was to find the right teacher and embark on a proper course of study. Despite my living so far away – had he even noticed where the letter came from? – the school that he recommended was his own, where he could be my teacher. At that age, and in my impressionable state of mind, a suggestion from W.E. Logan had the force of a command."

She paused to pick up a glass of water from the table and take a small sip.

I was astonished. How was it that Logan's biographer hadn't known this? And why had Logan himself tried to cover it up, with his little fantasy about Helen's prophetic dreams? "I'd love to see your sketches from that time."

"They're gone."

"Oh, no! What happened?"

She lifted her narrow shoulders. "I don't know what became of them. They're long gone. I didn't take them with me when I left Glasgow. I suppose Willy – or his wife – might have destroyed them."

It was on the tip of my tongue to tell her about the painting in the car. "Maybe not all of them."

She shrugged. "They're nothing to me now. And they weren't then, or I would have kept them, wouldn't I."

"Like you kept W.E. Logan's letter to you."

"Letters. There were several, tucked inside my diary. I took that with me to Paris."

"*Paris*? You left Glasgow for Paris? Why?"

Her smile this time included her eyes, which narrowed so much they nearly disappeared. "Why Paris?" she repeated slowly. "My dear, it was 1929. I was an artist, I was an American, cut loose, without much money but free – where would *you* have gone?"

I met her eyes and smiled back. "Paris," I agreed. "Of all the places and times I wish I could see for myself – Paris, in the Twenties."

"Well, then. You understand."

"Tell me – what was it like? What did you do there? Did you know anyone?"

She raised her eyebrows and looked away. "So many questions! My, my. Where to begin?" She reached with a hand that trembled slightly for her water glass. I waited until she had taken another tiny sip and put the glass back down before I repeated, "Did you know anyone in Paris when you arrived?"

"No. Not personally. But I knew a few names, and it was not hard, then, to fall in with the expatriate crowd. There were certain cafés and hotels where they gathered. And, as a young woman, unaccompanied, reasonably attractive, it was easy to make new friends."

VIII

For the next hour Helen Ralston kept me entranced and fascinated with anecdotes from her years in Paris. She name-dropped without restraint. I could hardly believe my luck, to be sitting in the same room, talking to someone who had actually attended some of Gertrude Stein's famous salons. Picasso and Hemingway were both, by then, *much* too grand to be known – she said – she'd seen them around, though. And she'd been friendly with Djuna Barnes and Man Ray and Marcel Duchamp and Brancusi, Caresse and Harry Crosby, Anais Nin and Henry Miller, and she'd taken tea with Sylvia Beach and James Joyce and his Norah . . . so many evocative names.

At one point I remember thinking *she's a living time machine* and at another I could have cursed myself for not having brought in the tape recorder, however idiotic it looked. How could I remember all the details? Would she be willing to relate all these stories again another day? It occurred to me that maybe there wouldn't *be* another interview – not that she'd be unwilling to talk to me again, but simply because she could drop dead at any minute. At her age, especially, you couldn't count on anything.

I wanted her to go on talking forever, to soak up as much of her remembered experiences as I possibly could, but after a couple of hours it was clear she was running out of energy. The pauses for tiny sips of water became more frequent, and her face seemed to sag, and she stumbled often over simple words. Even aware of this, I was too selfish to let her stop; it was only when Clarissa came in and exclaimed at the sight of her mother's obvious exhaustion that Helen finally fell silent.

"Time for a break," said Clarissa.

I jumped up guiltily. "I'm sorry, I've just been so fascinated—"

"I'm all right, I'm all right," Helen said, flapping a hand at her daughter. "Don't *fuss*."

"You're tired—"

"Yes, of course I'm tired – what's wrong with that? It means I'll sleep. I'll have my rest now, and eat later."

I chewed my lip, watching as Clarissa helped her mother rise from the chair.

"I'm fine, I'm fine, don't fuss me."

"I'll just come upstairs and see you into bed. Excuse us," Clarissa said as she and her mother moved slowly across the room.

When they had gone out, I wandered aimlessly around the room, gazing out the window at the birds and then looking around at the pictures on the walls – they were highly-detailed drawings of plants, like illustrations from an old-fashioned botany book. I had noticed a bookcase in one corner, and now gravitated towards it. A few familiar spines caught my attention immediately – *Nightwood*, *The Rings of Saturn*, *Hallucinating Foucault*, *Possession* – all dear friends which I had at home – and then the breath caught in my throat at the sight of a familiar pink and blue spine, the letters of my own name written there above the title. I had to put my hand on it and draw it out, and yes, it was one of my own short story collections.

I was still holding it, bemused and pleased, when Clarissa came back in.

"Out like a light," she said.

"I'm sorry—"

"Oh, that's all right, she loved it! But she can't take much excitement, that's all. Sad when talking about the past is the most excitement you can know." She noticed the book in my hands then and gave me a different sort of smile. "I liked your stories. I didn't think I would – I don't read sci-fi or fantasy – but yours aren't really sci-fi, are they? They're more like myths. I especially liked that one where the mother is born again – what's it called? – where she becomes a little baby, and her son has to look after her."

"Thank you." Always nice to meet a reader, but I couldn't help the quick stab of disappointment. "I thought maybe this belonged to Helen."

"Of course it does. She has all your books. That's just the only one I've read – but now I'll be sure to read the others," she said quickly.

"Helen Ralston has read all my books?" This was better than winning an award.

"Of course. Why do you suppose she was so excited to meet you? Didn't she tell you?"

"The conversation didn't go in that direction."

Clarissa shrugged and rolled her eyes. "Well. Would you like another coffee? There's a pastry in the oven. Mum has a sweet tooth, and normally I take a break and join her about now." As she spoke, we had been drifting together towards the kitchen area, where she now took a cinnamon plait from the oven.

"What sort of work do you do?" I asked.

"Writing – but not like yours or Mum's. It's mostly catalogue copy and travel brochures. I used to work in marketing. This is handy because I can do it from home."

We settled in against the counter, sipping coffee and nibbling the warm, sweet soft pastry while we traded information about our lives, laying the foundations for a friendship. After about a quarter of an hour, her eyes strayed to the clock on the stove and although I wanted nothing more than to go on talking to Clarissa, I knew I was interrupting her work, so I said, "I should be going."

"You're welcome to stay," she said, hesitating slightly. "If you wanted to wait and say goodbye to Mum when she wakes up . . . only I don't think she'll have the energy for much more than that."

"No, that's all right, as long as I can come back – how about the day after tomorrow? If that's not too soon?"

"That should be fine. I'll call you if there's any problem. I've got your number."

As soon as I got back to the car, I remembered "My Death" still in the boot. I thought of taking it up to the house and handing it over to Clarissa, just to get the problem off my hands, but then decided that wasn't fair. I'd make a point of mentioning it to Helen next time. I felt I could count on getting a fairly rational response, although whether she'd be happy to have this strange painting back in her possession again, I didn't know.

Before starting on the long drive home, I went shopping. I bought myself a neat, unobtrusive mini-cassette recorder and spent some more time in the bookshops of Glasgow, this time concentrating on memoirs and histories of Paris in the 1920s and 1930s, searching for and finding Helen Ralston's name in index after index.

The next day, two of the books I had ordered – *Hermine in Cloud-Land* and *The Second Wife* – arrived in the post, so the time passed pleasurably in reading. I was not very impressed by Willy Logan's first book. The pictures were charming, but by comparison the text strained after charm and achieved only a kind of dated, fey whimsicality. I didn't care for it and, having met the original of Hermine, I didn't think that she would have either.

The Second Wife, Helen Ralston's fifth novel, was a revelation: understated, subtle, psychologically complex, ambiguous and faintly sinister . . . it was just the sort of novel I aspired to write myself, and reading it now, at this fallow period of my life, stirred a creative envy in me. For the first time in ages I wished I was at work on a novel and, although I knew I wasn't anywhere near ready to start one, I could believe that one day I would be, that the roads of fiction weren't forever closed to me. Maybe, after I'd finished with Helen Ralston, I'd be inspired by her example to write fiction again.

That night, the unseasonably dry, mild weather broke, and a gale began to blow. I lay awake listening to the keening wind, the rain flung like shot against the windows, and worried. I hated driving in bad weather; I was nervous enough about the narrow, twisting roads in this country when they were dry and the visibility was good – had it been anyone else I was going to meet, I would have phoned to suggest rescheduling. But at Helen Ralston's age, any day might be her last. I felt I had to go.

By six o'clock in the morning the winds had died, but the rain had settled in, falling heavily and relentlessly from the laden sky. A few hours of that, and the road I lived on would be flooded, impassable. I made a thermos of coffee and a peanut butter sandwich to take in the car along with my heavy weather gear, a flashlight, and the shoulder bag with *The Second Wife*, notebook, new tape recorder, extra batteries and tapes, and drove off without giving myself time to reconsider. "My Death" was still in its wrappings in the boot, awaiting delivery.

I was tense and cautious, and although the rain had scarcely lessened by the time I reached the outskirts of Glasgow, and the traffic reports on Radio Scotland warned of problems on other roads, my way was clear. Drawing up in front of Clarissa Breen's house I felt the happy relief of the traveller who has, against all odds, battled safely home again.

"Home is the sailor, home from the sea," I murmured to myself as I hurried up the walkway. Clarissa, opening the door to my knock, looked surprised and pleased.

"I thought we'd be getting a call from you to say you weren't going to risk it – this rain is dreadful!" she exclaimed, letting me in.

There was the same smell of coffee and something sweet baking, and the black and white photographs displayed against the mauve walls of the entrance hall looked as familiar as if I'd been coming in through that front door for months. I sighed happily. "Oh, the roads weren't bad, really. How are you? How's Helen?"

I had not spoken loudly, but my voice must have carried to the back of the house, because the old woman shouted, "Waiting for you so we can get started!"

"Very bright today," said Clarissa, behind me, and then murmured, closer to my ear, "A little over-excited."

"Tears before bed-time?"

"Let's hope not."

"What are you *talking* about out there? She's *my* visitor, Clarissa! Let her come through, don't you keep her gossiping!"

We exchanged a glance, and I was split between enjoying our conspiracy, and guilt over betraying Helen, and then I went on ahead into the big, bright, room.

"Hello, Helen. It's good to see you again. How are you?"

"Not getting any younger," she said crisply. Her eyes were sparkling; she looked pleased with herself. "You see, Clarissa, didn't I say she would come? I knew she wouldn't be scared of rain!"

"I couldn't live in Scotland if I were."

I was soon settled into a chair beside Helen, with a cup of fresh, strong, hot coffee close at hand, and my unobtrusive little tape recorder pointing in her direction.

"I thought we might talk a bit about your childhood," I said. I had decided to be organized and chronological about my investigations, even though, after reading *The Second Wife*, I longed to talk about that.

A small sigh escaped her, and I felt I'd disappointed her in some way. "Very well. Ask your questions."

"Well . . . do you want to start by telling me your earliest memory?"

She looked vague. "I can try. Mostly what I remember are *things*, not events, so it's hard to put a time to them. The first house where I lived, where I was born – we were there until I was about eleven – all my memories are there. I could close my eyes now and take you on a tour of that house, describing every room, all the furniture, every nook and cranny, not just how it looked from every perspective, but the texture of the rugs and the painted walls and the bathroom tiles, the smells and tastes as well – but that would be far too boring."

I felt my heart beat faster in sympathy. In fact, this was exactly how I felt about my own first childhood home, which remained more clear in my memory, more *real*, than anywhere I had lived since. Those first ten years of life, in which I had so exhaustively explored my surroundings, had given me a depth of useless knowledge, made me an expert in the geography and furnishings of the house at 4534

Waring Street, Houston, Texas, between the years 1952-63. I supposed that other people – unless, like my first husband, they'd moved house every year or two – carried around with them a similarly useless mental floor-plan and inventory – but until now I'd never heard anyone else talk about it.

"I remember, there was coloured glass in the window, a fanlight, above the front door, and when the sun shone through it made a pattern of magical, shimmering colours against the wall. I remember trying to touch the colours, to catch them, and feeling frustrated that they slipped through my fingers – I was too young to understand.

"And there was a wonderful, old, dark wood chest that I was always trying to get into. It didn't matter how many times I saw inside, that it was only blankets and linens and so on, I would still imagine it was hiding some treasure. That was one of my fancies . . . my dreams and my fancies, now, I remember some of them as clearly as the things that were real. Perhaps my earliest memory was a dream.

"I had a toy. It might have been my first toy, maybe my only one – children didn't have so many toys in those days, you know, we made do with bits and pieces, cast-off things our elders had no use for, a wooden spoon with a face for a doll, but this was a ready-made toy, it had been manufactured for no other purpose but play. It was a doll made of rubber, an ugly little thing really I suppose, but it was my baby and I loved it dearly. Sometimes I'd put my finger into its mouth to let it suck – because its mouth would open if you squeezed it, and close again when the pressure was released – and sometimes I'd take its whole head into my mouth and suck on it – not very motherly behaviour, but I wasn't much more than a baby myself, and perhaps I resented having been weaned – at any rate, I wanted something to suck. Once I bit off a piece of its nose – something about the colour and the texture of it convinced me it would taste nice, but of course it didn't; it tasted of rubber, nasty, although the sensation of chewing it, feeling it slide through my teeth and then catch, again and again, was intriguing enough that I was in no hurry to spit it out. After I'd chewed a hole in it, of course the doll no longer worked properly, the mouth wouldn't open and shut like before, but that didn't bother me, I still loved it and carried it around with me everywhere until one day I suppose I must have dropped it when I was out, and my mother didn't pick it up, and so I lost my baby, my treasure, my first child, you might say."

She looked at me as if expecting some comment, but I could not respond. I felt almost giddy with *déjà vu* – only this wasn't merely *déjà vu*, but something much stronger and stranger, and it had cut the ground right out from under me. I didn't know what to think about what I was hearing: could it be coincidence? Lots of children in the past century must have owned rubber dolls and sucked and chewed them to destruction. She hadn't even described it very well – my doll had been a sort of clown, but hers presumably was a baby.

When I said nothing, she went on.

"I don't remember when I lost it, how it happened, when I noticed, if I was upset, and I don't know how long after that it was that he came back to me in a dream."

I noticed the switch from "it" to "he", and saw my own long-lost clown doll in my mind's eye.

"It wasn't a detailed dream, it was just him. He had come back. But instead of being glad to see him, I was frightened, and I screamed and woke myself up. I woke the whole house up with my screaming.

"When I told my mother about it I began to cry. She thought I was unhappy because I missed my doll. She didn't understand. To have the doll back was the last thing I wanted. I was terrified in case I did by some chance find it again, because I knew . . . I knew it would be like the dream. He would have changed. He wouldn't be my baby anymore. What the dream had shown me was the familiar become strange, how frightening the ordinary can be. You understand?"

I stared back as if hypnotized and just managed to nod my head. But I didn't understand. How could this person – a stranger, and of another generation – have had the very same dream as me? Even her interpretation, although different from my own, rang true, so that I thought yes, that was the real reason my dream had scared me.

As I still said nothing, after another little pause, Helen went on talking about her childhood. I hardly listened. I was in a swelter, all confused, frightening emotions as I tried to make sense of this impossible connection between us. I could not accept that it was mere coincidence, that *both* of us had shared the same experience as children – an experience which had given rise to the same dream, which had been significant enough for both of us to remember it all our lives. There had to be a reason for it; some link, an explanation . . .

And suddenly I remembered what I had, of course, known all along. That dream of mine, that highly significant, personal memory, was no secret. I had written about it. I had put it into a short story which anyone could read – I knew that both Clarissa and Helen had read it, because it was in the volume I'd found in their bookcase.

But what did Helen mean by telling me back my own story as if it were one of her own memories? Was it a joke? A tease? A veiled compliment?

At any rate, unless she was genuinely senile, confused enough that she couldn't sort out her own experiences from things she'd only read about, she must have expected me to recognize what she was doing, and comment on it. I recalled her suggestive pauses, the way she had looked at me and awaited a response, and I almost groaned aloud.

What an idiot she must think me!

Maybe she was feeling foolish herself, knowing her joke had misfired, thinking, perhaps, that my dream was not real, but something I'd made up, a passing notion which meant so little to me that I'd forgotten it and took her "memory" at face value.

I couldn't say anything now – she'd reached high school in her recollections, and it would be far too rude to interrupt her to say that I'd belatedly got her joke – I'd have to wait until she gave me an opening.

Maybe it was because I was concentrating so hard on not missing my chance to speak, but I could not get involved in what she was telling me. It seemed remote and unreal, second-hand, as if she was just retelling a tale she had memorized. Maybe that was my fault: perhaps she felt it was her duty, to get things right and in the proper sequence, and had prepared this potted history for me. But I missed the lively, spontaneous jumble of impressions which had come bubbling up the day before when she'd talked about her years in Paris.

We had soon reached the point where the young Helen Ralston made her dramatic, life-changing decision to leave America and go to study art in Glasgow.

"But you know all that," she said briskly. "And I've told you about Paris . . ."

"Wait, wait." I held up a hand. "Slow down and back up. You *didn't* tell me about your time in Glasgow – not at all. I sort of understand why you went, but not really—"

"What do you mean 'not really'? I told you, it was because of his letters. I suppose I fell in love with him. Well, it wouldn't be the first time such a thing has happened. I still have those letters, you know! I can show you."

"I'm not doubting you," I said quickly. "But what happened after you got to Glasgow – you haven't told me any of that."

She gave me a long, hooded look – very like a bird of prey considering whether it was worthwhile to pounce – before she spoke. "But you know, don't you." It was hardly a question.

"I've read one side of the story. I'd really like to hear yours."

"I don't know why. I'm sure you can imagine it well enough. Why is it people are only interested in women because of their connections to some man, some famous man?"

"That's not true."

She wasn't listening to me. "The letters I've had from people wanting to know *the truth*! That's what they say, but it isn't the truth they want at all, just gossip. Did Helen Ralston try to kill herself because Willy Logan wouldn't stay with her, or was she trying o get away from him? Or was it nothing to do with him at all, and he only happened to be there? Something happened – it happened more than seventy years ago – does it matter *why* it happened?"

"It matters to me – *your* story is the one I want to hear."

Her eyes flickered. "Then why keep asking about Logan?"

"I'm not – I don't mean to. I want to know what happened to you. How you felt about things. Everything. Your childhood, your youth, the time you spent in Glasgow, and Paris, and everything else. I know you weren't with Logan for long. Not even two years. Out of ninety-six years, that's not much. But it is a part of your life – the things that happened to you in your early twenties—"

"The truth."

I shut up.

She leaned forward, fixing me with her deep-set, faded blue eyes, her hands like claws clutching the chair arms. "The truth is that I don't know why Helen Ralston jumped out of that window – or if she was pushed. It happened to someone else. I don't remember anything about it."

I knew that serious accidents could sometimes result in memory loss, but I thought of the way she had given me back my own dream as if it were her own, and I wasn't sure I believed her.

"Okay. But you mentioned a diary—"

"Yes, and I'll let you see it. You can see all of them, in due course."

"Thank you. That will be very helpful. And we'll leave that day in August. But – would you mind talking about something else that happened before you left Glasgow and W.E. Logan?"

She shrugged her shoulders slightly. "What is it you want to know?"

"About the island. Achlan. I wonder if you could tell me about that."

There was a sharp click, and we both looked at the tape recorder, which had switched itself off.

"It's okay," I said, reaching for it. "I've got another cassette in my bag."

"I'd like something to drink. My mouth is so dry."

I stood up. "Shall I get you some more water? Or something else?"

"Why don't you go fetch Clarissa, and we'll take our break now."

It was too early; we'd had barely an hour together, and I knew that after the break she'd be bound to go for a nap. My disappointment must have shown, because she gave a small, thin-lipped smile. "Oh, don't worry. We'll get back to the island. I promise you, we'll get back to Achlan."

Clarissa did not seem surprised when I knocked at her door.

"She was up at six this morning, rummaging through her papers, sorting things out, making notes, muttering to herself. Getting ready for you. Nearly bit my head off when I dared suggest you might not come today, because of the weather. 'Of course she'll come! She has to come!'."

Strangely, a shiver ran through me at the idea of the two of them talking about me in my absence, although there was surely nothing odd or sinister in it.

"Such a shame, when you've come such a long way for such a short visit . . . tell you what, why don't you stay for lunch today, and talk to Mum again later on?"

"That would be wonderful – if she's up for it."

"I'm sure she'll tell you if she's not." Clarissa grinned.

Over fresh coffee – decaffeinated for Helen – and slices of apple tart, talk about Helen's life went on, leap-frogging a couple of decades to London during the Blitz, and the brief war-time love-affair with Robbie, a much younger fighter pilot. He was Clarissa's father, although he'd not lived to see his only child. I was surprised to learn that Clarissa was sixty – I told her honestly that she looked much younger – but she'd been born during the war, to a grieving single mother.

"I named her after *Mrs Dalloway*," Helen informed me. "I was reading that book during my confinement – in fact, I read it three times. It was the only escape I had, a window into the world before the War, London before the bombs fell, before . . ." she trailed off, blinking rapidly, and her daughter stroked her hand.

Helen's memories of the war years in London were vivid, her descriptions of that time of fear, tedium, deprivation, and passion full of the circumstantial detail I'd missed when she had talked about her earlier life. People said that when you got older the past seemed more immediate and was easier to recall than more recent years, but in every life there must also be periods you would rather forget, and others that you kept fresh by constantly reviewing. Obviously Helen had not wanted to lose a single, precious moment from her short time with Clarissa's father – from the way that Clarissa listened and smiled and chimed in, it was clear she'd heard it all before – but the affair with Willy Logan was different. Maybe it had been too unhappy, maybe her feelings and her actions then didn't suit her older self-image. I could well imagine her not wanting to remember what a reckless and troubled young girl she had been, whether she had seduced or been seduced by her teacher. In my experience, such an affair at such an age was too intense and life-shaping to be forgotten, but if anything could wipe the slate clean, I thought, it had to be a near-death experience.

Although Helen announced her intention that we should carry on talking, her energy was clearly flagging, so I chimed in with her daughter to insist that she have a lie down.

"I'll stay," I promised her. "Clarissa's invited me for lunch. I'll read while you're resting. We can talk all afternoon if you're up to it. I've brought plenty of cassettes."

Helen accepted this. "Come upstairs with me. I'll give you something to read. I'll show you those letters."

Clarissa went back to her work while I went slowly upstairs after Helen.

"I've kept diaries," she told me after she had paused to catch her breath at the top of the stairs. "And there's an autobiographical novel. I never wanted it published, before, but now, maybe . . . You could let me know what you think."

Her room was a dim, narrow space – an ordinary bedroom whose dimensions had been shrunk by the addition of bookshelves on every wall. There was one window, shaded and curtained. The shelves were deep, double-stacked with books, notebooks, and box-files. The other furnishings were a single bed, a small wardrobe, a bedside table, and something which might have been either a writing desk or a dressing table, but it was so cluttered with a mix of toiletries, papers, medicines, notebooks, tissues, books and pens that it seemed unlikely it was used for either purpose now.

"My memories," said Helen. "We got rid of a lot when I moved up from London, but I had to keep my favourite books, and all my papers." With a heavy sigh, she sank down onto the bed. Then, with a groan, she struggled to rise again. "My diaries. I was going to show you . . ."

I put a hand on her shoulder, pushing her gently down again. "I'll get it. Tell me where to look."

"Thank you, dear. If you don't mind . . ." She lay back, putting her head down on the pillow with a sigh of relief. "They're on my work-table. Desk. The whole lot. You're not ready to read them all, not yet, but you could look at one now, I think. Well, why not? Let me think. Which one? Hmmm."

Her eyes closed. I watched her uncertainly, feeling a mixture of affection, amusement and exasperation as I realized she was falling asleep. I opened my mouth to call her back, but just then she gave a tiny, stuttering snore.

I turned to look at the table, and saw the pile of notebooks she must have meant. She had been intending to give me one to read. I picked up the one on top, a hardbound black and red book with lined pages. There was nothing marked on the cover to indicate its contents. I opened it to the first page, a flyleaf where she had written her name and the year, 1981. Oh, far too late.

I put the notebook down carefully to one side and reached for the next in the stack. This one was much more battered and obviously old. It had a blue and white marbled cover with a square in the centre of the front cover where it said COMPOSITIONS. I'd had one just like it in high school in the late 1960s, and had used it to record my most intimate feelings, all the daily emotional upheavals, the first stirrings of sexual interest – to my misery, unreciprocated. How I'd poured my heart out, the protestations of my elaborate and undying love for the golden Yale – sometimes, long ago as it was now, I could still remember the particular bittersweet flavour of that feeling, the ache of unrequited love. And then, in the same year – things happened so rapidly in youth – there had been the mutual attraction between me and Andy, and the pain of being unloved had been assuaged by passionate love-making in the back of borrowed cars. My descriptions of what we'd done must have verged on the pornographic – even now, the idea of someone else reading about my first love affair horrified me. I suppose it was the thought of the contents of my own, so similar-looking diary, which made me set this one aside without even opening it to check the date.

As I did so, I dislodged a stack of photographs lying on top of the next notebook; they slithered in a watery rush down the side of the notebook-tower.

Shooting a quick, nervous glance at the figure in the bed behind me, making sure that she still slept, I gathered them up. They were all old, black and white snapshots of people, most of them posed in some outdoor location. They were identified on the backs with pencilled dates, names or initials.

LONDON 1941 ROBBIE

I recognized Helen, skirted and hatted amid pigeons at the base of some statue, holding on to the arm of a uniformed young man. As I peered into the distant grey shadows of his face my heart gave a jolt: in the curve of his mouth and the line of his jaw I thought I could see a resemblance to Allan. The likeness to Clarissa was obvious, and it dawned on me that this was why I'd felt so immediately drawn to her. Her father looked a bit like Allan, and she reminded me of him, too.

I glanced quickly through the other pictures, usually able to pick out Helen by her distinctive looks. Some of the other figures were also familiar: Djuna Barnes, Peggy Gugenheim, James Joyce. I caught my breath. In an English garden Helen Ralston stood, beaming triumphantly beside a tall, shy, elegant, faintly bemused-looking woman. There was no need for me to turn over the photo to check the name written on the back – Virginia Woolf was unmistakable.

Brilliant! My heart pounded with excitement. I wondered if she'd let me use these pictures in my book and immediately knew the answer. Of course she would – why else had she sorted them out, if not to give to me? With so many well-known names to toss into my proposal, I felt the biography was a done deal. *Helen Elizabeth Ralston, The Forgotten Modernist.* As I gathered the pictures up and stacked them neatly again my eyes turned greedily to the pile of old journals.

The one now on top was a slightly odd size, narrower than the contemporary standard, bound in some stiff black cloth, and as I reached out to touch it I somehow *knew* that this was one of her earliest notebooks, from her Paris years.

Without even pausing to question my right to do so, I picked the book up and opened it.

There was no date on the first page and, as I flipped through, I got the impression that it was one continuous narrative, for it wasn't broken down into entries like a diary. It seemed to be told in the first person, and there were long passages of description, but also conversations, set off with single quotes and dashes. Maybe this was the autobiographical novel she had mentioned?

Helen's handwriting was small, neat and angular, but despite its regularity it was not easy to read – especially not in the dim light of her bedroom. I flipped ahead a few pages and moved a little closer to the covered window, trying to find something I could make sense of. I saw that, despite the cramped and careful handwriting, she used her notebooks the same way I did, writing on only one side of the page. (I wondered if she had continued this profligacy during the war, with paper rationing.) The blank sides weren't wasted; for me they provided a space for notes, second thoughts, later comments, trial runs at complicated sentences, reminders, lists of interesting words and of books I wanted to read, occasionally quotations from the books I was reading, or ideas for stories, and as I flipped through the book, concentrating now on the 'other' pages, I could tell that Helen worked just like me.

These pages were easier to read since there was less on them. I managed to puzzle out a few quotations: there were lines from Baudelaire – his French followed by her rough translation – a paragraph from *The Golden Bowl* and two from *The Great Gatsby*. A list of British and American authors might have been one of my own "must read" lists, with the difference being that all of them were still alive in 1929. I wondered if she was reminding herself of books to look for, or people she wanted to meet.

The next list was something else. I read it again and again, trying to make some other sense of it than the personal meaning it had for me at first glance:

YALE
ANDY
IRA
MARK
JOHN
JIMMY
PATRICK
JOHN
CHAS
ALLAN

Nine masculine forenames, one of them repeated twice. The names of the ten men I had loved.

How could Helen Ralston have known that?

She couldn't; it wasn't possible; not *all* of them. My husbands were a matter of public record, and plenty of people knew that I'd lived with a man called Mark for three years. Although my affair with Ira was ostensibly secret, I had dedicated my first book to him, and, invited to contribute to a magazine feature called "The First Time", I hadn't bothered to disguise Andy with a pseudonym. But Yale? Or the fact that I'd been involved with two different men called John? And *nobody* knew about Chas.

Could it be coincidence? Another writer, drawing up a list of names for characters, stumbling so precisely on those most meaningful to me?

I couldn't believe it.

I saw stars and jags of light in front of my eyes as I carefully replaced that notebook with the others.

Somehow, I got out of that stuffy little room, filled with the sound of an old woman's shallow breathing, without bumping into anything or falling over, and made my way down the stairs. I was halfway to the front door, driven by terror, before I remembered my bag with all my things, including my car keys, was still in the kitchen.

Although I desperately wanted to sneak away, I couldn't. I went back to the big room to fetch my things, and then, after a moment of concentrating on my breathing, knocked at Clarissa's door.

The sight of me took the smile off her face. "What's wrong? Is it Mum?"

"Your mother's fine, she was sleeping when I left her. I'm afraid I've got to go – something's come up—" Unable to think of a convincing lie, I patted my shoulder bag as if indicating the presence of a mobile phone.

Clarissa's expression relaxed, but still she frowned. "Oh, dear. I hope it's not anything—"

"Oh, no, no."

"You're so pale."

I tried to laugh. "Really? Well, it's nothing terrible, just – kind of crossed wires, complicated to explain, but I have to be back there this afternoon. So – if you'll apologize to your mother?"

"Sure. You'll come again?"

"Oh, of course." I turned away from her as I spoke. "I'll phone in the next few days to arrange a time . . ." I felt like crying. I had liked her so much, and now I wondered if her seeming friendliness was part of some Byzantine plot, if she'd somehow been helping her mother to gather information about me, if they were stalkers, or planning something . . . but what? And why?

I stopped at the Little Chef in Dumbarton, not because I was hungry, but because I'd had to realize I was in no fit state to drive. I needed to stop and think.

The café was soothingly anonymous, and, so late on a weekday morning, almost empty. I ordered the all-day breakfast and coffee – although I felt jittery enough already – and got out my pen and notebook to write down the list again.

It was a list I thought only I could have made. These weren't the only lovers I'd had in my life – in fact, two fiancés were missing – but they were, to me, the most significant. Yale hadn't even been my lover, except in fantasy, and I wasn't sure there was anyone now alive who knew how I'd felt about him. I'd never told *anyone* about my two-week fling with the man I'd called Chas – which wasn't even his real name! Only I had called him Chas, the personal nickname adding another layer of secrecy and fantasy to the forbidden passion.

I wondered, as I dug into my eggs and bacon, if I'd ever written down this list of names I knew so well. Perhaps, one lonely night, on a piece of paper, or in a notebook which had later gone missing . . .? That might explain *how* she knew it, although not why she would have been driven to copy it down on a blank page in one of her old notebooks. Was it possible that she'd become obsessed with me? That she, or her daughter, had been spying on me for some strange psychological reasons of their own, eventually manoeuvring me into the idea of the biography . . .

No, no, that just wasn't possible. There had been no outside influence – I had suggested Helen Ralston's name to Selwyn, not vice versa. Even if Alistair Reid and "My Death" could have been a plant, no one could have influenced, or predicted, the chain of thoughts which had led to my decision. If I'd had some other idea on the journey to Edinburgh, or if I'd decided to go shopping instead of look at pictures . . .

Another possibility, which I thought of as I pushed my varifocal specs up on my nose and frowned in a futile attempt to make out the headlines on a newspaper at the other side of the room, was that I hadn't seen what I thought I'd seen. It was not unheard of for me to misread a word or two even in the best conditions, and in the dim light of Helen's bedroom I might have read "Dale" as "Yale", "Ivo" as "Ira", and been fooled by that into imagining a list of perfectly ordinary male names was something uniquely personal to me.

I'd written too many stories about people with weird obsessions. It did not follow that just because Helen had read my stories, that she was obsessed with me.

IX

By the time I'd finished eating I'd convinced myself there was a wholly rational, non-threatening explanation for it all. Yet some fearful, pre-rational doubt must have remained, because although I wrote a note to Helen, apologizing for rushing off as I had done, and promising to be in touch again soon, I did not suggest a date for our next meeting, and I was in no hurry to arrange anything.

For the next two weeks I didn't write or think about writing. Instead, I cleaned house. I had a major clear-out, giving my own piles and stacks of stale belongings the same treatment I'd forced myself to apply to Allan's things a year earlier. I burned and recycled box-load after box-load of paper, made donations to the charity shops in Oban, and invited a Glasgow bookseller to come up and make me an offer. It wasn't easy, getting rid of so much stuff – I had to steel myself to it. But this was the obvious and necessary first step towards a major life-change. If I was going to be moving, I didn't want to be laden down with clutter, paying to shift box after box of stale memories, books, clothes and other stuff I had not used in years.

The rain had been short-lived; the weather that spring was magnificent. It was the warmest, driest March I could remember since I'd moved to Scotland, and I took a break from my chores indoors to work outside, sanding down and repainting the window-frames, and clearing and cutting back the normally wild and over-grown garden, getting everything ready for the change that I felt sure was coming, although I did nothing to make it happen.

And then it was April, with blue skies, fresh winds, and a warm and welcoming sun that seemed to say it was already summer. One morning the telephone rang, and it was Clarissa Breen.

A great wash of guilt made me hunch down in my chair, as if she could see me, and my cheeks began to burn. "I'm sorry I haven't been in touch, I was meaning to call," I said, and came to a sudden halt, unable to think of an excuse for my silence.

"That's okay. Mum was pleased to get your note. I did wonder . . . is everything all right?"

I couldn't remember what I had said, or hinted, about my reason for rushing out of the house. "Yes, yes, I'm fine. Everything's fine. I've just been busy, you know."

"That's good. Look, I don't want to bother you if you're busy—"

"No, no, I didn't mean – it's good to hear from you. I'm glad you called."

"I just wanted to let you know – there's no pressure, and I'll understand if you're busy – but we're going to be in your part of the world this weekend."

This news was so unexpected that I didn't know how to respond. "Do you need a place to stay?"

"Oh, no! That's not why – I didn't mean – only, if you'd like to meet for coffee, or a meal, some time. We'll be staying at the Crinan Hotel."

"That's great – of course I want to see you! You must come here for dinner one night. How long are you staying? Have you made a lot of plans?" All at once I was eager to see them again.

"Just for the weekend. Three nights. I really can't take any more time off right now, but Mum has been so desperate to get back up there lately, and with the weather being so fine, for once, and the forecast good – well, the time seemed right. I haven't made any plans yet; there's just one thing Mum really wants to do. I thought I'd ask at the hotel after we arrive. They might know someone who could take us out sailing one day."

"I'll take you out." I didn't even stop to think, although my heart was pounding so hard, I knew this was no light promise. I'd already guessed where Helen would want me to take her.

"Really? You have a boat?"

"Yes. And I'm fully qualified to sail her, so you don't have to worry. I haven't been out since . . . I haven't been out yet this year, and the forecast is good, as you say. It'll be fun."

In fact, I hadn't been out since Allan's death.

We arranged that I would meet them at their hotel at nine o'clock Saturday morning and go out for a sail. I would bring provisions for a picnic lunch.

After her call, I went straight out to the boatyard, to find out if *Daisy*, to whom I'd given no thought whatsoever in more than a year, was in any state to be taken out on the water in a mere two days' time.

Fortunately, the manager of the boatyard, Duncan MacInnes, was the best friend Allan and I had made during our years in Scotland, and without needing to be told, or intruding on my grief, he'd taken as good care of *Daisy* as if she'd been his own, doing everything Allan would have done, and a bit more.

With the arrival of spring and the approach of the Easter holidays even our quiet little boatyard was all bustle and go as everything was made ready for the start of the tourist season.

When I set eyes on *Daisy* she was back in the water after her long winter's sleep, barnacles scraped, rigging and sails repaired, the engine recently serviced, all neat and tidy and absolutely ship-shape, ready to go at a moment's notice.

I turned a look of wonder on Duncan. He stared at the boat, not at me, and rubbed his chin. "I thought, if you were interested, I could lease her out this season. There's always a demand for a sweet little boat like this one, and it can be a good way to make extra money."

"Thanks, but I think I'm going to want her for myself." I had thought about selling *Daisy* once after Allan's death, but she had been so intimately a part of our marriage that I had been unable to go through with it, even though keeping a boat, even one that you *do* use, is, as they say, a hole in the ocean for throwing money in.

Now he looked at me, still rubbing his chin. "Oh, aye, but we mostly do short leases anyway. One or two weeks at a time. You could book her for when you wanted her for yourself, and the rest of the time, you get paid. There's the upkeep, of course, but you could pay me a commission and I'd take care of that, and the expenses would all come out of the rental fees. I handle three other boats like that. All you have to do is say the word, and I'll add *Daisy* to the list."

As he spoke, I thought that perhaps he had mentioned this to me before, but I had been too deep in grief to take it in. I maybe hadn't understood, and he would have been too different to persist. Now I saw immediately how sensible it was, and how useful it would be to have another source of income. I told him so, and agreed to a meeting early the next week to agree the details and fill in the paperwork.

I went home and surprised myself by actually writing a book proposal. It was only three pages, and it hinted at more than it explained, but I thought it might pique an editor's interest. I sent it as an e-mail attachment to Selwyn without agonising further. The time for procrastinating and running away was over. I was going to write Helen Ralston's life.

X

Saturday morning was bright and dry, the sun warm and the winds westerly and not too stiff, a perfect day for a pleasant little sail down the coast. The sight of Helen and Clarissa waiting for me in the lobby when I entered the Crinan Hotel made my heart beat a little faster, partly with pleasure, and partly with fear.

Helen Ralston fascinated me; she also frightened me.

If my feelings for Clarissa were uncomplicated, the emotions Helen aroused were anything but.

This time, I didn't run away. It would have been easy enough to go forward, smiling and falsely apologetic, to claim there was something wrong with my boat and offer to take them out for a drive instead. Clarissa, I knew, would be on my side – I sensed she wasn't thrilled with the prospect of taking a ninety-six-year-old woman onto the ocean in a small boat – and Helen's anger, annoyance, disappoint-ment could all be weathered.

The whole sequence of events for a safe, dull, socially uncomfor-table day flashed through my mind in a split-second. I had only to say the word to make it happen, but I did not.

I decided instead to confront my fear and the mystery at the heart of Helen Elizabeth Ralston, and when she announced that we were going to pay a visit to the isle of Achlan, although my heart gave a queasy lurch, I still did not back down.

"Oh, yes, *Eilean nan Achlan*. The island of lamentation. I have your painting of it – it's in the boot of the car. I brought it to give back to you."

The old woman looked at me with her hooded, hawk's eyes, unreadable. "I don't want it. You keep it. It's yours now."

Clarissa was frowning. I thought she would ask what we were talking about – I was eager to explain, ready to get the painting out of its wrappings and show it to her – but she was following her own train of thought.

"Mum, we can't go there. It's an uninhabited island. There's nowhere to land. You told me yourself how you had to swim ashore – I hope you don't imagine we're going swimming today!"

"*You'll* get us ashore, won't you?" Helen put her cold, claw-like hand on my arm and gave me an appealing, almost flirtatious look with tilted head.

I spoke over Helen's head to her daughter. "There's a dinghy on board, a little inflatable. We can go ashore in that."

"There, you see?" Helen looked as triumphant as she had in that old photograph with Virginia Woolf. This was a woman who liked to have her way.

"I still think it sounds like too much trouble," Clarissa said, offering me another chance to back out. "It's up to you, of course."

I was as curious, and almost as eager, as Helen to visit Achlan.

"It's not far away, and it's somewhere I've always meant to go. We – Allan and I – always meant to go ashore and explore, but we never did. I think it was because it was so close, too close – once we were out in the boat we wanted more of a sail."

"Well, if you really don't mind," Clarissa sighed.

I looked at Helen. "I'd like to get a picture of you there, today. For my book."

"You mean *my* book, don't you?"

"That's what I said." I gave her a bland, mock-innocent smile, and she snorted delicately.

I could see she was happy. And why not? I felt happy, too. It was only Clarissa who looked a bit out of sorts.

"Do you sail?" I asked her.

She shook her head. "No, I'm sorry. Is that a problem?"

"No, of course not. I can sail *Daisy* single-handed." Despite my long absence from her, she seemed to welcome me, and the old skills came rushing back. It was all very easy and smooth, pulling away from the dock, and putting slowly out of the busy harbour until I was able to cut the noisy engine and felt my own spirit crackle and lift like the crisp white sails as we went gliding through the Sound of Jura.

There are treacherous waters there, whirlpools and rocks of legendary fame, but I knew my way and was going nowhere near the local Scylla and Charybdis. I knew I had only a short and easy sail ahead of me, never very far from shore. As I breathed in the fresh, salt air and eased *Daisy* along the familiar sea-lane, I imagined Allan close beside me, his hand resting lightly atop mine on the tiller. He had taught me to sail. I felt an unexpected ease in the thought. I still missed him badly, but the memory no longer crippled me with sorrow. I could take pleasure in the good memories, and there were many of them, so many aboard this little boat.

Helen murmured, "Allan would have loved this."

It was as if she'd spoken my own thought aloud. I whipped around to stare at her, deeply shocked, but she didn't even notice, staring out at the water.

I thought of the list in her journal, and I moistened dry lips to croak, "Who?"

She turned to give me one of her filmy, blue-eyed stares. "Your husband, dear."

"How did you . . . I didn't know you knew him."

"Oh, yes." She nodded. "I met him in London. This was years ago – before you were married to him. He worked for Collins at that time, I think. My agent introduced us at a party, I do remember that. I was very struck by him. A lovely young man, so kind, yet so witty. That combination is rare, you know. And he reminded me more than a little bit of – but never mind that."

This was plausible. Allan *had* worked for Collins in the 1970s, years before I had known him, and he'd been a stalwart of the publishing party scene. And it was not surprising that Helen Ralston should have been drawn to him, recalling the photograph of Clarissa's father.

"But – how did you know—"

"That he was a sailor? We talked about it, of course! He told me about his holidays with his family, when he was a child, and how he learned to sail in the very same place where I came on holiday with Logan."

What I'd meant was how had she known that the man she'd met once, thirty years ago, had been my husband, but I realized there was no point in asking her. She might have claimed that I'd told her, or maybe she'd read it on a book-jacket. Anyone might have told her; it wouldn't have taken much effort to find out.

Plausible though her story of meeting Allan was, I didn't believe it. Allan had a wonderful memory for the people he'd met over the years, and he knew how much I loved *In Troy*. If he had ever met its author, he would have told me.

I was sure that Helen was teasing, just as she had been with the story of "her" dream, and that I would find out why before too much longer.

Eilean nan Achlan came into view within a few minutes, but I waited until we were much closer before pointing it out. Clarissa shaded her eyes with a hand to look. Helen turned her head with no change of expression.

"Did you ever come back?" I asked her.

She shook her head. "Never. I didn't want to, until now."

I steered *Daisy* into the little bay at the south-westerly end of the island and after some finicky manoeuvring, hove to. I had judged it very well, I thought: the view from here was just about exactly what Helen Ralston had been looking at when she'd painted "My Death" more than seventy years before.

When I got a chance to rest after hauling in the sails and making everything tight, I looked at Helen to see how she was responding.

She was sitting very still, staring up at the gorse and bracken-covered hills. Feeling my gaze upon her, she turned to meet my eyes. "Thank you," she said quietly. Something about her look or her tone sent a shiver down my spine.

"You're welcome. Shall we go ashore?"

"Yes. Let's."

Clarissa fought one last-ditch effort, casting an uneasy eye on the little rubber dinghy. "You know, I really don't think that's such a good idea, Mum . . ."

"Then you can stay here."

"That's not what I meant."

"I know. You meant that I should sit down and shut up like a good little girl. I'm not your child, Clarissa."

"No, but you do act like one sometimes!"

"It's my right."

"Why won't you be sensible!"

The two women glared at each other, driven past endurance by the unfair role-reversal which ageing forces upon parents and children. I felt sympathy for them both, but gladly removed from it all. This was not a situation I would ever confront: I had two sisters, better qualified by geography and temperament to look after our parents (both still in good health) if the need arose, and I had no children. When I was as old and frail as Helen Ralston, assuming I made it that long, there would be no one left to care if I looked after myself properly or not. And unless I had the money to pay for it, there would certainly be no expedition for the elderly me like today's.

Although I thought Helen had every right to do what she wanted with what remained of her life – even if it hastened her death – I felt a terrible sad empathy for Clarissa. I thought we both had guessed the real reason for Helen's determination to visit the little death-island again, and I wondered how we would manage if the old woman simply refused to leave it.

Something like that must have been going through Clarissa's mind when she broke the stalemate with her mother and asked me, "Will I be able to get a signal on my mobile phone out here?"

I shrugged. "You can try. I've got a short-wave radio on board for emergencies."

The tension left her shoulders. "That's good to know. Shall we go?"

There were a few minor hair-raising moments still ahead, helping Helen into the dinghy, but we finally managed to make land-fall on Achlan, and I was the only one who got even slightly wet.

"Shall we have our picnic on that big flat rock over there?" asked Clarissa. "It looks like a nice spot."

"We can rest and eat at the shrine," said Helen. "I'm not stopping now." She turned to me. "You can take my picture there, nowhere else."

"Do you remember how to get there? Is it far?" I looked at the thin, blue-veined, old woman's ankles above the sensible sturdy shoes, and recalled Willy Logan's description of the long, slow, torturous descent over rough, rocky ground, leaning heavily on his lover and suffering many stumbles and painful encounters with brambles, nettles and rabbit holes which he was unable to avoid in his blindness.

"How far can it be?" Helen replied unhelpfully. "Anyway, we'll follow the water-course; that will take us to the source."

I followed the direction of her gaze and realized when I glimpsed the fresh water tumbling over rocks to spill into the bay that I had been hearing its roar, subtly different from the rumble of the waves, ever since we'd landed.

Following the stream might have been sensible, but it wasn't easy.

Even so early in spring there was a riot of vegetation to slow our progress, wicked blackberry vines which snatched at our clothing and scored our flesh, roots and unseen rocks and hollows to trip us up. Clarissa and I led fairly sedentary lives and were not as fit as we might have been, but we were still relatively supple and capable of putting on the occasional burst of speed.

Helen, so much older, had fewer reserves. It must have been many years since she had walked for more than ten minutes at a stretch, or over anything more taxing than a roughly-pebbled drive. Within minutes, her breathing was sounding tortured, and I knew she must be in pain, pushing herself to her limit. Yet, no matter what we said, she would not consider giving up or turning back. A little rest was all she needed, she said, and then we could go on. And so, every three or four minutes, she would give a gasp and stop walking, her shoulders rising up and down as, for a full minute, she marshalled her resources to continue.

Of course we stayed with her, standing in harsh sunlight or in buzzing, leafy shade, during her frequent rest-stops, and then continuing to creep up the gentle slope of the island, plodding along like weary tortoises.

I recalled Helen Ralston's comment as a young woman that in this island she had seen her death, and Willy Logan's conviction that "death" meant something else. But maybe he was wrong. Maybe death was just death, and Helen, now so near to the end of life, had finally come to meet it.

We crept along in silence except for the whine and tortured pant of Helen's breathing and the laughing bubbling rush of the stream, and the background sough of wind and sea. I kept my eyes fixed on the ground, mostly, on the look-out for hazards. The sounds, our unnaturally slow pace, my worries about what was going to happen all combined to affect my brain, and after awhile it seemed to me that the earth beneath my feet had become flesh, that I was treading upon a gigantic female body. This was bad enough, but there was something stranger to come, as it seemed I felt the footsteps upon my own, naked, supine body: that I was the land, and it was me. My body began to ache, but it seemed there was nothing to be done. I lost track of time, and my sense of myself as an individual became tenuous.

"Is that it?"

Clarissa's voice cut through the feverish dream or self-hypnosis, or whatever it was that had possessed me, and I raised my head with a gasp, like someone who had been swimming for too long underwater, and looked around.

The stream had become a little, bubbling rill between two rocks. Nearby I saw a large tumble of stones, partly overgrown by brambles and weeds. Impossible to say now what it might once have been – a tomb, a sheep-fank, or a tumble-down cottage – but clearly they had been piled up deliberately by someone sometime in the past.

"Look at me. Now."

It was Helen's voice, but so different that I thought maybe I'd heard it only in my head. Yet at the same time I knew that she was speaking to me. I looked around and met her eyes. What happened then I can't describe, can barely remember. I think I saw something that I shouldn't have seen. But maybe it was nothing to do with sight, was purely a brain event. I flail around for an explanation, or at least a metaphor. It was like a lightning bolt, fairy-stroke, the touch of the goddess, death itself, birth.

The next thing I knew, I was lying on the ground, naked beneath the high, cloudy sky. I heard water sounds, and the noise of someone weeping.

There was an awful, dull ache in my back. I opened my eyes and sat up slowly, painfully, wondering what had happened. I smelled sweat and blood and sex and crushed vegetation. I remembered looking at Helen, but if that had been seconds ago, or hours, or even longer, I had no idea. The other two women were gone. I was alone with a man – a naked man huddled a few feet away from me, beside the cairn he'd named a shrine, and weeping. I recognized him as Willy Logan.

Then I understood who I was.

I was Helen Ralston.

XI

Now, more than a year later, I am still Helen, as I will be, I suppose, until I die.

I avoid mirrors. It gives me a sickening, horrific jolt to see those alien, deep-set eyes glaring back at me out of another woman's face, even if the terror I feel is reflected in hers.

Of course I keep what I know to myself – I certainly have no desire to be locked up in an early twentieth century loony bin – and, as time goes by, it has become somewhat easier. Memories of my other life and of that other world which I suppose to be the future are growing dimmer, harder to recall and to believe. That's why I decided to write this, before it is forever too late. The words in this book, which I intend to keep safe, will ensure that what happened once doesn't have to go on happening into an infinity of futures – unless I want it to. I will show it to myself when the time is right, seventy-three years from now.

The feeling of dislocation, of alienation and fear, which I had at first, has eased with the passage of time. The strangeness has faded like my impossible, disturbing memories, and the sense of being embarked upon a great adventure – a new life! – has become more powerful. After all, this is not such a bad time or place to be young and alive.

—Helen Elizabeth Ralston
Paris
22 September 1930

That was all she wrote. Although there were two more pages left in the notebook, she'd left them blank, her testimony complete.

XII

The interview – my one and only interview with Helen – had not gone exactly as she described. For one thing, she'd been more disabled by her stroke than the story indicated, and the conversation between us had been painfully repetitive, slow and circular. She did mention a few famous names, people she had known in Paris and London in the 1930s, but her anecdotes had a way of petering out rather than coming to a point, and one story would frequently blend into another, so that an incident which took place in pre-war Paris would segue abruptly into something that had happened to her in post-war London. I felt sorry for her, and rather frustrated, as I realized that I was unlikely to get much first-hand information from her for my book.

After about an hour, Clarissa took her mother upstairs to bed. When she came back down, she gave me the notebook.

"Mum wants you to have this," she said. "She wants you to read it."

I took the old, hardbound notebook with a feeling of great privilege and excitement. "What is it? Did she say?"

"She said it has the deepest, most important truth about her life."

"Wow."

We smiled at each other – the charge of sympathetic, affectionate sympathy between us was very real – and she invited me to stay and have a bite to eat. We spent maybe an hour over coffee and cake, talking, getting to know each other. I left, then, and after a detour to do some shopping at Braehead, drove home.

I remember the details of my arrival home – putting away the groceries, looking through the mail, heating up a Marks and Spencer Indian meal and then eating it while listening to *Front Row* on Radio 4 – as if they were incidents from a lost Eden of innocence. Afterwards, I brewed a pot of herbal tea and took it upstairs to my office. There, at my desk, I pushed the keyboard aside, set Helen Ralston's book where it had been and pulled the reading light forward and angled it down to cast a strong cone of light directly onto the page. I began to read, and fell into the abyss.

It was after midnight when I finished reading, my neck and spine aching from the tense crouch I'd maintained for hours at my desk as I struggled to decipher her cramped, narrow writing. I was trembling with exhaustion, terror and bewilderment.

How was this possible? Could her story be true?

If it wasn't, how did she know so much about me? How was she able to write in my voice, including so many accurate details about my life, and everything that had happened starting with the chain of events which had caused me to decide to write a biography of Helen Ralston up to our first meeting?

I didn't sleep that night.

At eight o'clock the next morning, so blank, cold and numb that I could have said I was feeling nothing at all, I telephoned Clarissa Breen and asked to speak to Helen.

In a voice that wavered slightly, she told me her mother was dead.

"It happened not long after you left. Or maybe . . . maybe before." She took a deep breath. "She was sleeping when I left her to come downstairs to you. Normally, she'll sleep for about two hours. At lunchtime, I went upstairs to check on her. As soon as I went into her bedroom I knew. She was gone."

All my questions seemed suddenly insignificant, and the terror which had gripped me loosed its hold. I rushed to sympathize, uttering all the usual, insufficient phrases of sorrow and respect.

"Thank you. I was going to call you, later today. I wanted to thank you – for coming when you did, and making Mum's last day so special. She was happy, you know, really thrilled to be meeting you. Not just because of the biography – of course it was great for her to know she hadn't been forgotten – but because it was *you*. She loved your work, you know. She'd been reading your stories since you were first published – she always felt there was a special connection between you."

I shivered convulsively and gripped the phone hard. "Did she *say* that?"

"Oh – it was obvious how she felt. Didn't I tell you, that's why I read that book of yours, because you were obviously so important to her. Anyway, I wanted you to know how much your coming meant to her. It was the first time I'd seen her happy and excited in – well, the last seven months were very hard for her. Since the stroke, and having to leave London, no longer able to live on her own. I – I really thought this was going to be the start of a new phase for her, I can't quite – I'm sorry . . ." she stumbled, then recovered herself. "I can't quite believe she's gone. But it was the best way, to go like that, suddenly and all at once, it's what she wanted – she hated the idea of another, even more crippling, stroke – so did I – of dwindling away in a hospital bed, dying by inches."

We talked for a few more minutes. Clarissa had a lot to do, and promised she'd let me know about the funeral.

I went to Glasgow for it the following week, and took the notebook and the painting to give back. I found my chance after the cremation when we few mourners – most of them Clarissa's own friends and extended family – gathered in her house to eat the traditional cold food. I took the notebook out of my bag, but she shook her head and told me it was mine.

"Mum wanted you to have it. No, I mean it; she couldn't have been more clear about her wishes; she left instructions in her will. In fact, not just the notebook, but a painting as well. It's called 'My Death', she said it's a watercolour, but I've never seen it – I'm sure Mum didn't keep any of her early works, she never mentioned it before, and in the will she didn't explain where it was or anything."

I launched into a rushed, stumbling explanation of how I'd come into possession of "My Death" until she stopped me with a hand on my shoulder. "That's all right. That's fine. I'm glad you've got it. It was what she wanted."

"I've got it in the car – I was going to give it back to you—"

"No, you must keep it."

"Well – would you like to see it? Just before I go. It's in the car."

She nodded slowly. "Yes. Yes I would. Thank you. I know Mum was an artist before she was a writer, but I've never seen anything she painted."

We left the house and walked down to the street where my car was parked. My heart began to pound unpleasantly as I took the wrapped parcel out of the boot, and I wondered if I should try to warn her, to prepare her in some way. But the words would not come, and so I unwrapped it in silence and laid it down, face up, inside the open boot of the car and we looked down upon "My Death" in silence.

A watercolour landscape in tones of blue and brown and grey and green and pink, a rocky island in the sea. Tears blurred my vision and I looked away in time to see Clarissa dash her hand across her eyes and give a soft, shuddering sigh.

She turned away, and I put my arms around her.

"Thank you," she murmured, returning my hug.

I kissed her cheek. "Let's stay in touch."

NEIL GAIMAN

The Problem of Susan

ALONGSIDE HIS ADULT FICTION and comics work, Neil Gaiman has also produced a number of books aimed at the young adult market. His short horror novel *Coraline* won the Hugo Award, the Nebula Award and the Bram Stoker Award and is being filmed by Henry Selick, while *The Day I Swapped My Dad for Two Goldfish* and *The Wolves in the Walls* are two graphic children's books produced with artist Dave McKean.

More recently, Gaiman has scripted McKean's debut feature film *MirrorMask* for the Jim Henson Company/Columbia TriStar. It is accompanied by a large-size tie-in book featuring art, observations and the complete script; a 12,000-word "graphic novella", and *The Alchemy of MirrorMask*, which focuses on McKean's artwork.

"When I was a boy I loved the 'Narnia' stories," Gaiman recalls. "As a parent, I've read them aloud twice, ten years apart, and I found more to like; but also found some things I disliked and one, the treatment of Susan, that I found extremely problematical.

"Over the last few years I've accumulated a second career as a children's author, and have been fascinated by the shapes and effects of children's literature – the differences in the way children's books affect adults and children; the part they play in our lives.

"I wanted to write a story that would talk about that. Since it's been published, 'The Problem of Susan' has been, I think, the most contentious short story I've ever written: people have spent a great deal of time online discussing it, arguing about it, refuting it and so on. I read a review of it recently by someone who said that they might have enjoyed it, but found it impossible to get past the blasphemy."

S HE HAS THE DREAM *again that night.*
   In the dream, she is standing, with her brothers and her sister, on the edge of the battlefield. It is summer, and the grass is a peculiarly vivid shade of green: a wholesome green, like a cricket pitch or the welcoming slope of the South Downs as you make your way north from the coast. There are bodies on the grass. None of the bodies are human; she can see a centaur, its throat slit, on the grass near her. The horse-half of it is a vivid chestnut. Its human skin is nut-brown from the sun. She finds herself staring at the horse's penis, wondering about centaurs mating, imagines being kissed by that bearded face. Her eyes flick to the cut-throat, and the sticky red-black pool that surrounds it, and she shivers.

   Flies buzz about the corpses.

   The wildflowers tangle in the grass. They bloomed yesterday for the first time in, how long? A hundred years? A thousand? A hundred thousand? She does not know.

   All this was snow, she thinks, as she looks at the battlefield.

   Yesterday, all this was snow. Always winter, and never Christmas.

   Her sister tugs her hand, and points. On the brow of the green hill they stand, deep in conversation. The lion is golden, his hands folded behind his back. The witch is dressed all in white. Right now she is shouting at the lion, who is simply listening. The children cannot make out any of their words, not her cold anger, nor the lion's thrum-deep replies. The witch's hair is black and shiny, her lips are red.

   In her dream she notices these things.

   They will finish their conversation soon, the lion and the witch . . .

There are things about herself that the professor despises. Her smell, for example. She smells like her grandmother smelled, like old women smell, and for this she cannot forgive herself, so on waking she bathes in scented water, and, naked and towel-dried, dabs several drops of Chanel toilet water beneath her arms, and on her neck. It is, she believes, her sole extravagance.

Today she dresses in her dark brown dress suit. She thinks of these as her interview clothes, as opposed to her lecture clothes or her knocking-about-the-house-clothes. Now she is in retirement, she wears her knocking-about-the-house-clothes more and more. She puts on lipstick.

After breakfast, she washes a milk bottle, places it at her back door. She discovers that next-door's cat has deposited a mouse-head, and a paw, on the doormat. It looks as though the mouse is swimming through the coconut matting, as though most of it is submerged. She purses her lips, then she folds her copy of yesterday's *Daily Telegraph*, and she folds and flips the mouse-head and the paw into the newspaper, never touching them with her hands.

Today's *Daily Telegraph* is waiting for her in the hall, along with several letters, which she inspects, without opening any of them, then places them on the desk in her tiny study. Since her retirement she visits her study only to write. Now she walks into the kitchen, and seats herself at the old oak table. Her reading glasses hang about her neck, on a silver chain, and she perches them on her nose, and begins with the obituaries.

She does not actually expect to encounter anyone she knows there, but the world is small, and she observes that, perhaps with cruel humour, the obituarists have run a photograph of Peter Burrell-Gunn as he was in the early 1950s, and not at all as he was the last time the professor had seen him, at a *Literary Monthly* Christmas party several years before, all gouty and beaky and trembling, and reminding her of nothing so much as a caricature of an owl. In the photograph, he is very beautiful. He looks wild, and noble.

She had spent an evening once, kissing him, in a summer-house: she remembers that very clearly, although she cannot remember for the life of her in which garden the summer house had belonged.

It was, she decides, Charles and Nadia Reid's house in the country. Which meant that it was before Nadia ran away with that Scottish artist, and Charles took the professor with him to Spain, although she was certainly not a professor then. This was many years before people commonly went to Spain for their holidays; it was an exotic and dangerous place in those days. He asked her to marry him, too, and she is no longer certain why she said no, or even if she had entirely said no. He was a pleasant-enough young man, and he took what was left of her virginity on a blanket on a Spanish beach, on a warm spring night. She was twenty years old, and had thought herself so old . . .

The doorbell chimes, and she puts down the paper, and makes her way to the front door, and opens it.

Her first thought is how young the girl looks.

Her first thought is how old the woman looks. "Professor Hastings?" she says. "I'm Greta Campion. I'm doing the profile on you. For the *Literary Chronicle*."

The older woman stares at her for a moment, vulnerable, and ancient, then she smiles. It's a friendly smile, and Greta warms to her. "Come in, dear," says the professor. "We'll be in the sitting room."

"I brought you this," says Greta. "I baked it myself." She takes the cake-tin from her bag, hoping its contents hadn't disintegrated *en route*. "It's a chocolate cake. I read online that you liked them."

The old woman nods, and blinks. "I do," she says. "How kind. This way."

Greta follows her into a comfortable room, is shown to her armchair, and told, firmly, not to move. The professor bustles off, and returns with a tray, on which are tea cups and saucers, a teapot, a plate of chocolate biscuits, and Greta's chocolate cake.

Tea is poured, and Greta exclaims over the professor's brooch, and then she pulls out her notebook and pen, and a copy of the professor's last book, *A Quest for Meanings in Children's Fiction*, the copy bristling with post-it-notes and scraps of paper. They talk about the early chapters, in which the hypothesis is set forth that there was originally no distinct branch of fiction that was only intended for children, until the Victorian notions of the purity and sanctity of childhood demanded that fiction for children be made . . .

". . . well, pure," says the professor

"And sanctified?" asks Greta, with a smile.

"And sanctimonious," corrects the old woman. "It is difficult to read *The Water Babies* without wincing."

And then she talks about ways that artists used to draw children – as adults, only smaller, without considering the child's proportions – and how Grimms' stories were collected for adults and, when the Grimms realized the books were being read in the nursery, were Bowdlerised to make them more appropriate. She talks of Perrault's "Sleeping Beauty in the Wood", and of its original coda in which the Prince's cannibal ogre mother attempts to frame the Sleeping Beauty for having eaten her own children, and all the while Greta nods and takes notes, and nervously tries to contribute enough to the conversation that the professor will feel that it is a conversation or at least an interview, not a lecture.

"Where," asks Greta, "do you feel your interest in children's fiction came from?"

The professor shakes her head. "Where do any of our interests come from? Where does *your* interest in children's books come from?"

Greta says, "They always seemed the books that were most important to me. The ones that mattered. When I was a kid, and when I grew. I was like Dahl's *Matilda*. Were your family great readers?"

"Not really . . . I say that, it was a long time ago that they died. Were killed. I should say."

"All your family died at the same time? Was this in the War?"

"No, dear. We were evacuees, in the War. This was in a train crash, several years after. I was not there."

"Just like in Lewis's *Narnia* Books," says Greta, and immediately feels like a fool, and an insensitive fool, "I'm sorry. That was a terrible thing to say, wasn't it?"

"Was it, dear?"

Greta can feel herself blushing, and she says, "It's just I remember that sequence so vividly. In *The Last Battle*. Where you learn there was a train crash on the way back to school, and everyone was killed. Except for Susan, of course."

The professor says, "More tea, dear?" and Greta knows that she should leave the subject, but she says, "You know, that used to make me so angry."

"What did, dear?"

"Susan. All the other kids go off to Paradise, and Susan can't go. She's no longer a friend of Narnia because she's too fond of lipsticks and nylons and invitations to parties. I even talked to my English teacher about it, about the problem of Susan, when I was twelve."

She'll leave the subject now, talk about the role of children's fiction in creating the belief systems we adopt as adults, but the professor says "And tell me, dear, what did your teacher say?"

"She said that even though Susan had refused paradise then, she still had time while she lived to repent."

"Repent *what*?"

"Not believing, I suppose. And the sin of Eve."

The professor cuts herself a slice of chocolate cake. She seems to be remembering. And then she says, "I doubt there was much opportunity for nylons and lipsticks after her family was killed. There certainly wasn't for me. A little money – less than one might imagine – from her parents' estate, to lodge and feed her. No luxuries . . ."

"There must have been something else wrong with Susan," says the young journalist, "something they didn't tell us. Otherwise she wouldn't have been damned like that – denied the Heaven of further up and further in. I mean, all the people she had ever cared for had gone on to their reward, in a world of magic and waterfalls and joy. And she was left behind."

"I don't know about the girl in the books," says the professor, "but remaining behind would also have meant that she was available to identify her brothers' and her little sister's bodies. There were a lot of people dead in that crash. I was taken to a nearby school – it was the first day of term, and they had taken the bodies there. My older brother looked okay. Like he was asleep. The other two were a bit messier."

"I suppose Susan would have seen their bodies, and thought, they're on holidays now. The perfect school holidays. Romping in meadows with talking animals, world without end."

"She might have done. I only remember thinking what a great deal of damage a train can do, when it hits another train, to the people who were travelling inside. I suppose you've never had to identify a body, dear?"

"No."

"That's a blessing. I remember looking at them and thinking, *what if I'm wrong, what if it's not him after all?* My younger brother was decapitated, you know. A god who would punish me for liking nylons and parties by making me walk through that school dining room, with the flies, to identify Ed, well . . . he's enjoying himself a bit too much, isn't he? Like a cat, getting the last ounce of enjoyment out of a mouse. Or a gram of enjoyment, I suppose it must be these days. I don't know, really."

She trails off. And then, after some time, she says, "I'm sorry dear. I don't think I can do any more of this today. Perhaps if your editor gives me a ring, we can set a time to finish our conversation."

Greta nods and says of course, and knows in her heart, with a peculiar finality, that they will talk no more.

That night, the professor climbs the stairs of her house, slowly, painstakingly, floor by floor. She takes sheets and blankets from the airing cupboard, and makes up a bed in the spare bedroom, in the back. It is empty but for a wartime austerity dressing table, with a mirror and drawers, an oak bed, and a dusty applewood wardrobe, which contains only coat-hangers and a dusty cardboard box. She places a vase on the dressing table, containing purple rhododendron flowers, sticky and vulgar.

She takes from the box in the wardrobe a plastic shopping bag containing four old photographic albums. Then she climbs into the bed that was hers as a child, and lies there between the sheets, looking at the black and white photographs, and the sepia photographs, and the handful of unconvincing colour photographs. She looks at her brothers, and her sister, and her parents, and she wonders how they could have been that young, how anybody could have been that young.

After a while she notices that there are several children's books beside the bed, which puzzles her slightly, because she does not believe she keeps books on the bedside table in that room. Nor, she decides, does she have a bedside table there. On the top of the pile is an old paperback book – it must be over forty years old: the price on the cover is in shillings. It shows a lion, and two girls twining a daisy chain into its mane.

The professor's lips prickle with shock. And only then does she understand that she is dreaming, for she does not permit those books into her house. Beneath the paperback is a hardback, in its jacket, of a book that, in her dream, she realizes she has always wanted to read: *Mary Poppins Brings in the Dawn*, a book which P.L. Travers had somehow neglected to write while alive.

She picks it up, and opens it to the middle, and reads the story waiting for her: Jane and Michael follow Mary Poppins on her day off, to Heaven, and they meet the boy Jesus, who is still slightly scared of Mary Poppins because she was once his nanny, and the Holy Ghost, who complains that he has not been able to get his sheet properly white since Mary Poppins left, and God the Father, who says,

"There's no making her do anything. Not her. *She's* Mary Poppins."

"But you're God," said Jane. "You created everybody and everything. They have to do what you say."

"Not her," said God the Father once again, and he scratched his golden beard flecked with silver. "I didn't create *her*. *She's* Mary Poppins."

And the professor stirs in her sleep, and afterward dreams that she is reading her own obituary. It has been a good life, she thinks, as she reads it, discovering her history laid out in black and white. Everyone is there. Even the people she had forgotten.

Greta sleeps beside her boyfriend, in a small flat in Camden, and she, too, is dreaming.

In Greta's dream, the lion and the witch come down the hill together.

She is standing on the battlefield, holding her sister's hand. She looks up at the golden lion, and the burning amber of his eyes. "He's not a tame lion, is he?" she whispers to her sister, and they shiver.

The witch looks at them all, then she turns to the lion, and says, coldly, "I am satisfied with the terms of our agreement. You take the girls: for myself, I shall have the boys."

The girl understands what must have happened, and she tries to run, but the beast is upon her before she has covered a dozen paces.

The lion eats all of her except her head, in her dream. He leaves the head, and one of her hands, just as a housecat leaves the parts of a mouse it has no desire for, for later, or as a gift.

She wishes that he had eaten her head, for then she would not have had to look. Dead eyelids cannot be closed, and so she stares, unflinching, at the twisted thing her brothers have become. The great beast eats her little sister more slowly, and, it seems to her, with more relish and pleasure than it had eaten her; but then, her little sister had always been its favourite.

Presently the witch removes her white robes, revealing a body no less white, with high, small breasts, and nipples so dark they are almost black. The witch lies back upon the grass, spreads her legs. Beneath her body, the grass becomes rimed with frost.

"Now," she says.

The lion licks her white cleft with its pink tongue, until she can take no more of it, and she pulls its huge mouth to hers, and wraps her icy legs into its golden fur . . .

Being dead, the eyes in the head on the grass cannot look away. Being dead, they miss nothing.

And when the two of them are done, sweaty and sticky and sated, only then does the lion amble over to the head on the grass and devour it in its huge mouth, crunching her skull in its powerful jaws, and it is then, only then, that she wakes.

Her heart is pounding. She tries to wake her boyfriend, but he snores, and grunts, and will not be roused.

It's true, Greta thinks, irrationally, in the darkness. *She grew up. She carried on. She didn't die.*

She imagines the professor, waking in the night, and listening to the noises coming from the old apple-wood wardrobe in the corner: to the rustlings of all these gliding ghosts, which might be mistaken for the scurries of mice or rats, to the padding of enormous velvet paws, and the distant, dangerous music of a hunting horn.

She knows she is being ridiculous, although she will not be surprised when she reads of the professor's demise. *Death comes in the night*, she thinks, before she returns to sleep. *Like a lion.*

The white witch rides naked on the lion's golden back. Its muzzle is spotted with fresh, scarlet blood. Then the vast pinkness of its tongue wipes around its face, and once more it is perfectly clean.

STEPHEN JONES & KIM NEWMAN

Necrology: 2004

AS ALWAYS, we continue to note the passing of writers, artists, performers and technicians who, during their lifetimes, made significant contributions to the horror, science fiction and fantasy genres, or left their mark on popular culture and music in other, often fascinating, ways . . .

AUTHORS/ARTISTS/COMPOSERS

One of Britain's most distinguished authors of adult and children's fantasy and ghost stories, **Joan** [Delano] **Aiken** OBE died on January 4th, aged 79. Best known for her "Dido Twite" or "Wolves Chronicles" alternative history series for young adults, which began in 1962 with the novel *The Wolves of Willoughby Chase* (filmed in 1988), she was the daughter of American poet and writer Conrad Aiken. The author of more than ninety volumes, including *Midnight is a Place*, *A Bundle of Nerves*, *A Whisper in the Night*, *A Goose on Your Grave*, *Give Yourself a Fright*, *The Haunting of Lamb House*, *A Fit of Shivers*, *A Creepy Company*, *The Cockatrice Boys* and *The Scream*, she was co-Guest of Honour at the 1997 World Fantasy Convention in London. *The Whispering Mountain* won the *Guardian* Children's Book Prize in 1969, and she also won an Edgar Award in 1972 for the YA mystery *Night Fall*. Her final book, *The Witch of Clattering Shaws*, appeared in 2005.

British-born poet and SF author **Norman Talbot** died of a heart attack in Australia on January 8th, aged 67. A co-founder of independent press Nimrod Productions, his books include *The Book* *of Changes* and *Every Sonnet Tells a Story*, and he had a story in the 1998 anthology *Dreaming Down Under*.

Forty-year-old horror and suspense writer **William Laughlin** died of bone cancer on his birthday, January 13th. He also worked for independent comics and was the writer/creator of *Macabrella*, a horror anthology in the EC tradition.

American author and teacher **Jack Cady**, best known for his collections of supernatural stories, died of bladder cancer on January 14th, aged 71. Cady worked as a tree high-climber, an auctioneer, a long truck driver, and in the Coast Guard before becoming a writer. His books include *The Burning and Other Stories*, *The Well*, *The Jonah Watch*, *McDowall's Ghost*, *The Sons of Noah & Other Stories*, *The Off Season*, *The Night We Buried the Road Dog*, *The Hauntings of Hood Canal* and *Ghosts of Yesterday*. Horror novels *Dark Dreaming* and *Embrace of the Wolf* were published under pseudonym "Pat Franklin". Cady's fiction won the *Atlantic Monthly* "First" Award, the Nebula, a Philip K. Dick Award special citation, the World Fantasy Award, the Bram Stoker Award and the University of Iowa prize for short fiction, amongst other awards.

Horror and mystery author and scriptwriter **William Relling, Jr.** committed suicide in Pasadena, California, on January 22nd, aged 49. His novels include *Brujo*, *New Moon*, *Silent Moon*, *Sweet Poison*, *Deadly Vintage* and *The Criminalist*, and his short fiction has been collected in *The Infinite Man* and *Along the Midway of the Carnival of Souls and Other Stories*.

Welsh-language author **Islwyn Ffowc Elis**, whose books include the 1968 SF novel *Y Blaned Dirion* (*The Fair Planet*), died the same day, aged 79.

American arranger and composer **Billy May** also died on January 22nd, aged 87. Best known for his work with Frank Sinatra, he composed the theme for *The Green Hornet* TV series.

Indian-born British historical novelist and children's writer **M. (Mary) M. (Margaret) Kaye** (aka "Mollie Kaye"/"Mollie Hamilton"), best known for her 1978 novel *The Far Pavilions*, died on January 29th, aged 95. She wrote at least one children's fantasy, *The Ordinary Princess* (1980).

Walt Disney artist **John Hench**, the official portraitist for Mickey Mouse, died of heart failure on February 5th, aged 95. He began his career at Disney in 1939 as a sketch artist on *Fantasia*, and went on to work on *Dumbo*, *The Adventures of Ichabod and Mr Toad*, *Peter Pan*, *Alice in Wonderland*, *Cinderella*, the unfinished Salvador Dali collaboration *Destino*, and was the lead special effects artist for the Academy Award-winning *20,000 Leagues Under the Sea* (1954). As one of Walt Disney Imagineering's chief designers, he played a key role in the creation all the theme parks and was working on designs for the latest, Hong Kong Disneyland, at the time of his death.

American academic and SF author **Donald Barr**, best known for his 1973 space opera *Space Relations: A Slightly Gothic Interstellar Tale*, died the same day, aged 82.

British cartoonist **Norman Thelwell**, best known for his fat little girls riding plump ponies in *Punch* magazine, died in his sleep on February 7th, aged 80. He had been suffering from Alzheimer's disease. His will included an unusual clause precluding his son's ex-wife benefiting from it in any way.

Multiple award-winning American comics editor and literary agent **Julius Schwartz** died of complications from pneumonia on February 8th, aged 88. He had been hospitalized for several weeks following injuries sustained in a fall. In 1932, with Mort Weisinger and Forrest J Ackerman, he launched *The Time Traveler*, credited as being the first SF fanzine to achieve a wide circulation. Two years later, again with Weisinger, he co-founded the first literary agency to specialize in science fiction, Solar Sales Service. His clients included Ray Bradbury, H.P. Lovecraft, Edmond Hamilton, Stanley G. Weinbaum, C.L. Moore, David H. Keller, Leigh Brackett, Henry Kuttner, Manly Wade Wellman and Robert Bloch. As an editor for DC Comics during the late 1950s and '60s, he was responsible for the "Silver Age" of comics by creating Adam Strange and The Metal Men, as well as reinventing such superheroes as The Flash, Green Lantern, Hawkman, The Atom and The Justice League of America. He is also credited with restoring the flagging fortunes of Batman in the mid-1960s, before going on to edit the Superman family and Captain Marvel in the 1970s. After his retirement in 1987, he continued to consult for DC. In his 2000 autobiography, *Man of Two Worlds: My Life in Science Fiction and Comics*, co-authored by Brian M. Thomsen, Schwartz wrote his own epitaph: "Here Lies Julius Schwartz. He met his last deadline."

Scriptwriter **Robert Thompson** died of complications from pneumonia on February 11th, aged 79. His credits include *Ratboy*, *Brave New World*, *The Hound of the Baskervilles* (1972) and episodes of *The Man from U.N.C.L.E.*

Novelist and biographer **Martin Booth** died on February 12th, aged 59. His books include two children's novels in the proposed "The Alchemist's Son" trilogy, *Doctor Illuminatus* and *Soul Stealer*, plus the biographies *The Doctor, The Detective and Arthur Conan Doyle* and *A Magick Life: A Biography of Aleister Crowley*.

Conductor and composer **Samuel "Sandy" Matlovsky**, whose credits include TV's *Star Trek* and the movie version of Ray Bradbury's *The Illustrated Man*, died on February 17th, aged 82.

Hugo-nominated artist **Mel [Joseph] Hunter**, best known for his "robot" covers on *The Magazine of Fantasy & Science Fiction*, died of multiple myeloma cancer on February 20th, aged 76. He also contributed to *Galaxy, If, Life* and *National Geographic*.

Composer **Bart Howard**, whose best-known song is the 1960 hit "Fly Me to the Moon" (written in 1954 as "In Other Words"), died of complications from a stroke on February 21st, aged 88. He also wrote songs for performers such as Peggy Lee, Eartha Kitt and Johnny Mathis.

Specialist bookseller, bibliographer and publisher **Bradford M. (Marshall) Day** died on February 25th, aged 87. Under his own imprint, Science Fiction and Fantasy Publications, he began publishing bibliographies of Talbot Mundy, Edgar Rice Burroughs, Sax Rohmer, H. Rider Haggard and others from 1951 onwards. He also edited the anthologies *Past & Future and the Last Generation, Olden Tales, Old by Old* and *Ghost Stories from Where and When*.

Science Fiction bibliographer **Keith L. (Leroy) Justice** and his wife **Hilda Virginia Savell Justice**, both aged 54, were killed instantly when their car was hit from behind by a pick-up truck in Mississippi on February 27th. A major collector of Robert Silverberg material, in the 1980s Justice compiled *Science Fiction Master Index of Names* and *Science Fiction, Fantasy & Horror Reference: An Annotated Bibliography of Works About Literature & Film*.

Playwright **Jerome Lawrence** died on February 28th, aged 88. Among his credits is *Shangri-La*, a flop Broadway musical version of *Lost Horizon* which was produced on TV in 1960 starring Richard Basehart and Claude Rains.

British clinical psychologist and SF author **Peter T. Garratt** died from a probable heart attack on March 2nd, aged 54. His nearly forty published short stories appeared in a number of markets, including *Interzone, Asimov's Science Fiction* and anthologies edited by Mike Ashley and Maxim Jakubowski.

Film and TV writer **Drake Sather** committed suicide on March 3rd, aged 44. Best known for co-scripting *Zoolander* with star Ben Stiller, the *Saturday Night Live* writer and stand-up comedian was working on a comedy remake of the TV series *Mr Ed*, on which he was also executive producer, when he shot himself in his Los Angeles loft.

Composer **Arthur Kempel** died of stomach cancer the same day, aged 58. His credits include such films as *Double Impact* and *The Arrival*, and episodes of the TV series *Twilight Zone*, *Tiny Toon Adventures* and *Ripley's Believe It or Not*.

Author, lyricist, teacher and critic **Joel E. Siegel** died of spinal meningitis on March 11th, aged 63. His study *Val Lewton: The Reality of Terror* was published in 1973.

American fanzine publisher **Jon White**, whose 1962 incarnation of the fanzine *Inside* continued as Leland Sapiro's *Riverside Quarterly*, died of a cerebral haemorrhage after a long illness on March 12th, aged 57.

American animation and computer games writer **Katherine Lawrence** (aka "Kathy Selbert") apparently committed suicide in Arizona on March 25th, aged 49. Her body was found two days later by a group of hikers. Lawrence's TV credits include such shows as *Dungeons and Dragons*, *Conan the Adventurer*, *X-Men Evolution*, *ReBoot*, *Mighty Max*, *Beetle Juice*, *Stargate Infinity* and *Jim Henson's Muppet Babies*. She also worked on the video games *Stratosphere* and *Mario is Missing*, and co-scripted the animated movie *Secret of Mulan*.

Oscar and Emmy-winning film and TV composer **Fred Karlin** died of cancer on March 26th, aged 67. His credits include *The Stalking Moon*, *Westworld*, *Chosen Survivors*, *Futureworld* and TV's *Kiss Meets the Phantom of the Park*, *Vampire* and *Man from Atlantis*.

Algerian-born French author **Robert Merle** died of a heart attack on March 27th, aged 95. His books include *Un animal doué de raison* (aka *The Day of the Dolphin*) and the John W. Campbell Memorial Award-winning *Malevil*, both filmed. He was awarded the Prix Goncourt in 1949.

Fifty-year-old Sherlock Holmes scholar and collector **Richard Lancelyn Green** was found dead in his bed the same day. He had been garrotted with a shoelace tightened by a wooden spoon. Although the coroner said that suicide was most likely, there was no note and he was unable to rule out murder and the death was left open. He added that garrotting was a painful and very unusual method of suicide. Green had earlier expressed fears for his safety after claiming that a batch of long-lost personal papers belonging to Sir Arthur Conan Doyle – sold at Christie's in London on May 19th for almost £950,000 – was part of an estate willed to the British Library by the author's daughter, Dame Jean.

British actor, director, composer, novelist, playwright and broadcaster **Hubert** [Robert Harry] **Gregg** died on March 29th, aged 89.

Of his more than 200 songs, the best known is "Maybe It's Because I'm a Londoner", made famous by Bud Flanagan in 1947. From 1953–60 he directed Agatha Christie's stage play *The Mousetrap*, which has been running in London's West End since 1952.

American author **Roger Dee** (Roger D. Aycock) died on April 5th, aged 89. His stories appeared in SF magazines from the late 1940s until the early '70s, including *Planet Stories*, *Super Science Stories*, *Amazing*, *Analog*, *Astounding*, *Galaxy*, *If* and *The Magazine of Fantasy and Science Fiction*. His short novel *An Earth Gone Mad* was published as half an Ace double in 1954.

Jerry Burge, who was art director for the magazine *Witchcraft & Sorcery* (1971–74), died of congestive heart failure on April 6th. With fellow fan Carson Jacks, Burge published the first hardcover history of SF fandom, *The Immortal Storm* (1954) by Sam Moskowitz, through ASFO Press.

L. Ron Hubbard collector and publisher **Virgil Wilhite** died following a brief illness on April 11th, aged 62. During the late 1970s and early '80s, Wilhite's Theta Books published Hubbard's *Buckskin Brigades*, the short story collection *Lives You Wished to Lead But Never Dared* and the non-fiction collection *The Way to Happiness*.

Author and Los Angeles newspaper reporter **Will Fowler**, reportedly the first journalist on the scene of the infamous 1947 "Black Dahlia" murder, died of cancer on April 13th, aged 81.

Veteran Disney animator **Harry Holt** died on April 14th, aged 93. He helped design *Snow White and the Seven Dwarfs* and *Lady and the Tramp* before joining Hanna-Barbera Studios, where he worked on *The Flintstones* and *Tom and Jerry*. He later became chief designer of Walt Disney World in Orlando, Florida.

Manga comics artist **Mitsutera Yokoyama** died in a fire on April 15th, aged 69. Many of his works were animated, including *Tetsujin 28*, *Giant Robo*, *Gigantor*, *Sally the Witch* and *Red Shadow*.

American composer **John Seely** died on April 23rd, aged 88. He worked on TV's *Looney Tunes* and also *The Hideous Sun Demon*.

American author **Hubert Selby, Jr.** died of lung disease on April 26th, aged 75. Best known for his books *Last Exit to Brooklyn* (the subject of an obscenity trial in Britain in 1966 and filmed in 1989), *The Room* and *The Demon*, Selby scripted the 2004 horror film *Fear X*.

American screenwriter **Nelson Gidding** died on May 2nd, aged 84. He worked with director Robert Wise on such films as *The Haunting* and *The Andromeda Strain*. His other credits include *Skullduggery*,

Beyond the Poseidon Adventure, *The Mummy Lives* and episodes of such TV series as *Suspense* and *The Inner Sanctum*.

Australian-born poet, short story writer and editor **Robyn** [Meta] **Herrington** died in Canada after a long battle against cancer on May 3rd, aged 43. She was an acquisitions editor for *Edge Science Fiction and Fantasy* and her stories appeared in a number of magazines and DAW anthologies.

American horror writer **Brian McNaughton** (aka "Mark Bloodstone") died on May 13th, aged 68. The author of more than 200 short stories, his third collection *The Throne of Bones* won the World Fantasy Award and the International Horror Guild Award in 1998. McNaughton's other books include *Satan's Love Child* (aka *Gemini Rising*), *Satan's Mistress* (aka *Downward to Darkness*), *Satan's Seductress* (aka *Worse Things Waiting*) and *Satan's Surrogate* (aka *The House Across the Way*), along with the earlier collections *Nasty Stories* and *More Nasty Stories*.

American comics writer and artist **Gill Fox** died on May 15th, aged 88. During the 1940s he produced covers for *Police Comics*, featuring Jack Cole's Plastic Man, and backgrounds and scripts for Will Eisner's daily newspaper strip of *The Spirit*.

Romanian-born composer **Marius Constant**, best known for his memorable theme to *The Twilight Zone*, died the same day, aged 79.

American horror writer **Rex Miller** [Spangberg] died on May 21st, aged 65. He had spent the previous six years in hospitals and nursing homes. Starting with his Bram Stoker Award-nominated *Slob* in the late 1980s, he published a series of novels featuring detective Jack Eichord and/or serial killer Daniel "Chaingang" Bunkowski. These included *Frenzy*, *Stone Shadow*, *Slice*, *Iceman*, *Chaingang*, *Savant*, *Butcher* and *St Louis Blues*. His short fiction appeared in the anthologies *Splatterpunks*, *Stalkers*, *Borderlands 2* and *Narrow Houses*, while *Rex Miller: The Complete Revelations* was a 1993 biographical study by T. Winter-Damon.

Known as the "Spectre Inspector", freelance parapsychologist and "secular exorcist" **Andrew Green** died the same day, aged 76. The author of fifteen books, including *Ghost Hunting: A Practical Guide*, *Shire Album of Haunted Houses*, *Our Haunted Kingdom*, *Ghosts in the South-East*, *Phantom Ladies*, *Haunted Sussex Today* and *Ghosts of Today*, in 1996 he was famously asked to investigate reports of paranormal sightings at London's Royal Albert Hall.

53-year-old British literary agent **Rod Hall** was found stabbed to death in his South London flat on May 23rd. He was the former film and TV agent for such SF authors as Brian W. Aldiss and Christopher

Priest. While working at Penguin Books, he created the UK's first film/ TV tie-in department in 1978. A twenty-year-old student was subsequently charged with his murder.

American biographer, critic and editor **Edward** [Charles] **Wagenknecht** (aka "Julian Forrest") died on May 24th, aged 104. Born at the turn of the century, his books include *Utopia Americana*, a 1929 monograph on L. Frank Baum's *Wizard of Oz* series, plus *Edgar Allan Poe: The Man Behind the Legend*, *The Letters of James Branch Cabell* and *Seven Masters of Supernatural Fiction*. A regular contributor to *The Arkham Sampler*, he also wrote biographies of Nathaniel Hawthorne, Washington Irving and three works on Henry James, as well as also editing *Six Novels of the Supernatural* and *The Fireside Book of Ghost Stories*.

Author and artist **Raymond Bayless**, best known for his covers for Arkham House's four revised reprints of H.P. Lovecraft during the late 1980s, died after a long illness in Los Angeles on May 25th, aged 84.

Roger W. (William) **Straus, Jr.**, co-founder of New York publishing imprint Farrar Straus & Giroux, died of pneumonia the same day, aged 87.

American SF and thriller writer **Alfred Coppel** (Alfredo José de Araña-Marini y Coppel, aka "Sol Galaxan", "Robert Cham Gilman", "Derfla Leppoc" and "A.C. Martin") died on May 30th, aged 82. He made his writing debut in 1943 and contributed more than forty stories to *Astounding*, *Planet Stories*, *Super Science Stories*, *Fantastic Adventures* and *Future Fiction*. His novels include *Dark December*, *Thirty-Four East*, *The Dragon*, *The Hastings Conspiracy*, *The Apocalypse Brigade*, *The Burning Mountain*, "The Goldenwing Cycle" (*Glory*, *Glory's People* and *Glory's War*) and the young adult "Rhada" series as "Gilman" (*The Rebel of Rhada*, *The Navigator of Rhada*, *The Starkahn of Rhada* and *The Warlock of Rhada*).

Australian small press editor and publisher **Peter** ("Mac") **McNamara** died of brain cancer on June 1st, aged 57. He was diagnosed in early 2002. His mid-1980s SF magazine *Aphelion*, cofounded with his wife Mariann, led to the creation of Aphelion Publications, and he co-edited the anthologies *Alien Shores* and *Forever Shores: Fiction of the Fantastic* with Margaret Winch (who also died in 2004). McNamara also edited *Wonder Years: The Best Australian Stories of a Decade Past* and had reportedly completed *Future Shores* at the time of his death.

The severed head of 91-year-old blacklisted American film and TV writer **Robert Lees** (a.k.a. "J.E. Selby") was discovered on June 15th in the home of his neighbour, Morley Hal Engleson. Sixty-seven-year-old retired physician Engleson, who lived about two miles from the gates of Paramount Studios, had also been stabbed to death by a 27-year-old homeless man while trying to book an airline flight on the phone. Kevin Lee Graff was arrested after he was recognized from a TV news conference by a studio guard. A former extra in such films as *Rasputin and the Empress* (1932), Lees' credits (often in collaboration with Frederic I. Rinaldo) include the scripts for *The Black Cat* (1941), *The Invisible Woman* and the Abbott and Costello comedies *Hold That Ghost*, *Meet Frankenstein* and *Abbott and Costello Meet the Invisible Man*, plus episodes of TV's *Alfred Hitchcock Presents* under a pseudonym.

Eighty-two-year-old American screenwriter **Tom Rowe** died in Greece of heart failure the same day. His credits include the story for Disney's *The Aristocats* and he worked on the scripts for *The Green Slime*, Jules Verne's *The Light at the Edge of the World* and John Derek's *Tarzan, the Ape Man*. Rowe also wrote several episodes of TV's *Fantasy Island*. During the United States' occupation of Japan, he was General Douglas MacArthur's chief translator.

British-born pulp author **Hugh B.** (Barnett) **Cave** (aka "Justin Case", "H.C. Barnett", "Jack D'Arcy", "Rupert Knowles" and "Geoffrey Vace") died in a Florida hospice after a short illness on June 27th, aged 93. Cave emigrated to America with his family when he was five. He sold his first fiction in 1929 and went on to publish 800 stories in such pulp magazines as *Weird Tales*, *Strange Tales*, *Ghost Stories*, *Black Book Detective Magazine*, *Spicy Mystery Stories* and the so-called "shudder" or "weird menace" pulps, *Horror Stories* and *Terror Tales*. Cave left the field for almost three decades, moving to Haiti and later Jamaica, where he established a coffee plantation and wrote two highly-praised travel books, *Haiti: Highroad to Adventure* and *Four Paths to Paradise: A Book About Jamaica*. He also continued to write for the "slick" magazines, such as *Collier's*, *Cosmopolitan*, *Esquire*, *The Saturday Evening Post* and many other titles. In 1977, Karl Edward Wagner's Carcosa imprint published a volume of Cave's best horror tales, *Murgunstrumm and Others*, and he returned to the genre with new stories and a string of modern horror novels: *Legion of the Dead*, *The Nebulon Horror*, *The Evil*, *Shades of Evil*, *Disciples of Dread*, *The Lower Deep*, *Lucifer's Eye*, *Isle of the Whisperers*, *The Dawning*, *The Evil Returns* and *The Restless Dead*. His short stories were also collected in a number of volumes, including *The Corpse Maker*, *Death Stalks*

STEPHEN JONES & KIM NEWMAN

*the Night, The Dagger of Tsiang, Long Live the Dead: Tales from
Black Mask, Come Into my Parlor, The Door Below* and *Bottled in
Blonde*. *Pulp Man's Odyssey: The Hugh B. Cave Story* was a
biography by Audrey Parente; *Magazines I Remember* was a perso-
nal memoir by the author, and Milt Thomas' biography, *Cave of a
Thousand Tales: The Life & Times of Hugh B. Cave*, was published
by Arkham House the week after the author's death. Cave received
Life Achievement Awards from The Horror Writers Association in
1991, The International Horror Guild in 1998 and The World
Fantasy Convention in 1999. He was also presented with the Special
Convention Award at the 1997 World Fantasy gathering in London,
where he was co-Special Guest of Honour.

Seventy-three-year-old British playwright and screenwriter **Peter
Barnes** died on July 1st after suffering a stroke. His films include *The
Ruling Class*, based on his own satirical 1968 stage play, which
featured Peter O'Toole as a crazed Jack the Ripper figure. He also
scripted a number of Hallmark TV projects, including *Merlin, Alice
in Wonderland, Noah's Ark, Arabian Nights, A Christmas Carol*
and *The Magical Legend of the Leprechauns*.

Illustrator **John Cullen Murphy**, best known for his work on the
King Features Syndicate *Prince Valiant* comic strip for more than
three decades, died on July 2nd, aged 85. He took the strip over from
its creator, Hal Foster. Murphy retired in March 2004 and handed
Prince Valiant, which appears in more than 300 newspapers
throughout America, to Gary Gianni. Murphy's own comic strip,
Big Ben Bolt, about a boxer, started in 1949 and ran for nearly a
quarter of a century. Murphy was inspired to become an illustrator
when, as a child, he was asked by his neighbour, artist Norman
Rockwell, to model for a *Saturday Evening Post* cover.

Stevie Wonder's former wife and collaborator **Syreeta Wright** died
of complications from breast cancer on July 6th, aged 58. Together
they wrote "Signed, Sealed, Delivered (I'm Yours)" and other hits.

Prolific American children's novelist **Paula Danziger**, whose books
include the SF romance *This Place Has No Atmosphere* (1986) and
the "Amber Brown" series, died on July 8th after suffering a heart
attack in June. She was 59.

Canadian-born child actor and illustrator **Sam McKim** died of
heart failure on July 9th, aged 79. Best remembered for his roles in
Hollywood Westerns and serials of the 1930s and '40s, including
The Lone Ranger and *Dick Tracy's G-Men*, in 1954 he joined Walt
E. Disney Enterprises (later Walt Disney Imagineering), where he
became Master Map Maker, drawing the first souvenir maps of

Disneyland. His sketches helped design such locations as Main Street and Frontierland, and his paintings introduced the public to the Haunted Mansion. McKim later worked on such Disney films as *Zorro*, *The Shaggy Dog* and *The Gnome-Mobile*, and he came out of retirement to draw maps for Disneyland Paris.

Seventy-five-year-old Emmy and Oscar-winning American composer **Jerry** (Jerrald) [King] **Goldsmith** died in his sleep at his home in Beverly Hills on July 21st after a long battle with cancer. Goldsmith, who was nominated for seventeen Academy Awards and won only one for *The Omen*, is still probably best known for composing the themes for *The Man from U.N.C.L.E.*, *Star Trek: The Next Generation* and *Star Trek: Voyager*. He also worked on episodes of *The Twilight Zone* and *Thriller*. Goldsmith's numerous other film scores include *Seven Days in May*, *Satan Bug*, *Seconds*, *Our Man Flint*, *In Like Flint*, *Planet of the Apes* (1968), *The Illustrated Man*, *The Mephisto Waltz*, *The Other*, *The Reincarnation of Peter Proud*, *Logan's Run*, *Damnation Alley*, *The Swarm*, *Capricorn One*, *The Boys from Brazil*, *Coma*, *Magic*, *Alien*, *Star Trek The Motion Picture* and four sequels, *The Final Conflict*, *Outland*, *Psycho II*, *Supergirl*, *Explorers*, *King Solomon's Mines* (1985), *Poltergeist*, *Innerspace*, *Twilight Zone The Movie*, *Gremlins*, *The 'burbs*, *Legend*, *Leviathan*, *Warlock*, *Gremlins 2 The New Batch* (he also has a cameo), *Total Recall*, *Matinee*, *The Shadow*, *Congo*, *Mulan*, *The Mummy* (1999), *The Haunting* (1999), *Hollow Man*, *The Sum of All Fears* and most of *Looney Tunes Back in Action*. Goldsmith also wrote the cantata "Christus Apollo" with words by Ray Bradbury, commissioned by the Los Angeles Philharmonic for *Fireworks: A Celebration of Los Angeles* (1999), and the duo were collaborating on the opera *Leviathan '99* at the time of the composer's death.

Italian film composer **Piero Piccioni** (a.k.a. "Piero Morgan") died in Rome on July 23rd, aged 82. A former radio jazz pianist, he composed more than 170 scores for such films as *The 10th Victim*, *Matchless*, *The Witches* (1967), *The Light at the Edge of the World*, *Agent 077 Fury in the Orient*, Paul Naschy's *Jack the Ripper*, *The Monk* (1973), *Sisters of Satan*, *Camille 2000*, *The Nuns of St Arcangel* and numerous Euro-Westerns. In the 1950s he was connected with the sensational murder of a young girl at a Roman beach community. Although he was completely exonerated, the scandal forced Piccioni's father to resign his position as Italy's foreign minister.

Scottish actor and SF novelist **Michael** [Aiken] **Elder** died on July 28th, aged 73. Best known for his role in the long-running soap opera *Take the High Road* (which he also novelized), during the 1970s he wrote fourteen novels in the "Barclay" space opera series that were primarily published for the library market by Robert Hale.

American TV writer **Arthur Alsberg** died on August 7th, aged 87. His credits include episodes of *I Dream of Jeannie*, *The Ghost and Mrs. Muir* and *The Jetsons Meet the Flintstones*. With long-time collaborator Don Nelson he wrote the Disney film *Herbie Goes to Monte Carlo*, and in 1981 the duo also scripted and produced the TV movie *The Munsters' Revenge*.

Blacklisted Hollywood film composer **David Raksin** died of heart failure on August 9th, aged 92. Best known for his haunting theme for the classic *film noir Laura* (1944), which with lyrics by Johnny Mercer remained on radio hit parades for fourteen weeks, his more than 400 other credits include Charlie Chaplin's *Modern Times*, *The Adventures of Sherlock Holmes*, *The Hound of the Baskervilles* (1939), *Mr Moto's Last Warning*, *The Missing Guest*, *Sh! The Octopus*, *The Gorilla*, *The Undying Monster*, *Dr Renault's Secret*, *Whispering Ghosts*, *The Secret Life of Walter Mitty*, *Whirlpool*, *The Next Voice You Hear*, *Night Tide*, *The Ghost of Flight 401*, *What's the Matter With Helen?*, *The Day After* and the 1953 animated film *The Unicorn in the Garden*, written by James Thurber. Raksin's autobiography, *If I Say So Myself*, was awaiting publication at the time of his death.

Oscar-winning film composer **Elmer Bernstein**, best known for such scores as *The Magnificent Seven* and *The Great Escape*, died in his sleep after a long illness on August 18th, aged 82. His more than 200 film credits also include the 3-D *Robot Monster*, *Cat-Women of the Moon*, *The Ten Commandments* (1956), *Blind Terror* (US: *See No Evil*), *The Amazing Mr Blunden*, *Saturn 3*, *An American Werewolf in London*, *Heavy Metal*, *Spacehunter*, *Ghostbusters*, *Slipstream*, *The Black Cauldron*, *Wild Wild West* and the 1991 remake of *Cape Fear* (when he adapted the original 1962 score by his friend Bernard Herrmann). Bernstein also started the Varese Sarabande recording label.

Editor, folklorist, film collector and founder of the Bram Stoker Society in 1980, **Leslie Shepard** died in Ireland on August 20th, aged 87. As well as editing the anthologies *The Dracula Book of Great Vampire Stories* and *The Dracula Book of Great Horror Stories* (later reissued as the omnibus *The Book of Dracula*), he also edited (with Albert Power) *Dracula: Celebrating 100 Years* and the two-volume *Encyclopedia of Occultism and Parapsychology*.

Film and TV writer **George Kirgo** died of kidney failure after a long illness on August 21st, aged 78. He scripted the TV movies *Brenda Starr*, *The Man in the Santa Claus Suit*, *Angel on My Shoulder* (1980) and *Massarati and the Brain*, as well as episodes of *Kraft Suspense Theatre* and *My Mother the Car*.

Oscar-nominated film and TV scriptwriter **Robert Lewin**, whose credits include episodes of *The Man from Atlantis* and *Star Trek The Next Generation* (which he also produced from 1987–88), died of lung cancer on August 28th, aged 84.

Fred [Lawrence] **Whipple**, American astronomer and co-author of *Conquest of the Moon* with Wernher von Braun and Willy Ley, died on August 30th, aged 97. The 1953 volume was awarded a Retro Hugo for Best Related Book just four days after Whipple's death.

Songwriter **Russell Faith**, whose film credits include *Voyage to the Bottom of the Sea* and *Beach Party*, died of a stroke on September 1st, aged 75.

American political scientist **Harvey Wheeler**, who co-wrote the nuclear war thriller *Fail-Safe* with Eugene Burdick, died of cancer on September 6th, aged 85. Their 1962 novel was filmed two years later with an all-star cast and again in 2000.

Frank (Franklin) [Rosborough] **Thomas**, one of Walt Disney's "Nine Old Men" of animation, died of a cerebral haemorrhage on September 8th, aged 92. In his forty-three year history at Disney he worked on *Snow White and the Seven Dwarfs*, *Pinocchio*, *Bambi*, *The Adventures of Ichabod and Mr Toad*, *Lady and the Tramp*, *Cinderella*, *Alice in Wonderland*, *The Legend of Sleepy Hollow* (1958), *Sleeping Beauty*, *Peter Pan*, *The Sword in the Stone*, *Mary Poppins*, *The Jungle Book*, *Winnie the Pooh and the Blustery Day*, *The Aristocats*, *Robin Hood*, *The Rescuers* and *The Fox and the Hound*, amongst other titles. Thomas retired in 1978 and co-authored several books about animation with Ollie Johnston, including *Disney Animation: The Illusion of Life* and *Disney Villains*.

Tony Award-winning musical lyricist **Fred Ebb**, who wrote the words for Frank Sinatra's "New York, New York" in 1977, died of a heart attack on September 11th, aged 76. With long-time collaborator John Kander, his other credits include the hit Broadway musicals *Cabaret*, *Kiss of the Spider Woman* and *Chicago*.

L. Ron Hubbard scholar **William J.** (Jerome) **Widder** died on September 16th, aged 78. He wrote *The Fiction of L. Ron Hubbard: A Comprehensive Bibliography & Reference Guide to Published and Selected Unpublished Works* (1994) and the Hugo-nominated *Master Storyteller: An Illustrated Tour of the Fiction of L. Ron Hubbard* (2003). He also helped launch the Writers of the Future contest.

Seventy-four-year-old Harvard professor and UFOlogist **John E. Mack** died in a car accident in London on September 27th. The Pulitzer Prize-winning author's books include *Abduction: Human Encounters with Aliens* (1994) and *Passport to the Cosmos* (1999).

TV scriptwriter and playwright **Shimon Wincelberg** died after a long illness on September 29th, aged 80. His credits include episodes of *Lost in Space*, *Time Tunnel*, *Logan's Run* and the original *Star Trek* series.

American songwriter and theatre director **Jacques Levy** died of cancer on September 30th, aged 69. He collaborated with Bob Dylan on such songs as "Hurricane" and "Joey", and also worked with Roger McGuinn of the Byrds ("Chestnut Mare"). He directed the 1969 New York production of Kenneth Tynan's *Oh! Calcutta!* and the 1983–84 stage musical of the comic strip *Doonesbury*, created Dylan's 1975 tour the Rolling Thunder Review, and as Professor of English and director of theatre at Colgate University, Hamilton, New York, mounted productions of *Marat/Sade* (1994) and *Frankenstein* (2000).

Eighty-one-year-old Japanese translator, writer and fan **Tetsu Yano** died on October 13th after a long battle with cancer. Invited by Forrest J Ackerman to attend the 1953 World SF convention in Philadelphia, he went on to translate more than 350 books, including work by Robert A. Heinlein, Frank Herbert, Frederik Pohl and Edgar Rice Burroughs. He co-founded the Science Fiction Writers of Japan in 1963.

Comics artist **Irv Novick**, whose career began in 1940 and who illustrated *Batman* from the 1960s until the 1980s, died after a long illness on October 15th, aged 88.

British writer and broadcaster **Vincent Brome** died on October 16th, aged 84. His many biographies include *H.G. Wells* (1951).

Bill Liebowitz, the founder of Los Angeles' influential comics store Golden Apple, died of complications from the flu on October 27th, aged 63.

Pioneering electronic music composer **Gil Mellé**, whose credits include *The Andromeda Strain* and TV's *Night Gallery*, died of a heart attack on October 28th, aged 72. Also a jazz saxophonist and respected digital artist, Mellé scored *The Andromeda Strain*, *You'll Like My Mother*, *The Ultimate Warrior*, *The Sentinel*, *Embryo*, *Starship Invasions*, *Blood Beach*, *Starcrossed*, the first four episodes of *Kolchak: The Night Stalker*, the pilot of *The Six Million Dollar Man* and such films and TV movies as *The Curse of King Tut's Tomb*, *The Questor Tapes*, *Killdozer*, *Frankenstein: The True Story*,

A Cold Night's Death, *The Intruder Within*, *The Last Chase*, *World War III*, *Night Owl* and *From the Dead of Night*.

Walt Disney animator **John Parr Miller**, who worked on *Pinocchio*, *Fantasia* and *Dumbo*, died on October 29th, aged 91.

Eighty-four-year-old American fan and pulp collector/dealer **Richard H. Minter** died of complications following gall bladder surgery on November 6th. He received the Lamont Award at the 1993 Pulpcon.

Canadian-born romance author **Elizabeth** [Eileen Moore] **Chater** died on November 10th, aged 94. Under the name "Lee Chaytor" she had a number of stories published during the 1950s in *Fantastic Universe* and elsewhere.

Prolific Italian film-music composer **Carlo Rustichelli** died on November 13th, aged 87. His more than 300 soundtracks include numerous costume dramas such as *Giants of Thessaly* and *Siren of Atlantis*, plus *The Day the Sky Exploded*, the 1960 *The Thief of Baghdad*, *Hercules Against Moloch*, *The Long Hair of Death*, *Operazione Paura*, Fellini's *Satyricon*, *And Then There Were None* (1973) and *Ator 2*, along with three seminal Mario Bava titles: *The Whip and the Body* (aka *What?*), *Blood and Black Lace* and *Kill, Baby . . . Kill!*

American comics artist **Harry Lampert**, who co-created *The Flash*, died of prostate cancer the same day, aged 88. He also worked on *Popeye* and *Betty Boop* cartoons.

American writer-producer **Richard Alan Simmons** also died on November 13th, aged 80. His credits include the 1969 TV movie *Fear No Evil* and he reportedly worked uncredited on *The Incredible Shrinking Man*.

Another writer-producer, **Seeleg Lester**, died on November 14th, aged 91. He worked on *Change of Mind* and the TV series *The Outer Limits* and *The Invisible Man*.

French-born composer **Michel Colombier** died of cancer in Santa Monica the same day, aged 65. His more than 100 film and TV scores include *Colossus: The Forbin Project*, *Impulse*, *Buried Alive*, *Strays*, *Foxfire*, *Purple Rain*, *The Golden Child*, *Barb Wire* and HBO's *Tales from the Crypt* series.

American academic and H.G. Wells expert **W. Warren Wagar** (a.k.a. "Ira Walker") died on November 16th, aged 72. His publications include *H.G. Wells and the World State*, *H.G. Wells: Traversing Time* and *Terminal Visions: The Literature of Last Things*. He also published fiction in *The Magazine of Fantasy & Science Fiction* and *Asimov's Science Fiction*.

Sixty-two-year-old American music producer **Terry Melcher**, the son of actress-singer Doris Day, died after a long battle against melanoma on November 19th. He wrote the hit "Move Over Darling" for his mother, produced "Mr Tambourine Man" and "Turn, Turn, Turn" for The Byrds and co-wrote "Kokomo" with the Beach Boys. Melcher always suspected that he was the actual target of Charles Manson's drug-crazed followers, who murdered pregnant actress Sharon Tate and four others in his former Hollywood Hills home on August 8th, 1969.

Broadway composer and songwriter **Cy Coleman** (Seymour Kaufman), whose credits include the musical *City of Angels*, died of heart failure the same day, aged 75. He had been taken ill earlier in the evening at a post-premiere party at New York's Tavern on the Green. With lyricist Carolyn Leigh he wrote such classic songs as "Witchcraft" and "The Best is Yet to Come". He also wrote the musical *Sweet Charity*.

Caldecott Medal-winning American artist and writer **Trina Schart Hyman**, who illustrated more than 150 books, many for children, also died on November 19th, from cancer, aged 65.

So, too, did young adult author **Willo** [Louise] **Davis Roberts**, from congestive heart failure, aged 79. Her more than 100 books include the fantasies *The Girl With the Silver Eyes* and *The Magic Book*.

British actor and playwright **Stephen Mallatratt** died of leukaemia on November 22nd, aged 57. In 1987 he adapted Susan Hill's ghost story *The Woman in Black* for the stage, and it is now the second longest-running play in London's West End (after *The Mousetrap*).

Comics writer **Bob Haney**, who scripted many DC "Silver Age" titles from the mid-1950s onwards, died on November 27th, aged 78.

Irwin Donenfeld, who became editorial director and publisher of DC Comics following the death of his father Harry in 1965, died on November 29th, aged 78.

Canadian journalist, broadcaster and novelist **Pierre Berton** died of heart failure on November 30th, aged 84. He wrote the 1961 children's fantasy *The Secret World of Og*, which sold more than 200,000 copies and was made into a cartoon TV special.

Bestselling British author **Arthur Hailey** died in November at his home in the Bahamas, aged 84. He had suffered a stroke two months earlier. Hailey's eleven books, which include *Hotel* and *Airport*, sold more than 170 million copies, and the film of the latter is regarded by many as ushering in the modern disaster movie trend of the 1970s.

Locus magazine editorial assistant and reviewer [Thomas] **Scott**

Winnett died of AIDS-related pneumonia on December 12th, aged 42. He worked at the magazine from 1989–94.

Film and TV composer **Arlon Ober** died on December 20th, aged 61. His credits include *Eating Raoul*, *Bloody Birthday*, *Hospital Massacre* and *The Incredible Melting Man*.

Cultural commentator and human rights activist **Susan Sontag** (Susan Rosenblatt) died of leukaemia on December 28th, aged 71. She wrote influential essays on science fiction films ("The Imagination of Disaster") and Nazi chic ("Fascinating Fascism") and appeared as herself in Woody Allen's film *Zelig*.

PERFORMERS

African-American singer and actress **Etta Moten Barnett** died of pancreatic cancer on January 2nd, aged 102. She toured in the 1932 Broadway show *Zombie* and dubbed Ginger Rogers' singing voice in *Professional Sweetheart* (1933). However, she will be best remembered for singing a segment of "My Forgotten Man" in Busby Berkeley's musical *Gold Diggers of 1933*. When she sung the song the following year at President Franklin Roosevelt's birthday, she became the first black woman to sing in the White House.

Canadian-born actor **Philip Gilbert**, the voice of the computer TIM in TV's *The Tomorrow People* (1973–79), died on January 6th, aged 72. He also appeared in *The Frozen Dead*, *Superman III* and an early episode of *The Avengers*.

Swedish film actress **Ingrid Thulin** died of cancer on January 7th, aged 77. She made eight films with Ingmar Bergman, including *The Face* (aka *The Magician*) and *The Hour of the Wolf*. She was dubbed by Angela Lansbury in the 1962 Hollywood production *The Four Horsemen of the Apocalypse*.

American-born British stage and screen actor **Lyndon Brook**, the son of actor Clive Brook, died on January 9th, aged 77. His film credits include *The Clue of the Silver Key*, *Invasion*, *Who?* and *Defence of the Realm*.

Al Jolson's widow **Erle Jolson Krasna** (Erle Chennault Galbraith) died of cancer on January 11th, aged 81. She was Jolson's fourth wife and thirty-six years the junior of the legendary entertainer (who died in 1950). During the 1940s she was a contract player at Columbia Pictures.

Blaxploitation actor **Ron O'Neal**, best known for his starring role as cocaine dealer Youngblood Priest in the 1970s movies *Superfly* and *Superfly TNT* (which he also directed), died of pancreatic cancer on January 14th, aged 66. His other credits include *When a Stranger Calls*, *The Final Countdown*, *Red Dawn*, *HyperSpace*, *Hero and the Terror*, *Puppet Master 5* and the 1980 TV movie *Brave New World*.

German-born Broadway stage actress **Uta Hagen** died in London the same day, aged 84. Her occasional film appearances include *The Other* and *The Boys from Brazil*. Her first husband was actor José Ferrer.

British-born blonde actress **Elsa Buchanan** (Elsie Winifred Buchanan) died on January 17th, aged 95. In the 1930s she moved to Hollywood, where she appeared in *Charlie Chan in London*, *The Mystery of Edwin Drood*, *Peter Ibbetson*, *The Thirteenth Chair* and *The Invisible Enemy*. She was a character in *Gosford Park*.

Two days after her birthday, 42-year-old porn star and single mother **Rebecca Steele** (Jeannette Dee Rogers) died on January 19th of a drug overdose while in the final stages of AIDS. She began her career as an underage junior high school dropout, and her numerous credits include *Young Cheeks*, *Bi Bi Baby* and *Butts Motel 5*.

Bernard Punsly, the last surviving "Dead End Kid", died of cancer on January 20th, aged 80. He appeared in *Dead End*, *Angels With Dirty Faces* and *Junior G-Men* before leaving the group after nineteen films to go to medical school. Punsly practised medicine in Los Angeles for almost fifty years.

Veteran Hollywood musical star **Ann Miller** (Johnnie Lucille Ann Collier) died of lung cancer on January 22nd, aged 84. Although best known for her dance routines in such films as *Easter Parade*, *On the Town* and *Kiss Me Kate* (RKO insured her legs for $1 million in the late 1930s), her final appearance was in David Lynch's *Mulholland Drive* (2001). Her autobiography *Miller's High Life* was published in 1972 and she also wrote *Tapping Into the Force*, a book about her own psychic abilities.

59-year-old French actor **Ticky Holgado** died the same day, of cancer. He starred in *City of Lost Children* and Jeunet and Marc Caro's 1991 black comedy *Delicatessen*.

Emmy Award-winning children's TV presenter **Bob** "Captain Kangaroo" **Keeshan** died after a long illness on January 23rd, aged 76. From October 1955, for almost thirty years on CBS-TV and a further six on PBS, he and his puppet friends – Mr Green Jeans and Bunny Rabbit – would present wholesome entertainment from their Treasure House each weekday morning.

Olympic gold medal American swimming champion **Eleanor Holm** died on January 31st, aged 90. After being sacked from the American Olympic team in 1936 for over-indulging in champagne while on board the liner bound for Germany, she appeared in a few films, culminating with *Tarzan's Revenge* (1938) playing Glenn Morris' "mate". She also appeared alongside Johnny Weissmuller and Buster Crabbe in the 1939 New York World's Fair musical and water stage show, *Aquacade*.

Steely Dan/Doobie Brothers sax player **Cornelius Bumpus** died of a heart attack on February 3rd, aged 58.

Actor and broadcaster **Dick Von Hoene**, better known as Cincinnati TV horror host "The Cool Ghoul", died of a heart attack on February 4th, aged 63. The Cool Ghoul made his debut as the host of *Scream-In* on independent station WXIX-TV, Channel 19, in 1969. A twelve-year-old Tim Lucus, future editor of *Video Watchdog*, was The Ghoul's official #1 fan.

Actor, singer and environmental activist **Jason Raize** (Jason Raize Rothenberg), the original Simba in the Broadway production of *The Lion King*, died of an apparent suicide in Australia on February 6th, aged 28. He also voiced the character of Denahi in the Disney film *Brother Bear* and appeared on Broadway in *The Rocky Horror Show* and *Jesus Christ Superstar* (as Pontius Pilate).

Fifty-six-year-old **Tony Pope**, the voice of Disney's Goofy for more than eleven years, died of an arterial rupture during heart surgery on February 11th. He worked on numerous films and TV shows, including *Who Framed Roger Rabbit*, *Back to the Future*, *Spaced Invaders*, *Shrek*, *Metropolis*, *The All-New Scooby-Doo and Scrappy-Doo Show* and *Vampire Princess Miyu*. Pope also voiced the Cheshire Cat and the King of Hearts in Disneyland's Alice in Wonderland ride.

Gospel singer **Doris Troy** [Higginsen], who had a 1963 hit with "Just One Look", died in Las Vegas of emphysema on February 16th, aged 67.

Les Gray, lead singer with the British 1970s Glam Rock group Mud, died after two suspected heart attacks in Portugal on February 21st, aged 57. The singer, whose hits included "Tiger Feet", "Lonely This Christmas" and "Oh Boy", had been suffering from throat cancer for several months and had a voicebox.

Blacklisted character actor and social activist **John Randolph** (Emanuel Hirsch Cohen) died on February 24th, aged 88. His open defence of accused figures during the McCarthy era led to his being blacklisted by the House Un-American Activities Committee. One of the founding members of the Actors Studio, his film credits include John Frankenheimer's *Seconds*, *Pretty Poison*, *Little Murders*, *Escape from the Planet of the Apes*, *Conquest of the Planet of the Apes*,

The Poseidon Adventure, Earthquake, The New Original Wonder Woman, King Kong (1976) and *Heaven Can Wait* (1978). On TV he appeared in *The Invaders, Lucan* (series regular), *Darkroom* and the memorable "They're Tearing Down Tim Riley's Bar" episode of *Night Gallery*.

American actress **Sheila Darcy** (Rebecca Heffener, aka "Rebecca Wassem"), who portrayed "The Dragon Lady" in the 1940 serial *Terry and the Pirates*, died of a heart attack on February 27th, aged 89. Her other credits include *The Big Broadcast of 1938, Zorro's Fighting Legion, Jungle Man* and *Arrest Bulldog Drummond*.

Singer and actor **Carl Anderson**, best remembered for his portrayal of Judas in the 1973 movie *Jesus Christ Superstar*, died of leukaemia on February 28th, aged 58. During the 1980s and '90s he released several albums.

Singer **Gene Allison**, whose hits include "You Can Make it if You Try", died of liver and kidney failure in Nashville on the same day, aged 69.

Academy Award-winning actress **Mercedes McCambridge** (Charlotte Mercedes Agnes McCambridge) whose raspy voice was used – initially uncredited – for the demonically possessed Regan in *The Exorcist* (1973), died on March 2nd, aged 87. A former alcoholic whose economist son killed his wife, two daughters and himself while wearing a Halloween mask in 1987, McCambridge's other films include Orson Welles' *Touch of Evil, The Scarf, Suddenly Last Summer*, Jess Franco's *99 Women* and *Justine, Echoes* and *The Concorde – Airport '79*. Welles described her "The world's greatest living radio actress," and she contributed to the *I Love a Mystery* radio series (1939–49). She also appeared in episodes of TV's *Tales of Tomorrow, Climax!, Lost in Space* and *Bewitched*. McCambridge's autobiography *The Quality of Mercy* was published in 1981.

TV actress and casting director **Cecily Adams**, who had a recurring role as "Moogie" on *Star Trek: Deep Space Nine*, died after a four-month battle against cancer on March 3rd, aged 46. The daughter of *Get Smart* actor Don Adams and singer Adelaide Adams, she also appeared in *Total Recall 2070* and cast such series as *Third Rock from the Sun, Bone Chillers* and *Eerie Indiana*.

Character actor **Walt Gorney**, who as "Crazy Ralph" warned the unlucky campers that they were "All doomed" in the original *Friday the 13th* (1980), died on March 5th, aged 91. He was back in the sequel and also narrated *Part VII*. Other credits include *Heavy Traffic, King Kong* (1976) and *Day of the Animals*.

American leading lady **Frances Dee** died of pneumonia and

complications from a stroke on March 6th, aged 96. In 1933 she married her co-star Joel McCrea (who died in 1990), and they eventually became amongst the richest landowners in California, rumoured to be worth between $50–100 million. Her best-known role is as nurse Betsy Connell in the 1943 Val Lewton classic *I Walked with a Zombie*. Dee retired from the screen in 1954. One of her three sons is actor Jody McCrea (Joel Dee McCrea) from the "Beach Party" films.

Dominican Republic-born singer **Peggy DeCastro** who, with her younger sister Cherie, had a #1 hit in 1954 with "Teach Me To-night", died of lung cancer in Las Vegas the same day, aged 82. Protégés of Brazilian star Carmen Miranda, the DeCastro Sisters made TV history when they appeared on the first live broadcast of Los Angeles station KTLA in 1947.

Emmy-winning African-American actor **Paul Winfield** died of a heart attack on March 7th, aged 62. Discovered by Burgess Meredith while a contract player at Columbia Pictures, his film credits include *Brother John*, *Damnation Alley*, *Twilight's Last Gleaming*, *Star Trek II The Wrath of Khan*, *The Terminator*, *The Serpent and the Rainbow*, *Mars Attacks!*, *White Dwarf*, *Dead of Night* (1996) and the TV movie *The Horror at 37,000 Feet*. He was a regular on the 1987–88 TV series *The Charmings* (as the Mirror) and also appeared on *The Man from U.N.C.L.E.*, *Spider-Man*, *Babylon 5* and *Star Trek The Next Generation*.

The body of **Spalding Gray** was found the same day in the East River near Brooklyn, New York, after he apparently jumped off the Staten Island Ferry. The 62-year-old actor and monologist was identified through dental records and X-rays. Gray was last seen on January 10th at his Manhattan home and was listed as officially missing on the 19th of that month. The author of *Swimming for Cambodia*, *Monster in a Box* and *Gray's Anatomy* (filmed, respectively, by Jonathan Demme, Nick Broomfield and Steven Soderbergh) had been suffering from depression since sustaining injuries in a car accident in Ireland two years earlier. He had reportedly attempted suicide on at least two occasions since then. Gray appeared in the films of his own work and also had featured roles in *Ilsa Harem Keeper of the Oil Sheiks*, *Little Orphan Dusty*, the remake of *Diabolique*, *Kate & Leopold*, *Beaches*, *The Killing Fields* and others.

Forty-nine-year-old American actor and former boxer **Robert Pastorelli** died from a drug-related death at his Hollywood Hills home on March 8th. Best known for his recurring role as house painter "Eldin Bernecky" on CBS-TV's *Murphy Brown*, he also appeared in several films, including *A Simple Wish*, *Michael* and the 1998 vampire comedy *Modern Vampires* (aka *Revenant*), in which he played "The Count". His 25-year-old girlfriend Charemon Janovich was found fatally shot to death in the same house in 1999, reportedly following an argument.

Former German heavyweight boxer turned actor **Wilhelm Von Homburg** (Norman Grupe) died of cancer on March 10th, aged 63. He appeared as the long-haired Lord of the Underworld in *Ghostbusters II* and also had roles in Hitchcock's *Torn Curtain*, *The Wrecking Crew*, *The Silence of the Hams* and *In the Mouth of Madness*. He spent five years in jail on drugs and prostitution charges.

Sixty-six-year-old Russian actor **Borislav Brondukov**, best known for playing "Inspector Lestrade" in the Soviet series of Sherlock Holmes films, died the same day of a heart attack.

Canadian actor **Jack Creley**, who played "Brian O'Blivion" in David Cronenberg's *Videodrome*, also died of heart failure on March 10th, aged 78. His other credits include *Dr Strangelove*, *Rituals*, *Change of Mind*, *Reincarnate*, *The Only Way Out is Dead* and *Welcome to Blood City*.

Dave Blood (Dave Schulthise) bassist with the American punk band The Dead Milkmen, best known for their 1988 song "Punk Rock Girl", committed suicide the same day, aged 47.

Seventy-seven-year-old French actor **Philip Lemaire** committed suicide by throwing himself under a Paris metro train on March 15th. He appeared in *Mystery of the Red Jungle*, *Spirits of the Dead*, *The Blood Rose* and *Beyond the Grave*. His first wife was singer Juliette Greco.

Former nude *Playgirl* model turned actor **Brian Bianchini** committed suicide in San Francisco on March 16th, aged 25. He appeared in the vampire film *The Brotherhood* and also *The Black Magic* shot in Thailand. A few days before his death he was subdued by police with taser guns while attempting to take his own life on a beach.

Sixty-two-year-old **J.J.** (John) **Jackson**, a long-time Los Angeles radio personality and one of the original MTV VJs in 1981, died of an apparent heart attack while driving in L.A. on March 17th.

Russian-born British character actor **Richard Marner** (Alexander Molchanoff-Sacha) died on March 18th, aged 82. Best known for his role as the bungling German Colonel Kurt von Strohm in the BBC-TV comedy series *'Allo 'Allo* (1982–92), he also appeared in *The Man Who Knew Too Much* (1956), *The Mouse on the Moon*, *Where* *the Spies Are, You Only Live Twice, The Boys from Brazil, The Last Horror Film, The Sum of All Fears* and TV's *The Avengers*.

French-Russian ballerina and choreographer **Ludmila Tcherina** (Monique Tchemerzine) died on March 21st, aged 79. She appeared in *L'atalantide* (as "Antinea"), *The Red Shoes, Tales of Hoffman, Salome, Sign of the Pagan* and *Agent 38–24–36*. The youngest prima ballerina ever at the age of fifteen, Tcherina was also the first western-born dancer to star at the Bolshoi in Moscow.

Motown singer and producer **Johnny Bristol** (John William Bristol) died on March 22nd, aged 65. His biggest hit was "Hang on in There Baby" in 1973. He also recorded the original "Someday We'll be Together" in 1961 (with Jackie Beavers) and later produced such acts as Michael Jackson, Stevie Wonder, Diana Ross and Marvin Gaye.

Irish-born character actor **Richard Leech** (Richard Leeper McLelland) died on March 24th, aged 81. His many credits include *Night of the Demon* (US: *Curse of the Demon*), Hammer's *Terror of the Tongs* and BBC-TV's *Doctor Who*.

Japanese actor **Utako Mitsuya** died of pneumonia the same day, aged 67. His credits include *Atomic Rulers of the World, Evil Brain from Outer Space* and various episodes of the *Super Giant* series.

Hollywood *film noir* star of the 1940s and '50s **Jan Sterling** (Jane Sterling Adriance) died of complications from a broken hip and a series of strokes on March 26th, aged 82. Often cast as conniving blondes in such films as *Ace in the Hole* and *The High and the Mighty*, Sterling also co-starred in the 1956 film of George Orwell's *1984*. She was the widow of actor Paul Douglas (who died in 1959) and long-time companion of actor Sam Wanamaker (who died in 1993).

Sixty-two-year-old singer and songwriter [William] **Jan Berry** who, with Jan & Dean partner Dean Torrence, helped popularize the Southern California surf sound of the 1960s, died after suffering a brain seizure the same day. The son of a millionaire, he had never fully recovered from a car accident in 1966 that resulted in partial paralysis and irreversible brain damage. The duo's hits include "Surf City", "Dead Man's Curve", "Little Old Lady from Pasadena" and various collaborations with the Beach Boys. In recent years Berry weighed around 300lb.

British stuntman and actor **Peter Diamond** died of a stroke on March 27th, aged 75. He choreographed the lightsabre duels in the original *Star Wars* trilogy and his other credits include Hammer's *Kiss of the Vampire, The Gorgon, The Devil-Ship Pirates, The Evil* of Frankenstein, Curse of the Mummy's Tomb, Rasputin the Mad Monk, The Reptile, Frankenstein Created Woman, Dracula Prince of Darkness and The Witches, Children of the Damned, A Study in Terror, The Psychopath, The Legacy, Superman II, An American Werewolf in London, Lifeforce, Raiders of the Lost Ark, King Solomon's Mines (1985), The Princess Bride, Highlander and Who Framed Roger Rabbit.

Oscar-winning British actor, playwright, director, novelist and raconteur Sir **Peter** [Alexander] **Ustinov** died of heart failure in Switzerland on March 28th, aged 82. He had suffered from diabetes for many years. Ustinov wrote, directed and produced the 1947 film of F. Anstey's body-switch fantasy Vice Versa, and his other genre credits include Blackbeard's Ghost, Hammersmith is Out, One of Our Dinosaurs is Missing, Logan's Run, Appointment With Death, The Thief of Baghdad (1978), The Great Muppet Caper, Charlie Chan and the Curse of the Dragon Queen, The Phoenix and the Magic Carpet, Alice in Wonderland (1999), Animal Farm (1999) and the 2003 CBS-TV movie Salem Witch Trials.

Thirty-eight-year-old stuntman, personal fitness trainer and former Navy SEAL **Scott Helveston** was one of four private security contractors ambushed in Fallujah, Iraq, and beheaded by insurrectionists on March 31st. His credits include Raise the Titanic and Face/Off.

Fifty-seven-year-old American film and TV actress **Carrie** (Caroline) **Snodgress** died of heart failure while awaiting a liver transplant on April 1st. Following an uncredited role in Easy Rider, she appeared in such films as Diary of Mad Housewife (for which she was nominated for an Academy Award), Brian DePalma's The Fury, The Attic, Trick or Treats, Pale Rider, Ed Gein and The Forsaken. Her TV credits include episodes of Friday the 13th, Shades of L.A., Touched by an Angel and The X Files. She is survived by her son, Zeke, whose father is musician Neil Young.

Musician and recording executive **Paul Atkinson** died of liver and kidney failure the same day in Santa Monica, aged 58. From 1963–67 he was the guitarist with British band the Zombies, who had hits with "She's Not There", "Tell Her No" and "Time of the Season". They also briefly turned up in Bunny Lake is Missing.

German-born supporting actor **Herb Andress** (aka "Herbert Andreas") died of cancer in Munich on April 8th, aged 69. He made his film debut in The Ghost in the Invisible Bikini and also appeared in Lady Frankenstein, Who? and Enemy Mine.

Harry Babbitt, the lead vocalist with Kay Kyser's Band, died of heart failure on April 9th, aged 90. Babbitt sang on such Kyser hits as

"Three Little Fishes" and "On a Slow Boat to China", and he appeared in the 1940 horror/comedy *You'll Find Out* opposite Boris Karloff, Peter Lorre and Bela Lugosi. His most famous solo recording is "All I Want for Christmas is My Two Front Teeth".

Nick and **Mary Yankovic**, the parents of singer "Weird Al" Yankovic, were found dead the same day in their suburban San Diego home. Aged 86 and 81, respectively, the Yonkovics apparently died of carbon monoxide poisoning as a result of a closed flue in a fireplace.

Nineteen sixty four *Playboy* "Playmate of the Year" **Donna Michelle** died of a massive heart attack on April 14th, aged 58. She appeared in such films as *Beach Blanket Bingo* (as "Animal"), *Mickey One*, *Agent for H.A.R.M.*, *One Spy Too Many* and *The Spy With My Face*.

British stage and screen actor **Philip Locke** died on April 19th, aged 76. Best known for his role as silent assassin Vargas in *Thunderball*, his other credits include *The Plague Dogs* and TV's *The Avengers*, *The Champions*, *Doctor Who* and *Box of Delights* (1984). He apparently spent much of his time in his pyjamas.

Patrick "Pat" [William] **Moore** (a.k.a. "Terrence Moore"), a child star of silent films, died on April 25th, aged 91. A discovery of Cecil B. DeMille, he was the last surviving cast member of the 1923 version of *The Ten Commandments*. After retiring from acting, Moore became an assistant editor on such films as *War of the Worlds* and *When Worlds Collide*.

Ecuador-born character actor **Albert Paulsen** died of Alzheimer's complications in Los Angeles the same day, aged 78. His many film and TV roles, usually as suave villains, include *The Manchurian Candidate* (1962), *How to Steal the World*, *Search for the Gods*, *The Man from U.N.C.L.E.*, *Kolchak The Night Stalker*, *Wonder Woman*, *Galactica 1980* and *Knight Rider*.

British actor **Anthony Ainley** who, from 1981–89, took over the role of Doctor Who's arch-nemesis "The Master" following the death of Roger Delgado, died on May 3rd, aged 71. He also appeared in *Naked Evil*, *You Only Live Twice*, *Blood on Satan's Claw* and *The Land That Time Forgot*.

TV and film character actor **Johnny Mann** died of cancer the same day, aged 73. He had a recurring role in *Highway to Heaven*.

Former disc jockey **Zulu** (Gilbert Francis Lani Damian Kauhi), who played Detective Kono Kalakaua for four seasons (1968–72) on TV's *Hawaii Five-O*, died of complications from diabetes also on May 3rd, aged 66. He was the only actual Hawaiian actor who was a cop regular on the show.

Acerbic American comedian and character actor **Alan King** (Irwin Alan Kniberg), a protégé of Milton Berle, died of lung cancer on May 9th, aged 76. The MC at president John F. Kennedy's inauguration, his occasional film appearances include *I the Jury* (1982), *The Bonfire of the Vanities* and Stephen King's *Cat's Eye* (ironically, given his cause of death, in the "Quitters, Inc." episode), and he was a producer on *Wolfen*.

Fifty-five-year-old R&B singer and songwriter **John Whitehead**, who had a disco hit in 1979 with "Ain't No Stoppin' Us Now" with Gene McFadden, was shot dead while working on a vehicle in a Philadelphia street on May 11th. Police had no suspects or motive.

Billed as "The British Bombshell", actress **Anna Lee** MBE (Joan Boniface Winnifrith) died of pneumonia in Los Angeles on May 14th, aged 91. Reputedly a goddaughter of both Sir Arthur Conan Doyle and Dame Sybil Thorndike, in 1933 she married director Robert Stevenson who, three years later, gave her her first leading role opposite Boris Karloff in *The Man Who Changed His Mind* (US: *The Man Who Lived Again*). After she appeared in *The Passing of the Third Floor Back* and *King Solomon's Mines* (1937), the couple moved to Hollywood in 1939, where Lee appeared in such films as *Flesh and Fantasy*, *Bedlam* (again with Karloff), *The Ghost and Mrs Muir*, *Jack the Giant Killer*, *Whatever Happened to Baby Jane?*, *Picture Mommy Dead* and *In Like Flint*. Paralysed from the waist down following a car accident, for twenty-five years she played matriarch Lila Quartermaine from a wheelchair on the daytime soap opera *General Hospital*, until she was unceremoniously fired by ABC-TV in 2003 in an effort to cut costs. Her third and final marriage was to novelist Robert Nathan (from 1970 until his death in 1985).

Spanish character actor **Narcisco Ibáñez Menta** died on May 15th, aged 91. His many credits include *Witchcraft* (1954), *Master of Terror*, *El Fantasma de la Opera* (which he also directed), *The Dracula Saga* (as the Count) and *Return of the Wolfman*. He was the father of director and producer Chicho Ibáñez-Serrador (*Island of Death*).

Egyptian-born German film star **Marika Rokk** (Marie Karoline Rokk), who appeared in the 1933 British production of *The Ghost Train*, died of heart failure in Austria on May 16th, aged 90.

Singer, actress and songwriter **June Carroll** died of Parkinson's disease the same day, aged 86. She appeared in *An Angel Comes to Brooklyn* and was the mother of genre author Jonathan Carroll.

Urbane stage and screen actor **Tony Randall** (Arthur Leonard

Rosenberg) died in his sleep on May 17th due to complications from pneumonia following heart surgery. He was 84. Best remembered for his Emmy Award-winning role as the obsessive Felix Unger opposite Jack Klugman's slovenly Oscar Madison on ABC-TV's *The Odd Couple* (1970–75), his film credits include *The Brass Bottle*, *7 Faces of Dr Lao*, *The Alphabet Murders* (as Hercule Poirot), *Hello Down There*, *Everything You Always Wanted to Know About Sex* *But Were Afraid to Ask*, *King of Comedy* and *Gremlins 2 The New Batch* (as the voice of "Brain Gremlin"). On TV, Randall co-starred opposite Boris Karloff in NBC's "Hallmark Hall of Fame" production of *Arsenic and Old Lace* in 1962. Broadway dimmed its lights in memory of the actor.

American character actor **Lincoln Kilpatrick** died of lung cancer on May 18th, aged 73. He appeared in *Brother John*, *The Omega Man*, *Soylent Green*, *Chosen Survivors*, *Fortress* and the TV movies *Dr Scorpion* and the remake of *Piranha* (1995).

Forty-four-year-old TV actor **Richard Biggs**, best known for his portrayal of Dr Stephen Franklin on the SF series *Babylon 5* for five years, died of an apparent stroke shortly after waking up at his home on May 22nd. He also appeared in episodes of *Twilight Zone*, *Touched by an Angel* and *Tremors*.

Canadian-born character actor **Austin Willis** also died in May, aged 86. His credits include *The Mouse That Roared*, *Goldfinger*, *Dr Frankenstein on Campus*, *The Boston Strangler*, *Firefox* and the TV movie *Death Takes a Holiday*. His first wife was actress Kate Reid.

Aloha Porter, who portrayed the Devil in the 1935 film *Dante's Inferno*, died on June 1st, aged 93. He also appeared *in The Campus Vamp* and *Thirteen Women*.

Sixty-nine-year-old Mexican comic actor and director **Sergio Ramos** "El Comanche" died June 2nd of kidney failure related to diabetes. Since 1965 he appeared in more than 125 films and TV productions, including *Santo contra la invasion de los Marci*, *Mi fantasma y yo* and the 1985 movie *Chiqui Dracula* (Little Dracula).

British character actor **Harold Goodwin**, who played the burglar surprised by a masked Peter Cushing in the opening scenes of *Frankenstein Must Be Destroyed*, died on June 3rd, aged 86. His other credits for Hammer include *The Mummy* (1959), *The Ugly Duckling*, *The Phantom of the Opera* (1961), *The Terror of the Tongs* and *The Curse of the Mummy's Tomb*, along with *The Man in the White Suit*, *Die Monster Die!*, *Jabberwocky* and TV's *Quatermass and the Pit*.

Ronald [Wilson] **Reagan**, the Hollywood actor who was the former Republican Governor of California and became the 40th President of the United States (1981–89), died of Alzheimer's disease and complications from pneumonia on June 5th, aged 93. He had suffered from the illness for nearly a decade. His credits include *Secret Service of the Air*, *Code of the Secret Service*, *Bedtime for Bonzo* and *The Killers*. He also appeared in news footage in *The Atomic Café*, *Head*, *Brimstone*, *American Psycho*, *Alien Nation*, *Witch Hunt* and *Faces of Death 2*. His first wife was actress Jane Wyman in 1940, and in 1952 he married Nancy Davis, who became First Lady. He survived an allegedly *Taxi Driver*-inspired assassination attempt when he was wounded in a 1981 shooting incident by drifter John Hinckley.

Italian actor **Anthony Steffen** (Antonio de Teffe) died of cancer in Rio de Janeiro the same day, aged 73. He began his film career in the 1950s as a studio messenger for Vittorio de Sica, before making his name as the phantom gunslinger in the spaghetti Western *Django the Bastard* (which he also co-wrote). His other credits include *The Invincible Maciste Brothers*, *An Angel for Satan* (with Barbara Steele), *The Night Evelyn Came Out of the Grave*, *The Crimes of the Black Cat* and *Killer Fish*.

American character actor **Jimmie F. Skaggs** died on June 6th of lung cancer, aged 59. Part Choctaw Indian, his credits include *Ghost Dad*, *Ghost Town*, *Puppet Master*, *Solar Crisis*, *Oblivion*, *Oblivion 2*, *Hollow Man*, *Dead End* and episodes of *Buffy the Vampire Slayer*, *Twilight Zone*, *The Flash* and *Star Trek: Deep Space Nine*.

R&B and gospel singer **Ray Charles** [Robinson] died of complications from acute liver disease on June 10th, aged 73. He released more than 600 songs on sixty-five albums, and his hits include "Georgia on My Mind", "Hit the Road Jack", "What'd I Say" and "I Can't Stop Loving You". Diagnosed with congenital juvenile glaucoma when he was seven years old growing up in poverty in west Florida, the blind musician battled marijuana and heroin addiction in the 1960s. He was married twice and fathered eleven children. He sang the theme song of ABC-TV's *Three's Company*, appeared in *The Blues Brothers*, *Spy Hard* and *Limit Up* (as God), and he was portrayed by Jamie Foxx in the 2004 biopic *Ray*. Charles' 1978 autobiography was titled *Brother Ray*.

Graeme Kelling, guitarist with the Scottish group Deacon Blue, died of a tumour of the pancreas the same day, aged 47. During the late 1980s and early '90s, he played on such hits as "Real Gone Kid" and "Fergus Sings the Blues".

Radio announcer **Danny Dark** (Daniel Croskery) died on June

13th, aged 65. The voice-over announcer on such shows as *Bonanza* and *Bewitched*, he was also the voice of Clark Kent/Superman on the *Super-Friends* animated TV series.

Prolific American character actor **George "Buck" Flower** (aka "C.D. Lafleur") died on June 18th, aged 66. Usually featured in cameo roles (often playing a drunk), he appeared in more than 100 films, including *Ripper Man*, *Circuitry Man II*, *Tammy and the T-Rex*, *Skeeter*, *Warlock: Armageddon*, *Munchie*, *Waxwork II Lost in Time*, *Sundown The Vampire in Retreat*, *The Dead Don't Die*, *Escape from New York*, *They Live*, *Starman*, *Village of the Damned*, *The Fog*, *Escape from New York*, *Ilsa She Wolf of the SS*, *Ilsa Harem-Keeper of the Oil Sheiks*, *Sorority Babes in the Slimeball-Bowl-o-Rama*, *Back to the Future*, *Back to the Future Part II*, *Pumpkinhead*, *Spontaneous Combustion*, *Maniac Cop*, *Puppet Master II*, *976-EVIL*, *Wishmaster*, *The Nightstalker* (1987), *The Capture of Bigfoot*, *The Time Machine* (1978), *The Alpha Incident*, *The Witch Who Came from the Sea* and *Bates Motel*. He also worked behind the camera in various capacities on such productions as *Teenage Seductress*, *Takin' it All Off* and *Hell's Belles*.

Hollywood supporting actress **Doris Dowling**, the sister of actress Constance Dowling, died of a series of strokes the same day, aged 81. Best known for her role as Ray Milland's bar-room pick-up in *The Lost Weekend* and Alan Ladd's murdered wife in *The Blue Dahlia*, she also appeared as Bianca in Orson Welles' *Othello*. On TV she starred in the 1964 series *My Living Doll* and guest-starred in episodes of *Wonder Woman* and *The Incredible Hulk*. Married three times, from 1952–56 she was the seventh of bandleader Artie Shaw's eight wives.

Actor **Peter Blythe** died after a short illness on June 27th, aged 69. He appeared in Hammer's *Frankenstein Created Woman*, *Jane Eyre* (1970) and *Merlin and the Sword*. His TV credits include *The Avengers*, *UFO* and the "No Such Thing as a Vampire" episode of *Late Night Horror*.

Considered by some to be America's finest screen actor, two-time Academy Award winner **Marlon Brando** (Marlon Brandeau, Jr.) died of lung failure on July 1st, aged 80. He was diagnosed with pneumonia in 2002 and could only breathe with the aid of an oxygen cylinder. Best known as a proponent of the "Method" school of acting since making his film debut in 1950, his best films include *A Streetcar Named Desire*, *On the Waterfront*, *The Godfather* and as a rebellious motorcycle gang leader in *The Wild One* (banned in the UK for twelve years). In later years the often eccentric performer openly derided his public and professional image, allowed his weight to balloon to more than 350lb, and encouraged a reputation for being difficult to work with. Although his crazed Colonel Kurtz in Francis Coppola's *Apocalypse Now* was a rare latter triumph, more typical projects included *The Nightcomers*, an odd prequel to Henry James' ghost story *Turn of the Screw*; *The Formula*, and the underrated 1996 version of H.G. Wells' *The Island of Dr Moreau*. He reportedly received $3.7 million for a few days work as Jor-El on *Superman* (1978), and a month before his death he recorded vocal tracks for the animated film *Big Bug Man*. His 1972 Oscar for Best Actor was collected on his behalf by actress Sasheen Littlefeather as a protest against Hollywood's treatment of Native Americans. Brando fathered at least eleven children with four women, and his son Christian was sentenced to ten years in jail for the 1990 shooting of Dag Drollet, the Tahitian fiancé of his pregnant half-sister Cheyenne. She in turn committed suicide in April 1995, after three previous attempts. Although one of the highest-paid actors of his generation, Brando spent his fortune on his son's legal bills and a bitter palimony dispute. He was widely reported to be broke and living on social security and a pension from the Screen Actors Guild at the time of his death, and his ashes were scattered on the island of Tahiti and in California's Death Valley. The actor's autobiography, *Songs My Mother Taught Me*, was published in 1994.

American character actor and TV writer **Frank Chase**, best known for his Western roles, died on July 2nd, aged 80. He also appeared in *The Creature Walks Among Us*, *Beginning of the End* and *Attack of the 50 Foot Woman* (1958).

British character actor **John Barron** died on July 3rd, aged 83. Best known for his later comedy roles, he also guest-starred in such TV shows as *Plateau of Fear*, *Out of the Unknown*, *The Avengers*, *Timeslip* and *Ace of Wands*. He was a regular on *Doomwatch* (1970–72) as The Minister, and his film appearances include *The Day the Earth Caught Fire* (uncredited), *Incense for the Damned* (US: *Bloodsuckers*) and *Whoops Apocalypse*.

Forty-six-year-old stand-up comedian and bit-part actor **Eric** [Anthony] **Douglas**, the youngest son of Kirk and half-brother to Michael, was found dead of acute intoxication in his Manhattan apartment on July 6th. He had spent years battling drug and alcohol addictions. He was sentenced to a month in jail after an air-rage incident on a 1996 cross-country flight and pleaded guilty in 1997 to cocaine possession. The younger Douglas appeared opposite his father in the 1991 HBO pilot *Two-Fisted Tales*, based on the EC comic book. After small roles in such films as *The Golden Child* and *Delta Force 3: The Killing Game*, he gave up acting to try his hand at comedy and song-writing.

Hollywood actress and former model **Dorothy Hart** died of complications from Alzheimer's disease on July 11th, aged 82. Her credits include *Down to Earth*, *I Was a Communist for the F.B.I.* and *Tarzan's Savage Fury* (as Jane).

Fifty-five-year-old punk rock star **Arthur "Killer" Kane**, bassist with the 1970s band New York Dolls, died in a Los Angeles hospital of complications from pneumonia and leukaemia on July 13th. The alcoholic Kane was named after a character in *Buck Rogers* and had been working for the Mormon Church. He was predeceased by three other band members.

Former British and European heavyweight wrestling champion turned stuntman-actor **Pat** (Patrick) **Roach**, died of throat cancer on July 17th, aged 67. After making his film debut as a Cuban bouncer in *A Clockwork Orange*, he appeared in Disney's *The Spaceman and King Arthur*, *Clash of the Titans*, *Never Say Never Again*, *Conan*, *Conan the Destroyer* (playing Thoth-Amon and two other roles), *Red Sonja*, *Willow*, *Kull the Conqueror* and the *Indiana Jones* trilogy (as four different characters). In 1976, Roach was auditioned for the role of Darth Vader in *Star Wars*.

Former ballerina and model **Georgine Darcy**, who played "Miss Torso", one of the objects of James Stewart's voyeuristic obsession in Alfred Hitchcock's *Rear Window* (1954), died on July 18th aged somewhere between 68 and 71. Her other film credits include *Don't Knock the Rock*, *Women and Bloody Terror* and *The Delta Factor*.

Dependable German-born British character actor [Manfred] **Frederick Jaeger** died after a long illness in Spain the same day, aged 76. His film credits include *The Seven-Per-Cent Solution* and he appeared in three episodes of TV's *The Avengers* during the 1960s, *The New Avengers*, *Doomwatch*, *Jason King*, *Out of the Unknown*, *One Step Beyond* and three episodes of *Doctor Who* (including playing the creator of robot dog "K-9"). He retired in 1996.

Suave French singer **Sacha Distel** died after a long illness on July 22nd, aged 71. A former jazz guitarist who had a brief but high-profile relationship with Brigitte Bardot in the late 1950s, his biggest hit was the 1970 cover of "Raindrops Keep Falling on My Head".

The last British silent movie star, **Joan Morgan**, died the same day, aged 99 or 105 (accounts vary). At the age of 16 she was offered a five-year contract starting at $100-a-week by Hollywood's Famous Players-Lasky, but her director father Sidney turned the offer down.

After appearing in such films as *The Cup Final Mystery* and *The Crimson Circle*, in later years Morgan reinvented herself as a playwright, screenwriter, novelist (under the pseudonym "Joan Wentworth Wood" in the 1930s) and property developer. Ivor Novello wrote the song "I Wonder Will My Dolly Miss Me?" for her.

Quorthon (Thomas Fosberg), co-founder of the "Black Metal" music group Bathory, died in Stockholm of heart failure in July. Fosberg and video director Jonas Akerlund created the band in the mid-1980s, and they are acknowledged as a major influence on artists such as Metallica, Marilyn Manson and Billy Corgan.

Meanwhile, four members of the Italian "Black Metal" group Beasts of Satan, led by a plumber named Nicolas, were charged in July with the murder of band-mates **Chiara Marino** and **Fabio Torris** in a drug-fuelled Satanic ritual.

Bass viola player **Abraham Luboff**, who played the memorable shark theme in *Jaws*, died on July 26th, aged 87.

Best known for the classic "It's a bird! It's a plane! It's Superman!" radio introduction, 92-year-old voice-over artist **Jackson Beck** died on July 28th from complications following a series of strokes suffered five years earlier. The son of silent film actor Max Beck, he not only narrated more than 1,600 episodes of the *Superman* radio show from 1943, but also played various characters including Beany, the *Daily Planet* copyboy. Beck also voiced such characters as the Cisco Kid and Philo Vance, he was the announcer for TV's *Tom Corbett, Space Cadet* and voiced the bully "Bluto" in over 300 *Popeye* cartoons from 1944–57.

American film and TV character actor **Eugene H. Roche** died of a heart attack the same day, aged 75. His credits include *Slaughterhouse-Five*, *They Might Be Giants*, *Oh God You Devil!*, *Crawlspace*, *The Last Halloween* and the TV movies *The Possessed*, *The Ghost of Flight 401*, *Airwolf* and *Roswell*. He also appeared as the "Ajax man" in TV commercials.

American character actor and voice artist **Sam Edwards** also died of a heart attack on July 28th, aged 89. A radio star during the 1930s, he voiced Thumper the rabbit in Disney's *Bambi* and sang "The Wonderful Thing About Tiggers" on the studio's record. He also voiced minor characters in *The Flintstones* and appeared in *Captain Midnight* and Disney's *Escape to Witch Mountain* (1975).

American leading lady **Virginia Grey** died of heart failure on July 31st, aged 87. She began her film career as a child in silent films directed by her father, Ray Grey, before becoming a notable MGM player. Her many credits include *Whistling in the Dark*, *Tarzan's*

New York Adventure, *House of Horrors* (with Rondo Hatton), *Unconquered* (with Boris Karloff), *Who Killed Doc Robbin?*, *Unknown Island*, *Jungle Jim*, *Target Earth!*, *Black Zoo* (with Michael Gough) and the TV movie *The Lives of Jenny Dolan*. She was at one time romantically linked to Clark Gable.

Seventy-year-old Italian actress and jazz singer **Laura Betti** (Laura Trombetti) died in Rome the same day of a heart attack following surgery. She was director Pier Paolo Pasolini's favourite actress and constant inspiration, and she championed his memory after his murder in 1975. Her films include *La Dolce Vita*, *The Witches* (1965), *Teorema*, Mario Bava's *A Hatchet for the Honeymoon* and *Twitch of the Death Nerve*, and the TV movie *The Word*.

"Punk-funk" singer, songwriter and record producer **Rick James** (James Ambrose Johnson, Jr.), "the bad boy of Motown", died in his sleep on August 6th, aged 56. Best known for his 1981 hit "Super Freak" (which was sampled by MC Hammer on his 1990 song "U Can't Touch This"), the diabetic James had a pacemaker and a history of cocaine addiction.

Canadian-born Hollywood star **Fay Wray** (Vina Fay Wray) died in her Manhattan apartment on August 8th, aged 96. The lights of the Empire State Building were dimmed for fifteen minutes in her honour. Forever remembered as Ann Darrow, the object of the giant ape's adoration in the classic *King Kong* (1933), she also appeared in such films as Erich von Stroheim's silent classic *The Wedding March* (1928), *Dirigible*, *Doctor X*, *The Mystery of the Wax Museum*, *The Vampire Bat*, *The Most Dangerous Game* (UK: *The Hounds of Zaroff*), *Black Moon*, *Bulldog Jack*, *The Clairvoyant* (US: *The Evil Mind*), *Rock Pretty Baby* and *Dragstrip Riot*. Her first husband, John Monk Saunders, the first writer to receive an Academy Award, killed himself after they were divorced. Wray reportedly declined an offer to appear in a small role in the 1976 remake of *King Kong* because she disliked the script. Her 1989 autobiography was entitled *On the Other Hand*.

Vaudeville comedian **Paul** "Mousie" **Garner** died the same day, aged 95. He was believed to be the last survivor amongst those who played one of The Three Stooges. He replaced Shemp Howard for a while in 1930 and, along with Jack Wolf and Dick Hakins, took the place of the original team on Broadway the following year. The latter trio later changed their name to "The Gentlemaniacs". Garner toured with nine different Stooges and during the 1970s appeared with "Curly" Joe DeRita and Frank Mitchell in the comedy team's final incarnation. He had roles in *Gift of the Gab* (with Karloff and Lugosi), *Saturday the 14th*, *Avenging Angel*, *Stoogemania*, *Radio-*

land Murders and such TV series as *The Munsters*, *The Monkees*, *Get Smart* and *I Dream of Jeannie*. Garner was also involved with satirical musical group Spike Jones and his City Slickers.

Eighty-four-year-old retired US Air Force general **Charles W. Sweeney**, pilot of the plane that dropped the atomic bomb "Fat Man" on Nagasaki on August 9th, 1945, died on July 16th. Sweeney was 25 years old when he flew the B-29 bomber mission in World War II. Japan surrendered six days afterwards.

British character actor **Peter Woodthorpe** died on August 12th, aged 72. Best known for his stage work in the original productions of *Waiting for Godot* and *The Caretaker*, his film credits include Hammer's *Hysteria* and *The Evil of Frankenstein* (as the evil hypnotist Zoltan), *The Skull*, the animated *The Lord of the Rings* (1978, as the voice of Gollum) and TV's *A Christmas Carol* (1984), *Jane Eyre* (1996), *Tale of Sweeney Todd*, *The Odyssey* and *Merlin*. Woodthorpe played Quasimodo in the 1965 TV version of *The Hunchback of Notre Dame*. He also voiced "Pigsy" in the dubbed Japanese TV series *Monkey* and Gollum again for the thirteen-hour BBC Radio adaptation of *The Lord of the Rings* in 1981.

Exotic leading lady of the 1940s **Acquanetta** (Burnu Acquanetta/ Mildred Davenport) died in an Arizona care centre of complications from Alzheimer's disease on August 16th, aged 83. Best known as "Paula Dupree", the Ape Woman in Universal's *Captive Wild Woman* and *Jungle Woman*, "the Venezuelan Volcano" (who was apparently born on a Arapaho Indian reservation in Wyoming) also appeared in *Arabian Nights* (1942), the "Inner Sanctum" mystery *Dead Man's Eyes*, *Tarzan and the Leopard Woman* and *The Lost Continent* (1951). The former New York fashion model subsequently married a car dealer and moved to Arizona.

British character actor **Hugh Manning** died on August 18th, aged 83. He had small roles in Hammer's *Quatermass and the Pit*, *The House That Dripped Blood* and *The Elephant Man*.

Silent film child star **Charles Eaton** died on August 22nd, aged 94. He performed on stage with the Ziegfeld Follies and made his movie debut in 1921. He was in the 1929 talkie *The Ghost Talks* and *The Phantom Strikes*.

Eighty-one-year-old announcer **Al Dvorin**, credited with saying "Elvis has left the building," was killed in an automobile accident near Ivanpah, California, the same day.

American "B" movie actress **Lyn Thomas**, who starred in *Space Master X-7* (1958), died of lung cancer on August 26th, aged 74.

Grammy nominated singer **Laura Branigan**, best known for her

1982 hit "Gloria", died of a brain aneurysm the same day, aged 47. A former back-up singer for Leonard Cohen, her songs were used in *Flashdance* and *Ghostbusters*, and she recorded a duet with David Hasselhoff in 1994 for the soundtrack of *Baywatch*. Branigan also appeared in episodes of the TV series *Automan* and *Monsters*, and she reportedly had an affair with William Friedkin (who directed her video for "Self Control") while he was still married to actress Lesley-Anne Down.

American actress **Suzanne Kaaren** [Blackmer] best known for her role opposite Bela Lugosi in *The Devil Bat* (1940), died of complications from pneumonia on August 27th, aged 92. She also appeared in Tod Browning's final film *Miracles for Sale*, *Phantom Ranger*, *The Ghost Comes Home*, *I Married an Angel* and a number of *Three Stooges* shorts. She married actor Sidney Blackmer in 1943, and in later years won a lengthy legal battle against Donald Trump, who wanted to raise the cost of her rent-controlled New York apartment.

KTLA Los Angeles newscaster **Larry McCormick** died the same day after a long illness, aged 71. He appeared (often as a newsman) in *The Punisher* (1989), *Terminator 3: Rise of the Machines*, and the TV movie *The Murder of Sherlock Holmes*.

American actress **Susan Peretz** died of breast cancer also on August 27th, aged 59. Her credits include *Oh God You Devil!* and *Poltergeist II The Other Side*.

Carl Wayne (Colin Tooley), lead singer of The Move, died of cancer of the oesophagus on August 31st, aged 61. The group's hit "Flowers in the Rain" launched BBC Radio 1 in 1967, and he also sang the theme song for *Percy's Progress*. Wayne's £1.4 million estate was apparently the result of advertising jingles, TV roles and starring in the West End musical *Blood Brothers*.

French actor **Serge Marquand** died of leukaemia on September 4th, aged 74. His numerous credits include Roger Vadim's *Blood and Roses*, *Tintin and the Mystery of the Golden Fleece*, *Spirits of the Dead*, *Barbarella*, *Quartet*, *Les Raisins de la Morte* and *Frankenstein 90*.

German-born **Tiny Doll** (Elly Ann Schneider/Tiny Earles), the last surviving member of the Doll family, died of heart failure on September 6th, aged 90. Along with her siblings, Frieda, Kurt and Hilda (who changed their names to Grace, Harry and Daisy Earles in the 1920s), the 3-foot, 6-inch midget actress appeared in Tod Browning's *Freaks* and played a Munchkin in *The Wizard of Oz*. After decades of touring with various circuses, the family retired in 1960.

Thirty-two-year-old British actress **Fritha Goodey** was found dead of multiple stab wounds at her home in London on September 8th. Several notes were reportedly found, and the police did not suspect foul play. Best known for her role as Hugh Grant's ex-girlfriend in *About a Boy*, she also appeared in the TV movie *Case of Evil* (a.k.a. *Sherlock*) and an episode of the revived TV series *Randall & Hopkirk (Deceased)*.

British stage and TV actor **Glyn** [Griffith] **Owen** died of cancer on September 10th, aged 76. A former London policeman, he made his television debut in *The Trollenberg Terror* for the BBC in 1956 and appeared in episodes of *Doctor Who*, *Doomwatch*, *Survivors*, *The Invisible Man*, *Out of This World* and *Blake's 7*.

Fifty-three-year-old **Norman** "Dinky" **Diamond**, former drummer with the 1970s pop group Sparks, hanged himself in the loft of his Berkshire home on September 10th because his neighbour played her music too loud. Diamond performed on three Sparks albums, including such hits as "This Town Ain't Big Enough for the Both of Us" and "Never Turn Your Back on Mother Earth".

Following in the steps of Joey and Dee Dee, who died in 2001 and 2002 respectively, 55-year-old **Johnny Ramone** (John Cummings), lead guitarist with the influential New York punk band The Ramones, died in his sleep after a five year battle with prostate cancer on September 15th. The band recorded sixteen albums and their hits include "I Wanna Be Sedated" and "Sheena is a Punk Rocker".

Izora Rhodes Armstead, one half of the signing duo The Weather Girls, who had a novelty disco hit in Britain with "It's Raining Men" in 1984, died of heart failure on September 16th, aged around 62.

American actor **Tim Choate**, best known for his recurring role as the alien "Zathras" on TV's *Babylon 5* (1994–97), was killed in a motorcycle accident in Los Angeles on September 24th, aged 49. His other credits include *Ghost Story* (as the younger incarnation of Fred Astaire's character), *Blow Out*, *DefCon 4*, *Not of This Earth* (1991), *Creep Tales* and the TV movie *Blind Witness* (1989).

American musical-comedy actor **Ignatius** "Iggie" **Wolfington** died on September 30th, aged 84. His film credits include *Herbie Rides Again*, *The Strongest Man in the World*, *Telefon*, *Hex*, *The Legend of Lizzie Borden* and Steven Spielberg's *1941*.

Fifty-eight-year-old former topless actress turned celebrity astrologer **Joyce Jillson** died of kidney failure on October 1st. After appearing in such films as *Superchick*, *Slumber Party '57* and *The Happy Hooker Goes to Washington*, as the official astrologer for Twentieth Century Fox she chose the opening day for *Star Wars*. The silicone-breasted blonde, whose forecasts ran in more than 200 newspapers around the world, had a Los Angeles TV show, an 800-telephone number for zodiac readings, and advised US president Ronald Reagan to only give press conferences during full moons.

Canadian-born **Bruce Palmer**, the original bassist with 1960s band Buffalo Springfield, died of a heart attack the same day, aged 58.

Janet Leigh (Jeanette Helen Morrison), best known for playing Norman Bates' shower victim "Marion Crane" in Alfred Hitchcock's *Psycho* (1960), died on October 3rd, aged 77. She had been suffering from vasculitis, an inflammation of the blood vessels. Discovered by actress Norma Shearer in 1947, her other credits include *Angels in the Outfield* (1951), *Prince Valiant* (1954), *Touch of Evil*, *The Vikings*, *The Manchurian Candidate* (1962), *Hello Down There*, *The Spy in the Green Hat*, *The Monk*, *Night of the Lepus* and the TV movie *The Deadly Dream*. Leigh was married to her third husband, actor Tony Curtis, from 1951–62, and starred opposite their daughter, Jamie Lee Curtis, in both *The Fog* and *Halloween H20: 20 Years Later*. She published her autobiography *There Really Was a Hollywood* in 1984, and her book *Psycho: Behind the Scenes in the Classic Thriller* appeared in 1995.

American comedian **Rodney Dangerfield** (Jacob Cohen) died on October 4th, aged 82. He had undergone heart valve replacement surgery on August 25th but, after suffering from a small stroke and then infection and complications, was unable to recover. He briefly awoke from a coma the week he died. Best known for such hit comedies as *Caddyshack* and *Back to School*, his other films include *The Projectionist*, the animated *Rover Dangerfield*, *Natural Born Killers*, *Casper* and *Little Nicky*. Dangerfield was credited with launching the careers of many well-known comics, including Jim Carrey, Tim Allen, Roseanne Barr and Jerry Seinfeld. His 2004 autobiography was titled *It's Not Easy Bein' Me: A Lifetime of No Respect, but Plenty of Sex and Drugs*.

Fifty-two-year-old **Christopher Reeve**, who starred as The Man of Steel in four films during the late 1970s and '80s, died of heart failure on October 10th. Nine years earlier he had been left paralysed from the shoulders down by a horse riding accident, and he became a world-wide advocate for the rights of the disabled and a campaigner for controversial stem cell research. Reeve had been suffering from a pressure wound that had become severely infected, and he fell into a coma after having a heart attack the day before he died. Along with *Superman* (1978) and its three numerical sequels, Reeve also starred in *Somewhere in Time* (based on the novel by Richard Matheson), *Deathtrap*, John Carpenter's 1995 remake of *Village of the Damned*, and the 1998 TV remake of *Rear Window* (which he also directed). More recently he guest-starred in two episodes of the revisionist Superboy TV series *Smallville* as enigmatic scientist "Dr Virgil Swann". Reeve's 1998 autobiography was entitled *Still Me*.

Scottish-born character actress **Sheila Keith**, the closest thing Britain had to a female horror star, died on October 14th, aged 84. During the 1970s she appeared in such low budget exploitation films for Peter Walker as *Frightmare*, *House of Whipcord*, *House of Mortal Sin* (US: *The Confessional*) and *The Comeback* (US: *The Day the Screaming Stopped*). As a reflection of her cult status, she co-starred with Vincent Price, Christopher Lee, Peter Cushing and John Carradine in Walker's *House of the Long Shadows*, and her last appearance was in an episode of Steve Coogan's 2001 BBC-TV series *Dr Terrible's House of Horrible* ("And Now the Fearing . . .").

African-American actor **Julius W. Harris** died of heart failure on October 17th, aged 81. Best remembered for his role as the evil pincerhanded "Tee Hee" in the 1973 James Bond film *Live and Let Die*, his more than 100 other credits include *Shaft's Big Score!*, *King Kong* (1976), *Looking for Mr Goodbar*, *Mystique*, *The Enchanted*, *Darkman*, *Maniac Cop 3*, *Shrunken Heads*, *Harley Davidson and the Marlboro Man* and episodes of TV's *The Incredible Hulk*, *Voyagers!* and *Amazing Stories*.

Betty Hill, who with her husband Barney was allegedly abducted by a UFO in 1961, died of cancer the same day, aged 85. She was played by actress Estelle Parsons in the TV movie *The UFO Incident* and also appeared as a character in the series *Dark Skies*.

Eighty-one-year-old actress **Katherine Victor** (Katena Ktenavea, aka Katherin Victor), best known for her roles in Jerry Warren's bargain basement horrors, died following a stroke on October 22nd. After making her debut in *Mesa of Lost Women*, she starred in Warren's *Teenage Zombies*, *Curse of the Stone Hand*, *Creature of the Walking Dead*, *Wild World of Bat Woman* and *Frankenstein Island*. Other credits include *Cape Canaveral Monsters*, *House of Black Death* and the TV movie *Fear No Evil*. Her final screen appearance was in *Superguy: Behind the Cape* (2002). For forty years, beginning in 1960, she worked as an animation checker for such cartoon studios as Hanna-Barbera, DePatie-Freleng, Filmation, Don Bluth and Walt Disney TV Animation.

Influential British radio disc jockey **John Peel** OBE (John Robert Parker Ravenscroft) died of a heart attack on October 25th in Cuzco, Peru. He was 65. The Liverpool-born Peel began his career in the early 1960s in America, before returning to the UK in 1967 to work for offshore pirate radio stations. That same year he joined BBC Radio One on a six-week contract and never left.

Hollywood dancer and actress **Peggy Ryan**, who as a teenager often tap-danced on screen with Donald O'Connor, died from two strokes on October 30th, aged 80. Her film credits include *That's the Spirit* and *Shamrock Hill*.

Sixty-one-year-old disc jockey and singer **Terry Knight**, who managed and produced the band Grand Funk Railroad, was stabbed to death by his daughter's boyfriend on November 1st during a domestic dispute in the Texas apartment all three shared.

Eighty-four-year-old **Ed Kemmer**, who starred as "Commander Buzz Corry" of the 30th Century on the live ABC-TV series *Space Patrol* (1950–55), died in New York City on November 5th after suffering a stroke. Kemmer, who was initially paid just $8.00 a show, also appeared in the movies *Giant from the Unknown* and *Earth vs. the Spider*, and he played the pilot who tried to calm down William Shatner in the classic *Twilight Zone* episode "Nightmare at 20,000 Feet".

American keyboardist **Pete Jolly** (Peter Ceragioli, Jr.) died of bone marrow cancer on November 6th, aged 72. As well as touring with the Pete Jolly Trio since 1964, he also contributed to the themes for such TV series as *Get Smart*, *The Love Boat* and *I Spy*.

American film and stage star **Howard Keel** (Harold Clifford Leek, aka "Harold Keel"), best known for his musical and Western roles, died of colon cancer on November 7th, aged 87. He appeared in the Rodgers & Hammerstein musical *Carousel* on stage in both the US and UK, and starred in the Arabian Nights musical *Kismet* and the 1963 film of John Wyndham's *The Day of the Triffids*. Later in his career he guest-starred in an episode of *Fantasy Island* and portrayed "Clayton Farlow" on the hit TV series *Dallas* for ten years.

Stage and screen actor **Norman Rose** died after a brief illness on November 12th, aged 87. Best known for more than a decade as the voice of Juan Valdez in the TV coffee commercials, his credits include *Pinocchio in Outer Space* and *Message from Space*. He narrated a radio adaptation of Ray Bradbury's *The Martian Chronicles* and was the voice of God in Woody Allen's movie *Love and Death*.

Thirty-five-year-old **Russell T. Jones**, better known as rapper "O.D.B." (Ol' Dirty Bastard), "Osirus" and "Big Baby Jesus", a founding member of the Wu-Tang Clan, died of the combined effects of cocaine and the painkiller Tramadol after collapsing with chest pains inside a Manhattan recording studio on November 13th. He had recently completed a prison sentence for drug possession and was posthumously featured in a three-episode reality TV show. He had children with eight different mothers.

Hollywood swimming stuntwoman **Patricia Dean Hulsman**, whose credits include *The Creature from the Black Lagoon*, died on November 16th, aged 81.

Actress **Marion Schilling**, who toured with Bela Lugosi in the stage version of *Dracula*, died on November 18th, aged 93. Her film credits include *The Clutching Hand*, *Captured in Chinatown*, *A Shot in the Dark* and *The Red Rider*.

Comedian and actor **Dayton Allen**, best known as the voice of cartoon characters "Deputy Dawg" and "Heckle and Jeckle", died the same day after suffering a stroke. He was 85.

Scottish character actress **Molly Weir** (Mary Weir) died on November 28th, aged 94. She had suffered a bad fall four years earlier and was living in a nursing home. Having made her radio debut in 1939, the four-foot, ten-inch actress' film credits include *Hands of Orlac*, *What a Whopper!*, the 1970 musical *Scrooge*, Hammer's *Hands of the Ripper* and *One of Our Dinosaurs is Missing*. She portrayed Hazel the McWitch for four years on the 1980s TV series *Rentaghost*.

American actor **John Drew Barrymore** (aka John Blythe Barrymore, Jr.), the son of the legendary John Barrymore and Dolores Costello and reclusive father of Drew Barrymore, died of undisclosed causes on November 29th, aged 72. In a wasted career, he appeared in a number of "B" movies and Westerns in the 1950s. During the 1960s he starred in several Italian films, including *The Night They Killed Rasputin*, *Death on the Four-Poster*, *War of the Zombies*, *Les possedees du Demon* and *Weapons of Vengeance*. Barrymore battled alcohol and drug abuse for much of his life, and he retired from acting in the 1970s after a small role in *The Clones*.

Spanish actress **Maria Perschy** died of cancer on December 3rd, aged 66. She appeared in *The Mad Executioners*, *Witch Without a Broom*, *The Castle of Fu Manchu*, *Murders in the Rue Morgue* (1971), *The Hunchback of the Morgue*, *Exorcismo*, *The People Who Own the Dark*, *The House of Psychotic Women*, *Espectro del Terror* and *Horror of the Zombies*.

American actor **Carl Esmond**, who appeared in added scenes for *Kiss of Evil*, the TV version of Hammer's *Kiss of the Vampire*, died on December 4th, aged 97. His other credits include *The Catman of Paris*, *Mystery Submarine*, *From Earth to the Moon*, *Agent for H.A.R.M.* and the two-part TV show *Hardy Boys and Nancy Drew Meet Dracula*.

Jerry Scoggins, who sang the theme song to TV's *The Beverly Hillbillies*, died on December 7th, aged 93. He also appeared in a number of Western movies.

Thirty-eight-year-old heavy metal guitarist "Dimebag" **Darrell Abbott** was shot to death on stage in Columbus, Ohio, by a crazed fan on December 8th. The gunman, 25-year-old Nathan Gale, was apparently upset that Abbott had left Pantera to form his own band, Damageplan. The guitarist was shot six times at close range and three audience members were also killed before a police officer shot Gale to death. Abbott's music was featured in such films as *Tales from the Crypt: Demon Knight*, *Heavy Metal 2000*, *The Crow* and *Dracula 2000*.

Sixty-five-year-old Filipino superstar **Fernando** [Ronald Allan Kelley] **Poe, Jr.** (aka "FPJ") died on December 14th after suffering a stroke. Best known as the star, writer, director and cinematographer of the "Ang Panday" series, based on a comic book about a blacksmith who forges a magic sword, Poe also starred as action hero "Da King" in 282 films over forty-six years. An attempt to run for President of the Philippines in 2004 ended in failure.

Actor and stuntman **Frank Orsatti** died of acute respiratory failure on December 23rd, aged 61. His credits include *Planet of the Apes*, *Soylent Green*, *Rosemary's Baby*, *The Poseidon Adventure*, *The Beastmaster*, *Highlander II: The Quickening*, *The Terminator* and *Star Trek V: The Final Frontier*. As well as directing several episodes, he was stunt co-ordinator and Bill Bixby's stunt double on TV's *The Incredible Hulk*. Orsatti was also second unit director on the TV movie *Sherlock Holmes Returns*.

Country, rock and jazz guitarist [Walter] **Hank Garland** died of a staph infection on December 27th, aged 74. He started playing the guitar at the age of six and he worked with Elvis Presley from 1957–61 on such hits as "Little Sister" and "Big Hunk of Love". A suspicious car crash in 1961 put him in a coma for months, and the resultant injuries and more than 100 shock treatments left him a shadow of his former self. He also played with the Everly Brothers, Roy Orbison, Charlie Parker, Patsy Cline and many others.

American TV and film actor **Jerry Orbach** died of prostate cancer on December 28th, aged 69. Best known in recent years for his role as Detective Lennie Briscoe on NBC-TV's *Law & Order* and its spin-off *Trial by Jury*, his movie credits include *The Sentinel*, *F/X*, *Universal Soldier*, *Upworld* and Disney's *Beauty and the Beast* (as the voice of singing candelabrum "Lumiere"). He also appeared in episodes of TV's *Buck Rogers in the 25th Century* ("Space Rocker") and *Tales* *from the Darkside* ("Everybody Needs a Little Love"), and was a voice on *The Adventures of the Galaxy Rangers*.

Big band leader and clarinet player **Artie Shaw** (Arthur Arshawsky) died of complications from diabetes on December 30th, aged 94. He had a hit with Cole Porter's "Begin the Beguine" in 1938, followed by "Dancing in the Dark" and "Stardust". After a brief Hollywood career in the late 1930s and '40s, he retired in 1954 to take up writing full-time. His wives included actresses Lana Turner, Ava Gardner, Evelyn Keyes, and novelist Kathleen Winsor (*Forever Amber*).

FILM/TV TECHNICIANS

British-born film and television director **Brian Gibson** died in London on January 4th, aged 59. For two years he had been suffering from Ewing's sarcoma, a rare form of bone cancer. As well as working for the BBC and HBO, Gibson's film credits include *Breaking Glass* and *Poltergeist II The Other Side*.

American TV director **Allen Miner**, whose credits include episodes of *The Twilight Zone* and *Mission: Impossible*, died on the same day, aged 86.

Paul Cadeac, producer of the 1960s *Fantomas* films and the *OSS 117* sci-spy series, died of heart failure on January 8th, aged 86.

Eighty-seven-year-old American actor, songwriter and TV director **Sidney Miller** died on January 10th after a two-year bout with Parkinson's disease. A former contract actor at Metro-Goldwyn-Meyer and long-time comedy partner of Donald O'Connor, he directed episodes of *My Mother the Car*, *Get Smart*, *The Monkees*, *The Addams Family*, *Bewitched*, *My Favorite Martian* and more than a hundred *Mickey Mouse Club* shows.

Hollywood film producer **Ray Stark** died on January 17th, aged 88. He formed Seven Arts Productions in 1957 with Eliot Hyman and his own Rastar Productions in 1966. Among his many credits is *Somewhere in Time*, based on the novel *Bid Time Return* by Richard Matheson.

Film producer and sales executive **Harry Blum** died of heart failure on January 18th, aged 71. His credits include Brian De Palma's *Obsession*, *At the Earth's Core*, *The Magician of Lublin* and the 1976 Russian-American fairytale *The Blue Bird*.

Influential German fashion photographer **Helmut Newton** was killed on January 23rd when he lost control of his Cadillac outside the Chateau Marmont hotel in Los Angeles. The 83-year-old apparently suffered a heart attack at the wheel. His photography was featured in the 1978 thriller *The Eyes of Laura Mars*.

Director-producer **Andrew J. Kuehn**, credited with creating the modern motion picture trailer, died of lung cancer on January 29th, aged 66. As the founder of Kaleidoscope Films, he conceived the advertising campaigns for such films as *Jaws*, *E.T. The Extra-Terrestrial*, *The Exorcist*, *The Empire Strikes Back*, *Jaws 2*, *Aliens*, *Back to the Future*, *Jurassic Park* and the *Indiana Jones* trilogy. His other credits include the 1984 feature documentary *Terror in the Aisles* hosted by Donald Pleasence and Nancy Allen.

Prolific American TV director **Bernard McEveety** [Jr.] died on February 2nd, aged 79. After working as the assistant director on *The Return of Dracula* (1957), McEveety moved to episodic television, where he directed for such series as *Wild Wild West*, *Planet of the Apes*, *The Incredible Hulk*, *Buck Rogers in the 25th Century*, *Blue Thunder*, *Misfits of Science* and many others. In 1971 he returned to the big screen with *The Brotherhood of Satan*, starring Strother Martin and L.Q. Jones.

TV director **Larry Elikann**, whose credits include *The Haunted Mansion Mystery* and *The Big One: The Great Los Angeles Earthquake*, died on February 4th, aged 80.

Oscar-winning costume designer **Elois Jenssen** died on February 14th, aged 81. She was nominated for an Academy Award for her work on Disney's *Tron*, and she also designed for the TV series *My Living Doll* (1964–65) starring Julie Newmar.

Two-time Academy Award-winning film editor **Ralph E. Winters** died on February 26th, aged 94. The Canadian-born Winters co-edited *King Solomon's Mines*, plus *Ben-Hur*, *Gaslight* and *King Kong* (1976).

Dana Broccoli (Danjaq Natol) who, with her late husband Albert "Cubby" Broccoli, controlled the rights to the James Bond film franchise, died of cancer on February 29th, aged 82. As an actress, she played "Queen Bonga Bonga" opposite her previous husband Lewis Wilson in *Wild Women* (1951) and also appeared in *Moonraker*.

Canadian film producer and exhibitor **Nathan A. "Nat" Taylor**, the creator of the Multiplex movie theatre, died on March 1st, aged 97. He produced the 3-D horror film *The Mask* (aka *Eyes of Hell*, 1961), the first Canadian film to be distributed in the United States by a major studio. His other movie credits include *The Reincarnate*.

French film director **Rene Laloux**, best known for his 1973 animated film *La planete sauvage* (*Fantastic Planet*), died on March

14th, aged 75. His other credits include *Gandahar* and *Time Masters*.

Fifty-year-old American art designer **John Vallone** died as a result of a drowning accident on March 15th. He worked on *Star Trek The Motion Picture*, *Brainstorm*, *Streets of Fire*, *Predator* and the TV miniseries *Firestarter Rekindled*.

Film editor and actor **Fima Noveck**, who re-edited *Ganja and Hess* into the inferior *Blood Couple*, died on March 30th, aged 86.

Film director **H. Gordon Boos**, whose credits include *Red Surf*, died of brain cancer on April 3rd, aged 45.

Veteran British film editor **Ralph Kemplen** died on April 5th, aged 91. His many credits include the 1933 *The Ghoul* (with Boris Karloff), *Scrooge* (1935), *The Triumph of Sherlock Holmes*, *Man in the Mirror*, *Uncle Silas*, *Pandora and the Flying Dutchman* and *The Dark Crystal*.

American TV and film director **Allen Reisner** died of Alzheimer's disease on April 8th, aged 80. His numerous credits include episodes of *Twilight Zone*, *Night Gallery*, *Green Hornet*, *Great Ghost Tales* and *Tales of the Unexpected*.

Fifty-one-year-old **Micheline Charest**, the co-founder of Canada's children's TV production company Cinar (*Are You Afraid of the Dark?*, *Mona the Vampire*, etc.), died on April 14th from complications from plastic surgery.

Olga Druce, producer/director of the TV series *Captain Video* (1949–56), died on April 18th, aged 92. Her other credits include the *House of Mystery* and *Superman* radio shows.

Britain's top casting director, **Mary Selway**, died after a long battle with cancer on April 21st, aged 68. Her more than 100 films include *Death Line* (US: *Raw Meat*), *Alien*, *Superman*, *Rollerball*, *Flash Gordon*, *Ladyhawke*, *Aliens*, *Dracula* (1979), *Excalibur*, *Outland*, *Return of the Jedi*, *Raiders of the Lost Ark*, *Indiana Jones and the Temple of Doom*, *Gothic*, *Fairy Tale: A True Story*, *Lost in Space*, *Thunderbirds*, *Harry Potter and the Goblet of Fire* and *The Chronicles of Riddick*. She also produced the 1992 version of *Wuthering Heights*.

Italian cinematographer **Franco Delli Colli** died on April 22nd, aged 75. His numerous credits include *The Last Man on Earth* (with Vincent Price), *Frozen Terror*, *Revenge of the Dead*, *Rats*, *Night Child*, *Macabre* and *Ghosthouse*.

Pioneer children's TV producer **Lee Orgel** died of emphysema on May 12th, aged 78. As creative head of UPA Pictures, he produced the first animated prime-time network special, *Mr Magoo's Christ-*

mas Carol, and the musical cartoon feature *Gay Pur-ee*. Through his company Jomar Productions, Orgel developed *The New Adventures of the Three Stooges* and the *Abbott and Costello* cartoon TV series, and he scripted episodes of *Batman* and *Scooby-Doo Where Are You?*.

American producer-director **John Braden**, whose films include the low budget *The Day It Came to Earth* and *Revenge of Bigfoot*, died of pneumonia on May 22nd, aged 55.

Movie art director and production designer **Robert Burns**, whose credits include *The Texas Chain Saw Massacre* (1974), *The Hills Have Eyes*, *Tourist Trap*, *The Howling*, *Full Moon High*, *Demonoid*, *Don't Go Near the Park*, *Time Walker*, *Microwave Massacre*, *Mausoleum*, *Reanimator*, *Future-Kill*, *Play Dead*, *The Outing* and *Nightwish*, committed suicide by carbon monoxide poisoning on June 1st, aged 61. He had terminal cancer. An expert on actor Rondo Hatton, Burns starred in and designed *Confessions of a Serial Killer* (1985).

Ed DiGiulo, who received an Academy Award in 1978 for helping to develop the Steadicam camera, died of congestive heart failure on June 4th, aged 76. He worked closely with Stanley Kubrick on all his films from *A Clockwork Orange* onwards.

Former musician turned Emmy Award-winning cinematographer and TV director **Charles J. Correll** died of pancreatic cancer the same day, aged 60. As leader of The Corrells he had some regional instrumental hits and released an album of beach party music. After becoming a camera operator on *Dragnet*, he shot such films as *Star Trek III The Search for Spock* (in which he had a cameo), *Dr Scorpion* and the mini-series *The Dark Secret of Harvest Home*, and directed a number of made-for-television movies along with episodes of *Stargate SG-1* and *Seven Days*. His father was Andy Correll, of the infamous "Amos 'n' Andy" blackface radio team.

Special effects technician **Donald** [Edmund] "Pappy" **Trumbull**, winner of two Academy Awards for Scientific and Technical Achievement, died on June 7th, aged 95. A designer of process projection systems, motion control camera systems and special equipment for film production, he started his career as a special effects rigger of *The Wizard of Oz* (1939), and his subsequent credits (often working alongside his son, Douglas Trumbull) include *Silent Running*, *Star Wars*, *The Little Prince*, *Firefox*, *Star Trek The Motion Picture* and *Close Encounters of the Third Kind*. With John Dykstra and others he was a partner and chief engineer in Apogee Productions.

American-born film producer **Max J. Rosenberg**, the cousin of independent film-maker Doris Wishman, died in Los Angeles after a long illness on June 14th, aged 89. A former attorney and film distributor, in 1956 he teamed up with Milton Subotsky (who died in 1990) to produce the teen musical *Rock Rock Rock*. After having their idea for a *Frankenstein* remake bought out from under them by Hammer Films, the duo formed rival company Amicus Productions in the early 1960s and made a string of successful low budget horror and SF movies in Britain, including *City of the Dead* (US: *Horror Hotel*), *Dr Terror's House of Horrors*, *Dr Who and the Daleks*, *The Skull*, *The Psychopath*, *Daleks' Invasion Earth 2150 A.D.*, *The Deadly Bees*, *The Terrornauts*, *They Came from Beyond Space*, *Torture Garden*, *The Mind of Mr Soames*, *Tales from the Crypt*, *Asylum*, *Scream and Scream Again*, *The House That Dripped Blood*, *I Monster*, *Vault of Horror*, *—And Now the Screaming Starts!*, *Madhouse*, *The Beast Must Die*, *From Beyond the Grave*, *The Land That Time Forgot* and *At the Earth's Core*. After Rosenberg split with Subotsky in the 1970s, he produced *Welcome to Blood City*, *The Incredible Melting Man*, *Bloody Birthday*, the 1982 remake of *Cat People* and *Invasion Earth: The Aliens Are Here*. He also distributed Hammer's *The Satanic Rites of Dracula* and *Legend of the 7 Golden Vampires* in America.

Japanese film director **Noriaki Yuasa** (Noriaki Uyasa), who directed seven of the eight original *Gamera* films during the 1960s and '70s, died of a stroke the same day, aged 71.

American film producer **Dan Cracchiolo**, whose credits include *The Matrix*, also died of June 14th, from injuries sustained in a motorcycle accident in Los Angeles. He was 39. Cracchiolo was Joel Silver's assistant on HBO's *Tales from the Crypt* series and his other credits include *Demon Knight*, *Bordello of Blood*, *House on Haunted Hill* (2000) and *Thir13en Ghosts* (2001).

American TV director **Seymour Robbie** died on June 17th, aged 84. His numerous credits include episodes of *Lost in Space*, *Kolchak: The Night Stalker* and *Wonder Woman*.

Infuential Indian film producer **Yash Johar** died of chest congestion on June 26th, aged 76. Along with his own globe-trotting Bollywood productions, he was also associate producer on Disney's *The Jungle Book* (1994) and his company handled production services for Michael Bay's *Armageddon*.

Anthony J. "Tony" Hope, a former director of business affairs at Twentieth Century Fox and the eldest adopted son of Bob and Delores Hope, died on June 28th after a brief illness. He was 63 and in 1986 ran for Congress as a Republican in California.

Award-winning cable TV executive **Alexandra "Alex" Midden-dorf** died of Lou Gehrig's disease on June 29th, aged 52. Earlier in her career she was an actress and stuntwoman, and appeared as a Bond girl in *Moonraker*.

Italian cinematographer **Carlo Di Palma** died after a long illness on July 9th, aged 79. His credits include Michelangelo Antonioni's influential *Blowup*, *Terror Creatures from the Grave*, *The Monster* and eleven films with Woody Allen, including *Shadows and Fog* and *Manhattan Murder Mystery*.

Puppeteer **Peter Baird**, whose credits include *The Muppets Take Manhattan*, *Howard the Duck* and *Howling III*, died of oesophageal cancer on July 16th, aged 52.

Seventy-eight-year-old German-born film director **Irvin S.** (Shortness) "Shorty" **Yeaworth, Jr.** died in a single automobile accident in Jordan on July 19th. He reportedly fell asleep at the wheel. Yeaworth's credits include the cult favourites *The Blob* (1958), *4D Man* (aka *The Evil Force/Master of Terror*) and *Dinosaurus!*. He later became a tour guide in the Holy Land and was an expert in evangelical media presentations and motivational films (financed by Billy Graham).

British aerial cinematographer **Peter** [Leslie] **Allwork** died on July 30th, aged 76. The founder of Aerial Camera Systems (ACS), a leading supplier of specialized facilities to film and TV companies, his credits include Hitchcock's *Frenzy*, *The Land That Time Forgot*, the 1978 *Superman*, *Indiana Jones and the Last Crusade*, and such Bond films as *For Your Eyes Only*, *Never Say Never Again* and *A View to a Kill*.

Fifty-one-year-old film editor **Geraldine Peroni**, whose credits include *The Last Temptation of Christ* and the TV special *The Buried Secret of M. Night Shyamalan*, committed suicide on August 3rd.

Spanish film editor **Pablo Gonzalez del Amo**, who worked on *The Spirit of the Beehive*, *The Blood-Spattered Bride*, *Leonor* and *A Candle for the Devil*, died on August 4th, aged 77.

Mexican writer, producer and director **Ismael Rodriguez**, who co-directed *The Beast of Hollow Mountain* and *The Mighty Jungle*, died of renal failure on August 7th, aged 83. He also directed the surreal horror/comedy *Autopsia de un fantasma* starring Basil Rathbone, John Carradine and Cameron Mitchell.

American special effects supervisor **Martin Becker**, co-founder with Jim Gill of Reel Efx, Inc., died of pancreatic cancer on August 13th, aged 49. His numerous credits include *Star Trek II The Wrath of Khan*, *Friday the 13th II-VIII*, *April Fool's Day*, *Mac and Me*, *Suburban Commando* and *The Muppet Movie*.

Thirty-five-year-old **Neal** [Leslie] **Fredericks**, cinematographer of the influential 1999 independent hit *The Blair Witch Project*, was killed in a small plane crash on August 14th, while filming Daniel Zinilli's horror film *Cross Bones* off Key West, Florida. Fredericks was trapped in his camera harness and dragged underwater by the wreckage of the single-engine Cessna after the engine apparently failed. Four others on board escaped. His other credits include *Laughing Dead* (1998), *The Curse of the Blair Witch*, *The Shadow of the Blair Witch*, *The Massacre of the Burkittsville 7*, *The Blair Witch Legacy*, *Killer Me*, *Voodoo Tailz*, *The Legend of Diablo* and *Abominable*.

Actor, director and playwright **Charles Rome Smith**, co-founder of Ray Bradbury's Pandemonium Theatre Company, died of lung cancer on August 16th, aged 77. Beginning in 1965, Smith staged such adaptations of Bradbury's work as *The World of Ray Bradbury*, *The Wonderful Ice Cream Suit*, *Falling Upward!*, *Bradbury × 2*, *The October Country*, *Fahrenheit 451*, *Let's All Kill Constance* and *Next in Line*, which premiered in June 2004. Bradbury publicly acknowledged "The debt I owe this remarkable man".

Canadian-born film and TV producer/director **Daniel M. Petrie** [Sr.] died of cancer on August 21st, aged 83. The Emmy Award-winning director's credits include *The Neptune Factor*, *Sybil*, *Resurrection*, *Cocoon II The Return* and the TV movies *A Howling in the Woods* and *Moon of the Wolf*. In 1957 he directed Richard Burton as Heathcliff in a TV version of *Wuthering Heights*.

American cinematographer **David Myers** died of complications from a stroke on August 26th, aged 90. Best known for his work on such music documentaries as *Woodstock* and *The Last Waltz*, he also shot George Lucas' debut feature *THX1138*, *UFOria* and the TV specials *The Making of Star Wars* and *Mysterious Monsters*.

American-born studio executive, film producer and scriptwriter **Lawrence P. Bachmann**, died on September 7th, aged 92. After scripting such movies as *Fingers at the Window* and *Shadows on the Wall*, he moved to Britain in the 1960s, where he produced *Children of the Damned*, *Night Must Fall* (1964) and the "Miss Marple" series starring Margaret Rutherford for MGM.

Lester Berke, who directed *The Lost Missile*, died on September 17th. He worked as an assistant director on such TV series as *Thriller*, *The Munsters* and *Night Gallery*.

Legendary sexploitation filmmaker **Russ Meyer** (Russell Albion Mayer) died of complications from pneumonia on September 18th, aged 82. He had been suffering from dementia. Best known for his subversive softcore sex films of the 1960s and '70s such as *Vixen!*, *Beyond the Valley of the Dolls* (co-scripted with Roger Ebert), *Supervixens*, *Up*, and *Beneath the Valley of the Ultra-Vixens*, his other credits include *The Immoral Mr Teas* (banned in the UK until 1987), *Motor Psycho!*, *The Seven Minutes*, *Blacksnake* (aka *Sweet Suzy*) and the 1965 cult favourite *Faster Pussycat! Kill! Kill!* Married six times (including to *Playboy*'s first playmate Eve Turner and actress Edy Williams), Meyer's three-volume, boxed autobiography, *A Clean Breast: The Life and Loves of Russ Meyer*, was self-published in 1992 and cost $350 apiece.

Canadian-born film editor **Robert Lawrence**, best-known for cutting epics such as *Spartacus* and *El Cid*, died on September 19th, aged 90. His later credits include the 1983 Bond film, *Never Say Never Again*.

British stop-motion animator **John Hardwick** died in a bicycle accident on September 24th, aged 67. With business partner Bob Bura, he created such popular childrens' series as *Captain Pugwash*, *Toy Town* and *Camberwick Green* via their company Stop Motion for BBC-TV.

Former Walt Disney Pictures president **Richard L. Berger**, who launched Touchstone Pictures, died of lung cancer on September 29th, aged 64.

British film producer-director and former production designer **Michael** [Leighton George] **Relph** died on September 30th, aged 89. Usually working in collaboration with director Basil Dearden, Relph was at Ealing Studios during the 1940s and '50s before becoming chairman of the Film Production Association of Great Britain and then chairman of the British Film Institute's production board (1972–79). The son of stage actor George Relph, his credits include the classic *Dead of Night*, *The Halfway House*, *My Learned Friend*, *Rockets Galore*, *The Mind Benders*, *The Assassination Bureau*, *The Tempest* (1979) and *The Man Who Haunted Himself* (which he also scripted).

Marvin Michelson, Los Angeles' most famous (and most feared) divorce lawyer, also died in September.

Eighty-one-year-old celebrity and fashion photographer **Richard Avedon** died of a cerebral haemorrhage while on assignment for the *New York Times* on October 1st. He was reportedly the inspiration for Fred Astaire's character in the 1957 movie *Funny Face*.

British-born stop-motion puppet animator **Ivor Wood** died on October 13th, aged 72. After working with Serge Danot in France on *The Magic Roundabout* (*Le manège enchanté*) during the mid-1960s, he created such children's series for BBC-TV as *The Herbs*, *The Adventures of Parsley*, *Wombles*, *Paddington* and *Postman Pat*.

Sound editor **Dale Johnson**, who won an Emmy Award for his work on Steven Spielberg's *Duel*, died on October 26th, aged 71. Johnson's other credits include TV's *The Six Million Dollar Man*, *Play Misty for Me*, *Return of the Living Dead*, *Time Walker*, *Critters*, *Return of the Living Dead Part 2*, *Society* and the Oscar-nominated *The Shawshank Redemption*.

American cinematographer **Charles F. Wheeler** died of Alzheimer's disease on October 28th. His numerous film and TV credits include *The Bubble*, *Silent Running*, *The Cat from Outer Space*, *Freaky Friday*, *Charley and the Angel*, *She Waits*, *Matt Helm*, *The Day the Earth Moved*, *Mystery in Dracula's Castle* and episodes of *The Twilight Zone*.

Forty-seven-year-old film-maker **Theo van Gogh**, the great-great grandnephew of painter Vincent, was shot and stabbed to death in an Amsterdam street on November 2nd. He had reportedly received death threats after making *Submission*, a documentary film about how women are treated in Islamic society.

Production designer **Charles Koon**, whose credits include KTTV's *Space Patrol* in the 1950s, died on November 11th, aged 85.

Australian film and television director **Ken Hannam**, who made the 1981 BBC-TV series *The Day of the Triffids*, *Moonbase 3* and *The Return of Sherlock Holmes*, died of cancer in London on November 16th, aged 75.

Tony Magro, the sound effects technician who created the voice of Cousin Itt on TV's *The Addams Family*, died of pneumonia on November 17th, aged 81. He was also associate editor on *Attack of the Giant Leeches*.

Former MCA executive **Albert A. Dorskind** died of prostate cancer on November 28th, aged 82. In 1957 he negotiated the purchase of 378 acres of Universal's loss-making "back lot" and in 1964 created the successful Universal Studios Tour. Dorskind also went on to develop Universal City and Universal CityWalk.

American writer-producer **William Sackheim**, whose credits include *First Blood*, *Pacific Heights* and the *Night Gallery* and *The Flying Nun* TV series, died of a degenerative brain disease on December 1st, aged 84.

Low budget exploitation director **Larry Buchanan** (Marcus Larry Seale, Jr.) died of complications from a collapsed lung on December

2nd, aged 81. A Twentieth Century-Fox contract player and an assistant to George Cukor during the 1950s, he later directed such cult favourites as *The Naked Witch*, *The Eye Creatures*, *Curse of the Swamp Creatures*, *In the Year 2889*, *Zontar – The Thing from Venus*, *Mars Needs Women*, *Creature of Destruction*, *It's Alive!* (1968), *Mistress of the Apes*, *The Loch Ness Horror*, *Goodbye Norma Jean* and *The Trial of Lee Harvey Oswald*. Only a few weeks prior to his death, Buchanan completed *The Copper Scroll of Mary Magdalene*, a film about the life of Jesus Christ, on which he had been working for thirty years. His 1996 autobiography was entitled *It Came from Hunger! Tales of a Cinema Schlockmeister*.

British film editor **Richard Best** died on December 19th, aged 88. He worked on *The Chairman*, *Psychomania*, *Dominique* and *The Blood on Satan's Claw*.

Composer and music editor **Arlon Ober** died on December 20th, aged 61. His credits include *Q The Winged Serpent*, *Eating Raoul*, *Child's Play*, *Superstition*, *Legacy of Satan*, *The Incredible Melting Man*, *Bloody Birthday*, *Sherlock Holmes and the Leading Lady*, *Robotech*, *Hospital Massacre* and *Nightbeast*.

Fifty-three-year-old German film and TV writer-producer **Werner Possardt** died as a result of the Asian tsunami on December 31st. Despite surviving the flood and being buried under debris for two days, he died while undergoing surgery in Thailand. Possardt's credits include the SF spoof *Xaver* and the psycho drama *The Pool*.

USEFUL ADDRESSES

THE FOLLOWING LISTING OF organizations, publications, dealers and individuals is designed to present readers and authors with further avenues to explore. Although I can personally recommend most of those listed on the following pages, neither the publisher nor myself can take any responsibility for the services they offer. Please also note that the information below is only a guide and is subject to change without notice.

—The Editor

ORGANIZATIONS

The British Fantasy Society <www.britishfantasysociety.org.uk> was founded in 1971 and publishes the bi-monthly newsletter *Prism* and the magazine *Dark Horizons*, featuring articles, reviews, interviews and fiction, along with occasional special booklets. The BFS also enjoys a lively online community – there is an e-mail news-feed, a discussion board with numerous links, and a CyberStore selling various publications. FantasyCon is one of the UK's friendliest conventions and there are social gatherings and meet-the-author events organized around Britain. For yearly membership details, contact The BFS Secretary, c/o 201 Reddish Road, South Reddish, Stockport SK5 7HR, UK. E-mail: <secretary@britishfantasysociety. org.uk>. You can also join online through the Cyberstore.

The Ghost Story Society <www.ash-tree.bc.ca/GSS.html> is organized by Barbara and Christopher Roden. They publish the superb *All Hallows* three times a year. For more information contact PO Box 1360, Ashcroft, British Columbia, Canada VOK 1A0. E-mail: <nebuly@telus.net>.

The Horror Writers Association <www.horror.org> is a worldwide organization of writers and publishing professionals dedicated to promoting the interests of writers of horror and dark fantasy. It was formed in the early 1980s. Interested individuals may apply for Active, Affiliate or Associate membership. Active membership is limited to professional writers. HWA publishes a monthly Newsletter, and organizes an annual conference and the Bram Stoker Awards ceremony. Apply online or write to HWA Membership, PO Box 50577, Palo Alto, CA 94303, USA.

The London Vampyre Group <www.revamped.co.uk> is an organization founded in 1995 aimed at fans of the undead from all over the world. A one-year membership includes four issues of the glossy magazine *The Chronicles* and the quarterly newsletter *The London Vampyre* (which includes lists of events etc.). They meet the second Thursday of every month from 7:30 p.m. at The Ben Crouch Tavern, Wells Street, London W1. For more information on events and membership details, send a stamped addressed envelope to: The London Vampyre Group, PO Box 487, London WC2H 9WA, UK. E-mail: <chronicles_ed@hotmail.com>.

The Lost Club <www.lost-club.co.uk> is an informal society of book lovers dedicated to celebrating cult, neglected and forgotten writers in a variety of genres. The group publishes a booklet, *The Lost Club Journal*, and material from this is also available online. For more information, contact: Roger Dobson, 182 Barns Road, Oxford OX4 3RG, England (E-mail: <rogerdobson@hotmail.com>) or Mark Valentine, Stable Cottage, Priest Bank Road, Kildwick, Keighley, West Yorkshire BD20 9BH, England (E-mail: <markl. valentine@btinternet.com>).

World Fantasy Convention <www.worldfantasy.org> is an annual convention held in a different (usually American) city each year, oriented particularly towards serious readers and genre professionals.

World Horror Convention <www.worldhorrorsociety.org> is a smaller, more relaxed, event. It is aimed specifically at horror fans and professionals, and held in a different city each year, so far only in North America.

SELECTED SMALL PRESS PUBLISHERS

Aardwolf Press <www.aardwolfpress.com>, PO Box 14792, Durham, NC 27709–4792, USA. E-mail: <aardwolfpress@aol.com>.

The Alchemy Press <www.alchemypress.co.uk>, 46 Oxford Road, Acocks Green, Birmingham B27 6DT, UK. E-mail: <info@ alchemypress.demon.co.uk>.

Babbage Press <www.babbagepress.com>, 8740 Penfield Avenue, Northridge, CA 91324, USA. E-mail: <books@babbagepress.com>.

Blackstone Audiobooks <www.blackstoneaudio.com>, PO Box 969, Ashland, OR 97520, USA.

Borderlands Press <www.borderlandspress.com>, PO Box 1529 Grantham, NH 03753, USA.

Chico Kidd <www.chico.nildram.co.uk>, 113 Clyfford Road, Ruislip Gardens, Middx HA4 6PX, UK. E-mail: <chico@chico.nildram.co.uk>.

Darkwood Press <www.fairwoodpress.com>, 5203 Quincy Avenue SE, Auburn, WA 98092, USA. E-mail: <info@fairwoodpress.com>.

Earthling Publications <www.earthlingpub.com>, PO Box 413, Northborough, MA 01532, USA. E-mail: <earthlingpub@yahoo.com>.

Elastic Press <www.elasticpress.com>, 85 Gertrude Road, Norwich, Norfolk NR3 4SG, UK. E-mail: <elasticpress@elasticpress.com>.

Endeavor Press <www.endeavorpress.net>, PO Box 4307, Chicago, IL 60680–4307, USA. E-mail: <rogerrange@endeavorpress.net>.

Hill House, Publishers <www.hillhousepublishers.com>, 491 Illington Road, Ossining, NY 10562, USA. E-mail: <peterschneider@hillhousepublishers.com>.

IFD Publishing <www.ifdpublishing.com> PO Box 40776, Eugene, OR 97404, USA. E-mail: <respond@ifdpublishing.com>.

MonkeyBrain Books <www.monkeybrainbooks.com>, 11204 Crossland Drive, Austin, TX 78726, USA. E-mail: <info@monkeybrainbooks.com>.

Necessary Evil Press <www.necessaryevilpress.com>, 2722 South Hill Road #31, Gladstone, MI 49837, USA. E-mail: <info@necessaryevilpress.com>.

Necro Publications <www.necropublications.com>, PO Box 540298, Orlando, FL 32854–0298, USA.

Nemonymous <www.nemonymous.com>.

Night Shade Books <www.nightshadebooks.com>, 3623 SW Baird St, Portland, OR 97219, USA. E-mail: <night@nightshadebooks.com>.

Prime Books, <www.primebooks.net> PO Box 36503, Canton, OH 44735, USA. E-mail: <saw@neo.rr.com>.

PS Publishing <www.pspublishing.co.uk>, Hamilton House, 4 Park Avenue, Harrogate HG2 9BQ, UK. E-mail: <crowth1@attglobal.net>.

Raw Dog Screaming Press <www.rawdogscreaming.com>, 5103 72nd Place, Hyattsville, MD 20784, USA.

Sandglass Enterprises <www.sandglass.com.au>, 44 Bellotti Avenue, Winston Hills, NSW 2153, Australia. E-mail: <mark@sandglass.com.au>.

Sarob Press <www.home.freeuk.net/sarobpress>, "Ty Newydd", Four Roads, Kidwelly, Carmarthenshire SA17 4SF, Wales, UK. E-mail: <sarobpress@freeuk.com>.

Savoy Books <www.savoy.abel.co.uk>, 446 Wilmslow Road, Withington, Manchester M20 3BW, UK. E-mail: <office@savoy.abel.co.uk>.

Small Beer Press <www.smallbeerpress.com>, 176 Prospect Avenue, Northampton, MA 01060, USA. E-mail: <info@smallbeerpress.com>.

Subterranean Press <www.subterraneanpress.com>, PO Box 190106, Burton, MI 48519, USA. E-mail: <subpress@earthlink.net>.

Tachyon Publications <www.tachyonpublications.com>, 1459 18th Street #139, San Francisco, CA 94107, USA. E-mail: <jw@tachyonpublications.com>.

Tartarus Press <www.tartaruspress.com>, Coverley House, Carlton-in-Coverdale, Leyburn, North Yorkshire DL8 4AY, UK. E-mail: <tartarus@pavilion.co.uk>.

Telos Publishing <www.telos.co.uk>, 61 Elgar Avenue, Tolworth, Surrey KT5 9JP, UK. E-mail: <david@telos.co.uk>.

Twilight Tales <www.sales@twilighttales.com>, 2339 N. Commonwealth 4C, Chicago, IL 60614, USA.

Wheatland Press <www.wheatlandpress.com>, P.O. Box 1818, Wilsonville, OR 97070, USA.

Wildside Press <www.wildsidepress.com>, P.O. Box 301, Holicong, PA 18928–0301, USA.

DVD DISTRIBUTORS

EI Independent Cinema <www.SeductionCinema.com> produces low budget horror (Shock-O-Rama Cinema) and erotic genre movies (SeductionCinema). 10 Park Place, Building 6A, 2nd Floor, Butler, NJ 07405, USA. E-mail: <eicinema@aol.com>.

Mondo Macabro <www.mondomacabrodvd.com> distributor of obscure European and other foreign horror and exploitation movies. Boum Productions Ltd., PO Box 3336, Brighton BN2 3GW, UK. E-mail: <video@boumproductions.com>.

SELECTED MAGAZINES

Alan K's Inhuman Magazine is an attractive digest fiction publication with an old-time pulp feel. Cover price is $6.95. For more information (no unsolicited manuscripts) e-mail: <outreart@aol.com>

Black Gate: Adventures in Fantasy Literature <www.blackgate. com> is a nicely designed magazine devoted to the best in epic fantasy. For sample issue and subscription rates check their web site or write to: New Epoch Press, 815 Oak Street, St. Charles, IL 60174, USA. E-mail: <john@blackgate.com>.

The Bulletin of the Science Fiction and Fantasy Writers of America <www.sfwa.org> is published quarterly by the Science Fiction and Fantasy Writers of America, Inc. You do not need to be a SFWA member to subscribe, and the magazine features many interesting and important articles aimed at professional genre authors and would-be writers, including market reports. Single copies or a full year's subscription are available from: SFWA Bulletin, PO Box 10126, Rochester, NY 14610, USA. You can sample articles or purchase back issues and subscriptions on the magazine's web site <www.sfwa.org/bulletin/>. E-mail: <bulletin@sfwa.org>.

Cemetery Dance Magazine <www.cemeterydance.com> is edited by Richard Chizmar and Robert Morrish and includes fiction up to 5,000 words, interviews, articles and columns by many of the biggest names in horror. Cover price is $5.00. For subscription information contact: Cemetery Dance Publications, PO Box 623, Forest Hill, MD 21050, USA. E-mail: <info@cemeterydance.com>.

Charlton Spotlight <www.charltonspotlight.com> is dedicated to the wonderful world of Charlton Comics Group. Through interviews, memoirs, reviews, surveys, checklists and commentary, Michael Ambrose's magazine examines the range of Charlton's comics line, especially its many horror titles. For a two-issue subscription by US cheque, money order and credit card via PayPal contact: Argo Press, PO Box 4201, Austin, Texas 78765–4201, USA. E-mail: <mikeargo@flash.net>.

Locus <www.locusmag.com> is the monthly newspaper of the SF/ fantasy/horror field. Contact: Locus Publications, PO Box 13305, Oakland, CA 94661, USA. Subscription information with other rates and order forms are also available on the web site. Sterling equivalent cheques can be sent to: Fantast (Medway) Ltd, PO Box 23, Upwell Wisbech, Cambs PE14 9BU, UK. E-mail: <locus@locusmag.com>.

The Magazine of Fantasy & Science Fiction <www.fsfmag.com> has been publishing some of the best imaginative fiction for more than fifty years, now edited by Gordon Van Gelder. Single copies or an annual subscription (which includes the double October/ November anniversary issue) are available by US cheques or credit card from: Fantasy & Science Fiction, PO Box 3447, Hoboken, NJ 07030, USA, or you can subscribe online.

Rue Morgue <www.rue-morgue.com>, is a glossy bi-monthly magazine edited by Rod Gudino and Jovanka Vuckovic and subtitled "Horror in Culture & Entertainment". Packed with full colour features and reviews of new films, books, comics, music and game releases, single copies are $7.95 (USA/Canada). Subscriptions are available from: The Rue Morgue House of Horror, 2926 Dundas Street West, Toronto, ON M6P 1Y8, Canada, or by credit card on the web site. E-mail: <info@rue-morgue.com>.

SF Site <www.sfsite.com> has been posted twice each month since 1997. Presently, it publishes around thirty to fifty reviews of SF, fantasy and horror from mass-market publishers and some small press. They also maintain link pages for author and fan tribute sites and other facets including pages for interviews, fiction, science fact, bookstores, small press, publishers, e-zines and magazines, artists, audio, art galleries, newsgroups and writers's resources. Periodically, they add features such as author and publisher reading lists.

Space and Time <www.cith.org/space&time>, the magazine of fantasy, horror and science fiction is published twice a year by editor-in-chief Gordon Linzner. Single issues are $5.00 plus $1.50 shipping (USA). Subscriptions are available by US postal money order or cheque to: Space and Time, 138 West 70th Street (4B), New York, NY 10023–4468, USA. In the UK order from BBR Distributing, PO Box 625, Sheffield S1 3GY, UK.

Supernatural Tales <www.chico.nildram.co.uk/SupernaturalTales .html> is a small press magazine of stories and non-fiction edited by David Longhorn. A four issue subscription is available from: Supernatural Tales, 291 Eastbourne Avenue, Gateshead NE8 4NN, UK. E-mail: <davidlonghorn@hotmail.com>.

Talebones <www.talebones.com> is an attractive digest magazine of science fiction and dark fantasy edited and published by Patrick and Honna Swenson. For a four issue subscription (US funds only or credit card) write to: 5203 Quincy Avenue S.E., Auburn, WA 98092, USA. E-mail: <info@talebones.com>.

The 3rd Alternative <www.ttapress.com> is a quarterly magazine of new horror fiction, interviews, artwork, articles and reviews edited by Andy Cox. Cover price is £4.00/$7.00. Six and twelve-issue subscriptions are available from: TTA Press, 5 Martins Lane,

Witcham, Ely, Cambs CB6 2LB, UK, or by credit card via the secure online web site <www.ttapress.com/onlinestore 1.html>. E-mail: <ttapress@aol.com>. You can also visit the TTA Press message boards at: <www.ttapress.com/discus>.

Video Watchdog <www.videowatchdog.com> is a full colour monthly review of horror, fantasy and cult cinema on tape and disc, published by Tim and Donna Lucas. Described as "The Perfectionist's Guide to Fantastic Video", the award-winning digest-sized magazine is $7.95 a copy. An annual twelve-issue subscription is available in US funds only or VISA/MasterCard to: Video Watchdog, PO Box 5283, Cincinnati, OH 45205–0283, USA. E-mail: <orders@videowatchdog.com>.

Weird Tales <www.dnapublications.com> is the latest large-size incarnation of "The Unique Magazine". Edited by George H. Scithers and Darrell Schweitzer, it is published by DNA Publications, Inc. and Wildside Press, in association with Terminus Publishing Co., Inc. Single copies or a six-issue subscription is available (in US funds only) from: DNA Publications, PO Box 2988, Radford, VA 24143–2988, USA. Submissions should be addressed to Weird Tales, 123 Crooked Lane, King of Prussia, PA 19406–2570, USA. An e-mail version of the magazine's writers's guidelines (no electronic submissions) is available from <weirdtales@comcast.net>. You can also visit the message board at <www.wildsidepress.com>. In the UK contact: Cold Tonnage Books, 22 Kings Lane, Windlesham, Surrey, GU20 6JQ, UK <andy@coldtonnage.co.uk>.

BOOK DEALERS

Borderlands Books <www.borderlands-books.com> is a nicely designed store with friendly staff and an impressive stock of new and used books from both sides of the Atlantic. 866 Valencia Street (at 19th), San Francisco, CA 94110, USA. Tel: (415) 824–8203 or (888) 893–4008 (toll free in the US). Credit cards accepted. Worldwide shipping. E-mail: <office@borderlands-books.com>.

Cold Tonnage Books <www.coldtonnage.com> offers excellent mail order new and used SF/fantasy/horror, art, reference, limited editions etc. Write to: Andy & Angela Richards, Cold Tonnage Books, 22 Kings Lane, Windlesham, Surrey GU20 6JQ, UK. Credit cards accepted. Tel: +44 (0) 1276–475388. E-mail: <andy@coldtonnage.com>.

Ken Cowley offers mostly used SF/fantasy/horror/crime/supernatural, collectibles, pulps, videos etc. by mail order at very reasonable prices. Write to: Trinity Cottage, 153 Old Church Road, Clevedon, North Somerset, BS21 7TU, UK. Tel: +44 (0) 1275–872247. E-mail: <kencowley@blueyonder.co.uk>.

Dark Delicacies <www.darkdel.com> is a friendly Burbank, California, store specialising in horror books, toys, vampire merchandise and signings. They also do mail order and run money-saving book club and membership discount deals. 4213 West Burbank Blvd., Burbank, CA 91505, USA. Tel: (818) 556–6660. Credit cards accepted. E-mail: <darkdel@darkdel.com>.

DreamHaven Books & Comics <www.dreamhavenbooks.com> store and mail order offers new and used SF/fantasy/horror/art and illustrated etc. with regular catalogues (both print and e-mail). Write to: 912 West Lake Street, Minneapolis, MN 55408, USA. Credit cards accepted. Tel: (612) 823–6070. E-mail: <dream@dreamhavenbooks. com>.

Fantastic Literature <www.fantasticliterature.com> mail order offers the UK's biggest online out-of-print SF/fantasy/horror genre bookshop. Fanzines, pulps and vintage paperbacks as well. Write to: Simon and Laraine Gosden, Fantastic Literature, 35 The Ramparts, Rayleigh, Essex SS6 8PY, UK. Credit cards and Pay Pal accepted. Tel/Fax: +44 (0) 1268–747564. E-mail: <sgosden@netcomuk.co.uk>.

Fantasy Centre <www.fantasycentre.biz> shop (open 10:00a.m.-6:00p.m., Monday to Saturday) and mail order has used SF/fantasy/ horror, art, reference, pulps etc. at reasonable prices with regular bi-monthly catalogues. They also stock a wide range of new books from small, specialist publishers. Write to: 157 Holloway Road, London N7 8LX, UK. Credit cards accepted. Tel/Fax: +44 (0)20–7607 9433. E-mail: <books@fantasycentre.biz>.

Ghost Stories run by Richard Dalby issues semi-regular mail order lists of used ghost and supernatural volumes at very reasonable prices. Write to: 4 Westbourne Park, Scarborough, North Yorkshire YO12 4AT, UK. Tel: +44 (0) 1723 377049.

David Wynn's **Mythos Books LLC** <www.mythosbooks.com> is a mail order company presenting books and curiosities on Lovecraftiana, Cthulhu Mythos, horror and weird fiction releases with regular e-mail and web site updates. Write to: 351 Lake Ridge Road, Poplar Bluff, MO 63901–2177, USA. Major credit cards accepted. Tel/Fax: (573) 785–7710. E-mail: <dwynn@LDD.net>.

Porcupine Books offers regular catalogues and extensive mail order lists of used fantasy/horror/SF titles via e-mail: <brian@ porcupine.demon.co.uk> or write to: 37 Coventry Road, Ilford, Essex IG1 4QR, UK. Tel: +44 (0)20 8554–3799.

Kirk Ruebotham <www.abebooks.com/home/kirk61/> is a mail-order only dealer, who sells out-of-print and used horror/SF/fantasy/crime and related non-fiction at very good prices, with regular catalogues. Write to: 16 Beaconsfield Road, Runcorn, Cheshire WA7 4BX, UK. Tel: +44 (0) 1928–560540 (10:00 a.m.-8:00 p.m.). E-mail: <kirk.ruebotham@ntlworld.com>.

Bob and Julie Wardzinski's **The Talking Dead** offers reasonably priced paperbacks, rare pulps and hardcovers, with catalogues issued regularly. They accept wants lists and are also the exclusive supplier of back issues of *Interzone*. Credit cards accepted. Contact them at: 12 Rosamund Avenue, Merley, Wimborne, Dorset BH21 1TE, UK. Tel: +44 (0) 1202–849212 (9:00a.m.-9:00p.m.). E-mail: <books@thetalkingdead.fsnet.co.uk>.

MARKET INFORMATION AND NEWS

Although the weekly **DarkEcho** <www.darkecho.com> newsletter for horror writers and others ceased publication several years ago, editor Paula Guran still sends out periodic, personal e-mails whenever time and whim allows. It doesn't cover horror news comprehensively or list market news, but it's still worth subscribing to for free by e-mailing: <subscribe@darkecho.com>.

The Gila Queen's Guide to Markets is an e-mail newsletter detailing markets for SF/fantasy/horror plus other genres, along with publishing news, contests, dead markets, anthologies, updates, etc. The newsletter comes out every three weeks. For a sample copy or subscription (US funds only, credit card or PayPal), contact: Kathryn Ptacek, PO Box 97, Newton, NJ 07860–0097, USA. E-mail: <GilaQueen@worldnet.att.net>.

Hellnotes <www.hellnotes.com> is described as "The Insider's Edge to Horror!" Judi Rohrig's weekly newsletter offers reviews, interviews, news, and commentaries, and is available through electronic delivery. Subscriptions are payable through PayPal or to: Hellnotes, 4212 Derby Lane, Evansville, IN 47715–1568, USA. E-mail: <info@hellnotes.com>.